I0822329

The Independent Bookworm

About the Book

A force of ancient Despair stirs again and twenty centuries of peace in the Lands of Hope are shattered. But in the chaotic Percentalion, evil's return goes unnoticed by all but a few. The grim young scholar Solemn Judgement, sails and walks a circuit of the northern kingdoms, in search of lore to fend off the plague of undeath. Meanwhile, the Woodsman Treaman struggles to guide his adventuring party to safety, but instead encounters deep loss and inherits a quest to pit all of their lives against desperate odds.

The demon Kog, formerly ruler of these lands, searches for his lost Eye which will render him again invincible. His uneasy ally, the liche Wolga Vrule, schemes to expand his undead army and overwhelm the unsuspecting kingdoms in his own bid for power. What part can a discovered scepter or a missing crown, a dwindling holy order of knights, a ghoul-guarded tomb, or an ancient prophecy play in the chance to ward off such threats?

The quest begun in Judgement's Tale reaches its climax

About the Author

Will Hahn has been in love with heroic tales since age four, when his father read him the Lays of Ancient Rome and the Tales of King Arthur. He taught Ancient-Medieval History for years, but the line between this world and others has always been thin. The far reaches of fantasy, like the distant past, still bring him face to face with people like us, who have choices to make.

Will has written about the Lands of Hope since his college days (which by now are also part of ancient history). He chronicled the adventures of Solmn Judgement dilligently in two tomes of over 1000 pages each. It is now being published as an eBook series and in print. His Shards of Light series, a sword and sorcery story, begins with "The Ring and the Flag" and continues with "Fencing Reputation". The concluding volumes "Perilous Embraces" and "Shards of Light" will be published soon. He also chronicled stand alone stories like "The Plane of Dreams" or "Three Minutes to Midnight." More of Will's tales of Hope are available at several online retailers.

Find out more on his website: www.WilliamLHahn.com

The Eye of Kog

The Sequel to Judgement's Tale

William L. Hahn

The Eye of Kog: The Sequel to Judgement's Tale

published by the Independent Bookworm, USA und D
this book is also available as eBook at various retailers

If you find typos or formatting problems in the book, please contact the publisher (www.IndependentBookworm.de).

editor: Ethan James Clarke
printed On-Demand Publishing LLC, 100 Enterprise Way, Suite A200, Scotts Valley, CA 95066, USA, www.createspace.com

ISBN-13 978-3-95681-081-7

Find more information on the publisher's website:
http://www.IndependentBookworm.de

To that most remarkable hero
who dares the perilous voyage over an ocean of words,
walks the length of the tale entire,
braves whatever monstrous distractions the Alleged Real World may raise,
and perseveres.

To you, the readers.
Because you want to know what happens next.
To you, Hope Forever.

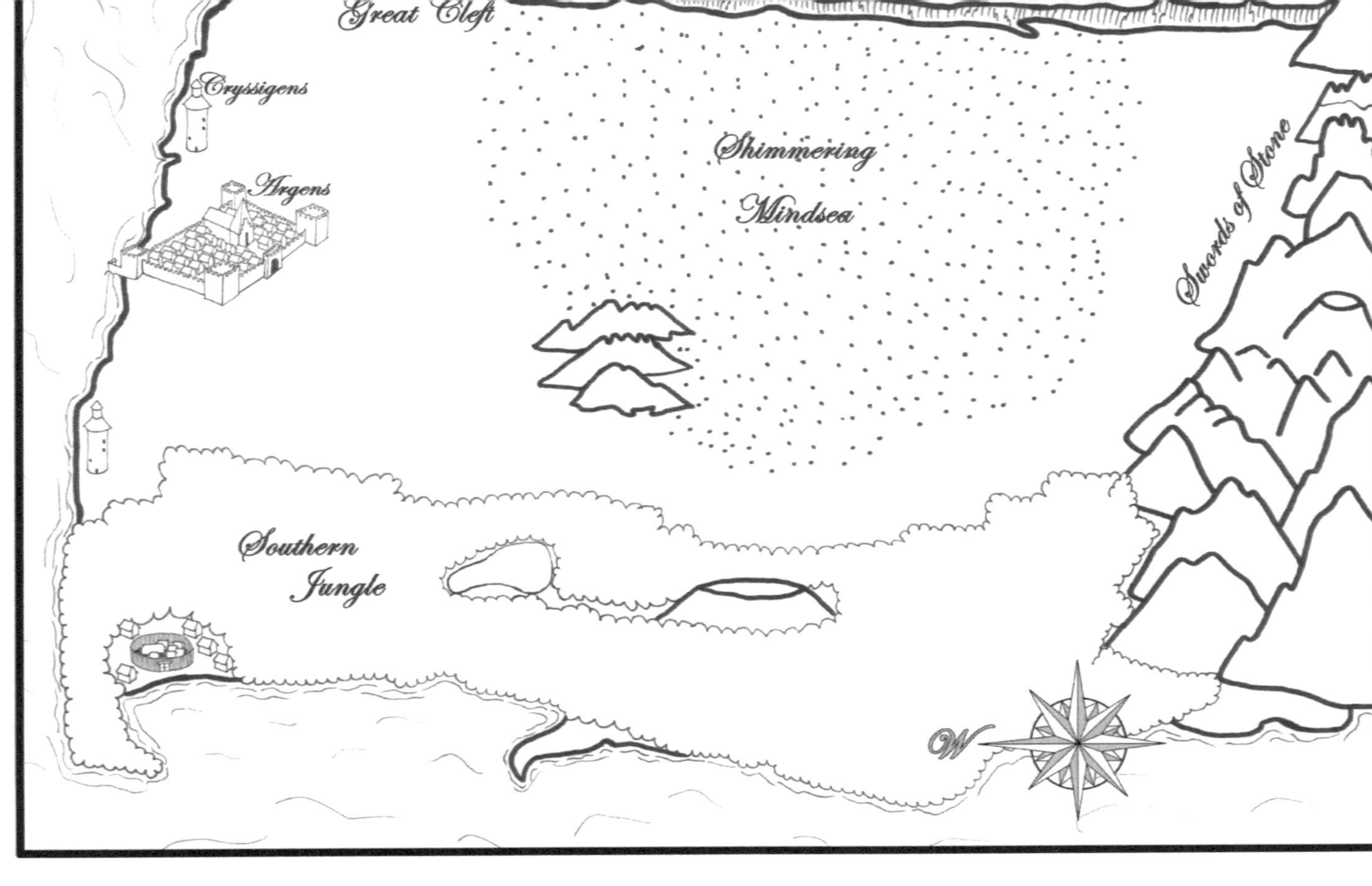
Great Cleft
Cryssigens
Argens
Shimmering
Mindsea
Swords of Stone
Southern
Jungle
W

The Lands of Hope
Northern Wastes
Novar
Halfwoods
Conar
City of Wonders
Trainertown
Stream Crossing
Cil-Ciluion
Shilar
Plains of Bordbeyonds
Skysword
Percentalion
River Sweeping
Eldaport
Araluntir
Mendel
Mendel

Table of Contents

This book is the sequel to *Judgement's Tale*, and it is highly recommended that you begin the story with that epic. It is available in one volume, or you can begin with "Games of Chance" which is the first chapter of that tale.

Landfall

The ax-bearing timberman strides through small brush and between tree-rows with the regular gait of the soldier he had been. The west-slanting sun pushes argent arrows of glimmer through the pine-boughs, lighting a thousand gems of the recent rain nestled in cone and coven, and occasionally from beneath the timberman's rough-weave tunic. The chain shirt, almost completely obscured, is another inheritance from his days with the Conarian Lances. He leaves it unhooked down the middle, though it is hardly small on his broad frame.

The timberman pauses at the crest of a tree-sown berm, to look onward into that westering orb with eyes that do not flinch or narrow. Behind him, a group of like-dressed woodcutters hails, headed back across the wide brick bridge to Oncario, but he waves them off and they laugh, expecting it. They are well accustomed to his evening jaunts and will not remark on his absence until he has been gone a week or more. For he is solitary though friend to all the city; a sole survivor from the outer Lands of Hope and proven warrior. He works hard and cheerfully, and they whisper he is beloved of the Primara herself. "Moonstruck," they chortle to each other as he leaves for another nocturnal round of the district. And in this they are more right than they know.

He sets off downhill and beyond the sight of men, those happy mortals returning to fire and family, who will spend the night under sheets, see the moons above without fear, and sleep with only such dreams as normally come to fathers and husbands. He cannot be one of them, and so seeks solace without them. He will check the kilns, a thankless task with leagues of lonely tramping in it, and hunt his dinner fairly, and stay as far as he can from the city for the next three nights. He tells himself at times that he is guarding his new home. He seldom asks from what—he knows the most mortal threat without seeking.

The smoke-trails from the kilns are easy to see by dusk, and the sky looks clear, so the timberman will be able to keep working late. Seldom indeed would a kiln-fire escape its chamber to threaten the forest, absent wind or freak storm. But better safe, and he enjoys the work. The banked clay ovens give off heat from almost a furlong; now the glints of rain drops and armor links are orange echoes of the glowing charcoals as well as the setting sun.

He breathes deep, hears the owl and the occasional pop of embers; the scent of charring wood is redolent. The river is nearly a league away, but he can still feel its might, the slow churn it makes on its course between nowhere in this chaos-land. He has work, has found love, and is alive against all odds as are none of his troop sent into the Percentalion these many weeks ago. The timberman strides on, reflecting that if his future holds no hope of dispelling his curse, yet perhaps he can leave it hidden; banked like these charcoals in a safe remote place where it may do no harm until the time is right.

Young nights like this, before the moons he dreads have risen, are happy for him. Why can he not laugh tonight? Why does his marching stride shorten and slow, the ax hop from shoulder to second hand in easy reflex? Why is there no sound either from all the glade about, why has even the breeze seemingly fled this dark place? Perhaps because it is not yet far enough from the last kiln, to spot a ruby glint in the bracken ahead, fired by neither star nor lantern.

He should not, but the grip of some mania is already upon the timberman. Four sharp hacks, and the way is clear to a slightly-smoking spot beneath the grass-draped thornbush, where sits a ruby the size of a fist, glowing of its own accord. A small voice inside him, one that listened to his parents and his commanding officer back in Conar, tells him to hack once more, and sunder the jewel. But the ax is laid aside instead, and the gem touches human flesh again for the first time in more than three thousand years.

It is, of course, power. From his palm, the raw energy like buckled lightning jerks up the arm and assails his neck, skull, spine. The jewel-thrall can see forever now—there is no night, no distance. Protected from harm, sustained against fatigue; the jewel relays to its thrall a dozen senses of its abilities, all well beyond what mortal frames can long withstand.

For the jewel's power serves itself, or rather its master, not the thrall. Since the separation, it has been handled with anxiety and brevity, only by those of heroic stature able to resist its allure. Freed now from crystal column and otherworldly prison, it calls to its master, ordering the thrall to carry on as long as it lives. With a mortal, perhaps a day, perhaps two, but more likely less. Another porter will come along shortly.

But the timberman, he is not truly a mortal, not anymore.

Clutching the giant ruby he runs towards the north screaming in pain. It is the general direction of the master, made distant by the chaos-land itself. But the timberman knows, as the foul jewel does not, that the moon he formerly feared to see is now his only hope. He threshes down through the vale and forges up the next slope, scattering the underbrush like feather-down and careening off tree boles in his tortured haste. He cannot throw or drop the ruby, it does not allow that. But a few moments more, and he may gain power of his own. Time, perhaps for the embers to come forth and work for good instead of evil.

He screams and his palm is beginning to char, but—yes! The top of the rise, and a small bald spot in the barren of pines. The former lancer holds out his arms, calls to all the heroes, begs with tears for the curse from which he normally hides.

His salvation arrives in silver, as the rim of Aral grows quickly to a disk and clears the northern horizon above the tree-line. The timberman shouts with joy and agony, howls the long call that brings a measure of freedom from the ruby's spell. His chain shirt is no longer loose upon him, and his felt-lined boots are only tatters around the claws that now protrude. With his intellect fading, the timberman thanks the heroes, and that hoary wolf he slew several moons ago. His human mind escapes the jewel's command; crouching low the silverwere relies now on instinct.

Dimly it knows power, for it has always wielded unthinkable strength under the moons. No thoughts, no plan, but the beast thinks of power now. This red stabbing glass wishes to be brought where power is. And that is the woman, she who rules the city across the river as well as his heart when the moons have fled. He will use her secret way, the cave-path that shelters the bats, and smells of her; she will know what to do. A final howl of greeting and triumph while clutching the jewel to its chest; the silverwere lopes off on three feet like a creature of hell.

The wagon rocked dangerously, a wheeled, covered galley heeling in the storm of claws battering its port side. Treaman nearly stumbled over a box of quarrels, to one side of the treasure-chest the party had just plundered. Voices drowned beneath the grinding din of the helldogs outside; battering paws gashed the reinforced wall as the beasts howled for death to anyone inside.

Bildon slammed the shining sword back into its sheath and held it out to Haltar. The strapping leader grasped the jeweled scabbard with his left, unwounded arm, and directed Treaman to the arbalest. Cupping his right hand around his mouth he shouted instructions.

"On signal—out the door, get to the side. First Bildon—above, just distract. Use everything. Best you can."

Mhoral reached to his upraised visor as he drew the bent wooden club. His strange, knowing smirk showed beneath the recent scars, as he shouted, "We knew—come to this someday. Glad, glad we saw that—" gesturing to the artefact in Haltar's grasp, "before the end."

Treaman nodded to the Elf, now helmed, and stuffed another two quarrels into his belt; because he was an optimist, he told himself. Haltar braced against the rocking and faced the port wall, the sword still sheathed and held awkwardly in both hands. He waved the others to the rear door, shouting "They sense this—can't swing well anyway—give time—get in position."

Bildon climbed the stack of boxes to the roof-hatch with a dagger in his teeth. When Treaman, Linya and Mhoral reached the wagon's rear door, the Woodsman and Stealthic caught each other's eye. With a mischevious grin around the blade, Bildon quickly flashed signals in the hand-cant he was teaching Treaman.

'risk life good'

'with you honor' Treaman flashed back, hoping the compliment was conveyed. Then Haltar nodded for the signal, and Linya, with an ashen face, threw open the door.

The chaos-storm had passed but thick clouds cut the light to nearly dusk. The pair of enormous helldogs continued to rend and claw the splintered side of the armored wagon; one of the suspending bars snapped under the weight of their assaults, making it list toward them. The tilt nearly took Bildon over the edge and into their mouths as he emerged from the smoke-hole. Careening for balance, he laughed, threw his dagger striking one harmlessly between the eyes, and called out in a mocking tone.

"Here puss-puss!"

Distracted, one helldog—without the spiked collar—tried to leap to the top of the wagon after the annoying Halfling. Claws bigger than human fingers missed the Stealthic by inches; overcome by the beast's foul breath, Bildon staggered back and fell as the creature slid down the ruined wagon-side, and recalled its original target.

Treaman and Mhoral stood just in front of Linya, their usual formation. Treaman struggled with the heavy arbalest, finally getting the dropstand in position to brace it and taking aim. The helldogs were punching holes in the wagon now, the entire side looked ready to collapse on top of the wounded party leader within. His plan had worked to perfection, giving the three of them plenty of time to get in position. Treaman's bow was at point-blank range; he hesitated because he knew the slim chance it would wound the monsters, and was clinging to the hope that ignorance brings.

It could not have been long, yet the time seemed to stretch absurdly, as the trio waited for something to happen. When the thought came to him from Hallah, Treaman yelped in surprise.

{*"Everything dead. Badsmell dogs go."*}

"Hallah!" Treaman called aloud in his haste, "Where are you?"

{*"Hallah on wagon, far from badsmell dogs. Burnt man move."*}

{*"Stay safe,"*} he managed to think; so concerned for his friend, Treaman's concentration flagged and he looked away from the helldogs out into the circled caravan.

It was just as Hallah said. Everything was dead.

When he was only nine, Treaman saw the result of an attack by the fierce Northmen of his native Novar, on a neighboring village. His father had taken him on just his second hunting trip and was stopping over to barter for supplies. The ice-fort walls were broken through in two places and over a dozen men lay slain in the wake of the failed raid, which also left one of the barbarians' enormous montori bulls dead, filled with spears and arrows and fallen before the breach it had made. As a boy, Treaman was sure it was the most disastrous battle in the history of the Lands. But the frozen cold stopped the smell of death, and some of the corpses were already neatly arranged beneath tarps before he arrived. The rest had been slain by neat weapon-strokes in honest combat, and would be burned under a starry sky with the thin smoke that deep winter allowed.

Here, the burning had preceded death. Torn corpses still sparking with stubborn flames, horses and guards and children together in sticky piles, gouges and wrack across the ground and its new carpet of flesh. The shifting breeze brought a reek as noisome as the helldogs' howl; Treaman nearly fell, gagging. The entire caravan, four or fivescore persons and their livestock destroyed; part-eaten mules propped up in their traces, three inch-thick stockade walls shattered like kindling, a soldier's intact body lying on its back, with the head beyond sight, driven completely into the earth.

From the corner of his eye Treaman saw the burnt man—Braja, covered in blood and shreds, still struggling to crawl and holding a thick coil in one hand. The sight of one moving thing made Treaman's heart jump; but as he debated whether to go to the man's aid, the perfect, doomed plan went directly to hell.

Both helldogs barreled against the wall, breaking through and exposing a glimpse of Haltar's form inside, flailing the Sword of Air still sheathed.

With a sharp snap another strut gave way; one wheel broke off its axle and the entire wagon keeled over to crash on its side, obscuring the dogs and the foot-knight from view. Behind Treaman, Linya screamed, now that Haltar was beyond help. Mhoral took a half-step in that direction and looked back at his friends. Bildon rolled to the ground like a sack of wheat and bounced half-up, regaining consciousness and apparently still unhurt. Within the wagon, the sound of biting-growls, Haltar's bellow, and more splintering ended with a blinding flash of light shooting from every crevice. A torn howl of hurt, more cracking; suddenly the entire wagon fell to pieces under the strain, throwing jagged wood poles and broken boards in all directions.

Haltar was still up, screeching in pain as he raised the Sword of Air in both hands. The sight of the full blade was more painful than looking directly into the sun; Treaman could see beneath the light-haze, red blood sprayed from Haltar's reopened shoulder wound as the leader brought the weapon down in a weak strike on the hound with its teeth buried in his side. It yelped and let go as the pair fell to the earth. Treaman's hands convulsively clenched, setting off the arbalest only half-aimed; but with less than thirty feet to travel it plunged directly into the ribs of the other, collared helldog. A quarrel thicker than his thumb traveling fast enough to penetrate any armor, but it bounced off as if a straw tossed by a child. The impact did shift the beast a few steps stumbling to one side; the helldog noticed the trio for the first time, growling and leaping in their direction.

Its stride was far longer than a man's. There would be no time to reload. Treaman clawed out his pioneer blade and just braced his body against the stock and stick of the arbalest, hoping to slow the impact and get in a stroke, perhaps at its belly. Mhoral tried to utter the incantation to enchant his weapon but stuttered. Behind him Linya called out the syllables of a spell Treaman had never heard, gesturing large with both her arms. The beast plowed straight into the trio scattering them to the ground like lawn-pins. Rolling free and half-up, Treaman saw with horror that it had both forepaws directly atop Linya's prone form, howling in her face as she lost consciousness despite the pain of her wounds.

As the helldog drew its next breath, however, it staggered and coughed under some unseen influence. Linya's spell, not able to put it to sleep, yet dazed and slowed the beast; it growled again but seemed unaware of its surroundings, forgetful that a victim lay helpless beneath it.

Treaman scrambled to his feet, his only thought to get the monster off of Linya: Bildon's shouts and the growls of the second monster were a strange discordant backdrop to his desperation. Just as he raised Gutter, his blade, he heard again the voice of his friend.

{*"Burnt man move."*}

Hallah flew past and glided above the helldog, screeching in a scaly tenor of fear and distaste Treaman had never heard her use before. Again the helldog reacted slowly, looking up and chuffing in hatred, half-jumping to reach the miniature dragon but unable to come close, or leap up as it had a moment ago. The Woodsman looked back, and saw Braja at the end of a ruby smear in the grass, crawling now towards the group and trailing the thick red rope. Treaman took two steps to reach him and saw that the giant black was unable to speak, throat and mouth too torn and filled with blood; he gestured with the rope-hand, and the woodsman took it, a large bullwhip incised deeply on the leather in strange symbols.

Mhoral was up and banging the helldog over the head as hard as he could with his mundane club; the creature snarled and bit at him, but just slowly enough that the Elf could evade. Linya lay still but breathing a few precious feet away, as safe for now as this occupation could afford. Treaman uttered a quick prayer as he advanced, coiling and raising the whip in his off-hand to bring it down at the beast.

The strike missed by a foot, but the resulting snap of the whip was cacophanous, and accompanied by red sparks of sorcerous energy. The spike-collared helldog spun immediately, ignoring Mhoral with a face bearing rage and even outrage to the human before it. Dropping his sword, Treaman quickly recovered the coil and raised it to whistle in the air before striking again. This time a hit, with a shower of reddish flame; the monster howled and recoiled, a stripe of burnt orange ichor leaking from its neck where the whip had scored. Again it advanced a few paces; Treaman stepped back to keep the weapon's range, but that seemed to return its sense of rage.

He struck quickly again, and this time the monster's roar was accompanied by a small step back, though the wound was not nearly as bad as the first. Treaman's hand felt hot and somehow also dirty, as if he held a stick of manure. Staying his ground, he coiled and struck again. Now the helldog tried to avoid the strike, no longer seemed to think of attacking. Its roar was more distressed, still angry but with an edge of panic.

Risking a look around, Treaman saw Braja collapsed, perhaps dead. Rising smoke from the ruins of the wagon showed where Haltar lay, only one knee visible and the Sword of Air no longer shining. But the greatest racket came from atop the circle of remaining wagons. Bildon, through whatever means, had grabbed the sheath of the Sword of Air and climbed up, teasing the uncollared beast into a chase across the roofs.

With a half-crack at the helldog before him, Treaman produced another step back, and this time he advanced, coming across the way to stand over Linya. Mhoral joined him, and without hesitation Treaman tossed him the whip.

"I don't know how—"

"And I did? Hold him, kill him, do your best. I'm going to save Bildon."

With no weapon in either hand, Treaman sprinted towards Haltar, passing close to the helldog but not attracting its attention. A moment later, he heard behind him the crack of the sorcerous lash and another howl from the monster, this time tinged with pain.

Haltar lay in an impossible position over the ruins of several boxes, his shoulder joint an open horror and the bite-wound in his side smoking with the bubbling-hot saliva of the helldog. Instead of screaming like any sensible person, the leader forced his breath in even gasps in and out and clutched the blade of the Sword of Air between red-stained fingers. When he saw Treaman kneel over him, Haltar nodded as if to say "what kept you" and thrust the blade up at the Woodsman. Unable to do anything to help, Treaman took it by the hilt and stood. In his hand,the sword felt like a struggling fish and the nerves in his arm raced with flaming pain. The searing light of the sword blazed forth again, and Treaman held it high like a torch to keep it from blinding him as he scanned the wagon-tops for Bildon.

The Halfling had made nearly the entire circuit already, vaulting the space between wagons and running as if he were in his exact situation, fleeing from hell. Haltar had wounded this beast near the top of one foreleg, which slowed it enough, along with the Stealthic's natural grace and reduced impact on the wagons, to keep him barely in the lead. Seeing Treaman move into the center of the circle with the sword, Bildon whooped and vaulted off the final wagon, rolling up from the grass and charging directly past the Woodsman. Treaman had just a moment to check that Mhoral was plying the whip with vigor, beating his opponent into a frenzy. Then the remaining monster leaped from the last wagon, covering almost all the distance to Treaman in a single bound.

Clapping both hands to the hilt and ignoring the sharp tingling pain that wracked him from palms to shoulders, Treaman took aim and brought the blade down onto the helldog's skull. There was a clap of thunder and whatever lay beyond his hands was impossible to see for the light. When his vision cleared, Treaman found the blade buried four inches deep in the monster's head, his blow having stopped it in its tracks from a full run. He yanked back and when the lightning-tinged blade came free, the monster fell to earth like timber. No longer able to hold the weapon, he dropped it with a cry. The bright blade faded to its normal silversteel hue at once.

Mhoral's scream brought him around, and Treaman could see the Elf going down with the remaining helldog clamped to his whip-arm. Rushing there he felt Bildon to his left; the little one leaped to side-kick the monster in the ribs for distraction. Treaman got to Mhoral's side and wrenched the whip loose as the Elf screamed in pain from the helldog's worrying jaws. The beast had several more sparking, oozing wounds from where Mhoral had plied it, but nothing looked mortal, though Treaman knew all guesses were equally good with a beast from hell. Cracking the whip in haste, Treaman missed again but the dog let go at once and snarled in his direction with hate and some alarm. Treaman sensed its attitude had come back to the same spot as when he first attacked it. On a hunch, he backed up and cracked the lash from distance across the monster's haunches. A howl of agony, a step back; in a flash Treaman realized the truth.

He stepped forward constantly and shouted "Hai!" cracking the whip above the beast's back. The helldog snapped up at the whip but on the sound of its crack it cowered a bit and backed away. Not for killing, but breaking the spirit, Treaman realized. He stepped up and cracked again, and the monster now seemed much more subdued, ducking its head a bit and snarling but without much prospect.

"What are you doing?" Bildon demanded, still trailing alongside him as he advanced.

"Driving it off, I hope," the Woodsman answered, "Get out! Go, go!"

Two more cracks, then a third which scored just lightly on its head, and the collared helldog turned with a yelp and fled, bursting through a wooden barrier on the opposite side of the caravan and rumbling into the gathering dusk.

"Well, I'll be a sore loser," Bildon murmured. "That worked."

"Let's see how many of us are left." Treaman responded grimly, stowing the whip-handle in his belt and wiping his hand constantly on his pants.

"I'll see to Linya," Mhoral said, gripping a smoking arm and tottering to his feet.

Bildon gestured to Braja on the ground and Treaman nodded, before trotting toward where Haltar lay. His left foot felt damp, some unseen stump hole, and now that the immediate combat was over he felt sheathed in sweat from the neck down. Behind him, the baying howl of the helldog-pack still stabbed his heart with fear, and he thought of the man in black, running or hiding out there in the waste beyond the circle of ruined wagons.

Haltar was trying to sit up, blood still seeping from his shoulder where white showed through the wet red.

"Sit still, you great oaf!" Treaman scrambled to find anything to bind the wounds. "Everyone made it. So far."

"That… wasn't supposed to happen," Haltar hissed through a clench-jawed grin.

"I said stop moving! Save your glorious suicide for next time, we'll handle things." Treaman heard his voice rise, too young to conceal his true feelings the way Haltar could.

"Pelian's wagon," Haltar managed. "Healing, probably." Then he fell back at last and either rested or passed out.

"Yes, master," Treaman muttered, rising and looking over to the green wagon-fort which served as the caravan master's personal quarters. From the grassy sward near the center, he could see Mhoral supporting Linya as she sat, groggy but awake. Bildon knelt over Braja's form; when Treaman caught his eye and flashed a thumb's up, the Stealthic responded with a neutral hand-waggle. Perhaps the giant black was still alive, maybe dying: from the wounds he saw, Treaman wasn't sure how any man could survive long. He'd be lucky to save Haltar, except the party leader always seemed to come through. Treaman's mind skirted around the thought of losing him.

{"Hallah?"} he thought carefully, {"Where is Hallah?"}

{*"Hungry! Hallah is eating."*}

{*"Good work, Hallah is very brave."*}

{*"Yes, and now hungry."*}

A momentary glimpse of a downed mule was all he needed to reassure him for now. Treaman scooped up Gutter from the place he'd dropped it, and marked the Sword of Air lying edge-up in the grass. Wouldn't do to lose that, he mused as he reached Pelian's green wagon. Using the broad, saw-backed blade as a lever, he forced the lock and went inside, lighting the lantern just inside the door.

Everything in its place, he mused while quickly scanning the lush interior of the wagon. Papered walls, carpeting clearly imported from Argens, bedding that looked like silk. Treaman spent an extra moment there, catching the sight of something black and metallic—each corner of the large bed had a short iron chain ending in a leather cuff.

But thinking ill of the dead was easy; Treaman flashed on the memory of Pelian's half-corpse and returned his mind to the task at hand. One corner held items that clearly spoke of the magician's art, including a large heavy book on a stand and certain glass containers. Later, Linya would investigate that. The Woodsman turned to the set of small drawers along one wall, too narrow and shallow for clothing. Pulling one out, he saw neat rows of small potion bottles, all capped with the mark of the Serpent who understands healing and sealed with Pelian's sign of the hoarding squirrel. Treaman simply grabbed the entire shelf, yanked it out of the wardrobe and turned to go.

With a shock he saw bloody boot-prints on the carpet; only then did he feel his wet left foot throbbing with pain. Something had sliced right through the pants and across the shin; now that he saw the blood, the Woodsman no longer felt he could walk, and the battle-strength ebbed from him. He sat down, gasping and chuckling by turns, and popped open one healing bottle to use on himself as a test.

Thin liquid would have meant a drink, slower to act but more deeply efficacious. Tipping the bottle, Treaman saw a thicker syrup nudge out—a salve then. Laving it on the cut, he felt the marvelous tingle and watched as the wound closed over in seconds, leaving behind only a thin scar that might or might not last. His boot was sopping with blood; Treaman noted he'd better move slowly for awhile, and not stand up too quickly. Still chuckling, he made his way back to the group bearing his tray of plunder. Hallah pipped contentedly to spot him leaving the wagon; she landed around his shoulders, falling asleep in moments.

Mhoral's arm bite was fairly straightforward: Treaman was relieved as he poured salve on, to note that the helldog saliva did not appear to be resisting its effect. Though it burned and popped when touching flesh there was no apparent poison defying the unguent's touch. After Mhoral rubbed it in, Treaman could feel no heat from infection beneath the scar.

"You want to… try some, on your face?" he asked hesitantly.

Mhoral reached for a jar, then drew his hand back and shook his visored head. "Perhaps later. If there's any left." Even without eye contact, Treaman knew the Elf agreed with his guess—the draining touch of the revenant in the haunted keep, which left those white facial scars, was beyond the reach of this ointment. Just as with the arbalest, not to know was the happier course.

Treaman left a salve with Linya, rather than try to apply it himself. She nodded and turned away with one arm crossed, keeping her torn tunic and scarred breasts from view. The Woodsman could not imagine how much that must hurt, and found he couldn't even wish her well without feeling guilty. He shook his head vigorously and turned to Bildon kneeling next to Braja in the turf.

"Give him two or three," he said, handing several jars to the Stealthic. "I have to get back to Haltar."

Over by the ruined wagon, he saw the strapping warrior again working to sit, and even stand despite his injuries. Jogging up, Treaman lightly kicked one heel out from under his leader, dropping him back to the ground with a grunt.

"You will do as you are told, Hope damn you."

"Tired… of waiting," he grouched through his pain. Treaman put one jar's worth on Haltar's side, then scrounged cloth strips for a binding before slathering two doses beneath a bandage he rigged for his shoulder. He pulled the dressings as tight as he could, evincing another gasp from the tall warrior as he sat on a chest, and tied them snugly between Haltar's shoulderblades where he couldn't reach them.

"I will change those tomorrow. If you're not dead, by which I mean you haven't been such a raging nuisance that I decide to kill you. You will leave those alone until noon tomorrow at the earliest; then we'll see if more will do any good."

"I'll be fine," Haltar said with characteristic indifference, as if he could continue adventuring without his right shoulder and arm. He stood and experimented with flexing his limb; when Treaman kicked him, he only grinned back and started in the party's direction. After a couple of steps, he relented enough to rest his left hand on the Woodsman's shoulder. Treaman spent the time muttering curses under his breath, while Haltar laughed and suggested better ones.

Back with the others, the laughing stopped. Braja lay half on his back—as far as the Halfling could force him alone—hardly breathing and with a ragged scar across the right cheek and jaw that almost ignored the salves. So much skin had been torn out; the bleeding stopped but teeth were clearly visible above, and a bit of jaw below. Braja was either sleeping or unconscious. In the distance the helldogs bayed again, and it sounded like a dirge indeed for the giant black warrior.

"He crawled all this way, look," Treaman muttered, "to bring us the whip. Probably saved our lives."

Haltar eased to the ground nearby. "Pelian may have had more powerful salves in his wagon. Check that out."

"Soon," Treaman responded. "First, I'm pitching that tent he offered us."

Haltar nodded and settled back on the grass. "Might want to sheathe the Sword of Air, after you clean it."

Linya stood with her cloak on backwards to cover the damage. "I'll check Pelian's wagon. And perhaps find some new clothes."

"He was a wizard alright," Treaman said to her, turning back to unfold the center pole and spread the canvas with Bildon's help. He erected the tent centered between Haltar and Braja, staking out the sides and directing Bildon and Mhoral to bring gear and firewood inside it as he flipped up the smoke hole he'd been shown. By Braja, he reflected grimly.

"This won't do anything if those three-legged horrors come back," Mhoral pointed out.

"A wagon with reinforced sides didn't keep them out," Treaman countered. "This is for the rain." The Elf nodded; no one mentioned the idea of leaving the Sword of Air far away while they slept. But once the blade was retrieved, wiped clean and sheathed, Treaman handed the lash to Mhoral and put the sword next to his bedroll. Go down swinging.

He started a small flame and set some water on. As night fell, Bildon scampered quietly around the camp and relayed back with armloads of useful things, dumping them to one side of the entrance flap. Linya returned hauling two sacks filled to their rims. From one, she produced various odds and ends of clothing, not the guard uniforms but soft colors and weaves matching a set she had chosen for herself. Treaman guessed the other held some of Pelian's sorcerous inventory worth keeping; from near the top she withdrew a set of long parchment-wrapped bands. Breaking one open she drew out a flat linen strip; consulting a small set of papers, Linya carefully laid three strips directly across Braja's ravaged jaw; Treaman smelled something sharp, but not unpleasant, like a fruit from the Southern Empire.

"Is that going to help, you think?" Mhoral asked.

"Oh no," Bildon quipped, "it's an aphrodisiac, Mhoral; because you know, the tongue is the sexiest part—"

Mhoral threw a tankard and hit the Halfling in the head, producing a curse and a chuckle.

"I'm not certain," Linya replied. "These instructions indicate the strips are for serious healing. I think if it does work, we could try it on Haltar's shoulder."

"I'll be fine," came the leader's voice from his prone form in the shadows.

The others took turns expressing doubts of that, in various degrees of pungency, then exchanged inquiries after each other's health. Treaman reflected they were the walking wounded, excepting Bildon as always. For all the risks he embraced, Treaman could count on the fingers of one hand the number of times the Stealthic had taken a serious injury. But his own leg no longer hurt and he hadn't felt dizzy, so he should count himself among the able-bodied.

"If our fearless leader can walk tomorrow," he said while sitting at the flap facing out, "we'll need… to make a decision." Everyone glanced at Braja. "The corpses here, and those monsters still around."

"The two we slew were definitely looking for the Sword of Air," Mhoral pointed out.

"Based on what I saw," Treaman said, "through Hallah, I mean. Based on that, they all were. Ten, maybe twelve of them."

"You say the others chased after the man in black?" Linya asked wonderingly.

Treaman recounted what he saw of the battle from his miniature dragon's view, hardly able to believe his own words. But Bildon confirmed from his scavenging, there were at least three dead beasts beyond the one Treaman slew with the Sword of Air.

"I have never, never seen a man fight that well," the Woodsman sighed. "He was… like one of the heroes returned. From the stories I heard as a child."

"A martial wizard," Mhoral asserted, "I'd bet the dragon's treasure on that. Fighting with the bare hand is a lost skill, they say, outside the Crystal City. He might even be one of The Five who rule Araluntir's capital."

"Yet," Linya murmured, "how could he still be alive? Out here for who knows how long, alone, and now with a hell-pack on his trail."

"We can't worry about that," Bildon said, "he's a better fighter against these things than we are, if I can believe my own eyes. Astor willing, he survives—maybe we meet someday, stranger things have happened. But we need to take care of ourselves."

"Right," Treaman replied, "so where to? Tomorrow, let us say we can leave. Reghalion? Or back to Trainertown."

The question hung in the semi-dark of the tent; either Haltar was asleep or he chose not to answer.

Treaman stood. "Get some rest, I'll stand first watch." He slipped outside and let his eyes adjust to the night. The clouds had started to clear and stars showed through. He wasn't certain but Treaman thought he could make out the dim bulk of Skysword to the south and east. No way to know which direction Pelian had traveled, during the previous day while they slept inside the wagon. And traditional orientation wasn't worth spit in the wind here in the Percentalion.

Yet Pelian managed it somehow. The thought of the caravan plowing slowly through this chaos-land, the captive collared helldog in the box, Braja's whip; what had one of the men called it, the lead-beast. Suddenly it made sense. Who knew how, but Pelian had been able to capture and subdue a helldog; by plying it with the whip, he forced it to direct him across the Percentalion, around or through the changes that so bedeviled other travelers.

The more he thought about it, the more it seemed like very bad news to Treaman.

"What's on your mind?" Bildon asked quietly from immediately next to him, and Treaman cursed, punching the chuckling Halfling.

"I'm thinking, after I murder the Stealthic, that we are lucky to be left alone here."

"The helldogs? Yes, a good break that they were distracted. With luck we'll soon give them the slip when the next chaos-shift occurs."

"I don't think so," Treaman replied grimly, and he repeated his thoughts for the Halfling's benefit.

Bildon whistled in appreciation. "So they should be able to track us as long as we carry the Sword, over anything."

"That would be my guess."

"Then answer me this, great sage. Why did the pack stop following the Sword of Air?"

"Better than that," Treaman countered. "What would they have done had they gotten it?"

Neither friend had any answers to that. But after a time, Bildon's chuckling became audible and only grew.

"What is the matter with you?" Treaman demanded testily, though he half-expected the answer.

"The indices of danger are quite strong," Bildon said through a fierce grin; saluting with two fingers he went back inside the tent.

Treaman shook his head a long while, for no one's benefit, and then started to stroll around the faintly-glowing tent within the ring of death. He pictured a helldog, having slain the party, snatching up the Sword of Air in its teeth. Fetch. But who could have sent them?

He wondered about the man in black, and uttered a prayer to Helmon, to guide him safely through the wilds and away from the monsters on his trail. A different black man lay within the tent. Treaman thought it might be foolish to trust him, but Braja's sacrifice had probably saved the group, and the Woodsman wanted desperately for him to survive.

The lower moon Aral started its fast rise to the north, confirming Treaman's sense of direction at least for now. No dark cloud banks showed in the sky; perhaps the party could gain a few hours' rest.

The helldog pack bayed in the distance, rageful and aroused; Treaman froze completely, body and soul. He heard the echo, felt the gentle breeze from what would be the east of north in a sane world. The sound itself, the precise direction and distance choked him with confusion and fear. It might have been several minutes before he heard Linya saying his name; only then could he turn his head. The look on his face reflected in alarm from hers.

"What's wrong? Are they near, are they coming? Treaman, are you alright?"

"Linya," he croaked at her, heart racing faster even than fear could make it. "How—how far away would you say that was?"

"I? I have no idea, you are the outdoorsman here."

"Was it closer than last time, just tell me your opinion? A league away?"

"I thought it was further. But I could be wrong. A league? Perhaps. Why, what's wrong?"

Treaman nodded, his mouth dry, staring off at the horizon and straining to see in the growing light of rising Aral. He sniffed the breeze and rubbed his fingers together.

"Do you see—in the distance there northeast, does that seem like a ridge to you?"

"I can't see anything, Treaman. Tell me, what's the matter."

"I agree with you, Linya. That helldog pack was a league away, maybe further. And they were on the track of that man in black. I could hear it, they have raised his scent or seen him."

"That poor man."

"That poor man can take care of himself. But I heard them. You heard them."

"Yes, so?"

"Linya. From a league away."

"Treaman!"

"Linya, we are in the Percentalion. Every step we take we could be swept a hundred leagues. What weather, what terrain have we ever seen that lasted as long as that chase has already? I can make out a low ridge there in the distance: I think it is driving the echoes of the hunt back to us. Linya, as I make it out… that's three leagues away. And the breeze, the weather. It feels like autumn here, now."

He faced her as some of what he was saying sank in.

"You mean," she said slowly, "things are returning to normal?"

"Or we are already in a place, near a village, something like that. Or… or the area has become more normal, around us, because of… I don't know what. But we should not be able to hear the sounds of a chase in this blasted land, or see terrain at this distance. That's all I know."

The young mage patted his arm as if in thanks. "Perhaps this is good news. Tomorrow you'll take us the best way."

Treaman swallowed his doubt and tried to look confident. "Good night, Linya. Sleep well."

The flap closed behind her, and Aral was almost fully up. Treaman was sure he could make out the ridge in the distance. Once more the distant pack bayed in brash, hateful unison; they were getting close, impatient for victory. But before the echo fully died, Treaman whirled in the opposite direction, for a howl—or scream—he had never heard before. Further off, so far he couldn't be sure at first, rising in pitch and horribly changing in tenor even as it grew. Solitary, agonized, fighting and surrendering at the same time.

The Woodsman could sense without looking that the party stood behind him, all of them drawn to that awful keening cry.

"A wolf?"

"A man, dying."

"Another helldog? No, different."

"And so far away," Treaman breathed in wonder.

They waited nearly an hour after that solitary wail died out, but nothing further occurred to disturb the night, except that Aral made it a third-way up the northern sky and Unal behind it began to rise. The others went back to bed and Treaman paced, straining to see in all directions and convinced, at least once or twice, that he could.

Twenty-Fifth Fire Ant, ADR 1995

My Dearest Kia,

No airy words, no attempt at wit to cover my blame and the anguish I suffer. I realize full well the unseemly length of our separation, now more than three weeks longer than either of us had thought. And the blame rests fully with me, as you justly point out—though your tone was lighthearted and meant merely to tease, I must tell you I felt the point keenly. I deny in all seriousness what you accuse me of in jest—Conar, this City of Wonders and capital of Hope, holds no allure for me and I desire nothing so much as to return to Mendel, to the land of time-proper, and to you dear heart.

But the commands of Kings cannot be put aside! It stuns me to write that, but you know full well not only Conantis XXI but also our own Ageless Monarch Tithalis have instructed me to remain in Conar, though I hope as ever to see the end of my detention now. Three weeks they have kept me here, repeating to the Board of Sages every fact I can recall from our adventure— that word!— in the Hopeward, poring over the ancient texts in the theater's scriptorium for further clues beyond what Natasha and Alendic had found, consulting with high lords, mages and preachers on the possible meaning of all that intrepid pair had uncovered.

My fondest wish, aside from my return to you, is that I might never have to think on this nightmare again; instead, I relive it each day, finding new aspects of horror and loss and reopening old wounds until they become scabbed in layers like the shingles of a thatch roof. My dear, had you only met Natasha, you would know why the nation of Men grieves her as if dead—as indeed to them she is, for the gate will not open again until all but the youths have passed away. I speak to knights and wizards now, whose sons and successors will join me in 2045 for the return visit. I shudder at that prospect—what shall we find of her... how wise and ageless they will all think me then, and how utterly inadequate will I be to serve as the focus of their hopes. I have no earthly idea how I shall bear it, and have had not a single hour's respite to meditate on the path I must take to that august wisdom. Please help me in this.

It is, on balance, the very worst of times to be completely alone in the world. I weep without you, dearest, and do not blush to admit it.

Even the loss of Solemn Judgement weighs heavily on me now. Over a fortnight since I saw his sail leaving the Bay of Conar, and yet his memory is fresh. It is too soon, perhaps, for even a fortunate and skillful sailor to have hailed the Mendelian coast, but I hope every day that some word will come. I have left instructions, via the blessed few who are allowed to travel in an instant from Conar to Mendel by gate, that any missive from him should be sought for and relayed. I live in dread that my inaction, my idiotic lack of foresight, left him alone in the challenge he faced, and which he brought off so brilliantly but at such cost to himself.

We hear word, from the far north, that young Pron Dedicar already distinguishes himself in the defence of Novar's borders and is risen in fame and stature among those brave and hard-pressed settlers of the snow-bound colony. That knight is free, and fighting for his future place and the hand of his betrothed, because my young protégé foresaw his dilemma, and stopped at nothing to quietly unravel the knot of the Law, giving him a chance to transform his penance into redemption through a custom that nearly all the people had forgotten.

I think of Dedicar and resolve to fight, in my own way, for my people, for the rescue of my dear friend, and of course for your hand, beloved. I must do so with mere words, spoken well or translated properly; I fight to bring light to dark histories, and to defeat the threat posed by the secrets of our past.

And the mention of secrets reminds me—why, when I already suffer the lack of you, would you seek to amplify my misfortune by writing so enigmatically of a surprise that awaits my return! Your tone seemed friendly, as indeed I should hope from the love of my life! Yet you withhold the substance, as if it were some trivial matter. Be not so cruel! Or else be minded that you are not possessed of the knowledge of Rallantan in all matters wise. I too, harbor some small fact, of the particulars I shall not yet write more fully. See to it, madam, that you are more forthcoming with me unless it should chance that you miss some news from my side.

But under no circumstances let us quarrel, love. Hold close whatever news you may wish—perhaps your uncertainty, like mine, whispers it better to risk delay than disappointment in a matter not fully decided. Hold my love for you even closer, and believe as I do that the days of our separation will end soon. It may even—but no, I shall not risk the chance of being wrong in something so important to my life and hopes.

Until I may hear from you again, soon, I remain
Yours,

Cedrith

After-Word: in haste—Our secrets both sprung! And I fear to my ruin. By inveighing upon the authorities in all diligence, I was able to secure permission for a brief leave, and to my joy also allowed to use the gate from Conar's palace to Mendel. So I pen these words to you from the land of time-proper, whose air I have not breathed in half a year. I stand but a handful of leagues from where you are! Yet no sooner arrived than I heard of the death of your mother-sister, whom I knew only distantly but of such support to you and your parents for so long. I grieved, even as my selfish heart thought it would occasion an excuse to see you, for surely the funeral rites would demand my attendance. Alas! The officials here have received word of some discovery or other in the texts of the scriptorium, almost as soon as I had left the City of Wonders. Now the King's own Chancellor, meeting me—me!— in person, has politely but firmly "requested" that I return at once, close upon the end of my official business.

I pleaded the seriousness of the family death, asked for just a single evening's furlough, and was denied. I pointed to my inadequacy with the Ancient texts, but was answered that my experience of the Hopeward trumped all other considerations.

So close to you!

And I heard the outcome of your news as well, relayed by a comrade here in the Sages Guild. Your mother-sister, meeting her end without direct issue, graciously decided to will to you her home. I am overcome—and I cannot name the emotion that whelms me. I am torn in two.

They demand my return on the instant. For my part I have commanded—yes!— that they bring this letter, with all speed to you. The high powers of the lands respond to my wishes now, so important they think me. I feel guilt at their respect, and wish for nothing more than a well-deserved anonymity that would bring me to my love the sooner. In Grief and Haste, Yours, C.

⊕⊕⊕

The lightning-spiked midnight storm is the kind sane folk flee. Only the very brave, or the completely unhinged, stay and gape at this joust of nature's crushing majesty, holding drenched and drawn as sheets of icy pins hammer against the head, until they are blown down by the gusts or perish in shivers. No animal, no Child of Hope would remain an instant on this exposed runnel of rock in the face of such deafening fury; not many trees have resisted its land-gouging force this night.

But for the garruk, nothing trumps the call to war.

Seven-score males had met, an hour ago at dusk when the chaos-skies over the Percentalion still showed clear. The separate bands came in mutual sight at the whim of some perverse intent under late autumn stars. Since that moment, only the code of battle mattered.

No thought of numbers or death deters the garruk male at war, no chance for escape or plan for alliance interferes with the driving need to fight and kill. By preference, they would slay humans or elves, had chance brought them within reach. But the Percentalion runs nearly empty of such goodly victims— and their Despairing masters of millenia ago, those with the sorcery to stifle and channel the battle-rage, are beyond even the vestigal thought of such short-lived reavers.

Heedless of rain-spiked gale above and churning earth below, despite blasts of fire from heaven that strike in their midst, the garruk battle on, stabbing and chewing each other with ferocious concentration. Two tangled shrub-oaks roll directly through the melee, gnarled branches snared in an embrace of wood that imitates the combatants. A lance of white light destroys a boulder at the periphery, spitting lethal shards of granite through limbs and necks. The garruk battle on.

And none of them notice, at first, the golden shimmer of a portal unseen by any eyes in precisely five years. The lightning stutters, offering a glimpse of dark-white sticks tumbling through the door, mixed with tattered cloth and leather strips, supernatural trash dumped from another world.

On all sides the combat rages, and less than half the garruk are still alive. Growls, curses, the clash of metal—this mortal clamor barely carries beneath the pounding howl of the wind; each few seconds the blinding light presages a deafening crack that strikes like a blow. Yet through the unearthly, urgent din it becomes increasingly apparent that someone is cackling.

Now shines a cluster of silent purple flashes, originating from the heart of the battle. No fog or dust could fight this wind and water, but an indigo haze spreads out contrary to nature. Those garruk still living at once break their death-clenches and flee howling to the nearby ridge, where they stand hunched and gasping in the grip of an unaccustomed fear. Behind them, the defeated dead now rise from the rain-battered ground, shuffling after former foes and kin alike. The living turn and rally into a rough line, temporarily banded against a common enemy: but hacking a face does little to deter an enemy already missing an arm. Sorcerous bolts dart in from the cackle of bones in the back, and steadily the ranks of undead warriors swell. Soon, only the lifeless are still moving.

The storm is passing, but Wolga Vrule was never in danger. Moving among the ranks of his army, the liche reaches into a garruk's chest. The bones of his one good hand carve through muscle and ribcage with scarcely any resistance; as the undead thrall jerks in spasms that its brain no longer records, he clenches and withdraws a shapeless, beating blob already bereft of blood and regards it with the satisfaction of a taste long denied, a habit too much forborne. Raising his other arm he gestures in a complex motion—this limb lacks a hand and Wolga Vrule grimaces, muttering with the unwonted concentration required. But the shadowed veil parts at last, and he thrusts the heart within, to rest in a crystal globe prepared at the very beginning, now holding only a thick layer of ash on its bottom, from myriad previous servitors. As the liche moves on the portal remains open, showing a cave where the light-stones faded long ago and the entrance has been blocked with stones. Vrule moves along, carving out hearts to feed the sphere in the faraway cave.

The hour and more it takes to complete his gaunt-company flies by for the liche who has waited nearly four millenia for his freedom. Everything amuses him— an unaccustomed stumble over rough rock, the way one of his loyal servitors limps on a half-severed leg, the distant call of reaver-birds, frustrated that no meal awaits them from the still-moving garruk band. It is all hilarious, even the need to draw breath for laughter is a source of delight.

Only one body still lies atop the ridge where the last living made their stand; an enormous red-cloaked specimen ribboned with gashes and gasping through its tusks. Pleased, Wolga Vrule approaches and speaks to him in a useless lisp, chuckling at each failed sentence and shuffling a step closer as the dying war-leader claws to shift away.

With gestures from his bony arms, the liche makes clear the subject of his speech as his dried lips and stump-tongue no longer can. A wave, to indicate the ranks of his bodyguard; one glance skyward from his ebony eye-stalks, to gauge the moon's position and orient himself. Then he turns and scribes a great circle to southward, pausing to indicate the stops ahead in his path of conquest, on a mind-map that only Wolga Vrule can see. He mutters and lisps in glee, then kneels paternally next to the near-corpse of the garruk chieftain in agony. He gestures without the missing hand, and continues garbling his condolences as he twists off a replacement from the giant foe.

While its body writhes in shock beside him, Vrule incants and calls; the still-twitching hand smokes with heat against the night chill, its leaking blood turns thick and darkens even further. Placing it against his stump, the liche calls out tones backed by eldritch force; taking his bony hand away, he flexes new fingers experimentally and chortles, well satisfied. He sniffs the unclean flesh, takes an experimental nibble, shrugs and turns again to regard the dying donor. Placing his new-won hand against its former owner's face, he stifles the final groans and draws life forth from the massive frame with steam and scarring.

Again and again the liche calls out, pumping more vitality from skull through hand to self. Suddenly, a blast of sheer lightning arcs from the clear sky and strikes him directly, as if the heavens protest this abomination and try to clear him from the earth. Vrule ignores it, standing tall and filled with energy denied him these many centuries. As he turns and bellows his exultation, the corpse of the handless war-chief draws up behind him to glide over the ground, a glint of hunger in its eyes nearly hidden by an inch-thick layer of spider-webbed scars. At a signal, the revenant surrenders its cloak to its master the liche, covering a multitude of patches and rot in its fulsome folds.

The liche sets out now, marching south for the moment and followed by a band of gaunts with a gliding, ghostly chieftain for lieutenant. The autumn stars speak of the harvest, and Vrule nods in agreement that the first fruits have been good. The leagues are long, but time means little when death's door already lies behind.

At intervals, the weather threatens, the enormous mountain looming under starlight to the southeast quavers. The master of death merely laughs, incants and points skyward; tides of cloud roll back, vision steadies, the land obeys him and those he leads. Ahead, separated only by distance, lies the hamlet where he sent his catspaw. Kog, despite the demon's chaos-nature, could be counted on to react with a spasm of destruction on its first taste of freedom. Surely, ahead lies a village-worth of new recruits for his army.

From there, marching steadily through the chaos that turns all mortals askew, he will set his course more directly east, for the great mountain. On the way, practically in Skysword's shadow, lies the brick city by the river, the old outpost of Despair's rule. His army will grow to thousands there: and the few left in the capital Reghalion are already dead.

Vrule did not spend the ages in prison idly. Studying his flesh-made maps and observing the movement of these insect-foes, he carefully crafted his plans. The prison-gate finally opened this night, releasing him despite all those mortals could do. Now he gazes at the stars above and reflects that the heavens augur his victory. The year of the Sun is appropriate to a time when great mysteries will at last be revealed. The cycle is Death, which could hardly be more apt to his coming, and the season presages Convergence among the elements, a process Vrule intends to hasten. His feckless ally the Earth Demon plays its part and helps him without knowing.

Poor Kog, shunning any plan, yet so easily predicted. Believing the earthly chaos it creates trumps all, the demon no doubt spends its time chasing the lost Eye, leaving the Tridium in play until too late. Kog's mistake lies in thinking that Despair can never find power through the law. Yet Vrule and his band remain unharmed, moving through this cursed land in obedience to Vrule's mind, his strategy and lore.

Five days, perhaps six, will bring them to the village where his rook left him recruits. Another week will bring him to the city of brick; the proud woman holds a replacement for his recently-lost scepter; the lawful might inherent in that tool can be bent to his needs. It, and she, will make excellent additions to Vrule's power by the end of the month. Perhaps, he thinks with another ghastly hiss of laughter, there may even be the chance to settle accounts with that dung-monkey in grey before the end. Yes, thinks the lord of undeath, by rights that one should be last.

I am Kog.

Beneath a bright sunlit sky, surrounded by crumbling ashen walls and the remnants of smoking corpses, a crimson thing chews its way to birth. As it emerges from the vaguely-female shell that held it, the red horned being is barely the size of a housecat. By the time it rips clear of its moaning birth-mother, it stands as tall as a teenaged boy. It turns, and feasts—and with the last gobbet lobbed into a cask-sized jaw, the demon stands over eight feet tall and nearly half as broad.

All evidence of its inception now consumed, the creature immediately forgets ever having been smaller or unborn, and believes in its own identity and purpose.

Lord of the center kingdom, I rule this land. Only my whim is law.

With a mind awakening to the ages of its past life, the demon gazes about the wrack of Hollinsfen with both eyes, and knows with certainty that this was its handiwork, and well done indeed. Only Kog created the flame waves, destroyed these humans for its pleasure, only Kog summoned the hell-pack and set them on the trail of Law a few days ago. To Kog shall they report when all who guard that Hope-trinket are dead, to him they will surrender it. Then the Percentalion will be fully under its rightful rule once again. But first—

There is an imposter.

The demon knows of this other self, and hates it more even than Areghel and Hope. It dwells on the effrontery, the blasphemy committed by the fraud, and new waves of flame wash off him in all directions. This substitute pretends to be Earth Demon, asserts that Kog is but offspring.

I am eternal! No beginning for me, and to my rule there will be no ending. I am Kog!

And Kog can feel it, knows generally where it is now. Just one of several things the imposter cannot know.

Kog alone is able to follow such a trace, because this is my kingdom. I see already, yet it is too weak to sense me—has already lost an eye fighting with some mortal, a further sign, and now chases my prize to improve this pretence.

I, Kog, will take it in ambush and show it true strength, force its submission before I consume the imposter to grow my own being.

With a deep grinding chuckle, the dread demon stomps off on its trio of trunk-legs, tail lashing in anticipation and new arm-limbs sprouting, falling off, wriggling back to rejoin the body as it plays with new shapes. Tripling its head, the demon looks in all directions and its three maws chatter in counterpoint, praising Kog and hailing its return to rule. Dimly, briefly, this young Kog reflects there is perhaps one thing forgotten, a fact its mind cannot bring to the fore like a familiar name not heard in ages. It is surely of no importance.

The massive body plows directly through a segment of the wood-and-wattle wall surrounding this deserted village, whose name the demon never bothered to learn before destroying it. Kog will resume control of the hell-pack, hunt down the three points of Law, and slaughter all in its path before resuming rule in the capital.

But first, the imposter.

One head is startled to spot a group of beings slowly approaching from the distant north. Only a ragged band of garruk, about to be disappointed in their attempt to raid. No harvest of earthly wealth here, and the invaders are not worth the effort it would take to suborn them now, when there is puissant death to be effected. Perhaps later, if Kog decides to invade the outer kingdoms. At the moment, the lord of chaos is in a hurry, and may decide to gate itself anyway. Besides, this band looks broken, moves as if they were dead. Destroying the imposter is much more important, as impulses go. More important, it feels, than any such desire it has felt before in ages.

Little does the demon realize this craving, but an hour old, is indeed the desire of a lifetime.

⊕⊕⊕

The broad-fletched marine arrow arced down from the Mendelian merchant ship to lodge in the hull of the corsair pursuing her, not a foot from where Captain Vonn gripped the rail. Smiling, he noted the design of the haft and feathers—three stripes of green, one of yellow—and made a note of it for later. Just like the lazy greedy Elves to mark all their goods, saved them the work of making new ones. And the pirate lord held nothing against the unseen archer, for wanting to slay the most dreaded vandal on the Western Ocean. Only death awaited the entire crew of the merchant in all events, now she had dared to run instead of striking sail at the first hail of his *Shrike*. But Vonn would see to making this corpse personally.

He bellowed for his first mate, and the hump-backed thug snapped around from the foredeck to answer. "A point to windward, Stirno, let's not give her a chance to escape us around that cape ahead."

"Aye, captain."

"No flame, let us take her entire. And Stirno—three green-to-yellow, that bravo's mine."

"Aye, sir" the first mate replied with a predatory grin, which all the boarding party shared.

"Ho, below decks!" Vonn yelled in Elvish at the captives furiously laboring the galley-oars to the pound of the metal drum-sheet. *"Pull now for yer lives, or sharks will eat well before sunset. Remember, slaves, this bounty will be yer third; serve well and ye'll exchange places with yon merchant crew."*

Vonn smiled benignly on the chained men below, happy that the tavern-tales the pirate league spread through its spies did so much work for so little effort. Three plunders to freedom, the merchant crews all swore—more liable to surrender at first, more willing to work hard the while, and all the more amusing, when a captain lost count, or fed the sharks despite the tale. No witnesses, there was the main thing.

On cue, the first mate pointed astern and called back, "What about him, then?" and Vonn, so near now to his prize, was jerked to recollection. Turning, he sighted carefully against the western sun and spotted again the distant blot of his pursuer. Nothing new about it, now as ever since the day he'd first seen it a week ago. A one-man craft, wending its way through the treacherous waters of the Bay of Ma-Eldar, between the rocky cliffs and haunted isles, on a voyage somewhere between Conar and Mendel as few sane captains attempted in this age without a naval escort. When he saw the loon at first, Vonn gave pursuit, despite the puny prize, on general principles; but the sailor aboard was quite adept at seacraft, and more, was clearly willing to run west, into the open ocean, where the *Shrike* lost its advantage. The corsair turned back into the shipping lanes then, and the skiff had seemed content to amble after him, in the general direction of Mendel south by east.

Some in the crew grumbled it was a scout, sent by one of the crowns to track them to the lair that formed the backbone of the pirate league's strength. The first mate, before Vonn had stared him down, was heard to comment mayhap it was a great mage from the City of Glass, seeking adventure. That was an ill thought indeed. Vonn had been just a second mate, two dead men away from his captaincy when the pirate fleet attempted to storm Araluntir in the spring of 1990. Twelve vessels sunk for their trouble and no ship came within bowshot of the docks; the pirate league nearly foundered that day. But the mages were not known to venture forth from Araluntir, content to shelter behind their walls of mystic protection and brew their wizardry apart from the world.

While the league regained its strength— and filled many vacancies, fortunately for Vonn and the next generation of pirates— the mages made no further move. Yet rumor insisted one among them had recently snuck away, by devious means and without the leave of The Five. If this lonely mariner were he, Vonn was in no mind to give further chase. But if true, why did he flee at all? It was a conundrum beyond the corsair's impatient mind to resolve.

So Vonn had ignored him, moving generally south by east towards Eldarport through the isles and back to hunting larger game. The skiff seemed to follow, though at too great a distance to make out many details. There it was still, but Vonn's blood was up now for the fight, and if the sole sailor was a great mage, it had been time enough for him to show his mettle. Through the glass, Vonn was unable to decipher even if it were an old man, by the glint of his hair, or a youth, by the spryness of his movements. Old or young, he was only one man.

The elvish archer aboard the *Moon of Plenty* was so moved by his near-miss that he actually cursed aloud, drawing the attention of Captain Thiel. Though the merchant also felt the miss keenly, he knew a loss of composure among his crew would be the end of them today, so he ignored the profanity and strolled down deck as if checking the depths, casually coming nearer his crewman, clapping him lightly on the back in consolation.

"An excellent shot, Lianon, who can handle the swells on two craft at this distance?"

The archer nodded curtly in understanding, but his face was still a shade too angry.

"We'll need our best shot in the crow's-perch above," the captain continued, looking him clear in the eye to convey the praise and then gesturing as much in permission as command. The young elf leaped to the rope-ladder with none of the sullen bravado that clouded the mind of most Man-crews, or an argument that he needed to be closer to the action. Thiel smiled to see once again his drop of honey work so much better than a shouted order, or an upbraid. It was how he had run his crew since he started at sea three decades ago, and if this was the day he died, he would rather meet his moment than change his command style.

He ran his fingers through hair still vigorous and untouched by the age that would have overtaken any of his man-brethren in Conar, and turned his sea-green eyes to look ahead at the island coast so near his port side, then back at the corsair angling for his starboard stern quarter. Forgamon's Isle on the charts, and Thiel knew it well. No inhabitants, as no being was brave enough to willingly shelter on any island in the Bay. Once or twice Thiel had weighed anchor near the shallow beaches on her northern, windward side and sent ashore by noon's light to gather water or even wood. But the southern shore he coasted now held only rocky cliffs higher than his foremast, and shoals he could never hope to draft above. At the cliff tops, tough blackened pines clung tenaciously to the edge, growing half-aslant as if frozen in mid-dive to the waters below. The shade of those tree-lined cliffs loomed over both hunter and hunted, in silent, lifeless anticipation of the battle in the offing and closing off the northern gusts that might have given him a chance at escape. Half a league to the wind, and it might as well be halfway to Argens.

"Shall we try to round the cape then?" Thiel asked Gannet his first mate, who looked at the oncoming pirate and nodded grimly.

"They'll overtake us, more than likely, sir, but it's our best chance. A point to windward?"

"Yes, and two points if she'll let us, though I doubt it," Thiel responded in a fey humor. "He's a mariner, this one. I think we'll probably—"

"Sail ho, Captain," came Lianon's voice from the perch, and everyone snapped to see his arm pointing astern. Even the helmsman, in the midst of his course-change, looked back, each sailor straining with elvish sight to make out the chance of hope on the horizon. Few saw anything, but their lookout insisted. "A one-man craft, sir, I don't know how she's out on these seas at all, but she's hugging the cliffs like a stone-crab."

Thiel caught a brief sight of her, not even the size of a fishing yawl, and his heart sank. His crew required some statement, though; striding back to the reardeck, he called out.

"We shall at least have a witness to how we acquit ourselves today."

The sailors grunted in agreement, then returned to the frantic business of tying off loose gear, limbering their weapons, and taking a few more judicious arrow shots as the corsair closed in. The oarsmen changed shifts on cue, as if they were not under imminent attack, the new men happy to lend their fresh strength to increase speed and the old rowers willingly taking up pins and knives to defend them. Lianon struck a member of the pirate boarding party full in the chest, and cried out in triumph as the crew cheered. But Thiel could not take his eyes from the beak on the prow of the pirate vessel churning just beneath the water, showing a wicked iron hook above the foam, making straight for his own rear quarter with the promise of violence to his hull. Perhaps the moment had come for all of them, he thought as he uttered a prayer to the Hopelord of Elves. Ma-Eldar, whose islands here had formed the first capital of Hope before the ruin. Captain Thiel prayed that if their spirits still haunted these places in search of the lost promise of their landing, that the first Elves of Hope might be assuaged to some small degree by the courage their children displayed today.

Vonn saw at once that the Elvish captain ahead was trying to make his way past the lee of the small island they both tacked southeast of, to catch some wind and amplify the efforts of his rowers. The merchant galleas had that advantage, but it would have mattered more on a windy day; as it was, its crew had too few oars, and too much weight, to get away from the sleek corsair, whose one mast was stepped down now for extra speed. It was either stand clear of the island's rocky shore, which would take the merchantman too far off the wind, or wreck on the unknown shoals in an effort to keep it. Vonn preferred the former, for he wanted the ship as a prize, not merely to plunder its best and sink her. Thus his new course took him closer to those rocks, but he depended on the skill of his helmsman and the shallower draft of the *Shrike* to see him through.

As the two larger vessels hove relentlessly closer he could make out individuals on deck; the arrows came thicker now, but he sheltered behind the rail and chuckled to hear them stick harmlessly in the *Shrike's* side. His boarding party, all the crew except three men to mind the chained slaves below, crouched ready as well, firing back on occasion but mainly waiting with swords, boat-hooks and pins for the ram to do its work. With a fleeing foe, the impact would be gentler, the hole smaller; plenty of time to patch her up once the crew was slain. His men outnumbered the Elves nearly two to one.

Looking back one last time, Vonn could not at first make out the skiff; it was hugging the island cliffs, and everything aboard her seemed the same hue as the stone behind. The lone sailor was wending among those same shoals, his draft nearly nonexistent and darting through rocky places even Vonn did not know well. A dangerous, and stupid game that; for safety, he may as well turn and flee as use the double-edged blade of the island's coast to shelter him. It was as if the man aboard wished to watch the fight, and risked his craft and life for the privilege of a front-row seat.

The boarding fight went almost exactly as Vonn expected. The merchant galleas, clearing the windward cape a few lengths before the pursuing corsair, rapidly put up both sails to catch the afternoon breeze. But that would hardly have added to the speed of its oarsmen, and the pirates responded with their acid-bearing arrows, striking the sheets before they were even full and spreading holes the height of a man until they resembled the rags of a beggar, or the torn dress of a helpless woman.

The exchange of bow-fire continued as well, and Vonn lost three men before the ram, moving just three or four knots faster than its target, nosed almost gently into the stern quarter. It barely broke the hull, less violent than a ravisher's kiss, and its hook held the victim close, disallowing escape while plugging most of the leak for now. In this love-bout, the climax would come with a rush of men, not water. Only after the rapture, when the pirate vessel disengaged, could the rounded, feminine hull begin to fill and sink; they'd patch her. But now the joyous time of rapine was upon the crew, and they swarmed aboard looking for blood as much as pillage. The slave-rowers below, knowing their job and the penalty for shiftlessness, held oars against the waves to keep the two boats locked in their embrace of rape and death.

Vonn swung alone by rope to the center of the merchant, and hewed the Elven marines left and right with the skill he'd gained from eighteen years as a pirate, even before he murdered the former captain during a prize-fight four years ago. Learning from his predecessor's mistake, Vonn always took care to come aboard amidships, while the main pirate crew took the prow-end. The audacity served to break the resistance of the victims and heighten his own reputation; the amulet under his tunic, which warded his skin against light and glancing blows, did nothing to allay those impressions.

Vonn slew the merchant sailors without mercy, and his spite for these enemies grew with every stroke. The crew were mostly sailors, without a scrap of armor and wielding short, light weapons with an almost total lack of skill. Vonn could see, as each one was outfought, wounded and finally slain, how they all struggled to maintain that cool look of composure the Elves were famous for. Unaging beyond a certain year that differed with each one, the elven people placed great store on the ability to hide their age from those younger, including of course all Men. Every sailor he fought, for all he knew, might be his age, ten years his junior, or a century older. Each one, with the scimitar in his heart, tried to look as if he knew his moment had come, had sought it deliberately. It infuriated Vonn, made him slay in ever-crueler and more surprising ways in an effort to see a shriek of terror, a shocked face, a twitch of retreat in a body given to panic.

The shouting on all sides made a pleasant din, and he could have listened to it beyond sunset. As it was, most of his victims perished in mere minutes, far too soon to suit him. Most marines had died in the first wave of combat, and without protection, the weaponless rowers fell like ants underfoot; some asked for quarter, but refused to beg or kneel, which angered Vonn even further.

Only the merchant captain and a few marine-guards still held out from the elevated reardeck, where the solid rail protected them from arrows and the narrow stairs made attack impossible. Up on the foremast crow's perch closer to Vonn, a lone archer still huddled as well, with perhaps two shafts left in his quiver, each one with more green than yellow on its fletching. Vonn smiled, and was deciding which pleasurable feast of fear to take first, when he vaguely realized that the shouting had not died out. The merchant was tense and quiet, but noise still came from behind him.

Spinning back, he saw from the merchant's higher vantage down into the waist of the *Shrike* where all was a roiling mass of struggling flesh. His ship, no longer holding steady against its prey, was lolling in the swell so that the ram-end in the merchant's stern was becoming the point of a "v" shape. Off the stern rail, Vonn noted a rope belayed his vessel to the prow of a one-man skiff. And down in the hold, a man in grey wielded an iron-bound cudgel against the chief of Vonn's oar-guards while the slave crew reached to finish off the others.

The oar-chief, a scar-striped veteran named Dulag, wielded both knife and bullwhip with deadly skill—on quieter days, he won bets from the crew for his ability to snap off a slave's hair-lock, or a piece of an ear. But now the gleeful killer was backed against the lower stairs and trying to keep the intruder at bay: he ripped out a current of oaths with every blow, every slippery backstep, each stair yielded. But his grim unspeaking foe seemed quite familiar with how to combat this odd weapon, and fell prey to no trick or feint as he relentlessly pressed him back and sought an opening.

Vonn knew the control of his ship was slipping fast; the boarding party, looking to hostile elves on both sides, were growling in fear without his presence. The enemy on the reardeck watched their chances in open surprise that gave Vonn scarce comfort. The pirate captain was torn between the need to regain his vessel, and keep his own men in line. As he hesitated, Vonn heard the twang of bowstring and felt a deep stabbing pain in his back, from the foremast crow. His amulet protected him from all but a scratch, yet the sting of it made him scream and flinch, and he tore out the arrow where it lodged limply in his tunic and furiously snapped it in half.

Now his main chance was already lost to distraction. The grey warrior had maneuvered past the oar-boss's guard and pummeled him once to the head with the end of his staff, felling him in a heap down the stairs back into the hold. Eager slave-hands grabbed for the keys on his waist, and a ragged cheer began to rise in waves, like a singing round growing stronger with added voices.

If there was any chance to save his own ship, Vonn knew he had to board it at once; and his crew, huddling in fear of the unknown, would not precede its captain in this. But when he stepped to the rail and gripped a furling rope, the pirate captain froze as his lone foe mounted the upper deck and came to stand directly across from him. He looked upon the lithe, thin frame, beheld the varying shades of ash, steel and mist in cloak, high leather boots and broad-brimmed hat, saw the staff's metal ends flare with silver when gripped in both gauntleted hands, and took in the argent points of light that were the stranger's eyes. The reaver of the Mendelian Bay felt his knees begin to leak.

Then he caught sight of the odd holy symbol jangling below his neck; a preacher of Conar, or one of the other heroes. If Vonn had heard another pirate tell of facing a preacher, he would have laughed and thought his fellow fortunate to find such a fool, so likely to have money and so certain to be disappointed when his faith failed him. Now Vonn gazed away from those burning eyes, to the smooth skin of the interloper and the easy stance he took as he awaited the assault, and sensed a faith that had already been tested, and not found false.

He hesitated again, and as he did he lost his ship. The *Shrike's* beak tore free of the *Moon of Plenty* as the two hulls came nearly parallel in the swelling surf, and while the pirates looked on, their prize-hull began to fill more rapidly with water. Splashes from the stern apprised Vonn that the elven captain and his crew had abandoned ship and now swam, with floundering struggling strokes, to the pirate vessel where eager hands free of their chains lowered ropes and planks to help them aboard. Vonn tried to will his body forward against his lone foe, in revenge if not for his fortune, but he was unmanned. Looking hatefully at the grey intruder again, he realized with a shock that the mist-grey hair was a disguise, masking the youthful face of a lad not two decades old. This, combined with the knowledge that behind those eyes lay no actor, but a hardened warrior who had slain Dulag without mercy, nor indeed with much effort, froze Vonn in his place on the rail. He stirred only when a body flashed in front of him, as the elven bowman dived within reach from the crow's perch into the bay waters and struck out for the corsair as well. This one swam with a more confident form, rare even to the sailor's experience, and the grey man reached down an arm to help him aboard.

Then Vonn gave vent to his profane rage in curses and clenched fists, halting only to draw breath again and again, until his seaman's legs told him the heel of his ship was growing dangerous. The rape of the merchant woman was complete, and the male member withdrawn left behind a wounded victim, fast growing pregnant on seawater together with the abandoned, sword-armed seed truly responsible for her condition.

Captain Thiel hauled up aboard the *Shrike* with grunts and chokes of salt-water, but smiling nonetheless like a mortal Man at the unexpected stroke of fortune. Turning to help his old crew, he had them on deck in a few moments, surrounded on all sides by the slave rowers, all of them also Elves. Across a widening length of sea-swell, the pirates raged and cursed aboard the listing merchantman, and their captain was kicking and stabbing them to start bailing even as her new helmsman tried to bring her to ground on a safe beach towards the island's other side. The ram had done its work well, and Thiel knew they'd be fortunate to ground her before sinking; and then ahead lay the task of patching that leak and limping off to wherever their secret hide-out lay. If he even dared go back in that weakened and disgraced condition, the merchant mused.

So distracted, Thiel never quite pinpointed where the laughter began; somewhere between rowers amazed at their escape from death and his surviving marines delighted at their foes' humiliation, a carnival atmosphere spread in moments across the deck of the former murder-craft. Elves who had never met clapped each other on the back as fast-made brethren; and a few who knew each others' family markings whooped with most unseemly delight. Youngsters, he thought—but still Thiel smiled.

Along the opposite rail, the grey stranger braced his feet on the deck and helped Lianon the archer up to safety. Attention slewed to the pair standing close by the rail, and as more and more took in the stranger the laughter died. Crewmen old and new fell silent as all eyes clung to his straight-backed form, alien dress and stern bearing. Lianon, after shaking his hand, seemed to catch the general fear and disengaged, crossing the waist amidships and skipping over the mast-socket to stand with the others. The grey man—no, a youth Thiel realized in shock—stood neutrally facing forward, able to take in the pirates to starboard and the Elves to port with minimal turns of his head. As it became clear the marauders were no further threat, the stranger turned to face the Elves more fully.

Thiel began to speak, to thank, to ask some of the many questions he had for this mortal mariner. All words stumbled on his lips as he took in the clean, lithe frame, the brim-shadowed unblinking gaze, and the fearsome set of the grey man's jaw. It was as if the youth still expected combat, was tensed for renewed warfare on the moment. Thiel glanced into the rowing-hold, where the slavers lay dead on a deck stained with many layers of aged blood, and some now fresh. The silence had stretched for an absurdly long time, and still the youth offered no word, made no move; he seemed as one awaiting orders, or the signal to fight.

Scanning his face again, the merchant captain was struck with awe to see no hint of gladness or relief on his savior's face. By the moment, this youth had seen a fraction of his years, and had just freed a crew, defeated pirates. Thiel looked in vain for the tiniest fleck of ease, or comradery; he saw instead an unbroken wall of vigilance and purpose, that chilled him more than his sea-drenched clothes. What could a young life have been, Thiel wondered, that this lad should bear himself in such contentious fashion. The youth offered no answers, but only nodded his head slantwise towards the rest of the ship, as if to say "cease looking on me, instead get on with your life, that I may leave it."

When Thiel spoke at last, it was to his first mate. “Gannet, step up this mast. Let the wind work for honest men awhile.” Some among the rowers cheered this thought, though only his previous crew moved to do his bidding. “And lighten this load, men,” the captain continued, raising his voice to include everyone, “lest we meet another pirate, or some foul weather before we learn the feel of her. We can start with those three worthies there,” he said meaningfully pointing to the dead slavers, and added, “and I think we’ll have no use for those chains either.”

That brought a loud cheer from all his men, as they jumped to do such pleasant bidding. Thiel was clearly captain from that moment, and turned to the helm to bring her about for Eldarport. He could have mourned the loss of his cargo; just as easily, he might have rejoiced at the gift of his life, and the prize of a fine warship the Mendelian navy would surely buy from him. But Thiel felt none of those emotions, only a stabbing chill, as once again his view fell across that of the grey stranger on the opposite rail. A moment their eyes held, conveying no secret he ever chose to tell another soul; then the youth turned astern, stepped quickly to the rail where his skiff was tied, and gauging the distance, leaped over the side and beyond sight.

Gannet came to stand with his captain by the helm and remarked, “There, we’re lighter by another corpse, I’d reckon sir.”

“Aye,” Thiel nodded, “and some chains as well.”

Heeling dangerously close to the island cliffs, Vonn screamed every order and punctuated each instruction with a blow, till his crew learned that on your duty and out of reach were best. The bailing was tolerably effective, but left only a handful for the oars, and they made dreadful slow time. Mid-evening, at best before they could reach sandy shore; and once aground, he couldn’t be sure of enough strength to clear her off, even with the tide. Untorn sails would have come in handy, Vonn thought in self-reproach, and his reddened rage at the bizarre turn of events left him choking for curse-words rich enough to suit the occasion.

Holding the helm hard against the ship's list, and minding the swells with the urgency of a death-grip, still his anger and curiosity made him glance back, time and again, to his former vessel. It was making away towards the Mendelian mainland at a slow, stately pace under the sole sail. Vonn was lucky the Elves held no mind to take vengeance; for now their numbers were nearly equal, and with the damage he'd already taken— that is, given— putting this hull under the waves would be easier than scooping seaweed from the tide.

To have come so close! And to lose ship, plunder and all, because of a boy. A lucky, mad youth who played with fortune's wheel when any sane sailor would have fled. Vonn saw the skiff now, making off also easterly and at a smart clip, catching all the wind with its clever close-set sail and trim rig, as if the grey youth snared a different, stronger air, a breeze from another ocean. Almost, the pirate captain wished him aboard again, without his skiff—he could use another crewman no matter how hostile. But there had been no compromise in those eyes.

The Elves upon the *Shrike* were throwing bodies overboard now, and Vonn could hear the sound of singing. The buccaneer caught sight of the archer on the nearer rail, carefully plucking arrows from the hull and returning them to his quiver. Another rush of fury seized him then, and large veins stood out on Vonn's neck and forehead as he raged against his luck. If only he had a few more men... and a patch for this hull.

⊕⊕⊕

An octet of eyes watching from the clifftop pines had viewed the sea fight below. The dwarf ran his fingers across the top of his axe, unable to stop shaking his head and chuckling into his beard. Crouching by his shoulder, a tall muscular human warrior stared down at the hostile crews that had mysteriously changed decks, and said nothing but grinned slightly the while. Behind them, at the fireless camp, a black-skinned wizard was actively giggling, something to which his fellows seemed inured. From a high branch leaning out over the rock-spiked water four rods below, a lithe slim Halfling strained to see through a silver-rimmed monocle held to one eye, taking in every detail of the pirates and their new, wounded craft.

The little one remarked, "Perhaps the heroes favor us—the plan we scratched together is now working out better than we could have hoped."

The spry Halfling leaped down easily as the former merchant vessel began to limp around the cape to the northern side of the island. The four companions stood together awhile, laughing and pointing as the one craft desperately heaved over bailed water and heavy cargo, while the other threw off dead bodies and chains. The newly-won elvish ship made under small sail for the east and Eldarport, safe from any attack as the pirates focused madly on keeping their chins dry.

"And here we thought we'd have a hard time of it," the wizard announced, grinning as he voiced the thought of all. "Sitting on this island and signaling to passing pirates, hoping to be taken on with some story about being shipwrecked. Pretty thin before—not so bad now, eh Morinack?."

"Now," the halfling Stealthic agreed, "they'll be coming to us, Melvod, and in sore need of more men, whatever their suspicions."

"Better get back to our boat soon," the human warrior warned, "and sink her, or else we'll arouse suspicion."

"Leave the starboard side alone, Hansen, put the holes to port," the Halfling said, "our new employers can use that to fit the patch they'll need."

"How fortunate for them!" the wizard chortled.

The tall warrior in chain and spiked helm, realizing he was elected by default, muttered a gruff curse and headed off down the northern side of the hill to the cove.

The Dwarf, still watching the seas below, held back an unseen hand.

"Let me have the Far-Sight lens again, Morinack."

"Here you are, Yula."

Once more the Dwarf looked down on the lone sailor in the skiff. He saw him closely as he sat straight-backed at his tiller and adjusted the sail by ropes, looking ever onward toward his unknown destination. The others came to view him standing behind the Dwarf, and the wizard at last commented, "That fellow's got courage, I'll give him. Less sense than me, but brave as Hansen," looking briefly back to see if their companion was out of earshot.

"Very clever," the Stealthic added, "waiting here in the shoals until just the right moment. No idea why he took the risk he did, but it paid off—though it didn't pay him."

"He's well paid," the Dwarf averred thoughtfully, "you can see it from this distance, he's a paladin of some kind. Got a charge on him to do the right thing. He's paid now, because he can continue on his way—before this, he could never have left that pirate with a crew in chains. I bet you my share of our commission, the hardest part for him was waiting his time."

"Too bad he's not coming with us, Yula," the wizard mused, "he's handy in a fight. No fun at all, looks like... but when we win, we wouldn't have to pay him!"

"Lord Orual'n C'ellinor, who hired us— that is hired me," the Stealthic corrected, "said nothing about my method, or how many I brought." The little leader shrugged and turned away from a chance that would never be. "Let's go over the plan again; it's the first hour that will matter most, so we all must say the right things."

"Which for me," the wizard moaned, "means saying nothing."

"The less the better," the Halfling agreed with a small grin, "but then, that's always true for you, Melvod."

Still the dwarf Yula looked on the lone sailor; it was not often he wondered what adventures another might be facing. Normally he and his companions were at the edge of life, seeking danger in comissions like this foolhardy attempt to infiltrate the pirate league. What could be more heady, more life-threatening or rewarding than discovering the secret lair which had sheltered these sea-brigands for decades, protecting their strength while they leeched the shipping of the northern kingdoms?

Now that the Percentalion had fallen into chaos, no communication of any kind between Mendel and Conar was both safe and quick, except for the powerful few who could still use the mystic gates between the capitals established more than twenty centuries ago. No trade or commerce, no intercourse between the common classes, unless it took the risk of piracy on sea or chaos on land; only a small ferry station far upriver allowed transport from Mendel to Shilar, and the journey from the elven kingdom to Conar by that route was more than two months.

So it had been that the lord of Eldarport, Mark of the elven kingdom of Mendel and speaking in the name of the Ageless King himself, had approached Morinack to undertake this commission. Rumor held that many had been employed before, and none heard from since; common opinion in the port city was that these had been slain or else traitorously joined with the pirates. Thus the lord had offered material support, but no money in advance, and of course let no word of this out to his navy, to preserve secrecy.

So Yula and his companions were minutes away from achieving the initial infiltration of the pirate league, a task where so many others had failed. Most likely, that was due to the tremendous difficulty and suspicion the brigands exercised, but they had to get new recruits from somewhere; and if any captain were minded to bite his lip and take in strangers, this one was tailor-made. Had been tailor made, rather, thanks to the efforts of one heroic fellow, come from nowhere and now headed off again. The Dwarf stared through the enchanted glass lens at the thin, hard mariner by the helm of the sturdy little skiff, and wondered whether they should ever hear of him again.

As if in answer to his thought, the sailor turned and looked back, directly at the place where the watchers camped atop the cliffs. Yula fancied he caught the sailor's hawk-eyed gaze even at this distance, and on an impulse raised his arm in salute to the youth's courage. A long moment the grey sailor looked back, without responding and with a face of stone, yet Yula could not doubt he had been seen. Then the grim determined mein turned away, and the dwarf heard the warrior Hansen returning. He reluctantly put down the lens and turned back to hear once again the Stealthic's plan.

The plains beyond the River Sweeping were intimidating by their infinite width, for the unvarying vista they ceaselessly imposed on the eyes. The flat grassy scape had swallowed the last word from the two Shilarian knights the previous day.

The need to speak existed, certainly—but a sudden decision to leave, sneaking quietly from the capital palace, and searching out the northern ford in constant anticipation of pursuit left little time for reasoned argument. The armored pair had ridden forth with visors down while in view of their fellow Shilarians, trying to look like knights busy under orders, rather than the heir and his squire in furtive flight. No scope to bicker whether in the code of chivalry, honor trumped duty. But those were old arguments, the end of such puzzle-talk already known.

Now beyond the river and riding steadily, uselessly across the never-ending grassy flats, the only words that would do needed the genius of poetry, to describe sights unseen by civilized men in centuries. This measureless steppe, the occasional sight of birds and herd-animals made tiny with distance, an added thickness on the southern horizon promising a forest primeval, and the stony, untouched heights barring the way east: what bard born could describe these things, the cutting chill of morning on a desolate disk without end.

Lacking such eloquence, the knightly pair never ventured to begin. Replacing human tongue was the hammering heartless wind, the tree-bare, black Swords of Stone in the utter east, and a steadily growing fear, of being out in the open. The Plains of the Bordbeyonds gathered them in, two motes under the eye of heaven, cantering with haste yet proceeding more slowly than the Fire Ant of the tenth month staring down on them at night.

They traveled light, and everything they carried performed double-duty before long. Swords cut the whipgrass for twisted firelogs, lances served as walking sticks in the times they led their mounts, and silver spurs helped gouge the campfire trench when they stopped. Cloaks had been blankets before of course, and the rucksacks now empty of food could stand for pillows, with the buckles folded toward the rock-hard earth. Lying beneath the brilliant panoply of starlight, one of the knights would frame the lower moon as it passed, pretending to push it along (low chuckles, they were not forbidden). Or the other might point to the tiny crimson disc, still there throughout the season like a hanging lantern signaling menace. At times each would try to measure with outstretched hand the even-blacker outline of the Swords of Stone in the eastern sky, to see if indeed they had become any larger with the pair's approach. Evidently not; but the Plains worked an awful sorcery on the eyes, and by day when they stopped, it needed only a few moments' staring at the sharp, titanic rocky peakline, to make it seem that they were growing closer of their own accord, to overtake and crush every mortal thing in their path.

So it was, on the third hungry day beyond the border of Shilar, riding steadily south-by-east toward the guessed-at center of the Plains, the two knights were taken. One moment entirely alone, the next hauling up hard to stare at a loose ring of two score helmed warriors on all sides. The squire put visor down on instinct, but the prince raised one hand to forestall further action, and neither youth reached for the lance in its socket. Perhaps, the two on foot to the left could have lain flat behind that tuft of grass. And the half-mailed knight behind, if patient, might—but it was impossible. They were everywhere at once, without a spoken signal, and the mounted men wore nearly as much metal as the Shilarians. The prince sat back and waited, and the squire followed his cue.

The silence stretched for a time matching the limitless plain around them. Even the horses stayed quiet, still and ready. The knights had time to wonder if their captors spoke by magic. The first words were so sudden and sharp, such a violation of the Plains' forbiddance, that the horses shied. But the Bordbeyonds spoke only to each other, rapidly and in words with slicing edges.

The squire, hearing nothing familiar, whispered to the prince, "What do they say?" All conversation around them ceased a moment, and every helm in the ring seemed to scowl at the two. The prince shook his head, and with furrowed brow listened intently when the conversation began again. But after a moment, he shrugged and sat back, looking to his squire with a gentle smile. Back to waiting then, as the Bordbeyonds had evidently finished conferring and stood as still as the mountains behind the risen sun.

It was a crisp autumn day, and wind propelled puffy clouds overhead at that stately speed which sends a thrill to see. The Swords of Stone reared beneath and above much larger rings of cotton, the size of knighthoods yet looking like decorative lace about the throats of those sky-sweeping rocks. The bright sun was not quite enough to dispel the cold, as it did in more sheltered lands, and when the breeze gusted it bit through the skin. The squire, not daring to show weakness by gathering the cloak, held still and waited on the prince of Shilar. For his part, the young knight seemed content, almost happy to be apprehended with no further duty at the moment. The waiting game favored him, having no clear plan beyond the spot where his horse now stood.

If a verdict was reached, the plainsmen did so silently; the horses and men in front of the knights turned and the entire party started moving again, south by east on a path toward the center of the plains, not far from the ever-encroaching edge of the Great Forest.

The squire dared to murmur again, "Is this a prison-guard or an honor guard?"

The prince's gentle smile was never far away, "I get the impression that the Bordbeyonds don't think there is much of a difference. To be a prisoner here, better than to be free further west, yes?"

Just past mid-day, and the horses had been walked twice, when the entire party halted at a broad, clear strip of grey earth cutting across their path left and right. To the southwest it pointed at the forest-line, seemingly centered between two verdant bumps on the far horizon. But their escorts scanned only to the left, toward what seemed an even-darker gash in the mountains. After a long moment, the squire started in recognition.

"The Scratch of Desolation!"

A horseman spurred closer and struck the squire hard across the plated shoulders with his two-stick flail.

"Silence, Sheltered!" he hissed.

The youth, nearly knocked from the saddle, was even more astonished to be so insulted. But one hand atop the pommel was stayed by another; the prince's eyes flared urgently as he mouthed the word "*wait*". The squire settled slowly back, then turned to meet the assailant with resolution, lifting the visor to show a face to such effrontery.

More waiting, without evident purpose. The Elves, perhaps, would have time to squander compared to a mortal Man, but the Bordbeyonds were cursed as half-Elves, none of them aware which parent their blood would favor. So much more a sacrifice, then, to burn candle without knowing the length of the wick.

This time, the Bordbeyonds again appeared to act as one, but the prince detected a slight lead from a mounted warrior on the left side. They slowly raised their visors an inch, as every man spat onto the barren scar of sod. Understanding this gesture of resistance, the Shilarian knights quickly followed suit, defying the memory of Despair's final march through the Lands of Hope, when its invading army brought such potent sorcery and raw malice in its wake, nothing grew there in the score of centuries that followed.

The squadron proceeded across the arrow's flight of naked earth as if it no longer existed. On the other side, the foot soldiers of their guard split to move in opposite directions, as though the Scratch was a defensive wall. The mounted men, still more than a dozen, broke into a trot and continued southeast.

There was as yet no chatter; but a few words here and there passed between their guards, and as a large herd of sheep came in view, a hail to its flock-minders. A slight sense of relaxation entered the atmosphere, or perhaps vigilance against foes turned to anticipation of their judgment. The prince spurred slightly forward nearer the leader.

"Protector," he asked quietly, on instinct using the other half of the ancient formula, "is it permitted that we may speak?"

His squire exclaimed aloud behind him, that the heir to the throne should claim a rootless shepherd as his superior in any way.

The leader's helm did not turn, but after a moment the voice echoed inside it. "Permitted, yes, Sheltered. Not encouraged."

"Encouragement," the prince rejoined in good humor, "is not what brought me this far. Will you consent to tutor us, that we do or say nothing more which is forbidden?"

The slight tilt of the helm was not a refusal, but hardly betokened friendliness. They rode on in silence another league as the sun moved into the western sky. The Great Forest grew ever-more substantial to their right; like the Swords of Stone, its tree line seemed too large for the distance it claimed. It became harder and harder not to stare at the two fingerlike tree-bald hills within its border, by legend the site of the Battle of the Razor.

When they stopped to rest the horses before walking on, the prince decided to try again. He strolled to where the leader stood and bowed.

"I note that your armor is somewhat lacking, compared to your companions."

As the Bordbeyond stiffened in surprise the wind gusted and blew back his cloak to reveal only two battered pieces of metal plate atop his chain hauberk.

The prince of Shilar reached up and unbuckled his own shoulder-piece, and handed the paldron to the leader, saying "I would be honored if you could accept this small gift, a token of hoped-for friendship."

None of the others moved, but a couple of them barked a chuckle. After pausing only a moment, the leader stiffly received the piece and slapped it hard in place, buckling it to his neck and below the armpit with an angry tug.

A quiet voice behind them said "The given gift is never refused." Though the words formed a harmless truism, the tone was clearly one of condolence.

They rode faster now, and for longer periods, but night still found them short of the unknown destination. The leader declared a halt, but none of the soldiers arranged a camp, instead waiting for moonrise to continue by night. Dry meat made the rounds, and much later after the thirst had passed, water in skins. The prince took no larger a sip than his hosts, and the squire risked no shame after him. The stars bore down from a sky cleared of clouds, and the stillness seemed more determined to freeze the men than the gusty winds of day. The lack of conversation was astonishing, and the knights of Shilar could no longer keep up.

"They are taking us to judgment I presume," the squire suggested quietly, and his lord nodded.

"I don't know if we transgressed merely by coming, but I hope we can make our case clear in time. One sure wager, you cannot accuse these folk of rashness."

"Nor of warmth. What did we do to them?"

"What did their ambassador do, when he came among us?"

A silent space, and then "Aye."

Some time later, when the Men of Shilar could barely see each other's face, the squire began again.

"You really intend to—to go through with it?"

"If she will have me, yes."

"You mean, if she's pretty enough."

"I mean, if it will prevent war between our peoples. Like an idiot, I made the Bordbeyonds believe that I offered myself in marriage. Their embassy came back merely to accept, not to hear of delays and maybes."

The prince rubbed his face and sighed. "But it's too late for that; today we heard how they believe. 'The given gift is never refused.' So it's marry this princess of the Shepherd Folk, or be remembered as the one who caused a war between the Children of Hope. My aim now is to avoid that war. For that purpose, I guarantee, she'll be as pretty as Elosira. And I, not half-bad looking either."

"Duty and honor, after all. But we had a year, by the terms the ambassadors gave us."

"To what purpose? My father was decided, and saw whichever stars supported his decision."

"Gareth! The king would never—"

"Hob, I know him better than you. He was horrified at the very idea, and covered it with temporizing. Talked of taking council with the crown of Mendel, but mark my word, he'd bring one or two knights with him, the most deaf of his retinue. The answer he came back with would only affirm the one he already has."

"He loves you."

"Yes, and shows his favor by risking war, rather than let me act with justice. And further—when this deadline had passed, if the Shepherds came west across the river to avenge the insult, what then Hobsel?"

"Battle, certainly?"

"Most certainly. And my good lord the Baron of Hirion would have at last the excuse he needs to exercise his temper so long restrained."

"You mean, the king would provoke war, as a favor to his vassal?"

"Nothing so obvious, milord the king need do nothing on his own. But my point, Hob—fathers would die, and their children grow into hatred for generations. Not just a battle, a state of unending war with those who should be our brethren. Not someday, but right now."

The squire nodded, then coughed and voiced a more immediate fear. "But how do you think we can make this match before the pursuit arrives?"

"Some weeks yet, I wager."

"Weeks? Do you think so little of your father's love, that he would wait so long?"

"Hardly that, dear Hobsel. The morning after we left, I imagine."

"Then why—"

Pitch black, yet the squire could hear the prince smiling again.

"I left him a note. Said we were headed to Mendel."

"Gareth!"

"Perhaps I implied it. I begged his pardon, said I could not bear to wait for the wisdom of our allies, and promised to return across the river as soon as I heard his answer."

"You proven liar!"

"Not a bit of it. At least, not yet. I intend to forge an alliance here, if I can, Hob. And if I fail—well, it seems the penalty could well be death, so I would be off the hook."

"Why, Gareth, why now?"

For answer the prince of Shilar looked up to the stars. "Because, Hob. There is a war coming—not this one, something bigger. And it will be here sooner, I can feel it. Not by accident is this the month of the Fire Ant: all of us, the Bordbeyonds, Shilar, Conar, Mendel, the wizards, we must be marching to war before this year is over."

The squire swallowed hard and pointed into the unseen east. "Do you mean, from out there, from beyond—"

The prince shook his head slightly, in confession of ignorance rather than denial.

The rise of Aral took less than a minute; everything on the Plains cast faint, immense shadows to the south, which rapidly shrank as the lower moon climbed the northern sky. The Bordbeyonds mounted up and continued to ride in a loose ring around their prisoner-guests. Within an hour, they had passed through or near three enormous herds of sheep, and the men on foot tending them saluted the leader. Towards dawn when both moons were up, the light for shapes was nearly as good as day, and they could see ahead of them a city of cloth, some of its edges already moving, breaking down, creeping south with the season.

The final rest-stop accompanied the sunrise. As Solar's orb cracked bright and sharp over the towering peaks of the mountain range that at last looked closer, the helm of the leader swiveled slowly to regard the two foreigners. After a pause, the words rang forth clearly but gently.

"Sheltered, speak truth to the chieftains. I am tasked with thy chastisement, should you lie."

The prince's gentle smile dimmed a bit at last. "Even in the western kingdoms," he replied, "we value honesty above our lives. *Ar Aralte*."

The Bordbeyond's visor hid any reaction on his face, but the raised hand indicated tired dismissal. "*Ar Aralte*, a Child of Hope, aye. But all die, soon or late." He tapped his new armor piece. "Take none else with you."

The prince considered. "You are my Protector. Responsible for me. Because of the gift." Two nods, and the wordless ride resumed.

The cloth city held no pattern to its manifold faded colors, yet their arrangement was ruler-straight, with wide streets and a central open space like a plaza, where tents of extra size faced each other. The detail rode to within a textile-block, dismounted and came forward in a group, but without yet binding or seizing the outsiders.

They stopped before a tent facing east, yet still deep enough to shadow its interior from the rays of rising Solar. The patrol leader stood with both knights at the front and the others arrayed behind. Another long pause, and this time it seemed more than ever that the Shilarians were tested. The youths did not speak aloud, but the prince turned to grip his squire's arm and give a single clap to the back.

Risking the offence, the prince dared to whisper quietly. "Thanks, whatever happens, for coming this far."

The squire seemed to choke, but managed back, "I'm with you to the end."

When things began to happen, it was all too quick.

From the tent emerged several tall proud Bordbeyonds, one in the center with age-weathered hands and white hair extending below his helm; just behind him a slender warrior in leather, whose helm could not adequately disguise gender, and wearing a blue-and-silver brooch pin at her shoulder. Her hair, long black and braided, disappeared down her back and she held a flail in one hand as easily as a man.

The prince stepped forward, even as others continued to file out of the tent. Bowing to the elder, he began, "Son of He Who Must Not Be Named, I am Gareth of Shilar, come to deliver my hand to your princess, if she be willing."

The woman behind the helm stood still, and neither by hand or word gave any sign of her reaction.

The chieftain gestured and called, "The Shilarian, bring, to speak Man-speech clearly." Behind him stepped up a youth whose hair and face carried a more familiar stamp than that of a countryman. Without question, here was a native of Shilar, and by his bearing the son of a knight. In another moment, his prince would have recognized him.

But behind Gareth, the squire gasped and fell flat to the ground as if struck by a stone. Crying out, decorum and peace forgotten, the prince knelt and scooped his arms under the neck and shoulders.

"Hobsel! Are you well, what has—"

His squire, breathing but unresponsive in the prince's grip, was strangely relaxed, with a face now softer in its features than Gareth had seen before. The face before him now could have been a copy struck from that of the one the chieftain had just called forth. Gareth was dazed with wonder, his initial fear now submerged in a strange reluctance; he did not call out again.

Two hands gripped Gareth's shoulders, pulling him back not roughly but irresistibly. Even at this close range, the familiar face of the sandy-haired youth did not break through the prince's panic and stupor.

But the words he spoke worked wonders.

"Leave my sister to me."

⊕⊕⊕

HARVEST

Excerpt from The Kingdom Chronicle 1995 ADR

IN SUM, THE TENTH MONTH *of the year was marked chiefly by these two events, the continuing depredation of pirates upon peaceful shipping in the Western Ocean, and the sudden distressing disappearance of the prince of Shilar. Herein lay a tragic irony as the Elves of Mendel found themselves beset by dissimilar yet equally undeserved crises.*

For on the seaward side, the kingdom was constantly distressed as reports of ships taken or sunk increased with the stormier season. This hardship was a familiar one, growing steadily since at least the year 1992 and now nearly in the nature of a blockade. There were rumors of captains paying tribute to avoid plunder, and others of action taken by wizards from Araluntir, neither of which can be confirmed. And whether an accustomed pain's increase is worse than the onset of a new agony, only the sufferer may say.

For to the east, the kingdom of Mendel was now afflicted with another dilemma, again through no fault of its own. The heir to the throne of Shilar, Prince Gareth, having taken a hand in the affairs of state despite his tender age, in the middle of this month did disappear, either taken or fled. None doubted that the recent imbroglio with the savage Bordbeyonds was at the heart of this mishap. The nomadic half-Elven people had taken it into their minds that Gareth, who gave a token gift in all innocence to their ambassador that summer, should marry the daughter of their chief. Now the popular report was that the prince had fled to the kingdom of Mendel, there either to seek counsel or sanctuary against being forced to the deed by his royal father. By month's end, it was evident that Shilar's crown would indeed visit with Mendel, far sooner than originally intended. But whether to search for his son or to demand his return has not been made clear.

And certainly with restive savages on their border likely to take offence at any reasonable decision, one could hardly envy the position of our Eldest brethren among the Children of Hope. For who knows where calamity or death may strike, in this month when the bolt of the Arbalest in heaven finally falls to earth.

After-Word: Here ends the tenure of the Kingdom Chronicle's most ardent, long-lived and dedicated archivist, the sage Valenthur of Trainertown. He kept the Chronicle from the second day of Serpent in 1943 through the last day of Fire Ant, 1995; by eight years and more, his hand lay on this chronicle the longest, since its beginning.

Though charged with carrying on the record (until some worthier hand should be appointed), I find my heart is too heavy with grief to alter a single word of what he so lately penned here. For the facts and of the month they are accurate enough. That he—and his city—should have borne so fully the ravages he referenced just weeks later, cannot be laid at his feet, for indeed none of us can know when or where the bolt of the Arbalest will fall. Let the record show only that I, once Valenthur's student, am resolved now to carry on for him as best I may. In token of my pledge, I append his name to my own forever. I take up the duty now. May I keep the record well, however long I am tasked to do so.

-Anteris Valenthisson

⊕ ⊕ ⊕

The Mark of Eldarport was a very busy man, on a good day. But as Orual'n cast gloomy eyes around his silent office chamber, the elven lord reflected that today did not appear auspicious.

Curtains back, sills up, plenty of light and air, and as bright a carpet on the floor as he dared. Still the sheer age of the place was oppressive when alone, carrying centuries of decisions made by wiser lords, those fellow Elves who came before him. Orual'n sat gingerly in a dark-stained oak armchair made just after the First War of Liberation, his composure under assault to imagine how his ancestor the first Port-Mark sat here on this very piece of salvaged wood, four millenia ago. The Hopelord Ma-Eldar stood in this room, centuries before the Dagnor Rokan; conversant with heroes of that generation, deciding the fate of nations with inerrant foresight. Now Orual'n glanced at a slender pile of papers, already signed into orders, mundane decisions regarding slip-fees and guard shifts. He doubted every one of them. Having only seven decades to his credit, he felt totally inadequate to the task left him by his mother, who had governed Eldaport with such confidence and popularity since before he was born.

And in his center drawer, where he dared not peek today, a copy of the letter of marque drawn up just a month ago, sending another band of adventurous souls to their deaths against the pirate league. His mother would never have taken such drastic steps. But the attacks grew only worse, word from the Crystal City as rare as it was polite, its wizards both noncommittal and brief. He had acted alone, but to break with precedent in secret brought him no joy.

The knock interrupting these reflections sounded slightly rushed; perhaps there was some hope for the next hour. Orual'n recited the rhyme of patience and bid entrance in a voice both measured and lordly, his eagerness to hear the news masked from everyone. Only Katel'yn could tell the truth—he would never wish to hide his thoughts from his wife.

"Milord Mark, the Boatguilder to see you," the custodian said with one hand on the knob.

"Send him in." Another dispute, no doubt, about pecking order in the building rolls; two merchants who each wanted a lost hull replaced sooner. Orual'n sighed and stood, starting to search the bookcase for the proper precedent tome where his famous ancestors—or perhaps one of their assistants—resolved such issues while defeating the Garruk tribes so prevalent before the Age of Peace, or something equally momentous and pressing.

A painted wood panel silently pivoted to admit Katel'yn, and Orual'n moved to take his wife's hand with visible relief, another emotion those of noble rank could seldom share.

"I could feel the disquiet from the manor." Her smile held the barest shade of coy as she exaggerated in glee. Orual'n stroked the white locks near her cheek and reflected that only a lover could tease him this way. From the manor, indeed; but in those wondrous eyes, from the planes of her dignified, perfectly middle-aged face emanated her concern for a husband too much bothered by his legacy, his duty, the immeasurable burden of time-proper. Orual'n inwardly cursed the very thought of his own face, barely twenty-five by the glass, shouting to the world his inability though he was five years the elder of his spouse. She knew his thoughts as he did, and gently tweaked him to return his sense of humility.

"Sorry to disturb your morning, dearest," he returned with his manners in perfect place above his own smile. "But then, there may be some prospect; the Boatguilder has a question."

Nodding at once, Katel'yn moved to the rack of tomes, while Orual'n returned to his chair. In matters of their partnership, running the Mark containing the kingdom's only port, they danced in perfect silence. When the custodian returned with the craftsman, he spared only a quick glance and bow for the room's new occupant; though the office had no other exit and the panel's hinge was invisible, he knew more than to question the proven abilities of his betters and elders.

The Boatguilder, ignorant of this minor miracle, bowed deeply to them both and launched into his question.

"I hesitate to trouble you, milord," he said as Orual'n's hopes fell. "It has been so long, and I was unsure."

"What is the matter, sir? Someone seeking a higher place on your building rolls?"

"No milord, I could well handle that I think. I've been offered a boat for sale."

"For sale!" For a moment Orual'n could not restrain his tone, and cursed the loss of composure. His heart quailed, to think that perhaps the merchants were at last becoming discouraged, quitting the seas rather than face such risks. He thought them better than that. Katel'yn set a hand on his shoulder as she laid the roll-book down; the slight squeeze was enough to restore him, bless her.

"What draft, and which house may I ask. The next arrival was to have been the *Moon of Plenty*, Thiel I think."

"He's not returned yet, sir," the guildsman shifted a bit and looked aside. "A few days overdue. No, this is just a two-man skiff, only one aboard, came in this morning. This elderly wanderer, or so I take him to be, hops off to tie up at the fishing quay and asks where he might sell his hull. Doesn't need it anymore, he says."

Orual'n began to relax at this news. The loss of a fisherman was not nearly so bad.

"Well, men retire from the sea, dear guildsman, I see no—"

"He's a mortal, milord," the craftsman interrupted, ducking his head at the embarrassing loss of manners but too moved to wait. "And he's none of ours, nor his keel. Not from Eldarport, it's the first day I've laid eyes on the Man. And I hope the last," he ended with a mutter.

"Not from here? Whence does he hail, then?"

The silence was not long, but it was complete. Orual'n felt his spirit stir for that nameless moment, one with perhaps no precedent in it.

"He says, from Conar, milord."

Katel'yn's hand on his shoulder tightened in a spasm of pure fear. That helped Orual'n to swallow instead of shout.

"The Conarian merchant fleet comes to us under heavy guard," he managed in a level tone. "They arrive twice a year, and this is not the season. Now you tell me a lone seaman, elderly and feeble, made it past the pirate isles in a ship smaller than this room?"

"Oh, I don't believe him either, sir," the builder hastened to assure. "Eight hundred leagues, it won't pass muster. Though his craft is quite trim, I'd wager. And I never said he was feeble, milord," he added on a note of apology. "Looks quite the fighting man, despite his hair."

"Be that as it may, why would he lie to us? Is he related, perhaps, to one of the human families in the city? Someone we've missed, or did he steal a boat and now seeks a quick profit?"

"I'm sure I don't know sir. I told him he would need permission for any sale or purchase, and papers to show ownership of the craft. He just looked me in the eyes then, and I thought he might—well I'm sure I don't know as I said, milord. But after a moment he asked about the rental fees for the slip. I told him, he drops a gold coin in my hand and strides off without waiting for his change. So I've come to ask, milord, if anything should be done."

The Boatguilder trailed off, until his lord raised an eyebrow in question. Then he blurted, "Maybe this fellow should be questioned or followed."

"I dare say. A fighting man you said?"

"Aye, from his look, milord."

"Was he bearing a sword and armor, then?"

"Neither, sir. I mean his look. You speak to him and he stares you directly back, and he doesn't blink or hardly, and you feel—well, as if anything could happen. He spooks me and I don't deny it."

"Could he be from the Southern Empire?"

"Cryssigens is near as far as Conar, milord as you know. And those Argensians, even the poorest dress like peacocks. Not a drop of color on this fellow; he looked like he had sailed all his life and just stepped ashore this morning. It's a mystery, milord." Silence for a space, and then the guilder added, "It wouldn't surprise me, sir, if he were one of the pirates."

Orual'n thought that an idea worth considering. He nearly grinned to recall, here he had sent those adventurers on a hopeless quest to try and infiltrate the league of his enemies. Why not, in a turnabout, might they send one back? Or more plausibly, an older seaman who had lost his usefulness to the buccaneers, now cast adrift and deciding to try his luck among lawful men rather than starve on one of the uncounted dot-islands in the haunted bay.

"We should indeed locate this fellow, and bring him—"

The second knock was more sudden and followed by the custodian's unbidden entrance, already accompanied by another. Orual'n was too struck to remonstrate at this unseemly haste. In his heart, he was starting to feel glad.

"Milord Mark, this is a messenger from the River Gate, some kind of disagreement, he says it is urgent."

"I'll hear him." Orual'n managed through his irritation, to be pulled away even momentarily from such an interesting problem. It was a long walk from the River Gate perched at the river's mouth north of the city walls. Another scrap over boat-precedence, no doubt; the fishermen arguing pride of place, as they departed for the day from a district just beyond the gate on the river's southern bank. Minding the affairs of immortal Elves could be tiresome, when even the poorest peasant might have centuries of pride behind his work.

The new plaintiff wore the livery of the Riversweep's guard, tasked with defending the boom blocking the great river from unlawful traffic.

"The Riversweep sends his greetings, milord—and milady I'm sure—and asks your advice what to do if this fellow comes back."

"Which fellow? Some fisherman arriving before the opening hour?"

"No, milord, a human mage. Came across the bay at dawn, tried to access the river."

"What! Do you mean he came from the ocean?" Orual'n was so startled he nearly interrupted. The pirate seas formed something close to a blockade in this day, how could there now be two ships slipped through overnight? Katel'yn, having already found the second unneeded tome, set it down to distract him, alongside a cup of steaming tea, which helped restore his composure while the messenger continued.

"Bold as a sword-edge, sir, straight from the west as if he had every right to be there. Not a one of us on duty had ever seen this craft before. He stood off from the harbor awhile, looking things over it seemed, and then made straight for our tower and demanded we raise the boom, let him pass upriver."

"A craft, you say; what draft, perhaps a fathom, how many crew?"

"No, milord. A one-man boat, there's the odd thing—barely the draft of your knees."

"And the length?"

"Perhaps twice his height, or a shade more, milord. Smartly rigged, I'll admit. Still, an amazing feat to have come all the way over the bay from the Crystal City alone. I expect that's why the Riversweep figures him for a mage."

"Indeed," Orual'n rejoined, covering the fact that he could not devise a better explanation. No one attempted nearly two hundred leagues across the open ocean alone, even with sorcerous lore to assist them. "What words passed between them, where is he now?"

"I was there to hear, milord. This wizard sails up, as I said, and calls out to us to open the boom. As if that were all! The Riversweep tells him no, and demands to see his papers. The fellow just looks him back in the eye, and I thought he might start to fight right then; so cold a look as I've not seen from a Man, sir in my lifetime. And the strangest man! All in grey he was, broad hat, long cape, thick staff. He keeps sailing closer without a word, until I think he'll try some spell to break the boom. But then he turns her about, like a cat around a chair just spins her, and heads back towards the harbor. So the Riversweep sends me, milord, to be sure you hadn't perhaps made any arrangements with the Crystal City, with the mage-lords of Araluntir, and he wants to know if he did well."

Orual'n had learned waiting from the ladies in his life. He thought of his mother now, departed these last eight years, and of Katel'yn by his side. They would always pause, just so, before responding no matter how marvelous the news.

"Tell milord Baron he did well to bar the river. But say also that this mage is of interest to us and should be brought in. Both men," he said taking in the first petitioner.

"May we… have guards, milord?"

"Well, if you believe he—"

With a brief presage of approaching tumult, the thick office door burst open this time to admit several of Orual'n's town guard hauling a prisoner between them, barreling ahead despite the weight of the protesting custodian in their way. The Port-Mark leaped to his feet, taking in the unprecedented chaos to storm this room, and felt a guilty thrill that almost made him smile. What ancestor could point to the custom for this?

"Milord, this villain assaulted the guard in full daylight—"

"There he is!" shouted the petitioners in unison.

All eyes turned to the prisoner. Orual'n, battered by several tales in short order, at first saw three men before him. From the high leather charcoal-grey boots and the smell of salt he recognized a seaman; one of the guards, still furious, shoved him hard from behind, and the prisoner braced himself as against a rolling deck. The long ashen cape, the double-row of silver buttons on his jerkin, and mismatched misty gauntlets told of an imperfect uniform, a soldier of some ghostly regiment the sole survivor. Sweeping off his broad-brimmed slate-hued hat, the grey-haired man bowed deeply over straight legs, then stood as one who expects interrogation.

Orual'n felt the nape-hairs crawl at this apparition. One of the soldiers held an iron-shod cudgel of stony petrified wood. "Give this fellow his staff," he said, following protocol as he had not heard a formal accusation yet. Had it been a mage's tool, it would have exploded in another's hands.

But when the stranger, still wordless, took it in his left hand, all the metal bands flared from iron to bright silver. Katel'yn gasped behind him, the custodian fell back and the soldiers clenched their spears. But the Man in Grey only turned back to face the Port-Mark, and behind his gaze the Elf saw, if not a mage's power, certainly a reservoir of lore not to be trifled with.

Before he could take any further action, the stranger spoke.

"Eldest, Mark of Eternal Tides, defender of this most western city in the land of time-proper."

Now the three men of moments ago disappeared into a sole person, unique and unprecedented and invaluable. Not even his own barons addressed Orual'n so correctly.

"Sibling," he responded, returning the formal address between Elf and Man, "you have surely set our day against the wind in short order. Barely mid-morning and already there is much to answer for."

He expected a start, some protest, perhaps even a shift to use his weapon. But Orual'n watched incredulously as the stranger, with hardly a flicker from his eyebrows, drew a long breath which he then let out to the soundless words of the Elvish meme of patience. Here, in the seat of power this mortal intruder and the source of so much offence was holding his temper as if aggrieved himself. As if accustomed.

Only then, while the Mark of Eldarport, tenth-highest ranking immortal in the kingdom of Mendel, searched for words to trump the unspoken insult, did he realize he had avoided the man's gaze. Since the first bow, the grey stranger rested his eyes only on the Mark. Returning the look, Orual'n realized with shock that this hawk-like glare blazed from a face of less than twenty winters. This composure, formality, the righteous defiance—from a youth.

Orual'n turned a moment and saw in Katel'yn the steady face that he knew she wanted him to see. Beneath the surface, decades of loving marriage showed him her fear, which moments ago drove her hand. His wife knew how her man hungered for decisions without precedent, free from the burdens of his ancestors, filled with the chance of adding a deed to the record of time-proper.

Orual'n turned back to face the prisoner, and decided that Hope should guide his course even before an enemy.

"I can bid you but poor welcome to my city, in light of the deeds set against you prior to our meeting."

There may have been a flicker of something in the youth's lip, annoyance or even amusement.

"If I may be so privileged, eternal lord, let me hear the record of these accusations."

"First, the order of things, if I may, sir. You sailed to Eldarport this morning."

"Aye, milord."

"You went first to the River-Gate and bid entrance."

"Sooth, if asking be a crime, I must beg pardon."

"No, young… sir, not the asking. But then to sell your craft without record—"

The youth only looked back and waited, until Orual'n applied the same logic as to the first case. He nodded and smiled at the youth, who nodded once in return.

"To the third matter then. How did you fall into dispute with my guards?"

"Certes, milord," the youth replied with a touch of excitement in his most courteous speech, "I trow that yet again the asking of a question didst embroil me."

"And what dangerous question did you ask?"

"I chanced upon an elder in the street, and asked why he should be left to starve."

"Milord, do not hear him!" The angry guard pushed forward, and Orual'n recognized Kall'stan, captain of the Theme guards and heir to House Me'ld. His face held such pain as was nearly a slap to see, and he spoke low in the Elvish tongue to match his torment at justice delayed.

"Milord, he fed my father bread and water."

Behind him, Orual'n heard Katel'yn choke; it seemed not a breath stirred in the room despite the open windows. He faced Kall'stan fully and put a consoling hand on his shoulder.

"You are quite sure? You saw him?"

"With my own eyes, and a dozen more of my company. It was the dawn hour milord, his last request—the last time he spoke to us, he wanted to be brought to the courtyard where he could see the sun rise. I swear, by my Moments, his time was here, perhaps even—and suddenly this uncouth warrior steps into the Theme court, directly into the family district. He looks about, because of course the fool is lost, and I thought as everyone, that he would leave and no one would have to break silence or speak before one who is choosing his Moment. But then he sees my father in his sitting-booth and, and before I have time enough to think, he…"

The horror of it kept washing into Orual'n, waves of an incoming ocean, tidal dismay too strong to stand against. Meir'kall Me'ld, most respected Theme of the city and among the oldest beings in all the Lands, had awaited his chosen death now for over a week. Agony to his son and family, of course, but another pall of advance mourning for all in Eldarport, even before the whispers that always came with such sad events. For an outsider to interfere, so abrupt and ill-considered: the Port-Mark knew there would be no purpose to search for precedent here. Yet drenched in remorse, he felt only an unaccustomed longing for mundane, trivial matters again.

"We must extend our patience, Captain. This mortal is but a youth, with no knowledge what transpires here."

"Milord, no peasant is allowed within the Theme—much less a mortal! Were it not my father's last request he would have been safe inside the estate, attended by his servants. What evil chance brings this pirate outcast among us? Find him guilty of this crime, I demand, or give me justice in the arena."

With a heavy heart Orual'n turned back to the stranger. Interfering with an Elf's chosen Moment was among the few crimes that merited death. Theme Me'ld was a preacher of Ma-Eldar, versed in foresight and the proper selection of the hour. Quiet isolation and time to bid the world farewell, these were his rights. The damage done to his spirit, and that of his family were beyond reckoning.

He returned to the Common Tongue to interrogate the accused.

"I must try to apprise you of the weight of your misdeed, young man. You have interfered in the free choice of our eldest and most revered—"

"I trow I have gained some small knowledge of the custom, milord." The youth spoke smoothly like the student repeating his lessons, and Orual'n was struck at the contrast with the sailing man or soldier he appeared. "Sooth, 'twas why I asked him if I could do aught for him."

"You spoke to my father! You dared, you reaver!"

The grey youth faced the Captain then, calm yet with an edge of holding his patience still.

"He said nothing to me, and I were minded of your custom, aye, and bethought me that mayhap this were such a one as I had read of in my teacher's books in Conar."

Piling tall-tale upon blasphemy; Orual'n realized there would be no course to save him now, even were he minded to grant the lenience. But the accused had a candid, truthful way about him despite his oddly contained anger. Orual'n had the impression of righteousness that did not fit the facts.

"Thus," the youth continued, "I drew out a flask and a heel of bread and showed them, merely, to make my intention plain in case my words had not. For it was in my mind that he might be willing to live, yet too weak to answer."

"Black-hearted peasant!" cried Kall'stan, "You have seen your last day, and I shall set your corpse adrift for the birds to pick at."

"Captain, gainsay this loss of composure, it does not become the Theme's legacy."

"He knew the custom, milord, he is convicted from his own speech."

"He says he merely asked a question."

"He lies! He fed him from his own hand, standing close upon my father. And when my men accosted him, he became violent."

"Not I."

"He threw the first punch!"

"Landed, perhaps."

"Quiet, you have no r—"

Kall'stan choked on his words, and Orual'n realized with a chill that the prisoner was also conversing in Elvish.

"You understand," he continued in Common, "somewhat of the gravity of this offence. All depends, you should grant, on your ability to establish the truth of your claims. Any claims."

Once more the youth, though sorely accused, showed no upstart; in his face Orual'n detected the stranger's reaction, the set of his jaw and fractional shrug of his shoulders, that this was rather expected.

"What is your name and country, stranger?"

"I am Solemn Judgement, milord, last son of Final Judgement. I have no country."

"What mean you, no country? Are you indeed a pirate then?"

The young man's eyes snapped to him, and Orual'n saw genuine shock, though whether in naivety of the logic or guilt at the discovery, he could not tell. Something tickled at the back of his memory, a grey man whom all should in some way beware of. Was it news in a letter?

Before he could continue, Kall'stan spoke.

"Did you displease your pirate captain, to earn expulsion from his deck?"

There was a pause as the youth framed his words. "Wast no captain of mine. But I trow, I may have indeed displeased him upon his deck. Wast fain to do so."

"Guilty then, again by his own words," Kall'stan pointed to the accused in triumph. "He attempted mutiny of some sort, lost and was marooned."

"Tis not so! An' I miss my guess, ye may ask the merchant crew when they arrive."

"Which crew?" the Boat-guilder broke in. "Do you mean the *Moon of Plenty*? Did you see her?"

Judgement turned to him to speak. "A galleas? With both sail and oar? If I reckon true, she is sore punctured by the ram and most like has sunk."

After a moment, he added casually, "Yet the captain will know for certes. Ye may question him as he arrives."

Orual'n put out a hand to restrain Kall'stan then, who was reaching for the throat. Still, the boy made no defensive move, not even putting his staff on guard. He was trusting to the procedure here, a marvel.

"So," Orual'n managed through the pounding din in his temples, "you claim to have crossed the ocean from Conar. Angered pirates, yet escaped alive. Seen a Mendelian merchant ship rammed and likely sunk, but did not help. Yet their crew will be here presently to verify your tale."

Again there was a moment of profound silence. The youth turned to Katel'yn and bowed again, saying *"Mistress, are thou the Mensor, who tests for truth? I pray, bring on your miracle then, to make assurance of my word. As I am not of the noble class, 'tis no insult to mine honor."*

The lady actually laughed in response, tight and high. The Boatguilder and Riversweep guard stood in the corner with mouths agape, hardly drawing breath for fear.

"Clear this room," Orual'n barked with a touch too much volume. The two petitioners, custodian and other guards backed away, and the Mark of Eldarport turned to Kall'stan to murmur, "and you as well, Captain."

Kall'stan's face fell, then curdled toward rage. Orual'n gave him no chance to speak but kept his eyes close on him. "I will settle this matter in accordance with justice, Captain Me'ld. Return to your post, and see to your beloved father."

Disbelief and fear salted the nobleman's face, spices to a flesh of grief now bubbling above the heat of a most unwonted anger. Three long breaths, the meme of patience, and finally he could master himself enough to head last for the door. With his back to the room, he ground out a parting word.

"By my father's name, reaver, you shall not pass this door unpunished."

Orual'n turned back to his desk, clearing both hands through his hair to compose himself and draining off the tea in a gulp. He glanced again toward Katel'yn for support, then drew breath and faced the accused.

"I cannot punish any man who remains ignorant of his crime." Orual'n paused for the sense of that to settle in. The Man in Grey simply waited, as if learning a lesson about someone in another country. "This case—the gravity of this offence, and the circumstances, you must understand, are unlike anything in our rolls."

The youth nodded. "Your decision, then, will add to the record of time-proper."

At these words a flush suffused Orual'n's body from head to vitals; it was several moments before he realized his jaw was open. This lad!

"Where did you study Elvish customs, to hold such knowledge at your age?"

"My teachers in Conar were, I trow, among the best, milord. Most prominently, a very patient Sage, your countryman, was my especial tutor."

A slight something buzzed again at the back of the Port-Mark's brain; he thought irrelevantly of a letter, but brushed it aside.

"This is the lady of the Port, my wife Katel'yn."

"My sincere apologies, milady Marchess, to mistake your station." Orual'n saw her smile and wave in dismissal, but take a half-step further from the staff-bearing youth.

"Are there none, then, who may interrogate me to discern the truth of my tale?"

"We have preachers with this skill, but do not employ them thus. The precedents serve us well, of course, in all but a few cases."

The youth nodded in grim acceptance. "Verily, such as this one." Again that fractional shrug, a gesture which conveyed familiarity with the threat of imprisonment or death.

Orual'n felt strangely moved against his better instincts, to explain, to seek further explanation in turn.

"How could you dare to risk interference in our most cherished custom, knowing as you claim how deeply personal, and painful—the subject of a Life Moment, it is—it is not for mortals to involve themselves."

The youth considered briefly, then responded, "Milord, if he were at the right moment to die, how be it that he still lived?"

Hot anger suffused Orual'n's face, and he felt as Kall'stan must have, wanting to strike the mortal down.

"Blasphemer! You dare question the wisdom of the eldest among us."

The youth looked vaguely puzzled. "The eldest, milord? Do you mean the heroes themselves?"

His candor could not be doubted, and the simple piety of the question brought Orual'n up short.

"The heroes, of course not. Their will is not to be frustrated by a stripling like yourself, whatever your motives. And the Heroes of Hope do not urge us to our deaths—rather they inspire us to better lives. I refer of course to the revered elder, once head of house Me'ld, whose sacred right it was to die at a time of his choosing. A nobleman who had lived well in excess of five centuries.

"Think you, boy—his title was resigned, his will announced, his son whom you so deeply angered is the new Theme in all ways that matter before the law. Meir'kall Me'ld had spoken no word, taken no food, nor had any direct impact on another being for nearly a fortnight. The Captain is his eldest son and heir. By your action it is, it is as if you raised his father from the dead."

On this, the youth's eyes blazed again, with that restrained and righteous fury.

"Milord Mark, with respect. Hast seen the dead raised, sooth?"

A second time the Mark of Eldarport felt his mouth open in shock. The youth nodded at this denial.

"Certes I have, and thereunto is no likeness either of deed or intent."

"Ne—nevertheless, you—"

"Milord," the youth ground on, so human to interrupt, "bear with the logic of this accusation. I ask again, whose will ordered this holy man's death, that I should have frustrated it. The heroes? You say yourself they do not send a man's end, and I agree. The eldest one himself? I trow we speak not of suicide, for that is against Hope."

"Of course not. But by his wisdom, this immortal had decided his Moment had come. His purpose in life served, he awaited its end."

"But had he so decided, wherefore could he not ignore me, milord? In what way, by offering life did I enforce it upon him?"

There was no good answer, and the entire strain of conversation was painful to Orual'n; he could not stop thinking of his mother's end, blessedly less than two days in duration. A thought peeked out, whispering that Theme Me'ld had not the same foresight, that he might have been mistaken; the Port-Mark shivered in his full body at the idea.

"Must it not be," the Man in Grey continued, "that above me, and you milord, and the revered Theme, and yea, even above the heroes themselves, that there is another, and a sole, source of will, of intent, that properly directs such a purpose? Else to whom did Conar and Ma-Eldar look, for direction and inspiration, when they didst pray, that they taught their children in turn to do the same?"

Orual'n felt his head spin as such bizarre and irreligious thoughts cascaded upon the ears. He had an urge to strike the youth, and another to flee the room, to hug Katel'yn to himself and hold her an hour in some hidden place. These words from a mortal lad, just quiet words, yet they hunted his mind with horn and hound behind them.

"Milord Mark, only such an authority could be offended in mine actions, if they were truly against the course of Hope. If all be merely chance, mine presence there, the time, the meeting a mere flicker of fortune, whereat is there to be offended? Neither can it be the revered elder's will which is aggrieved. For certes he were free, at every moment I trow, to refuse, to ignore me. And for my side, it has ever been in my heart to support life, not to end it. If there is a will that guides the heroes to guide us in turn, it could not be unaware of my intent, my habits. So again, how could I have been there, lost as is averred, if it were not to the purpose?"

For a long silent space Orual'n simply stared at him. The air seemed too scarce, he had to look again to confirm the windows were open.

"What are you saying? Did he speak to you?"

"Not in words, no. When I did ask him wouldst fain aught assistance, he looked back at me in grief and fear as it seemed. Methought I had broken custom, as indeed I had feared afore then. Yet were naught to do but ask, for surely the failure to render succor were a worse offense. So I determined to draw forth the food and water, and showed them merely, to make my intention plain."

"And then?"

"Then, milord, a look of wonder overcame the pious elder Elf. He looked beyond my hands, through me I trow to some far-off light. By my father's name, milord, his countenance did brighten, and he sighed. He seemed to see me again, and all the world about him, like a man awakened. And he did gesture most clearly, that I should approach to deliver the water and bread I had shown to him."

Orual'n was touched with wonder at the youth's words, and only belatedly thought to doubt the tale itself. A sly part of his mind, still sheltering in a dark corner from the hunting-call of thoughts about something higher than Ma-Eldar, suggested the Mark could dismiss the youth at once. Down the hallway, past the door waited Kall'stan with his promise, and then the arena, and there no doubt an end to all these problems. He turned back such an unworthy idea, but it roused him to be peevish. He paced away from the stranger as he spoke.

"This spider-web of rhetoric avails you nothing, to excuse your crime. Can you begin to imagine, in your two decades of life, what it means to lose a loved one? What can you know, boy, of the heartache that comes of—". He broke off as some of those distracting thoughts and images suddenly coalesced in his memory. The tragic news from Conar, the Healers Guildmistress lost, left to die in some horrid underworld, these three weeks ago.

And the tales told of a grim grey adventurer, a coward who abandoned her. Suddenly chilled, he spun back to see the boy's face, still staring straight ahead but cracked with a knowing pain as at an unbidden memory.

Orualn's voice broke as well, when he resumed pacing and continued his accusation.

"And then too, mayhap other mortals have lost a friend… by some means… but what of a father, answer me that. Did you think of Kall'stan when you acted, that there would be a son left behind, who had buried his sire once already…to bear the brunt of his loss anew, and all that was owed him, to have that memory brought before you again?"

He drove his words harder than intended when he started out, and once again there was no reply. Spinning away triumphant, he saw the pain not from the stranger, but in Katel'yn's face first, as she looked on the youth. With returning steps Orual'n saw that outwardly calm mien, like stone but veined with grief-fissures across the surface.

When he spoke, the Man in Grey was quieter, almost subdued.

"Milord Mark, would it please you that I sit?"

Orual'n gestured to a side chair, and saw the youth sink to it and sag slightly, looking to the floor between his boots, his shoulders bearing the burden of some nameless weight. Before this, Orual'n had never considered a lad so young might have known a father's loss; seeing him sit unspeaking, he no longer doubted it. Shame washed through him, to realize this one and Kall'stan had more in common than either would admit.

Katel'yn moved at last, to the side table where with shaky hands she prepared a cup of tea and hesitantly set it down beside the stranger. Several moments after she retreated, his head slowly rose to regard it there, steaming and real at his right side. The youth seemed to come back to himself; recalling his manners he nodded soberly and took the cup, not drinking but merely drawing it to his center to hold in both hands. Orual'n, with no idea what dread precedent to set, stood and watched the Man in Grey.

The youth's voice when he spoke was clear in the silent chamber.

"This tea—the aroma reminds me of my tutor. Perhaps, if it is not too great an imposition, I might write him a letter before my sentence is passed."

"Certainly, young man, and I shall see it posted if you can give me enough information to locate him. He was a sage, you said?"

"Aye, a member of my order."

"You!" Orual'n no longer had the strength to restrain this constant rhythm of surprise. "You have earned membership in the Sages Guild of Conar? You mean, as an acolyte I suppose."

For answer, Solemn Judgement reached into the collar of his double-buttoned jerkin and let out a necklace with the silver symbol of an owl, beloved creature of the Sages' hero Rallantan. The size and silver composition denoted the rank of full Guildsman, not attained by Children of Hope before their thirtieth year. Something again tickled the back of his mind, but Orual'n was becoming fatigued with news and recollection. To stave off thinking further, he asked a question.

"This alters the picture somewhat. If the Conarian Guild acknowledges you as member, do you wish to claim the protections they can offer?"

"None will speak for me," the youth returned with flat certainty, causing Orual'n's worst suspicions to flare again. Something about the serious, driven nature betokened a man against whom he might prefer to be judging a pirate.

"Well then, this tutor."

"He is Senior Guildsman Cedrith Fellareon, but I know not where—"

"Sage Fellareon!" Orual'n physically stumbled as he turned back to his desk. The letter! More pieces fell in place, and any certainty the Mark of Eldarport had felt an hour ago was now fully dissolved.

"My dear," he managed to Katel'yn, "in my correspondence, near the top, it is very recent. Read it out again for me."

Katel'yn found the sheaf at once, unfolded it and silently scanned the superscriptions showing whose lawful authority lay behind the writer's words. Her glance snapped up to meet her husband's, and Orual'n nodded in appreciation: even the Mark of Eldarport seldom saw a document bearing the royal stamp of two kings.

She read out the letter itself.

To All Who May Read this, Greetings.

Though well aware I bear no authority in my own right, still I Hope the seals affixed hereto will be sufficient to engage your attention.

By this letter be apprised that one Solemn Judgement, Sage of the Conarian Guild, is to be looked for in the event that he makes landfall in any kingdom of Hope, and rendered all reasonable assistance as a stranger to your polity. He is likely engaged in a course of research, possibly involving tomes not often read; these he should be allowed to access.

Let this letter stand as my word, in the unlikely event that my name should be known to you, and if not, rely upon the power of those offices whose seal it bears. Whatever personal quirks or eccentricities he may present to your eye and ear, Judgement's task is worthy and should be supported as possibly among the most important in the recent history of our order.

Though likely worth nothing, accept my personal gratitude for any such aid or forbearance you may offer. And should he desire to write to me from wherever you find him, I beg that you accede to his wish, posting his message to the address I subscribe here.

May Hope watch over all your Moments,

Cedrith Fellareon, Sages Senior Guildsman

Orual'n spoke to Judgement, who had stood and once again seemed infused with resolve. "The seals referred to are those of the Kings of Conar and of Mendel. I have never seen such authority vested in a single document since the days of my youth."

"Mayhap then, before sentence, I may be allowed to write to him?"

Chuckling despite the situation, Orual'n nodded and Katel'yn set the writing desk before the youth. He briefly admired the quality of the quill and the desk itself, then reached to his side-pouch to produce a tightly-rolled set of parchment sheets, each one light grey. Orual'n and Katel'yn looked to each other in wonder, then withdrew to give him privacy to compose.

"He is… so fully grown, for a human," she murmured.

"Indeed, I fear he has seen much. Too much, perhaps; and I no longer doubt the main features of his tale. This lad sailed alone from Conar, beyond the shoaling reaches and across the pirate sea."

"Remarkable. Yet he evidently knows Cedrith Fellareon, the hero of this tragic tale we've heard, about the Hopeward and the lost Guildmistress."

Orual'n could hardly bring his mind to bear on the story, noised all about the kingdoms this past month, yet with the character of an ancient tale, mythic and horrid and daunting.

"Does he know him! My love, you understand, here is the third of those survivors if we can credit the tale at all."

Her eyes widened. "You mean—he is the one who abandoned the Healer Natasha to a fate worse than death, marooned in that far-off prison? The one who returned with Cedrith, but of whom we know so little?"

They stared awhile on the lad, earnestly writing without pause as if he would not waste his host's time before facing execution. Orual'n was up against the awful moment now, his foolish wish come true. A precedent would be set by his next words, and he never desired more sincerely that someone, anyone else were now the Mark of Eldarport. He prayed a moment for guidance from Ma-Eldar, and Katel'yn's hand in his own buoyed him. He looked her in the eyes as they shared a flicker of utter clarity, and she nodded though gulping at the consequence.

The youth had finished his letter, made use of the sealing wax provided, and pressed it closed with a small ring bearing the signet of the scales of justice. He handed it to Orual'n, who saw it bore the address, "To the Most Learned Sage Senior Guildsman Cedrith Fellareon" and on the line beneath that, "To be read at his convenience". Taking the letter, Orual'n laid his other hand on the boy's shoulder.

"It is my decision that obedience to my king and the king of Conar outweighs whatever crime you may have committed here today. Where were you last bound, Solemn Judgement?"

"To the capital of Mendel, milord Mark. The libraries there have resources, I understand, more complete with regard to the elder times, than any even in Conar."

"But—such tomes, they would all be written in Elvish. Or Ancient."

The silver eyes of the Man in Grey did not so much as flicker, and Orual'n learned a deeper respect for the incredible ambition of the youth. When was the last time, he wondered, a mortal Man had so much as entered the Tome-House of Mendel?

"You shall have a horse to speed your journey."

The youth bowed, but said, "With respect, milord, I cannot ride. I had hoped to sail somewhat closer to the capital before setting out on foot."

"The way to the river is closed, young man. I can of course order the boom to admit you, but there is the matter of Lord Me'ld. I must consider his honor, and he has given his word regarding you."

He turned to Katel'yn. "The Marchess will conduct you via a private corridor to our estate within the city and you may proceed on foot from there. It is the best I can offer you, I'm afraid—even the coach will be watched and I wish to avoid the appearance of friction with my vassals. The private explanation will be difficult enough."

"A copy of this letter, bearing written reference to the royal seals and signed by myself, shall go with you." He nodded to Katel'yn who knew where all the proper materials were and signed in his name more often than he, to observe the formality of one being's rule. She gestured Judgement to the side-panel, and he stayed only long enough to don his hat and bow low once more before the Mark.

"The road to Mendel is long, young man, but I suspect you will master your pace as you have so many other wonders. Whatever dark cloud lies over your past, I urge you to think of the high repute you have won from such distinguished persons. May Hope watch over you."

The Man in Grey nodded once to acknowledge these words, saying only, "If it please milord, accept my skiff as poor recompense for your assistance. And mercy." Then, the youth spun on his heel, to follow the Marchess from Orual'n's life forever.

Suddenly infused with energy akin to joy, Orual'n moved to the bookcase and drew down the tome regarding criminal law. Opening to the first blank page, he set the volume on his desk and simply stared at it. The words themselves, whereby he declared a rare exception to the punishment of death for interference in a Life Moment, would likely take months of contemplation to word correctly. To bow before the kings was merely an excuse of the moment; Orual'n needed to set a precedent that would apply with no such recommendation. The speech of the Man in Grey, which echoed so clearly from these walls just minutes ago, an argument about a higher power—those words now seemed wispy and impossible to follow. Indeed even his presence faded quickly; the Man in Grey, like the things he said, defied easy belief.

Kall'stan opened without knocking, and Orual'n saw his look darken when he found them alone. He rose with unexpected calm to face this storm of accusation and grievance; though he had not a scrap of evidence that would pass muster, the Mark knew he was right.

But the custodian interrupted them both.

"Milord! A pirate ship approaches the harbor."

"Alert the fleet. Is it alone?"

"Alone, milord, and flying our flag!"

Even Kall'stan was swept up in the news. "A trick" he guessed.

"An unusual one, milord, it also flies the symbol of the *Moon of Plenty*. And the ensign for Captain Thiel, sir!"

The Mark and his Theme stared to one another in shock. The guard of Kall'stan's watch had to address him twice, after stepping up, to gain his attention.

"A note for you, milord Theme."

"From whom?"

The guard shook his head as if struck dumb, and backed away at once. Preparations to receive the rogue corsair-turned-merchantman resounded in the corridor as Orual'n walked, Kall'stan beside him reading. The young Theme finished the note and dropped it to the ground as they emerged from the office and ran now downstreet to the harbor overlook walls. There was the pirate hull, looking trim and standing safely off while Mendelian war-galleys pushed out to examine her. Smaller fishing boats, with crews too curious to wait, had swung closer and were returning to port; a rising cheer from the docks betokened the miracle. Thiel and half his crew, alive after a sea-fight with the buccaneers.

A victory over the pirates, by a mere merchant ship, however hard won; this would encourage more trade, Orual'n thought; further risks, and no doubt more precedents for the Mark. With a sudden wonder, he thought perhaps his mother had also covertly hired adventurers, after all. Why was he the only Mark to have made decisions in secret?

Kall'stan at his side looked as one defeated by grief. Turning to face the Mark, the Theme spoke with great, formal difficulty.

"Milord Mark, the mortal youth in grey, where is he now?"

"Theme Me'ld, my decision is made and you must brace yourself for further disappointment, much though I would wish to avoid it."

"Milord," he grated again in pain, "I must know where he is."

"Why is that, Theme?"

"My—my father, milord. He notifies me that he will live on, now, a few more years, to see—see what he calls the new age beginning.

"He wishes… wishes to write to him."

⊕⊕⊕

The one-eyed Earth Demon lumbers through a petrified hedge in an ever-worsening humor. Though his trio of legs propel him forward nearly faster than a man can run, the lord of the Percentalion is angered that he must walk at all. The Law, still it bears down on him, and always at the worst of times. The hedge ignites in hellfire from the touch of his crimson, chitinous skin in passing.

Through the bramble lies the stony trace of an ancient dried riverbed, more than a furlong across. Kog never bothered to name the waters when he ruled; whatever Areghel's ilk may have called it could not interest him. All that matters is the instant, and just now Kog can feel the weight of order has lifted. The space ahead is in its proper state of chaos now. The enormous maw grins, and he is there, on the other side in an instant.

But here, near a stand of scrubby woods, a pocket of Law still clings. The trees—Kog cares not what type—their roots and leaves throw off a horrid reek of reason, exuding seasonality, burrowing and cultivating and promising the same, next year the same, always coming back. With a deep gravelly roar, the Earth Demon blasts fire to all sides, incinerating the boles with a heat that reaches to the core in moments, drilling down to char the thinnest tendrils in the earth and blasting up through the stems to sear the air above. Within moments, a rain of blackened dust patters to the scorched earth. Kog feels this black snow of blissful destruction, snorts the ashes of trees that had managed to survive for centuries until he came, and laughs, his mood improving.

He draws breath to laugh some more, and realizes that he is breathing again. Regular respiration, the sustenance of life and order, this pattern is still everywhere set against his will which should be the only law. Kog creates another mouth, that he might howl the louder with both of them.

Calming himself at last, Kog looks up from the depth of a two-fathom crater, and realizes that several hours have passed during his tantrum. Or perhaps a day and several hours—he neither knows nor cares. Now is all. Throwing out his mind-vision, Kog seeks after those distant points of light, those hateful remnants of Areghel's work he must destroy to secure his reign and end this spotty tyranny of law. One, the jeweled circle, is still there where it always remained since the elder days; hidden, unreachable. The metal stick… Kog sniffs the dusty air, then snaps to one side. It is very close! And…yes, the Eye, his missing eye is also there, though no longer carried. Both in one room, convenient, so that should be next. But there was a third thing…

The blade, Kog thinks—he cannot immediately locate it, and beyond a few moments of effort, he once again ceases to care. The demon gazes absently at the thick ash around his three massive, cloven feet, trying to recall something important he had thought of. Suddenly he comes back to it with a bark—he destroyed the trees! He looks about hungrily for more copses to devastate, the Tridium completely forgotten.

By gating himself through any area where chaos rules, Kog covers a hundred leagues in an hour. His lava-hot flames char several more stands of trees and brush, pulling down their echo of order and helping his kingdom along to its proper, hellish state. The great peak of Skysword has moved from east and south of him, to directly west, when Kog's ears prick and bend with the sound of a wounded baying.

One helldog limps across the grassless wastes, growling in fury, then whimpering in pain as it comes. Catching scent of its master, the beast yowls and doubles its pace. Kog awaits, his maw in its eternal grin and both his current arms reaching out. The helldog is more than four feet tall at the shoulder, but in Kog's enormous embrace it is a terrier, and its excited barks and bites, the clawing of its two shovel-sharp front paws are but playful joy. Kog holds the beast still with his talons as he gazes over its many wounds, and that maw-grin slightly hardens. The spiked collar is the work of mortals; thoughtfully Kog snips it off and gently, carefully turns it sharp-side down before placing it over the top of the helldog's skull. Growing a new limb for the purpose, Kog grips the collar, pulls its head close, and as the nails press into its skull, he begins to probe the mind for news of these crimes.

First, the wide, shallow cuts about its back and head. Kog rubs those as the helldog whines in pain, and to his mind-vision comes the sight of wrack and burning, mortals wielding a whip. An Ego-Lash! Someone has laid hands on a tool of Kog's former allies; but the faces the demon sees are clearly the clean, disgusting visages of Hope's puny descendants.

Now the two deeper gashes at the foreleg and side; boring his claws into them, Kog hears the helldog scream in agony and dismay. Its lone back leg is driven into the hard earth, then folds awkwardly as the fetlock snaps. The beast squirms now to escape its master, but Kog bears down harder and continues to tighten the skull-collar. The helldog is completely pinned to its suffering now; and Kog sees a flash of blinding light. The blade! The blade of light, held by a towering warrior who goes down, and then by a slender youth in brown and green.

Mortals have uncovered the blade, against all sense and chance—Kog's grin turns lethal, and the spikes now press an inch into the helldog's iron hide. Creatures of the lower depths are immune to normal weaponry; that law, which stands even in hell, is easy for the lord of this kingdom to modify. The nails punch into the skull, and russet blood spurts as the helldog simply hangs on, weakly gurgling and vainly clawing for leverage to break free. Kog sees more flashes of the fight, and glimpses of the creature's years of servitude, captured by chance and forced to work for a mortal insect now dead. But some survive, and the blade is free.

Under the pressure of Kog's two arms the helldog's back slowly breaks, in several places. Kog roars with satisfaction as the collar-spikes reach fully into the beast's head; its eyes burst into flame and bits of sizzling brain exude from between its clenched teeth. Kog embraces his loyal servant until he is holding a calf-sized rag, which flops into a leathery puddle at his feet when he rears back to roar his disgust with weakness. Waves of fire coruscate to all sides, flaming ripples that remake the land leaving cracks and lava behind.

For a moment, all else is forgotten; more play destroying trees, the need to escape walking and breathing, the other items of power, a momentary memory-flicker about a man in black who also escaped his pack. Kog becomes focused on one purpose now—recover the blade and kill the insects who dare to hold it. But this plan is not order—this is the will of Kog.

This time, the demon thinks with a wicked grin, the whim may last awhile.

The man in black squatted atop a boulder and calmly regarded the helldog on his trail. The twin moon light bore down on the long, bare-rock ridge, Unal nearly full plus a slice of Aral ahead of it, illuminating the craggy landscape. Wind was not a factor, but the Martial Wizard could tell that smell and sight were irrelevant to the beast on his trail. The monster padded along steadily, its head swaying side to side but neither looking sharp nor sniffing strongly for its prey. Its eyes, like coals in a breeze, flared whenever the head crossed the spot where he bent low. And the crouching warrior looked back into those eyes, certain that he felt the same tingle the beast did when their visions crossed. He thought there was surely something there to study, gazing into the eyes of death.

The monster froze, bearing directly at him though still too far off to make out his form against the rocky background. Quivering with hatred and the need to bite and rend, the helldog stayed its ground, rocked back on its third leg and bayed.

The Martial Wizard Pol watched with interest, as the creature howled again; from a great distance, the pack responded. This had not been their habit at first. When he encountered them within the circle of wagons two nights ago, their assault was overconfident, haphazard and even competitive as they all vied for the chance to bring him down. With his mastery of the Thunderfist, Pol had taught them fear; yet yesterday the pursuit was still grouped and massed. When he had tempted the lead-beast then, it provoked another rush, enabling him to slay one more of their number.

Now, they had perhaps learned craft; but he surmised this was unlike the hounds of chaos. Precious little to base a guess on, but Pol assumed without false modesty that by fighting a pack of helldogs three days ago, and still being here to reflect on the experience, he probably outstripped the knowledge of any man alive. The monsters were driven by passions, and perhaps had some means to sense his presence despite stillness and distance. That one would forebear to attack could mean respect, but it could also signal a greater fear. The beasts of hell belonged in Hell, whatever the state of this cursed land. Pol suspected the monsters had a master, and if a master then instructions. If not quite a plan, yet a desire; and knowing Despair, dread consequences for failure to meet it.

Pol lithely hopped down from the boulder and walked without hurry toward the lone helldog before him. Its lack of startlement proved out one of his assertions. The creature flinched with repressed hatred, and alternated vicious, earth-shaking growls with more urgent baying as the Martial Wizard came within a few rods on open ground. Just as he sensed the thing would retreat rather than risk fair combat, Pol stopped.

He knew from the past two days of alternating flight and rest, he was just faster than these things over open ground, in the long haul. From the first day, he learned that their hunt was not accidental; he could not shake their pursuit and they never gave up. Running the rest of his life would bring him no closer to the center he sought;

better death than to give up the search. But Pol was close enough now, to read the beast's mind.

Focusing and gently intoning a few syllables of nonsense-sound, Pol reached out and felt for something behind the wall of hatred and fear riding on the growls. There, yes, fleeting visions of things that inspired strong response from the helldog. He pushed the thought of *when* across the space between their minds. Fires everywhere, and torment for rulers and subjects alike; then a crack to the bright sky, freedom and a colossal figure with deep crimson hide. Pol shivered and nearly lost contact with the beast's mind. Such power, and malice unleashed—in the daylight, here in this kingdom?

A mission, orders, a search to find… not himself, Pol realized with a small shock. He pressed further, sensing that the beast before him had ceased baying; probably confused at this mental probe. A search for *what?* Pol could see only light, blinding like lightning; as he trained the helldog's thoughts to this blazing memory, Pol sensed the monster's fear and revulsion of it, but to his mind the sight was oddly exciting, yet comforting. The helldog knew nothing of this flaring white thing on its own; forced to think on it now, the beast audibly whined as at an important obligation forgotten.

Surely, Pol thought, there was something here. He had called out, when he fought inside the circle of wagons, and heard no response. But in his mind, he doubted, still felt there might have been survivors. Focusing harder, ignoring the strain and calculating the risk for his own safety, he pushed in again, boring after the riddle of this chaos-beast and its willingness to follow orders, to cooperate, to stay with the plan.

At the circle of wagons, he pushed the memory at the helldog, alongside questions of *why* and *what*. For a long time there was nothing except the din of many helldogs, the pack on the hunt. Pol maintained the contact, longer than he had with any human, he was not even sure how long. Then, even over the sound of several monsters growling and baying, he saw. The wagon-fort, that was their goal. Something there, he realized, was the white light's source. And the helldogs turned aside from that to him. Again, he pushed the thought in one word, *why*.

And saw an image of himself, surrounded in blazing white light.

The pack had turned on him, followed him, hunted him, because the beasts sensed something akin to their target in his person. And surely, most surely, there was something here…

Pol snapped the contact and opened his eyes. The moons above had moved too far, the time slipped by while he cast. And half-around him, the howling hell-pack was arrayed in a loose semi-circle, all assembled now and moving in with deliberate steps.

Dropping to a defence-retreat stance, Pol breathed in for seven counts and out for six. Too long he had maintained the thought-contact spell; now he had insufficient stamina to summon the Thunderfist. Behind him, the boulder was within a sprint's reach, if he could feint and freeze them here for a half-step's lead. From height, they knew better than to attack less than three at once; and as they regrouped, he would leap beyond the circle and head off, using surprise to gain away from them with his long-distance gait. Irrelevantly, Pol thought of food—not because he was hungry, it had only been three days. But because a lifetime of running would eventually lead to hunger. And because, as he delivered the feint and ran, Pol realized the helldogs also did not eat, not truly. Despite their glowing eyes and triform legs, they took animal forms suggesting weaknesses they did not possess.

Already on the boulder, Pol watched them approach, carefully yet predictably, and prepared for his leap on the first rush. He should not have maintained the contact so long. If this pack kept its discipline, it was only a matter of time before they broke his resources and took him down. And death, Pol knew, was nowhere closer to the center he sought.

Still, he thought as he executed his flipping leap, there was surely something here.

⊕⊕⊕

When Treaman awoke in the pre-dawn gloam, he didn't make a sound despite the stab of terror he felt. Falling asleep on guard duty was unforgivable; everyone was wounded and he had let his pride get the better of him. They could all have been slain before rising.

But Treaman cried out as if gashed, bringing everyone piling out of the tent, when he saw where they were.

"Treaman!" Mhoral cried with his bent club ready, looking around at the destroyed circle of wagons surrounding their tent.

Haltar was standing and held the sheathed artefact in one hand. As it became clear there was no immediate threat, he leaned down and quietly hissed "Cark" to no one in particular.

Linya watched Treaman looking left then right, and put a hand on his shoulder to interrupt. "It's the land, like you said last night, yes?"

Treaman nodded, and swallowed to get his words back. He pointed north by east and challenged them, "See the ridge?"

Swinging around he pointed south, between two of the wrecked wagons. "There, that's a forest."

"And there's the sun," Bildon quipped from beneath Treaman's elbow. "And puffy clouds, and there's the mountain."

Treaman looked down on the Stealthic, then popped him on the skull with his fist.

"Yes, and it's the same mountain, you stubby dolt, in the same place. All of it is in the same place."

The group looked at their Woodsman as if he had started speaking the Dwarvish tongue.

“Are you saying,” Linya suggested slowly, “it was all here before last night? Treaman, the fight, no one could tell—”

“No. I saw.” Treaman realized he was remembering the visions he had through Hallah’s eyes. That quickly became the second thing he decided not to tell the group. “This terrain—it was all like this, when the fight began, throughout the night, and now. Skysword, the forest, all of it.”

He turned to the leader, “Haltar, the map shows a forest, called the Tallwoods, around the capital. At the base of the mountain.” He watched as the leader straightened up, unconsciously flexing his injured shoulder while his lip stitched back in a momentary grimace.

Their eyes met and Treaman spread his hands to deflect the responsibility. “We may never be closer.”

Haltar gave a single nod that indicated understanding, not agreement. “We eat. How is the Nubian?”

“I’m surprised he’s still alive,” Mhoral declared. “He slept like the dead.”

“Can we rig a wagon, or some gear, to carry him?” Haltar asked, as Treaman made a fire and started to lay out food.

“He’s enormous, Haltar. All the mules are dead. Even you couldn’t haul him far alone.”

The leader sat on a box, rubbing his face. “We don’t know how long the land will… stay solid, like this.”

“We don’t know,” Bildon put in, “why it happened at all.”

“Or if it actually happened,” Mhoral droned, as was his nature.

“What about the man in black?” Linya asked. “He saved us, and he’s all alone out there.”

Treaman could hear the crackle of his cookfire, and the gentle rustle of morning breeze moving little things among the wrack of the caravan. No one had any liking for the hard choices ahead of them.

The meal passed in silence. When Treaman's eyes crossed Bildon's he was shocked that the Halfling winked at him. In answer to his unspoken puzzlement, Bildon made momentary mime-show of falling asleep, which no one else caught. Treaman had to grin, recognizing that his friend had few flies on him. Hallah glided down from her joyous romp around the camp to settle on his shoulder and arrange herself for sleep—so sated by remains of mules that she did not even ask for fish.

Haltar ate less, finished first, and dusted his hands.

"We are not leaving Braja behind."

Mhoral drew breath to argue, but everyone jumped at the rustle of the tent flap behind them. Braja loomed in the aperture, then came forth, slow but steady with a face handsome on one side, ruined on the other. Linya hopped up with a cry and the Nubian knelt, allowing her ministrations. None of the others came within arm's reach.

There was precious little Linya could do for him, and the giant black stood again, to tower over the party. Wounded and pained as he looked, Treaman still felt a tangible thud of fear at his sheer size and strength. He said nothing but stood as if awaiting orders, or perhaps for sentence to be passed.

Haltar stood also, and held out his arm, which the Nubian gripped. Then Haltar gestured out at the body of Pelian, or rather to the bloody left half of Pelian's corpse, where the flies and bravest of reaver birds still swarmed.

"Leader," Haltar said. Braja did not respond, but when Haltar pointed to himself and repeated the word, he nodded with a one-sided smile.

"Mhoral, get some of the currency gems we found."

The Elf produced a small bag as Haltar gestured everyone to gather around. Pouring out the bag on the ground between them, Haltar again said just one word.

"Equal." Braja watched him with brows knit. Haltar pointed around to each member of the group and himself, and said again "equal".

"He doesn't know the word," Treaman offered.

"Equal," Haltar repeated. "The same."

"Same," Braja nodded.

Haltar squatted down, took a handful of gems and began placing one at each person's feet including Braja's. Mhoral started to protest, but Bildon stepped on his foot hard and pointed to the Nubian, who watched the growing piles with interest.

Haltar finished, stood, pointed to Braja's pile and said again, "Same."

Braja stared down at his pile for a long moment. Looking up with a serious face, he put his fist to his heart, then pointed to Haltar.

"Leader."

Then he turned his proud, ravaged face to Treaman and pointed to his pile of gems, flashing that one-sided grin.

"Same."

Treaman grinned and nodded.

Bildon said, "You have the soul of a diplomat, great leader. Two words, and we have a new recruit."

"Gather up anything we might need," Haltar said, "we're leaving before noon." He nodded meaningfully to the south towards the line of trees.

"But what about the man in black?" Linya breathed.

Haltar shrugged. "Let's not overestimate the extent to which the chaos is receding. We might run into him as likely that way as any other." The foot-knight's calm gaze did nothing to assuage the worry on the mage's face, but it did establish that his decision was final. The group broke up in varying directions to forage, with cloths over their faces against the growing stench.

It was past noon before they could finally leave. They spent three hours arguing about what to bring along.

There was enough treasure, in coins and gems, to make up half what they had split from the dragon's hoard. Mhoral even volunteered to carry more of the gold, on top of his share of the party-load: as he spoke, Bildon stared slack-jawed at the Elf in a mime-show of amazement until Mhoral pushed him down and Haltar had to break up the tussle. After much acrimony, ten votes and several half-measures, they moved everything they thought valuable into one of the least-damaged wagons and boarded it up. Everyone's face showed how hopeless they thought the gesture.

As the morning wore on the stench of corpses became overpowering; Treaman found vinegar among the cooking supplies and soaked thicker rags they could tie around their faces as they worked to pull the dead together for burning. The humans lay together on two enormous biers, reinforced by all manner of broken up wood and cloth, while the mules were dragged two-on-each to another pyre. Treaman looked up at his companions, stalking around the wagon-circle with faces covered like masked bandits. Indeed, there was little difference, he thought, except that they had not caused this carnage. He shied rocks at the reaver-birds and reflected that scavengers differed only by degrees.

Bildon came out of one wagon with a small barrel, perhaps a foot high, tightly sealed and marked "Oncario". No one had heard the name; shrugging, he shook the cask to be sure it did not contain liquor and then tossed it on the pyre. Perhaps ten counts later, the area shook to an enormous explosion; Bildon and Treaman hit the ground together as Hallah squawked and took to the skies. Hot burning bits rained down on everyone and all was confusion for a time.

They each took turns recriminating the Stealthic for his carelessness.

"You keep shrugging like that," Treaman said, "your shoulders will freeze that way."

"What do you wish from me!" Bildon shouted back with some heat. "I don't know what in the Hells of Despair was in it, flour felt like, it was just something for the flames."

Haltar held out his cape to one side, with three singed holes in it, and Linya smeared another healving salve on the back of his leg.

Braja, who had been inside a wagon, came striding over then with a question on his face. All attempts to ask him about the cask produced a blank look , but when Haltar repeated the name "Oncario" his torn countenance lit and he pointed to the south toward the forest.

Treaman looked over the enormous black, dressed now in a thick black animal skin with silver-white spots, perhaps a nocturnal feline from the southern jungles of his home. Braja carried a long spear nearly his own height and thicker than three fingers on the haft, plus a stretched-skin tower shield of long oval shape. Across his broad back lay a recurved bow that was taller than Treaman and looked like grey, petrified wood with layers of something dull white, perhaps horn. He had secured one pack to the back of his waist with a broad belt, and when Haltar pointed to another on the ground, the Nubian grinned and snatched it up like a small book.

Braja slapped Treaman's backpack and said "Same".

Treaman grinned and nodded, then pointed to the tent. "We are not leaving that behind." He and Braja broke it down in a matter of minutes; it rolled into a bundle just larger than a blanket-pack, and Braja slung that over his shoulder as well.

Bildon nudged Mhoral with his elbow. "Who says we're not bringing a mule?"

There was nothing more to be done, but none of the group made a move towards leaving. Treaman settled his pack, waited, hitched his belt, and waited more. Everyone naturally gazed toward the body-bonfires. Mhoral had his visor down, seemingly unaffected. Haltar looked reflective, as if someone else would give the signal to march.

Treaman saw Linya's face streaked with tears, and for a moment he thought of her as a tender and compassionate young woman. Then he remembered how she had once set a tree lion ablaze, all eight feet of it from toe to tip. Another time she laid ahold of a bravo trying to stab Mhoral in the back, seizing him with her bare hands that spat off arcane tendrils until black smoke dribbled from the attacker's mouth. Just a flash-thought, of her standing in the open field when they were all naked, was enough to complete Treaman's confusion, and he fell into a fit of coughing.

That made the others turn to look at him. Haltar stirred from his thought-walk, slapped a newly-scavenged plain broadsword at his belt, and nodded for Treaman to take the point. Treaman hefted the spear he'd found, and set out.

They strode off towards what appeared to be south, by just a point west, adopting a ragged, narrow triangle shape without speaking. Within several rods the land around the wagon circle changed, to the cracked, grassless steppe they knew; back by the caravan, Treaman noted, it seemed still barren but somehow less parched and dead. He could not recall whether that had been the case when he first came out from their wagon, during the fight. There had been other things on his mind. But yes! The Sword of Air, when he dropped it, had lain in grass. There was more grass where Pelian had camped, or else it somehow came there.

Treaman from the front kept swiveling, taking backwards steps while spotting the landmarks behind them. His heart took a deep plunge down, when he saw the distant ridge east of the wagons had disappeared. Their stark outlines and the thick pillars of black smoke now stood against a blue sky; that raised horizon formerly so real had melted away. Treaman had dared to hope, perhaps things were changing for the better, or that they were already on the outskirts of another safe-haven. But he saw the grey-chalky soil beneath his boots now, smelled the peculiar tang of dust in the breeze, that taste which reminded him of constant threat, and almost longed for the charnel reek again. The forest ahead seemed no closer, and Treaman felt a surge of panic, lest it too disappear and leave them completely stranded.

Driven by that thought he plunged ahead at force-march pace, and the group behind him had no breath for banter while keeping up. After perhaps a half-hour, the forest ahead was bigger and closer, with some individual trees standing out —pines or spruce, most likely. Suddenly remembering, Treaman stopped and spun about to look back.

Half the tiny distant wagons, and all the smoke, had disappeared.

Everyone stopped and followed his gaze; Treaman expected curses and shouts, but instead they all looked back to him with puzzled faces.

"So, it's gone," Haltar said, "we've seen it happen before."

"It's not all, there are, I see," the Woodsman stammered. Everyone looked at him blankly. "Don't you see some of them, the wagons?"

Bildon said, "There's nothing there anymore, friend."

Treaman charged to the back of the party and tried to count. Six, no seven still in sight, not all on the near-side; it was as if some wandering Titan had lifted half of the enormous carriages and put them in his pocket before silently moving on. Treaman stepped to his right, to see if the angle changed anything. Two more wagons disappeared from plain view, erased.

"No!" he cried, not sure why this gradual loss to chaos should distress him so. Treaman ran back left in an effort to restore them, but another winked out in the space of time he took his eye from it. Only four remained, for certain.

Haltar's arm latched onto his shoulder, arresting him in place. "What do you see?"

"The wagons, they're still there, some of them, but we're losing them."

"We never had them," Haltar said gazing down steadily. "Treaman. We have all we can carry. Finding this place again, even assuming it stays a place. Very unlikely."

Haltar took his hand away and waited until Treaman turned south. The leader nodded once, and added, "No sense losing the forest too in this hell-hole."

Ten minutes' hard hiking later, they reached the edge of a huge pine barren. Treaman never looked back again, and now his nose caught a scent on the shifting wind. Looking to his left, he saw Braja, who had also stopped.

"Water," he said and the big black warrior nodded. It was one more proof, that they were beyond the clutch of the Percentalion's chaos and in a place of relative order. Treaman craned his head to the southeast; the treeline obscured much of his vision, but most of the rest was taken up not by crisp sun-dappled turquoise sky but by the deeper, more choate blue of that unthinkably large mountain, Skysword, the object of their quest in the far, but suddenly finite distance.

Treaman led the party on under the boughs, trying to maintain a healthy skepticism in the face of the mounting evidence that they had escaped the Percentalion. Some parts of the wasted lands held scrub-forest with stunted, gnarled pines or gorse often covering the space of a ten minutes' hike: but now the tall straight boles thickened and widened throughout an hour of steady marching. It started to snow, gently but steadily with large flakes, something else that had never happened in the curse's grip. Treaman felt sure they were somewhere. It seemed beyond credit. To judge by Skysword's looming bulk, still visible to the southeast through any break in the trees, they had come more than a week's journey in less than two days.

The pines stretched high overhead, changing to other varieties of conifer as the land rolled and occasionally broke into a clearing in the dells. On flat spaces, the trees that had won the fight for sun over many decades shaded everything beneath them, leaving only small patches of brush, fern and thorn below with lots of open space, covered by a thick bed of needles. The trunks stood naturally spaced, constantly suggesting a layout in rows but never looking planted. At times the woodsman could see down a near-straight avenue for a furlong or more; yet blind-spots tickled his nerves and kept him on his guard.

There was a healthy smell about the forest, too—resins and the musk of varied animal life were keen to Treaman's senses. Something more, a smell made by man which he recognized instantly though he saw nothing as yet—smoke. The snow flecked needles underfoot muffled even Mhoral and Haltar's steps, whereas Linya walked without skill but lightly, with almost a dancer's grace. The giant Nubian was clearly more at home here as well—except for a shiver-chill, probably from air he'd never known as a youth—stepping with surety and making little sound. Bildon, had it not been for his mouth, might as well have been invisible. But conversation lagged from all of them, drowned as they were in the sheer size and majesty of this pine barren.

Braja noticed the first tracks, and Treaman the worst of them.

The Nubian was already ranging near the front and a bit to the left of where Treaman normally led, when he grunted and pointed down. Gathering, they could all see the wolf-tracks in mud; much smaller than helldogs or even the hexavores, not bearing as deeply into the soft ground. Treaman chuckled at the normality of it all. But his sense of release tightened back up when he spotted a patter of prints at the edge of a clearing. He called the others over and wordlessly gestured. Small, splay-toed marks of many somethings that went about on two feet.

Bildon hooked a thumb at Braja and said "I like his tracks better."

"Are these Halflings?" Linya asked, and everyone compared from Bildon's feet.

"We're doomed," Mhoral's voice echoed within the helm, "a tribe of him lives here?"

"Why do you assume they would be enemies?" Bildon challenged with a grin.

"Based on experience," came the response and everyone laughed.

Treaman had knelt close to a particularly clear specimen in the snow.

"So, what are we up against, Woodsman?" Haltar said.

"Forced to guess—"

"You are."

"I would say garruk children."

"Children!" Mhoral cried, raising his visor a moment.

"You don't think they have them?" Treaman challenged, "Anyway, that's what the tracks suggest."

Bildon pointed to a round hole, and Treaman nodded. "Spear butt, most likely. So they carry weapons from an early age perhaps."

"Where are the females, or adults?" No one could answer Mhoral on this.

"There could be a dozen here, or more," Treaman said, "they don't seem to be taking much care. Hunting, maybe."

Haltar leaned in for a second look, then shrugged. "The warbands, like the ones we met, are only males, everyone agrees on that. We'll need to stay on guard, is all."

They kept on, moving generally south by east in the direction of Skysword into the late afternoon. Treaman sought a place to camp, but was drawn by the increasing smell of water nearby. The party almost never got to rest near a pool or stream. The hill country was mainly behind them, and the trees had become predominantly cypress and a kind of low-clustered thick bush he could not name.

Footing was poor with knobs of root-wood thrusting up from the ground like hundreds of chess pieces on an acre-sized game board.

In places where pines and some birches still showed, they were curiously short and clustered together with many trunks rising from the same spot, looking more like bushes. There were clear signs of cutting on older trunks near the center of these tree-clumps, and the smell of burning was unmistakable.

"What happened here?" Bildon asked, and Treaman shook his head.

"Charcoal," Haltar stated matter-of-factly. Everyone stared at the foot-knight. "I read about the practice, these trees have been coppiced to produce more wood in less time."

"He read a book," Bildon said to Mhoral, and they both started chuckling until Haltar, turning to go, accidentally bumped one into the other and down, still laughing.

"That explains the smoke," Treaman agreed. A short time later the group came upon a kiln of brick. Nestled in a grove of clumped birches, the dome-shaped structure emanated heat that could be felt from twenty steps away and glowed redly through its visored door like an eye. Several cords of neatly cut sections were stacked nearby, waiting their turn. The heat melted the snow even as it hit the ground, and fine black powder lay everywhere.

Bildon sidled up to the slits in the door and peered within a moment.

"They are cooking wood in there," he said with emphasis, as if resolving a great mystery.

Treaman pointed to a clear flat space upwind. "Let's camp here. Whoever built this may come by and answer some questions."

After setting up the tent Treaman took his spear and headed out, as always to try hunting, but also to scout around further south and east. The party was well out of hearing behind him, and almost out of sight, before he realized that Braja had followed. He waited for the enormous warrior to catch up and they grinned and nodded to each other before continuing.

Hallah woke and looked around at the trees with some interest before announcing her hunger. Treaman's hand automatically went towards a pouch holding some riddy, but then froze, as he realized the clear space ahead was a river.

Creeping up with Braja a step behind, Treaman came to the bank of the largest body of water he had ever seen. At first he was sure it was an enormous lake, but then he saw the slow, massive current moving southward to his right. The river entered from the east, and just north of his position it swept about to southward in a great curve. The trunk of a tree floated by, larger than the Woodsman could have put his arms around yet looking like a stick. If Braja had fired an arrow across its flow, and then walked over water to pick it up, he might not have reached the opposite side with his second shot. That far bank rose up a sharp bluff, five furlongs of high rock studded with cave-mouths and a few hardwoods clinging stubbornly to crevices here and there.

"Big water. Hungry!"

"Would Hallah like to catch a fish?" Treaman offered, pointing to the river and sending a thought of something jumping out of the water. The miniature dragon cocked her head to gaze into his eyes a moment, then cooed excitedly and darted off his neck to soar above the river, poking her head down to both sides in earnest search. Treaman chuckled, and it was several long moments before he realized Braja was staring at him. Not fear, but a kind of respect sat on the warrior's features. Unsure what to say, the Woodsman shrugged, gestured out to the little flier.

"She's my friend." Braja nodded once, perhaps in understanding, and then the two men settled in on the arching roots of a large cypress extending out over the bank. Treaman could see the river bottom below and spotted several kinds of insect and reptilian life, as well as fish, while keeping a weather-eye out for Hallah.

He breathed deep the marshy smells of the near bank, until a breeze off the water carried the odor of fallen leaves from the other shore. What a wonderful place, he thought. The snow kept falling but it wasn't quite cold enough to allow much accumulation. Almost as warm as spring back north in Novar; Treaman hadn't been in a forest without struggling to survive in more than a year, and never this far south. The new trees, certain wefts of the weather, even the strange tracks and the signs of man, all seemed thrilling yet comforting. Beyond the Percentalion's chaos, Treaman felt he could handle whatever a merely wild country threw at him.

Hallah dived at the water two or three times and came up empty; the last time her plunge was inexpert and she floundered in the current for an anxious moment before managing to get aloft again. Treaman congratulated his friend on her strength and courage, then told her to come back for food. To his surprise he was saucily informed that Hallah was not afraid and would find her own fish. He grimaced at her independent streak, then wondered why even an infant dragon would do anything a mortal told her to.

He fell to examining the opposite bank, but it was too far to make out many details. Braja grinned and reached into his pouch to extract a short metal tube. Turning and pulling he extended a smaller tube from within and put it up to one eye, gazing across at the opposite bank awhile. Spotting something, he pointed and handed the tube across to Treaman. The Woodsman noticed that the elegant brass fitting on the bottom bore the mark of the hoarding squirrel.

"You clever dog," he said, "you looted this from Pelian."

Braja grinned, a few extra white teeth showing through the hole in his cheek. "Same" he chanted, while gesturing that Treaman should look.

Through the spyscope, Treaman could see that while some caves on the far side were natural, ragged and small, others were more rounded with signs of wood bracing, ladders, and walkways set into the sides of the bluff. One of these was where Braja had pointed.

"Hallah win! Get fish!"

Treaman had a flash of something silvery and struggling, pinioned by claws just above the water's edge, still roiling and churned by the strike. This was encouraging—Hallah would grow more independent with time, and if anything happened to him, the Woodsman had hope she could survive. He didn't want to think about losing her, but it felt the right thing to do. No matter how small, no dragon could ever be a pet.

The wind shifted to blow upstream and at once Treaman caught a strong scent of smoke. He turned his glass south and nearly fell off the root into the water. Just in sight beyond the curve of the near bank more than a league away sat a large island in the middle of the giant river, banked by rock cliffs like those on the far side rising a hundred feet above the flow.

And on the island stood the largest city Treaman had ever seen.

He pointed for Braja, who grunted in surprise as Treaman clapped the spyscope to his eye again. The city filled the island to its edge, walled in red brick over three stories high, with more buildings than he could count extending three, four, even six stories above that. The edge of a massive brick bridge led from the east-facing gate out of sight to the shores on this side of the river. If there were other bridges, Treaman could not see them. But from fivescore points across the rooftops, thick black smoke streamed up into the darkening dusky sky.

"Oncario," he breathed to himself. "It's a city, an entire city here in the chaos land." He turned to Braja, handing him the glass so he could look. "There must be ten thousand people living there, or more."

"Hallah big, coming, win, tired. Hallah come."

Laughing, Treaman turned to see his friend laboring along with a fish half her size, still squirming. Hallah's wingtips were less than a yard above the water, and Treaman held out his arms to make it easier for her to land.

It didn't make sense that the water below should still be churning.

Before he could think, Treaman cried out and launched himself beneath Hallah's line of flight, crashing clumsily into the sinuous, scaly, tooth-studded thing that lunged up from the chop. Its strike, aiming for the dragon, missed as the Woodsman's body deflected it, jaws shutting with a sharp snap. Treaman plunged into ice-cold water with one arm half-around the body of a monster nearly as thick across as he was, and horribly longer. He cried out in panic, and an agony of freezing wet in his throat was the result.

Sputtering and flailing, he managed to clear the surface, but the body of the monster was wrapping itself around him now, as the head shook and snapped again, turning back to face its new prey. Both the hilt of his sword and the arm he used to draw it were beneath a loop of something scaly yet eel-like, and as Treaman kicked his legs half to swim, half to hurt, he felt talons beneath the water cutting into that same calf wounded by the helldogs. The monster's head arced fully around, missing on its next lunge due to the thrashing of its victim. Rearing back, the thing squeezed hard, forcing what little air Treaman had out of his lungs.

The head above him suddenly sprouted a stick from its tongue, as the creature flailed and hissed in outrage. The coil loosened and Treaman fell free. Another stick appeared in one of the monster's eyes, while Treaman discovered the water was not above his waist. Threshing fully free, he drew Gutter and slashed down hard, hitting a bit of trunk and possibly some submerged leg, enough to draw inky blood. With a convulsion as quick as thought, the snake-thing was back under water and the smooth current erased all sign of its passing.

With one hand still on his bow, Braja reached down with the other to haul Treaman bodily from the river. Together they doctored the scrape, which was not deep but would certainly leave a scar layered onto the previous wound like that.

"You saved my life," Treaman said, not sure if anything would be understood. "Thank you."

Braja looked at him blankly, then gestured vaguely out to the river several times with a dismissive hand. Finally he said just, "Friend. Same."

They clasped arms then and Treaman stood to test his leg.

{*"Hallah good hunter. New fish good."*} The little dragon crouched on a cypress root, joyously tearing into its prize.

{*"Treaman saved Hallah. You should be more careful."*}

{*"Treaman fall in water, but not catch fish. Learn from Hallah."*} As Treaman stood there with his mouth open, the creature looked up at him a moment, then tore off a piece of fish and held it out in one foreclaw. Braja started to laugh without hearing a thing, rolling low and deep, and there was nothing more to be said.

Back at the camp everyone was quite interested in Treaman's report. But as they discussed plans to approach the town the next day, the Woodsman became concerned not with what lay ahead, but what lay above. Mhoral searched for a city anywhere on the journal maps, while Linya tried hard to recall all she could about one isolated reference to an "under-capital" near Reghalion. Bildon found easy targets to mock in all the bickering, but it became the buzzing of flies to Treaman, as he stepped away from the fire's light to focus in growing horror at the night skies.

"Treaman," Haltar said, in repetition the Woodsman realized. "What is the trouble?"

Treaman turned back to see them all sitting around the fire twenty steps away. He tried to frame his fear, but couldn't find the words.

"Aral, see? Do you see her?"

"Well, hardly," quipped Bildon, "she's at the thumbnail phase."

"Nearly new, yes." Treaman said heavily.

"What of it," Haltar demanded.

"Last night, after we fought the helldogs, by the wagons. She was just past full."

"What!" Mhoral cried, "Hold, what day is it?"

"We left Trainertown the morning of the tenth," Linya said, "and the first night out was, it was the ruined keep." Everyone held peace for a time on that.

"And Pelian," Treaman continued for her, "we met his caravan after midnight, so the eleventh. He kept us in the wagon most of the day. Last night, we rested after the fight: I saw the moons that night, today must be the twelfth."

"So it's the twelfth," Bildon repeated, "what's the fuss?"

"On the twelfth of this month, the lower moon should be just past full, not nearly new."

Not a sound except from the campfire.

"It's the twenty-fifth or twenty-sixth of the Fire Ant. We have lost two weeks somehow out there."

"Impossible!" Bildon cried with heat, "You must have made some mistake."

Mhoral didn't say anything, but leaped up to walk past Treaman as if those few steps could take him close enough to Aral for surety.

"Wait, wait a moment," Haltar insisted, "If Aral is almost new, then Unal would be new this month as well—isn't that right?"

Treaman nodded. "And by now it should already be up, still a little ahead of Aral at this hour." He held an arm out to the heavens. "Does anyone see it?"

Not a word from the party.

"Braja," Treaman said, making a gesture like pulling open a spyscope. Braja produced the item and handed it over. "There," the Woodsman said after a moment where everyone around him held their breath. "The vague outline, you can see it there." And he handed the glass to Haltar who followed Treaman's site-arm.

"Maybe Pelian drugged us," Bildon said weakly, looking ill. "He might have kept us in the wagon—"

"I saw the moons the night after the fight, Bildon. It was the evening of the eleventh."

Mhoral turned back to face the group, and nodded in confirmation.

"Two weeks," Haltar breathed, impressed and letting it show for once. "Cark me hollow."

After a while, Linya said, "That's about as long as we might have taken, to reach the center of the kingdom. If things were normal."

No one had anything further to add, but they all drifted back around the campfire as if for company. Treaman couldn't shake the feeling of horror and loss; part of him never wanted to return to the chaos-land again.

When the explosion sounded, everyone jumped as if struck. A deep boom with lasting echoes that seemed to take forever to die down.

"From the bluffs across the river," Treaman said.

Bildon made a shape with his hands the size of that small cask.

Braja looked at the Stealthic, and then quietly said "Oncario."

The Twenty-Eighth of the Fire Ant, 1995 ADR

My Dearest Kia,

Every letter I send you, it seems, must begin with some hackneyed phrase that a schoolchild would hesitate to use. But I cannot lie to you for my life, and the truth is, I can truly bear it no longer.

{Having said that, let me assure you, this rope you find in the packet is not from my suicide. Though my mortal friends here all joke that it comprises enough rope to hang myself! It is indeed, a binding rope for marriage. Patience.}

Separation from you, when I first agreed to a "temporary" posting here, was a grim prospect. I have wished for seven years to ask for your hand, but we both recognized the moment was not right. All that spring, I heard in my heart "soon". I thought the assignment would further my understanding (it has), that it would advance my position in the Guild (oh, indeed it has! would it had not) and perhaps if I endeavored to make myself busy with study that the time would fly (no, I cannot even attempt a jest at this last).

I swear, my love, time seems now to have stopped; my chest is tight, I hold my breath every second, like a man underwater throughout the day. That first month following my arrival here in Conar—six long months ago!—the sun seemed to crawl, and the nights alone among sleeping humans stretched on. Thinking back, I admit I took a purely selfish pleasure in the company of young Judgement, may the Heroes protect him. At first the effort to keep him from arrest, and later the doomed attempt to fill his bottomless thirst for knowledge, these were great diversions. I missed you as much as ever, and even more as time went by. But I confess without shame (or much), the example of that incredible youth, his courses of study and also his deeds—they made some of those days slip by like his gliding, silent skiff on the bay, covering hours before I could remember my emptiness, and giving me labor to fill the void. We even wrote of him in our correspondence, and I recall you said you desired to meet him. How unlikely that prospect seemed, in the summer.

But my protégé, or dare I say my friend, Solemn Judgement has left us now. Out to sea in that tiny craft, purposing as I hoped for the south and Mendel, but I fear perhaps lost forever. And I, in that time, am bereft, dear Kia. There is nothing else I can use to buffer my heart from the staggering distance between us, the shearing pain of our separation. I love you! With all my life I do—this is so unworthy, such words should be spoken, should be heard, faces seen, hands clasped. But I love you, and without you I wither.

The seventeenth day today, since the end of that awful ordeal in the Hopeward; filled like all the others with monotonous interrogation, ceaseless repetition of trivial, meaningless details, and not one hint that it will ever stop. Visiting officials keep arriving, quietly spirited to the city of Conar from every kingdom in the Lands, to be apprised of this wondrous discovery (their words!). And of course for a Mark, or a Baron, a High Mage or Curate, nothing will do but to hear it from the sole survivor.

They will repeat these words to their children and successors, with heroic decoration and manly purpose, to inspire the next generation for that day five decades hence, when the awful portal shall open again. I have told of the Arms of the Earth, of sentient marble statues, of water with a face and shattering walls of glass, a thousand times. I have relived Alendic's death, and shuddered again to think how Eddoran horribly survived it for a time. And Natasha—no, I refuse to burden even you with the thoughts I have of her, that dear, great woman, so burdened with loss yet saving our Hope at the price of her life.

I returned to my cell today, dear Kia, beaten and beyond thought for my future. I had ceased to care if I lived or died this very evening. Yet what should I find awaiting me, but your letter, dated more than six weeks ago! Sent by messenger overland to Eldarport, and thence by some daring vessel across the pirate seas; a month and more these words have waited to speak to me. What fate, I might have grumbled, delayed your voice on paper from sounding again in the ear of my mind. But then I read what you had written herein…

Nothing of the recent news, of your dear aunt's decease, my misadventure by the gate and foiled attempt to see you. These were all in our future when you wrote. Your missive predated all the hubbub of this fortnight's frustration, it was a sweet birdcall of beauty, composed in all innocence before there was any shadow across my life from that dreadful prison, and the loss of my companions, and the horrid sight of that undead, skull-like face. In the merciful chance of time, you wrote of the heat of summer, the search for a house, of the taste of my cousin's matchless wine—and I was transported by your words, back to the land of time-proper, to the bliss I always knew by your side. I caught myself cursing (mildly, I promise you) to read that you had again the taste of Kira-Ashton wine! And then I recalled where and when I was, and laughed, fully laughed, for the first time in two weeks.

Most would say it was mere chance that brought your words to me, just when I needed them. But I know in my heart, it is the voice of time-proper. You, Kia, will always be the speaker I need to hear, and your words always the guide by which my skiff will sail. We are five hundred leagues apart, and a pair of crowns conspire to keep us separated. But I know the customs of our land, that a house too long unoccupied and a couple too long unmarried or unhoused will bring poor fortune. Your sweet words of the daily, wholesome life, sent so long ago, have decided me. I never wished to wait, but knew I must. Now, though, I recognize that time itself will no longer tarry, for us, or for the countries and powers of Hope.

I intend, Kia Weitherton, by this letter to ask for your hand in marriage.

I am well aware of the customs, which demand that the couple be present, in private interview when the traditional words are spoken. To that I say, firstly, that we have never been more intimate, nor further from the prying concerns of others, than when we write as we have this half-year and more. Here, in the words we both admire from the Guild of Sages to whom we dedicate our study, on the pages of letters we have poured out our minds to each other. So it is best, I think that I ask you in writing, as no Elf to my recollection has ever done. So be it, the woman is exceptional and deserves a new precedent in her betrothal.

Then too, I am now a lawless adventurer, am I not! Reckless of custom and niggling adherence to rules which run contrary to the common good, I dare to ask a maiden's hand in the way I see fit (and in a letter, I find a testing ground to my liking).

But I will have you know, madam, I do not ignore the most important elements of tradition here. I am, though you must accept my word for this, dressed in traditional white which I purchased today for the occasion. The winding-rope is about my wrist. And as I prepare to write the words of my proposal, I shall be on my knees, here in my cell in the city of Men. See to it that you, my love, are on your feet as you read these words, and that you take this same winding-rope enclosed, around your wrist in turn.

Are you standing, then? Very well. The writing desk is somewhat high, but I shall manage.

Kia-aWithr tn Ced aronn ereby humb uts y ur hand s your hnd i filfullmrnt a ime pr r et the etrnul stars s t we sh

I have been reduced to the final indignity, a resort to my Diligent Quill, that it will take dictation of my proposal. I am still on my knees, I swear by The First!

Kia Weitherton, Cedrith Fellareon hereby humbly requests your hand in fulfillment of the mandates of time-proper. Let our hearts and minds be paired, let the eternal stars bear witness that we shall remain even as they, fixed and constant until our final moments. And may Hope watch over us and our love.

It is done, and never more poorly done I avow. I curse and laugh in turn, my love, even as I prepare the packet to send this ludicrous literary outrage to you. So fitting, is it not, that I should make a hash of this most important moment of my life. Yet even now I could not be more certain of the rightness, not of my own poor actions, but of the object to which my thoughts tend. You, and only you Kia, can well understand the meaning in my mistakes, sound out the sincerity in my foibles. None other is a fit mate for my remaining years. None other could put up with them! And if you say yes, then I would wish my years to be many indeed.

One thing will go right, I am certain. This missive, as all our correspondence in the future, shall go by the gate to Mendel and reach your hand in less than three days. That much, at least I have won from a fickle fortune set in all other ways to humiliate me. No more voyages! May I step through that gate again myself, dear one, and soon. Never to return. Never to seek adventure again. Never to desire another favor from someone high or low, except to abide with you.

Until that blessed day, I remain
Yours, with all my love,

Cedrith

⊕⊕⊕

Renan had the vigil-watch on the night Brother Farivaine was slain. He sprang up from prayer when the bridge of light returned, throwing its silvered glow over the Farsight Chamber as the bell in the tower above thrummed deep and long. From the upper entranceway, he saw his comrade's body partway down the mystic span, strapped across Harbinger's saddle. Striding down on solid light, he took the leads from the young woman whose life his companion had saved. With one hand he guided the stallion, while his other arm offered support to the survivor. She was still too choked with tears and wonder to speak, and this suited Renan well. He had not spoken to anyone outside the Order since leaving his family.

He had been with the Chosen Wanderers nearly a month, learned all the mysteries, taken his shifts and sallied forth several times to aid those in need. His victories were the source of much remark, especially the destruction of the Light-Drinker, of whom no legend told. Renan was known as the one who never returned with an unbroken lance. The loss of precious wood marked an occasion for good-natured jokes, but no one questioned his worth to the company. Now the Order's newest knight found his happiness shattered on the loss of a companion, but his inner peace remained intact. This was the full circle of his oath and commitment, and most likely his own future he witnessed now; for death had come among the brotherhood before this, as it would to them all soon or late.

Within the Watchtower, squires summoned by the bell's toll took charge of Farivaine's corpse, while another led Harbinger down the stone ramp to the stables. The weeping woman gave the name Dematha, and Niles escorted her to the compound's southern quarter, where she would be housed and fed until the Brethren met to determine her parole. Jeceb, the older fighting man who had greeted Renan on the day he joined the Order, nodded to him and put a hand on his shoulder.

"The body will lie in the chapel until dawn, and you may come to attend the funeral if you wish. A squire will watch from here and summon you if the bridge appears again."

"Thank you, Jeceb."

After stroking Quester briefly, Jeceb descended. Renan turned to face out the unrailed aperture of the third-story view-chamber, where the bridge of light had gone as quietly and quickly as it appeared. Gazing over the nightscape to the east, he searched his heart and felt torn, as usual, between dread at the call and desire for its challenge. The will of the Watchtower was beyond the knowledge of its occupants; despite constant threat in the Percentalion, the bridge of light followed no pattern they could discern. Farivaine, like most of the Brethren sent forth, returned within the hour of his summoning. A second bridge in one night was rare, but not unexampled. As few Brethren as were left, each must be ready. Renan looked east for those moments of vision that usually preceded the bridge's appearance, and murmured a verse from the oath they all had sworn.

"Before defeat, my life—only victory or blood can dispel shame."

Both moons hung to his right, the stars bore down in their late-autumn configuration, mostly above the clouds, but a few on the eastern horizon peeked between them. The bracing chill of oncoming winter kept Renan alert, as the sadness of loss focused him. Whether in this evening's watch, or whenever the Heroes saw fit, he was resolved to offer nothing less than his departed Brother had done. Renan glanced back to see his chamber glazed with silver moonlight, and briefly wondered if the day would come that Unal and Aral illumined an empty chamber here, without one Wanderer left to keep the vigil. Better to fight hard and die in defence of the helpless, rather than survive until such a day.

The bridge of light did not return, yet visions came to Renan many times before dawn, as they often did. He kept this secret to himself, as certain comments from his peers led him to believe they were not so frequently visited. He saw distant people, monstrous beings, the abandoned capital Reghalion by moonlight, convulsions of the earth and enormous wings against the slopes of Skysword.

These were seldom the kind of views that presaged the light-bridge; nothing of immediate combat or destruction requiring aid to innocents. Rather, he saw fell creatures roving alone, or folk in an isolated village looking west, or a spate of harmful weather over empty terrain. Renan came to believe he was made witness to the tale entire, the gradual decay of the proudest and largest of Hope's kingdoms. Should he chronicle all this, he wondered? What mind could encompass such a colossal task? And why would someone attempt it with no comfort in view?

Renan saw the scattered towns, and became only more despondent as dawn approached. Stathos, the walled city where the peasants gave each adult a vote, held their own against the giants in the nearby hills. Their grain could feed many in Delvehold, that is, if any of the colony of miners there still lived. Oncario's stacks poured smoke into the sky, from an abundance of wood that Maladon so sorely needed. From Hollinsfen, neither Renan nor any of the Brothers had news for a week.

The evil of the land's blight lay here, in this lethal separation enforced upon the Children of Hope. The crowns of the northern kingdoms took no action, not even sending embassies as the curse over the Percentalion had worsened. And the nobility would obey only orders from a king. The Children of Hope no longer believed in special missions such as that of the Wanderers; Niles had told Renan he was the first recruit in more than a year. However many of Despair's ranks the Wanderers slew, still this mazed web upon travel and the mortal weather would kill all its people in time. The bridge of light defeated chaos while it shone, yet even if the Order survived, there would soon be none to save in the largest Hopeful kingdom which was their special charge.

Suddenly eager to break from such reflections and escape the gnawing despair in his chest, Renan looked after the declining moons, to the south. Yet his visions continued, this time the strangest of his young career.

Briefly, he glimpsed the broad River Sweeping, the Percentalion's southern boundary a hundred leagues away, and on into the verdant expanses of Mendel still enjoying the warmth of autumn. His eye traversed the land as if in flight, seeing warm cottages of the farm country with windows dark; a lone wagon under the moonlight carried two men east on the deserted road toward the capital, and suddenly Renan's view swerved up the escarpment surrounding the city itself. In a small but exquisite chapel, an Elven couple before the altar took the vows of marriage in the blackest hour of night. Guards stood nearby, evidently to arrest the groom upon completion of his vows. Yet the couple both laughed and kissed in joy. Renan could not imagine why such a strange sight would be brought before his eyes, yet neither could he doubt the truth of every detail.

Onward his vision flew, across southern Mendel and for a dizzying moment above the deep canyon of the Great Cleft. Renan gasped and stepped back from the sheer height, but before he could do more he was soaring across flat, baked-earth desert lands, sheering somewhat westward and back into more settled, fertile country in the empire of Argens. His vision flitted past hamlets and towns, coming to rest on a quiet camp in the hill country where a small group of persons slept. Renan could make out few details, but one slender man stood guard while another, an elven female, knelt in prayer.

In one thunderous beat of his heart, Renan recognized the reason for his vision: to see this preacher and know her from afar.

Her devotion was clear from the lateness of the hour. He marked her shield, battered and in need of replacement, bearing the symbol of the tower, like yet not the same as his own. An adherent of Aballe, most likely; Renan was pleased at once, to think there could be a connection.

She looked young, and yet as an Elf there could be no certainty. Renan was strangely drawn to her face, at first plain but bearing such even, delicate features and so beautiful in prayer. Renan thought irrelevantly of the noblewoman his parents had intended for him to marry, back in Conar—what was her name? The same delicacy and fine devotion he sensed in their one very brief meeting, when he came to explain why he refused to take his brother's place. But this Elven preacher—Renan saw the bandage on her arm, the other marks of wear and hard living and was struck with wonder at the evident contrast.

He fell to wondering if the southern foefdoms were at war. News was scarce in the Tower of the Wanderers, and anything without direct bearing on their mission was of little interest to the brethren. Women fighters were rare but not unheard of—the Order had several in its own history, though none at present, as female knights were scarcer than a dragon's goodwill. Could this be a future recruit? Why would he need to see that?

The warmth from his left hand distracted him, and Renan glanced down to see his house bond-ring. As shock coursed through him, he remembered that while he tore off his family crest on the day he arrived, he had not taken off his ring. He had never even thought of it until this moment. The only function of this jewelry was to seal a betrothal between noble houses. Yet Renan had renounced any such claim on joining the Order. What had the Watchtower-guard, Niles, said to him then? The Tower saw the truth of his claim, yet somehow he was and was not destined to marry. Renan reached to his left hand, yet a sense of awe near dread stayed him, and he left the ring in place.

So deep in thought, he hardly knew the passage of time until dawn's first ray struck his eyes.

When the duty-squire arrived, Renan tousled Quester's head and gave him a tuber-root before descending. The warhorse acknowledged his master with joy, sensing that the two of them were on alert with another battle to come before he returned to the stables below. He flinched and shook with impatience; like Renan, he knew nothing of the hour they would be called, only that they were next. To everyone else, even the squires who helped handle him every day, Quester was barely patient, often nipping or stamping at shows of affection.

In the chapel, Renan saw Farivaine's body laid out under samite, his shield atop his chest and the blood washed away, as if sleeping in the presence of all his fellows. Taking a place in the pew behind Niles and next to Brother Broders from Shilar, Renan was shocked as always to see how few of the Order still survived. Less than twoscore knights stood on the left-side of the chapel, barely filling a third of the benches there.

And his dismay rose to see Pallus now standing with the squires on the right. The Brother whose turn had preceded Farivaine's held his right arm still bound in a sling from his battle with the garruk. He met Renan's glance with determined sorrow, the mark of a man who has considered his course of action. Funerals, Renan recalled from his reading, were a moment of assay for the Brotherhood. Knights in training could avow their readiness to join the Wandering Order by crossing the aisle at the death of a Brother. In the same way, older fighters could signal their retirement from the active Order by standing with the squires. In this castle, the assistants were all older than their knights.

The ceremony was spare and sincere. For a quarter-hour they all stood in silent prayer, each man reflecting on his memory of the fallen. Then Niles stepped forward to speak for him, briefly recounting his many victories in a half-decade's career.

"Say not that he was ever defeated," Niles concluded as the rising sun peered through the nave window and descended toward the altar. "Say rather he kept to the strictures and returned to us with its commandments fulfilled."

The Brethren nodded and chanted in unison, *"Before an innocent life, mine and my steed's—for without their succor, there is no Order."*

Niles censed the draped body with aromatic oils, while squires turned the stone wheel that opened the chapel roof, just as the sun's light hit. Whether by the shape of the window-glass, or the properties of the oil, or perhaps the sanctity of the church, Farivaine's body ignited nearly at once into bright, consuming flame. Within moments, as the Brethren sang of Hope for the future and their dedication to Wandering, his ashes were carried by heat and draft into the sky. The company looked on until the roof-gate closed, then exchanged embraces with their neighbors and filed out for the morning meal.

Renan sat next to Broders, eating without a false need to make conversation. Niles joined them after a few minutes, having checked in on the woman who survived Farivaine's last quest.

"Dematha has rested—not slept—but seems rational and ready to tell us her story. We shall convene the parole board at noon. It was indeed Stathos, as we believed. A pair of giants attacked her family as it foraged."

"The others?" Broders asked.

"She thinks they got away. But the second giant, though wounded, also survived."

The Shilarian knight growled and clenched his fists. "Such an offence, that any of these creatures still live."

Renan noticed for the first time that Broders, too, wore the bond-ring of his house.

"Was it not in the days of King Gareth," he said gently, "that your ancestors defeated their tribe in Shilar?"

Broders looked at Renan sharply, as if sensing an insult. "A great victory, or so we thought, because we believed it final. The life of our king, and my… most famous forebearer, were accounted a worthy price. But now, to know there are still some of that ilk to survive! Here in the heart of chaos."

"So," Renan prompted, "you still wear the ring of your house. For its unfinished business."

"Aye, until I have concluded the quest to end the plague of giants or given my life as my ancestor did."

Niles leaned in to grasp the Shilarian's arm.

"Counsel Broders was a rare knight and the finest of women. She no doubt looks down with approval on your courage."

"Whenever the bridge of light calls me to Stathos," Renan added, "I shall remember your oath, and carry it as my own." He looked down on his own bond-ring then, and dwelt for a time on the matter of oaths without speaking or eating further.

The bell's toll broke into all such reflections, and Renan leaped to his feet, moving to the door before Jeceb appeared.

"Brother Renan, garruk in the wilds."

Through a row of hands clapping his back and to the sound of calls for his success, Renan ran from the chamber as he pulled on his gauntlets. Racing up the tower stairs, he arrived in the Farsight Chamber where the duty-squire struggled to hold an impatient Quester in place, that it would not charge down the glowing span without his master aboard. Renan mounted as easily as sitting in a chair, and saw down the endless bridge a group of seven garruk warriors moving across broken ground, perhaps hunting or in pursuit of human plunder. It mattered nothing, the will of the Tower was all; an opportunity to strike a blow for Hope was the prop of his existence. Grasping the offered lance, he grinned down at the squire.

"Best start carving a new one."

"If there is any wood left to use, Sir Renan!"

Then the knight lowered his visor and loosened the reins a bit, allowing Quester his desire, and cantered down the bridge of light towards the distant foe.

Less than one hour later, Renan returned from another victory, to tell briefly of seven garruk slain. In his right arm he held the stub of his shattered lance, but behind Quester he dragged four straight saplings, stripped and suitable for use as replacements. In jest his fellows made more of the second prize than the first. There were no signs of any Children of Hope to rescue, no nearby habitation to investigate. Renan wondered if he should even bother to jot an entry for the chronicle in the library. Sir Hagemon of the Conarian headlands region took his place in the Watchtower, while Renan bathed and dressed cuts and scrapes which had gone unnoticed until his return. He thought of Sir Pallus—now Squire Pallus—whose arm had no doubt set improperly and ruined him for fighting service. If only Healers were less rare, or if the Tower would call one to the Order. But perhaps the risk of death and the body's ruin kept them sharp.

At noon, Renan attended his first parole.

The Order obeyed its injunction to rescue innocents from threat, but especially in recent years, the chaotic nature of the land east of the Tower made it unthinkable to leave such folk behind. The Brotherhood had long ago agreed it would be sometimes needful to bring them here, provide shelter for the briefest possible time, and then return them to the Lands. None could stay with the Order unless called.

The young woman had been kept apart since the previous evening, fed, bathed and rested in a stone-cut guest room that was easily isolated from the rest of the compound. As Dematha came into the council hall normally used for deliberations, Renan felt the same shock as his brothers around him showed. Here was someone from the outside, who did not obey the strictures. He glanced away as her gaze swept the room, avoiding her palpable gratitude and admiration. As Niles advanced and led Dematha to a chair, she gazed on him with something that she would call love, if still here in a week. Her dark straight hair and even features accented skin that showed the tan of outdoor labor. Renan doubted she could be eighteen yet.

As a squire to one side scribed the words, Niles asked Dematha about the recent fight and rescue, more to settle her to the sound of her voice echoing from granite walls without interruption.

"I hail from Stathos, sir knight," Dematha's voice was clear, her manner intelligent. She dressed a peasant, but Renan could tell that she was educated as all from that town were said to be.

"Milady, now tell us what happened. We wish only to be clear on the deeds of the departed Sir Farivaine, and to leave a record for those who follow us. Have no fear then of the truth."

"When the giants attacked us, my father and brother stood with grounded spears while the rest of us ran, as we had agreed. I could see one giant wounded but they both brushed aside the men with only short delay. I, I determined then to split from my mother and little sister, and draw them after me if I could."

This brought a quiet sigh of approval from the company.

"Because," Niles prompted, "you sensed the giants wished to take a woman prisoner."

Dematha nodded, her head high and gaze straight. "They attack the walls of the town when they try to plunder wealth. When we must hunt or forage near the hills, they usually ignore us. But it would have been no great matter for these two to kill my father and brother. I ran to one side of the path back to the city, and they both followed me."

Her breath caught in her throat a moment.

"I had the speed to escape them, but the torn paths and gullies there… I lost my way, and ended in a high narrow place with the giants behind me. I thought, I believed the end had come. Then, there was a light, a solid bar of sunlight as it seemed. The bridge, and the sound of a charging horse."

Dematha described the fight in lay terms but with concision: one giant slain by lance in the initial charge, the second fell back with grievous sword-wounds but only after laying in several blows with its massive club that broke through Farivaine's guard and battered his middle. The knight had enough strength to set his horse on the bridge back, with Dematha alongside him, before swooning in the saddle.

Only at the end, when her mind returned to the living, did her age and awe of the Order betray themselves.

"He saved my life. Just as in the stories we were told. I cannot hope to repay—"

"We thank you for your testimony," Niles cut in gently. "It is our intention, Mistress Dematha, to return you now to your people. Before one of our squires leads you down the mountain, we require an oath. Though you will be blindfolded throughout your trip, we wish you to swear that you will say no word about what you have seen here, or by what ways you came from the Watchtower. You must swear and then promise in the Ancient tongue. Do you understand?"

Dematha swallowed, but nodded and repeated the words, concluding with *"Promissar"*. It was clear to Renan that she would have much preferred to stay among the Brotherhood, and also clear that this would be catastrophic. Boy or woman, farmer or smith or even healer could never dwell among the Wanderers whose focus must be on the next watch, the call to Hope, the chance of death. Even a mate who fought alongside one of them, he reflected, would be a terrible strain, a mark of difference.

The young squire with a black silk head-sack in one hand bowed to Dematha and she followed him from the chamber. The air seemed under less pressure at once, and the Brothers stayed a moment in their usual silence, thinking of their fallen comrade. They rose almost as one to return to their duties, and still that sense of peace remained, the calm that comes of determination and settled intent.

Three weeks later, Renan was again on stand-by in the Farsight Chamber, this time for Niles. The bridge of light appeared and his heart rose higher in his chest as at first his sight could not make out the traveler. When the mystic properties of the span brought the view close enough for recognition, still Renan could not force his eyes to match the apparition before him. Though distant, it was enough to pierce him to the core, and now his inner peace was shattered indeed.

Against the backdrop of a fiercely burning pyre, he could see Niles on foot, holding only the reins of his mount Siara, whose body immolated behind him. Though he walked slowly as one in a trance of sleep, the bridge brought him home in a few long moments. Wordless, he stared at Renan with a face hammered into horror, shoulders slumped, gear dangling carelessly askew, broken sword in his belt. Renan seized his comrade and held him tight as the knights shook with grief.

Niles murmured the words of the code he had broken, *"Before my horse's death, my life—let my saddled corpse speak for me"*.

⊕⊕⊕

"Now then, Mun'lir," Katelynn cooed soothingly, "it is only one further letter, nothing you could feel in your pack."

"It isn't the weight, milady," the courier addressed the Marchess with stubborn respect, "but I mislike me the seal, is all." Mun was never enthused about changes to his routine postal run, and being addressed by his full name only increased his disquiet.

"Look you," Katelynn said after a moment in which she pretended to think and used the time to silently recite the meme of patience, "the seal of Eldarport is only for the priority, not the address or business. Here, next to it, a private seal, so you see the letter itself is quite mundane."

"That's as may be, milady," Mun admitted grudgingly as he stowed the light grey parchment in his pack with the rest of the port's correspondence, "still and all, the noble seals mean noble business. And noble business means changes for the rest of us."

It was one of Mun's sayings Katelynn could have recited from memory, but she did not rise to the bait this time, seeing as the letter was accepted. Mun had been courier on the capital-city route for as long as the Marchess could remember; he was certainly much older than she, and habit was his life's breath. He hated it even when the snow was early, not from the trouble of moving his mail-wagon through the drifts, for he never shirked the work. But Mun disliked all change or variation, especially with the mail itself; he seemed to believe that carrying the scroll with a new law or announcement or even news made him responsible for disturbing the unbroken flow of time-proper.

"A safe journey to you, courier, as always," Katelynn offered and Mun doffed his cap to make a formal bow before mounting the frontboard of his wagon. She watched him click to his mare and smiled as they pulled away from the city precinct toward the eastern gate. A random thought made her start and she called out, "Mind you, there will be a mortal Man ahead on the road. He's bound for the capital."

"On foot? That fellow," Mun snorted over his shoulder, "I saw him this morning, and shall likely see him six more times, if his goal is Mendel." The courier made a face as if he already abhorred the prospect of sharing his road.

"Courier! Wait, courier!" The guardsman at a full run bore the badge of Theme Me'ld and waved a folded parchment. Mun neither slowed the wagon nor turned to look, but when the soldier reached his side and held the letter in view he calmly took and stowed it, in the same manner as a preacher accepts a belated donation. Into the bag it went, as Mun's mare handled herself quite well without his guiding hands. The breathless guard grumbled after the courier, then turned with a face of disbelief to Katelynn seeking agreement, remembering too late her station and bowing to her. The Marchess waved him off with a light laugh, then shivered with something beside the advancing chill of autumn before turning back into the urban manor house, away from anything to do with the morning's business.

It wasn't quite sunset of the first day when Mun's wagon caught up to the Man in Grey. The cloaked mortal with high leather boots and tall quarterstaff set such a strong, regular pace that the courier wagon only overtook him slowly. To pass him by absorbed a long minute, and while Mun stole a few disapproving glances in the direction of the walker, the Man for his part seemed immune to curiosity. One slight turn of the head, an unhurried tip of his broad-brimmed hat and he marched on as if the wagon was invisible. A ride, it seemed, was as unthinkable for the stranger to beg as it was impossible for the driver to offer. Against regulations, of course.

Mun made his usual stop at an inn in the third village along his route. Nothing from Eldarport was bound for these hamlets, but three notes and one small package were brought to him headed for the capital. Mun weighed every parcel and quoted charge-rates from memory: change for coin was not offered, the next trip would do as well for him as this. In autumn the menu featured corn and apples, which in autumn suited Mun just fine.

He was on the road again early when he once again came in sight of the grey mortal. This was entirely too much; as the wagon breasted the hiker Mun upbraided him.

"Did you walk through the night then; what do you think you're up to, going without sleep?"

The Man in Grey spared one glance and another respectful nod without breaking pace. "I slept, Eldest. In an ungathered haymow just east of that last village."

"For an hour perhaps!" the courier scoffed; but since this was not a question he went without answer. "I shall have you know, there has not been a mortal to walk this road in King Tithalis' reign! Embassies and merchants, at times, but in a carriage where they belong."

The youth did not seem to take the scolding as intended, but walked on with the rhythm of his boots and staff too regular for comfort. The wagon was again slowly passing, when the mortal spoke unbidden.

"Eldest," again using a formal title to upset Mun further, "thou art versed in the way ahead. Where might one offer a few days' labor, in return for food and board?"

Looking slightly back, Mun detected no outward sign of discomfort or privation in the intruder, yet he was so spare of frame it was difficult to say what might be his normal size. Something mean and unkind rose up in Mun then, and he told the covered truth when he spoke.

"The next manor on the way is Theme Tenethel, where Master Vauci has extensive holdings. You might reach it before sundown."

Once more the grey man tipped his hat, hardening Mun's heart even further. Everything about the mortal overset Mun's comfort and routine, and he could feel the fury boiling within. He suddenly wanted to run the Man off the road. No, as he looked more closely in passing, he saw that for all his measured speech and stiff manners, this was a boy, with an elder's hair. More affront—Mun resolved to warn the freak no further, and touched his mare with the reed whip to produce a short trot of surprise. Again, out of all custom, and now Mun was so angry he grumbled curses the rest of the day.

And a fine day he was missing too. Resplendent sunlight washing the brilliant colors of fall upon all the rural trees. Even a light vest served to ward against this chill, and the breeze was as nothing. Another round trip from the capital, or perhaps in two, he would need his heavy coat and maybe his boots if the snow came early. But it had better not. This wondrous day Mun ignored was fall, as it was supposed to be. If only he could rid himself of the image of this stranger, marching like a soldier and holding his face like stone. The courier spent the rest of the day trying to imagine how he could avoid the sight of him on the return trip. It was all he could do not to look back on the straight rural way, and spit.

There was no inn or hamlet within two days' distance from Eldarport, so Mun had settled on the habit of staying at Manor Kaullith. He passed the turning for Manor Tenethel, where a metal sign-post showing the arms of crossed staves sat atop a tight split-rail fence barring entrance. Mun rode beyond this fence and took the next turning a league further on, where an ancient oak tree stood by the road as the house symbol and the only boundary. Theme Kaullith offered a friendly manner, comfortable accomodations, excellent fare and a true respect for time-proper. Mun knew that his arrival would always go just so: the enormous brown mastiff galloping out to greet him on the cart-path to the manor, a groom for his mare, hot food, and a gorgeous sunset by the look of things. Dasil Kaullith boarded the courier as part of his feudal obligation: any messages he wished to send went free.

Supper had been cleared and the courier now sat with his host in the fire-chamber where a small blaze was kindled just to provide the light, rather than heat, needed to ward the gentle cool of autumn.

Mun did not require much conversation, and after a few amenities was delighted just to rest, as always, while Theme Kaullith read from a book about the northern kingdoms, in which he had showed a lifelong interest.

That anyone should visit was most unusual. That a visitor would bang on the door like a marauding garruk from legend could mean but one thing, that Kaullith was again to be burdened with some argument from his neighbor, Theme Tenethel. Sighing and smiling apologetically, Mun's host arose and went to the door, waving off the butler. The courier followed to lend support—such interruptions were unwelcome, but not unprecedented, and as such his sense of routine was not disturbed. Even the dog growled before the door was open, sensing who stood on the other side.

"Theme Tenethel, to what may I ascribe the pleasure of—"

"Dasil, I've come to warn you." The neighboring manor owner was as hard and straight as his fences, his face the sharpened end of a portcullis already slammed against further debate. "I have hired on a beggar, a mortal, and I've given him just one job. He is to catch your mongrel in the act of killing my conies and slay him for it."

Mun never saw such shock on his host's face.

"You would—my Tasker, he, he has never assaulted your rabbit cages, I have told you."

"And I have told you, a thousand times to chain that maurader, or sell him, confine him to the house. But you will let him run the grounds at his pleasure."

"But he—"

"Every time, every single time he starts to bark and howl I know there's trouble. No matter how fast I run back to the hutches, there's been a broken slat and he's slain six or eight of my lovelies."

"Tasker would not kill a caged animal! I have dozens of fowl in coops."

"And whose tracks, then, leading back into the woods behind us. Enormous prints, you have seen them with me, Dasil. The next morning, who comes slinking back all scratched and with blood still on his jaws! He's a menace, and it's a miracle he hasn't slain one of my workers."

Dasil Kaullith hugged himself a moment, gathering his patience with a slow breath.

"Theme Tenethel; Vauci, my neighbor, think a moment. Our families held these lands since before the millennium. Our workers have married, we celebrate Darksebb together. When my Maurilenn took the prize last month at the county fair with her stew, she used potatoes from my plots, but where did she get her meat?"

"From my stock, of course."

"And she shared the prize with your tender-man!"

"This is of no bearing, Dasil. All would be well excepting your blind disregard for the depredations of that giant beast!"

"I tell you he would never slay a helpless animal. Do you doubt my word?"

"Your judgment, Dasil. Since the passing of your dear wife, I regret to say, you have indulged that animal beyond reason and now he's become a killer. For three seasons I warned you, but my staff are all fully employed and he finds the times no one is watching. Now I have hired on an able-bodied fellow and in three days, a week at most, he will have done his job."

Mun was stunned. His few dealings with Vauci Tenethel had been brusque and formal, but this plan of retribution seemed out of all proportion. His host drew himself up and Mun could see him now shaking with rage.

"I have tried to reason with you, Theme Tenethel. I must ask you to leave, and if any of your hirelings come onto my property to do harm I will have the reeve bring you in as well as he."

"Never fear, Dasil," the manor owner returned implacably. "The beggar is well instructed and even now is on watch. It will be on my land that the intruder is caught and slain. At which point you will answer before the circuit judge yourself, for the clear and extensive damages that mongrel has caused me. This is a final warning. Chain him or lose him."

So saying, Tenethel reached inside and pulled the door shut on himself.

Mun tried to frame his condolences as an apology, while his host deliberately moved to where Tasker lay and stroked him with defiant affection. Now came the part where Mun must stay and listen, as long as required, to whatever unaccustomed remarks his host might choose to make in his anger and grief. It was all very much beyond habit, and the courier was nearly as out of sorts as the manor owner to have to face it.

"He is right of course, in that I have great love for this fine fellow. But what my neighbor refuses to recall is that with love comes knowledge."

Mun nodded and grunted appropriately and almost wished he had boarded elsewhere this trip.

"Tasker knows his friends, and would defend this house fiercely against an intruder. And he hunts, yes, quite well though I don't as much… and he would never kill an animal who could not give him chase, there is no sport there."

A long pause then, and Mun shifted in a way that could begin retirement for the evening. But Theme Kaullith was sitting now and staring out at the gorgeous sunset, its classic color ruined by the unique memory that would accompany it. The host sighed and continued speaking.

"Ah well, Tasker is in for the night, and tomorrow we shall just have to be careful. But he must run, you know, it is a part of him, Tasker is no lapdog."

Mun could not help a short laugh at the notion of this enormous hound with its body crammed across his master's middle in the chair. A sudden thought came to him and he spoke before he could stop himself.

"He said he had hired on, good Theme. A mortal. Isn't that unusual?"

"Eh? Why no, really, Theme Tenethel has had season-workers in the past, when his wheat or barley has been bumper. Rom, sometimes, and once or twice Men. Once, I recall he had a mortal youth with him as a fosterling. Sent out from the capital, perhaps you saw him?"

Mun had, now that he recollected. A remarkably calm and intact young fellow it was easy to forget he was not an Elf. Doing all sorts of work and living in the manor house.

"I could see him at times, beyond his master's fence, doing some kind of exercise when chores were through. Often in the evening, for Tenethel has all kinds of work, and never enough workers it seems." Kaullith's smile was fond but tinged with spice, and Mun knew the neighbors differed about the treatment of their peasants.

"So," the courier offered, with a spark of mean desire, "it's likely he will run this new fellow rather hard. Get his money's worth from the mortal."

"Oh, dawn to dusk, I do not doubt. And he will be held accountable, poor fellow, whenever there's another coney lost for any reason."

The Theme finally rose on this, finishing the last of his wine and giving Mun free rein to do the same. But as the courier turned the host did not, still gazing out the window lost in thought. It wouldn't do to precede him, so Mun waited unhappily, eager for this exceptional night to end.

It pleased him, as he waited, to think that the grey ghost, evidently too poor to afford a coach, would be laboring here for his food under a master who would wear him out for a time. With luck, the boy would give up and just disappear.

"Milord, what did happen to that other mortal youth? I seem to recall he stayed on for several seasons."

"Hem? Yes, yes until he was fully grown. Some kind of arrangement, I think, with his guardians. I always had the impression they were highly placed, somehow. Was it five years ago? Perhaps longer, the boy went on, and I heard Vauci say it was to the Crystal City. He was studying to be a mage."

It all came back to Mun then; another series of special notes, which he of course had had to carry, between Theme Tenethel and the capital. And sometimes between the capital and Eldarport too; one of the city Themes, Me'ld surely, had some part in this conversation. That last note, run to him by the guard, had also been from Me'ld. It was all a bit sour in the stomach, and Mun was hardly even polite as he bid his host good evening. Tasker slept quietly on a bolster set to one side of the fire, and Mun felt a twinge of something like guilt to see him there. Whatever else, the grey youth had the look of a fighter about him. Despite Tasker's size, Mun doubted the friendly hound stood much of a chance versus that iron-shod quarterstaff. He expected on his return to hear more tales of sorrow from his host. Curse that boy, the whole autumn's routine was like to be ruined.

Over the next four days, Mun's trip to the capital went back into expected channels and his mood slowly improved. His final approach up the long, gradual escarpment below Mendel was a glorious, endless landscape of the autumnal bloom, since the slopes of Tel Ma-ar were thickly dotted with trees almost like a forest. Each bole, perhaps a child or grandchild of the First Invasion, had its own place in the sun and seemed to vie with its fellows for the brilliance and completeness of its turning. It was the peak, the utter apex of the season with hardly a leaf on the ground below and a stillness in the air that had lasted more than a week. A perfect fall, one that Mun swore to himself to remember all his days, the autumn of 1995 ADR.

Coming to the broad mesa top, Mun saw more trees dotting the way to the city itself. Mendel was named for its founder, first son of Hopelord Ma-Eldar after his sire's retirement; five times the size of Eldarport yet its wall was barely half as high. Here was the end of Mun's run, at least in his own mind. The coast to the center and back, more times than he could recall (though he could easily calculate it if asked). But Mun had set out from Mendel on his first day, further ago in time than it was polite for even his superiors to ask. Many other royal couriers rotated duties, happy for the variety of new roads and people. But the capital-to-coast route was never available.

Of course there was some to-do about the letter under Mark seal, as Mun expected. Addressed to a minor Sage on the Roamsedge route, it bore a tag from the Mark of Eldarport directing the Chancellor's office to handle delivery. Personal message indeed, Mun thought—no doubt some coded missive about a big change coming. Nothing could tempt the courier to betray his duty and break the seal, but the sooner this grey parchment was out of his hands the better. He brushed off the usual questions from other members of the staff and sought out the Chancellor in the palace at once.

"Ah, something for our hero Sage Fellareon," the Chancellor exclaimed happily. "We were told to expect a communication. It would appear his, em, companion, this Man in Grey, survived a long voyage after all."

Mun was not willing to admit the truth to himself, but his heart sank to think the object of his ire was somehow highly placed. He bowed to leave but the Chancellor detained him.

"Did you see the fellow when this letter was entrusted to you?"

"No milord," the courier replied, telling again a covered truth. But his mouth betrayed him, adding "A mortal, all dressed in grey then?"

"Yes, so I am told. Named Solemn Judgement, a fearsome veteran and a reckless adventurer—as best I can understand from Sage Fellareon on his last visit, he worsted some monstrous demon. You have certainly heard the tales."

Mun had not, as matters of the high and mighty concerned him little, and tales of exceptional adventure not at all. But the thought of how he had come so close to both irked him as he completed his delivery rounds. And when he came to the Sages Guild, Mun could not help but notice the address on his last letter, the one from Theme Me'ld that barely made time. His heart sank even further: *"To Solemn Judgement, the Man in Grey"*.

Mun cursed so loud that the nearby scribes looked up in alarm. He was trapped. Of course he could leave it here as addressed, but that only meant on the next trip he would find it waiting for him, forwarded to Tenethel and still on his route. Better now than later, and so the courier stuffed the message back in his bag and stomped home in a foul humor.

When his two young children ran to hug him and Mun had taken a kiss from his wife, he felt again the welcome touch of habit and custom that he missed so much. But when his little ones laughingly asked him whether there had been any news from his trip, Mun said no as always. And they laughed again, but Mun did not join them, for he had lied. Out of sorts once more, and his wife noticed but could get nothing from him the rest of the evening.

In the morning Mun returned to the courier's office and limbered up his mare to the wagon. Gauging the weather, he brought forth his coat and laid it on the sideboard as the mail cart moved out. He fussed with the placement of his food-box, the mail bag with that cursed letter near the bottom now, and other matters. The mare knew well which way to go without his hands on the reins.

The days which follow the peak of autumn can be disappointing to many. Cloudier, a tad windier and thus colder on two counts, the leaves begin to drift down and thoughts turn to the advent of winter. But Mun found all as it should be; followed the dimmer lights in the trees with his gaze as he rode, noted the mixed palette of colors on the ground, still yellows and reds with only a light spice of brown. The deeper chill after the first sunset and before the next sunrise were not less pleasant, but expected and welcome to the courier who took the proper steps to warm himself, in things mulled and woolen.

He approached Manor Kaullith with some trepidation, and was both anxious and relieved to hear Tasker's meaty bark as the mastiff pounded down the road to greet him and startle his mare. Theme Dasil's manner was as courtly as always, with just a touch of underlying stiffness to signal his disquiet in the week since Mun was last here. The food was just as good, but the conversation significantly less than usual. Mun noticed his host on several occasions stroking and speaking quietly to his dog, in the way one might to a relative who is ill and uncertain of life. Sunset was clouded and bedtime came a tad earlier than Mun would have liked.

His delivery next morning would add a few precious moments to his trip, so Mun rose early and left without waking the Theme. Tasker the mastiff looked up from his bed by the fireplace and it seemed to Mun that there was a heightened seriousness in the animal's eyes. Certainly he showed all the signs, in his tangled coat and scratched face, of recent running in the woods. So his doom was set, Mun reflected, as he drove the wagon up to the fence-gate of Theme Tenethel and struck the gong, to be admitted and deliver a letter to the dog's executioner.

Tenethel himself answered the manor-door, and sent his overseer to fetch the mortal. While waiting he passed a few polite sentences with the courier in Elvish, then rather artlessly came to the point.

"So! A missive for my worker from Theme Me'ld in Eldarport. I wonder what weighty business concerns him—actually, I thought he had passed, may the Heroes bless him."

"We just deliver the mail, milord. The contents don't enter into it, only the question of a reply."

"Naturally, of course you are right. Perhaps, though, there is news there that will draw this fellow forth. To leave. Possibly." The manor lord cleared his throat and leaned in a bit. *"Between us, I shall dismiss him as soon as the hound is dead."*

"Not a good worker, sir?"

"Just the opposite! Most industrious fellow—spry, for an older man—always seeking out what there is to do, and manages to keep the hutches in sight the while. I've loaded him with food to assuage my conscience! And he saves a portion, for the road ahead he says. Sleeps less than—that is, nearly as little as the rest of us. My other workers, they're running a bit short of chores, excepting the harvest in the far fields. Suffice to say I shall be glad to have my conies protected and see the back of him."

With a start, the courier and the gentleman noticed the Man in Grey standing nearby, hat doffed, staff in hand, waiting. Mun held out the note and felt his skin crawl from the lad's intent, comprehending gaze. He wondered if despite the foreign tongue they used, the mortal had taken the gist of their distaste. If so he showed no sign as he examined the envelope, then opened and read the note. Mun could see only that it was short, one side of a single page, and was not officially interested in the rest. The mortal finished reading and looked up and away slightly, his eyes seeing something far off.

After shifting his feet several times, Mun cleared his throat and asked "Well? Is there a reply, boy?"

The recipient swung his gaze around, and the courier flinched. But the mortal shook his head, and then addressed the owner of the manor.

"Milord, did you have someone here several years ago? A ward, perhaps, sent from the city?"

"What business of yours, sirrah!"

"I am instructed," the mortal said simply, gesturing with the letter, "to find him."

Mun realized the open mouth he saw had a twin, and coughed to cover his confusion as the Theme found his voice.

"That's quite enough, never mind these mad ideas, you. Back to the hutches and your job."

The grey Man donned his hat and tipped it to his master, responding calmly. "As you will, milord. I shall ask the servants for his description."

"You see?" Tenethel cried angrily as his worker withdrew, *"Nothing but trouble with him, every minute it seems. The sooner done the better."*

Mun could see nothing to add, but wished the Theme well and returned to his wagon. Near the barn on the far side of the rabbit hutches, the grey youth crouched over the ground as if examining something. As Mun's mare took the path back to the road, he could see the youth measuring with his hand, then standing to look at the distant forest beyond the fields.

The remainder of the trip to Eldarport was completely without flaw by the courier's lights; weather, distance, duties all as he would expect. Mun found himself fidgeting atop his wagon, rearranging his kit and looking around him more often than he had in decades: not from fear, as he slowly realized, but something a bit like boredom. The sky and trees were losing color, and for the first time Mun regretted it. In the city there were no strange parcels, or noble-sealed missives or other taints of the unusual to deal with, just letters and a few packages whose senders and receivers he well knew. The Marchess was there to see him off as usual, and she frowned a bit when Mun took up his load and departed with no guff, and just a small sigh. The courier felt something building inside him, a tightness in his stomach that he believed might be anger.

Within the first day of the trip back, the weather had turned. A stiff breeze rattled the sills in the inn all night, and the morning even brought a touch of frost. Mun's coat was sufficient, just, but his hands were cold and he thrust them beneath his arms for warmth. The wind always seemed to be head-on regardless of the turns, and trees that had shown burnished gold against blue skies not three days ago now were skeletal beggars spiking the grey sky from a cloying skirt of fallen leaves already faded near to brown. Leaves blew against the wagon wheels and swirled to the height of giants near him. Mun got off several times to clear them from his axles, while the mare plodded on with her head down.

He made slightly slower time, and then too the sun went down a bit earlier. Dusk arrived at Theme Kaullith before Mun did, and he saw torches and lights ahead from the various workers' homes as well as the main house. The way was eerily quiet, and as they came in sight of the manor house Mun felt very low indeed; for there was no great bark, no pounding of large feet to startle the mare or put his heart back in its place.

But there was a bonfire, such as was used to inter a person of great status. Around the man-high flames stood a crowd of manor workers, from both estates to judge by its size, talking quietly and occasionally embracing. Mun could feel the heat from the front stoop, nearly a furlong away. But he felt colder still than he had on the road, as he stared at the interment flame, and the nightmare thing propped up and dead beyond it.

A beast from the land of the mad, with six legs and protruding eyes, as many hands high as Mun's mare and looking twice as bulky. Its back-spines and enormous, hanging jaws seemed to quiver and snap in the unsteady firelight, and he could not discern how much red was truly blood, or whose. Mun could hardly breathe, though twoscore workers stood between him and the creature's corpse showing no concern. Unable to bear the strain any longer, Mun scrambled off his front board and crossed the porch without waiting for the groom. Not daring to knock, he instead opened the portal himself and eased inside, nearly gasping in fear of what he would find.

From the fireplace chamber he heard laughter and the clink of crystal. Mun saw Dasil Kaullith and Vauci Tenethel toasting good fortune and drinking from a bottle that bore the label of the famous Kira-Ashton vinyard.

"Mun'lir!" cried Kaullith his host, "come, celebrate with me." And using a small tumbler he handed a few drops of the precious elixir to the stunned courier.

"Milord," he managed, "when I saw the fire outside, and that, that horrible beast—"

"I am so sorry, Dasil," Theme Tenethel said with one arm on his neighbor's shoulder. "I was wrong, completely wrong. And my stubborn hatred has cost your beloved dog."

"I have lost a dear friend," Kaullith agreed rallying, "but I have gained back my good neighbor, and for that I shall always be grateful."

Mun did not dare ask the details, and was hardly sure he cared to hear them. But in dribs and drabs the story came out, supplied by the two Themes and spiced by the servants who shuttled in with more firewood.

"When I heard the howling, I was sure the mortal would be on guard. I ran to the hutches together with some of my men, and what did we see but a patch of torn ground, gouged and muddy with some great struggle. The tracks led away, not to the fence-line but back to the open woods; and still I heard howls to gel my blood. So I ordered torches and followed."

"I cursed the day at first, friend Vauci, I don't deny it. I heard Tasker baying and the cook ran in to say that my boy had watched his moment, and then bowled him over as he came in with water. I ran after him, seeing his tracks run parallel to your fence, and every so often the marks he made on the rails, as if he were barking at something beyond it."

"We found them in the woods, milord, that monster and the beggar. Great Moment, what an enormous beast! But that Man, he was quite game though bleeding from both arms already. His staff, it flared all silver in the torch-light, some kind of magic weapon. And the monster took blow after blow on its head, began to bleed some as well. It bore him back, and in the exchange the creature seemed to have the best of it."

"I threw a torch at it, sir, and it just sparked and fell away I swear. The fellow next to me let go with his hayfork and it bounced off like a sack from a wall."

"There was no hurting that thing, except through sorcery."

"Finally it got the fellow pushed up against a tree, and lunged with its jaws. All my man could do was jam his stick side-wise into it, holding back with all his strength but grinding against the trunk till he cried out. And the monster started raking him with its extra claws, got him hard across the hip and the blood gushed out."

"And then Tasker, milord, from nowhere it seemed, came thundering in from the side. He got the beast right underneath, near the stomach, and took it by surprise. The heroes must have blessed that dog, milord; he ripped the beast open with his jaws and never minded the gashing he took in return."

"He was a hunter to the end, Tasker, I've always said it."

"Noble animal! A toast to his courage."

"So then the monster howls and pulls back. The warrior, or the mage, whatever he was, draws up his weapon high and brings it down with both hands and a great shout. I heard the most awful crunching sound of my life, and I don't mind saying it. First the thing falls dead, and after the Man."

Mun waited as the servants drifted back to the bonfire, and just the two lords were left in the fire-room. He glanced at the empty pallet where the great hound should have lain, and his chest felt tight again, throat aching. This was news, a great event, a long feud ended, loss and blood and things not at all in custom.

"So, the fire then, milord, I suppose I should pay my respects to the poor fellow."

"A great dog, indeed," Theme Tenethel averred, and Mun's heart kicked a bit.

"You mean, the Man?"

His lords shared blank faces a moment.

"What, the warrior!" his host cried, and then laughed. "He lays in my barn right now. Stout lad—a young man, did you see that Vauci—they brought him to me along with Tasker's body, and I insist, he stays with me now until he's well."

"I shall add some coin, to his pay," Tenethel nodded.

"He wouldn't stay under my roof, can you imagine? Aplogized to me, said he had failed to save my hound, spoke of staying on to work the winter in payment. It was all I could do to convince him to sit still. Moment in time, he lost buckets of blood. My Maurilenn went in there to tend him and came out screaming, said it was too horrible. And him lying there muttering strange words beneath his breath, insisting all would be well."

"He'll sleep tonight, I wager," Vauci chuckled, "at long last. A week at least, before he's walking anywhere."

There was a long moment of uncomfortable silence following this. Vauci Tenethel bid farewell and embraced Dasil Kaullith again with many warm words. The butler showed Mun to his room, and the deeper chill of autumn went nowhere, despite the thick bolster on his bed.

Mun rose early in the giant stillness of a great house following celebration. The cook gave him rolls and a large mug of tea, and he limbered the wagon himself, rather than disturb his host. The winds had blown a light snow into small drifts, covering only the odd patch of ground near a corner or hollow. Wheeling out of the barn, he saw at once the odd pattern of tracks along the path; two ovals, one round.

Mun pulled his wagon to a halt and looked down the road ahead, where the tracks diminishing to the distant oak pointed the way to end of all his habits, his routine and comfortable life. The courier did not feel the cold of morning, did not see the sun peeking through breaking clouds. The level road suddenly seemed to him like the edge of a cliff. His chest was still tight, too small for the rising anger he held there. Work for food—Mun had sent the boy here.

He wanted to go back. He wished there were some way to go back. After several white breaths and muttered curses, Mun left the matter up to his mare with a click of his tongue. In no time at all, it seemed, the wagon was rounding the corner by the giant oak and heading on toward Mendel.

At once, Mun could see the grey cloak and hat ahead, limping with horribly truncated gait towards the east. With one arm the Man leaned hard on his staff, which made an unsatisfactory cane or crutch; in his other hand he clutched a simple sack of provisions, that slipped treacherously whenever it banged his side. Even at its leisurely pace Mun's wagon caught up with him as if standing still.

The boy would have walked on forever but Mun pulled hard on the reins and shouted to him.

"You!" The grey youth turned his head to look up at the courier, only the puffs of his rising breath obscuring the view. Mun thought about spring and fall, and the inns and people of his route, and all the comfortable habits of time-proper now destroyed. His anger reached his throat, and he wondered if he might even strike the mortal down.

"You!" he cried again, holding out an accusing finger and showing his own breath. Mun thought about the size of that monstrous beast, and Tasker's funeral, and his children asking the same questions after his every trip. The youth looked back steady as stone and waited as if quite accustomed to the punishment of others.

And the tightness finally came out of Mun, through the eyes and all over his cheeks. He dropped his arm to pat the bench next to him.

"You… you come up here, lad. You come sit by me."

The mortal managed it without bending at the hip too far, and looked as much at attention when sitting as he had standing up. Mun suddenly felt the cold quite keenly—his cheeks refused to dry despite the sunlit breeze—and he hugged himself hard for the rest of the morning. But a click to his mare was enough, she knew the way.

At Mun's regular stops folks all stared as if he had the monster's carcass on the seat beside him. But the courier paid no heed, and even became more jovial as the days passed. Whenever anyone was brash enough to question the breach of regulations, Mun just raised his eyebrows and whispered "noble business" in a confidential tone. Which was most likely just the covered truth in any event.

By the third day the grey-clad youth was well enough to walk at his usual pace, for perhaps an hour at a time. He helped make camp the last night in the open. The entire trip the two men exchanged less than fivescore words. But when they reached the capital the youth walked alongside the wagon, thus removing a potential source of embarrassment. And he bowed formally to Mun when they passed through the gates, asking only directions to the Tome House, then turning on his heel and disappearing before the courier could think of anything more to say.

When Mun came home, his children ran to him for a hug and asked if he had heard any news. Winking first to his wife, Mun paused and drew their attention before nodding his head. The children took in breath for so long he thought they would both fall over. And after a dinner peppered with begging and promises, he sat by the fire and told them such a tale of mystery and horror that they screamed and swore they would never sleep again.

The next week, Mun put in to take the southern route to the Great Cleft, claiming he wanted to keep the warmth in his bones for a few more days if he could. He quickly scouted out the best places to post and rest, and never truly liked it when his routine had to change. But every time he returned to Mendel, he always, always had a story to tell his children. They came to regard it as part of their routine. And Mun never forgot the autumn of 1995 ADR.

⊕⊕⊕

The Fourth of the Lion, 1995 ADR

My Dear Guildsman, Good Solemn Judgement,

How marvelous to receive your letter, how dreadful to read it! The paper and penmanship declared instantly that you lived, beyond all credit had survived that perilous voyage south from Conar's harbor where I saw you last. Yet every word in your too-brief missive spoke only of the threat of death, the ultimate penalty to be levied for breaking our most sacred custom. My friend, you tear me asunder. Send two letters next time, and separate such gloom from what should have been my unalloyed bliss to confirm that you live.

I write this reply at once, on the faith that your life continues. Of the matter regarding your meeting with the great and revered Theme Me'ld, I shall say nothing. I have never met the young Mark Orual'n but I trust his good sense, aided perhaps by my letter to which you referred, will have governed in this case. Indeed, I can only live in hope, it being unlikely I shall hear from you soon enough to suit me.

I am at this moment in Mendel the capital, arrived through the miraculous agency of the gates, which everyone knows about but so few have ever used in centuries. I have been allowed a few days' grace from my imprisonment in Conar to formally marry the lovely and otherwise most sensible Kia Weitherton. The circumstances of my proposal were in truth too ridiculous to repeat in writing, though it would make a priceless joke in person; suffice to say she has assented and I am most content.

If you have set out for Mendel as I surmise you purposed in your letter, you should reach us in somewhat around two weeks of traveling, and perhaps two or three days from today. How I regret you could not have waited just a few days, or I would have arranged a coach to ease and speed your journey. It embarrasses me to write these words, but I seem to have become a rather important person among many in power—thanks, as you well know, to no virtue of my own! And I will certainly bend my efforts to assist you in any way I can. As things stand I must wait with tapping foot for your arrival. There can be no question of a faster trip, I fear: the official couriers are bound by regulation and may not accept passengers. But in all other ways they are pleasant fellows to my experience and you may pass some happy hours on the road in their company.

One appointment we must keep, my friend. The date of my wedding is set, for the Eighth Lion in just four days' time. I trust you will have arrived in Mendel by then, but before you begin your researches (of which I shall say a word below), I pray you to attend the ceremony. It is unusual of course for a Man to witness an Elvish wedding, yet there is no other Man, no better man I would wish to have by my side at that happy moment. Indeed nothing else could increase my joy on that fast-approaching day.

You see? I have already constructed such a happy future for us both—you still alive and safely here in study, myself freed from the bonds of royal commands and married to my love. Surely if I wish hard enough, as children are wont to do, it may happen. Even the fond desire, in itself, is a makeweight for happiness in a heart as harangued and tested as mine has been.

So take cheer, my friend, that matters are at last improving. I urge you not to speak so casually of death. Or at least, thus I would urge you—had I not been witness to that horrid place, and seen with my own eyes how you faced death itself, in that malignant skull. I hope I may never see such steadfast courage, hear such brilliant defiance, benefit from such miraculous skill, or survive such a tragic pass in the remainder of my days. How useless it is, what a misfit I am to offer you any advice, friend Judgement. It should have been Natasha who survived the Hopeward, to properly guide your further instruction and provide you with an example more suited to your heroic talents and determinedly active bent of mind.

Enough. I will write no more of the event on which staves and crowns require me to dwell daily. I wish the best speed to your studies, dangerous though they are, and despite the misgivings which fill me to know of them. I shall leave word with the Sages Guild and the Tome-House here to expect your arrival, and lend my recommendation to ease your access. I do this not because the subject of your study wins my approval, but because you do, in your person and the worthy manner in which you have conducted your young life. Indeed, I owe you my life, Solemn Judgement, a fact which I can hardly face but, like the worst of that nightmare, I doubt I shall ever forget.

Do take good care of yourself, my friend. May your trip to the capital be pleasant and filled with charm, your studies uneventful, the outcome happy and your future filled with rest and peace. I cannot wait to see you again; I shall await you in the chapel with my bride to be (who is also most eager to meet this hero of my personal acquaintance).

Ar Aralte,

Cedrith

Post-Script: Remember, make sure your next letter only pleases me! Nothing appalling to report, not in the days before my wedded bliss. Farewell.

Post-Script, in Haste: Ruined! Always my plans come to ruin! Just now I understand that my furlough is once again cut short, and I am summoned to return to the capital of Men for another interminable, dreadful, useless conference. I fear I threw quite a fit, demanding the right to marry, which produced this comedy that I now unwillingly star in. No parole to wed was vouchsafed me, but instead a hasty ceremony in the middle of the night, with no witnesses beyond an honor-guard charged to see me directly to the gate instead of my bride's arms upon completion of the vows. I am bound again for Conar, and separation, and that same frightful monotony which has been the curse of my life since we parted. But I shall insist this letter be left at the Guild for you first. I go to marry now—all fortune to you, since I have none myself!

The Sixth of the Lion, 1995 ADR

Eldest,

I thank you for your good wishes, which have all been realized, by my reckoning.

The road here was indeed sufficient and uneventful. I arrived somewhat early of your expectations and set to work at once, guided by your advice and admitted on your endorsement.

My studies advanced quickly, and I have found what I sought. My path from here lies north and east. I shall leave at once.

And you, I read, have indeed wed, also in advance of your estimates. If it please you, I offer my heartfelt congratulations, and ask you to convey them as well to your lovely wife. I regret not being here in time to attend, but your happiness should never be delayed, nor tainted as it no doubt would have been with my presence.

As for lives, your letter no doubt saved mine in Eldarport, so I account us even at best. In truth, I remain in your debt and shall labor to repay you and all my hosts in this land with my poor efforts, delayed at sea but now renewed. You spoke of wishing as a child, but I am unwilling to stray where neither memory nor habit can assist me. For today, I have work and a road ahead, and in this I have found happiness, or its nearest neighbor.

I cannot say when or if we shall meet again, Eldest, though I reflect that we had been but a handful of hours and steps apart. One thin wall or a thousand leagues, separation is a condition not measured in distance alone. That you should express the wish to see me again is in itself a gift, and that one I can repay in kind. With paper and ink we create gates to cross the distances: let us use ours in future more freely than the great folk of the nations have seen fit to use theirs to date. If I gain the opportunity I shall write again, but I go now to remote and hostile places.

I seek the Tombs Thanazun, which lie indeed by the Plains.

Respectful Regards,

Solemn Judgement

Post-Script: You would please me greatly, Eldest, to write again if you have the convenience, with any news or none. I must ask you not to refer to the Guildmistress Natasha Ioki as dead; we all of us survived our trial in the Hopeward and I insist that you keep this in mind. The Heroes willing, we shall stand together, on a night fifty years from now when next the portal opens, and there I trust we shall all meet again.

⊕⊕⊕

In seven years among the Bordbeyonds, the Shilarian youth had always been made to feel inferior, that he carried no Elvish blood. But staring up at the fading lights of dawn he reflected that at last, he knew what it was like not to sleep. Six nights out under the ebon-chilled stars, and trying to decide, the longest week of his new life.

He lay on his back near the strangers' tent, outside as many of the nomads did except in full winter. Pretending to guard the guests in this, he perhaps earned a minim more respect among the tribesmen. Seven summers ago he ran here, leaving behind name and country for love of his sister. The Shilarian refugee was willing to bear up under the harsh seasons and harsher testing of the nomads. Their scorn for his known race and settled upbringing was a challenge he rose to with fierce joy. Until a handful of nights ago he had thought himself one of them, not fully accepted but no longer dismissed. And they had given him a name, though it was meant to demean.

All that shattered like a breastplate of frost, at Tossa's first sight of his countrymen.

He stood up to pace around the tent and keep warm, scanning east to the star-blocking mountains as a Bordbeyond did by habit. One look at the prince, that morning before the chieftain's tent, sufficed. Mortally tired and dingy as he had appeared, Gareth's upright stance, noble speech and above all, that mature, kindly face brought the comforts and beauty of Shilar surging back to Tossa, not to leave him for a moment since. Roaring fireplaces, broiled meat, the smell and swirl of autumn leaves and the laughter of court, jousting and mattresses and pets, encouraging claps on the back, and jokes—how he had missed the jesting.

But hard on that moment, the squire, his twin had fainted, and Tossa reacted without thought. His sister, grown and in armor! He had moved forward on sentiment and impulse, reaching for her and for all his soft, civilized past life together. Just like a settled man, despite seven years of diligent effort to be hard and calm.

And now her secret was out, thanks to him. How was he to know, she had kept the truth even from her lord?

Tossa stopped before the tent flap and scryed the sky, trying to wring from the heavens a cure for heartsickness. In his school days, the Shilarian named Hobsel had not learned how to tell the future in stars; unlike so many of the Bordbeyonds he could not see this red light in the east, the one to trigger their first embassy nearly half a year ago.

Tossa recalled how his sister recovered from that swoon within moments, but the knight and the squire only stared to each other as at strangers. The prince turned back to address the Bordbeyonds, hauling with him a face twisted in confusion and pain. Tossa's sister, writhing away from his embrace, was stone to any whispered question and stood apart as though guarding the prince against an attempted escape. Their hosts thought them admirably tough, little suspecting, but Tossa saw it all.

The chieftain's daughter, Sidrathay the Combatted, bowed to Gareth and accepted his proposal without awaiting her father's leave, as she never tarried for any man. Concluding a betrothal was evidently no good reason to raise her visor. The interview came to a close comically soon, and the guests were given quarters to stay at night, a place in the marching-order by day as the tent city crawled south towards the Lesser Fields by the Great Forest.

But if the Shilarian son, the one the Bordbeyonds called Tossakateu had expected a warmer welcome from his former countrymen, he was disappointed. Prince and squire hardly spoke in each other's presence since that debacle before the chieftain's tent. The secret so long and carefully kept was out; words were no help to a lord so confused, or a vassal so mortified.

Now they both walked as if with boards strapped to their backs, and spoke almost as little as their grim, stoic hosts. Tossa chuckled drily, to think how they accidentally won further renown, drew higher in the estimation of the Bordbeyonds even as they fell further apart from each other. His sister, he could tell, was close to tears every waking moment.

But today, Tossa knew, that would have to end. As the tribe approached the Lesser Fields their guests would be left behind, the half-elven nomads moving on to their dread mission near the Great Forest. He must go with them, if he would remain one of them, and might not return. There was no speaking to either prince or squire, before the rift between the pair was settled; Tossa resolved to confront whoever came out first, though he had no idea what he might say.

The sun was not yet up, but the prince of Shilar slipped through the flap into the predawn gloam, and Tossa turned to greet him at once, lest he seem a spy. Bowing, he approached and knelt in a gesture of fealty. Looking up, he could dimly make out the prince's face, studying him with a mien mild yet determined, a steel blade in a velvet sheath.

"Am I to accept your service, sir?" he asked without challenge or anger, a simple question. "Do you claim loyalty to my father's kingdom despite your years here?"

Tossa rose and put his hands behind his back as he answered. "My absence, milord, was due to no lack of love for Shilar. I loved my sister more—and then too, it helped me to escape."

Gareth's eyebrow rose in comprehension and he nodded. "Ah yes, an unwanted marriage. Hob—or em, Hillel I suppose—" a grimace writhed across his handsome features a moment, "That is, she mentioned your father's wishes of a quick match for, for her. But it was you who left instead of she."

"He would have married me off as well, shortly," Tossa replied, "I think—though he never told me, milord—but he saw his end coming in the stars. And he wanted us settled before we were ready, so we made this plan."

Under the prince's soft, thoughtful gaze he flushed but felt only camaraderie, not embarrassment. "A hare-brained scheme, I admit it. Your Highness has no experience, I'm sure, of a father who ignores your wishes."

This brought an honest laugh from the prince of Shilar. "Certes, sir! My squire and I merely thought to take in the air of the plains, as it were."

Tossa laughed too and felt the air thawing by degrees in morning light. "By sojourning among the Bordbeyonds, I thought I might prove myself, have some adventure before settling down. I never realized, how difficult it would be to get word—and then I heard my father had indeed died, and that you, milord, that em—"

"That I had taken an injury in the company of my newly famous friend," Gareth chuckled. His smile waned even as the dawn arrived, his face returned to a kind of wounded half-grin of disappointment. He murmured to himself, "So of course, you could never return after that. Well and truly stuck, poor fellow; a knight's conundrum indeed, honor versus a given word. And she was always trying to tell me, in a way, how your sister wanted to be a knight."

"All she could talk about, milord, from our earliest days. When father, when he told her of the marriage, she was desperate."

"And you agreed to help her," Gareth mused, "which speaks well for the bond you have. I'm glad my blundering has brought you two back together, at least. Light of day, how much alike you look. And yet I don't think I could ever mistake her for—that is, well, I've been wrong before."

He smiled more fully then, and Tossa was struck to the heart, remembering festivals and dancing, eating more than one needed and long conversations over chess. Everything about the prince of Shilar, so human and so noble, bespoke a giving nature that made one want to exceed others in giving. Like his sister, Tossa too hoped to earn the prince's favor and respect, and did not know how.

"So then, sir, how shall I call you? By rights your name is Hobsel Parrey, and you stand to inherit your father's lands in a year."

"Call me Tossa, milord, that's the name the Bordbeyonds have given me," the youth said, holding out his arm to grip. "Short for Tossaketeu."

Gareth returned the grip as his face frowned with the effort to translate the variant of Elvish in the syllables.

"Words, many, talking?"

"Speaks Often," Tossa said with a grin.

"Not a hard name to earn here," Gareth returned and they both laughed.

The squire suddenly emerged from the tent and for a moment both young men froze. Tossa felt his arm on Gareth's was a betrayal, and he broke free to hug his sister. Her return embrace was tight, but stiff, and when he released her she was still staring at the prince.

All around them the tent city was coming to life, as people folded the cloth strips and prepared to continue the southward migration. Gareth's face at first was brimming with pain and confusion, but he forced a more good-humored mask in place to ask gallantly. "And what name have our hosts given to the two of us, Tossa?"

"You milord, they call Diamemne. Keeps His Word."

The prince studied the ground, and his smile was both grateful and proud. He quietly repeated the name, and it seemed to help him decide something. Looking up at the young woman, he crossed in a few steps, bowed to her, and then lightly laid a hand on her shoulder. She shivered at the contact of glove and gaze, but stood straight before her lord.

"I should be proud to live up to that name, and keep my word as present company have. Tell me then, Tossa, what name do they use for this—" and here he paused with a smile that looked whole again, "my loyal squire here?"

Even as he watched her cover a gasp with her hands, Tossa felt a twist in his gut. He might have stood where his sister did now. But a choice was made, and Tossa could not regret it. Clearing his throat, he said "They call her Brakthula; Never Says."

The girl's face clouded at the harsh syllables, but Gareth said "It's surely a compliment around here. We shall try it. Perhaps 'Thula'? I apologize, milady, but I doubt I could ever call you Hobsel again."

The three broke down the tent and their few supplies, carrying them to a wagon before seeing to the mounts. Tossa noticed that Gareth, formerly determined to fend for himself, now acquiesced once more in allowing his squire to equip him and bard his horse.

These mundane chores, routine for any squire of Shilar, drew stares from the Bordbeyonds as "Thula" took them back, but her smile was proof against all mute frowns.

"It's part of their way," Tossa remarked as they mounted up, "Each one does what he is capable of. All are equal here—unless you act settled or human."

"Yet surely they can see," Gareth returned, "how much more one can do when assisted by another? Plus, how do they train for war?"

"As nearly as I can make out," Tossa responded with grim glee, "they are ready for war from birth. I haven't solved the riddle in just seven years, and seventy might not be enough." He paused and huffed a breath into the morning air as they rode: another two hours before a small meal.

"I can tell you this," he continued, "the boys, and sometimes girls too, go off on their own for a few days at a time, when they're about as old as we were, Hill, they year we, ah, made our promise."

"What could they learn by themselves?" his sister asked.

"That I cannot tell you. But when they come back, they're treated as adults. And they don't always come back."

Thula choked at that, stammering, "That's barbaric! They let their children leave? While they are still… and to go where?"

Tossa waved to the east where the mountain shadows still eclipsed them. It was difficult, he could see, for either of the Shilarians to look the mountains straight on, now that their path had veered this close to them. The sheer faces, rising so abruptly from the plains, the incredible height of the entire range was indeed a sight to stab the vitals. Tossa could do it, from long practice, but not steadily, not to truly see anything.

"They climb among the lower cliffs, hunting or seeking, I'm not sure." Tossa was practically whispering now. "Sometimes they return with a kill, beast-skins of a kind I have never seen, and all different.

Their capes and helms," Tossa gestured to several nearby Bordbeyond warriors, "they sometimes wear them. But others return with nothing, at least that I can see, and the respect they win is still the same. I've thought about going myself."

His sister reined in sharply and reached out to hold Tossa's bridle in panic. Gareth pulled up as well, and the three let the tribe flow around them awhile.

"Up there?" she gasped. "To climb the Swords of Stone, for what? No, Hob, you must never—I'm your family now, I would never leave a child of Hope to face—and to—"

Gareth turned a tart grin to the squire. "Indeed, and sometimes they never return."

She nodded at her lord, then glared with understanding, then had to laugh. The three resumed their pace with the nomads, who still steered clear of them as if their conversation was a catching disease.

"Well, I know with us it was our idea."

Tossa looked on them dubiously, not sure if his sister was joking.

"At least, Highness, your father will come for you."

"Yes. A settled custom, our hosts might say."

Tossa nodded, but Thula interrupted him.

"The king is looking, alright, but in the wrong country. Gareth sent him to Mendel."

Now it was Tossa's turn to stare, while his sister laughed. Gareth gave an embarrassed shrug.

"I needed time to get away, not knowing how long before I could find you. That is, to find our hosts here. Another week and I might have missed them; we are now well below Shilar's southern border."

Tossa gestured to the right, where the eastern edge of the Great Forest was clearly visible, individual trees standing out and the twin mounded hills rising behind them like a pair of children crawling under a leaf-colored carpet.

"Our maps did not show the trees coming so close to the Swords here," he remarked. Ahead of them was only a narrow pass of grasslands, less than two hours' ride across. "I believe the Forest has been growing, beyond the limits that the Elves of Mendel noted to the west and north."

Gareth nodded, then pointed straight into the gap in the south. "Through there, the road to Mickhel I believe?"

Tossa nodded, then cleared his throat. "I've never been, the Bordbeyonds have as little contact with the Dwarves as with Shilar. But they come this far every year. The nation will pitch camp tonight and then move on at first light to gather wood and salts. You will be staying behind."

His sister looked at him sharply. "We? Not you?"

"I'm determined, Thula. The Bordbeyonds don't, they don't discuss things, you simply stand up for yourself. I know what they're doing is dangerous: some of the warriors haven't come back. I already decided, before you arrived, I will go with them. But I'm sure they won't let you come."

"This is insane, Gareth. They have to fight, for wood? Against who! Tell him he cannot go. Milord." Thula looked down, remembering her rank.

The prince rode on alongside the siblings, saying nothing but with a slow growth of grin that made Tossa feel happy and worried at the same time. He leaned to his sister and whispered, "What is he planning?"

Thula's shrug was an angry twitch. "You think I can guess? Gareth does what he likes, polite and all, but stubborn as a mule on a one-plank bridge." She raised her voice a bit. "He will likely fit in well here."

The prince did not respond, except to bow slightly to her side as they rode. Thula blew out her breath in frustration and Tossa had to laugh out loud, despite the angry glares he drew from the nomads around them.

On the rest of the day's ride south, the three spent the time speaking of lost years, familiar comforts of home and relatives rather than the hard unknown ways of the Plains. Tossa ached with every word his sister spoke, and longed to hear her voice again whatever it cost him with their hosts. From his eye-corner he saw the prince listening, hearing the tales anew and nodding along in recognition. Now and again the lord of Shilar looked to his squire with that same gentle smile, affirming the loyal heart beneath a changed countenance.

The day waned, and the westering sun splashed its rays onto the gorgeous dark rock faces of the Swords of Stone, revealing cracks, canyons, black defiles and copses of twisted trees near the ground. With just this fringe of normal terrain, the range sprang from the earth to nearly touch the heavens. Tossa found it difficult to take a full breath whenever the tribe came this close. Yet he had still not broached the conversation he must with the prince of Shilar.

He reined in near Gareth's horse and the three of them stopped close by each other as the human tide again flowed around them.

"Milord, you must know this. The Bordbeyonds will encamp here, and tomorrow morning before full light the warriors will leave to forage, first to the Forest and then across, into the lower mountains."

Gareth quietly took in the news. "We should accompany them, as a sign—"

"You will not be allowed to come."

"Is this some secret place they go to?"

Tossa shook his head and shrugged. "In the Great Forest they seek wood; straight poles they can use for tents, spears, the like. There is fighting, against some creatures they call Bents. They never come back with as much wood as they need."

"After that," Tossa gestured to the mountains, "There is a place in there they can find strange colored salts, with uses I have not seen. I don't think there has ever been fighting, but they do not remain long. Waiting here with the young and the shepherds, I have seen the people just as tense as at first, until the warriors return. They call it Tumekheo Gantargor: The Grave of Giants."

Gareth looked thoughtfully to the mountain-side as if he could make out the path the nomads would use. "Tumekheo Gantargor. The histories tell that during the Battle of the Razor, the Dwarves were beseiged in their city by the Giants, subborned by Kun to Despair's side. In the final days, the Dwarves broke free, killing many Giants, and fell on Despair's flank to help break their battle-line. My namesake and ancestor hunted down the rest," the prince said with a touch of pride.

"But—do you mean to say," Thula hissed, "that these salts are their bones? From so long ago?"

Tossa shrugged. "I've only caught glimpses, brightly shaded powder, wet at first but dried in the sun and then stowed away."

Gareth's face was thoughtful as the halt was called and they dismounted to set up the tent again.

"We know the Giants took up with Despair from an early age, perhaps were even created by them in the first place."

"So burial in the ground would have been their custom." Thula added.

"Or it may have been a killing-field where the bodies were left after the battle." Gareth smiled brightly. "Or just a superstition. In any event, they are valuable to our hosts and we should offer our help to obtain them."

"Milord," Tossa's face was pained. "You cannot. These are the Bordbeyonds; one does not, you do not make an offer. They only state the facts here."

Gareth looked on him seriously, trying to understand. "Do you mean they never negotiate, or argue?"

"That would be 'a settled matter'," Tossa replied, "a sign of mortal life, an insult, do you see?" He pulled closer to speak low. "They are obsessed with Elven heritage. Our tales tell that half of them are born Men, half Elves. But they must behave at all times as if they are undying. Each is pretending he's centuries old, do you see? I'm saying this all wrong, but one must not ask, not debate, one simply knows or else…" Tossa held out his hands.

"Or else he is a human." Gareth finished for him. "And not worth listening to."

The prince stood awhile with hands clasped behind him; facing east directly into the towering sheaf of granite, he knelt and prayed in words aloud that Tossa knew, asking Shilar for guidance. Gareth rose and looked back at the siblings with his smile returned.

"My thanks, Tossa. If you are both willing to trust my addled brain in this?"

The two held out their arms simultaneously and Gareth clasped them both.

"Good, my thanks. Come with me and let us speak to the chieftain." He stepped away, then turned back to Tossa.

"They don't do much fishing, do they?"

Tossa could only shake his head, and so close to the center of the tent city, there was no chance to discuss it further.

They stood outside the leader's tent even as the rest of the canvas town came into being around them: the grass-tufted piazza where they waited looked as if the Bordbeyonds deliberately cleared it to stay away from the settled knights. The northerly breeze was chilled, and its snap against cloak and tent flap was by far the loudest sound. Gradually, some of those finished with their chores drifted in to stock the outer edges of the open space, an uneven hedgerow of visored helms staring at the guests.

Gareth managed perfect ease in all this, gazing around as if no great period of time were passing and smiling like a man who is welcome. Tossa knew how to stand straight at attention when scrutinized, to which the Bordbeyonds could give grudging respect. Thula fidgeted, yet had the sense not to speak now. Tossa flogged his mind but could derive no reason for the prince to show such confidence even in bluff.

The hale, elderly chieftain emerged with his family and two advisors, one of whom had a Shilarian plate paldron on his left shoulder. The chieftain rested his eyes steadily on Gareth. Behind him, the anonymous mask of the prince's Protector and former guide seemed to shift slightly, as if hoping to catch his gaze and silently warn him away.

Gareth bowed deeply to the chieftain and raised a solemn hand in greeting to Sidrathay. Her visor lowered in a nod, one hand rising to rest akimbo as she assessed her new husband. When it was clear that the prince would not speak first, the chieftain proceeded.

"The Half-Elven encamp here tonight. Tomorrow our warriors leave. To hunt. You—"

"We of Shilar will be pleased to accompany our hosts." Gareth's voice broke in strong and quick, a human interruption but Tossa knew the prince had little choice. If the chieftain had finished his statement it would impossible to gainsay him. Now Gareth had stated a fact; he knew how to play.

In the dead silence that ensued, Tossa felt something important balanced on a sword-edge here. Slowly, the old chief held up the short staff he had rested in one arm, offering it out for someone to take. Tossa felt a charge run through him; his prince must be told. He leaned in to quietly whisper.

"Milord, it is the Talking Stick, you must—"

Gareth cut him off with one rising hand; his face was bright with surprise, but also pleasure. Turning the gesture, he waved to one side as if deferring to others.

The Protector with Gareth's paldron stood forward, touched the staff with one hand and said "They will be seen."

Nods of agreement all around, an accepted fact. Tossa felt a wave of dismay and inwardly cursed himself. How could Gareth have known, but Tossa should have guessed. The caution, their furtive departure and return. The Bordbeyonds were using their fabled powers of invisibility to forage in these dangerous places. And Tossa had never discovered their secret way. All was surely lost.

Gareth waited a moment to see if anyone else wished the stick after the Protector stepped back. Striding forward with confidence and one eye always on his bride, he reached and clasped the top of the staff before responding.

"The People of the Plains will not need to leave off their foraging so soon. The attention of their enemies will be drawn by three knights who ride alone to one side." He looked sincerely over the chieftain's shoulder to add, "And the prince of Shilar will not leave his bride to face the danger alone."

Bait! Another correct guess, Tossa realized, one the Bordbeyonds had not considered. Gareth released the staff and remained before the chieftain. More silence as the growing shadows and snappy breeze bore down on the group of mortal specks, urging the need for fire, and cover, and other ways to stave off the approach of death from the cold.

Tossa could not resist looking around at the cordon of faceless metal, straining to see if one of the warriors would advance to touch the staff and state the obvious. If but one of them said "They would die", the matter was ended. The honor of a foreign prince could not outweigh a statement of fact. These proud Bordbeyonds would not countenance either one of their own to be called a liar, or their guests to be killed. Gareth and the others would remain behind, tied to a wagon if necessary.

The chieftain held the staff out at an angle that would have tired Tossa's arm long ago. The Bordbeyonds could wait for truth; Man or Elf, they all pretended they had ages, in the Hope that it was true. Gareth also could wait, having spoken last. Thula no longer bothered to conceal her restlessness, and did not return Tossa's urgent glances. The Protector wearing Gareth's gift nodded tightly once, in answer to an unspoken request. Sidrathay stepped before her father then and tapped the staff once in perfunctory fashion before speaking.

"We leave before dawn. Gleimharn will guide you to a useful position. Fight well, husband."

"Remain well, Sidrathay. I would hear your voice again soon."

She showed no sign of hearing the prince's voice, but turned to follow her father into the tent. Only one or two of the Bordbeyonds lingered to stare at the newcomers now, while the Protector approached Gareth. After a moment he raised his visor to show a hawlike, thin face of middle age.

"We shall ride south by east before first light. You will need your full armor."

Gareth reached out to arrest Gleimharn's hand at his left shoulder.

"My shield protects my left from horseback. That is a given gift, and you will move among your own ranks."

Gleimharn stood frozen a long moment, then dropped his hand in resignation. As he turned to go, he let his visor fall in place. Gareth was halfway to the siblings when he heard the warrior's voice and turned back.

"Prince of Shilar. The Bents are not large but very numerous. Wood harms them little. Use the sword."

"We will, my thanks. And later, at the graveyard?"

Gleimharn said nothing in response, slowly turning away again to enter the chieftain's tent.

Gareth rejoined Tossa and Thula with his face a study in contradictions.

"We are committed. That is, if you two care to join me?"

Tossa started to nod and speak, but Thula kicked Gareth in derision—evidently a habit with them—and spun to leave. Gareth smiled after the squire, or it would have looked like a refusal. Something in Thula's manner was definitely off.

"Sister, what is it?"

She shook her head, muttering, "Good thing."

"What good thing?"

"That I've learned to void standing up! Every time I even look at those mountains…"

She stomped around the corner with a more familiar haste, as the two youths laughed, then hitched at their drawers simultaneously.

"Shilar's Eyes," Tossa said, "she's right." Still chuckling, the pair broke in different directions by the light of cookfires and dusk.

That night was frosty cold, but the guest-tent was adequate for three.

As he lay again unsleeping, Tossa was astonished to discover that his sister snored so loudly. Fits of chuckling swept over him with each new burst. Gareth's face in sleep remained calm; it appeared a gentle smile was his mouth's natural position. Tossa lay back and wondered if the feeling within him now was peace.

A year ago, he stood with the children and the aged all day for the sixth time; it had triggered a disquiet and shame in him that lasted the entire year. He was grown, yet Bordbeyonds two years his junior, it seemed, had gone on this perilous secret round. None spoke to him of it then or since, as there was never a need among the nomads. So Tossa had determined to accompany the Bordbeyonds this time, though he knew nothing of the dangers they faced and would probably die. He swore to himself under Shilar, he would go, and thought his grim determination was courage.

Now he gazed on the sleeping prince—his prince, he realized again—and thought how the three of them would face this peril. In all chance, Tossa would be a part of great tragedy tomorrow, responsible for bringing the end of the current ruling line. What had the nomad seers said about this invisible red star in the heavens? *A crown is lost in water.*

Like a piece of bait. Tossa wondered why he felt no anguish, not sweating with fear and regret, but instead resting on his blankets like a gently rocking boat, swept along by a peaceful tide of loyalty.

Before, Tossa had crafted a conflict for himself. Determined to earn respect, he was willing to throw his own life into the scales. But now, seeing his sister again, so well used to her place as squire to a future king, he was like a hound hearing his master's voice after a long absence. Shilar trained him for this life as well; it had the customs and traditions he had learned to love, and forgotten to miss in his dogged efforts to fit in with the nomads. The duties, the charges lying upon a knight of the sword in Shilar, these were his life's habit, and the honor came naturally with them. A settled thing indeed.

This, to follow such a lord who inspired all he met with the spirit of Hope, was the path that avoided all shame. Death or victory, the morrow would find him by his sister's side and defending the prince all men burned to serve. Women too, to think of it; Tossa chuckled again and this time Gareth drowsed up toward wakefulness in response.

"Em, what?"

"All is well, milord. Not dawn for some hours yet."

"Ah. Well." Gareth closed his eyes and leaned his face to one side. After a long moment he spoke again, quiet and distinct.

"Your sister snores."

"That she does milord."

The quiet resumed, and Tossa lay still once more in the arms of peaceful rest. Better than sleep, to know one's place.

He dozed away to awaken in the gloaming, with his sister's bedroll empty. Outside, Thula was already at work barding Gareth's mount, and Tossa came to assist.

She glared up a bit sharply, and he assured her saying "You can arm him, I promise."

That brought her full smile, something he had not seen in seven years. "I'll arm you as well."

"We'll help each other," he said as they buckled and cinched the charger first with a thick woolen blanket, then the heavy chain coat, followed by the finely wrought connected plates around ears, nose, fetlocks and chest where blows would most likely fall in battle's heat. Tossa fell to musing; three or four Bordbeyond knights could have better protection than the centuries-old tatterdemalion suits they wore today, from just cutting up the length and quality of what a Shilarian prince threw on his steed. He had preserved only his plate pieces in recent years; seeing chain mail again, he felt under-dressed.

Gareth emerged and greeted them with good spirits, and Thula hurried to arm him. The prince had already donned the leather plackard extending to his thighs, and was shrugging into the back-laced chain shirt with the usual difficulty one person has. Tossa came to watch from safe distance as his sister slapped away all helping hands and straightened the heavy links in place, settling easily around his elbows and knees before lacing him up. Gareth looked on Tossa with that gentle smile, and gestured to the plate pieces lying strapped atop the long woolen tunic he wore now in the Bordbeyond style.

"No offence, sir knight, but your protection has suffered somewhat in your absence from court."

"I have endeavored, your highness, to make do," Tossa responded proudly, pointing to several places where old pieces had been hammered or punched with holes to stay in place. "This metal is all of Shilarian forging, but I could not keep the shirt from rust. Too much rain and too little cover. Besides, our enemies have been few—a rogue montori bull last month—the Wanderers tend to need speed foremost."

Gareth listened nodding as Thula knelt to strap on his greaves. "I am sure our hosts have learned how best to carry on their tasks. It is a wonder they maintain the plate, even with the somewhat, ah, uneven appearance it gives."

"Simple, milord. They sleep with it, attend to each piece every day, polishing away all trace of rain or melting snow as the moments between work allow. Steel is so rare here, it's almost sacred."

The prince of Shilar pondered this as his squire continued her rounds with pieces of plate, firmly hooked onto the chain shirt or buckled across his neck and waist to each other. The lack of a paldron for his left shoulder became increasingly obvious. When Thula wasn't looking he reached over her and donned his metal gloves, earning a cluck of disgust. Smiling, he recited the litany-verse of armoring that applied.

"The gauntlets protect the knight's intent, for without his hands he can neither aim his weapon nor direct his horse where Hope needs him."

Thula smiled back, but slammed the thigh-guard so hard onto his leg that the prince gasped. "The cuisse protects the knight from dastards," she recited, "and those on foot, and all forms of treachery together with the tasset." She slapped the sheet of ribbed plates across his pelvis, bringing a cry of sympathy from her brother.

"Have done, squire! Else you save the prince's life at the cost of his heir."

The silence following this joke made them all suddenly aware how alone they were in the midst of the tent-city. Gareth glanced about him, then met the looks on his companions' faces.

"It feels extra empty. I believe the war-party has already left."

With a quick glance up to the brightening skyline beyond the black looming mountains, Tossa pulled on his own gauntlets and retrieved Gareth's shield. Then he helped Thula shimmy into her own chain shirt and assisted with the pieces of her suit. He saw the weighty armor at close range hanging onto his sister's slight frame. Tossa gulped with apprehension; the uses of their armor, so long ago subjected to memory, were becoming fearfully real this dawn. Thula showed no effects, however, turning to mount her mare with smooth speed. Tossa did the same, and marveled at the strength she showed. With her helm on, she looked like a man. Or better, a knight.

The trio rode south from the tent city, noting the stares of children and older women rising for chores but hearing nothing louder than the distant bleat of the herds. Once clear of the tent-lines, they felt the strong cold wind from the west, bending the prairie grass and tussling in the tops of the trees ahead.

"South by east, they said." Gareth spurred into a trot and the siblings followed in a triangle behind him.

They rode nearly an hour into the narrowing gap south of the Bordbeyond cloth-capital, angling ever closer to the Great Forest and seeking any sign of the foraging party.

The Swords of Stone always loomed high behind Tossa's left shoulder. But gradually he became more aware of the great height of the trees ahead; and now the twin tors within the forest were clearly visible, sheening a solid, bright green in the dawn light crowning them before the rest of the forest world below.

"The two hills where the Battle of the Razor was fought," he said in a quiet voice.

"Or," his sister said, "if you believe the tales, the place on the plains where each side buried their dead, forming them."

"Perhaps a bit of both," Gareth said smoothly, "but either way, I never thought to see them myself."

"What are these Bents?" Thula asked as they continued at a steady trot, almost within hail of the trees.

Tossa shook his head, "The Shepherd Folk never say, in so many words. Something guarding the woods, or infesting it perhaps."

"Infested!" Gareth reined in to study the terrain.

The dry brown grasses reached above their horse's knees and led right up to a solid line of oaks and maples less than a league away. Hardly any tree Tossa had seen in his youth reached more than half as high as these massive towers in wood. Only a little bracken, brush or evergreens survived beneath their canopies, each of which covered more space above than a courtyard would have below. These were the oldest living things in all the Lands of Hope, older even than the dragon Callisse should anyone chose to believe she still survived. If Gareth had four more followers with him this day, they could not all link hands to reach around these trunks.

Tossa could see the constant movement of the upper limbs, which he judged to be nearly three hundred feet from the ground in many cases. Trees that had long ago fought and won the war for sunlight towered up, leaving enormous spaces between them, yet shadowing much in darkness. But not all—in many places a withered rotted bole stood broken off and disintegrating, creating a glade by itself where sunshine poured down on thin, dying grasses of autumn.

"Why are there so many blighted boles?" Gareth asked, and Tossa was shocked. He could indeed see more than a score of trunks near the edge that were bright with bare wood, almost devoid of bark. Yet they still wore a full head of leaves, and bounced in the breeze with the others. The forest's crown far overhead shimmered like the waves of an ocean, constantly wriggling and never settled, mingling leaves from trees that stood rods apart. Bits of wood and branch fell almost continuously in the stiff breeze, to perch a moment in the cleft of a neighbor before tumbling on.

Gareth spurred ahead at a walk now; Tossa expected to be at the forest before the sunrise touched them. Everyone was alert for trouble, but it was impossible to know what to look for. Thula pointed to a slight trace in the grass, as of something dragged in the same general direction.

"Perhaps the Shepherds came this way," Gareth said, "they may be ahead of us now and about their business."

"So how do we distract an enemy we cannot recognize?"

Gareth turned to Thula. "My most excellent squire, did you by chance bring your hunting horn with us?"

"Milord, I did indeed."

Thula raised her visor, waited for a calm in the breeze, then winded a strong blast on two notes that shattered the inhuman peace of the Plains. For the first moment, Tossa was as startled as by a crash of thunder; trees a bowshot away might have shuddered with its echoes.

The chill wind of Lion seemed stronger over the Forest, Tossa thought, however unlikely that was. Near the three knights it rose and fell by turns, but the branches of the colossal trunks ahead of them were always gently boiling with activity. He tried to look for signs of animals or other life on the ground level, but always his eye was distracted by movement in the mass of leaves above, predominantly shades of brown as if color was a rare offense.

"So many dead branches," he remarked after a time. Gareth looked to him and Tossa pointed up among the canopy, where stripes and blotches of brown wood could be seen between the waving leaves. Pieces fell to earth now while they spoke—whatever blight the Bents brought it was far advanced here, leaving the autumn wind to blow dying trees to pieces.

Thula signaled again with the horn, a three-tone of charge and attack. Gareth spurred his horse and the trio cut the distance to the edge in half.

"Shall we go in?" Tossa asked.

"Let us preserve our advantage here if we can," Gareth responded mildly.

"This is insane," Thula cried. "We'll be as dead as these trees before we see any Bents, whatever they are."

"And we will look foolish in the eyes of our hosts," Gareth said quietly, "if we fail to attract some nibbles as bait."

Tossa flinched at the sight of movement among some new-fallen bracken beneath the boles. Leaves, and perhaps dead vines, with bits of bark and wood, but animated by something beneath them. He called out and his sister pointed elsewhere to another source of movement. Suddenly Tossa heard the pelt of rain against his armor, and looked down to see long small splinters glancing away or sticking in the woolen undercoat. The horror began to dawn and in a moment he saw it all.

From the trunks above, the storm of flinders and chips increased, not dropping but jumping to the earth, wrestling and mingling in the thickets, and emerging now in craggy man-shapes. Dozens of beings, assembled from the woods, no taller than Halflings and thinner, flatter, jerking forward in a ragged line and hurling parts of themselves as spears toward the foe with unearthly strength. Tossa recognized one high on a trunk, as it ripped away a strip of bark and wood to slap to its own side where it stayed. Another landed on the ground with a leafy branch in its jagged wooden mouth, chewing and swallowing as it advanced.

“The Bents are come,” Gareth announced equably, and settled his visor in place, blocking the kindly smile and leaving the prince of Shilar to confront the foe. To one side, Thula put the horn to her lips and blew a third, long blast of defiance. Perhaps the Bordbeyonds would find the battlefield guided by the noise.

Tossa reacted on instinct, snatched his lance from the rest-socket, couched and charged.

Behind him Gareth was yelling, probably encouragement but Tossa needed to focus. He didn’t want the first action before his lord to embarrass the nation. Charging a grounded foe was normally a simple enough matter, but the creatures ahead were shorter than children. He held the lance steady, careful not to hit the ground at this speed: Tossa remembered fellow squires in the tilt-yard, vaulted to the earth with broken bones that way.

His chosen foe, just ahead of the crowd of others, obliged by running straight at his horse. It raised both arms with its splintered mouth open in a dry, crackling scream of rage when they met, and Tossa’s lance speared three feet through its hardwood frame. Tossa lifted the lance as his horse plowed through their ranks, raising a volley of snaps and cracks. He reined for the turn, looking around for more foes, and felt a prickling sensation all over his ribs and neck. Behind him, the wrack of his enemies was very satisfying, but that sense of pins and needles did not fade. Some of the creatures he overran lay still, others rose with one arm or leg broken and dragging. Tossa finally looked to the one he had slain, so light he doubted he would need to clear his lance before charging.

Except that it was not dead.

The Bent was writhing down the lance, squawking with rage and pulling the shaft through its chest. If anything it seemed even more furious at its current position; Tossa felt his hackles rise to see shreds of his weapon whittling off and entwining with the body of his foe.

In a flash, the thing choked up a wad of something black and sappish, and spat it full on his visor, obscuring his sight.

Tossa gagged on the stench of vomit-coated tar. Rough wooden claws groped at his neck, beneath the helm. The sound of nearby horses chuffing and trampling mingled with the staccato shouts of the Bents. Above the din, Gareth's voice cried out.

"Use the sword! Not wood!"

With a convulsive cry, Tossa brought the edge of his shield hard into his whittled lance. A loud snap and a hardwood shriek, as the weight of the broken lance dropped away. He threw down the useless handle and clawed at his visor, pulling away enough sticky tar to raise it. The bottom half of his foe lay across his crupper, oozing, and Tossa batted it off like a rodent too near his vitals. His sword was clenched tightly in his fist when he drew it, oozing slime between his fingers cementing it in place. Tossa wheeled his horse and tore back into the Bents from behind, chopping to both sides as he varied his mount's course with the pressure of his knees.

Gareth and Thula perched side by side, protecting each other's flank and chopping down as quickly as they could wield their blades. Tossa got up to a canter and plowed past Gareth, then wheeled to trample again on Thula's side. Turning, Tossa surveyed the wrack of battle.

Pieces of broken Bent littered the field, their quivers making a verdant chop of the grasses above. Two halves of separate foes staggered together, perhaps by accident, and welded into a single misshapen being before returning to the fray. Tossa's mount whinnied in distress and he looked down to see it festooned with scores of splinters, most hanging loose but a few drawing blood. Its flesh quivered in every exposed part as if it were covered in flies. Tossa wailed in horror and dismounted, trying to gently clear them from its chest and legs. He too was covered in wooden quills, though his woolen undercoat kept them down to an annoyance.

From ground level the danger was multiplied; though scores of Bents had been destroyed there were dozens remaining. But Tossa did not hesitate; dropping the reins he strode toward the combat on foot, for without his horse the knight does not long survive. The other steeds, he could see, benefitted greatly from their chain coats and superior plate.

Several loud cracks within the trees behind him told of the Bordbeyonds at work; it sounded as if they were several minutes' run away. At once, every surviving Bent snapped around to face the sound beyond Tossa, their faces showing a moment of horror before resolving back into their natural rage. Tossa turned to shout at his horse, getting it to jog a few crucial lengths further away. He spun back to hold the enemy as long as he could. Clots of wooden spines struck him; he slapped his visor back down before swinging in great sweeps to the front and both sides, harvesting enemies whose prime goal was to get beyond him.

The strength of his blows cutting through wooden waists and arms raised smoke, then sparks which began to catch in the sappy bodies of the Bents. Now Gareth came riding through, then Thula, and Tossa could rest a moment as more limbs spattered up from the carnage of their hooves. He turned again behind the flow of battle, and did ample execution upon the foes. One leaped on him from the side, and drove two grainy claws into his upper shoulder near the neck, before Tossa could shake it off. He chopped down three times with shouts, and saw his blood drip on its still form at his feet.

Two Bents had clambered up the flanks of Thula's horse, beyond her reach and panicking the mount into shying. With a shout, Gareth wheeled to sever one with his blade, but then had to fend off several more to the front. Was there no end to these devils? Tossa ran towards Thula, shouting and kicking at flinders in his way. But it was hopeless. Her horse shied even further off as the monster leaped over the scupper to land on Thula's back. She twisted in panic, but the Bent held on with one arm and scrabbled between the plates to drive a claw through chain into her ribs.

Thula's shout of pain was only a little higher-pitched than a man's. Maintaining her seat, she saw Tossa from one side and deliberately reined her horse around to present him her back. Tossa flung down his shield and seized the child-sized terror, ripping it red-handed from his sister. The Bent skittered in anger, twisting in his gauntleted grip to face and batter at Tossa with all its limbs. But the young knight was enraged now too, punching with his sticky hilt at the thing's head and shouting curses. Chips and splinters shot off the Bent in all directions; it tried to spit at him but Tossa ducked, all the while tightening with a grip to squeeze water from a spear.

The monster writhed more and more quickly under the steel gauntlet, until Tossa's hand felt oven-hot and sparks issued from its waist and out its mouth. With a final scream of fury, the creature burst into a popping, fiery mannikin. Still Tossa clenched its waist, until it was shedding cinders; then he threw the flaming body into two of its fellows, who also caught flame.

The Bents were now torn between hatred of the wood-choppers, and fear of the fire. The few survivors showed dismay and hesitated for the first time. Gareth, quickly sizing up the situation, cantered through with his shield held low, plowing four more bodies into the growing bonfire. Tossa saw, and chop-hurled several more. The last of the Bents, far enough away to flee, looked in horror at flames twice their height, yet leaped in, perhaps to save their fellows. Tossa was close enough to feel painful heat on his face, but his spine's chill overrode it.

The woody corpses began to explode in the fire's heat, shooting blazing body-embers out into the grass and sometimes catching on severed limbs there. Tossa ran to where his sister slumped in the saddle.

"I'm fine," she grumbled, but with a quaver from inside her helm, "just… stings."

Tossa could sympathize; his body was a mass of pinpricks and sweeping at the splinters a few times with his hands seemed only to aggravate the tickle-agony. Gareth's shout brought him around to see the grass catching fire in several places, and Tossa ran to step on embers closest to him. Real exhaustion swept in; he staggered but kept on. Fires on the Plains were forbidden, he knew.

Suddenly there were Bordbeyonds everywhere; six or seven within close range, and another dozen running in from the forest's edge. Without word or hesitation, the warriors threw themselves bodily on stray flames, rolling and slapping to arrest the fire's progress. More embers popped high from the central pyre, and nomads at a dead run leaped to catch them in bare hands before they could hit the grass. They spat into their palms as they fell, with hisses of steam and pain. Tossa marveled at their sacrifice, then got back to work with renewed energy.

The smoke from smothered cinders made it hard to see, even after he threw off his helm. But Thula's gasps to one side made clear she was still functional, also stepping on minor flames. The chill breeze periodically swept off the smoke, and each time it seemed to Tossa there were more Bordbeyonds and smaller fires. Still it was nearly an hour before the pyre ceased launching peril into the grass, and a ring of humans and half-elven stood watching its last flickers, darkly red then fully black at last.

It was high time to see to wounds on horse and human. Yet the circle remained in place like statues, only three without visors down. Tossa's legs were crying out with the need to rest, but evidently it was a moment for more testing. The wind of Lion bore down, the needling stings demanded that he pluck them, his horse still quaked as if terrified. Tossa felt a righteous anger rise—what could they expect, the blaze was not of their making. His sister's lip-bitten grimace tore at him worse than the Bents. But she was holding still, for Gareth's sake; and he was holding still for his own reasons, for the honor of their homeland before the judgment of the Shepherds. Duty must own the hour.

From the distant forest-edge several more Bordbeyonds emerged, dragging travois with piles of straight limbs taken from smaller trees deeper within. Ignoring the standing circle they headed north by west, back to the tent-city. At last, the nomad with a bright new paldron spoke.

"Many poles have been taken."

Nods from around the circle, and a voice. "Four times our usual load."

Another, to Tossa's left, said simply, "Five".

Another long stretch of silence, and Gleimharn spoke again, slowly and heavily.

"The Plains burned."

Tossa's heart fell. He knew the reverence which the Shepherd-people showed for their home; children barely able to walk were strapped for not minding a cook-fire. There was evidence of guilt in the Protector's words: looking around he could not see Sidrathay, nor the chief, though the latter was probably at home. Tossa closed his eyes and tried to ignore the needling pain.

Shilar Far-Sight, he silently prayed, show me the right course to honor my prince.

Tossa swallowed hard, then stepped into the center of the circle, deliberately stopping with his boots on the coals of the enemy pyre. Looking around defiantly he pointed to the ground.

"Many Bents are dead."

Gleimharn's helm slowly nodded.

“We faced them with blades, and drew the enemy at the risk of our lives, and the cost of much hurt”. Tossa pointed to his sister, her fist wedged atop her spine.

“The flame,” Gareth added quietly, “came of our use of steel edges.”

Another Bordbeyond grunted with folded arms. “With flails, we cannot kill so many.”

The breeze again picked up the conversation awhile, but Tossa could sense the verdict had passed them by. It was enough, and though he had no doubt spoken too much again, he was overjoyed to have served well.

As always, the Shepherds seemed to decide by magic, without visible signal. One by one they turned away, some to scavenge for unburned limbs, another to tend to Tossa’s horse. Gleimharn raised his visor at last, and the set of his mouth was far from unhappy as he gestured for a comrade to bring a pouch of ointment. Tossa shed his gauntlets and plucked at the hundreds of wooden nails while he walked to see about Thula’s back. The warrior with ointment went to her first, gently wiping a piece of drawmoss around the edges of the wound, which pulled away from the hole with a pitch black surface, leaving fresher red blood looking like the flush of health by comparison. The ointment clearly stung, but helped to close off the bleeding at once. Thula thanked him, gaining only a stony stare in return.

Gareth was marvelous little injured, his plate proof to the thorns of the enemy and just a few scratches above his wrist or behind his knees. Tossa’s mount was badly frightened and nearly exhausted, but suffered him to pluck out some, sweep away others of the splinters. Last of all, Tossa accepted some swabs of ointment for his neck and returned to the nearly useless task of clearing the wood from the wool of his undercoat.

Gareth chuckled at him good naturedly. "You look like an enormous caterpillar, sirrah. Or a wicker basket caught in a windstorm."

Tossa shrugged and grinned. "Now we know, milord, what a Bent looks like."

"Yes," Thula replied, "like the bottom of a fireplace!"

It was well after noon. The Bordbeyonds began to move directly east, across the grassy gap to the base of the Swords of Stone. The Shilarians walked their horses to rest them—in Tossa's case riding was not an option—and plied each other as they went, with questions about their enemies, what battle moves worked best, whether the other's wounds felt better. Thula insisted gruffly, but he could see his sister favoring the back to one side. Tossa had never experienced such a full-on fight before, and wondered if he would ever face such weird creatures again. If not for the fire… but that could not be a regular tactic around the Bordbeyonds. Surely the Great Forest would be a perilous adventure, if these were its outermost guardians.

"How could the heroes have let such a danger go unchecked?" he wondered aloud.

Gareth looked upon him mildly before answering.

"They had but twenty years, the legends say, before departing to the utter East. Dragons, demons, things much larger than Bents were their task. Or are these a more recent outgrowth, like the forest's expanding boundaries? Which would make them the responsibility of the Children of Hope." Tossa looked on the prince's face, seeing not a rebuke but something more like an invitation.

The black mountain walls loomed ever higher now, becoming even more frightening as the westering sun threw their cliffs into sharp relief. Tossa could make out a large defile or gorge almost directly ahead, leading steeply up and winding beyond sight. Gareth pointed further south along the range, where a broader, more gradual ascent led to a narrow shelf in the distance that sported a tiny set of square, regular shapes.

"There! That must be Mickhel, home of the Dwarves."

Thula and Tossa both stopped and exclaimed at this. Gleimharn, still visored, came up and said "The guard-towers only. Further in, the Crafters have their city, mostly inside the mountains." The Shilarians shivered at the thought of living underground. Gareth gazed longest in that direction; Tossa thought he perhaps contemplated a visit, or another alliance renewed. No one he knew had ever seen a Dwarf before.

Moving on, the band stopped before the sudden ascent into the eastern defile, barely three rods across and nearly steep as stairs.

Gleimharn gestured up the gorge and said simply, "Tumekheo Gantargor".

Gareth turned to him and said, "Here will we also accompany you."

The Protector nodded, "You have earned this right."

"What will our enemies be here? How may we prepare for them?"

Gleimharn's helm shook once, and he made no answer. Puzzled, Gareth signaled to his friends to mount up: Tossa bitterly repented the loss of his lance. Patting his horse for reassurance, he gently spurred onward, and the three Shilarians became the first civilized Children of Hope in living record to enter the Swords of Stone.

It was impossible to speak in full voice, but the solid rock to all sides carried a whisper as if shot from a bow.

"We ride into legend, milord," Tossa said.

Gareth nodded, and after a moment replied, "Unless you count Sir Ridevan."

Thula's high chuckle rebounded like a slap from the sides of the gorge; she cut off halfway with a gasp. Tossa looked askance at his companions, but their smiles and head shakes betokened a private joke. The horses walked ever more slowly of their own accord, not just from the steep grade. The knights used light taps of the spur to keep them onward, and stopped to rest whenever the Bordbeyonds did. The nomads also needed to pause frequently. More than ever, their lack of conversation seemed wise.

Tossa craned his head up to stare at the sheer rock faces to the north and south, extending more than two leagues, up into the patchy clouds and beyond. Here and there, tough spindled trunks perched at bizarre angles, shrubs or small trees without enough soil. The height of it, the unbroken planes of stone pointing to the sky: Tossa's head filled with motion and fear, and he tore his eyes away. Nearby, a Bordbeyond knelt to refasten a boot strap; struggling to see his laces through the visor-slits, he at last pushed it open a moment. Tossa saw a face chalk-white with unspoken fear. It almost equaled comraderie; but Tossa looked away before the nomad could notice him.

They wound up along the face of this outer ascent for two hours. It became nearly as fearsome a thing to look west and down, as east and up. Once while walking the horses, the gorge-path slimmed to the width of several men, its cut so shallow Tossa could drag his hand on the side like a rail. The stone was surprisingly warm in afternoon light, and he felt a kick in his groin to think he touched bedrock that joined in an endless slab with the clouds above.

"It is as if, as if someone built this," he whispered.

Gareth looked to him seriously. "Someone did, of course. The Heroes, chiefly Araluntir together with Rallantan, wrought this miracle in the Age of Balance."

"I know the tales, milord. But with respect, does it not seem unlikely, that two mortal men, whatever their lore or lineage, should cause all this?"

"It does indeed. But what can we say then? All the histories agree that once, in the first and second ages, there was no mountain range here. Do you think the Lieges of Despair erected this barrier?"

"Of course not," Thula cut in, "what for? They spent the next five centuries trying to break back into our lands. Despair created the Cleft, not the mountains." In the silence that followed, Tossa could tell that every still, helmeted ear around them was listening carefully. The slanted rock face beneath his gauntlet scraped like gritwool: he could not imagine the weight of the league-deep rock his hand rested upon.

"These mountains are new, as the age of the world goes," Gareth mused. "Have you ever seen the Snowdon Hills, or the Marble Swords in the west? Their peaks are much lower, of course, or else the sun would set an hour past noon! But more rounded, and there are grassy copses and groves of trees. These," the prince paused in his stride and looked upslope at the imposing peaks, "these mountains were thrown up yesterday. In the age of the world, that is."

"But if the heroes raised these mountains, why are they so…"

"Evil?" Gareth asked. No one moved to affirm or deny such a valuation. The prince shrugged before continuing.

"The Swords of Stone are surely imposing and fearsome, I do not scruple to deny it," here he smiled all around, and Tossa thought him the braver for it. "But our heroes had to use the world they lived in."

"Yet the Giants were drawn from the rock of these mountains."

"And also the Dwarves of Mickhel, though the legends say Ma-Eldar worked from stone on the surface, before the others raised this range." Gareth looked speculatively at Tossa a moment before adding, "Imagine how many steps beneath the earth, sirrah, must once have lain the rock you now have your hand upon."

Tossa felt a sting of panic and snapped his palm away; the nomads around him chuckled. He stared at a small piece of stubborn brush, jammed into a crevice and growing at an angle in a cleft of what was formerly hell. The sun, air, and time had just this much effect after twenty-five centuries. But Despair was kept out, locked into the utter East by this titanic barrier of itself.

The group emerged onto a long, narrow plateau, invisible from the ground. Tossa could no longer look back even casually at the heights they had achieved, and it seemed he never caught his fogging breath no matter how long he held still. Before them lay a pool upon the rock, more than two bowshots across and smooth as ice, yet steaming with tendrils of heat, or something worse. The taste of the air was acrid, and beneath his armor Tossa could feel the wool dampening with moisture in the air.

Gleimharn announced, "Tumekheo Gantargor. May the Visored One protect us."

The Bordbeyonds hurried now, following unspoken orders, but sometimes stumbling as they fanned out to the shores nearest the entrance. Each produced a wide flat woolen bag attached to thin ropes. They stood next to the water but careful to keep their boots dry.

Gareth rode north along the rocky western bank, staring into the pool. The water within was suspiciously clear, surely poison to drink. Tossa and Thula followed and kept their weapons ready despite the quiet. Soon, banks of rock rose to their left, cutting off the western view which was a relief. Yet the rock was seamed with juts and gaps, slices of ebon in the shade of the western sun. Tossa heard little pebbles rolling down at times, as if kicked or blown free but invisible to his searching glance.

"There," Gareth called pointing into the water as their horses stopped.

Tossa could see better without sun's glare; dim, white lines lying tightly parallel on the bottom an undefined distance beneath the surface. Across the pool, the Bordbeyonds were hurling their bags over the water, letting them splash and sink, drawing them back in.

"Are those, bones?" Thula whispered.

"Mayhap the water here has tides," Gareth answered quietly, "lapping higher and lower, and gathering these strange salts in rows."

It made perfect sense to Tossa. The idea that the bodies of Giants lay dead here, to sink and decompose in the water of this dread pool, centuries after the Battle of the Razor, was too strange to contemplate. That the Giants of those days had many extra bones, like ribs and elsewhere, was probably part of the legends concerning how hard they were to kill. And the suggestion before his eyes, that these lines in the water were slightly curved, or that a spine divided them…

Gareth spurred onward, as if fear was only a word in books; again the siblings followed and again the awful stillness of this rock-walled pool enfolded them; any stray sound seemed to herald an attack. Their path curled around the northern side, only one horse abreast in places. Tossa saw with a chill a crevice to their left, so black on black he had not noticed it with his eyes, just felt a slight draft on his cheek. The air could not decide if it were hot or cold, so muggy and wet, but it was foul in a way that cleared the breathing and hurt the skull.

The Bordbeyonds, now five furlongs away across the pool, were drawing back their sunken bags, with salts inside them. Signs of their haste were obvious because they were so unusual, and added to Tossa's near-panic.

"Milord, we should rejoin the Shepherds."

Gareth nodded, yet sat his horse a long moment before spurring gently onward, around the lake toward the easternmost reach of the plateau.

"Stubborn," Thula clucked as she rode to keep up.

Tossa drew in his reins, then froze at the sound of something larger than pebbles rolling free. The rock wall circling the lake now joined with the main peaks of the Swords, still in shadow. Too late, his eyes made out an enormous crevice in the darker darkness. The prince's horse pricked up its ears at the thick sound of something moving within the cave.

The roots of a twisted tree emerged from the cleft, followed by a holding hand the size of a torso, and the hulking shape of a man-like being towering over the mounted knights. His shapeless roar of fury slammed off tons of pure rock like a weapon itself. The prince's horse shied and cantered further down the slab-beach, even in panic avoiding the water.

Tossa reached for his lance by instinct, only remembering when his hand closed on nothing. Thula, now directly between the monster and the lake, brought her point down but had no room to charge. She spurred the horse, which jumped less than a full pace in the giant's direction, thrusting more like a spear into its shoulder, lodging lightly and arresting its advance a moment. Roaring again, the giant swept up with its tree-club, snapping off the lance point and nearly unseating the squire.

Tossa groped for his sword and dug in the spurs, still reacting on instinct. But Gareth was closer.

"Hobsel!" he shouted, as names of the moment yielded to years of friendship. Wheeling and dropping his visor in place, the prince of Shilar charged in on a short run, bringing the lance head down in perfect time for impact and putting at least a foot of steel-capped shaft into the chest cavity. Still the massive foe did not go down, and Gareth let go his weapon rather than risk a broken arm.

The creature turned to face this new foe even as Tossa closed with sword raised. Thula's horse staggered into the shallows and screamed, breaking past him to regain the dry rock and kicking up clouds of salty steam in its wake that obscured the view. Thula kept her seat but the lance-arm was clenched to her side, the wound still hurting her. Tossa stood in the stirrups to gain as much height and leverage as he could. He entertained no illusions that he would live where his older, more experienced forefathers often had failed. But he would die to save the prince, and perhaps his sister.

Coughing through the steam-cloud, he saw Gareth also with drawn sword, ducking the first sweep of the club and hacking into his enemy's waist raising gouts of blood and a shout of anger. How many men would be dead already from such wounds? Cantering in slightly behind the giant, Tossa hacked down at the hinge between shoulder and arm. Shilar must have guided the blow, for it struck as a well-aimed carver does the joint of fowl. Slicing more than halfway through bone and gristle, it stopped the sweeping blow aborning; the tree-club dropped uselessly from the hanging pillar of blood-gushing flesh and muscle.

The giant hunched the wounded arm forward and brought its working elbow around behind it, bashing Tossa's shield so broadly and hard as to bend it into a crescent. Tossa was thrown over the crupper and to the ground, within inches of the steaming water and completely winded. His ribs felt broken; unlike giants he did not have extras.

Gareth, blood spattered and breathless, drew back for another strike at the wounded foe. His horse shied again, in response to a sound from the cave.

A second giant emerged, of indeterminate sex or age but unmistakable in its twin fury. Before the prince could react, and as Tossa lay there near fainting or death, it swept its own club around in a level arc, batting the knight off his horse like a pot from a post and into the pool.

Tossa cried out as the first giant, perhaps dying, fell back across his thighs and pinned him beneath nearly a thousand pounds of flesh. Blood sprayed across his visor; tearing it open he could just see the armored form of Prince Gareth of Shilar, stunned and sinking into rising clouds of poisonous steam. There was no movement from his closed helm, as the crown sank last into water and was lost.

Nothing moves in the village of Hollinsfen. Even the chill wind seems to halt at the edge of its fields; the broken corn, the rotted doors hanging by a hinge, and every one of the torn corpses lies unchanged by the sound of airy moans around them. Days pass and flurries fall to rest on corn silk hair, in row or street; at the first touch the flakes freeze in place. By noon they sometimes melt but do not roll off. At night they are icy white again. The deepening cold of oncoming winter prevents even rot from pulling down the dead. It is only right and proper, that nothing should move when nothing is alive.

On this day, just after dawn in early Lion, the sounds of gentle snowfall and lonely breeze are drowned by tramping feet, a wooden gate's snap, and a self-satisfied chuckle. A warband of garruk marches into Hollinsfen, their order ragged but showing a discipline and obedience they never had before. Members of rival bands stand quietly side by side without a flicker of enmity, or rage, or even interest. Now there is a great deal moving in Hollinsfen: but it is far from right or proper, because still nothing there is alive.

Their red-cloaked leader turns to his fourscore garruk and garbles orders in words no one understands. It doesn't matter, the intent conveys through his necromancy, and they turn in groups to do his bidding. Corpses by the dozen are dragged and heaped before the central square. Every house feels the tramp of slat-booted feet and is plundered of any flesh.

The stable holds several ragged horses—poor things, not well attended since the hostler left town last month, they were forgotten when the panic took hold, and starved in their stalls—and they too are hauled out by garruk in pairs.

One dead man's corpse is still attended by a small, bone-thin hound. He has lain at his master's side for nearly two weeks now, and growls at the gaunts who drag the body away. They return with the man in their arms and his guardian biting at their heels. But even this loyal friend shrinks and whines, in the presence of Wolga Vrule.

Ever-amused, the liche leans down to pet the cowering dog, raising whimpers and steam from its head, before leaving it barely alive to witness the abomination. He rises and incants in a language few living ears could comprehend even if his tongue still worked. Waves of indigo miasma cascade from him, stealing across the ground like fog in counterpoint to the gently swirling snowfall.

None of the corpses nearby feel the cold anymore; but at the touch of the purple mist, there is still more movement in Hollinsfen. They rise, shedding flakes of snow, no longer worthy to feel water's touch as they had in death. The undead army of Wolga Vrule nearly triples, many too long dead to serve as the hardy gaunts, but still useful as skeletons. He moves among the ranks, carving hearts and adding to his store in the crystal globe beyond the veil.

Vrule's path takes him to a spot where the blackened, dried blood is slightly fresher, the earth churned by a set of enormous hooves, bearing a few shreds of a young woman's dress. Vrule examines the scene, noting some of the large prints overlay others, both sets heading off eastward as if the second pursued the first. He understands—in fact he anticipated this—and again he laughs in derision at the predictability of chaos. He seems to pity the loss of one more servitor here, but shrugs with a confident grin on his lipless face.

The horses too have been reanimated, and some among the skeleton class are ordered to mount up and carry motley poles and implements for weapons. The army takes up the march again, headed almost directly east toward the city of brick. More than seven hundred feet tramp behind Wolga Vrule, plus one enormous garruk who floats along behind the liche's right shoulder. Not their number, but the fear they inspire will be well enough to take the outpost by storm. Then Vrule will command thousands. No city among the weak, ignorant descendants of Hope can withstand an undead army of that size.

Behind the undead, Hollinsfen again lapses into silence and stillness. Just a slight tendril of miasma pools around the torn dress-shreds, still seeking. The purple wisp fades slowly from view, replaced by a silvery-white aura, the shape increasingly that of a pretty young girl. She looks upon her translucent form and utters a thin, barely audible shriek of horror, clutching her middle in remembrance of the wrong done to her. The silvery shape nearly dissolves from view, but steadies and moves off, fighting the breeze for headway but gliding further from its former home. She follows the undead army, and her face is set in a mask of hatred and pain.

Not a bone nor a hair of any animate being is left in Hollinsfen. Next spring, the grass and wild wheat will begin a decades-long quest to grow over the scene of multiple crimes Despair committed here. One frozen winter more to hold in the memory of the world. Nothing moving, no sounds: and that is again as it should be.

Downfall

Treaman needed no help staying alert on this night-watch. His recent encounter with the river-serpent was only a dull throb in his calf that persisted despite the salve. But the party was otherwise quite comfortable, ensconced in their tent and chatting before sleep, while the Woodsman stood post outside by the warm glow of the banked cookfire and nearby kiln. After his bizarre night in Pelian's wagon and the helldog fight, camping in the wilds felt as close to home as he had ever known. Hallah was curled around his shoulders as usual and wheezing gently. Treaman should by rights have been exhausted anyway.

Yet sleep never came near him, as he stared up at the new moons of Fire Ant, and shivered for the loss of time.

The last two trips, Treaman had been truly astray in the Percentalion, made nearly frantic by his failures. The burden of navigating for the group was still daunting, but he had started to feel guiding threads in his hands, clues and hints that held true. Yet those were matters of north and south, speed of march and when to stop. Now, to think that time itself could go awry: it chilled him, and made the Woodsman feel at fault.

The monsters and other dangers scared Treaman, as they would anyone. But he realized with a private grin, those were Haltar's responsibility, not his. He trusted the foot-knight to win through, he sensed, just as blindly as they all believed in him, to get them home. Each one did well at their chosen moment. Two years ago Treaman did not know any of them; now he willingly put his life in their hands.

He heard the sound of boots on bracken before the intruder sensed their encampment. It was too dark to discern more than an advancing shape. Soon, those footsteps stopped as the other made out a campfire's glow near his kiln; every nerve in the Woodsman's body jangled. He was debating whether to shout when Braja thrust his scarred ebon face through the tent flap. He looked off in the same direction as Treaman had.

"Man," Treaman whispered, and the black nodded, holding up a single finger.

Treaman gestured for Braja to stay before the tent, and the Nubian emerged with iron spear in hand. Taking up his own, Treaman padded off to the right in a lazy circle to get beyond the stranger. Walking toes-first and picking his way, the Woodsman glided between the cypress root-stumps on soft earth without a sound. He started downwind of the intruder, the kiln glowing between them; he was fairly sure he made out the other's position, a still shadow, perhaps crouching by that larger bole.

When Treaman was nearly past the spot to the right, the wind shifted slightly, and the dark shape with it.

"Hold there, stranger" came a deep voice speaking the Common tongue. "You are no *grinak*."

Treaman swallowed hard, "Where do you think you are?"

A chuckle from the shadow-shape, which lengthened as the man stood.

"No, wanderer, you are not in the Percentalion now. This is Oncario."

"Let us come together with our arms held wide."

"Alright then, agreed. I'll have a look at you."

Splitting the distance, Treaman walked on a diagonal path back toward the tent, as the intruder came on directly. He saw a tall man whose spread arms reached quite far, one holding an ax, a glint of mail peeking beneath his tunic. They stopped when close enough to make out features and assessed each other; Treaman marked certain signs of a man who knew his way outdoors, and noted the same glances and nods from him. Treaman liked the look of the ax-man at once.

"We are adventurers out of Trainertown."

"In Conar!" the tall ax-man cried. "So far away, how does the kingdom, tell me. And just the two of you? Light of the moons, he's a giant."

Treaman stood closer to Braja now, and rested his spear on the ground. "Braja here is a Nubian. My friend. I am Treaman."

"The leader?"

"The Woodsman." Treaman raised his voice just a touch, to be sure the others could hear inside the tent.

The intruder relaxed enough to rest his two-bladed axhead on the ground, but gave Braja a short glance, with a face that said 'not him either'. Treaman caught sight of a dark patch inside his left palm, a burn the size of a swan's egg, but the tall warrior did not seem to mind it. Looking at Treaman's campfire, the stones and level of it, he nodded in approval.

"Perhaps," he said in a light tone, "if the others are ready, I can meet them now."

Haltar emerged from the tent with Linya and Mhoral behind him. The stranger took a step back at the numbers, bringing his ax to both hands, but still smiled. Treaman scanned the area behind the kiln and made out a small form padding silently to the rear.

The ax-man looked to Linya and bowed. "A mage, by your dress, milady. Are you the leader of this expedition?"

Linya's eyebrows went high and she put her hands in her sleeves.

"Well met, sir," Haltar replied smoothly, "and perhaps you would do the courtesy of a few answers yourself."

"Your pardon, I am sure!" he chortled. "We get no visitors from the cursed land, excepting only the merchant Pelian. He is overdue."

"He is dead," Haltar responded crisply, adding "not by our hand," as if an unimportant detail.

The stranger's countenance fell, his good humor slain with the word.

"Dead! That is dreadful news. The Primara must be informed."

For a moment, he scanned the group as if the job entailed carrying them all on his back.

"We will gladly accompany you, sir," Haltar said, "if you can guide us to the town."

"Of course. I can be ready as soon as you are, just checking the kilns."

Haltar introduced the five members present, and the rangy timberman gave his name as Januelus.

"Januelus," Haltar said, as the two men stood on a level across the firepit. "That sounds a Conarian name."

"And Eltrinstar does not," he responded cheerfully, then added, "once of the Guard, sent here last year and now the sole survivor."

"You said I was not grinak," Treaman said, "what is that?"

"The curse of these barrens. The grinaki are a kind of stringy, weasel-faced garruk, about as tall as a Halfling." The timberman held his palm down at waist-level. "Do you know what I mean?"

Bildon, who had stolen up in silence, sheathed his knives and chose this moment to stroll casually past under the hand, making the timberman jump, then heartily laugh.

"I withdraw the question," he said, extending his arm for the Stealthic to grip. "You're as quiet as your guardsman here, sirrah."

"Much quieter," Bildon replied as his arm gyred so widely he needed his tip-toes to maintain it.

An eerie silence descended as the party limbered up in the midnight gloom. Treaman glanced sidelong at Januelus, who wore a look of good humor, but never moved to turn his back on anyone again after the Stealthic's trick. He helped Treaman kick dirt on the embers of the campfire, and then sidled toward the kiln keeping them all in sight as if for politeness' sake.

It was time for a gesture. Treaman poked his spear-butt into the soft ground to leave it standing, and strolled by the kiln, within easy reach of the timberman's weapon.

"So how long does it take, for charcoal?"

"Depends a bit on the type of wood you use," the timberman replied. "Cypress around here, usually two days." He opened a swinging door in the dome of brick, revealing the kiln's inner chamber where the firepit below still glowed with burning split pieces. Another large container within had a similar door, which he deftly unlatched with the blade of his ax; it swung open on the gravity of its angle; within were rectangular bricks of blackened wood, stacked in a kind of parquet pattern.

The timberman nodded; still glancing around at the group frequently, he reached for a long-handled shovel leaning against the kiln. Treaman saw several there, and grabbed one to help. The two of them in tandem cleared out the contents to a bin at the side, leaving a trail of thick black dust as they walked. The bricks were light for their size, yet Treaman found he could not carry half as many on his shovel as the Oncarian.

Januelus closed the bin and began to bring new-cut wood from stacked cords back to the kiln. Apparently unbothered by the heat of the fire below, he reached across the inner chamber to stack them in the same overlapping, rising circular pattern. Treaman brought more wood from the stack to heap at his feet, and by the time the party was packed up the kiln was reloaded. Januelus closed both doors and stuffed several armloads beneath the kiln, watching until they began to catch on the embers of the previous flame.

"The men will be out to wheel that load into town," he said. "There are too many kilns for one man to keep up, but I like to load them when I can. Mostly I just check to be sure the *grinaki* haven't been up to mischief. Evil bastards, but also idiots—they'd have burned the forest down long ago."

"Why so much charcoal?" Haltar asked, trying to sound casual.

"You shall see," Januelus said with a wink, "suffice to say, in Oncario the people are much occupied. Now, shall we go?"

Haltar gestured for Januelus to lead, but he stepped to one side pointing south. After a moment, the party slowly walked past him; he spun his ax over one shoulder and followed, calling out minor course corrections to Treaman in the front. The young woodsman could not shake the ridiculous feeling that the entire party had been taken prisoner. He noted a long blanket-wrapped item across Haltar's shoulders—good sense, not to show the Sword of Air under these circumstances.

They hiked through the barrens in unaccustomed silence, lacking even Bildon's habitual chatter. Treaman chose the paths where they existed, altered twice at instructions called out by Januelus as he guided them toward other kilns to check. During one of these stops, Haltar caught Treaman's gaze and gave him a look filled with consequence. The Woodsman could make no sense of the leader's urgency, and felt a stab of fear that they were going to ambush their guide.

Januelus shoveled and stacked without a visible sign of worry, leaving his ax to one side for long periods. Treaman could easily have taken it up; but then, the rangy soldier might beat him down with just the shovel. Haltar of course was another story, but still wounded. Treaman's mind raced with the possibilities, and he knew he had to do something.

Playing dumb seemed about right, so he decided to try that.

The next time Januelus called out a course correction, Treaman went the wrong way. When the guide called out for him to stop, Treaman turned back with a puzzled expression, trying to model his face after Braja when the others spoke.

I don't get it. What are you saying, this way?

"Oh here I'll show you," Januelus said and came to the front. As he passed, Treaman shot a serious look back at Haltar and held his hand out in a slowing motion. Haltar casually pointed to the bundle over his shoulder, and Treaman began to understand.

The city ahead would have measures to deal with adventurers.

Praise to Helmon, more grinaki tracks across their path provided the perfect excuse. Treaman knelt and studied them.

"I make out a dozen, maybe a score, and fresh" he said, looking up to Januelus for confirmation. "Do they always travel in such packs?"

"Sometimes much more," his guide assured him, "they are like an infestation of rats. But they would only attack a group like this if they were desperate. And not by day, only in full dark. A night like this." He scrutinized the sky through the pine boughs, confirming moonset with a deep breath that seemed strangely like relief to Treaman.

"So," the young Woodsman offered, "folk from the city only go about armed."

"The colliers and timbermen, yes. And once in a while, the bravest of us go fishing in the river."

"Yes! A scaly legged serpent—"

"You saw a hathlagor!" Januelus was excited and impressed. Treaman, moving south again with him felt comradery, and almost forgot to stay on the subject he had raised.

"So, when folks enter the city under arms, do they peace-bond?"

Januelus nodded, then stopped with arms akimbo and a wide grin. "Hah. So that is the matter that has your leader all aflutter."

He gestured to Haltar and stepped toward him.

"Let's have a look at your arsenal, then. Starting with that lovely blade you have wrapped up beneath the blanket there."

Too clever, this one, Treaman thought. His heart plunged when Haltar drew his broadsword instead. But the foot-knight moved to one side of Januelus, looking at something beyond the group. An arrow the size of a dart hit Linya in the arm. Treaman whirled to see the trees all about festooned with the smallest, thinnest, ugliest garruk-kin he had ever seen.

Everyone acted at once, in seeming chaos. Mhoral stepped to throw his wood-blade and tripped on a cyprus knee, sending the weapon gyring into the soft earth. Bildon drew his knives and stood next to Treaman, hefting one for a throw. Linya sank to her knees in shock, while Januelus and Haltar stood together facing back the way they had come. A hail of missiles, many of them rocks, stormed in to little effect now that the group was ready. Treaman estimated there must be at least thirty grinaki in the ring to all sides, chippering in their tenor gutterals and edging in and out on the verge of fear.

Bildon ran forward a few steps and hopped atop a cypress knee, catching his balance and hurling a knife into the mouth of one closest to him. A dozen grinaki on that side fell back in panic, while others to his flanks closed in. He jumped back and ran at full speed, which had the desired effect. A half-dozen of the most brave or least intelligent gave chase. Mhoral, rising with flail in hand, swung through as Bildon passed and knocked three of them over with the sound of snapping bones. Treaman stabbed at one, purposefully missing as he still could not feel truly threatened by these wiry man-grubs. The rest of the attackers fled, except one whom Haltar struck and cut in half.

This caused the entire ring to recede a rod or two, but not flee. The survivors reformed, gabbling nonstop to each other. The hail of homemade missles resumed. Braja unslung his longbow and returned shots, each one causing a cry of dismay from the enemy though he seldom hit. One shaft struck a knee of wood with such force that it skewered the grinaki sheltering behind it. His cries of agony were a din that crested all other noise, until one of his tribe-mates ran over and slit his throat.

"I don't understand," Januelus cried, "they must be starving to attempt this, it's insane."

"How long until sunrise?" Haltar shouted back.

Treaman and Januelus both said "Two hours," at nearly the same time.

Mhoral took a rock to the face and cried out more in rage than pain. "We can't wait that long, Haltar!"

"Linya, are you alright?" the leader's face was tense.

As Treaman glanced over, the mage stood and deliberately pulled the arrow from her arm with a scream. Clutching the bloody spot, she nodded, and quietly said something the Woodsman had never heard her say before.

"I'll handle this."

She stepped forward of the group in dramatic fashion, gesturing with her arms and shouting a nonsense syllable to draw attention. The grinaki obediently calmed, holding weapons and watching her every move. Linya raised light from her headband, shining before her and creating a clear target; still, none of her audience hurled a rock or dart. Taking the back-end of her wand, Linya drew a ragged circle in the earth several feet across, and two lines bisecting it. Stepping back from the circle, she cleared her sleeves above the elbow and threw them skyward, crying out a series of nameless tones.

For a tense couple of moments, nothing happened. Then the caster sagged a bit as if from exertion, and her headband gem glowed a fiery hue. Smoke and flame materialized within the circle, rising more than seven feet from the ground. The blaze hissed and crackled, sending out sparks that caused a few of the grinaki to run off in terror. Treaman felt the hackles on his neck spring to life; was Linya really summoning a dread beast of the netherworld?

Emerging from the fading smoke he beheld a thickly muscled, red-skinned creature with horned head and three legs, tail lashing and tusked jaws gaping with hunger. Linya drew a gasping breath, then cried out while pointing dramatically with one arm.

"Go! Slay them all!"

Grinning, the monstrous thing strode forth beyond the earth-drawn circle and toward the grinaki horde. Its feet made the muddy earth hiss and pop like branding irons, talons sinking inches deep and prints smoking in its wake. The grinaki were petrified in place, like so many more cypress knees, as it reached them. Seizing one scraggly fellow by the top of the head, the demon held him up a body-length off the ground. On reflex, the poor thing stabbed with its spear, which broke on the hell-born's invulnerable chest. He tossed it to one side like a cat, seven feet through the air smashing into a trunk and snapping its spine.

Almost as one, the two dozen or so who had so far held their terror broke into complete panic, screaming higher than children and dropping weapons in their haste to get away.

Treaman circled behind the demon to approach Linya, who seemed to need a nearby bole to support herself, one arm draped over her shining circlet and face. He didn't dare touch her; what awful lore had she studied, what horrible price had she paid to master this creature of Despair?

"Are you, are you alright?"

From beneath her draped sleeve, she quietly asked, "Are they gone?"

"Yes, but what about this—"

Linya looked up and straightened quickly, evidently no worse for having summoned a creature from hell and bending it to her will.

The slavering thing, stomping off after the rout, stopped less than a spear's cast away. Though she said nothing, it turned back towards the group now, smiled again, and came on in search of new prey. Everyone cried out in warning and alarm. Mhoral began to sing the Battle Song, and Haltar took position before the rest with his sword in a two-handed grip.

"Linya," he said with unaccustomed tension, "if you can call this thing off, do it now."

The mage only smiled wickedly, and Treaman feared the worst from this betrayal. His hands clenched—someone needed to destroy the sender of this threat, yet she seemed unconcerned about attack from her former comrades. And she had saved his life three times since they met. The Woodsman froze in indecision, as the monster came within sword's reach of the foot-knight.

At the last moment, the thing seemed to unravel in strips, red flesh and talons dissolving in many directions as Haltar's blade swept through empty air. And Linya could not contain her giggles regardless of who swore at her.

Looks all around. Haltar and Mhoral held their peace, while Bildon jogged over to retrieve his knife and examine some of the bodies. Treaman saw Januelus, his face filled with consternation and his confident good humor at last cracked wide open. The Woodsman helped the mage salve her arm, his mouth tingling with a thousand questions; but noting the warning eyebrows all around, he did his best to pretend that this happened every day.

In fact, Linya had never displayed anything like that kind of power; Treaman wasn't sure the ax-man was wrong to fear her. Looking up at her face, he saw the same delicate features and shy smile he had known, now with a spice of delight dancing in her eyes that only made her more beautiful. Her smile was contagious: the rest of the group seemed in high humor as they resumed the march, while Januelus dragged along doubtfully to one side. Braja was also impressed. Hallah, on the other hand, had slept through the entire affair, shouting and all: Treaman carried her weight on his shoulders without noting it anymore.

Bildon was clearly puzzled, signaling to Treaman in his hand-cant:

'Dead enemy not broken'

The Woodsman could not make out the Stealthic's point, and simply sent back:

'Dead enemy dead. Good.'

Bildon waved off the conversation with a curse and a laugh.

Dawn found them breaking from the barrens into drier pine-lands where the trees had been clear-cut. At first the ground was dotted with clustered stumps, later gouged with craters where they had been pulled. Beyond, wide fields with high, spike-topped fences created a squared off maze with lanes running between them. The closest were made of solid wooden slats, but most used brick, all of them effectively blocking the view. Some had large bolted doors set into their sides, opening only from within. In others, a small brick house built directly into a wall-corner provided the only entrance. The path beneath their feet was also paved in deep red brick: Treaman gasped when he thought of the sheer scale of production accomplished here in the isolated wilderness. There were scores of such walled-off fields, and Treaman detected the scents of fall harvests; late corn and pumpkins were everywhere though he saw nothing through the hemming walls.

"We shall reach the Colli bridge before mid-morning," Januelus assured.

"How many folk live outside the city?" Haltar asked.

"None, really," Januelus answered him. "Farmers take it in turns to tend and harvest the fields, spending perhaps a day, or sometimes overnight in the houses you see, which are reinforced. But everyone's home is in the city."

"Are the grinaki so fearsome then?" Mhoral asked.

"Them! Nearly a joke, they manage to steal food once in a season perhaps. If they were not so clearly cruel and debased, I might pity them." The timberman paused as they walked briskly along, thinking to himself. "But the people of Oncario follow traditions as old as the kingdom in this. And once in a while, well, you can never quite tell what the Percentalion will throw into our district."

Treaman knew he heard only half a story there. "But you are clearing new fields," he observed.

"All the time," Januelus replied with a smile. "We are growing, indeed."

"The population?"

The timberman nodded, then spread his arms wide. "And the land itself." He let that sink in a moment, before adding, "I have roamed the outermost borders of these barrens, and a bit of the Tallwoods, on the other side of the river. Oncario grows, and the chaos shrinks."

They walked in silence between high walls, almost on streets and probably as safe as they had been since Trainertown. Yet Treaman felt a chill at the timberman's words. Looking back to Haltar, he saw the leader mouth the one word, *we*. That didn't make him feel much better. Still, trusting Januelus was better than showing the Sword of Air to the entire city guard.

"Should we, that is may we peace-bond our weapons now? We have all the supplies with us."

Januelus nodded agreeably. "A bit particular, I see, about others pawing your blades? Mind you, the laws are very strict; break the seal for any reason and you'll be brought before the Primara."

"Excepting self-defence, of course," Haltar suggested from the back.

Januelus shrugged. "That will be for her to determine. But if you show me every weapon you have and bond it, I'll speak for you to the guards. They'll pass you on my word."

The party stopped and unlimbered their various weaponry. Treaman took out a length of sturdy cord and laid it over the hilt of his frontier blade resting in its scabbard, sealing the string on both sides in wax that he melted from a tube using tinder-wick. Once it cooled, it would be impossible to draw the weapon without popping open the seal or cutting the string. Mhoral tied the ends of his flail to the handle; they covered the sharp ends of both spears in cloth and bound cords around the shaft. Braja understood the matter through signs, unstringing his bow and peace-bonding both ends with blobs of wax.

And so it went: most party members had more than one weapon, as with Treaman's spear and pioneer-sword. Mhoral had quite a collection, and the bent wooden club defied all efforts; Januelus waved it off with a laugh. He glanced covertly at Linya's small wooden wand; she produced a cloth wrapping which she sealed before holstering it smoothly in her sleeve, and Januelus nodded in approval.

Last of all, Haltar—who had already bonded the broadsword taken from Pelian's caravan—knelt down and pulled forth the bundled sword from his shoulder-brace. Carefully unwrapping just the end, he exposed the gem-pommeled hilt and the very top of the scabbard, not showing an inch more than needful as Treaman quickly peace-bonded it. Januelus looked on with eyes alight in disinterested amusement.

"Quite a treasure," he said to Haltar quietly.

"A ceremonial blade," the foot-knight offered with a deadpan face. And that would have to do.

"Tell us something about the Primara you're taking us to," Treaman suggested, to break the mood. Januelus looked at him quickly, and in a flash Treaman saw there was much he would not say.

"The office of the Primar rules the city," he replied as they took up packs and continued on lanes now fully paved in brick. "In ancient days I'm told the king appointed them, but now we hold elections each five years. Vuthienne has won four times since succeeding her father, and probably will from now on."

"Essentially a queen," Mhoral observed.

Januelus grinned. "Technically, just the First among us."

Mhoral had more to say, but his mouth stopped in the open position, as the party crested a final rise and their destination came in sight.

Treaman's eye could not stay on the dozens of farm-fields in the shallow valley below, barely registered the brick roads converging like spokes to a large plaza, or the final wide street leading east to the bridge. His vision completely arrested by the view beyond that arching span, Treaman gazed in breathless wonder at the tight-packed, fortified city in the midst of the wide Cario River.

Oncario's wall seemed to grow directly from the island's top, its base of granite blocks and the rest built with man-high red bricks in a perfect interlocking puzzle-pattern. Mortar painted black only emphasized the impregnable strength, the towering isolation of the fortress city. Within its walls, gables and stack-chimneys spiked up toward heaven, some to five or more stories. Treaman saw lovely balconies, and connecting bridges between cupolas, colored tile roofs, banners and windows of marvelous stained glass. A few trickles of smoke already stained the blue morning sky and the looming profile of Skysword beyond. Distantly, Treaman heard the clash of metal and a deep chuffing hiss, as might come from a teapot grown to the size of a room.

He had seen it once already from a distance, but now Treaman was stunned. Looking back, he noted the effect was even greater on his companions.

"An entire city!" Mhoral exclaimed.

"No army could breach those walls," Haltar said.

"So many people," Linya whispered, "I cannot believe what I see."

Bildon stepped up and patted a friendly hand on her back.

"Yes, my dear, we all know how that feels."

At the plaza the party's road joined with four others, creating a huge five-sided space between the border walls of the nearest farms. On each wall was an archway set against the brick, leading nowhere but made of solid metal; silver and gold, Treaman guessed, or else cleverly painted iron. A few farmers heading out from the city passed with greetings for Januelus and open stares at the strangers.

As they crossed the plaza, Bildon asked, "What do these arches signify?"

Januelus shrugged. "They are called the gates, but no one remembers why." He pointed. "That one is for Conar, I've heard it said. But the others, I don't know." He grimaced with mock frustration. "A symbol of the unity of the ancient kingdoms, I suppose."

On the bridge-side a functional brick arch bore the words "Speak in Hope to Enter" in bas-relief. Januelus moved to the front to lead again, and spoke the ancient words *"Ar Aralte"*. He turned back and observed the party as they crossed the portal, each of them speaking the binding words as they did so. Linya drew everyone's attention, but said the words without a stammer. Treaman repeated the phrase for Braja, who dutifully spoke through his scarred mouth in a heavy accent. The party approached the gatehouse with the morning sun in their eyes.

Linya mused aloud. "How did Braja pass if he did not know the meaning of his words?"

"Maybe the sounds themselves do the trick," Bildon suggested.

"Or more likely," Haltar said, "there is no magic here, only custom. The sign is written in the Common tongue."

"A good custom, then," the Halfling rejoined. "No enemy of Areghel could knowingly say the words in Ancient, regardless. Just as we cannot say… you know, the opposite."

"Though no doubt, you've tried," Mhoral suggested.

The guards at the gatehouse were very interested to have a job, for a rarity. Camus, with a red beard and no hair, oversaw every weapon the party showed him to ensure the peace-bonds were in place: as the timber-man had promised, they asked to see no other, including the one wrapped in a blanket. Wiry little Pekar stood by with nothing to add, but glared up at the Nubian in a mix of fear and dislike. Linya caught the guardsman's eye and put her hands in her sleeves with an unsmiling face, effectively conveying her disapproval, which abashed him completely. The party was bid formal welcome to Oncario, and on the assurance that Januelus would guide them to the Primara's Palace, required no further escort. Treaman saw him watching the party again as they passed, with a new reluctance in his gaze and gait.

The span was wide enough to pass two wagons abreast. Treaman felt the usual tingle between his legs at the crest, three rods above the waters. Far below, the turgid Cario seemed to barely move, massive and deep against the island cliffs.

"Where does the river, ah, go?"

Januelus stopped by the stone balustrade and the party stayed with him to look out over the wide water.

"No one recalls anymore where the Cario sources," said the timber-man, waving upstream. "But it gathered strength in the north and east of the Percentalion, before flowing on into the River Running. From there to Eldarport and the Western Sea: Oncario was a port of some significance, so the records say."

"And now?"

"I myself have not seen. But the fishermen tell that in both directions, the Cario just fades. The course becomes shallower and swampy, until no passage is possible. Here, near the island, you can still see the current, though not what it once was. The water… I don't know how, or what happens, really. But this river, this city, I suppose it's too real to fall into chaos completely."

Januelus gave a friendly wave up to the guard-window when they approached the inner gate, and the portcullis rose as the thick wooden portals swung smoothly back. Treaman heard no rattle of chains, just the creak of wood and rope; no team of men manned the portal either. Silently, the party passed within to the shade of the under-wall. After a long moment, the doors and bars slowly slid back to closed, revealing some tightly-made mechanism at the hinges to either side. It was as Linya said, even with his eyes Treaman could not believe the city was fully real. Bildon dashed over for a closer look, tracing the hawsers through pulley and block and glancing about for a motive source.

A guardsman swaggered out to greet Januelus, and the two Oncarians chuckled at the Stealthic's puzzlement.

"Duty by yourself again, Barithul?"

"Mag, he had a late night," the guardsman claimed, as his eyes glittered proudly at Bildon.

"It's a *Makine!*" the Stealthic exclaimed, and the single word instantly doused all good humor.

"You shut your tongue, runt!" The guard brought his spear to bear, but Januelus caught his arm.

"Stay, Barithul, he's a rustic. Look you, Halfling, where is the mass of metal, aside from the bars? What destruction has it wrought?"

"And it stops and starts when I move it," Barithul added, still angry. "The work of Dexithilon is not for the likes of you to piss on."

Where any other in the party would have been apologetic, Bildon was only more curious. "Sure, fine, but what do you call it?"

"Call it? It's a gate, you club-headed runt."

Bildon's head-shake wasn't even polite. "Yes, but the mech—the driving force, whatever you prefer to call it."

Januelus looked down on Bildon with distrust. "The inventor named them *automakoi*, if you must know. But they are most certainly not—"

"Yes, yes of course not. Where is he?"

Now the Oncarians laughed again, but not as kindly. "Who, Dexithilon? Why, he's been dead for centuries."

"Conar's balls!" the Halfling cursed, and Treaman could see he was severely disappointed. "But wait! These ropes, and the gear is made mostly of wood."

"Of course, it's no *Makine*, idiot."

Bildon smiled, and Treaman knew he'd love to put a dagger in the guard's thigh. "So these things don't last for centuries. Who repairs the gateworks?"

A pause while the guardsman blinked. "Well, Enict of course. He studies all of Dex—"

"Time to be off," Januelus said firmly, "You lot have a report to make to the Primara."

Treaman could read on Barithul's face, that title brought the banter to an end. Januelus led them on into the narrow brick-lined canyons of Oncario.

Treaman gaped at the close-set buildings down long streets to either side, watched the bustling population—many of whom noticed the party as well—and smelled everywhere the odor of burning. He remembered the good-natured bustle of Trainertown, so small and quiet by comparison, more open and sunlit, and felt a little lonely even among the throng.

The chill of early winter could not reach inside the walls; at least three large, low buildings they passed were foundries of some kind, ebon smoke now pouring full force into the air and giving off enough heat to warm the bricks nearby. Certain alleyways appeared dedicated only to traffic in goods, running thick with wheeled carts pulled by one or two men and most often loaded with charcoal. Other, slightly wider streets were fairly empty except for a few folks on foot, residences with decorated doors and sometimes family name-stones on the house corners. Still more streets held nothing but shops, with signs hanging out emblazoned with the traditional symbol of the goods sold or crafts pursued within.

"May we quarter at an inn first," Haltar asked politely. "A chance to rest, and make ourselves presentable."

"And bring only what you need, of course" Januelus shot back immediately. "I have no secrets from the Primara, citizen Eltrinstar. Besides, Oncario boasts no inns, as we have few travelers in need of lodgings."

"You must not throw us on the Primara's mercy for shelter," Haltar pursued. "We will appear to be beggars or refugees."

"Or prisoners," Januelus replied with a tight smile. But he stopped walking a moment. "Yes, I can understand you might have some, ah, misgivings after all you're seeing." He looked down again on Bildon a moment. "I tell you what I propose. Enict the tinker has an enormous property, needful for all he does. No spare beds I know of, but—"

"Perfect," Bildon cut in, "we'll be fine, take us there."

Januelus shrugged and led the way at a brisk clip; from the man's face Treaman could see the wheels were turning as usual, but about what he had little idea. Januelus seemed to like and distrust them; the Woodsman thought that most in Trainertown had shown his party only the latter reaction, so perhaps they should be grateful.

Their way intersected a broad street running north and south through the center of the city; everyone exclaimed at the view of the ruler's mansion to their left, rising five stories and more behind a barred wall and gate.

"The Primara's palace," Januelus shouted over the passing crowds, "where you will have your interview. When she can find time to grant an audience."

Treaman had never seen the hall of a great lord, where justice was served, and he felt a strong jangle of distaste to think he would need to enter those gates, and surrender to another's will. Two lofty towers loomed from the rear corners, their highest windows connected by a thin arching brick bridge that struck the Woodsman with fear just to see.

Januelus kept moving across the avenue, through a throng of hundreds, perhaps thousands all up and about their business. No question, he was delaying for some reason. Januelus seemed almost gay now, as he described various other landmarks in the western half of town. Several blocks on, he turned right in a narrow street, one used for trade, except it was empty of traffic unlike the rest of Oncario's industrious tumult.

Hardly any doors or windows fronted this street, and there were no hanging signs. Some buildings had the marks of deep burns, and a couple of windows were shattered. Stopping at a pair of slanted cellar-doors, Januelus stomped on the metal, then pulled a lever set into the wall, causing a brass hammer to fall on its bell. The handle moved slowly back in place when released, and the hammer likewise raised up, resetting. Treaman heard the distant sound of another bell from deep within.

"Ho there, Enict Moaro, rouse yourself from your mad experiments! Primara's business."

A torrent of muffled language within, incomprehensible for words but clearly understood for tone, preceded a longish pause, the sound of steps on the inner stairs, and the sudden swing of the slant-wise doors. The slender man there was smudged, sweat-streaked and annoyed.

"Blast you with fire, Januelus, I have barely begun work for the day. Your mistress—"

"The Primara has guests," Januelus cut in, "and requires lodging for them while they await her pleasure."

The occupant thrust both hands into pockets of his leather work apron, his mouth agape as if he'd been asked to give birth to a horse.

"Did you run head-first into a tree, timberman? Go to the hells of Kog if you think—"

"Calm yourself, Enict. You will be amply rewarded for your service to the city."

"Everyone knows where the Primara bestows her rewards nowadays," the inventor replied with an angry smirk. "Push off with this rabble."

"We pay our lodgings in coin," Haltar interjected. As the inventor turned, the warrior produced a palmful of mingled gold and silver, enough to pay a month's stay at Fairnum's Tavern in Trainertown.

Bildon stepped forward, "And we could help you work."

"What would you know of my work, Halfling? I have no beds, no food!"

Haltar jingled the coins. Januelus said "Get Jaya to send over supplies, the food you need, blankets, anything. Stop whining over details, craftsman."

Enict switched to whining over important things. "How am I to further my labors while playing housemaid?"

Januelus adopted a straight face. "Ah yes, your work. I seem to recall several petitions with the Primara; improvements in the chapel tower, requests for yet more iron, added work in the caves. Some have lain on her desk for a month, or more."

Now Enict stood very still.

"If only I could recall," Januelus said quietly, "where exactly in the order of audience you stood at present."

Defeated, the thin inventor swung back like a door. "Welcome to my humble home."

"I shall return by days' end with any further instructions," Januelus was already moving away up the street as the party shuffled down the steps into Enict's basement.

The under-level was an enormous open space, peppered with worktables, barrels set against the wall, and two sets of stairs leading up. It was brightly lit, against Treaman's expectations, and smelly but neat. The distant sound of burning from other rooms and an occasional cough in metal punctuated the sight of Enict pacing around the party, staring at Braja and passing his gaze alertly but quickly over everyone else.

His last look was at Treaman before turning back to speak, but his head feinted double and cut off his words.

"I have no—th—what in Hope's name?" He snapped back to stare at Treaman, and the Woodsman knew it was Hallah he saw. The dragon roused under the unaccustomed silence.

{*"Odd-man is hungry? Treaman feed odd-man."*}

The image in his mind of lobbing a salted fish into Enict's open mouth was too much, and Treaman chuckled. Suddenly their host found his voice.

"Shit!"

"Citizen Moaro, please don't be af—"

"Shit. I'm sure of it. Wait, wait here."

The tinker fled the room through a door at the far end, and the sound of a latching lock echoed through the enormous basement.

"Did he say shit?" Mhoral asked.

"He did indeed. That is what he said." Bildon averred solemnly.

Braja tapped Treaman's shoulder, saying "Shit?" Everyone laughed at the task, but Bildon was happy to convey the sense through pantomime.

{*"Odd-man is afraid?"*}

"I don't know, Hallah, perhaps."

{*"Afraid of Hallah!"*}

"Well yes, I'm sure he was afraid of my big hungry dragon."

{*"Hallah will have fish instead."*}

As Treaman reached to his food-pouch, Bildon and Braja were laughing together and repeating the same word. Haltar levered his pack to the floor like a gavel, taking charge again.

"A meeting, everyone. Now."

"Are we prisoners here?" Mhoral asked at once.

"Januelus is hiding something," Treaman offered. "He wanted us delayed, and used this fellow's eagerness for his petitions to meet his own purposes."

"Simple," Mhoral answered, "he wants to visit his lover. We've been taken into custody by the queen's consort."

"Later, both of you. Bildon."

"Understood, captain, I'll have that door open in a moment."

"Bildon, sit down. Linya, a word now if you please."

Silence again, as everyone looked to the slender mage wearing a face both sheepish and impish, holding her stomach in both arms.

Haltar guessed correctly.

"An illusion."

She nodded.

"You enchanted the headband to summon a demon's form?"

"Not precisely," she said slowly. "The enchantment only enables a certain size."

"Wait," Bildon cried, "what about the grinaki it slew?"

Treaman remembered the ground of battle; during the fight he had seen the demon's talons crushing into the earth, he was sure of it. The foul smell of smoke, the loud hissing preceded the demon's attack. Afterward? He could not recall if the prints remained, and hadn't looked.

To answer Bildon's question, Linya pointed to her skull.

"There are spells to create mere images of things," she said, "they have no substance beyond vision and any physical test destroys them."

"And you can summon real creatures," Mhoral said quietly, "like the bear."

"Yes, exhausting but real and controlled, for a short time. But this is a kind of middle case, taught by only a few. The illusion does exist, there is light and power in it. But it works best when it suggests something real to your mind."

"So," Bildon said slowly, "the grinaki *believed* your demon could raise it off the ground, and throw it into the tree? So it could? Then how did it die?"

Linya shrugged. "I would say, of fright."

"I heard his back break!" To Bildon's accusation Linya only smiled again, as the thought sank in fully.

"The point," Haltar said heavily, "is that this spell fools us the same as our enemies."

"Haltar, I was joking a bit, I am sorry."

"Never mind that," Haltar said with a dismissive wave. "Can you make other things with this spell? Fire, a pit, a rain of acid such as we have seen out there?"

There was a long silence.

"Well, practice makes perfect I suppose. I could do some of what you say, Haltar, but with something separated, like raindrops… the façade would deteriorate, you could tell it was not real. And if you focus on the thing I create—with practice, again—you can undo it."

Haltar rubbed his chin for a few moments, always a good sign to Treaman's experience. He finally looked at her with his honest grin.

"It was well done at the time, Linya, do not misunderstand me. And you need not divulge everything you know to us."

"Your trusted friends!" Bildon cried in accusation.

"Remember in future that we are all affected, as you say. We will discuss further what sort of illusions you might attempt, when would be good times, so forth."

"First," Linya admitted, "I must refuel the headband's energies, and then sleep would be very good."

"Sleep where? Eat what?" Mhoral spoke up. "Our gracious host has left us in a cellar, no doubt for hours."

The rattle of the keys stopped the Elf.

Bildon looked over to ask. "Does it tire you, being wrong all the time?"

Enict had locked the inner door behind him with a large brass key hanging around his neck. The inventor lugged an enormous leather-bound tome to a side table and thumped it down, then advanced toward the party while alternately rubbing his knuckles and clenching them still. Once again, he paced entirely around the group, the way a man looks at a set of statues. He did not bother to conceal his interest in Hallah, but his head twitched in new directions every few moments, seemingly whether he wished it or not. Very very quietly, he clucked and whispered single syllables to himself. And still he paced, stopped, paced again while his hands wrestled with each other.

"Good sir," Treaman finally said to break the mood, "I used less energy today in coming to your city than you have in the last few moments."

The Woodsman's effort was rewarded with a high-pitched crack of nervous laughter. Their host's face rippled in indecision and then he shrugged.

"I shall be candid with you, strangers. In that service, I should like to say three things without interruption. First, I believe that my work here is one upon which the future of the Lands utterly depends. It sounds vain, I realize, but when I speak thus it is only a tribute to those who have come before me, whom I study and whose genius I hope to revive."

"Dexithilon." Bildon said confidently, earning him a stare of surprise.

"Just so, Halfling. Secondly, I wager you know I am eager to have my petitions heard before the Primara. No insult, powerful warriors! But I would never have agreed to shelter you without that, that arrant blackmail from Januelus as you all witnessed."

He resumed pacing back and forth, chewing his lip before speaking again.

"Furthermore—this is still my second point, I beg you to bear in mind—I miss my guess or you are not overly eager to butt in front of me in that particular line." He stopped pacing and sought a face who could answer him.

No one looked to Haltar; they all knew their part better by now. Still, without even moving the foot-knight gained the inventor's attention before speaking.

"We are guests in your city, and would not for the world dismay our host."

This speech delivered with a straight face brought a heartier, more honest laugh from Enict.

"Splendid! Then I think we may be able to find a common cause. I agree to feed and board you, in return for your word that you will not press to see the Primara before me, and to assist in my suit, to the extent you can exert any influence with that barbarian who dumped you here."

Haltar nodded once. "This is an acceptable bargain, sir. We shall of course pay for certain amenities we might require."

Enict was already waving off the words. "Of course, plenty of ale and beef, and I shall find bedding for all of you. Jaya can see to it." He seemed impatient of the agreement now that it was made, and began to pace and rub hands again.

"There is yet my third thing. This—is difficult."

"Perhaps, perhaps indeed it would be best to show you some of my work before going further. You may leave the gear in this room, which I shall deploy as your quarters." He moved toward another door, motioning the party to follow. "No need for your weapons where we are going."

"You mean," Haltar said casually, "that you intend us no harm?"

"I mean," Enict said with pride, "that my weapons are better."

Haltar's face acquired that crooked, dangerous grin which usually portended someone's death. Treaman cleared his throat and loudly dropped his spear, shield and pioneer sword.

"I want to see this," he said, and everyone looked his way at the implied challenge.

Haltar also glanced a moment, then shrugged and dropped his broadsword and pack.

"Braja," he said motioning, "stay here. He wouldn't understand anyway."

As everyone else put down their things, Treaman noted that Haltar's punch-blade remained behind his back; and no one was ever sure whether Bildon had surrendered his last knife or even what Mhoral's weapons were. As they filed in behind Enict, Treaman thought they were five to his one, and only Bildon was shorter. Yet the wiry little man seemed oddly confident, still nervous but elated to the point of laughter.

He opened this door with his key, and everyone exclaimed in dismay.

Treaman's first sensation was heat, from a chamber also brightly lit and smaller than the first. More work tables lined the walls, except the far end which was dominated by an iron forge with a chimney wider than a human, leading up into the ceiling. Surrounding the forge were a set of metal furniture, not chairs or tables, but some with several arms or trays, and lower areas filled with pulleys and toothed wheels that interlocked. Each was moving, slowly and gently, to no purpose that he could readily determine. But no hand drove their motion, and Treaman felt the hackles on his neck rise as the specter of his childhood tales surged up to blanket his heart with fear. Better weapons indeed!

"Calm yourselves, adventurers!" Enict's cry was dashed with conceit. "These are not *Makine* I assure you. They wreak no destruction, and I can arrest their workings with a single word, or by manipulating their controls."

"All that metal," Mhoral gasped. "Where did you acquire such wealth, and why bend it in such convoluted, horrid shapes?"

Enict looked on the Elf with disdain. "Perhaps it is better you not trouble yourself, sir. Suffice to say, I control the process completely and there is no conceivable way they threaten you, despite their appearances." He looked ruefully at the group. "Out there, of course, in the city, I must take ridiculous pains to construct devices of wood or stone, rope or cloth whenever possible. But here, in my sanctum, I am free to devise in the full light of what my mentor envisioned."

Treaman, still unable to pull his eyes off the constructs by the forge, began to wonder why the inventor would take a group of unknowns into his secrets so quickly. He could tell now that the *automakoi* were slowly drawing a piece of metal into and out of the fire, alternately heating, cooling and reheating it. The flame must have been white-hot to judge from the glow of the ingot, and the Woodsman felt no urge to draw closer to the source of that heat, nor to those innocuous, slow-moving metal arms.

"Can you repair my broadsword, Citizen Moaro?" Haltar asked. "It has acquired a notch—" whatever else the leader was going to say was drowned in a chorus of clucks and groans from Mhoral and Bildon.

"Repair! Aye, certainly warrior, I can. But mayhap you would prefer something better? How if you could wield again a longsword of old?"

"A longsword!" Haltar's face lit with unaccustomed enthusiasm, and the inventor cackled with delight.

"Come! The finishing room, see for yourself."

Once more Enict's key did service and he stood aside from a door uncomfortably close to the apparatus of the forge. Treaman edged by and could hear the inventor chuckling as the rest followed. This room was smaller still, and whereas the others had been filled with things, here was clutter in all its glory. Several other doors led into this chamber; Treaman felt a slight draft and realized that somehow Enict was able to bring fresh air even here, deep within his building. The inventor strode to the longest table, where something lay under a cloth covering. Catching Haltar's eye he pulled it back to reveal a wondrous weapon.

Enict gestured for the warrior to try it out, and Haltar took up the long hilt with his right arm. The weapon came to guard quickly, as if he held a rapier, but the blade was nearly as wide as his broadsword, and as long or longer than the bastard blades Haltar prefered. The pommel, guards and runnel were all plain and undecorated, but the darker steel gave off glints in the lamplight of the workroom.

Haltar swept the blade before him until it sang through the air. Then he smiled, let it fall point-down in his hand and held it out to Enict.

"A wondrous light weapon to fence with, sir. An honor duel, perhaps, to first blood. But the blade is too narrow for the work we do."

"You see the pommel," Enict replied, "take it in both hands just as you would your bastard sword, but faster now and with an edge you cannot improve by whetting."

Mhoral laughed out loud to hear this, and Haltar was stung by the challenges.

"It would snap on first contact!"

"Hah! Break something in here, sirrah, if you can!" Enict's eyes were lit with a fire close to madness, Treaman thought, as the inventor cast about and seized upon a high, sturdy stool and slammed it down before the warrior.

Haltar took up the blade in both hands, raised it smoothly overhead and brought it down hard. The seat of the stool was three inches thick, but the longsword rang off the floor as if he had chopped through a hay bale. Bildon cursed as a strut piece ricocheted past his head; a moment later, both halves of the stool hit the floor simultaneously. The slate flagging had a slight notch, but the sword was unaffected.

"Solid ash!" Enict crowed, and then held out his hands to take back his property. Haltar's reluctance was stamped on his face, but he gave it over.

"I want that blade." His voice was low and clear, and everyone smiled.

"Is that silversteel?" Linya asked.

"Of a low grade, admittedly," Enict replied, covering it again. "But yes, it is the magic metal, and even creatures of hell may be wounded by its puissance." He fussed with his hands some more before continuing.

"The ores are found only deep within the mines, in the hills over the eastern bridge. I must get more, of course, to further my researches—Swords! By Hope, hardly the best use of such precious metal, but I needed to demonstrate their worth to the city. This, the

Primara has already seen; but now, with what I intend…" Here the inventor trailed off with another glance at Hallah.

"I need. I need." Enict strode across the room to a large black pipe lying in a wheeled wooden rack. Patting it, he said, "I need for this to work."

The party looked over the enormous thing without much comprehension. Treaman could see the pipe-rim was more than an inch thick, and longer than he was tall. He doubted Braja and Haltar could lift it together.

"What does it do?" he asked.

"Nothing yet!" Enict shouted, then laughed at himself. "Or nothing much. I must, I, oh it's all too complicated to explain. This is a weapon, suffice to say, capable of winning great battles in the event of Despair's return, which I think likely."

"The return of Despair!" Mhoral cried, "You cannot be serious. Two thousand years since—"

"Citizen Moaro," Linya broke in, "how does this weapon work?"

"Jaya here? She's my first, you could say. I shall do better in time." The inventor moved to one end of the pipe and pulled back its cap on a hinge. He gestured to a pile of rocks nearby, each about the size of Bildon's head.

"This device, which I call a powderbow, creates tremendous force through a violent burning charge of my invention. Each charge will throw one of these rocks through the air in a straight line, like an arbalest bolt, but even faster and farther."

"Impossible," Mhoral cried, "those rocks?"

"Bah," Enict scoffed with his waving arms, "I have newer models in the next room, smaller, longer, using shot entirely made of iron. Those will be the real weapons which defend this city from any attack. Jaya here was my demonstration model. I need, I need better powder now."

"Those scorch-marks in the street," Treaman said, and Enict nodded as he opened another locked door with his master-key. "But how is this powder made?"

"All in time, sir. For now, just look you in here."

Standing back, Enict chuckled again as the group exclaimed at the stench from within. Long, wide tables covered in something dark and earthy gave off horrid odor; several large barrels stood to one side only partly full.

"Bat droppings," Enict explained as he closed the door, "one of the less appetizing steps in the powder-making process. The details need not concern you."

Through several more chambers Enict moved quickly, locking and unlocking as he went and leaving little time for conversation. Treaman saw heaps of different-colored powders, not smelly but somehow threatening. Bildon pointed ominously to a set of smaller casks the like of which the party had seen before. On a side table were several odd-shaped items, half of wood and half of metal, in various states of completion. Treaman admired the dark ash handle of one, curved to comfortably fit the hand and set cleverly into a metal frame holding three smaller pipes, each a little thicker than his thumb. He could make nothing of the various notches and levers above and below it, however and put it back down next to the pile of round metal balls where it had been.

Enict heard, and came back with an angry face.

"Do not touch when you are not instructed, sir!" The inventor's fury abated when Hallah raised her head and hissed at him. "That is, of course you could not be expected to know, ah, let me demonstrate."

Enict picked up the item by the handle and pressed a pair of buttons on its side with a sharp click; then he rotated the entire pipe construct a third-turn, as a single piece, bringing another one to the top of the device. The workmanship was clearly first-rate in every detail; Treaman still had no idea of its use, but somehow hungered to hold it all the same.

"It is in essence a smaller version of my powder bow, with the ability to take several shots in rapid succession. I came up with this design myself; I believe Dexithilon did not have access to the quality of materials required for its completion."

The inventor lovingly put it down on the table and turned back to face the group.

"Only a great noble should be entrusted with such power." He glanced at Treaman, and his face was apologetic. The Woodsman could sense his need, and knew it would be to their advantage, but the puzzle eluded him.

They emerged back in the main room by another door, and Braja turned to them with his torn smile. Enict walked to the table where his large book lay and stroked the binding while he gathered his thoughts.

"To business, then, citizens, my third point. I require more ores for my work, from the mines. Of late, the miners have grown fearful of sounds in the lower shafts, and there have been, ah, some accidents. Purely coincidental. But they refuse to assist me without further sign that the mines are safe. I have petitioned the Primara to order them back, but that document languishes on her desk," he grumbled to himself some unfamiliar curses, "along with others."

"I offer you, in addition to my quarters as a base, my services of introduction to merchants and crafters for any supplies you wish to purchase. Jaya will take one of your party around immediately, for food and bedding." He pulled a lever on the wall which had no evident effect.

"Finally, I will give your leader the longsword he so greatly desires. If you can meet my price."

"And what is that?" Haltar asked, impassive with arms folded.

"Two things. First, enough money to sway the workmen to return to the mines."

"You wish us to bankroll your venture?"

"In plain words, yes."

Haltar took a deep breath before continuing. "I believe we can supply your need in this area, sir."

"You can pay the workers?"

"We can lead them."

"Your pardon?"

"My party will descend into the mines with the city's workers."

Treaman felt ice in his spine at the thought of dark, enclosed spaces.

"We will protect them there from any threat. Your men will have access to the deepest levels and return with a bumper crop of ores, or however it is you describe such hauls."

Treaman could only draw half-breaths from the stuffy, acrid air, he could feel the painful tingling under his boots with every step; he heard sounds, distant and indistinct around each tight tunnel passage. Every strike of the pickaxes behind him made the Woodsman jump: he starved for breeze, and grass and life.

He shook his head hard. He was back in the cellar room with Enict Moaro and Haltar, dickering over his life's risk. The mines were still ahead of him. The deal concluded with a handshake and the transfer of two small bags of gems and coin. Treaman wiped away the sweat when he hoped no one was looking. He wet his dry mouth to ask.

"You said you wanted two things."

Enict nodded eagerly, his smile in place.

"Shit."

Everyone looked to each other this time, and Braja burst into laughter, waving one hand behind him.

"Shit!"

Enict moved back to his tome and threw it open to a bookmarked page.

"You saw my drying room, where I derive an essential ingredient in the charge-powder for my weapons. The island-caves below these walls are festooned with bats, and this has been my source until now. But there is a better one. I never thought to have the opportunity, until today."

He stepped back from a page and Bildon eagerly leaned forward to read.

"Men, dealing with dragons? What fairy tale is this? And what are 'fewmets'?"

Enict did not bother to answer but only stared at Treaman. Braja answered the question with a single word in his booming voice, and the laughter spread like a wave.

"You mean to say," Treaman asked, "my dragon's, er, leavings will fuel your powder-bow?"

"According to my mentor, it will produce charges of the highest efficacy. That, and your adventure to the mines, are my price."

Treaman looked at Haltar, already addicted to the weapon in the other room. Back in Trainertown he had taught Hallah to leave her feces in a small pot over in one corner; she even put the cover back on with her teeth and was very proud of his praise. But something seemed terribly wrong about this deal; he recognized in his heart that by refusing he could avoid the underground perils, and his breath drew short again at the very thought.

So the one way to stop Enict perfecting his *Makine* meant yielding to cowardice.

Treaman stroked Hallah a moment.

"Does Hallah want to give her poop to the strange man?"

She looked back at him with her gem-eyes a moment.

{*"Odd-man make big fire."*}

The Woodsman was shocked; Hallah never paid much attention to the speech of others and he assumed she was asleep all this time. But then his mind was flooded with brief, flickering images: great mages standing on blasted hillsides, leaning on staves and discoursing silently with great, adult wurms. Wagons of coins rolling toward the caves, returning without horses and piled high with manure. Not since the death of Maladon's dragon had Treaman felt this barrage of foreign images. But he was certain as he was of his own memories, dragons of the elder days had dealt with some of the Children of Hope in this way.

That would have to be enough.

"Yes, Hallah will help to make big boom."

{*"Because Hallah also big. BIG!"*}

"And no doubt hungry."

{*"Yes, also that. So Hallah can poop later."*}

Treaman laughed and nodded to the leader that the deal was done.

Banging on the overhead door brought Enict up the steps, to return with a middle-aged working woman of frank face, strong arms and skew-stranded hair. She was jibing the inventor when she came in sight of the party and stopped with her mouth open, showing slight gaps in her teeth. When her gaze fell upon the Nubian she gasped and clawed Enict's arm in fear.

"Calm yourself, Jaya, these are my guests, newcomers to the city and soon to be its heroes."

"Just a moment," Bildon quipped, "we already have one town convinced we're the Hand of Destiny."

"A hand with six fingers now," Linya murmured as she stepped forward to greet Jaya.

The washerwoman kept her eyes on Braja every instant. He stood gazing back for several moments, then suddenly thrust forth his hand with a hideous grin and shouting, "Shit!".

Jaya squeaked, jumped, laughed and fell down all in close order. Haltar extended one arm to heft her easily to her feet, and suddenly Jaya was able to look at someone besides the Nubian.

"Please go with one of these guests to the market before it draws too late in the day. Help them get whatever items they need. You will be paid to help cook and clean while they are here, just as I have done."

Jaya snapped her eyes away to look speculatively at Enict, then back to Haltar with a saucy grin.

"Aye, come along with me, sir knight, and I'll show you all." It seemed decided by mutual consent that the leader would fetch and carry the goods.

As they left, Mhoral spoke to Enict.

"Why did you name your great iron weapon after that woman?"

The inventor turned to look at Linya, who had joined Bildon by the book and was puzzling through the text.

"To honor her, my reliable neighbor," he said before turning back and dropping his voice so only Mhoral and Treaman could hear.

"And two more reasons as well." He suppressed a grin and said, "She is easily loaded from the rear."

Mhoral stuffed a hand in his mouth while the inventor held up one finger to finish.

"And shortly thereafter, a great deal of noise."

Treaman bit his lip as the inventor moved away, and he and Mhoral started to arrange the party's things.

"We'll tack up some blankets, I suppose," Mhoral sighed, "for our leader's privacy."

"It never takes him very long, does it?" Treaman mused.

The Elf stopped a moment and looked at Treaman with that strange, almost queasy look on his white-scarred face.

"Still think we are just stones rolling randomly in a box?"

"What's my alternative?" Treaman shot back. "The Hand of Destiny?"

Mhoral nodded, as if that was the answer he expected, but not the right one. He returned to arranging the gear and said "I don't like to see so much metal in one place. And this, this powder. The heroes never used anything like that cask Bildon threw in the fire."

"One job," Treaman suggested. "We lead these miners, clear out any dangers there, avoid dying; then we win the Primara's approval, get supplied and head on to Reghalion. We must be two days away, at most."

Mhoral nodded again, smiled and moved to a far corner with his things. Treaman sat back, half-listening to Bildon argue with Linya about the meaning of an antique word; he looked up when Braja quietly levered himself down nearby.

They looked at each other a long moment, and both spoke at the same time.

"Shit."

⊕⊕⊕

A librarian's shout is all the louder for the guilt in its echoes.

"Kastaliel! By the Moment, dear woman, am I glad to see you!"

"C'tellin, what under stars is the matter? You look stricken, are you well?"

"Kastaliel, I am, that is, thank the stars it's you!"

"Good sage, lower your voice. You shatter the peace here, I doubt we've ever had such noise in the Tome House. And you may release my tunic now."

"Apologies, friend, sincerely. But what a night. I have been beside myself with frustration."

"You? You have always loved night duty, my friend. Quiet evenings alone—"

"Yes, yes I do, but—"

"And if you should happen to consult a volume for your lonely studies, well, no need to register the withdrawal! No one the wiser for your ever-advancing erudition, as you showed me."

"On occasion, yes, on occasion. But tonight I am not alone. The Tome House has a visitor, Kastaliel, may the Ageless One wither him."

"What do you mean? Does not the Tome House exist to entertain visitors? What could possibly have fouled your mood?"

"You have not seen him! He's a curse, I tell you, here since before sunset and not one moment's peace."

"Calm yourself, friend. Sit, drink water, breathe more easily, then tell me everything."

"It is well. Why not, with all the hours he's murdering, I might have time to tell the full tale. Do you recall the rumors we've heard, of this mortal adventurer roaming in Mendel?"

"The grey Man? Of course, we spoke of nothing else. Do you mean—"

"The very same! He's back there now, with books piled over your head."

"Incredible. They say he is a murderer, traitor, who left the Healers Guildmistress behind in that awful Hopeward, from which our own Sage Fellareon barely escaped with his life."

"All true, I don't doubt to look at him! The old soldier shows up today, right before this desk I tell you, and bows so polite, and speaks Elvish like you and I, and asks to see *'a few tomes, mayhap'*. Mayhap! But all the while, those eyes, like silver ghost-lights, boring right into you. I swear he never blinks."

"Ghost-lights, be serious! Well and all, I hear he has protection of some kind."

"I should say! Look here, the letter he bore and gave over as proof. See the seals, Kasta."

"Winter stars, I can hardly believe it. And the text—this is Cedrith Fellareon himself whose recommendation I see. I wonder the hold this rascal must have on him, to wring such a concession. Still, what danger in books, my friend?"

"What danger indeed. Look, here is the list he left on the counter; see these titles Kastaliel."

A moment-layer of silence descended, and when sound resumed it was only in whispers.

"Well Kasta? Have you ever seen the like?"

"Moment in time, never. Histories of the kingdom, tomes of magical study; why, these three are in the Ancient tongue!"

"Authors I have never heard of, from the earliest centuries and every walk of study. How did he know they even existed?"

"Moment of Ma-Eldar! These two are from the archives. You let him take these?"

"What could I do? You see the seals."

"Do you mean, you guided a mortal Man within the inner sanctum of this library?"

"Not I, madam: insisted he remain here while I went, though it froze my throat to speak. But all the rest—traipsing back and forth to every wing and floor, helping him fetch and carry. 'A few tomes' indeed: the two of us together could not hold them in our arms at one trip. And always the originals, never copies."

"He will be here for days, reading all this."

"The last I saw him, he was sampling."

"Sampling! Whatever do you mean, C'tellin?"

"He's a sorceror I tell you! Or else insane. I watched him awhile. Opens one tome, his notebook at the ready, he flips to a certain page, jots a few characters, bookmarks it and on to the next one. History to magic, crafts to the bestiary, there's no order to it. Almost as if, as if he were hunting some clue or other."

"And he has been gone how long?"

"Four hours at least. Ten silver says the dawn will find him here."

"I shall not wager until I see him, young sir. Which way is he studying?"

"Through that arch, see his staff leaning in the corner nearby."

"Moments of life, what a grim weapon! Those iron bands, it looks ready to do murder on its own. Do you suppose he is a mage, in truth then?"

"You mean, is it safe to touch? I cannot say, nor shall I test it for love of life. Will you go to watch him, then?"

"Not I, not alone! Come with me."

"Never, if I see him once more before my life ends it will be too soon."

"You fear this old Man so much? Is he the Tome Spirit, then, whose tale I told you of so many years ago?"

"Kastaliel, dear woman, I promise you, if I were wandering in a darkened way and met this villain and the Tome House Spirit at once, I should flee to the Spirit for protection."

"Ah well, perhaps I shall just wait here with you a time. But C'tellin my dear friend, you must distract and calm yourself. Perhaps your studies."

"I cannot! The thief has taken my note-tome."

"He dared? What do you mean?"

"Well, assured that I cannot have it, at any rate, the same thing. By my life, Kasta, he took me so far back into the stacks I saw chambers I've never entered before. And what do you think? One tome he required sat beneath a shelf so badly damaged, it would collapse the entire row to remove it. I had to substitute my note-tome in its place! And now until he returns—"

"You are bereft, I see, poor fellow. Perhaps the chess game then? I see you have another match against the Archivist here on the desk, do you—"

"Hopeless also! See for yourself; I've stared at the board until my eyes are crossed. I so wished to have him, for once in all these years. But he has me in check next turn, leading to mate."

"Your Warrior is on the seventh rank, you can advance and promote him."

"Yes, but the resulting Queen does not place his King in check. One more turn, and I could force mate myself. My misery is complete, dear friend."

"What is this, C'tellin? A note here, on a scrap of vellum beneath the board, is that yours?"

"What, not mine, no. Let me… by the stars, this is too much! Even here, the ruffian taunts me!"

"Do you mean, the visitor left it?"

"The handwriting, see it matches the list of books."

"What does it say?"

"The effrontery! This crazy old Man, advising me about chess. Look you, in perfect Elvish script; *'Take Khoirah's path; the warrior must become a knight'*. Rubbish; I have lost both my Knights, and the matter before us is placing his King in check."

"Khoirah's path indeed, I confess I know not the rules of chess but that seems a dread augury."

"I shall waste no further time on thoughts of this fool. Some half-senile mortal dilettante—with hair as grey as the dust on the shelves—come to look at the funny marginalia in books far older than he is."

"You are unkind, my friend."

"Not harsh enough by half! At least this human will not escape without a tongue-lashing: the thoughtless, selfish dunce."

"Sage of the Guild, he is our guest."

"Respect for the guest-race be damned! The Conarian Guild sends forth amateurs and dilettantes, to judge by this one. Not a whit of serious intent, no coherent curriculum of study to follow; a pampered life as shown by this letter, clearly the product of an indulgent upbringing in his youth."

"C'tellin."

"And now he wastes his last year as badly as he no doubt did the first. Probably asleep, dreaming of women and wealth and youth."

"C'tellin, stop! I smell smoke."

"Ma-Eldar's Moment, we are doomed. Run, Kasta, get water, we must save the books!"

In his rather uncharitable thoughts, the scribe was at least one part correct. For a little more than a quarter-hour ago, the Man in Grey indeed fell asleep, for the first time in two and a half days.

After arranging the records and his personal journal for note-taking, Solemn Judgement had begun, just past the winter sunset, with the earliest tomes. The tallow candles gave off light that was warm to see by, but not bright enough to read small print or pick out details in the margins. The Man in Grey had learned to look for those. Quietly saying *"Luxar"*, he put a tiny moon of clean blue illumination atop a nearby shelf, and angled his work beneath it. Then his hunt began.

Yet for the first hour or more, he labored not to read or understand, but simply to repair the books. Mold-eaten edges were a source of shame to most Sages, but to the Man in Grey's quest they were a lethal threat. At the start of a chapter from the earliest histories, concerning a battle in which necromancy was deployed, the passage used an opening letter "V" with what appeared to be marginalia of pointed leaves. Yet the side of the page was torn and most of the pattern lost. The text of the passage did not name the sorceror, but described instead what tools he used to summon up Hope's dead and send them against their living comrades.

In haste, the mortal Sage set about repairing the end of the page. Cribbing extra parchment from his supplies, and tearing a piece to fit the destroyed section, he pasted it in with infinite care, as if setting a comrade's splinted limb. While waiting for it to dry, he sharpened his quill and scrutinized the margin of the following page, where a faint mirror-outline still showed the design. At last, he began to draw on the new margin. The floral motif extended from the outer edges of the opening capital together and down, the arrow-shaped leaves pointing to different line-starting letters on the page:

"V" for "Very few" which started the chapter, then
"r" in "remains",
"u" of "under",
"l"in "lineage" and finally
"e" in "estimation".

Even after the word-connection was made, the Sage continued, deliberately filling in every detail of vine and figure as faithfully as possible. Then the Man in Grey sat back and contemplated the passage, describing a necromancer's power without daring to openly pen his name. Sharpening his quill once more, Judgement signed the restoration in very small letters: after a moment's thought, he added the cryptic opinion, *Names are important.* That would do—the secretive habits of the forebearers of Hope were not his province to subvert or question.

His work yielded two treasures, not just the name of his for but the rough location of the battle where the liche had been seen. "North and east of Shilar's hold" the tome declared: at last the Man in Grey had a clue of where to seek the Tombs Thanazun. But what was Ranebruh, by what plane could he find it?

The next several hours passed in a near-silence filled with purpose. Each slight motion, closing one tome to open another, broke the stillness with the tenor of urgency. The Man in Grey, though only reading and writing, also sweated. Several times, the muttered curse of a distant librarian intruded on the student's concentration. The word in Elvish was constantly repeated but unfamiliar: he jotted it down for later definition and returned to the hunt.

The Elvish histories were a few crucial generations older than those of Man in Conar, the maps somewhat more detailed, though also poetic and floridly decorated. Everything seemed designed to show more and reveal less. As the evening burned on, the Man in Grey bore the signs of final fatigue: staring at a passage, shaking his head to clear it, beginning again. His mage-light faded, to be renewed with a word; his note-quill dulled and required a new point. Every interruption led to drops, wrong pages, repeated references. But though he slowed, the searcher never stopped. Completely alone, yet he straightened his back and looked about him as if watched.

In trying to fix the date of a promising scroll, he referred to the tome setting out the ruling line of the Percentalion, descendants of Areghel into the sixteenth century ADR. Each ruler was briefly described; Judgement's finger paused, for the space of two blinks, over a seemingly-irrelevant passage about royal garb.

Thus ascended to the throne in Reghalion Konre son of Pollin descended from Reghine herself the grandaughter of Areghel in ancient days. And upon assuming the kingship, Konre donned for his investiture the golden robes of the ruling house, putting aside his family's close-fit plain black garb, worn by tradition until one is chosen to rule. Thus arrayed in gold he took up the sacred Tridium and possessed the seat of his forefather the Demon's Bane, keeping the ways straight until his passing in the year 347 ADR.

Judgement turned from the book of rulers to his backpack, withdrawing a much-creased letter from the Elvish Theme of Eldarport, words that charged him to a quest.

Son of Man, you must answer that call of your destiny, which I sense lies heavy upon you. Forbear not to unravel the mystery of all the Lands in this present age, that is, the curse of the central kingdom, bereft of its heir. Recall the prophecy of Rallantan. And when once you have found what lore you seek, which I see lies near stone and snow beneath the searching Racoon, then return to the center, and there find the boy of black robes, straight-armed youth who once sheltered near the sign of the Oak, and then went unto the City of Mages. His line took refuge among Elvenkind until the time had ripened. By star-signs I see this has now transpired, and you, son of Man, a sign not least of all. Neither of you knows your place yet, and I see only dimly. But go you, north by east to find your purpose, and then return to the center to bestow his.

Judgement sat a long moment in stillness, then reached for a history-tome. Like many such, it was inscribed on the flyleaf with a series of ancient prophecies, uttered by heroes in the Third Age nearly thirty centuries ago. His finger stabbed down to the one treating of the Percentalion:

As Areghel's line sits the Kingdom's throne
Ways keep straight, Kog's day is done.
But failing the seat, hell's place repeat,
And no child of Hope alone
No branch of Conar's bone
May demon cheat, his eye align,
Or Tridium seat, till the heir assign
The fivescore castles his own.

The Man in Grey repeated the words aloud, but nothing occurred to smooth his brow. He turned aside, and sought once again for the first scroll, which held an excerpt of the Nameless Tome. But though old, this was merely a redacted abstract of Faltus Fanem; after a few moments of study, the Sage swept it aside with exasperation. At once, he retrieved his truant composure, straightening doublet and spine with a deep slow breath the while.

The very next tome, in the third of four stacks at the eighth hour of his study, contained the clue he sought.

Later histories of Hope's wars focused exclusively on the Battle of the Razor. Other skirmishes, campaigns that served mainly to neutralize thrusts or feints to draw off forces, merited no attention compared to the decisive ten-day Dagnor Rokan that broke Despair's strength and led to their expulsion at the start of the modern calendar. The volume in Judgement's hands now had been composed just before that fateful conflict; ignorant of history's merciless thirst for concision, it told of those minor battles in uncharacteristic detail; the young Sage's eye lit with gratitude for pedantry as he read. For the names of generals and casualty lists were as nothing compared to the mention of battlefields, and one in particular.

There: the clue left by Faltus Fanem in his madness, at last stood revealed.

As Elves under Ma-Eldar and his sons prepared the southern approaches near F'eilsttor and the large forest, in that same campaign Conar did send his vassals Dunedin with Ekhonon and Aballe north of the great river running between the hosts, east of hill and tree, there to engage with a force of Despairing Men and their unearthly thralls, the flesh-eaters, on the stony plains of Ranebruh, hard by the unseen horrors of the Tomb Thanazun.

The young Sage sat frozen a long moment, as tallow and magelight burned lower. With a shake and start he broke his fix into near-frenzied action, spilling parchment and scroll to the floor in his haste to retrieve his buried notebook and a map. He bent low above the ancient atlas, seeking among the dense décor of its northeastern quadrant, beyond where he knew the kingdom of Shilar was established thereafter. The very spot, amidst dark dense dottings on the page, in tiny letters stood the word "Ranebruh". He shook his head, opened his journal to a book-marked page, and made his amendment:

Seek ye the Tombs Thanazun, by the ~~Plane~~ *Plain of Ranebruh*

The Man in Grey was so intent on his task he did not at first note the books were moving.

He paused a moment, when finding the history tome closed, but did not question his memory, and simply thumbed it back to the proper passage. As he did so he rested his right finger on the atlas. When the wood-bound volume snapped shut, only his battle-reflexes allowed him to escape a broken hand. The *KLAOP!* reverberated strangely within the reading room, with echoes that only grew stronger. In rapid succession all the books about him closed; some fell or leaped to the floor around his feet. Scrolls unrolled and coiled again, snakelike darting at his face and slithering off to join one of two piles. Only Judgement's personal notebook refused to join the rebellion: the rest danced, bounced, rolled and flew. In a trice, the exit door was blocked up with books, while others began to stack and merge, scroll-sheets folding into bone-thin legs, a skull, a vellum sceptre in one hand, the other arm handless.

The Man in Grey stood and readied his aura, but his arm hesitated to wreak harm upon books, even in the were-form of his arch-foe. But his staff, useful for self-defence, lay too far away beyond the tome-choked entrance. The paper skull opened its mouth, a stub of binding for its tongue. Judgement took the one chance remaining, a minor miracle of his own study.

"Imperat silens"

For one moment, the scroll-liche worked its jaw and gestured without sound. Then the simulacrum of books silently disintegrated as if struck by a marble sphere. Components scattered in all directions, battering the human foe to his knees and obscuring his vision. Judgement huddled behind his arms and waited for the storm to subside. Once more the books around him moved away. Peeking from under his hand, Judgement saw the makings of second doorway in books, a portal leading nowhere against the wall opposite the entrance.

And in that portal built of learning, Judgement saw the same pair of high-topped dark grey boots that he wore himself. The same cloak that draped his own shoulders hung down now behind strong homespun breeks. The youth instantly gained his feet, on reflex, to stand straight and at attention in this company. But there was a pause, and a gasp of effort, before he raised his eyes above the wide belt, doublet and silver holy symbol, and returned the gaze of Final Judgement, his father, the man who died to bring him to another world.

"We continue, then, with the constellations and their impact on worldly events." He stood now framed in the bookshelf portal, confident in every fiber, relaxed and ready in each muscle, wearing that same visage crackling with restrained fury at the willful, daily ignorance which human beings of the world so gladly suffered.

"They are arranged, of course, by their elements in adjacent fashion; thus in Spring, the Water signs of the Whale, Dophin and Fisherman as would be the month today… but I see from your face that you have another of your interminable questions."

"By your pardon, sir, it is no longer so."

"Indeed?"

"Aye, sir. We are another world removed from our origin, when—of that day. Here, the elemental signs are scattered in a more complex pattern. Some are changed. Then too, time has passed since… we are at present in Lion, awaiting Raccoon, then Turtle in the next year of this calendar. Sir."

"Certes?" One word only from the teacher, yet the student shivered before nodding.

"And to the meaning of Water signs, art certes also that this is obsoleted?"

The son opened his mouth, but in the lack of certainty closed it again.

"Thou art wise to consider such a synthesis, Solemn. There are worlds aplenty, yet only a single Nature. The signs of Water always betide fluidity, change, travel, spiritual transformation such as with death. But I see yet another question before the teaching may continue."

"With respect, sir. Thou hast been dead a half-year."

"An accurate observation. Pray, what relevance?"

"Sir?"

"We have much to discover, beginning next with the meaning of the signs of Air. Canst discourse as to why my status should alter or delay the curriculum? Or wouldst fain learn from another?"

"No, sir—sir! Wast no one, or rather, I have endeavored to improve, to become less ignorant, through others, when the chance allowed. But wouldst thou consent, sir, to instruct me on the nature of death, and the condition in which I find thee now?"

Final Judgement drew a deep breath, enough to launch shouts like arrows, but only sighed, long and slow, with a hint of the actor's touch, shaking his head as if to say, 'ever the distraction, never the serious student'. He looked to the side of his son's face, and reached to touch locks gone grey while his still shone black. The youth flinched but held his place.

"Ye have had trials, youngest."

"There have been moments, not completely devoid of interest father."

"Such were my guilt."

"You, sir? You gave unto me life and the beginnings of wisdom, and above all a sense of duty. For whatever difficulties I have encountered, I blame chiefly my own indolence, then my rashness, and perhaps in some minor vein certain opponents have played a part. I am minded particularly of a liche that—"

"A liche! I had hoped to steer a course for a quieter land. One with no magic at all would have been best. And I planned to be alive, my son, for a part of the time after landing. I was weak."

The son began to protest, but the father held up a forestalling hand.

"Of death, my son, I can tell you only this. For men both goodly and villainous, it is not the end, though they may mightily wish it so. Look ye well to these studies of yours. Sooth, if this earth be as changed as the stars I can avail ye little in your search. But remember, the nature of the worlds is always the same. The use of Magic is double-edged, as no doubt ye know; it fatigues thy spirit even as it brings energies under thy control."

"Is there no difference, then, in magic between Hope and Despair?"

"Not so much in the magic as in the mages. Where Hope seeks to renew even from ruin, Despair only destroys, and in the end will encompass e'en itself in the catastrophe it hungers to manifest. Stand not in the way of that part of Nature, and simply endeavor to be elsewhere when the moment comes."

"Yet what of miracles, sir? The Heroes of these kingdoms knew much, but left it not behind. They passed from the world, yet the people are devoted to them."

"What of this? Did you not unravel the skein leading you to that horrid place upon yon map, and recover the chance to complete this miraculous ritual? T'was not hidden from thee, my son."

"But sir—if the people pray to their Heroes, and live their lives in imitation of their ways…"

"Aye, what then?"

"Then to whom did these Heroes pray?"

Final Judgement stood a moment, gazing at his son with a mixture of pride and dread. Before answering he reached over to take up the holy symbol on its chain around the student's neck. He admired the work, the addition of Hope's circle around the cross, leaving the bottom arm standing out below.

"This is the secret I had hoped to keep from you, Solemn. I have spoken to you so far of Nature, the underlying way of all worlds. But I did not speak to you, neither in this world nor the one from which we fled, of the author of all nature, which is not a part of it. Such thoughts bring danger with them: in our world, because the people spoke of them too much."

"And here?"

"Here, it seems, they think on them too little. Tis enough for now, I would say, that ye have discerned the existence of this creator."

"He is… the father?"

"I see ye stole glances at my holy book in thy youth, as I suspected. He is a father, Solemn, as much as he can be considered any single thing. The Heroes of this land prayed to him, thus to faithfully follow any one of them will suffice. For this land, at least."

"I would prefer to follow him, sir, but I know him not."

"Rest easy. I studied that book, tried to know and follow him my entire life, and I feel no less thirst than you, most like."

"In his absence, then, I will continue as I have."

"And that is?"

"To follow you, sir."

The elder man clenched his jaw then, his eagle-gaze flickered a bit in the fading lamplight. He reached across again to lay his hand on the holy symbol once his, and now his son's: beneath his palm the silver glowed to become the brightest light in the room.

"Wear ye this well, for certes I believe it shall be thy protection. Tis my only legacy to thee, son, that and whatever may rattle loose inside that stubborn and intransigent skull of thine. It may be that we never speak again. Know ye then, that I am well pleased in thee. My son."

"I shall remember thy face, father."

The form of Final Judgement took on the glow of the silver symbol like a catching flame. Judgement was battered by gusts laden with scrolls, and unnamed tools, sharp-pointed leaves, chess pieces. He pitched slowly forward as if riding an ocean swell, with the hissing roar of leaves, or waves, or flames, or perhaps the last indistinct words his father tried to convey.

Judgement came to on hands and knees, vellum and loose paper raining down on his shoulders in a pile upset from his table. The sound was flame; the magelight still showed a lamp overset and several parchments had caught fire. Lunging forward, the Man in Grey seized the lit wick in his bare hand to put it out, his body falling directly athwart the singeing paper. Smoke and coughing were all that could be heard or seen for some time.

The pair of Elvish Sages running down the corridor stopped, then fell back before the misty figure emerging from the smoke ahead. C'tellin thought at first he beheld the fabled Tome Spirit; when he recognized instead the blazing eyes of the Man in Grey, he was so struck with fear he forgot to cough. Kastaliel, seeing him for the first time, cried out and dropped the water-jug.

Solemn Judgement breezed between them with a gait that belied exhaustion, his pack already stowed.

"Fear not. The flames are out, no book has been destroyed."

"Fear not? See here, you!" The Elves stumbled after the visitor into the registry room, still choking and waving their arms as he retrieved his staff from the corner. He donned his gauntlets, covering the burns on his hands.

"For this damage, to harm the sacred books, you shall languish in prison to the end of your days!"

Judgement turned back to face his accusers, and they gasped at the sight of silver bands flaring on his staff. His words were soft but pitched to grind wood.

"I have left the cost of recopying on the desk. For myself I shall not tarry here. Disregard my letter if you wish, but do not assay my capture. I am for the northeast: the Corpse War shall soon begin, and I mean that the Children of Hope should not lose it."

Nothing in the education or years of either Sage would have sufficed to answer such a statement. The two Elves stood frozen as the Man in Grey turned back to leave. Pausing by the chessboard, he gently reached to move the advanced Warrior one space, then replace it with a Knight. He faced the pair once more and spoke as if explaining.

"'Twas the Betrayer himself, Khoirah, who innovated the rule whereby a promoted Warrior may become some piece other than a Queen. It is sometimes needful," he seemed to muse now for his own sake, "that a commoner take noble rank."

Leaving the Warrior piece on the counter top of the reference desk, the Man in Grey bowed low to his hosts, then walked out of the Tome House in a silence broken only by the ring of boots and iron-shod staff, whose echoes did not fade for a long time.

"C'tellin, the fire, should we not see?"

"Of course, Kastaliel, but the smoke already grows less, it is no doubt as he says. The villain! I shall summon the guard, before he can escape the city."

"C'tellin, my friend. The game, look you."

On the chessboard, the promoted Knight from its position on the eighth rank placed the enemy's King in check.

Chewing vigorously and in a good mood, the two-eyed demon emerges from the walled enclosure he found, blasting a new breach from the one he made going in. Drawn to the place by the disgusting scent of regularity here, a stain of order and law that nearly pained him, Kog felt surprise to see small garden plots, a few animals and a single family quietly carrying on as if the Percentalion's true state were of no concern to them.

Now that is remedied. The grown man, after fighting the hardest and feeling the greatest fear from watching the others, went last and Kog finds him particularly delicious. Females die too easily, he thinks, often with the first limb. And children, hopeless really, too small to bite into, hardly any taste at all. They are weakly kicking a bit in his gullet alongside the shreds of their parents, and there is some amusement in that.

Behind him every stalk and beast is scorched, the mark of flames blackening the stone and wattle walls to hasten their disintegration. Kog forgets them in an instant, wondering what he might wish to do next.

The imposter! In an instant he recalls his quest, from which this random discovery formed a half-hour's distraction. Still out there, still distant yet closer now than before, the object of his vengeance parades in Kog's own form, usurping his rightful place.

Kog reaches out stealthily with his mind to touch the imposter's thought, evidently distracted by some matter and thus not sensing the intrusion. It is powerful, this one-eyed charlatan, and Kog must exercise care to surprise it without discovery.

Kog senses the pretender's rage, dimly feels the broken helldog in its arms, and reads the same thoughts. The Tridium, parts of it are nearby, in the hands of mortals. This poser worries unduly about the part they play in matters, a clear sign of his unworth. The prophecy, indeed! Mortals are for eating, and nothing more.

But here is an opportunity, Kog senses, to trap and humiliate his one-eyed dopple. Softly pulsing the mind-link, Kog sends the thought that these mortals must be found at once. Defeat them before they can take any part in the prophecy—Kog must smother a burst of disdain to realize, this scarred weakling actually worries about ancient rhymes from long-dead heroes. And the pretender's lost eye, even better, that too is nearby. Recover them all in a stroke, Kog's mind whispers to the imposter. Summon the helldogs—your creatures, yes surely— get them back from whatever mischief they've gotten into, and hunt down the thieves at once.

A long moment, and then this effort is rewarded. The thought-wave Kog's pretender sends out is remarkably strong, quite impressive as it summons the hell-pack. Almost, Kog begins to doubt something about the relative place between the two of them. Kog nearly thinks of that lost eye—not simply an obvious sign of the imposter's weakness, but as an indication of age, and mighty opponents.

But then Kog feels the rage of the other, his ears hear the howls of the helldogs over any distance, and his spirit hones in on the place where the imposter is now heading. Too many slices of Law across Kog's path to close with it immediately but that will only increase the pleasure of the final victory. Any doubts Kog might have felt are drowned in a wave of confident lust for triumph and vindication. The plan is working perfectly, nothing can go wrong now.

After all, Kog recalls with a hearty chuckle, the rightful lord of the Percentalion was not born yesterday.

⊕⊕⊕

As fall turned colder, the children left off their nightly vigil beneath the south wall. Trainertown went about its business by day, no more populous than before but wealthy and busy, with plenty of need for new goods and plenty of coin to pay for them. The gang of children still raced to the southern pole and stayed a few minutes; but most of them ran back into the town now, leaving the veterans and a few of the least adventurous to watch. No one doubted the Hand of Destiny would return, Alaetar had guaranteed it. The others increasingly looked to the fleet scribe and the blacksmith's boy to meet their nightly demand for amusement.

In Lion, the game was street-racing and hunting for ghosts.

Among the tight corners and multi-alleyed ways of the western side, Anteris' speed gave less advantage. Forge's knowledge, strength and above all his insane appetite for risk most often crowned him the winner. Forge's father took little interest in his son's activities after the day was done: they agreed that he was free to leave his apprenticeship, and whether he was hurt playing, or in the Stealthic training that was the city's most open secret, made no difference to the smith. Anteris knew that if he returned with so much as a scrape on his writing hand Valenthur would keep him home for a week.

The speed and constancy of the racing harrowed down the gang of children to a reasonable number; the cold after sunset generally took a few more. By full dark, there might be just one or two little ones left, sniffling and shivering but determined to be one of the half-dozen "grown". When Forge got that twinkle in his eye, the others knew—it was time to see a ghost.

The signal passed between those who were in on it, and one or two peeled away from the group or claimed they had to get home. Forge led the rest among the more cramped empty streets, telling some tale or other about a restless spirit in the abandoned western side of town. Anteris knew as much as anyone what would happen; from the well-worn tales, he could usually guess where and when. But he still felt that tingle of apprehension as Forge whispered about the cheated mason or the sisters caught in the chimney-fire. They crouched now on the roof of the old Grechnon place, peering over the gutter at the gabled cupola across the way. There were eight of them left, including the pair who had still to earn the right to stay.

"Now the Widow Caney," Forge spoke low, "after her second husband died, lived right over there, and it was there that she took on the attentions of her third love, the sly young devil name of Malline."

Anteris kept searching his friend's face, for any sign of his charade. He never saw anything but that dead serious look that drew in the younger children—right now, Giri's little brother, who had forgotten why his sister had to leave tonight, huddling alongside the grocer's fourth next to the chimney. Forge told the tale as if his decorations were as old as the rest, his face firmly showing he didn't care if he was believed or not. Which of course only inspired belief, from those just old enough to want to belong. They had heard the stories.

"And all was going well with this third courtship, until she saw the paper in his jacket while he slept; there, in that bedroom below the window. Of course, the widow thought it might be his love poem, the verse a fellow writes out when he wants to seal his marriage. So she read it while Malline slept—and he never woke that night, the poor bastard—for the poem doomed him."

"You mean, it was poorly writ? But she should never have looked until he gave it her." Giri's brother was breathless and indignant.

"Oh, it was smooth and affecting alright." Forge returned with a shade of his impish grin. "But it used the name of another woman!"

"He was unfaithful to her?" One of the older children chimed in, with a face Anteris could easily read, too shocked, too pat.

"And before he had even married," Forge admitted with a shrug and a sigh. "Just after the widow's wealth, I imagine".

"What happened?" It was a natural enough question, the story was running itself now. Anteris was grateful Forge never asked him to participate in these games, he was sure he could never hold his part. Tricking the younger ones seemed so mean, but he held his peace in deference to that reluctance he always felt. Years ago had been his first week to stand the test; deep down Anteris knew this was an important time now for others as it had been for him. And besides, there was usually a laugh in it; he wanted to see what Forge would do.

"She paced all night, back and forth by that window, weeping and miserable, while the villain slept in the downstairs bedroom. It was a night like this one, cold and clear and full of stars so heaven could see what she did."

Everyone followed his gesture to the skies, and Anteris had a moment to spot again the red star of the east, which seemed bigger than ever in the clear night air. He shivered too, and it was nothing to do with the vengeful widow.

"They say sometimes you can see the light in the window still, moving back and forth. Folks as can, they're in trouble they say, for the Widow Tellfis, she doesn't care much anymore, who she takes out her fury on."

Forge sat against the raised gutter as he spoke, his back to the window across the alley. Everyone else saw the dim candlelight slowly cross the opening one way, a few moments later back the other, with black between. Everyone gasped; Anteris could not tell how many were faking. This was one of Forge's better notions.

"I see it!" Giri's brother squeaked.

"What? Where?" Forge turned to look as the black returned, then faced Giri's brother with a furrowed brow as the light came back. This happened several times, and Anteris had to admire the fellow's timing. The gang was worked up near a frenzy now, he had them in the grimy palm of his hand.

"If you've seen the ghost-light of the Widow Tellfis, you need to watch your step, or she'll do to you what she did to Malline."

"What did she do?"

"I thought you said she was the Widow Caney."

"She went back to her first husband's name, shut up now. After she paced all night, crying and raging and wondering, she stole downstairs, and took up the heavy skillet. And she went into the bedroom where Malline was still sleeping, and laid the love-poem gently back inside his jacket. And then she brought that iron pan down on his skull so hard… she broke the bed right to the floor. Dead as the crickets in winter he was. And the widow lived alone in that house the rest of her days."

"They said he died in a fall."

"Surely! A spry young man not twenty-two years old shows up in the street with a crushed skull, folks have to say something! But the letter, that told everyone what they needed to know. Accident, you believe that if you want to. I didn't see this light you talk about—"

A high-pitched shout of fury from across the road. A skillet pan cracked into the chimney stack not six feet from where Forge crouched. Everyone screamed, and Forge leaped up in terror, staggering backwards along the gutter-line into the darkest part of the roof.

"It's the widow! She's come for us all!"

Every child on that roof was venting their lungs, the two youngest frozen by their fear like the rest. Forge, already a near-shadow, suddenly cried out, gryed his arms, and fell through a hole in the roof with a fading cry of fear. Now the youngest fled back to the ladder on the opposite side, scrambled down and never returned. The echoes of their terror could be heard for some time. But the rest of the gang looked anxiously toward the roof hole, and one of them opened the lantern to reveal, just at the edge, a pair of dark grasping hands.

"Gone?" Came the voice of their leader.

"Gone, Forge. No one new in the band tonight."

"Couldn't be helped," the smith's son replied, kipping easily up onto the roof again. He moved to the gutter rail, and called down "Well thrown, Giri, come on up."

Anteris moved to grip Forge's shoulder in relief as everyone else bubbled with laughter.

"You could have died from that fall."

"This? Practice, my friend, practice everything, that's the key."

"In the dark? With the edges crumbling all the time?"

Forge shrugged and grinned. "Who knows, perhaps the heroes need me."

"The heroes! Of all the vanity. And if not, if Astor has plenty of followers already, what then, genius?"

Another shrug. "Why then, it could be my spirit that haunts this place, a year from now."

Giri returned, and took her bow, completing the circle of older children. Anteris could see from the lantern-lit sweat, most were not made privy to all of Forge's skit. Why, he wondered briefly, did they all love so much to be terrified? Would one get braver just from practice, as Forge argued?

"What shall we do tonight, Forge?"

"We have the evening free, with no new initiates. Giri, not a word to your brother now, let him figure it out on his own." He looked them over, assessing their breathless condition. "Perhaps something less dangerous awhile. Let's follow the will of our good sage here."

Anteris took the implied insult to his courage with a ready will, for he had indeed seen enough to last him.

"The weekly stage from Conar's Helm comes tonight. Let us visit Canith and help him with the horses."

No one in the gang ever disagreed with the word from one of their twin leaders. Besides, everyone liked Canith, and the boys could not stop staring at Piree. As they made their way down the ladder and across the haunted district towards the hostler's house, Forge leaned in a moment to whisper in the scribe's ear.

"Have you seen Canith's love-poem yet?"

Anteris was too shocked to say anything, and Forge nodded.

"I'll get it for you later. Conar's Hope, it's awful."

When the refugees Canith and Piree had escaped the Percentalion, Anteris' choice for their new home was the old Thatcherson manse. It was close to the western gate stables that Canith tended; unlike many other properties in the deserted quarter, the house held its coat of powder-blue paint very well and the trim was in good condition. At first, Forge had been angry that the scribe gave away their best hideout and meeting place. But the home boasted three floors, and its new owners never went above the first—there had been no second stories in Hollinsfen. A ladder from the old storehouse across the alley easily reached the upper window, and Forge decided he was well pleased, that the band could still gather and even spy on the trio.

They had to be careful. Piree thought the upstairs might be haunted.

Their business tonight was very brief, conducted by lonely candlelight. Everyone agreed that the Widow Caney was a keeper, though Giri thought it might be a little too hard. After that, candle snuffed, the band stole down the steep stairs to the second floor, there to peek in on the new couple and the baby. Everyone had a favorite hole or crevice, except Forge, who padded silently about and imperiously motioned for his turn at all of them. Anteris felt guilty watching anymore, but loved to listen to their infrequent speech and the sounds of the baby. Besides, their routine was so unvarying a sculptor could have told the tale in marble along the top of a theater.

Anteris crouched back in the corner by the stair-hatch and listened with closed eyes. There, the merry bubble of something stewish in the kitchen, and Piree's quiet hum as she cooked. The baby was still asleep or else she would be talking to him constantly, seeking his advice for what to add or how well along the chores were coming. The rattle of the stewpot lid; now Daston from his hole above the stove watched carefully, hoping to catch a better glimpse of her ample bosom as she leaned in to stir. He hissed with frustration, and Anteris knew she had primly covered, just as a lady would if watched. Not for the first time, the young scribe wondered at how practical was the bride's belief in ghosts. But Piree, a bit above twenty and very full of figure, was nothing short of a priestess to the teens, especially the boys; if she said haunted, that must be what she supposed.

Now the latch at the front door, as Canith returned from the stables. Anteris grinned at the endless scrape of his boots on the mat, the older man minding the dirt he brought into the house as a nervous guest would.

"Something smells very good, wife."

"Compared to the stink of horse dung, perhaps. Wash your hands, please Canith."

The baby's gurgle: he always awakened when Canith came home, and now the ritual play continued. Two or three bootfalls on the floor below, as the hostler moved towards the crib.

"Canith! Wash before you pick up the baby."

A chuckle, and the sound of pitcher-poured water while the child fussed impatiently. Canith knew by now how particular Piree was about dirt around the child, heroes knew why but everyone's mother was a source of wisdom that made no exceptions for time, and no deference for jokes. Giri watched intently from a crack by the wall just over the crib.

All this past month, the old man and young woman had never named the baby, their child though a son to neither. Time yet—some noble families waited a year—but there was something in their silence that hinted to Anteris of a sad story.

The flung towel resounding in the washbowl signaled that at last the baby was subject to capture, dandling and tickles. His shrieks of joy and ever-higher screams as Canith hefted him overhead did not quite drown the creak of the chair. Canith was tired, but playing with the baby might wear him down a bit, and get him to sleep, later in Piree's bedroom. And in this the husband harbored no selfish hope: without looking Anteris could see the blanket rolled in one corner behind the couch below him.

The ladling of hot food accompanied its aroma, and between the rhythmic bang of a wooden spoon filling a tiny fist the couple conversed. Praise for the meal, reports of words the child might have said. Canith's chair scraped back first, before Piree could finish. He had yet to allow her to wash a single dish, and always acted as if he owed for the meal.

She spoke with some hesitation.

"Another package left for us today. Some curtains and a nice pot."

Canith's sigh of frustration, then the crinkle of rummaged paper.

"All this charity," he muttered, "I shall never repay them, I could not live long enough." Yet he scratched down each item, doggedly recording his debt to others unlike a man who has worked all day.

Now the downstairs echoed with the pacing steps that accompanied puttering.

"Will you have some ale, Canith?"

"Thank you, no, wife. The stage is due in soon. May I get more wood for the fire in your room?"

"I have enough, husband. And I can light it myself."

"Aye, that you can. Chilly night, feels like."

Anteris could see them, sitting quietly as the baby nursed; across the second floor Daston was frozen in place, a line of drool from his open mouth. Another boy muttered as he strained to see from poorer vantage.

"I should keep her bed warm for her."

Forge cuffed the boy into the wall. "Shut your mouth, Flan." The withering look he gave to the rest was sufficient to still any protest. Like all of them, Anteris thought Piree the most beautiful woman in town; all the boys knew she and Canith had not shared in the rites of married folk, and naturally they dreamed of her. But the scribe would never dare, she was too grown up and imposing, and he was saddened to think Forge was possessive of this fantasy. He hoped the rash young Stealthic would leave her alone; Canith was unhappy enough.

The short note of a horn from the west gate meant the stage was on its way. Canith took his hat from the hook by the door, and the latch rattled once, but not again to indicate closing. Anteris was drawn to look down at last.

Piree, rising from her accustomed chair, had moved to the door and laid her free hand on Canith's arm. Arrested by this gentle touch, he turned back to his young wife with a face full of concern, even fear.

After a long moment, she said "Hurry home, husband. We, the baby always misses you."

"As soon as I can, my wife." Canith looked over her shoulder and slightly above her head. "Perhaps if I have help."

So, Anteris thought, at least Canith knew about the spies. Oddly he felt a bit better. But either way he did not want to miss the stage. Without waiting for Forge's order, the scribe scrambled up the stairs to the attic and led the way across the ladder-bridge, from there down and by side-streets to the stables, where they all saw Canith's lantern just coming to rest on its hook inside the door.

"Good evening, Canith," Forge said speaking for the group. "Can we help with the horses?"

"Hero-sent, the lot of you," he replied with a twinkle only Anteris understood.

Canith kept a good stable and there was little to do except wait, until the stage arrived. If it was in good repair, or bearing a hurried noble, changing horses would be an urgent task. But the next team was ready, fed and brushed; the children dignified petting and speaking to them with the name of work. Carriage horses were spirited but friendly to anyone with a bit of apple.

Canith enjoyed the children's company, for they never gave him anything and imposed no debt in return. A few minutes passed and the stage was evidently slow in coming, no second note to apprise them of entrance by the west gate. This was the Shilarian stage, bound for Cil-Cilurion nearly a week away. Most likely the passengers would spend the night at Fairnum's tavern. Plenty of time.

"Tell us again about the Light-Drinker!" Now the clamor began, and Canith set his face for a struggle, most nights a doomed one. The bald hostler never enjoyed telling of his nightmare-trip from Hollinsfen to safety, and he steadfastly refused to speak a word of it in Piree's company, later when the oldest children came home with him to play with the baby. But now, there was usually time; and children wear down refusals as sea-storms wash away the dunes.

Canith sat, rubbed his head before replacing his hat, and absently kicked at the low brazier to make the coals flare as the children gathered round.

"The Light-Drinker? No, I'll not trouble the world with another hearing of such a monster. Ask that Chosen Wanderer for the tale, if you see him someday."

Everyone looked around, sensing that he would still give them something, perhaps a new story if they waited long enough. Anteris was surprised to see Forge put one long arm around the hostler's shoulders, so like a grown-up, in companionship and support.

"I recall young Brig," Canith said low, "who led us out, and not much older than any of you. Such a brave lad, and so certain he was, that the heavens were telling him to go. A sign in the heavens, he said, and he pointed east when he did. I never saw it, but we went with him anyway, my Shelia and I."

Anteris looked out the stable door and saw at once the spot of red in the night sky that was not there last spring. He knew Alaetar the great seer from Shilar saw it too, and likely no one else.

"Straight toward this light in the heavens he led us, never turning nor stopping except for sleep. And all the way, he assured us, this confident lad, that we were on the path to safety and great happiness. Poor Brig. That first run-in with the ape-men, he fled straight onto the black-water pool, covered with tar on the bottom…"

Canith did not speak for some time after that, but absently reached down to check the soles of his new boots—a gift from Giri's uncle the tanner—rubbing the under-tread with his fingers but not looking, seeing another day.

"Dark, oily, slick but sticky, with a stench near to passing out," the hostler's voice came now from darkness beneath the brim of his hat. "I could not rub it from my shoes for a week."

He paused again, as if there were no more story to tell, but the gang all knew differently. Anteris could hardly breathe.

"Shelia, my wife, she ran right behind Brig. I stopped at the edge, and couldn't reach her." Canith's every breath had a wet tinge now, and he needed two or three to manage even a small batch of words.

"Had to run. Apes upon us. Heroes forgive. I, I ran with the others. And Brig, sank but waved us all on, go. East and north, he said."

"The ape-men, they had ropes."

He gathered himself for a final effort.

"With hooks."

Every face around the brazier was etched in horror. Forge patted Canith's shoulder in comfort, like an equal. When the gate-bell rang everyone jumped up with relief. Anteris felt there would be less interest in Canith's stories from now on.

Their steps echoed through the quiet, dark street between stable and gate. Forge sidled up to Anteris and slipped a folded parchment into his hand.

"What?"

"It's the love-poem," Forge replied in a whisper. "Copy it, quickly."

Anteris stopped, too shocked to think, until the bustle of the arriving stage broke in. He stuffed the paper into his sleeve, and moved to one side of the gatehouse, looking for light; he always carried some paper with him, and a capped quill on a string with some ink.

The gate-guards and Canith were discussing the state of the coach, whether the axles were breaking, and everyone else was gathered close by. Anteris hesitated a long moment, wracked with guilt but still unable to disobey Forge. He had never seen a man's love-poem before.

He unfolded the parchment, and copied so quickly he was half-through before realizing how dreadful it truly was.

You are a harvest brought to grace my house

It is a wonder to me, there was no better man to claim this prize

Your beauty

The boy

He could not begin to think of rewriting this good man's heart; the great thing now was to get the original back to wherever Forge had taken it. Scanning around the coach, Anteris spotted a pair of filthy sandals sticking out from beneath the rear wheel.

"Cracked, no doubt. You're lucky it didn't snap on you."

Forge slid out and hopped to his feet, talking back to the coachman with ease.

"My father can fix it. Two days, though, to do a proper job."

"Praise the Heroes," came a gentle voice from within, "a chance to heal my wounds."

First out the coach door was a mailed knight, with a surcoat of green and gold. He looked about, confirming no one of his rank was present, and turned back to hand down the second passenger. All the gang gasped, to see an Elf, dressed in plain robes and wearing the owl-necklace of the Sage's guild. He groaned quietly as he stepped down and kept one hand planted against the small of his back, yet he wore a smile and looked around at each person a moment, as if genuinely pleased to meet them. The knight, at first the more imposing figure, stepped back in deference, staying close as if the Sage might attempt to escape.

"Good fellow," the immortal said to Canith, "is there an inn here where I might rest?"

"Fairnum's, sir, just down the main thoroughfare, left at the church."

"I can guide you, ahm, Eldest!" Anteris blurted in an instant.

The Elf raised both hands in a warding gesture, still smiling.

"Please, lad, let us not resort to such formal titles. My name is Cedrith, and you?"

"Anteris, Ce—Senior Guildsman."

"Worse and worse! I am doomed to such treatment, even from the youngest, it seems. Very well then, Anteris, I am in your hands. I'll just retrieve my bag and then to the inn with us."

The knight announced his intention to stay and oversee the repair awhile, and the other children were enamored of armor and strength. Anteris heard a low voice, and suddenly found Forge just at his elbow.

"Remember, you've got to finish that poem. I'm counting on you."

"You!" Anteris hissed as he handed back the original. "I thought you wanted her for yourself."

Forge looked stunned and hurt, then punched Anteris hard in the meat of his shoulder where it would sting for a day.

"Me, you pig's knuckle, I'm for adventure and the world. Canith deserves to be happy, I thought you saw that."

Anteris rubbed his shoulder, and slowly grinned as the Elvish Sage returned with satchel in hand.

Just before going back under the carriage, Forge pointed a finger at Anteris and winked, and the scribe's heart fell. He knew now his friend's intent was good, but he quailed at the thought of playing muse for Canith.

The immortal's kind voice roused him.

"Shall we go, Anteris? Which way to your inn?"

The kind eyes of the Elf were unlike anything Anteris expected. A hot sharp stab shivered through him: the thought of this interesting Sage staying in an inn was painful. And soon he would leave, and never be seen again. The youth gulped and took charge of his own fate as never before.

"Sir! Sage, em, Cedrith, will you consent to come instead and meet my master? We would both be honored, I assure you."

"Honored!" the knight barked from over by the carriage. "No doubt, to meet the hero of the Hopeward."

Anteris had no idea what the noble could mean: perhaps it was a badge of rank, but the Sage wore nothing except the guild-symbol around his neck. Flustered, he tried to convince him.

"Honored, of course, to converse with a fellow Sage and one whose life—that is, with such a great store of wisdom…"

At first Anteris could barely meet anyone's eyes, convinced he had made a perfect mess of things. He saw the knight first, looking on with amused and scornful doubt. But Cedrith—his face was just as kindly as before, now crossed with puzzlement which cleared into delight. The immortal took in a deep breath and released it as if he were already at ease.

"To converse. Yes, what a pleasure that would be. Well, of course I should like to meet your master, the Sage—"

"Valenthur."

"—that is, if the hour is not too late for him?"

"Oh no sir, the sun is down earlier now of course, but my patron is often awake and reading by lamplight, even after I am asleep."

"And mayhap you can stay up later, eh, with a guest in the house?"

"It is Conar's Day tomorrow, sir, I shall have few chores in the morning. Please come."

"Of course, lead the way Anteris. I can make my way later to the inn."

"Oh no, sir, I'm sure Valenthur will insist that you abide with us, use the library, as our guest."

"Then I am doubly indebted to him, and to you as well."

"This way, Sen—this way milord."

"Milord now! Cedrith, I beg you."

The chatter of the stage-stop faded behind them as they ambled towards the scarce lights of center-town ahead.

The two turned a bit short of the main square, making their way by side streets towards the Sage's Quarter. Cedrith seemed in no hurry, a bit tired but smiling and looking about pleasantly at the darkened town. So unlike the visored adventurer Anteris had seen but briefly with Treaman; this immortal was surely hundreds of years old and that frightened him. But Cedrith appeared so friendly, almost normal.

"You seem a student by the look of you Anteris."

"Indeed sir, I am apprentice to Sage Valenthur of your order."

"Ah yes? Valenthur, that name seems familiar to me. Have I perhaps read some work of his I wonder."

Anteris was too surprised to be polite. "Why he is the Kingdom's Chronicler of course!"

The Elf stopped short in surprise, smiled with open mouth and put his hand to one side of his head.

"Valenthur? But surely, this is Trainertown!" He laughed, looking around with new eyes at this rest-stop, as if its identity had lain hidden until now. Anteris had to laugh too. He had always thought the Elves remembered everything.

"So then, Anteris, have you chosen a course of study?"

The boy shook his head, then shrugged. "At least, sir, I do not know that my master would approve."

"It will be our secret, you can trust me."

"Of course, sir, that is, I'm sure your word… I have always loved the tales of heroes, of the ancient days."

"I see, well you cannot go wrong with such a deeply religious subject. Why would your master disapprove?"

"It is only that—I should say, sir," Anteris felt again that famliar deep reluctance, to tell his heart's secret to this unknown immortal. Looking up he saw again that warm face, politely waiting and giving him, a scribe's assistant, his full attention. And for the second time that night his reluctance dissolved.

"I have always felt that the later tales, from our own age, were worthy of as much attention, sir. Or nearly. Everyone can recite the story of the Battle of the Razor, of Conar and Dunedin, Aballe and Areghel. But I find nearly nothing written of those worthy folk who came later and yet also risked their lives for Hope. Such as Percis, the great knight of Shilar."

"Yes, I see," Cedrith replied, clearly giving the thesis some credit. "Or the tale of Tarly, the Miller's Daughter. Tales that are often told, but seldom written down. A very worthy aim I should think."

"And more, sir."

"Cedrith, Anteris."

"Yes sir. Cedrith. Even before the most ancient tomes, there are tales, of the animals and such, do you know them? And the beasts and birds of those tales, they too show us about courage, and intelligence and faith. And I wonder, sometimes, if even the heroes of our day, those in the Hand of Destiny and who knows yet what others, if they will not be accorded the status of heroes in future ages."

Anteris took a deep breath, and plowed on before his courage fled.

"That is, if we should properly record their deeds."

Cedrith stopped walking, and Anteris feared everything at once: that the immortal would scold him, turn him in to Valenthur, have him put in jail. But all his fears dispersed when the kindly Elf put a hand on his shoulder in admiration.

"My lad, what an incredible idea you bring to me. I'm almost happy I made this abominable trip, just to hear such a notion. I confess I have no idea who this Hand of Destiny is you speak of, but I can say," and here the Sage paused searching for the proper words, "I can confirm with confidence, that there are indeed heroes in the world today. I travel to speak of one of them. Perhaps each in their own way, is doing what our great leaders of the Age of Balance would have done. And you remind me of the Animal Tales, why yes I did hear them as a child, but I never imagined—you bring me a whole new way of thinking, Anteris."

He looked to one side in thought, and then returned his gaze with an outstretched arm that the scribe gripped on reflex.

"I am very pleased indeed to have met you, Anteris. And if there is any way I can assist your efforts, I certainly will."

Anteris flushed with hot pride and something close to fear, hearing such words from this distinguished visitor. No grown-up had ever affirmed one of his ideas before.

"Thank you, sir. Cedrith. Thank you, for your kind words."

"Let us bring the matter before your master this evening. I shall lend my support to your theme and we can see how he receives it."

Anteris turned to lead the way and had no sense his feet were even touching the ground until he heard a voice far behind him.

"A bit slower, lad, I am somewhat older than you!"

Anteris passed up the outer stairs and knocked before opening, since he had a visitor with him. Within he saw that Valenthur already had a guest, and his heart leaped when Alaetar rose from next to his master at the table. Anteris took a breath and stood to one side revealing the Elven Sage.

"Master," Anteris said bowing, "may I have the honor to present the Senior Guildsman Cedrith, of Conar and Mendel. He is bound for Shilar on the stage and graciously came when I requested that he meet you. Senior Guildsman, here is my master the chronicler Valenthur, and may I also present the great preacher Alaetar of Shilar." He stepped back then feeling winded and almost dizzy as the three men greeted one another.

Valenthur was as pleased as Anteris had ever seen him.

"Will you take some tea, Sage Fellareon?"

"Tea?" Anteris saw Cedrith's face brighten with joy. "Recently brewed? And in such fine porcelain, may the heroes bless you, sir."

Anteris bustled to the cabinet for an extra setting.

That night was among the longest and most pleasant of Anteris' memory. Valenthur bubbled over with polite remarks and wit, looking ten years younger; Cedrith for his part appeared to Anteris the perfect conversationalist, widely versed and able to follow many topics but never needing to hold forth on his own. The Elf asked many questions about the history of the northern kingdoms, and Valenthur never needed to consult a tome to supply the answers.

The conversation only paused a moment when Alaetar spoke, for his voice was full of consequence and his words always seemed so final. Yet he was engaged in the talk and attended most closely when, as often, the topic turned back to the importance of recent events. To the Shilarian preacher, it was as if the stars were visible through the ceiling and still whispering to him of the future's shape.

"I can hardly believe," Valenthur said as Anteris refreshed the cups. "I have the honor to entertain an ambassador to Shilar. Have you met His Majesty Shilarion XXXI before?"

"No, I have not had that pleasure," Cedrith replied with some hesitation. "Indeed, four months ago I only saw a king for the first time, across the throne room in Conar. I thought that the height of my acquaintance with fame."

"Yet since then?"

"Since then, I have been disabused of the notion, about fame and several other things."

"He is a good man, the king," Alaetar intoned, "though he does not readily listen to advice freely given." The room again fell silent a space. "He seeks to preserve traditions, but the times are changing without his will."

"Well, that he should only hear me is all I ask," Cedrith said, "I have no need to be believed, since I am simply giving witness to… well, it is perhaps not important to mention here." And he looked on his host and the preacher with a sad face; to Anteris, he seemed for the first time lonely.

Valenthur nibbled his lip, too polite to indulge his curiousity. "That's as may be, sir, but I regret to say you will have to wait before the king will hear you. He is at present departed for Mendel to consult with the Ageless King Tithalis."

"Gone? But when? Moment in Time, this is dreadful news."

Alaetar sat forward, "He seeks the counsel of the Elves, for his son has fled there, most likely."

"What? When was this? I was in Mendel myself, only a fortnight ago. Oh, curse these customs, and my luck." Cedrith was clearly worked into anger now, and Anteris had no idea why. He waited with teapot in hand as the Elf recited something beneath his breath, recovering his temper but becoming even sadder as he thought.

"Forgive me, Valenthur, I am just a sedentary bookworm, used to his comforts and prone to complaining. It's only that, I had so hoped to complete this quickly. First I discover I cannot use the gates to Shilar's capital—"

"You have traveled by gates, sir?"

"I have, and most grateful for the chance I can assure you. Between Conar and Mendel they are maintained in good order, and our mages recall the rules of their use. To think, I could have stepped through from either city and arrived in Cil-Cilurion in a moment. And then my mission would at last be completed." Cedrith pulled a grimace. "But it seems our nations have fallen out of custom, the practice of travel in this way was never common and, absurd as it seems, there are rules governing the use of Shilar's gates that require their participation before a successful transit. So I, with one message to send, must needs travel overland to give it. Well, of course I would never have had the pleasure of this evening, and this marvelous tea."

"But sir" Alaetar asked, "why should you wish so soon to abandon your life's work?"

"My life!" Cedrith laughed to his face, something Anteris was sure Alaetar had never seen before. "You take me for an important person, sir, I surmise." He sipped some tea, and settled back with a chuckle. "My work, holy sir, was in languages, and a bit in history, and I dare say I was happy at it. Not famous, not in the least bit important: I could recognize some things in the style of a man's writing, and that is perhaps all. My greatest ambition, I assure you, was to marry, a lovely maiden named Kia. If nothing else, I accomplished that at least, and only last month."

Valenthur and Alaetar both rose to offer their congratulations and sat again. The fire burned lower; the tea was cool but still delicious. Anteris nibbled a roll from a stool by the stove and let the sounds of erudite conversation wrap him up and soothe him, as the quiet kind Elf told some of a tale that made him tingle where his legs joined. Gates and monsters, twisted magic, sacrifice and desperate fighting made echoes throughout the quiet room.

"Thus, even my wedding day was interrupted by this dreadful business. So you can perhaps understand my frustration, gentlemen. It seems only fitting, I must say, that I should find further delay in the completion of my duties." Cedrith sighed, no longer sad but wistful and resigned.

"Yet you are a part of great deeds," Alaetar intoned like a judge, "Of this Hopeward I have only heard rumors, and the loss of our great Healer was grievous. But it fits what I have seen in the stars. An age is passing, sir—mark you, good chronicler, the Age of Peace is ending, and today dawns another. The Hand of Destiny, now suffering the dangers of the Percentalion, will be a part of it, and I foresee even the King of Shilar will play a role. But I could not get him to hear me."

"I don't believe I understand you, holy sir. Who is this Hand of Destiny?"

Valenthur coughed, and said, "A rather grand name for a ragged band of adventurers, Sage Cedrith. No such ilk as you would wish to associate with, I assure you."

Cedrith smiled very warmly then and quietly said, "Ah, adventurers, I see. No doubt you would not wish to entertain them here."

"And yet," Alaetar said, "it was here they began to discover their true purpose, which as I believe is nothing less than to find the great capital Reghalion, and there to undo the curse that lies upon that kingdom."

"Here in this city?" Cedrith asked politely.

"Here in this very room." Alaetar responded.

"Anteris," Valenthur said quickly, "you should retire now, lad, tomorrow's the day of Conar."

Anteris felt the floor beneath his heart drop away; disobedience to Valenthur was unthinkable.

But the immortal spoke before the heart could drop an inch.

"Your pardon, Sage Valenthur, but I must speak to you about this student of yours."

Valenthur turned to stare at the Elf with wide eyes. "You flatter me, sir, to take such an interest."

"May I inquire as to his contract with you? Is he apprenticed?"

"Certainly, sir, since he was seven."

"And now, I gather he is fourteen or thereabouts."

"Correct, he turns fifteen in Turtle of next year."

"At which point he might choose to return to his family."

Valenthur remained indoors nearly every moment of the day; Anteris would not have thought his skin capable of blanching, yet it did.

"I had hoped," the elder scribe croaked, "hoped that he might agree to stay on. As my assistant."

"That is of course your business," Cedrith replied smoothly. "Should he remain on beyond his indenture, however, he must choose a course of study. And in that, as I am sure you know, the Sages Guild takes an interest."

As Valenthur turned a suspicious gaze to his apprentice, Alaetar suddenly spoke.

"What does the lad wish to study?"

All eyes were on Anteris now. He drew breath and tried to hold his voice steady.

"I wish to chronicle the deeds of the heroes of the Age of Peace, down into very recent times. Including living memory."

"Impossible. What sources could he use?"

"There are some, master, and other tales would have to be collected in the same manner as more, as more recent news is. Tonight's tales from the Senior Guildman, for example."

"Aye," Alaetar intoned, "to set down the deeds of the Hand would be a most worthy endeavor."

"Worship of adventurers!" Valenthur snapped, "I had hoped for better, Anteris."

"What better could there be?" Alaetar demanded not unkindly, and Valenthur looked trapped.

"If I may," Cedrith put in before Valenthur could think of a response, "I am minded of certain volumes, in the Conarian Guild and I believe also in Mendel, that could serve the turn for a start."

Valenthur was hardly breathing, entranced at the prospect of books coming into his orbit. Cedrith smiled as if to make light of his offer.

"I would be delighted to write to my colleagues and ask for them to be sent here on loan. The lad could perhaps fair-copy them—"

"Or put them to print!" Anteris exclaimed.

"As you wish of course. And in this way he will make a worthy addition to the collection here in payment of your indulgence, sir, for his choice of study."

The evident approval of these two guests was a powerful deterrent to the scribe's objections, and the prospect of new books a nearly irresistable lure. Anteris stepped forward now, still afraid but sure he would never feel reluctant again as he spoke his heart.

"Master, I would stay and obey you whatever you decide. In two months I shall no longer be your apprentice. But I will not return home, sir. I have come to think of you as my family."

The elderly man smiled then, a bit crooked but still happily, and nodded once to accept the bargain. And Anteris knew then that he would always be happy, now that his newest friend the immortal had found the way to keep his desire under the same roof with his honor.

The following week, when the band of older children gathered again in Canith's attic, they were concerned to hear so little noise from below. Stealing down to their accustomed spy holes, each one reported a darkened living-room and no one moving.

Forge looked as pleased as a mother cat, and forbade anyone from peeking into the bedroom. But Anteris knew, the bedroll behind the couch was gone, and Piree's bed was no longer empty. By the dying fire's light someone had left a sheet of folded parchment, but he did not need to look to see the words, or recognize the dual hands:

You are a harvest brought in autumn *to grace my* ~~*house*~~ *doors*

~~*It is a*~~ A *wonder to me,* ~~*there was*~~ *no better man to claim this prize*

Your beauty is beyond compare, I am honored to be yours

The boy will be our son, and joy to my eyes

Pol can see the red star is moving. Once stationary, and until last summer not visible, now it crawls across the clear night sky of early Raccoon with infinite slowness, far above the full disk of Aral and the needle-thin crag he clutches. And there is certainly something there.

But he cannot spare a thought for the heavens now. The helldogs are close. The bleeding from his back will not stop. Without food or rest, he knows tonight will be his last.

Gazing down at the talons and teeth beneath him, the man in black reviews how untenable his situation has become. The five remaining monsters take it in turns to launch up the rock face toward the spike where he crouches like a treed raccoon (an irony, he reflects; it is indeed Raccoon, winter has begun). If Pol does not attend to each assault, striking down with punch or kick, one foe might gain hold and haul itself to his crag. The rest would follow as he battled it. And he would die. The others howl while waiting their turn. Thus he gains no sleep, cannot muster the concentration to enter the trance state for even a moment. Without his technique, he is again a man; the blood flows, the body feels hunger. Death nears.

This realization is cold within him, as are all his thoughts. The life-chain has been broken, the balance of energy and technique no longer feed each other. Just so, another fact to log. The pain of his wound is as nothing, it still does not touch him. Lack of food, after a fortnight, has become serious, and dearth of water more so. Pol scrapes at the rock spire above his head, ferreting out a little snow and clenching it in his hand to melt it.

A helldog mounts the spire, but slips before coming within reach and skitters down into the pack. They abuse it for failing and another coils its legs to try. Pol feels the melted frost pool in his palm and licks a few drops. An icy trickle, a tiny charge of strength; he directs the flow to where the fluid can do the most good within him.

He risked everything yesterday, climbing this cliff through dense fog and using most of his focused strength in an effort to go where they could not follow. Nearly correct. In the first yard he earned the searing gash across his back, and climbed on. The helldogs whined and stumbled any higher than one furlong above the blasted terrain. Pol feared only that the rock beneath him might split, or shift, or disappear like everything in the mutable Percentalion. He gained away in his climb, began to plan for a trance state. Then the clearing mist revealed his narrow rock ending in a spire, and nowhere else to go. Beneath him death, and heaven above. He had lost his gamble, but the only choice had been to continue running. And there was nothing there.

The dogs indeed hate this height, constantly twitching and lurching. But the balance of fear in them still leans towards their unknown master's command. Now they smell triumph from the clinging meat above them. The largest of the five gathers itself, back end slightly swaying on its single leg and eyes glowing in the night like embers.

Pol takes a deep breath, ignores the bleeding, shuts out the exhaustion and the risk; draws his right arm in a circle clenching his fist. A glow of golden light encases his hand, sign of the Thunderfist lore he learned as a youth. The beast launches up the crag, its strength and momentum carrying it to the edge of his spire. With two forelegs clawing the granite the helldog hauls within a yard of Pol's neck and wails its hatred from lethal proximity.

Pol meets the lunging maw with an accelerating strike of the radiant Thunderfist punch. The monster's temple cracks, some of its fangs break loose, and the force of the arcane strike knocks it bodily back off the spire and onto its pack like a wagon wheel into a chicken coop. The russet blood on Pol's hand pops and crackles as the energy of the Thunderfist boils it away. The helldog pack shreds the dying beast, and their howls added to its screams are loud enough to move the moon.

Pol pays no heed, smoothly crumbling to the crag and settling his head to rest. The technique is shattered now, no energy left, no more blood, no time. The helldogs will eat him next. Just so.

But Pol is thinking; though his body has no more energy to move, his thoughts cannot help but travel. Pol thinks again of his youth, his sheltered days on the Elven manor near the sign of the oak, of idyllic labor and training. He ponders again the steadfast refusal of his caretakers to say anything about his parents, and of his admission to the Mages School in Araluntir.

Never questions, but respect and silence: since his earliest memory everyone treated him thus, and certainly, he thinks, there is something there. The combination drove him, to seek the center of himself. Has he at last arrived, is death what happens when one has made every effort?

Possibly, but there are other thoughts as well, amid the din of the feasting monsters below, to disquiet him. That these hell-beasts should run free, undefeated to vex the helpless, is troubling. That this kingdom is cursed—why, Pol wonders, did he feel any sentiment for a land he had never visited—but it seemed unjust. So he came here. Did he believe he would slay every chaos-creature by himself?

Whatever he has done, wherever he is now, Pol knows it is not quite the center. There is no sense to the logic. Yet he feels quite sure, somehow that he must live awhile longer.

The mental summons comes like a wave, a force so strong and sharp the helldogs below are slapped whimpering to the rock. Pol can feel it, not aimed at him yet attuned as he is to such sorcery: never has he felt thoughts of such strength, a being who simply is and has always been. Mewling and whining, the helldogs scramble up and leave the corpse behind, descending the cliff half in freefall to regain the broken blasted earth below. The thunderous patter of their feet echoes up through the night air. Pol can hear it for the length of time it takes the red star to move a hand's breadth above him.

He should have died. And there is without doubt something there.

⊕⊕⊕

Tossa lay beneath the giant's corpse, gasping through the stabs of pain from his broken ribs, and waited to die. The second behemoth raged about in the shallows, wielding a sapling-club and looking for the knight who had slain her mate. Gareth's horse was standing over the sunken armor, in steaming water to the knees but defending his master to the end.

Like me, Tossa thought. Surely he too had done all he could. The code of chivalry could demand no more than your life, and perhaps his sister would survive. The crushing weight, that was all he knew now, each breath harder to draw than the last, and smaller. Soon…

The war-cry struck him like another stab, high and strong and full of vengeance. In mid-air the leather-armored form appeared, the long braid of black hair trailing behind her as Sidrathay the Combatted leaped from the rocks above to land squarely on the giant's back. Quicker than thought, she wrapped the handle of her two-stick flail around the trunk-like neck and heaved back hard enough to make her foe stand straight.

Sidrathay was hissing in the giant's ear now as she pulled on the flail. Tossa could not understand all of the Half-Elvish cant, but he did make out the words for "death" and "slut". The Combatted princess evidently had no difficulty discerning her foe's gender and it seemed to make her only more furious. The neck of the giantess bulged square against the pressure, bones at both corners straining, bending, and snapping while choking her roars of anger.

Perhaps a little more could be required of a knight. Tossa brought his sword to bear and poked at the corpse atop him. It cost all his remaining breath but he managed to wedge it a bit beneath the giant's shoulder, enough to pant in half a breath at a time. His legs still pinned, he tried again, pushing the giant's body up perhaps an inch, but puncturing the skin as well so that his lever made no progress.

From behind him, Thula ran in on foot with sword raised, splashing heedless into the edge of the pool where the giantess had staggered with her hostile load. Thula swung at the back of the knee, severing a tendon as thick as a binding cord with an audible snap. Screaming in rage, the giantess sank to one knee and then both in the smoking waters. After scrabbling with one arm to dislodge the mortal on her back, the brute dropped her trunk-club and slapped both hands together behind her head, trapping Sidrathay there, bunching her muscles even while choking, in an effort to crush her unseen enemy.

Tossa heaved against the dead giant's body and shouted in agony as his legs moved at most a hand's width from beneath the crushing load. He could not feel them, perhaps they were also broken. But he would in no way rise in time to help. The Bordbeyonds from across the lake were also crying out and running up the western shore, but too far off still. Sidrathay was barely visible between the mattresses of flesh on either side, and screamed herself, but maintained the death-lock on her enemy's neck.

Gareth's horse shied as the armored form of the prince of Shilar rose from the waters, sputtering and with his shield arm hanging uselessly beneath a broken collarbone. But his sword was still clenched in his right hand, and Gareth stumbled forward to drive the point at the broad open chest, a few fingers deep into the heart where blood spouted like a broached cask of red wine.

The kneeling foe stopped struggling, frozen in place and quiet. Sidrathay shook herself like a wet dog, pushing free of the crushing palms with a cry of triumph; still she hauled back on the flail, and two more neck bones snapped making the giantess' head sag forward. Thula cocked her helm in doubt, then kicked the corpse from the side. It heeled slowly to the right and down into the pool. Sidrathay leapt lightly off and caught Gareth before he could fall back beneath the water.

Everyone was shouting, some more in pain than victory. Tossa's struggles were assisted by a pack of hands, as the Bordbeyonds came up at last to the north side of the pool. His legs still worked. Everything between his chin and his groin was in agony: holding still hurt, breathing deep or moving was the same as taking a knife in the ribs. Thula and Sidrathay stood closer to Gareth, his armor still streaming water from its hinges; hesitantly he laid his good hand on his squire's shoulder as they stepped up out of the shallows. Now it was Sidrathay's turn to tilt head a shade, but she raised no protest in words. Only then did Tossa realize, sloshing up to shore himself, that the waters of the pool were evidently not lethal, at least not immediately.

Items retrieved, horses recovered, the group gathered to marvel at the corpses of the giants. More than two feet of still water did not cover their bodies, lying almost athwart each other. Blood was everywhere, making shore rocks slippery and staining the rising smoke. Tossa was coughing more and more, despite the pain, and Gareth was also, though he tried to stifle the fits. He pulled back his helm, and Tossa could see his hair was nearly white with salts.

"Sidrathay," he said quietly, "you saved my life."

The Bordbeyond princess shrugged. "I thought I was avenging you."

"I believe," Gareth continued, "I shall imagine you all my days in gratitude. May I see your face, then, that I may match the mein to my memories?"

Tossa held his breath, and the only sound was the quiet froth of the waters as they bubbled around the floating tree-trunk clubs the giants had wielded. Sidrathay reached both hands to her helm and raised it off.

Gareth looked on her a long moment, then bowed slowly and gingerly, saying, "My imagination would not have sufficed."

Thula cleared her throat, moving a bit closer to assist the prince away. Sidrathay replaced her helm as they passed; when Tossa saw the two women look at each other he felt as if lightning would strike.

Gareth came up to Tossa between the two women and smiled.

"Perhaps it is indeed time to turn back now."

"As you wish milord." They both laughed, then winced.

From the edge of his vision Tossa caught movement. He looked up, directly at the sheer face of basalt stretching to the clouds. Too hard to look before but now, movement. From a cave overhead, from dozens of them, heads larger than barrels staring down at the ants below.

Tossa felt the arms of Bordbeyonds assisting him to his horse. Despite the shooting stabs of agony he swallowed his voice, until they heaved him aboard and he heard another small snap in his ribs. But the Shepherds were staying near, steadying him even as the boulders began to fall, helping a comrade, he realized, at the risk of their own lives when the path of retreat lay open to them. Likewise, Tossa reined in as he struggled to stay upright, looking back for Gareth.

The prince of Shilar lay across his crupper like a sack, evidently heaved there by the Combatted who held his belt in one hand and the bridle in the other. Thula led her mount and at last they were ready. A short cry, as two warriors were crushed by a single rock that bowled them down in turn. By the time they reached the western edge path, the majority of those thrown boulders were sending only waves of steaming liquid over the party.

At the entrance, Tossa looked back to see four giants clambering down the face, but they had chosen to throw for too long and were still hundreds of paces away across the roiling salt pool. The mist rising from disturbed waters obscured vision, and as everyone by now was drenched, there were tendrils of acrid-smelling smoke clinging to all of them. Coughing, crying, stumbling but not running, they left the graveyard and descended beyond sight and sound. A few moments spent breathing heavily at the first wide area revealed there would be no pursuit.

Tossa looked to Gareth with alarm; with no sound or movement from the prince, he thought him perhaps unconscious. But when Gleimharn rose from his place as if to continue, Gareth gasped and began to slide down from his seat. Sidrathay moved to hold him up, but he struggled weakly to the ground; holding his useless arm against his body, Gareth walked to the middle of the open area and stood straight. After a moment, he raised his good arm with another choke, and slowly lowered his visor.

Tossa understood in a flash. There must be judgment.

Lowering his own visor so that the tears would not show, Tossa dismounted too hard. He cried out and fell against his horse, while his insides told him of bits and grinding, and things in places they didn't belong. But he pushed himself upright and Thula was there to assist him to his place in the slowly-forming circle.

The time of waiting had never seemed longer; Tossa's every breath hurt him, and he was sure the next moment he would pass out. Sidrathay stood beside Gareth, not holding him up but with one hand clenched around her flail as if to say that anyone criticizing her betrothed would have to deal with the giant-slayer.

Gareth's helmet was turned to face Gleimharn's, and at last the Bordbeyond leader nodded. Gareth spoke at once.

"Two of the Shepherds are dead."

The echoes of this awful doom pattered about among the rocks of the shallow cleft. But quickly, for the nomad taste, another warrior stepped forward to speak.

"Two of the giants are also slain."

"And we have our salts in plenty," said another.

Gareth's helmet shook almost angrily in response. "Not in honest combat did our people die." His choice of words sent a shock through Tossa's heart, making him forget his own pain in a wave of sympathy and fear as his prince gave himself over to judgment.

"They died," Gareth's voice ground on, "because a lord of the settled lands did not see fit to turn back, and wished to explore."

The wind spoke very quietly for a long moment, and Gleimharn gave a small nod.

"There must be penance."

"I am ready," Gareth said without hesitation.

Thula stepped forward and raised her visor. "No! You cannot, Tossa don't let them!"

With his good arm Gareth barred his squire's path and weakly pushed her back to her place in the ring.

Gleimharn stepped in. "At dawn tomorrow, there is time enough."

"At this moment," Gareth responded, "there is time enough."

"As you wish. Come to the center, Diamemne."

Gareth limped forward, one hand behind warding Thula to remain. He faced Gleimharn, who gestured that someone take up station behind the prince.

When Sidrathay stepped forward, Tossa gasped. Thula clenched both fists, then slowly and silently drew her sword, but she kept her place as Sidrathay took her flail to hand and set the two sticks swaying rhythmically back and forth before her.

"May I know," Gareth said to Gleimharn, "the names of those who died to save me?"

Gleimharn said "Baleidos was second of the sons of his family. Creiton was last of his line, and set to be married in the spring."

"I shall remember them, and restitute their blood."

Tossa marveled, even in his horror, that Gareth's intuition was so close to true. These were noble thoughts, fit for the Shepherds; he had seen three chastisements in his time among them, and the words differed but not the spirit.

Gleimharn signaled and stepped back. Sidrathay raised her flail and set the twin sticks spinning until the air hummed deep. Stepping in, she brought them down hard, one on each shoulderblade of Gareth's back.

The right stick rebounded from the metal plate, denting it two inches deep where it would no doubt leave a bruise for days. But on the left, the missing paldron exposed just the chain shirt and the padded gambeson over the spot where the prince's collarbone was already broken. The snap of wood on bone was softer, but infinitely more horrible. Gareth released a sound like weeping, and his knees slowly sank forward until he pitched at full length upon the stone.

Nothing would stop Thula now. She dropped her sword with a clatter and rushed to the prince's side, screaming in anguish through her tightened teeth. The Bordbeyonds turned to move on, and Tossa could sense in their posture deep sorrow and respect. If Gareth lived, he would live in honor now.

After several seconds, Gareth worked his way back to two knees and one good hand, then levered slowly up to his feet again. Thula assisted him as little as he would allow, and when he shuffled off to his horse, she moved with cold deliberation to retrieve her sword. Sheathing it, she strode again to the former center of the circle and faced Sidrathay the Combatted, who tilted her leather helm down to her in puzzlement.

"This is how you care for your husband?" Thula asked cooly.

"He has paid the price," Sidrathay returned, "he is now one of us."

"That's wonderful news, I'm sure he will be pleased." Thula said and her gaiety held a sharp edge. "In Shilar we also have customs, to show how we care for those dear to us."

And without warning Thula shot her fist up into the leather helm so hard that Sidrathay lost her feet and hit the stone back-first.

Every Bordbeyond turned at the sound; Tossa ran forward to stand next to his sister. She raised her visor and her face was filled with a kind of frozen cheer. She faced the Shepherds to all sides as if someone had just welcomed her to their company.

"On my word as a squire," she said, "anyone of you who strikes milord Gareth again will get the same."

Gleimharn, after a long moment, simply nodded. Sidrathay, who flipped easily back to her feet, raised her visor, spat out a bit of blood, grinned, and also nodded.

Only the wind had anything to say the rest of the trip down the Swords of Stone.

It was full dark by the time they reached the Plains again. Tossa remembered Thula struggling alone to erect a lean-to from blankets and her lance, but he and Gareth could offer no help. Feeling alternately chilled and sweaty, he struggled dozing as the moons stared down.

When he awoke, Tossa felt he must have slept in the saddle, for he was gently moving again. But Tossa knew that was wrong, for he had never trained his horse to walk backwards. Through slitted eyes he saw he was lying flat instead of sitting, his sweat-soaked blanket holding him down by straps. Thula looked on him, but she also jogged and bumped slightly.

"He's awake!"

All around him Tossa could hear the party halt and Gareth, one arm resting in a rope sling, was the first to come in view.

"Praise the stars, we were quite worried about you."

"How lo—" too late, Tossa realized how dry his throat was and fell into coughing.

Thula brought him a waterskin. "Two days."

When he couldn't raise his hands to take it, Tossa realized at last, he was in a kind of cot strapped to the back of his horse, dragging him across the steppe at a walk. He had no leverage to rise. But even the effort of swallowing convinced him there was no use to try: everything in his chest felt shuffled into the wrong place. When Thula brought the water to his lips, he was sweaty and hot; as it chilled its way down his throat, he suddenly felt frozen to his toes. Tossa had no more fear of death in battle than anyone raised in a knight's household. But for sickness within, there was no stance, no shield or block to protect him. A surge of terror pushed past his wounded vitals to grip his heart.

"You said when he awoke you would heal him," Thula accused Gleimharn.

"I said that until he awoke we could not attempt it. There is still the chance of death."

"No,"Thula corrected tautly, "there isn't. He's awake now, so cure him."

Gareth looked to Tossa with concern. "The Shepherds will not tell us much, only that there is pain and danger. I have asked Shilar for guidance, but have seen only… well, it's likely nothing."

Gareth turned to face Gleimharn. "In my father's name as well as my own, Eldest, I appeal to you for aid. Name your price for healing my squire."

The Protector answered with a tiny shrug. "The salts are rare and dearly won, as you have seen, Diamemne. But we would use them willingly except for the risk. Tossakateu has never taken a step into Vision before, as have the children of the Nameless One. If he lives…" the Bordbeyond considered a moment, "he will then be one of us. And that is price enough."

Gareth nodded. "Tell us what must be done."

"Strip and clean him. We must work soon, he would not survive a Vision by night." He looked down on Tossa then, saying "Remember, it is day."

They used twisted grass cords to heat some water while Tossa groaned between a pair of blankets on the icy tundra. As Thula reached beneath to lave him with a warm rag, his skin jumped and bucked at each touch until he felt beaten with sticks. Tossa was not sure his consciousness would last, but jolted himself awake to think of the dire warnings he had heard. By the time Gleimharn with Sidrathay returned to his sight, he was breathless and prostrate.

"What will you do to him?" Gareth asked.

"He is too weak to ingest the salts," Sidrathay said tonelessly.

"The salts? You mean, those you recovered today?"

"Not the same," Gleimharn returned, "also from the Graveyard, yes. They are of various uses, as shown by their color. But for the journey to Vision, they must be eaten young, and only in small quantity."

"So now?"

"We must cut his skin, above the heart, and introduce the dream-salt to his blood."

Gareth looked on them as if the language they spoke had changed.

"Let me be clear. You intend to cut him. And then—pardon me, but then you will rub salt into the wound."

"It's a joke!" Thula shouted. "He will die if you do that."

"He may," Sidrathay commented quietly. "Without it, he certainly will."

Thula stared teary daggers at Sidrathay, then snapped around to look only at Tossa from that moment. She knelt by him as Gleimharn approached and gently drew back the blanket. Thula took his hand as he shivered in the cold wind blasting down off those titanic slabs of black rock crowding over his view of the sky.

"What was that song mother used to sing for us?"

"Stop prating, brother, you know I cannot sing." Yet Thula hummed a bit in the general direction of their mother's lullaby and for a time Tossa felt once again back in Shilar, as if out in the freeze of winter a moment while fetching logs for a warm fire within. He only knew the cut was made when his sister's hand clenched on his own.

Looking down, he saw with astonishment that Gleimharn had made two cuts, in a cross like the symbol of Hope, just left of the center of his chest. When his eyes saw the blood welling up, Tossa remembered to feel the sting at last, but it was far from the worst injury he had ever received.

Until Gleimharn drew a spilling handful of rainbow-glinting salt from his bag, and slathered it down hard across the wound.

With a scream Thula shouldered Gleimharn away and rolled over her brother's writhing body. Gareth hastily knelt and scrabbled with his good hand to hold, to comfort and reassure him as the sound of others filled his ear with words, too many words, *tossakateu.* He knew that his shout of anguish did not count, as long as it was only one, the Shepherds could excuse it. But Tossa's vision was drowned in a scarlet curtain worse than darkness, as he climbed the slippery cord of his agony up a black slope of pain and fear, beyond the world of the living.

People far below him in the darkness were still talking, concerned about a body lying on the ground. Tossa felt none of its pain now, but his wonder and disorientation cut him just as keenly. The tug of the rope outmatched his effort to climb, his hair stirring with the speed of his ascent. A sudden stop found him on a rocky peak of ebony basalt so vast and sharp that he felt pain through his soles and past the lids of his tight-shut eyes. Above him, a panoply of stars loomed larger, closer; he could not stop the sight of them with eyes already closed.

"But it was day," he gasped.

Like the flash of an enormous opening door, Solar's light flooded the world from his back, and he opened his eyes on reflex. The air was thin here, but Tossa needed less of it. All about him was the rock of the mountaintops, and clouds, snow, impossible height, and across the ledge a falcon the height of a horse staring him down. Tossa's need for air increased.

The light was passing again, like a single wave on a beach it faded and the stars of night reappeared to renew his horror. Turning away,

Tossa nearly stumbled a single step west and into the air. Across from him, he saw Aral the lower moon, barely above the level of his head, and he shouted in fear.

"It was day!" he shouted, remembering the warning of the Shepherds. "I am still in daylight."

On the echo of his words the light washed back in, and Tossa felt a rush of energy to think he had something to do with it. Gritting his teeth he held on with all his will to the light of day.

Behind him the falcon spoke.

"You are wise to resist the lure of all-seeing. By night-vision you could see all there is in these lands, and of the world of Despair. But children should cling to Hope."

Tossa regarded the being, not entirely like a large bird after all, but holding close enough similar. Thinner than he with its wings tightly folded, it stalked one slow step closer, with knees that bent only backwards. In two quick steps it could attack him, and its head was alert and cocking in several directions. Parts of its body had fur, not feathers, and the wings were still out of sight.

"Are we to be friends or foes, you and I?" Tossa asked.

"Yes," said the bird equably. "Or you may choose the third path."

"How so?"

"If friends, you and I may go on together, west or east and see the world from spirit-eyes. We shall use this body," the giant beak tapped its own chest, "and we shall never pass on, or know fear or pain again."

"And my… my self, below the mountain?"

"That body of course will cease, indeed it nearly has already. Come with me instead, man of the sheltered lands, and we shall be the first such spirit in millennia of your years."

"How if we are foes?"

“If we struggle, you mean, and I defeat you?” the thing preened a bit, and Tossa felt as if more time was passing than he saw. “Then you go to your reward as the Children of Hope believe, and I await Bastiel, the red-haired one who will climb next summer.” It sounded as if it could hardly care less which choice Tossa made.

“And if I defeat you?”

The thing sighed. “Back down the mountain on the western side, to your body, and a few more years of the life you have already known. But some part of my sight, my knowledge, shall come to you at need. It will not be often, child of the sheltered lands. And there will still be pain, and so much you do not know.”

Tossa reflected, still feeling as if these few moments on the mountaintop were longer back on the earth. The loss of pain he felt now was sorely tempting, he realized. Something like fear rose in him, at the idea of returning to that. But he thought of his sister, and the prince, and in a flash saw them hovering still above his body, back now inside a tent, and recognized pain on both their faces as well. It would be ignoble to choose their abandonment now. He loved them both.

“Let us be foes, then, and struggle for life as I knew it.”

The bird sighed long and heavily. “None ever hears the third path.”

Suddenly it squawked loud and deep, unfolding its wings—one feathered, another clawed—and launching across the small space at Tossa. He reacted with a defensive posture, as if still wounded, and only on contact with the large, light thing realized he had full use of his vision-form. Punching the beast several times, Tossa endured its clawing with scratches everywhere and got his arms about its neck, heaving back to snap it with surprising ease. As he fell away through the dream-air his tight grip came away with a mass of furry feathers, and he noted the thing’s talons had cut a cross into his chest.

He awoke to see daylight through the tent-flap and the prince of Shilar next to the cot, asleep on his knees. With one hand Tossa gingerly touched the scars in his chest, now just two red lines with an echo of the pain he loved to know, given his alternative. Quietly he lifted off the blanket, felt the cold, rejoiced again. In his other hand was a scrap of pelt, with a half-dozen black and white plumes nearly the length of his forearm springing from a deep russet fur.

Thula came in, shrieked, and there were too many words for some time.

"I still won't believe it," he said later to Thula. "Tell me a hundred times, but it cannot have been another two days."

They sat outside the tent by a wind-battered campfire, awaiting Gareth's return. Every few moments, another Bordbeyond adult walked up to exchange greeting and salute the new tribe member. Tossa felt the same thrill of pride whenever he put his hand on another's shoulder and felt the return clasp. Tossa wore his pelt above the cloak, never once unaware of it since his return. A few Shepherds gave their names, which was another sign of respect: but none spoke of recruitment, offering to become Tossa's Protector and accept his fealty in return. He mentioned that to his sister when they were alone.

She thought then shrugged. "They probably think you are pledged to Gareth."

"I am," he said, with a laugh at the simple solution. "But that will not hold, if he leaves to return to Shilar."

"When," Thula said with emphasis, "he returns, we will both go with him." She shouldered her cloak higher around her neck and edged towards the fire. "May Shilar grant we do not pass the winter on this table of ice."

Tossa grinned, and put on airs for fun. "This? The winter of '92 was much colder than this."

Thula stood to kick him, proving his tease a success; together they strode off to check the horses.

Both mounts were well cared for; a knight's life was short without his horse. Thula's mare was well used to her and kept on nibbling the sparse brown grass as she stroked its neck. But Tossa's stallion snapped up to look sharply at his rider, and threw his head twice before allowing him near. It was the reaction of a war-horse to a stranger, and Tossa knew the animal could sense a difference about him. Quietly he spoke and held out one hand; as suddenly as it started up, the stallion relaxed and allowed him in as if he had never doubted him. But he could not get enough of sniffing the pelt, and Tossa let him.

To one side of the keran, Gareth and Sidrathay were walking in quiet conversation. The prince always went about bare-headed with his hands in courtly clasp behind his back. The Bordbeyond princess was his opposite, helmed and visored with hands swinging free. Tossa burned to know every word, and feared to hear even one. Gareth sighted the sibling squires and gestured to them with his usual warm smile.

"I am pleased, Tossakateu, to see you so fully recovered."

"How fares my prince?"

"Well and better, thanks to the salves my wife supplied." Tossa could see that Gareth's left arm still moved slowly and carefully, but the prince was at pains—perhaps literally—to use its full range as he swept it before him in a bow to Sidrathay. Her visor showed no reaction, but her arms akimbo signaled disapproval or challenge at his chivalry.

"You may not fight another fortnight," she replied.

"The prince of Shilar," Thula bristled, "may do as he wills."

"Yes," Gareth replied brightly, "and I do recall how that worked out the last time."

Thula had nothing to say to that, and the quartet walked on for a while, beyond the limits of the tent-city and west, as if to catch the last warmth of sunset in early Raccoon.

"At all events," Gareth remarked, "I am loath to lose my life so soon after my marriage." Tossa could see the prince marking Sidrathay for any sign of a reaction, but as usual there was nothing.

"And perhaps, Sidrathay, it is of more import that we discuss—that we decide, not whether I shall live, but whither we shall live."

That brought a halt. Sidrathay turned her helmed head at Gareth for the space of a long breath.

"I live upon the plains, with my people."

"And I would not willingly be sundered from my wife. But neither of us can refuse our obligations, Sidrathay. I know you cannot love me, not yet. We are Children of Hope, yet no longer are we children. "

"I cannot let others hold the watch while I shelter behind stone."

"And I do not renounce the throne of my father by crossing the River Sweeping. I would not escape the responsibility if I passed the Swords of Stone."

From within the leather helm came a cluck of frustration, and it was all Tossa could do not to laugh.

"Then I must come with my husband," she announced like a sentence of death, "and live among the settled people."

"If you will it, Sidrathay," Gareth responded and Tossa could hear some doubt in his tone. "as your ambassadors have come among us before, without taking much harm as I hope."

"They were bound for a short time, and always intended to return."

"As are you, wife. We have but to set the intervals, and then we may properly visit all our people."

Sidrathay nodded, then turned to walk on.

"You would spend the winter among the settled lands, I imagine."

"With great pleasure!" Gareth replied with a laugh. "That is, Sidrathay, if you are prepared."

"Prepared to leave?"

"Prepared to marry me."

She snapped around at the insult. "You refuse our marriage?"

"We are married, among the Bordbeyonds. In Shilar, Sidrathay, there are… certain customs to observe."

"We will stand in a church," she said with some bite in her voice, "and a preacher will speak. This is a settled thing."

"It is indeed. Settled for several thousand years. And then," Gareth's voice broke, and Tossa realized with horror where this was going. "Then too, there are certain, em, certain other traditions…"

"Tell me of them."

"Well first, of course, there is—this is perhaps absurd—but I must write to you. A poem, in fact. Of sorts."

Gareth looked on the blank helm for several long moments, but Tossa could see, the prince's courtesy and honor showed him no path forward. In fact, chivalry forbade such rude mention. Even were he sure of Sidrathay's reaction, it would be ignoble. But the tall leather-clad warrior just stood there, waiting to hear the matter out.

"Oh, for the love of the stars," Thula broke in, stepping forward to take Sidrathay by the arm like a lingering child, back toward the tents. "Come with me."

Gareth followed the two women with his eyes, jaw open. After they were out of earshot, he seemed to snap from his daze, turning to Tossa with desperation. Without a word, Tossa followed after them, more to intervene should a fight break out.

Sidrathay wrested her arm free of Thula's grip, but the squire was in no mood for delay and simply grabbed her by the belt, breaking into a trot. It was either come along or fight, and Sidrathay chose the latter. Thula marched them into their tent, and the flap did not completely close behind the pair; Tossa stopped there to listen, and remain ready.

"What then, warrior of Shilar. Is this another time where you must strike me?"

"There are things you need to know," Thula said tightly, "about marriages in Shilar."

"You will tell me of them."

"I beg your pardon, lady?"

"You will tell me."

"I cannot hear you, lady, with your helmet on."

Tossa felt sure he would have to rush the tent. But after a frozen moment and a chuff of impatience, he saw the helm itself bounce through the flap. He knew Sidrathay stood there, two inches and more above Thula, with her arms as ever akimbo, and furious.

"I hope you can hear me now."

"Very well, lady. What my prince is too kind to say, what every silly child in Shilar knows, is that we court our mates by custom. A yes and a nod under the open sky is all well and good for you, I suppose. But to be married in Shilar, Gareth needs to send you a poem. Which you must read and accept."

"I do not read."

"What?"

"That is a settled thing." Sidrathay's voice dripped with distaste.

"Well, it's going to become unsettled. I shall have to teach you, I suppose."

"You!"

"Listen to me. Milady. There will be a poem, and it will be a good one. Gareth will think of little else until he can speak from his heart about this, so you likely have some time. But until he has sent it to you, and you have read it—out loud, do you mark me—you are not half-married."

"I cannot learn it."

"Oh, but you can wield a flail, kill giants, lead the entire tribe! You can read, and you will." Thula's voice at last gained an edge of humor. "I may have to beat it into you."

"And that will make me half-married in Shilar? What of the other half?"

Outside the tent, Tossa froze in fear. When did his parents tell him about this matter?

"You and Gareth, you must, to be married, after the ceremony you must lie together. As if to make a child."

The silence was filled with ice, the air seemed blocked with it. When Sidrathay spoke, it was with wonder in her tone.

"But you are his lover."

Tossa's knees gave beneath him and he stumbled toward the tent flap near falling.

"Say that again."

"Surely, you love him, that is plain."

Tossa barely deflected Thula's lunging form as she reached for Sidrathay's throat. The Combatted, needing no assistance to dodge an assault with warning, stepped back and viewed the twins in a tangle beneath her.

And at that moment, before anyone could speak, the horns blew.

Across the tent city, every horn of warning sounded. Gareth met the trio as they emerged from the tent, and pointed back north by west across the plains. The westering sun glinted off scores of armored suits trotting toward the Bordbeyond city. Already hundreds of warriors had appeared to either side, but the knights of Shilar rode on, shields and helms ready to repel assault and blowing their own horns in defiance.

"Arm and mount," Gareth's tone brooked no delay.

Tossa had seldom moved so quickly, yet his heart dragged on the steppe. Was this war at last, all Gareth's effort wasted? Even on celebration days he had never seen so many Shilarian lances gathered in one place. The Bordbeyonds of the area far outnumbered these invaders, but as the trio came into line with the tribal leadership, Tossa could see barely more mounted warriors than the invading party. The Bordbeyonds fielded ten walkers to every horseman, and few among the latter with true lances. Shilarian armor was a great advantage. Despite his years among the Shepherds, Tossa felt there could be no victory here.

When Thula displayed the banner of the royal house on her lance, the Shilarian brigade stopped at once, its lead knights dismounting to advance under the tri-branched flag of truce. Tossa's heart could unclench a bit, as Gareth, the chieftain, and Sidrathay moved ahead with Gleimharn joining Thula and him in the second rank.

"My good Baron Hirion," Gareth called out in high spirits, "I am delighted to—"

Hirion on foot pulled off his helm and knelt before Gareth's horse. With two words he shattered what little calm the dusk had gathered.

"Your Majesty."

Tossa looked to Gareth and saw the sudden advent of such pain as brought tears to his own eyes for his lord's sake.

Long live the king.

In the last days of the spring thaw, in a land with (among other things) a river and a king, the old ferryman of the east bank passed away. He left alone, after making the passage for one hundred sixty years; forever to the Men of Shilar across the great curve of the River Sweeping, but just an average career in the Elven land of Mendel. The people of Cambendom, the town on the Elvish bank, cast about for a successor, and a young Elf named Pakal volunteered. He had lost family as well, and at only thirty-some years was beginning to drift without work. He knew nothing of the river and had no particular aspirations of the job, but he was strong and agile, used to living alone, and inclined to the prospect of steady income and quiet days. At least, he thought, there was nothing to lose.

The duties were simple. When a fare comes to the boathouse, take the toll and pole them to the west bank. Whenever fares come the other way, cross with the empty boat and see if others are waiting. This old custom always kept one boat on each side. Other than that, the ferryman's time was his own.

On his first day, one of quiet sunshine and hinting breeze, Pakal passed the time settling in and inspecting the ferry. A sound boat, as far as he could tell, and simple in operation. A fixable rudder on the back, to hold her straight against the current; a side-oar for countering waves or extra speed; and a long pole to push her forward. She leaked a little, not enough to be serious, and the hole could not be found in any event. He was still looking for it, and beginning to wonder how long the old boatman had done the same, when he heard a distant bell from across the river. Looking up, he saw the other ferry slowly coming on, with three tiny figures aboard.

As he sprang to his moorings, he noted a similar bell on his dock. On a guess, he rang a hasty reply and hove to the oar. After clearing the pilings, he corrected course with the rudder, and locked it down. Then he took up the pole and pushed it clear of the dock's breakwater. He felt the gentle urge of the current and the tug of the pole as it stuck briefly in the mud. Alone, the boat was easy for him to push, and he felt a thrill to be actually out and doing, in this new place. It wasn't until he reached the middle that he remembered the other ferry, now near and passing on the port. He saw the mother and child making passage and, for the first time, the other ferryman with his back to him pushing the pole.

Pakal had been told that Man's name was Divalin, by coincidence a new hire as well, sent by the west bank village of Ostal as a replacement. Men were impatient creatures, of course, and could not stay with a job for long. This one seemed the same outward age as Pakal, though of course a mortal; a bit smaller perhaps, but apparently more used to the work. As the two sterns pulled abreast, both men came up from their poling and caught each the other's eyes. For a long time, it seemed to Pakal that they just stood there, poles in hand, staring. Suddenly, because he had to do something, Pakal nodded blankly. The other did the same and immediately returned to his work. Pakal too continued, wondering why he had felt so awkward. The thought of speaking to a stranger had caught him off guard. It was certainly not that Men and Elves never spoke, just that he had not once done so. But what was to be gained by simply saying something? Better not to break the stillness of the day by talking for no reason, Pakal assured himself.

He nearly hit the west dock before coming out of his reverie. There were no passengers waiting, so he paddled the rudder to spin the ferry and headed back, quickly. He had resolved to keep his head down and say nothing, but there was Divalin, poling back with an empty boat, and Pakal knew that something must be said. He noticed that the other boat listed slightly to starboard, and resolved to tell the man, for his own good. But when they came alongside, he found himself frozen again. There they stood, poles in hand, on boats slowly drifting by, with the sounds of tiny waves and hinting breezes in their ears. Pakal moved to speak, but the silence forbade it, and he mutely made a tipping motion with his arms and body instead, as if to indicate, "she'll go over one day, you know". To Pakal's surprise, the other suddenly smiled, as if he knew and understood, and in return pointed grimly to the water in Pakal's boat, meaning "and she'll sink first". They both laughed then, happy to know in that moment that they shared the same problem. But now they were passing by, and there seemed nothing else worth saying, so, as if by previous agreement, they poled on rather than lose the beautiful silence.

When he returned to the east bank, Pakal moored the ferry and sat on the dock, watching the sun go down over the west bank boathouse. He thought of his new life, the urge of the river, the hole in his boat, and other things. Occasionally his thoughts returned to the Man under the setting sun. He felt sure he should speak to him, but didn't know how to begin. No matter, he thought, he would think of something by the morrow.

The next day passed, and the several more, in much the same way. Pakal took his meals alone, read, worked on his boat (which he named *Leaker*), and watched the big boats on the river, sailing down and up with fares and passengers from far away. Sometimes after early morning a fare would come, a trader or messenger, or visiting relative, and there would be work to do; else, he would hear the distant bell from the Ostal side, and spring up to heave to. His young frame shed the aches of his work in a few days; the river's mud always tugged briefly at the pole, and its current always gently fought the rudder. And when they reached the middle, Pakal would see Divalin, and say nothing. Most often they would nod or smile, as do those who already know each other well. Or, when both boats were empty, they repeated the comic motions of tip and sink, as the joke never wore off for them. But somehow speaking felt taboo, and not a word passed between them, though both often seemed to try. At times the weather was too quiet to speak, as at first, sometimes too loud, sometimes dark. They simply poled on by, ten times, a score, a hundred, until the numbers disappeared.

In the later afternoon, when the fares usually stopped coming, Pakal would take out a book, or search for the leak. Somctimes on warmer days he moored the ferry at an angle to the dock, making a small breakwater where he could bathe. One slow afternoon, he took up a song, a melody from the town set to river lyrics, and listened to his voice as it rolled back from the western bank. To his surprise, a few minutes later he heard a far-off voice like the distant bell, Divalin, singing snatches that he remembered. Pakal immediately sang it again, correcting the stray notes, and then Divalin had it all. That evening, one of those magical few made of a stillness when the river slows and distance makes no echo, they sung it together from out of sight on the opposite shores draped in darkness. Divalin's voice could go higher more easily, Pakal's somewhat lower. Since it was his song, the Elf had the mastery of it. Yet in days to come, songs of both men could be heard rolling across the current as the ferrymen worked their ways.

One rarely warm, late fall, lazy, do-nothing day, as Pakal floated in the break-water pretending to doctor the pilings, he caught the motion of Divalin's boat as it moved upriver along the western bank. Divalin appeared to be struggling frantically, and his boat heeled lazily back and forth against the weaker current-edge. After watching a few minutes, Pakal decided he was either curious or had nothing to lose by investigating; lacking the determination to choose, he cast off and headed over.

Just as he was getting worried about what to say or ask, he recognized that Divalin was trying to execute a circular maneuver with the cumbersome, one-way boat. As Pakal watched, Divalin poled the boat to full speed against the current, then released the rudder with one hand and took the side oar with the other, and using them with alternating push and pull, tried to make his boat spin with the current. Just at the crucial point his boat began to list to starboard again, and Divalin had to desperately lock down the rudder to avoid capsizing.

Even as he laughed, Pakal felt the growing urge to try it himself, and he had no more will to argue with his idiocy than Divalin had. It became a race. Pakal used Divalin's idea while adding more pull to the side-oar, as Divalin's list prevented him from doing. Following many failures on both banks, and after soaking himself with spray from slapping the oars, Pakal finally executed a rather nice circle, and repeated it so Divalin could copy the rhythm. Then they both leaned on their poles in such a way that their boats stood still, and looked at each other, panting, through the heat shimmers rising from the water across the middle of the current.

For a moment, it seemed to Pakal that as soon as they caught their breath they would have to speak; then he heard the repeated shouts of a man who is being ignored. He looked over to see an impatient merchant with a laden mule on his dock, gesticulating furiously at this foolish delay. As they poled past at the middle of the river, with the fuming trader in Pakal's boat, Divalin stopped to make a circular motion with his arm behind his back, and Pakal had to concentrate not to show his embarrassment. The merchant stormed on to Ostal, and did not return.

That very night a thick fog settled down to sleep on the riverbed, and when a late traveller came for passage, Pakal turned to get the lantern from the boathouse. The cloaked man stopped him and murmured a quiet word, like a note from a song; slowly, a light grew from the end of the stranger's staff. It cast shards of illumination that poked their way through the fog in scores of places, like fingers through a cobweb, and drenching the two with light that silvered their clothes—or rather, did so to Pakal's clothes, as the stranger was already grey from his hair to his heels. He sat in the bow while Pakal rang the bell.

Pakal poled gingerly, as if he were sneaking away with an escaped prisoner, not wanting to make any more noise than needed. The distance to shore and center and sky and time were all lost, and he felt as if he were on an endless voyage, carrying his fare to another world. He began to imagine monstrous things looming up out of the river-fog, but eventually Divalin's prow jutted into sight to the port, like an island of sanity. As they passed Pakal could see Divalin's jaw hanging open. Again, he could say nothing to disturb this moment, but he slowed his poling a bit so they could share this strange and wondrous trip. For his part, the passenger also said nothing, seemingly at home with folk who did not address him. On the western bank, he disembarked and after tipping a broad-brimmed hat to his ferryman, strode off into the mist, towards the north. Like the merchant, he never returned.

So three seasons passed, through summer and fall into early winter, wind and wave and song and sun. Divalin and Pakal worked and watched, together while apart, knowing without speaking. Every day Pakal wondered if this would be it, if he would strike up a conversation on this pass. Sometimes he resolved to do so, for some excellent reason or other, each thought of in a flash and as quickly forgotten. Sometimes he merely hoped it would happen. The days escaped one at a time without words, and only an occasional song while they worked or watched the setting sun, or gazed at the clear stars at night.

Once a month a tall ship from south at the riverport would anchor midway between the boathouses, and Pakal would pole out for supplies. The sailing ship had two ladders, one port and the other starboard, so the two ferrymen never saw each other on the opposite side. In late Lion, Pakal learned from the captain that the king of Shilar would come, on a state visit from the land of Men to that of Elves. He intended to cross from Divalin's side to Mendel in a few days' time, and return on the following week. As always when an important person comes, nothing seemed good enough back at the dock. Pakal fell to work cleaning the boathouse, shoring up the dock pilings, and most importantly, searching yet again for the hole in *Leaker*. He once looked up at the west dock, wondering if Divalin knew of the king's coming. Before he could think of what he might say, however, he saw him attaching something, weights perhaps, to the port side of his boat. He knows then, thought Pakal, and continued searching.

When the big day came, Pakal was ready with clean house, solid dock and spotless boat. Nervously he bided his time, feeling guilty-glad that his friend would have to manage the royal visitor first—he could observe, maybe learn what to say, or not. But when a family of three walked up to request passage, his nerves took a hop higher on his spine. He rang the bell and crossed, and saw Divalin on his opposite course, with an empty boat.

To his horror, as he approached the west bank, Pakal saw the glint of steel and gold awaiting him.

Pole in hand, he bowed low to the king in his litter, borne by four knights. Shilarian horses and carriage, quartered now in Ostal, would be replaced in Cambendom. As the king stepped into the bow end, Pakal rang the bell, a little loudly, and pushed off. The king was clad in gold circlets and belts, and he had a box in the litter where the royal crown was kept. In addition, the knights were all in chain mail. Pakal found it a tremendous effort to even move the boat, and the pole sunk so deep the first time he planted it that it almost jerked from his hands. After a few times, it got a little better and the slow passage began. Almost immediately, the leak became evident (as it had never been found). Due to the added weight, the boat filled more quickly, and by the time *Leaker* reached the middle, there was fully two inches in the bottom. The king, evidently put off by this menial mode of travel, sloshed back to his litter; while the guards, having nowhere dry to stand, bore it with silent indignation.

Passing by on the port side, Divalin made a nervous reverence to the closed litter and gave Pakal a look that was reassuring in its apprehension. He knew what was happening, was guilty-glad it wasn't happening to him, and hoped to escape worse in a week's time, now that the order of passage was reversed. Still, Pakal half thought his friend might jump across to help him in that moment. And Pakal, who had never felt more alone and was ready to quit, knew instead that his silent friend understood. It gave him the strength to force *Leaker* to the west side dock. The litter debarked at once, leaving wet footprints on his boards. On the instant, the bell rang again and he saw yet another load of travellers coming on Divalin's boat. Pakal hastily bailed and headed back. As he passed Divalin this time he made the sinking motion himself at his own boat, to say "you were right—it did sink first". Divalin smiled, and replied with the tipping motion, meaning "not yet—I can't get mine to stay level".

It was a blustery early winter afternoon when the King of Shilar returned. Pakal felt that same chill for the rest of his life, whenever he thought about what happened. By the sheerest chance, there had been a passenger just a quarter-hour before, an elven lady on a pilgrimage, who required him to cross with her on board. He heard the bell from behind him, and looking back, saw the royal party boarding Divalin's boat at the eastern dock, and shoved off before the echo died. As *Leaker* cleared the dock, a gust pushed it upstream into the current, and Pakal had trouble correcting course. As he approached the center, he resolved once and for all to speak as inconspicuously as possible to Divalin about that when they passed, for he could see as he came on that the other boat was listing slightly to starboard still, with Divalin straining against the pole. "Careful of the gusts" "Watch the chop" "Wind is sneaky today": these and many other phrases ran through his mind as if chased by the weather itself. They were nearly abreast and Pakal was actually clearing his throat to call, when the king abruptly got out of the litter on the starboard side. At that moment, a strong gust slammed in from port, carrying heavy chop. The combination of added weight, wind and water flopped the boat before a man could even cry out. An instant later, Pakal hit the water and raced to the spot.

The king was still wearing his gold, the knights still clad in coats of mail. Nobles seldom learn to swim. When Pakal put his face to the water and opened his eyes, he could see them ahead and below, sinking like stones. Two kicking legs on the other side of the capsized ferry ahead caught his eye, and in one dive Pakal was under the boat and up on the other side, holding Divalin in his arms. Steadying himself against the slowly sinking craft, he held the man, coughing, above water while *Leaker* floated down near them. To one side, the wooden chest slowly turned lock-side down, sank and bubbled as the crown of Shilar followed its master into water and was lost.

Kicking off, Pakal made slow progress across the current after his boat. Divalin was totally spent from the work and the shock of the accident; he had to be carried under one arm. Pakal continually swallowed waves kicked up by the hostile breeze. Ten minutes later, he dragged them both aboard *Leaker*, and plopped down to catch his breath. With a dull shock he remembered the king of the land of Men, but he couldn't even summon the energy to look over the side; they were gone. Sliding exhaustedly up on an elbow, he and Divalin looked at each other, still gasping and coughing.

"How are you?"

"Fine. Thanks."

"I'm sorry."

"It's alright. Ostal owes me a better boat than '*Lister*' anyway."

With the stone anchor dropped over *Leaker's* side, they spoke far into the evening of themselves and others, of boats and songs and rivers and kings. Then, after dropping Divalin off at the west bank dock, Pakal poled back as they both went to tell their kingdoms the terrible news.

So it was that Divalin lost his boat and his country lost its king. The people of Shilar wept with the distant sorrow that one feels at the death of a famous man; while Divalin felt the sadness of he who loses something before he can finish with it. Which loss was the greater is hard to say, but it is certain that no gain would later have come without them both. For the prince of Shilar proved to be the greatest leader of Men in human memory. And in time, the people of Ostal gave Divalin the materials for a new boat, which Pakal spent long hours on the west bank helping him build. In return Divalin pulled with Pakal and dragged *Leaker* fully onto the shore, where they finally found and caulked the hole.

Nowadays things go on much as before; the passengers come and go, the river flows and the sun sets over the west bank boathouse. With time, however, some things are bound to change. Now, when the ferrymen pass by on the return trip with empty boats, they come alongside and, placing one foot over either rail, plant their poles and speak awhile of rivers and kings. And in the rare, magical evenings when the distance makes no echo, they still sing the songs, but now in harmony which must be practiced; Divalin higher and Pakal lower. And the people of Cambendom and Ostal wonder about the two ferryman, an Elf and a Man who often chat, who lost a king and yet carry on as though they have gained.

Reaping

Trapped, Treaman could see no way out.

The air was stuffy and the walls seemed to close in behind him. Glancing around he saw Mhoral unhelmed, Haltar without weapons, Bildon with no armor on. And he was already lost, the Woodsman with no sense of how to escape. The way forward was clear but not to his liking; no others seemed possible at the moment.

But worst of all was the group's morale, as they each spoke their thought despite the danger.

"Mage's mind, how did we get into this?"

"We should have left, I told you, before this got started!"

"Quiet, Bildon, all of you. Straighten up and look sharp."

"Surely, this will be an easy time! Another brilliant decision by our fearless leader. Trapped and surrounded, I'm telling you no good can come of it."

"Stop whining. Act like you've been to a celebration feast before."

Treaman looked again at the magnificent courtyard of the Primara's palace, and heard the deep clang of its metal gates closing behind them. The manse was brightly lit against the starry winter night, and the open double doors beckoned, attendants in livery standing by to receive them. Treaman could feel the absence of his sword-sheath, the missing weight of his shield and pack. Cleaned and dressed as never before, they were headed into the ruler's palace to be feted and perhaps rewarded for their service to Oncario.

All in all, he wished they were still back in the mines.

Hard to believe the adventure was nearly a fortnight ago: if Treaman just let his mind go free a step he could be back there in a heartbeat, and more often than not he woke up dreaming he was still in the under-earth. Several days of exploring, waiting out mysterious sounds, with one frenzied fight to the death sandwiched between endless stretches of not eating or sleeping. The Woodsman knew that wasn't the way Haltar would tell it, to the audience at this large and better decorated version of Trainertown's campfire gathering. But his leader knew the occasion as no one else he had ever met. Treaman trudged up the steps and felt at least this bit of encouragement, that a wondrous tale lay ahead of him. Despite his starring role, it was to be a story he had not yet heard.

As the servants stepped back and bowed, he felt another wave of unease at his situation. The party had been invited the previous day, and Januelus seemed more nervous than any of them, that they would finally meet the city's leader, his lover. New clothes, baths, hair brushed out; Jaya the serving woman even tried to press perfume on them, though Treaman finally drew the line.

Haltar humored her, as indeed he had done since their first night in the city. That coupling, at least, seemed acceptable; Jaya was full-grown and had no maiden's dreams dancing in her eyes. Treaman preferred the muffled sounds of Fairnum's Tavern to Jaya's screeching declarations beyond a thin blanket wall. Best of all, he liked Haltar on his feet, in the wild-lands and celibate. But it seemed poor manners to complain. Every time Treaman saw Linya these days he nearly dropped something.

The servant who led the way into the palace left them a moment in the antechamber, a room with five walls, three doors and an iron chandelier overhead. Now there were two portals between the party and freedom, and Treaman was already a bit short of breath. Haltar's orders came as a relief.

"Get hold of yourselves. Memorize this layout, I want to know everything before we leave here, understood?"

"What for? We're not coming—"

"Damn you, Mhoral!" Haltar seemed to Treaman to be playing a role, the anger a bit overdone, not that he'd want the leader yelling at him. "For once in your too-long life, just do as you are told. Remember how well you did with drawing the maps, and keep your sleepless eyes carking open."

The Elf was abashed at last, and doubly uncomfortable to be without his helm as the scars still showed from his encounter with the captain of the haunted keep. He nodded once, and snapped away to look in another direction as everyone did the same. Only Braja stood solidly at the back, not understanding enough words to follow orders but content to be with the group and out of the caves. The long scar on his arm was an honest red, earned when he thrust his massive steel spear straight through the monster at the height of the struggle.

The servant returned from the central door and gestured them to an entry hall with high ceilings and wall-lanterns that gave off no smoke. The group advanced directly into the palace; Treaman noted two patches of ceiling overhead made of solid glass, curving like portions of a gigantic arc and revealing a floor above. The architecture was as ornate as he had ever seen, replete with drapes and wall paintings, and the outdoorsman raised in frontier Novar could sense it was very old.

Through the next set of double doors was the main chamber, again a five-sided space and this time utterly huge, nearly an arrow's flight across. The center of the room was set with a U-shaped table six feet wide, with massive oak legs and endless yards of white cloth as covering, laid with candles and pewter settings enough to seat three score. Treaman realized he was gawking even as the assembled guests stood to applaud someone who must be standing behind them. He felt dizzy and tried to return his mind to the job Haltar had given.

To left and right were broad winding stairs, undulating up to a buttressed gallery that cut edgewise through the open space above this room, exiting on both sides. Further back on the ground floor were two large doors, and between them on a dais, a large throne of cut stone part-draped in velvet faced the open "U" of feasters. Januelus stood to one side of it, unlike everyone else still dressed for the outdoors, as if intending to leave any moment. Treaman might have given his share of the rumored reward to go with him. But a pleasant evening stroll through the pine barrens seemed further off than those mines tonight; Treaman followed the group to their chairs of honor high up on one side of the tables.

Braja tapped his shoulder and said "Floor hot."

Treaman grinned and nodded, "Yes, some kind of fire burning below." He thought only then to marvel at the comfort of this enormous stone cavern, no fireplaces or braziers but as warm as bed.

"Fire always burn, Oncario." Braja was getting better at making himself understood, but seldom chose to speak. Treaman wondered how much of the party's conversation he could pick up. He probably did the same as he had under Pelian, by listening hard.

The Primara was not in evidence and the feast began without her. Treaman only slowly put a finger on his instinct of what was wrong here. Servants coming and going severally, food laid out unevenly, the guests all dressed up yet conversing only in stops and starts: Oncario was not used to state occasions. Three times a wealthy-looking fellow stood to propose a toast to the courage of the outsiders; the response was hale and strong with relief, yet the words were almost identical. The food was just the sort Treaman loved, squashes and corn and venison, plenty of bread and as much ale as wine. Suddenly, in a space of near-silence while everyone simply ate and drank, he realized there was not one note of music.

Januelus stepped down from the dais to chat with Haltar briefly, and he seemed happy as the paintings on the walls, a smile frozen on his face with something cold beneath. The ax-man spared a glance and nod at Treaman, and the Woodsman answered with a raised tankard salute. But the timberman returned to the dais to oversee the feast and wait.

The door opened behind one side of the throne, and Treaman saw then, what they all had waited for.

His first impression, as he stood with everyone else for the Primara, was one of striking beauty. Vuthienne was tall and long-limbed, with a lustrous shock of red-brown hair spilling around a golden circlet and a slitted scarlet gown that left no doubt about the breadth of her curves. A smooth and unhurried pace allowed no choice where everyone should look, for whom everyone should wait to speak. She took Januelus' hand to ascend the dais steps and made it look as if no one had ever approached this chair before her. It was oversized, blocky and almost primitive; but when the Primara sat, the throne looked just the right size, well contoured and comfortable.

Vuthienne cradled a gold-chased sceptre set with bright stones. The instant Treaman laid eyes on it he felt a tingle to his core and a sympathetic ache up his right arm where he had held the Sword of Air weeks ago.

Linya laid a light hand on that arm, her whispered voice choking. "We have seen that style before."

Treaman could not think clearly—had they fought so hard to reach the capital, and nearly missed another piece of the Tridium right under their noses? His eyes met Januelus', which flickered with pain, and things began to make sense.

Around her neck, the Primara wore a bright ruby the size of a swan's egg in a simple gold setting. Vuthienne turned to lay the scepter to one side upon a velvet cloth. It could have been the glow of a nearby lamp, but Treaman thought he saw sparks around her hand, and twitching fingers when she let the rod go. The room was well lit and could be picking up reflections in the bloody gem round her neck, or the jewel could be giving off glints of its own. There was some darker decoration outside the setting, or perhaps make-up on her chest, but Treaman could swear the skin of her cleavage looked burned.

She raised a goblet and turned to gaze benignly on the party.

"Hail and well met, heroes of the world beyond the chaos." It was a voice as large as she was, the unstudied tone of an ancient orator. "Our reports of your valor were inspiring, and we hope to hear the tale from your own lips soon. Oncario with this feast only begins to repay its debt."

Haltar stood briefly to bow as she continued.

"Rejoice, citizens, for the mines are again open to our use as they were to our ancestors."

Everyone applauded and stood to drink, though Treaman noted several were smiling only politely. Ever since they had begun the quest a fortnight ago, his companions sensed the deep reluctance of most to be using the underground spaces. The miners' fear of a monster in the depths had proved justified.

Treaman muttered to Bildon at his side, "At first, I thought it was just my nerves, to be going underground." He shivered in remembrance. "But when we got to the entrance, and saw those broken wards…"

"Made by Hope," Bildon nodded, "Linya and Mhoral confirmed it. And very old. Our gracious and beautiful Primara took a loose view of Areghel's dictates, it seems, when she fulfilled Enict Moaro's desire for more ores."

Treaman shrugged and reached to stab a baked apple off the table platter. "He can do marvelous things with them. You saw how Haltar performed with that longsword; can't make them with regular steel." He chewed a while in silence, then chuckled. "And when's the last time you agreed with Mhoral's view?"

Bildon winked back. "Don't tell him. Poor fellow, he wouldn't know what to do with the news."

Feasting continued, neither Januelus nor Vuthienne eating but toasting along with the rest of the assembled crowd. Hallah demanded food, and Treaman handed her a slice of his baked apple. The dragon nibbled the tiniest bit then wrestled heroicially with the skin awhile.

{*"Taste bad."*}

"I don't think I've ever heard you say that," he mused while getting some riddy from his pouch.

Bildon excused himself to seek the garderobe, and Treaman knew the Stealthic would use that opportunity to scout. Enict the inventor came by, as pleased as a cat about to nap, and sat a moment in the Halfling's place.

"Splendid night! Marvelous feast; and the ores! So much to do now."

"Another powder-bow?" Treaman asked for courtesy and the inventor nodded while drinking deep.

"And more, better ammunition, perhaps even a new petard I've come in mind of." He winked at Treaman conspiratorily. "Never did I imagine I would access so much dragon-dung. You're sure you won't sell her?"

Treaman shook his head once, still trying to be polite. "We'll be back through, and I'll try to save it up for you." Or anyone else who knows the formula, he thought to himself. What could he give Hallah as a reward, he wondered, for this exploitation. She slept now on his shoulders and had never given the slightest indication she needed anything other than food and his company. Treaman stroked her smoothly and knew, he could never be willingly parted from her.

"That dragon-stock is drying now, and I'm keeping it safe I can tell you." Enict patted the large brass key around his neck. "It's all I'll have left," the inventor grumbled, "thanks to the new edict."

It took a moment for this to register on Treaman's thoughts.

"What? Your powder—"

"All moved to the palace here, while you were gone, along with my working powder-bows." He pointed to the floor. "In a basement storeroom, I've seen it, directly beneath this floor. Nothing left, excepting old Jaya, our Primara wants nothing to do with stone shot. After all my efforts for this city…"

Enict drank again and lurched away to his seat, becoming affected. Treaman kept half an ear on his fading complaints while looking around the room again. Against each of the five walls was set a gold-rimmed arch, missed at first because of this much larger space. He nudged Linya.

"See the arches, here again just like outside of town," he said. "What could it mean?"

"Januelus told us one was for Conar," Linya mused, then shook her head. "Symbolic architecture, he said something about the unity of the kingdoms."

"Oh come now!" Treaman cried with a wide grin, "You know there are no symbols, everything's a clue, right?" They laughed and toasted together, and Treaman looked into her eyes for a flashing space. Linya had laughed, because of something he said. His collar went flush with heat.

The burble of conversation died as Vuthienne stood. Bildon returned with a knowing smirk just in time.

"And now, brave heroes, let us hear the story of your marvelous victory. Tell us how you liberated the mines."

Haltar stood again and gestured to the group from his spot at the end of the table.

"Our method was to search and map each cluster of shafts, clearing their passages and enabling the miners to proceed. There is no puissance required, of course, and little courage to discover that nothing is there." He paused for the chuckles.

"But by the fourth day, we were in the shaft which I am told runs the deepest beneath the earth." That brought silence again, and Treaman could see even Vuthienne leaning forward in her throne. Something in her gaze seemed hungry, her hand continually touching the giant ruby, flinching away, coming back again. Januelus was standing nearby, staring straight, jaw set and slowly clenching his fists.

"As we broke through to the undiscovered depths, then we knew some evil thing was near."

Treaman snapped away from his reverie at these words. *Broke through*? That was how Haltar chose to describe the cave-in, the half-day trapped in a cul-de-sac smaller than the space of this table. Of course, he realized, no one wanted to emphasize lethal conditions—this was the uplifting story of how danger had been removed. The miners who recovered them, and cleared the rubble from the blast-hole Linya had created in their last desperate moments; those worthy laborers were not in attendance here tonight to give contrary testimony. Then again, no one knew the true risks better, or needed to.

"These were new tunnels—new, that is, to the Children of Hope, but created perhaps in the deeper past. By a different people." Haltar let his words hang in the feasthall, and it seemed the lamplight dimmed for lack of air. Farmers and tradeswomen with no stomach for delving beneath the sunlit lands were rapt with horror at the thoughts this outlander brought to them. Vuthienne was also staring, at a point just past Haltar with her gaze aglow; Treaman could not shake the impression that her ruby gem was a third eye, whose glance it would be wise to avoid.

"At once, we made out the creature's spoor, for it melted the rock by its passage. It could move up walls and across a ceiling as easily as the floor; in a large cavern, we saw rows of drip-rock from above where the molten stone pointed down before it cooled and turned solid again."

The Primara shifted eagerly forward in her throne and spoke in a thick voice.

"Which of my—"

Her eyes rolled up, as with a great sigh she sagged back against the throne. One arm fell upon the sceptre and her body twitched a moment. The clear gaze returned, her composure regained in a smaller space of time than it took Januelus to reach her side.

Waving him back, she asked "What sort of creature was it?"

Haltar blinked once and replied, "A Salamander, milady."

The sussuration of groans was just what they had hoped for, when Haltar and Treaman put their heads together beforehand. The avatar of Fire was thought to be as rare as it was dangerous. True, the monster they had fought lacked hands or even much of a head, far less speech. If the Woodsman had been forced to name the unnamed again, he might have said it was a Magma Serpent. Certainly the thing coiled and struck as a snake. But Haltar had judged the likely truth lacking in flair; and all the party agreed, best not to mention the eggs they found later, and smashed. This tale should bear no sequel.

"The heat of the monster was that of a forge," Haltar said calmly, "and we knew it could only be cooled in death. Our wooden weapons ignited on first contact—" Treaman rubbed his left arm where his incinerated shield had scored the flesh "and the only weapon that availed to harm the beast was of Oncarian craftsmanship." Here Haltar gestured across the table to where Enict slumped, and the applause for one of their own was sincere. The inventor, taken by surprise, rose a bit to one side with his grin tilting opposite for balance.

"But it was magery, as much as any strength, which essayed the creature's demise." Haltar nodded slightly to Linya, who gripped the tablecloth in both hands as if on the edge of a cliff. "Sorcerous water acted as blows to the beast, driving it back with clouds of steam to fill the cavern. That, and certain other talents we were able to employ, served to defeat it." Mhoral's battle-song and Braja's courage, Treaman knew, had been chief among them. But Mhoral cared nothing for fame, and Braja, though able to follow the gist of the tale, seemed similarly disinterested.

"As the monster fell, it burned still further into the caverns, opening a vein of ore which I'm told might be silver?" He turned to look quizzically down the table, then shrugged off the trivial detail. "We could not tarry, for our wounds were rather serious, and the air at that depth was hard to come by."

Treaman remembered, as the applause grew around him, how incredibly long a march back up it had been. His fear of closed-in spaces grew more powerful as that realization had born down on him. When they missed their way, it was Bildon who guided them all, as the Woodsman stumbled along with an unbandaged arm and chattering teeth. But the Stealthic was good at counting the turns and they were back to the surface before the soaking wet cold could set into their bones.

Plucks on his sleeve alerted Treaman that the rest of the party was standing to receive the applause of the gathered guests. It was as warm and sustained as one might expect from such a settled, well-fed group. Wine all around, and more toasts, including one for Enict, and finally one to the health of the Primara, founder of the feast and patron of the adventuring heroes.

As she stood again to speak, the ruler of Oncario left her scepter to one side. The sheer size and effulgence of the ruby at her chest was impossible to ignore. So tall, proud and profoundly beautiful, Vuthienne looked a true daughter of heroes, cut from an elder age. Yet that gem looked wet with desire, and wearing it she seemed a hollow woman. Treaman caught Januelus' eye as he grimaced beyond her shoulder; he knew what was coming.

"The city of Oncario has ever protected the realm from danger," she began grandly. "Its governors appointed in the ancient times by the line of Areghel warded the way to Reghalion and served as the heart of the kingdom's trade and glory. Think you well on how we have prospered here, even in the midst of the curse which hangs heavy over the rest of the kingdom, how our industry has restored the ancient glory and provided us with new wonders to amaze the world."

The applause was heartfelt, the first citizen who received them seemingly breathless with her vision. But more; Treaman sensed there was a punch-line in her knowing glances, to a joke not yet told.

"In the absence of the line from its throne, the leadership of the Percentalion falls to us, citizens of Oncario. We will uphold the law, as we beat back the chaos on behalf of the heroes of old. We know, we have seen in recent years, the expanse of our city itself has grown, as we settled new fields to the west, and explore again the depths of our mineral storehouse to the east. Now, I assure you, the size of our kingdom will continue to grow. In fact, it will double."

There: she had dropped a clue, and seemed pleased that no one yet guessed its meaning. Treaman wished he had used the privy already, or that he had an excuse to leave.

"Oncario honors its debts, brave adventurers. The payment you have already won is yours, and we shall add to it from the coffers of the city."

She gestured to a servant by one door, who opened a small cask filled with multicolored glints.

"Gems, which we are given to understand win preference among those of your vocation, for their lightweight value."

Everyone smiled, even Braja understood; he looked to Treaman and mouthed the word "equal" which made the Woodsman laugh despite himself.

"We know you seek the capital of our cursed kingdom," the Primara continued in a husky tone, "and though our own expeditions, capably and bravely led—" here a gesture to Januelus—"have failed to pierce the barrier of chaos between our cities, yet we do grant you passage through the eastern gate, to pursue your quest there, for the Order-Brow."

So there it was. The party's smiles snuffed out, and Haltar stood stiff, unsure for once how to answer. Treaman looked again to the timber-man standing slightly behind his ruler, face drawn with regret and determination as the Primara announced a verdict and sentence.

"The Sword of Air, of course, will remain safe here with us."

Now Haltar knew better than to say anything, and Treaman felt his heart sink; the feasthall no longer seemed so large and open as before. At the three doors, he could now see liveried men standing with spears. Several, he noted, had flour on their hands and one a wine stain on his pants. None of them looked happy to be here; but the party had no weapons and very little magic to hand.

Haltar opened his mouth and paused, to gain a turn to speak.

"With your gracious permission, Primara, we will retrieve the relic and take our leave of you." He turned and gestured with a smile for the group to gather.

"We are leaving. Treaman, Bildon, go and get all our things from the house. By the time you return, we will all be outside. Somehow. Go." While blocking the view from the dais with his body, Haltar laid one hand briefly on Treaman's arm and shook his head once. The Woodsman understood, and turned to leave the hall with his every nerve keyed up for battle. The Heart-Shaft of the Tridium seemed clearly beyond their reach for now.

But Oncario would not have the Sword of Air.

Treaman and Bildon dashed through deserted moonlit streets to the back-way where Enict Moaro's door jutted up from the ground level. At the head of the alley, Treaman stopped cold with remembrance.

"Cark me! The key, Enict locked his place."

Bildon kept jogging and laughed theatrically. "Please be serious, my friend. The key?"

At the door Bildon reached to his pant leg, withdrawing a set of slender rods from inside his boot. Selecting two, he muttered to himself as he worked the lock.

"Three notches on the key, standard pressure and turns, there!"

He heaved up the storm door with a triumphant cackle and leaped down the steps to the main room where they had all bivouacked this past month and more. Treaman moved to pack the group's belongings and Bildon went at once to the inner door, where they had agreed with Enict to leave some of their more valuable possessions.

One thing the Woodsman knew well was how to pack efficiently. By his example, most party members had learned to stow their gear in snug order, and everything they carried had a cloth handle or strap. Only Haltar was a determined slob; pulling down the blanket separating the leader's sleeping space from the room, Treaman could hardly find any one thing touching another. He exercised his own preferences about how much to stuff away, and where.

"How do you suppose the Primara came in possession of the Heart-Shaft?" he called across the room to Bildon.

Only mutters came his way at first.

"Three notches, carking lock, why doesn't it—erm, what? Well she's clearly crazy, who knows?"

"If there have been no expeditions to Reghalion, it must have been here since the curse fell."

"Cark me! Was it second, third, first, or… yes, I suppose, but then why is their realm expanding only now?"

"And what is that awful red gem, where is that from?"

Treaman could see next to where Haltar laid his head, a few trinkets of jewelry, a scarf, remains of baked goods. So perhaps Jaya was a bit sentimental of her liason after all. Treaman realized how embarrassing it would be for Haltar, if he left them behind and then returned someday, and thought maybe he would "forget" them. Then he thought about how heavy all the food scraps and other drek would be to carry, and gleefully stowed them away at the bottom of Haltar's pack.

"Oho!" Bildon cried. "The fox, a different pattern of turns, there we are." Bildon stood up from the open door as Treaman came alongside. "I give him credit," the Stealthic said, "same key for all doors, but unlocking one tells you nothing about the others. I'll bet he has a different pattern for each lock."

"And you weren't watching," Treaman accused.

"He used the same key!" Bildon protested with a laugh. "I've never seen that before, a lesson to me. Carking clever dog."

In this side room were Linya's cloth-wrapped wand, Mhoral's weapons and the Sword of Air in its blanket wrapping. To one side were some of the inventor's other creations, including the miniature tri-tubed powder-bow. Treaman could see next to it small piles of darker, fine-grained powder and pellets made of glinting metal.

Bildon whispered, "Should we take it?" and Treaman jumped, to realize he was being watched.

"No, it's not ours, and besides, we couldn't make it work. Hurry, let's get back."

They returned to the main room and began to arrange everything atop two sheets that they each could haul. Treaman took the Sword of Air from inside the blanket, thrilling to the sight of the decorative inlay and nervous to remember its jarring feel when out of the scabbard. Carefully opening the tent bag, he slid the weapon down between the poles and tarp and pulled the strings to close it again. Now it was hard to reach but invisible. Taking Haltar's old bastard sword from a corner where Enict put scrap pieces for melting, he wrapped the blanket around it in the same shape as before, and tied it with cord.

Donning their personal gear and weapons, they each gathered the sheet corners and hauled hard over-back to lift their loads perhaps three inches from the ground. Hallah climbed aboard Treaman's sack and flapped her wings to help. Then Treaman and Bildon bump-bumped their way out of the inventor's quarters and turned up the alley towards the palace of the Primara.

Their pace was glacial under the load of three per man. Treaman kept alert for other denizens on the street; only a few forms moved slowly down faraway alleys, carrying loads like they were, a perfect disguise. As they approached the central thoroughfare, moonlight from Unal across the wide flagstones and the glow of the palace itself gave them pause. The two let down their loads and huddled.

"How do we get the others out of there without a fuss?"

"Nothing easier," Bildon assured. "I had a brief word with Mhoral before we left; told him how to get to the second floor window there," pointing to the left of the main entrance, a wall still in shadow. "I've got rope here, they'll shimmy down."

"As long as everyone else is in the feast hall," Treaman countered. "And they'll never let us all out to use the privy at the same time."

"Give me Mhoral and Linya," Bildon grinned, "and we'll be fine. Just let those serving boys try to hold Braja or our gentle leader."

"No," Treaman said almost fiercely. A conviction grew inside him, and he only knew its shape as his lips kept moving. "None of these people have done us any harm; we can't kill them if we can avoid it. This is all on that Primara. Something is deeply wrong with her."

They crouched on the corner while they thought. Treaman realized that Bildon, for all his bravado, was waiting on orders.

"We stash these in the alley. You get to that window and try to let them down, don't be seen; come back here, gear up and wait. I'll talk to Januelus. He owes us some answers."

Five steps later, Bildon had disappeared, and Treaman wasn't even sure which way he had taken. The front door for him; trying to control his knees and his temper he approached the gate where the guards passed him on recognition. Something kept building inside him at the thought of speaking to Januelus; he owed him, he was angry with him, he liked the man too much. But his party came first. And Treaman knew their friendship would not be the timber-man's highest priority either.

The porter bowed and stepped back to let him enter the palace, but Treaman stood firm.

"Tell Januelus that I would speak with him."

Puzzled, the man closed the door. Treaman tried not to look too often down the way to where Bildon might be effecting his comrades' escape. The time stretched on and he imagined a squadron of spear-armed men coming to the door. Unal's light crept over one boot on the steps; the clatch of the door made him jump again.

It was Januelus, alone. He glanced at Treaman, then immediately up and over his shoulder at the night sky, and finally to the blanket-covered sword. His face was a study in pain; when he spoke it was with admirable directness.

"She is my lover. Not just the Primara, my loyalty to the city by itself I could weigh. But she owns my heart. I told you I keep no secrets from her."

"What has happened to her, Januelus?"

"You don't know her!" the timber-man growled, taking a step towards Treaman in real anger.

"I don't know you!" Treaman shot back. "We trusted you, Januelus, came into the city on your word. Now your leader wants to—"

"She wants to restore the kingdom!" The consort reached with one arm to grip Treaman's tunic. He looked down at it a moment later, half-bathed in moonlight, and released him, stepping back a bit subdued. Hallah hissed and clacked her jaw in warning.

"I am sorry, Treaman. I, I don't know what's come over her. She was always headstrong, but once she spoke with a clearer voice, she had a vision for the city and all was, but she was not so… now, she never sleeps, hardly eats, I find her talking to herself." He looked up in the Woodsman's eyes. "This city needs her to keep it safe. I trust her wisdom, but now, I can see she's slipping away and I don't know what to do."

"When did she come by that awful gem?"

To Treaman's surprise, Januelus shivered in response, looked down, and nodded his head in agreement.

"Was that it? Recently? Before she began to change?" Another nod, and a gurgle of something Treaman feared to ask about.

"Januelus, she won't let us go."

"She has given her word. Your freedom for the Sword."

Treaman just waited until Januelus returned his gaze, then held up the wrapped weapon.

"She will never let us go."

The timber-man stared as the words sank in.

"She will send the guards in search of you. I will lead them."

Not knowing the full intent, whether he was speaking to a friend or an enemy, Treaman slowly nodded. Januelus took the wrapping, and his face hardened as he felt its shape. Again Treaman realized, there was no fooling this one.

Treaman held his gaze for what seemed too long a time. Then the timber-man nodded and turned to call across the antechamber.

"Tell Haltar he needs to speak with his man here."

Turning back he spoke in low tones.

"You must hurry. I will make every effort to catch you. The trail will lead us deep into the barrens. Do you understand?"

Treaman did not, not yet, but he nodded dumbly.

"We won't seek you along the riverbank, not for the first day."

"We need to move east," Treaman protested, "towards Reghalion."

Januelus shook his head hard. "Impossible. There's no going on that way, I've tried."

"But we can—"

"You must make for the western bank, and cross the river there, to the caves below the city. There is a way, marked with scent, back up into the palace itself."

Treaman could see Haltar and Braja striding down the hallway to them. "You want us to circle back?"

"Get that gem away from her, I beg you. But do not touch it, try to destroy it if you can." Januelus clenched his fists, and Treaman remembered the deep burn on one palm. "It smells of Despair. Then, all will be well with her."

Januelus held up the phony sword as a reminder of their bargain.

"I will give you as much time as I can. Do this for me, and go with Hope my friend."

Treaman held out his arm as promise.

"We will see you again."

Haltar passed Januelus with a glance at his parcel, and turned to Treaman wearing his poker-face.

"It's fine, but we must hurry. Braja, this way."

They found their things in the alley and Treaman explained his half-plan while the others armed themselves and shouldered their loads.

"Mhoral told us about Bildon's window," Haltar said. "I let Linya go first, then him, and was just starting to wonder what to do next when the messenger came. Nice thinking, but I'm surprised Januelus is letting us go."

"He's in love," Treaman responded, "and he's desperate."

"The two are probably related."

"And you, of course have never been either!"

Haltar laughed heartily, taking no insult. Treaman handed the strapping foot-knight his heavy pack with a full smile of cheer. They heard the others' approach from the sound of Mhoral and Bildon bickering.

Treaman handed Linya back her wand and waited on them to limber up.

Braja said, "Red queen burns."

Treaman was caught in doubt by this. "She's, the ruby, it's evil yes."

"She burns. Below the floor, below the mines. Ovens in the woods, in working man's shop. Oncario all burns." Braja looked around in the darkness at flames only he could see, and Treaman wondered if this was some tribal superstition, or an attempt at poetry. The smell of charcoal furnaces was heavy even now, even before dawn, it had been constantly there for weeks.

Getting as far as the west gate was easy; no sounds from the palace behind them.

"Do we rush the guard-house?" Mhoral asked.

"No." Again Treaman's words were his first clue that he had an opinion. "We mustn't kill them if we can avoid it. Besides, it would raise the alarm. Let's tell them Januelus sent us, it's not even a lie."

"Better yet", Linya said quietly, "let him say it. Everyone, on my signal, walk out smoothly toward the gate, like you expect it to open on time."

She focused then and gestured slightly with her fingers. From behind the group, Januelus padded quietly past, flipping a two-finger salute and smiling. Linya watched him from around the corner, then signaled for them to start out.

The timber-man called up to the guardhouse next to the gate with the same friendly wave he used on their arrival.

"Ho there, Barithul! um Mag, open up there. These six have business outside, Primara's orders."

The group walked on as Januelus looked up to the guard-window. Treaman saw a face appear, nod and disappear within. The doors began to open just as the group walked through. Januelus stayed behind, and Treaman saw him raise his fist in friendship with a grin on his face that he earnestly wished was real. The portals closed again, and a few seconds later Linya let out a gasp, followed immediately by a muffled outcry within the walls.

"Run," she said in a low tone and the group trotted down the opposite side of the span.

They were halfway through the settled fields along the paved road closest to the river, when the alarm bells and horns began to echo across the way from the city of brick. Each had recounted their stories for the others, but agreement proved elusive.

"It is insane to go back," Mhoral cried, "that woman is mad with power, gem or no gem, and we would never see the outside of those walls again."

"I gave my word," Treaman said tightly.

"Yours, exactly. I got out on my own."

Bildon made an exaggerated cough, and Linya turned while walking to look archly on the Elf. From within his unmoving visor there was no sign, and everyone had to chuckle.

"You did your best," Haltar said with finality, "and I say well done, Treaman. But we are not yet at the point to make a decision. If we remain free until daylight, find a way closer to the river, then we can explore our options." The leader spoke in exactly the same tone as he might say "then I will decide".

As they moved, Treaman kept a weather-eye out for ways to get further east. But the land to the right of the north-bound road was very choppy, tangled and unmarked; his outdoor sense told him the bank would be a bluff here, too steep to get down. Somewhere back in the barrens further north beyond the road, a place such as the one he went fishing with Hallah would do. But if it were too far up, they'd have to build a raft.

They took a brief break at sunup, snatching a few bites and swigs while the gorgeous winter disk climbed over the massive shoulder of Skysword slanting a second shade of blue across nearly half the skyline from the east. To the north ahead, the land was dotted with stumps, the road just rammed earth pointing to the pine barrens across the horizon.

The group plodded on, still with no sign of pursuit behind them. Treaman mentioned this, and immediately regretted it.

"What should we expect," Bildon quipped, "the baying of dogs as if we were foxes?"

"Drums, horns, or singing while they march in step!" Mhoral chimed in.

"Go swim with your armor on," Treaman shot back. He imagined the timber-man coming for them alone on quiet tread. Quite aside from his unwillingness to fight Januelus, something about his confidence and demeanor made the Woodsman nervous. He kept scanning to the right as they entered the piney woods, and at last called out to see what looked to be a path.

"Stay here, rest, I'll check it out."

Wending along the narrow trail with his spear in hand, Treaman saw tracks of many-toed lizard-like beasts, and some feathers of fishing raptors. But no movement in the brush and cedars to either side. It was full winter now, the scaly things should be asleep. He noticed several puddles and small swampy inlets that were iced over. Perhaps the way to the island caves would be easier than he feared; that might be a point in favor of returning.

The way down to the banks was tangled and steep, but manageable. From a cove-shaped section of shore, Treaman could see most of the river was still liquid, but ice stretched out many feet from the banks. Just the northern edge of the city was visible from here; Treaman cursed as he remembered Braja's spyglass.

When the baying started Treaman felt no shred of vindication. It was not the howling of mortal dogs.

The first time he tried to rise and run back to the group, he failed. Forcing his legs to work, his teeth were chattering by the time he had them in motion. Hallah awoke and looked alertly ahead, saying nothing. His breath came in gasps, his fear rose higher than he had ever felt before.

By then, the world around him was changing.

The path was still there, twisting and rising exactly as it should. But icy puddles and cypress stumps thinned out, and in their place were cracks in the dry earth, bubbles of lava, smokey vents, burning bushes. It was an eternity before he saw the group, facing to all sides with weapons drawn, in a place that had been dense with evergreens, now less than ten in sight, black rain to the left, a defile that had not been there behind them. The hate-filled howls came ever closer, and seemingly from all sides at once.

An entire tribe of grinaki fled directly through the group, scores of wizened gangly midgets tripping over packs and bounding off bodies, dropping everything in their hands and shrieking like sawed glass. Treaman watched in horror as a dozen ran directly into the defile and disappeared.

A small rise that had obscured the view, perhaps a hundred feet away, just dissolved as sugar in rain. Coming through it was a massive trunk of flesh on three legs, five or eight arms of differing shapes sprouting unevenly from any part of its body, topped by a head itself the size of a horse, filled to both sides by a tusky maw that could never form words, yet did.

"The Sword, mortals, I will have it, and my eye." To one side of the face, a pulsing melon of wet red malice bore down unblinking upon the group, seeing any movement yet ignoring any threat. Treaman nearly fell to his knees from the sheer sight. He could not be sure he still held his spear, much less could form the intent to use it.

The baying grew louder and he saw a loose ring of hell-dogs closing around them like a garrotte. Treaman counted five, more than enough to chase down and eat them without their master. He thought of the tent-bag on Braja's back, but his mind could go no further.

Haltar drew his longsword as smoothly as if answering a yokel's insult.

"We have nothing you want, demon," he called out while circling a few paces to one side.

The giant brute snerked in derision and shot out a sharpened tentacle as quick as a thrown dagger, aiming to decapitate him. Wheeling and parrying, Haltar's blade moved faster than sight and four feet of writhing snake bled hot liquid into the ground, igniting dry leaves.

Angered now, the demon turned a bit more in Haltar's direction, withdrawing the wounded arm into its body and growing two more, club-ended like sledge-hammers. Haltar gave ground and ducked, but the third alternating blow caught him flush and laid him to the earth with a bounce of pain.

Braja cried out "Ju-lye-ta!" and hurled his solid steel spear with everything he had. The shaft bent and flexed as it struck and bounded away. Mhoral began to sing the battle-song but his voice was faint. Haltar shook his head and tried to stand in the space provided by these annoyances.

Still Treaman did nothing; Hallah left his mind awash in images of another day.

A full grown dragon coiling back, grounded and wounded, as seen between the triple legs of a massive beast that now looked quite familiar

Linya cried out and a small glow from her headband preceded the appearance of her demon. It advanced to meet the leviathan and looked almost frail by comparison.

Waves of smoke, a dragon fights with claw and flame as his mate lies dead to one side

The foe turned to face his smaller, more handsome kin with a gape of amusement; his sole eye glinted horribly, as strip by sliver the demon-thing peeled apart while Linya screamed and held her head.

He is Kog, he is eternal, chaos and fire without end

A lightning-loud crack tore the air, and Treaman saw a bright sparking welt appear across the demon's ribs. Before he could think, there was another, and he saw the end of the whip this time.

Bildon, standing atop a cypress stump, was wielding the ego-lash upon the lord of chaos.

Slowly the monster turned, even such an inhuman face plainly showing incredulity as Bildon continued plying the whip. With no respect whatsoever, he put a stripe across one knee, then another under the demon's maw. Treaman saw Bildon's hand flash quickly, and remembered his antic, self-pleased grin the rest of his days.

"Get moving, all of you, I can take—"

Kog caught the next strike in an almost human hand and held it sparking and popping while a quiver of pain worked its way up that arm. Treaman stood helpless to look away; the demon wanted to feel the pain of the ego-lash, it amused him to be angry and hurt. From his open maw came a roar deep as a quake, rising and growing until a column of pure flame shot from his mouth and engulfed the halfling completely. The spot where he stood held fire for several seconds. The end of the lash dropped limp to the ground and burned to dust.

Treaman fell to his knees, his mind filled with Hallah's fear and his mouth screaming the loss of his friend. The flame disappeared, and a small suit of charred, fire-proof armor dropped to stand on its shortened legs, as fountains of pure ash dribbled from the arms and neck.

Flame washed freely back and forth around the land, as waves of water in a child's tub. Everyone was hit, and the heat finally moved Treaman back into himself.

"Hallah, get out of here, fly, flee, now!" He staggered back to his feet, sobbing and choking, and ran to Linya and Braja. The tent bag was on the Nubian's back. Treaman did not know if he intended to protect him, or flee further, or rip the Sword from its hiding place and offer it on his knees. For now, running was all.

The helldogs were all close, none of them had a collar.

Kog was still shouting his rage, gazing at his scars either unable or unwilling to heal them.

"All of them, my pets. Rend them slowly, and bring the metal bits to me."

The defile cracked wider and deepened, emanating a glow from far below the world of Hope. Helldogs herded them all back toward it.

Mhoral had long since stopped singing, only gasping half words like the others. Treaman could not feel Hallah's weight on his shoulders anymore, and felt a little glad.

"Imposter!"

Through the burning trees came striding Kog, himself, angry, unwounded, and glaring with two eyes at his twin.

Bildon's murderer stared at the newcomer, laughed horribly and spread wide his many arms.

"My son! What worse time—"

"Liar! You use my power and now I have caught you. Die, weakling!"

Rushing in through a holocaust of flame, Kog slammed into his twin with a concussion that knocked everyone down. The sight of so much hot flesh, the roiling, generating limbs, the savage bites large enough to tear through a stag, wounds ripped open and healing. One mouth, stuffed full of its own torn-off limbs, could no longer bite its foe; the creature simply created a second face and chewed away half a neck in retribution. The pair fought to consume each other's mass first, the flames and explosions around them merely the cast-off of their glee and rage.

Even the helldogs cowered before such might, unsure which was their true master anymore. Treaman crouched there waiting to die, unable to move his mind's eye one step from the sight of his incinerated companion.

But Linya lay on the ground, bleeding from eyes held open by shock.

Hallah circled above, and lived and cried. And needed him.

They all needed him. Treaman staggered up, helped Braja, helped Linya. Saw the others. Limped away from the defile, slunk past the helldogs, moved and kept moving. Perhaps in a hundred steps, there would be a torn hill, some fallen trees. They could hide. He could stop.

Long before then, another concussion, and the land behind them went perfectly flat, a table of grey dust and stone. Demons, dogs, defile all erased, their fight not over but no longer here. All around them the pine barrens raged in flame. No river, no city, no promise to hold. Treaman hugged his middle and sank to the ground, allowed at last to weep.

Excerpt from the Kingdom Chronicle, 1995 ADR

Thus all in the kingdom of Shilar, formerly plunged in grief at the loss of their king in the first week of Raccoon, were raised again to Hope in the next week, by the recovery of their prince, alive and well and living among the Bordbeyonds. Here was surely where the fortunes of our ignorant lands turned again towards the light, though at first it seemed an evil omen.

By all reports the Baron Hirion, who took command of the search for his prince, was minded to make war upon our eastern neighbors, convinced as he was of their complicity in a kidnapping. Rumors of all flavors had run rife in Shilar since the loss of King Genel, and the good Baron was minded how the Bordbeyonds could make themselves invisible at will.

Prince Gareth, when found, hastened to apprise him of his error, and with tears did most openly and humbly beg his pardon to be the cause of his distress. Then Prince Gareth withdrew to his tent awhile, and returned with solemn face. All admired his demeanor at such tragic news—for the loss of a father is grievous indeed to any who have suffered it. The Baron summoned retainers to present the new king with his vestments and the sacred Talking Stick, yet the prince would not take it in his hands, crying "I shall be no king here east of the river". Nor would he accept the fealty of any knight present, despite their eagerness to be first among his vassals. But he did cause to meet the highest ranking lords and the chieftain of the Bordbeyonds, and bid them grip arms as allies. This they all did, even the Baron Hirion at his lord's explicit bidding.

They processed west at once, preceded by fast riders to carry the joyous news sooner to Shilar and accompanied by a great host of the Plainsmen. At the ford above Fort Hirion the prince beheld a wonder, for lo! The Baron had devised that a narrow bridge two planks wide be thrown across the River Running. With trunks of great trees driven into the river floor, and bindings of rope and wooden pegs set securely, then were twin planks laid into notch cuts across the top of each trunk. In this way his horsemen were able to cross into the Plains without need for a long detour or to wait the pleasure of the season; then too their retreat were more secure should occasion warrant. At this sign the Bordbeyonds were much consternated, whereat they anticipated the ease with which the knights of Shilar might return and do them harm.

In that place, known thereafter as the Accords of Grass just east of the bridge, Gareth did call for a formal council between the peoples. It was here, as night fell, that the prince did first see the red star visible to so many of the Bordbeyonds. He was much moved at the vision, and did kneel to pray, and at once it is said he prophesied.

"Look not to a point of blood, but for a crimson path
No crown may lead wanderers to walls
When heat moves north in winter"

Then did Gareth order Shilar's knights to follow him across the bridge. With him came his squire Hobsel Parry, while a young Shilarian lady, his sister Hillel whom they had come to find, abided still with the Bordbeyonds and their chieftain's daughter, for her desire to hear more of settled custom, and for the great love they had of each other.

When Gareth and his knights reached the western bank of the Running, there they entreated him most sincerely to let them do fealty. And retainers did bring the scepter of his forefathers, which still he would not take. But to those who knelt before him Gareth did clasp their hands, and of each man he learned his name and family, thanking them for their devotion and warning that soon their loyalty would be tested. And unto the Baron Hirion Gareth gave order that the bridge thus begun should be widened and strengthened, in all ways made permanent even unto the use of stone.

"Sooth milord, that we may better strike our enemies?" he asked with eager tone.

"Certes, my good Baron," Gareth replied, "Our enemies will have cause to regret your good work. Not eastward, for Despair that way lies only beyond the Swords of Stone and such a venture is not for a callow, hasty crownless boy."

The Baron was mazed and dismayed at such words, but the prince seemed again in the grip of prophesy, as indeed men do say of him he has the gift.

Gareth continued, saying "Such a quest lies under the brow of a greater king than I, though mayhap I shall follow him when the time comes. First, we must fight to see him crowned. And for that battle, we shall need help of our allies who ride the Plains. See to it that the building is well done, then, and soon, so that we may the quicker move as the day is right."

And all amazed and wondering, yet the Baron hastened to do his lord's bidding.

⊕ ⊕ ⊕

Tak ting-tak, tak ting-tak, a measured, relentless pace clicking closer and hinting at doom. Strangers always attracted attention here in the remote northern reaches of Shilar, and in winter they were as rare as warm days. Several dozen people had gathered between their cottages before they could even be certain whether it was man or woman who approached along the south road.

No one in the village of Barden had ever seen the Man in Grey before, but that made them only more certain what to do. The unvarying cadence off the hard-packed road rang with hostility—the figure bore a staff and traveling cloak, with a wide-brimmed hat above and high-topped boots below. And the color of him, top to bottom, from his long straight hair to his cold-smoldering eyes, was a symphony of stone.

Down the length of the single street, women called to their children, and men went within to return with a hoe, or a hayfork, or just a stick. Some even shushed their dogs, as the grey traveler approached, and the ring of his hard soles and staff on the frosty road could be clearly heard.

If the stranger saw the signs of his cold welcome on this cold day, he showed no reaction to it. Straight down the middle of the road he paced, neither slowing nor turning until he came level with the first house. He stopped then, and surveyed the entire scene with dark silver orbs that held no hint of his intent. No one spoke, to welcome or warn, yet with this the Man in Grey seemed perfectly at home. The world was awash in silence, and while the villagers felt they were drowning, the stranger seemed to bathe.

A silence stretched so long, the catastrophe when it struck took them by surprise. The girl and her brother playing tag out back did not notice the quiet until they came careening around the corner, still twenty feet from where the stranger stood. The girl, perhaps six, saw the crowd and tried to stop, but her brother was intent on making the tag and ended up bumping her forward to stumble onto the road, falling before the stranger's boots. Her mother let out a strangled cry of fear, and the man of the house lurched forward, his face as grey as the stranger's shirt, but compelled to try.

Looking down, the Man in Grey contemplated the winded child beneath him and then bent low, shifting his iron-shod staff to the left hand while extending his right. Suddenly, his staff flared silver its entire length—the father stopped despite his intent, while the rest of the crowd surged in, spurred by a nameless hatred and fear of the unknown.

But there was no chance, for any of them. Long before they could get within reach, the Man in Grey had bent down—and gently raised the child up, as if she were made of silk. Standing with her arm in his gauntleted hand, the girl looked into the eyes of the Man in Grey at close range. He did not smile, and she did not scream, but tears began to roll down her cheeks all the same. When he let go and pointed back to her parents, she turned to walk slowly and only started to bawl, with relief, when her mother swept her up in arms. The grey stranger stood like a statue, heedless of the boiling suspicion that assailed him closely from three sides now.

"What do you want, stranger?" asked the father, his hands still clutching his rake as if already in combat.

"Is there a healer in this village?"

Whatever answer the crowd had expected, this was not among them, and no one said a word for a time. They simply kept staring, as if looking for one speck of his clothing, hair, or eyes that was not ash, mist, slate, or smoke. As he waited, the Man in Grey shifted his staff back to the right hand, and its silver sheen faded to iron as before. As if he had not asked once, he asked again.

"What is your disease, then, stranger?" asked a young man in the front. "You think our healer would help you?" The crowd murmured in assent to this, but those foremost took a step back to think he might be contagious.

The stranger gave no answer, but asked only, "Would you prefer that I search each house?"

If it had been quiet before, now it seemed even the breeze stopped. One of the tallest villagers, the smith, stood forward a half-pace. "Ya'll not come a step across my door, ya, with me two babes inside." He pointed with his hammer as he spoke, the nearest thing to a true weapon any of them was holding. The Man in Grey turned his head to look at him, and without a word, the smith dropped his arm. Finally seeming affected by events, the stranger put his free left hand up to his brow for the time it took to draw a long, heavy breath and let it out. Even his frosted spirit seemed to have a tincture of ash.

"I mean no harm to any Hopeful being, and would not trouble you folk as much as I evidently have already. If I could be told off the turns to your healer's abode, I have questions for her, or him."

At this, the adults looked about between themselves; a poll was taken with head-shakes and shrugs, and at last the young man, touching his belted hatchet, gestured down the road and to the right. "There's a hut beyond the oaks, with a holly bush in front."

"We'll be watchen," added the tall smith, "So mind yarself—no one wrongs er Gelia and gets away with ut."

Still not dignifying any threat with a response, the Man in Grey began again his measured tread directly along the line his unwilling guide had pointed. The crowd scurried back on both sides as if the game was Poison Pill; some made half-threatening gestures, but not before he had passed their line of sight. The stranger paced on and out of view within a minute; returning the village to order took the rest of the morning, and no one was quite at peace until the next day, when the smith came round to report that he had left before the dawn, headed north over the just-frozen stream and into the Snowdon Hills.

"Treaman? Treaman, which way?"

The Woodsman looked up and saw Linya's slender, delicate face drawn with worry, against the background of the same blasted, featureless terrain that always lay there. Perhaps they were all born here. Maybe those thoughts of a family, and a land of snow in the north were just tales he told to distract himself. It could not possibly matter, which way. All ways were the same here. Loss was the only destination.

Still. Some of those faded tales told of a man with a job, he guided the others. Treaman somewhat recalled them, knew that Linya, at least, believed he had been that man once. She must be wrong, but she was pretty and kind, he still knew that much.

He roused himself to look around him. The sun meant nothing, of course, the terrain meant nothing. No mountain anywhere in front of him, too much trouble to look behind. Taste of jerky in his mouth, then likely it was later in the day, usually fruit for breakfast.

The man in the tales, what did he do? Checked the wind, perhaps; or was it running water? None of it mattered, there was only one place to go, but if he acted, pretended to try, Linya would no longer have to ask. And she might feel better for a while.

Hallah spoke to him, and he nearly awoke.

{*"Hallah hungry."*}

Fingering up the riddy was automatic, required no thought and little memory. But the sight of the friend on his shoulder, the connection he felt to her, was a bitter tonic and his tears began again. He could measure his loss by the remainder in these twin gem-orbs.

{*"Treeeman find caves of Men again. Treeeman can do anything."*}

He scratched the side of her head, to get those eyes to close in pleasure and cut off the burden of her trust. One more to fool, then. He looked around vaguely at the other beings standing behind him, and added just "group" to his burden of need.

He did not count them, he could not bear to.

Just for something to do, he set off in the lead. The cold was nothing, the wind was nothing, and the direction was the same. In the recesses of his instinct, he judged it was a slow pace, trudging by comparison to the man in the tales. Yet what was the hurry, with his destination? Only scraps of the conversation behind him drifted in.

"Lost" "-four days" "food, what do we" "Sun keeps shifting"

He felt so very tired, it was too hard to overhear the full sentences. In the tales, he knew the guide-man he pretended to be would have been stung, taken insult. Because he would be proud of something, his skill, this burden of need from trusted comrades would move him to his best effort. But Treaman was tired, even the charade of walking in front was nearly too hard. Dimly he sensed darkness coming on; when he saw the red star, he stopped. He may have slept. If so, then the memory he had, of needing to awaken in the morning, was a real one. He knew he had to get up the next day, to feed Hallah. Otherwise…

That morning he got up, and fed Hallah, and waited for Linya to ask him the way. Had she asked him yet, today? He wasn't sure. Sometimes Bildon would—

Treaman fell to his knees, the pain in his gut was too sharp. Once more he had arrived, at Loss. As he wept again, in familiar salt-tracks already well marked on his face, a new thought came to him, randomly as they did now. Instead of rejecting it with shock, or feeling disgust at its inappropriate nature, he let the thought in and wander lonely around his mind. He knew that like the others it would get bored and wander out again.

His thought was this. In the tales, the guide-man would pray in times of doubt. Just that, since he was on his knees already. The thought was that he could carry the pretense this little bit further. He could clasp his hands in prayer. For the others, because Linya especially was a good person and she too had been crying.

So. On knees, hands clasped, what else he wondered. Perhaps eyes closed would be better: tears, he thought, were not a hindrance in this case. Of course, for real prayers he needed to have desires, dreams. But the others could not see those, it was not needful. Just being nice to them, because they are good people. They do not… not deserve to wander lost, that was the sense of it Treaman remembered.

Before he realized it, he was actively wishing, that his friends, these other persons in the tale he recalled, were not lost, were instead safe. He could see them at an inn, or at least in a forest with the tent (there was a sword in the tent bag); he could dimly make out a campfire too, and food, a fresh meal made from the gathering of the guide-man in the story. It was all dim and misty in mind's-eye, for between Treaman and this happy thought lay a black curtain of subtraction. When he saw the group, he could not avoid counting them.

Yet it was a happy thought, over there beyond the dark curtain. He could hear the sounds of chatter, a deep voice learning a new word, someone giving orders. Laughter. He could see the flicker of firelight, and he could smell…

Treaman opened his eyes at the smell. It wasn't wood burning, or meat, or the latrine or sweat or fresh blood. It was a smell Treaman knew he could never have imagined. He only smelled it once before, back in the tales, and years ago.

He stood and faced due east.

"Treaman?" Linya asked again. "What is it?"

He turned to look at her, to see all of them. It meant counting, he could not avoid that. But he was too shocked by the smell to sidestep the pain.

"Cut grass."

"What?" That was a male voice, Mhoral's.

Treaman pointed east. "Do you remember the noble's estate, in Shilar, just after we… we first met. We slept under the trees there. In the morning, his servants, he liked his grounds kept neat. Like the Elves sometimes do."

They gawked at him as if he spoke in Sorceror's Tongue. Treaman heard someone laughing, dry and dusty, and suspected the poor fellow might be himself.

"Someone has cut the grass, over there."

The tall one stepped in—the leader from the tales, Haltar—and looked down on him with concern. And that was new, Treaman had never seen this before.

"That nobleman, he had his servants bring us food in the morning. Pewter plates, and real butter, and a silver knife to spread it with. For vagrants; they told us to move on after we ate."

Treaman shrugged. The tall one continued.

"You're telling us there's an estate over there, in the Percentalion, where the wealth and safety is so great they cut their grass for looks?"

"Could be herds," Mhoral said. "I don't smell anything."

Haltar looked at the ground, and shrugged, and nodded his head the way Treaman was pointing. They set off at no particular pace. Treaman took the lead, realizing he had to. No one else sensed the freshness, the newness in winter that he did. There stole over him a tiny, creeping tingle. All other directions, now, still led to loss. But this way…

The land very gradually rose as they walked over the next half-hour. When he felt a tremor in his gut, he stopped merely from habit. No one spoke. The sun suddenly shifted, just a point, but Treaman corrected at once and the group behind him hissed with whispers. The Woodsman was guiding them again.

A few tufts of scraggly grass were nothing unusual, though with winter they should have been thin and brown. As Treaman approached the top of the gentle rise, the clumps thickened and became greener, still normal length but very much like the start of somewhere. He assigned no belief to this, after all he had not tried, forgotten how to. But the smell of cut grass was alloyed now with scents much more floral, and a breeze nearly warm on his face.

"I can smell it now," Mhoral said, sounding excited. Where the party walked, the air still held flurries of snow, dim grey and hard flakes that fell to earth in a hurry and felt like hail on the hand. But to the east, a warmer breeze carried something so fresh it touched Treaman with fear. How dare he breathe this air.

He stopped, and the group with him despite their eagerness. The stillness normally would have jangled Treaman's inner sense in a familiar way. But this flavor of alone drew him, he suddenly hungered for it. There was something far away, over this rise and hiding from him, and the presence of the group was sure to spook it.

He had no idea what lay ahead. But Treaman knew who he was once more, the tales came back to him and settled in their place. Bildon was dead, that would never change—a spurt of tears overtook him to recall it—but there was more. There was something else besides the destination of loss.

He turned back to face the group, swallowing hard as he looked them all in the eyes once each. Counting them. He took a deep breath to speak in the place where he would have seen his friend.

"I need to go on alone."

Everyone except Braja said "No" at the same time.

Haltar carried on. "We can't risk you, Treaman."

The lies began.

"I'll be fine. I'll only explore a bit."

"You won't," Mhoral insisted immediately. "Look, Treaman, you haven't been yourself. This is the longest conversation you've held in a week. I know…" he stopped, then stepped up and raised his visor. "Bildon is gone, and I know it hurts. Hurts you."

The ante rose, another lie into the pot.

"I'm alright. You're right, Mhoral, but I'm not insane, I need to go ahead alone. Just a few moments."

"Let's have a look for ourselves," Haltar said, in the voice he used for final decisions.

"No!" Treaman flinched from the outright defiance, but this was too important. "I mean, we can't risk it, trust me."

Haltar stared down on him for what seemed an hour.

"Packs down everyone. We shall crawl to the top of the rise, and the Woodsman shall lead us by a length."

Treaman pictured it and the pain almost made him cry out, but he had no answer. Down with the packs, and he snuck to his position more than two lengths ahead, motioning for silence several times as they processed.

"This is absurd." Mhoral muttered, and Treaman almost kicked him in fear. The risk, he could feel the risk was too great.

He saw the tops of trees beyond the crest and dropped to a snake-crawl, motioning for the others to do so as well. Very slowly the vale beyond came in view, and it was several minutes before Treaman realized the party had come up.

Noise was not a danger here. None of them could have spoken for their lives.

In the glade, the sun shone down as if there was a paler copy being used out in the rest of the world. Beginning with the first downturn of the land beyond the crest, within arm's reach if one dared, the grass was thick and closely cropped within two inches of the turf. Dotting the glade were short, solitary trees with dark green upturned leaves more than the length of a man clustered together at the top. Flowers in bloom gathered by bunches whose color, height and shape suggested both wildness and arrangement at the same time. Fluttering between bole and bush were creatures too large to be songbirds, too quick to be insects, and too colorful to be believed.

Treaman had a creeping sense again, that his hero Helmon had walked here, centuries ago. And perhaps no one since.

A tap on his boot; he turned his head to see the others crawling slowly away, and reluctantly followed. Back at their packs, the group stayed seated. No one spoke above a whisper.

"It's… incredible." Linya.

"I felt, it's dangerous in there." Mhoral. "What if Treaman goes in, and then it just, disappears. Like the fortress."

"I must go alone. You have to let me."

Haltar looked thoughtful for a silent space. He spoke with his gaze fully on the Woodsman, as if daring him to raise the final bet.

"We shall tie a rope to our good Woodsman here. If he tugs it hard twice, or if it goes slack, we shall enter the glade. At all events, he may have one hour if things remain quiet."

Treaman's heart fell at the thought of the rope, but he could devise no alternative. It was only one more lie, so he nodded. As the group scrabbled for every length of rope and cord they had, a thought came to him. Without asking, Treaman opened the tent bag and pulled out the sheathed Sword of Air.

Mhoral froze like a statue at the sight, but no one said a word. Linya came to him and placed both hands on his shoulders, searching his eyes with fear in her own.

"You must be careful, Treaman. We can't, we mustn't lose you too."

Treaman smiled at her, knowing as he did that he would never be safer than in that glade alone. Or else, that if he did die, there was no better place for him to meet his end. She took his grin as reassurance and let him go. Braja and Mhoral held the nether end of the knotted rope-chain, and Treaman turned with a shiver of indrawn breath to crest the rise and enter the glade.

As soon as his steps took him below the horizon-line, Treaman felt a deep quiet descend all around him. He knew the group back there was talking, heard nothing. Mhoral's suggestion about the disappearing keep seemed weirdly right, but of no concern. For the Woodsman, being here was all.

He stepped smoothly and quickly to the nearest tree, to make Mhoral loosen his hold on the rope. Slinging the Sword of Air over his back, Treaman unknotted the line and transferred it to the smooth, birchlike trunk. Free of his lies to other humans, he stepped off into the perfumed air and began to explore.

The breeze was much warmer here, sheltered from the biting chaos of winter outside. Treaman estimated the glade was less than a league across; the trees that predominated the area were bound up like closed roses and not much above fifteen feet high, so the sight between and over them was excellent. He walked toe-first though nothing appeared to threaten him. Pausing to look at a brilliant stand of flowers, the Woodsman marveled as the blooms continually opened out, layers of complimentary shades a dozen deep. He came back to himself with a small start, and feared that an hour had passed while he stared. He resumed moving downhill, drawn by a need to reach the center, though what he might do there was unknown to him.

Hallah awoke and looked around with an air of satisfaction. She did not demand to eat, did not question or send any thought-pictures to him, but seemed quite interested in all the sights. The flying things were more like butterflies than any creature Treaman had seen, yet the size of jays and using three of every color in the rainbow apiece. Evidently his companion felt no desire to hunt them, as she had with every other flying thing she saw. Thinking on this, Treaman realized he would probably be unable to draw in anger himself. Yet he had brought the weapon of the Tridium with him: it still felt right.

Near the center of the glade ran a murmuring stream, where Treaman and Hallah both refreshed themselves. The water was as cold as the winter beyond the crest; at its first touch he cried softly and fully, finally tapping off some of his grief. The tight gut knot started to unclench at last, releasing deeper breaths and sobs, allowing a more honest sorrow. From his knees, Treaman ran both hands through the thick cropped grass in amazement. Something regularly cut this turf yet he had seen no tracks, no spoor, and no boot-prints of humankind. The cold water continued to move down his chest and into his stomach, a drink as filling as food, and his mind at last moved back, beyond the group and the pain of counting them, to face again the fire and the death of his companion.

With tears still flowing, Treaman fell back to sit and into a kind of sleep. He saw again the fight—no, the massacre, the casual expression of such power as there could be no thought of resisting. He saw the demon, heard the awful maw forming words, felt the heat and the glowing eyes of the flesh-eating hounds. And as if it happened again very slowly, he counted the welts appearing on the leviathan's body, the look of incredulity, and his reckless friend wielding the lash. Treaman cried out in his trance, no longer keeping the grief to himself, his seated frame shaking hard enough to slough off the useless, hope-less feelings he had dragged with him since.

He saw the demon start to roar, the fires of hell erupting from his mouth and again felt the terror of following the flame to where his friend stood unburned for one final second. Treaman remembered Bildon shouting, telling them to go, that he would handle things, as he raised his whip-hand for a futile strike. The scene unrolled with awful slowness. He spotted now what he had not marked before; Bildon signaling in the hand-cant that only one other person present could understand.

:: Honor. Farewell/ see you ::

In those two finger-flashes was Treaman's release. All the risks Bildon ever took, his cocky attitude and constant jokes; no one could believe he had any idea, really, what danger was. But the fingers told all. The Stealthic had known, probably had always known his risk, the cost of living as he did. He had not hesitated to offer his life, and had let Treaman know that death was no surprise.

The Woodsman was still deprived of his best friend, the death grew no smaller. But as he breathed deep and felt his crying stop, Treaman thought that perhaps tomorrow, his grief would at least begin to age, by one day.

Vaguely, his instinct-voice noted that despite the passing of time the sun had not moved. Treaman awoke from a thing like a nap, and could not tell if it was the first time he'd had such a thought. But now, he could hear another noise beyond the murmur of the stream. Thick, slow rustling, and the sound of grass being snapped off, and eaten.

Across the stream before him, perhaps thirty steps away, one of the trees was opening. He could not move from the turf, and watched as the wide green leaves turned out to the sunlight. In the middle, the trunk continued bereft of branches, bright and shiny like the inner fronds and nearly as thick as that below. The tip-top bulbed out again, and before the leaves were fully open the upper trunk began to sway and arch towards the ground. Two tiny branches worked free at the very end below the bulb, bracing the stem as it descended into the turf. A small, inoffensive maw protruded and the tree returned to grazing the rich grass.

The sound came from nearer him.

Treaman turned slowly and saw not two feet away a grazing tree-mouth. The silence was made clear by how far the munching carried. Each tree stood well-spaced to cover a similar patch of turf, and now the flying things fluttered and perched near the trunk-necks, where the collar of thick fronds held nests of dried grass and twigs.

Treaman reached one tingling hand out to the grazing tree's head. It quivered at his touch but continued eating, eyeless and earless and full of life. Treaman felt a charge surging through him, these unknown creatures awoke his wonder. In a flash he thought of the death-copse, with its lizard-things and reaver birds, the grass that clung and murdered the unwary. How could the same world hold both places?

Another timeless nap, or trance; Treaman saw the glade with all its wonder, yet sensed it was merely part of a Hope-ful land on all sides. The world was newer, even breathing this air made him feel he could do miracles.

A tall, sun-bronzed scout wearing only cloth about his middle strode through, petting the trees as they grazed and speaking to the bird-flies when they landed on his shoulder. The sound of hoofbeats caused every tree to clap shut, all other life to flee. A dismounted warrior in full armor and helm entered the glade from the north, with the symbol of the sun and fist on his tunic. The warrior saluted and spoke with the outdoorsman in earnest tones. Treaman beheld Areghel, first king of the Percentalion and Helmon, the hero of the Woodsmen.

Areghel made straight-line gestures from north to south, off to the horizon on both sides of them. Helmon's face fell, and he spoke earnestly pointing around them to draw his peer's attention. The king looked at small closed trees, seeing nothing, hearing nothing. The debate was short; Helmon bowed, acquiescing in the project of this land's lord. Areghel drew a sword with a blade like the noonday sun and faced north with it held before him, concentrating and shouting aloud in a language Treaman could not speak. Helmon turned to go, but stopped a moment to stare down directly at Treaman where he will sit, centuries later; his look carried much consequence. Certainly sadness. Perhaps even trust.

Areghel, left alone in the glade, shouted again, and turned to face south, directly at Treaman with the Sword of Air held before him. Its blinding flare struck like lightning. Treaman understood, the ways were made straight…

He awoke again. Surely it had been a day? He felt somewhat hungry, but refreshed and clear for the first time since… The trees were all still grazing, the color-flashes now everywhere like swirling petals in a light breeze. The weight of the Sword in its scabbard lay across his back like the coming blow of a lash he knew he must suffer.

Kneeling, Treaman prayed to Helmon.

Must I do this thing? Am I able?

There was no rumble of thunder, nothing parted or quaked or changed. Long minutes later, the breeze seemed to whisper back.

No one must. But only you are able.

He opened his eyes and looked around him, taking in the wonder of the kingdom's earliest days with a heavy heart. Were there any more of these in the world? Perhaps the choice was only to have both kinds of copse, or neither. But Treaman's hero obeyed the king. If the curse was lifted, the search for this glade could resume one day. If not, Bildon would have died for nothing.

Treaman petted the tree-mouth again, whispering goodbye, and slung down the Sword of Air. Still on his knees, he braced himself and took a deep breath. Uttering a loud cry spiced with sobs, he drew the Sword of Air and held it out before him directly to the north.

The jarring jangle of the unsheathed weapon threatened to shake his shoulders loose from their sockets. Treaman saw only lightning, faced north, shouted louder and louder, hung on.

Something like a warm beak nudged his forehead every few seconds, moving his head a little on the stone, waking him. Hallah's eyes at this distance seemed like small points of lightning in the cold winter sunlight.

"Treaman! Treaman, where are you?"

"There! He's down, over there!"

Treaman sat up on the hard ground, saw no stream, no thick turf around him. The Sword of Air was back in its sheath and lying on stone before his knees. Perhaps thirty feet away was a slightly pocked spot of ground where a small tree might have rested in ages past. More likely his mind was playing tricks.

The party came pounding up to him, panting and gasping beyond speech. Mhoral absurdly clutched one end of a rope. But with the glade gone, and the sun still unmoved, no one had a word to say. Treaman could not believe his eyes, even with the hard stone beneath his hands.

The straight way starting from his knees was eight feet wide and shot directly north, pointing back to Trainertown.

⊕⊕⊕

Nothing lives on the Plains of Ranebruh, men say. The rock-strewn waste beyond the Snowdon Hills, just below the northern tundra of the Montori-riders, holds leagues of thin grass clumps, eternally-dying, lightly dusted with blowing snow full nine months of the year. If life means comfort, warmth, a chance to grow, or any other kind of Hope, then indeed the plains are lifeless. But it would be false to say that nothing ever moves.

A solitary hawk circling high overhead scans down, hunting for one of the few remaining coneys the season may have left him. These scrawny nibblers, whom rustic people called the forlorn hare, can manage survival on the remote plain during summer, but by this month, most have moved to take their chances with the wolves of the wood-covered Snowdon Hills to the south and west. The raptor glides and scans and on occasion screams his disappointment. He sees, but cannot understand, the larger pattern below him, leagues across and written in the scattered stones. He marks, but does not mind, one larger, grass-free stone sitting hunched below him in the eaves of the wood. The hawk simply reads food/no-food, and flies on. As the sun sets, he circles one last time and heads for the higher trees of Snowdon, hungry but unruffled. When that larger rock stands up and begins to hike due east below, the hawk marks it, but still it is no-food, so there an end.

The Man in Grey strikes out into the Plains of Ranebruh in search of a legend of horror. If anything lives near the Tombs Thanazun in defiance of that legend, there is no sign; as night falls it becomes even harder to spot this intruder. The seeker takes a straight course, and in less than an hour is at the vista of stones, forced to slow and seek footing among the scattered knee-high rubble held captive by scrub-grasses. Eventually every step must be chosen with care; even where the grasses do not catch and clutch with their hardened, deadened strength, there is gravel out of sight beneath the powdered snow. Hiking a mountain slope would be faster. He churns on, head only occasionally glancing up and using his iron-shod cudgel as guide and crutch.

The moons rise and the landscape becomes easier, but no more pleasant, to see. In another hour he has managed to reach nearly twice as far as he had before sunset, but still the going is slow. His breath is visible and he hugs his free arm to his chest. Finally, he stops, looks about him, and sees a space large enough to curl up on the ground. Kneeling amid the stones, he rummages in his tunic and withdraws four small smooth pebbles. He turns one over in his hands, the symbol on either side visible by moonlight. After some hesitation, he thrusts them away, instead touches the silver symbol around his neck and closes his eyes for a time while still on his knees. Then he lays between the stones, with a flap of his cloak under his face and the broad-brimmed hat atop it, and for several hours more he is again a part of the landscape.

The second day draws old on the Plains of Ranebruh and the grey traveler is awake and moving, straight to the east through the endless scree. He pauses more and more frequently, it seems, to look around at the ground: he nudges a stone with his staff here and there, and once just leans on it as if in thought. His brow is furrowed as when a man thinks the view is familiar, that there is something about it he should recall. How would a grassy plain come to be strewn with rock? Is it imagination, or do many of them seem squared off at the corners, long ago? Did someone try to build here? But there are no foundations near these rocks,only earth.

He slogs ahead, tripping and turning over the bizarre terrain, until just as the sun is flirting with the Snowdon Hills at his back, the stony ground thins and stops within a single step. The man in grey is standing on clear terrain, flat, snowbound and grassy but completely rockless. He stops and turns back, looking left and right at what appears now to be a boundary-line, or an edge. Above him yesterday's hunting hawk screams in exasperation, but the man looks up with envy for the raptor's view.

The traveler scans back over the stony ground through which he's marched. His fingers tap, chin nods as he counts off hours and leagues. The eyes narrow as he realizes the sum. These stones strewn thick, then none, cannot be the work of nature. But to be the work of men, would be beyond thousands.

He hitches his belt and heads north along the line, hiking hard now to catch what daylight remains. In half a league, with twilight bearing down he stops where the stony ground cuts directly in front of him, stretching off to the east as if drawn with a builder's tool. Far above, the hawk issues a final cry before turning back to the hills, and its echo sounds like mockery.

The darkness falls, while the Man in Grey stands at the corner of stones. He sits on a larger, squarish rock for a time, then draws out something from his pack. In another moment, the Plains of Ranebruh suffer the first words spoken by a human voice in centuries: just a brief command in the Ancient tongue of power.

"*Luxar.*"

A small light grows on the end of the man's staff, the palest blue shot with silver. By its light, the man in grey holds up the book he has taken—black leather bound and square, not large but very, very old. He does not read it, instead contemplating the graven symbol on the front, the form of three bent legs joined at the center, the sign of Despair. Each lower leg follows the outline of the symbol itself, in a very gentle curve. The man in grey traces one such line, and then the straight upper-leg leading to its nexus. He stands, turns to look down the new angle of the stony ground, bearing directly east as he had been hiking, off into the darkness. He freezes, understanding what the hawk before him always scanned but never knew.

An enormous gust of breath chuffs raggedly from his throat with a cry; staring down, he regards the stones beneath his feet with a new look on his spell-lit visage—a gaze filled with dawning fear and revulsion. Steeling himself, he steps to the one he had sat upon, and with his free hand clears away the grass stranded on it. It is more than a foot across and strangely worn, but still suggesting a square. The top is uneven, with pocks and scars that could be weathering, or could be... the man searches the ground thereabouts, planting his staff so it stands upright and lights his terrain like a small lamp-post in the cities of men. He uncovers a half-dozen stones nearby, ripping away the clutching grasses with haste, pulling up candidates to examine, one so sharply it strikes him and sends a stream of blood down his cheek. Heedless, he seizes one at last that seems nearly as large as the first; hauling the prize up, he flips it, turns, puzzles over it, and then slowly sets it down atop the other. The fit is no longer exact, but it is clear. And on the side facing east down the straight path, there is faintly incised a number in the numerals of Despair. An enormous number.

He drops the marker, seizes his staff, and backs away from the grave marker as if the earth itself was poisonous. At the very edge of the rocks he staggers, stumbles and falls headlong onto the Plains. The Man in Grey sits up, and looks down both the endless angles of rocky land as if at two walls of an insuperable prison.

In a whisper, he utters just the second word spoken here since the ancient days. "*Kemetaria!*"

Then Judgement hears the howls of the ghouls. As he claps one hand to his bloody cheek, the light of his staff disappears, and all is covered in night.

Three long hours later, it is dark and the moons have set over the Plains of Ranebruh; nothing shows except the stars overhead. The orb Ma-Eldar, heavenly sign of immortality is highest now, shining over the end of the year and the changing of orders. Winter's onset is a roll call of survival. The slow frozen nights of Racoon are a time for beings to burrow to live. Behind that lonely silver planet near the eastern horizon rises the constellation Men call Sword in Crown, signaling justice and final decisions. But these stars, by themselves, do not speak.

In the mid-night without wind, the chill is almost strong enough to dampen sound on its own. Only the sharpest ear could detect, from less than ten meters away, the low sound of shivering pushing past clenched teeth.

Compared to that vestigial rustle of human breath, the sudden cry of the hunting ghouls breaks like a crash of cymbals, the grinding howl of a multi-headed behemoth. From the echo, they are a league distant yet, and perhaps not coming closer. In the blackness lying now upon the Plains, it is impossible to see. But from the place of shivering comes a quietly whispered word—the third spoken here since the Age of Balance—and now there is a patch of something less than black low to the ground, two inches across and lying on a leather palm. The stone with the sigil on its sides glows slightly, not enough to shed much light but still cupped protectively by the hand that holds it, turns it, sets it gently on the ground just west of a gravestone.

The pebble sits awhile on its own, glowing but not illuminating, and for a time the shivering continues, but ever quieter and then disappearing. Bare hands appear near the pebble from time to time, warming themselves by it and then withdrawing. Now there are other sounds, a tink of something metal and a light scraping, schunching. The edge of a tin cup packed with snow is set next to the stone; in several moments, despite the cold, the snow within has melted to a half-inch of water, which is then removed.

The ghouls howl again, in sequence after a leader it seems. All sound near the small stone stops, long after the echoes die away—closer, for a betting man, than last time. And every moment on the

Plains is a bet, at the highest stakes. Another cup melted, and then the stone's glow begins to fade. As the bare hands appear and rub themselves next to it one last time, the stone splits in four pieces and all illumination snuffs. The sounds of the owner of those hands and cup rising: footsteps now, in the blackness, and the sound of a staff rapping the ground ahead and fading to the east. A few more steps, perhaps the shadow of something cloaked seen against the lowest stars; then nothing, neither scrape nor shiver, remains. Until the ghouls howl again.

Renan never believed the Order of the Chosen Wanderers was ending, until the night he saw the red star moving toward him.

The bridge of light summoned a brother forth nearly every day, and sometimes twice. The hours merged into a haze of readiness, watchfulness, and worry. Sir Feil'n, an Elf from Mendel, volunteered for nightwatch as the rotation became more strained with injury and fatigue. Now the mortals could sleep, though no rest came to them. Renan rode out twice in less than a week; the first time Quester returned with a club-spike in his fetlock, and Renan was awash with anguish that he would need to sally out on foot before his stallion's wound could heal. At the next call, instead of just the chain coat and three or four front guards, he ordered his mount be girded in the full set of plate pieces, sacrificing speed and endurance for protection. As he noted in the days following, every brother did the same.

In fact, Renan became increasingly aware of his rising influence among the Order's ranks, despite lack of seniority. None had come to the bridge in the weeks since he joined; he was by all accounts the most junior servant of Dunedin. His family name counted for nothing, he knew; Renan had not given thought to the influence of the Altrindurs since entering the keep. But the others clearly began to defer to him as the days grew short and cold, and more so because

Niles was hardly ever seen after the tragic loss of his mount. This attention drove Renan more often away from public eyes to prayer, in the chapel or on watch. And his visions became more frequent, yet offered him no comfort, no answers; even the miracle of Farsight brought more burden.

The vale of Maladon had seen garruk bands brush by twice, unable to penetrate the main city walls but burning that secondary fort to the ground. Praise to Dunedin, the people had already ended their bizarre experiment with sundering men from women a month ago, in time to save what few late-harvest crops survived the dreadful insect plague. Massive flocks of reaver birds descended on Ashel to the far north. This was another threat a knight on horseback could do nothing to avert. Bands of ape-like raiders, snaky ebon monsters who melted the rock behind them and set wood aflame, and teetering-tall mantis bulls the height of a small tree roved freely in all parts of the kingdom. Renan had even seen a pack of helldogs from the days of legend, loping over the terrain and howling after some unseen prey.

All the knights agreed, sitting at meals and speaking new horrors with each sally, the animation of these creatures, their level of excitement was higher than ever before. Like wasps from a rustled hive, they spewed forth from dark corners of the chaos-land, looking for something and causing their depredations only in consequence of a summons beyond the Order's hearing. The brethren grasped arms more often, ate with fervor tasting nothing, and trudged off to another place as if at random.

In Renan's tower visions, the cloud to the southeast moved towards the center now, still obscuring his vision and arousing fear, though not triggering the bridge. In its wake, Hollinsfen lay destroyed. Sir Broders, summoned there to defeat an enormous wolf-thing with antlers and a split tongue, came back to report wrack and abandonment. Holes in the rampart walls, many houses collapsed, evidence of burning and the dimmed stain of blood everywhere. But no bodies, no sign of internment or burial. Across his crupper, Broders carried a small dog, shivering and nearly starved, with the sign of white scars across its muzzle that chilled Renan on first glance. Returning to the chronicles of the Order, he found reference to such wounds, even as Broders nursed the mongrel towards a semblance of health.

"A revenant, or perhaps a liche," he said as they watched the hound eating.

"I have heard no tale of these undead," Broders said gravely. "In the northern foefs of Shilar, some tell of the dread ghouls beyond the forest. They were tales to frighten children, the eaters of flesh and guardians of Despair's *kemetaria*."

"Perhaps I am a frightened child, then," Renan said with a smile. "For weapons forged without silversteel avail nothing against a revenant. It needs cold iron, or the miracle of destroying the undead."

"Are there any in the Order with such a weapon, or the skill?"

"Let us make quiet inquiry." Renan petted the grateful dog and left, his heart still heavy.

Two nights later, Renan felt the crisis descend. The bell of return sounded just past mid-night, and he awoke to pain as had become usual. Even in sleep, his muscles clenched with worry; he felt as tired as he had before lying down. Only the urgency of the bell pulled him groaning from his pallet. When a Wanderer returned victorious, there were shouts and cheers to accompany him, and resting brothers heard it like a lullaby. Tonight, the bell's echo died quietly replaced by no human noise. Renan ascended to the top chamber while the rest of the knights and squires waited the dread news in the bailey below.

Broders was on the vigil-watch and descended the bridge of light to retrieve the body of Sir Geharis and his mount. The two knights said much without words as he passed, and Renan remained to keep the vigil until the duty squire arrived for relief. Another funeral. Renan knelt to pray, hardly knowing whether to wish for the bridge of light to return at once. Unarmed and unhorsed as he was, a hopeless fight now might be better than to face again the loss of a brother so soon.

At first he saw nothing but the quiet night, the dark time after moon-set laced with the biting chill of Raccoon. The cold oozed through the aperture, brushing off the heat of the nearby brazier as it beat into Renan's bones with another reminder of things that could kill. As the slow minutes passed and no thoughts or comfort came to him, Renan realized he was too drawn with worry to concentrate. Something pressed against his spirit; he tried to clear his mind, and at once he noticed the red star.

For months, it had hung a hand's-breadth above the eastern horizon, a malignant promise of evil days. It was one of two secrets Renan kept from the order and never mentioned in conversation; since no one else spoke of it, he suspected the blood-light might be a mirage built of his fears. He had learned to ignore it; but now he felt his skin crawl as the distant crimson disk climbed the heavens westward, on a path to divide the sky. In awe and horror, he followed its slow movement, and it seemed to Renan from this great mountain height that the star did not circle his world, but grew ever so slightly larger, as if on a straight path toward earth. His mind's imagining at once suggested the impact would be here, directly upon the Chosen Wanderers and meting their destruction.

He addressed himself again to prayer, as if this would be his last.

Lords of Hope, send help in our hour of need.

The interval was but a moment, until Renan clearly heard the response in his mind.

More knights, perhaps for the Order?

Yes! Scarce able to believe he was not dreaming, Renan leaped without shame to affirm his plea.

Three, think you? Or mayhap six; no more or we would crowd the refectory.

In his mind Renan saw a strapping knight in plate mail, with the symbol of the Tower and Eye on his surcoat and shield. Dunedin, certainly, the founder of the Order of the Chosen Wanderers, known for courage, and loyalty. And also, Renan reflected, for a kind of fey humor as the children's tales went. The great knight's face held just a hint of a smile.

The form of the aid, great lord, he amended, *should be in your keeping.*

Indeed, as it has been, knight of Conar.

Renan was abashed though the reproof was mild. His sense of urgency and peril was not put off, however, so he kept trying.

Will you consent then to guide us, great Dunedin? Or to send just one who can lead?

A leader? Do you think, then, I have not done so?

But Niles is wounded in soul, milord. He is unhorsed—

Yes, a great loss to the Order. It should be redressed at once.

Redressed? You mean the leader will come soon?

That is up to the one I have chosen. I do not direct his steps.

Another long moment passed, and the voice in his mind added a parting shot that Renan sensed was also intended to amuse.

Indeed, I hardly speak to him.

The duty squire arrived as dawn lightened the east, to hold Sir Broder's place for the funeral ceremony. The red star leered at Renan as he rose to leave, seemingly tinting the chamber with a wounded hue for several steps down the ramp. Renan headed toward the chapel, dreading what he would find there.

It was worse than he imagined. As the brotherhood filed in to pay their last respects to Sir Gaheris, Niles was already standing next to Pallus with the squires. The face of his companion, formerly filled with goodwill and purpose, now showed a man adrift, sloshing between shame and loss. As Renan staggered to his accustomed place in the second row on the knight's side, he realized with a shock no one stood closer to the altar. When would Dunedin send the promised leader? Had he imagined the whole vision, in a bid to stave off the doom of his vocation?

There was a prolonged silence. No squire could officiate such a ceremony, and Niles had clearly abdicated his role in any event. Renan never considered taking his place, such an affront to the Order. Surely the main part of the proceedings consisted of prayer. Yet for Farivaine, and for all the others, one knight had stood forward to say a few words.

Prayer was becoming habitual with Renan, and he resorted to it now on reflex.

What can I do to honor the fallen, until the leader comes to us?

He heard no answer in words, but the image of a quiet, well-meant chuckle rose to his mind. Renan knew only that someone had to do something. His feet seemed to move of their own accord, as he rose from his knees, stepped around the altar and looked down on his slain comrade. He took in forty-odd expectant, anguished faces there in the total silence of the chapel.

Thinking on what speech could praise such sacrifice, on what others had said so much better than he could, Renan felt his spirits hit the bottom, the uttermost nadir next to which was only Despair. The words would not come. Renan did without them.

His arm moved as quickly as if it held a sword, and pulled back the samite covering Gaheris' torso. Before anyone could complete a gasp, he reached down with force, seized the collar and tore open the surplice and winding shroud, snapping the laces of his armor and scattering the pieces across the stone floor. In the growing light of dawn, the wounds on Gaheris were laid open to full view.

Renan pointed to them, one at a time, the old burgundy scars as well as those bright crimson with liquid stilled only in death. He became fierce inside, angry that a Chosen Wanderer would have insufficient eulogy. Renan's eyes fired around the chamber, taking in the others by turn, until they nodded their understanding.

Stepping back, Renan seized his chain shirt and began to disrobe from the waist up. Everyone followed suit, and the chapel rang with links and buckles dropping to the benches and floor. The room was a panoply of injuries: jagged scars across the shoulder, missing patches of hair, Pallus' arm-bone slightly mis-set, Niles still bandaged at the abdomen seeping brownish-red. But the faces: the order saw each other, and took full measure of what each brother had offered. Squires, too, bore proudly the faded rents and large blanched scabs of decades ago.

Everyone stood with white breaths rising into the chapel dawn light. The chuckle Renan had heard in his mind took hold of him, and soon the assemblage was smiling, like a pack of wolves.

Gently taking Gaheris by the shoulder, Renan rolled him up so that all could see his back, clear of any wound old or new. The inspiration for words finally came, a few at least that counted. Everyone knew them.

"Let my wounds show in front, may no enemy have the chance to strike from behind me."

Several members stepped forward then to help redress the fallen, and Renan gave the signal to open the ceiling. Dawn light through the windows did their work and Gaheris joined those members of the Order who had gone before in heaven.

In the courtyard as the others filed out, Renan accosted Niles, and both men stood holding their chest-armor in the frigid morning.

"Sir?" Niles stood patiently, his former mentor now showing obedience to a superior. Renan felt the injustice of it burn through the cold.

"Your duty."

"My duty, Sir Renan, is clear. I am needed in the stables."

Niles turned to go as Renan boiled. Something drew taut inside him and he walked briskly to catch up. They entered the stables together, and Renan pulled Niles away to one side. There was a fit on him, and he allowed it to take an unknown course.

They stopped abruptly before one stall, and everything became clear.

"Your duty, squire."

Niles stared in confusion. "Sir?"

"Since Farivaine's death, Harbinger has had no exercise, no attention."

"No," Niles breathed in horror, his face alive now but backing away. "You cannot—Sir, I beg you."

Renan pointed. "Your duty, squire. Keep this charger in repair and readiness. The Order demands every resource in its best condition."

Niles swallowed, then slowly approached the stallion who eyed him with suspicion. He slipped within the paddock, took a bucket of feed, and walked up on the mounting side, offering it before attempting to touch the proud warhorse. Harbinger nearly knocked the feed bucket from his hand, and the warrior laughed. The horse shied at the first touch, but after a moment would allow at least the brush, so long as Niles kept within side-sight. The stallion looked as if only the oats stood between its teeth and Niles' arm. Renan reflected that if the animal didn't burst with over-feeding, then perhaps, someday. Perhaps. He spun on his heel and returned to the refectory. Only after he arrived in the company of his fellow knights, did he realize he remained shirtless.

This ghoul is leader, not because of size or the length of his teeth or age (all of them are ageless, and none of them know it). He leads the pack because of his reach, and the hunger. His misshapen, garled upper limbs are even longer than his legs. So in any lethal contest over the decades, it was always his nails first, hooking in from the side of his foe, that gouged into the tendons of the upper thigh and lower back, snapping and incapacitating, then drawing his victim within reach for the single, mortal bite. The others have learned that he is not to be challenged, and followed him since the last such death-struggle over two hundred years ago. They ate a little then, but the taste of ghoul is against even their deep desire, and after they crunched the last bone of the loser, it failed to sate them. Perhaps, the leader apprehends in the back of his savage mind, perhaps the bald, hook-backed one will work himself up to a challenge in a decade or two. The leader neither fears the event nor plans for it. He vaguely... smells it, and for now as always the hunger rules. Always, always the hunger rules.

He squats atop a large stone, with the pack arrayed in quarreling disorder on all sides, and sniffs the night, trying to sense the living human nearby. The moons are set and light is no help to him in any event, as his orbs are desiccated and glassy with near-blindness. But the scent of blood is unmistakable—faint but sharp as the edge of ice: after the first powerful blast, it became muted but still leaks into the senses, taunting and ripe. Human blood, harbinger of fresh meat to be devoured and slain; the ghouls have been without prospect on the Plains for centuries, and their deathless hunger has held them just barely alive and not nearly sane throughout all those decades. All of them are insane but none know it. They know only the hunger, and it draws them now.

He howls, and lurches off in the direction of the scent. The human is still alive, and unbelievably, he approaches as if offering his meat to their hunger. Deep inside, the leader knows, every last organ and scrap of that flesh would not fill him, even if he could defeat his entire pack and have the mortal all to his own. The hunger cannot be defeated; but it drives him, and the thought of tasting again, even if it brings a moment's respite from the madness, this is worth any risk.

He sees the shape of the intruder now, and his instincts tell him more than his mind can grasp. The flutter of cloth behind the man, the smell of animal skins on his chest and hands: the ghoul slows his loping approach and feels at his own right-waist, where the knot of rope still protrudes from his skin. Long ago, a rope belt, and a pair of breeks it had held up; now the latter is worn away and his skin has grown over the former, still it rustles beneath his leathery flesh and rubs near his aching, empty belly. The man stumbles and slows—he hears, but cannot well see the pack of doom coming on him. He bears a bar of wood, and this troubles the leader as well as his fellows; the wood, shaped like a column, it once... meant something, something that equaled terror and obedience and not eating.

The hunger rises at the thought, and the ghoul's vision turns red. In the darkness he can see the man's face now. Everything about him—the misty breath, which means warm lungs and tender chest meat, the clear, glaring eyes, not seeing but wet with juice and the tang of salt, the mud-crusted cheek where blood still oozes like a small alarm bell for the nose—everything bespeaks a creature alive, a warm bag of flesh to be eaten before slain. Unwonted, the ghoul stops in his tracks and remembers...

...a dying night, a field of erect gravestones reaching almost to the Inner Band, where the Masters addressed the remaining unburied followers. Looming on all sides of the mausoleum that served as the only entrance to Thanazun, the Makine grunted and shivered with iron life and choking smoke. The leader of the Masters spoke from the door of the tomb, and words the ghoul could never understand today make their meaning plain on his memory. The City Below was at last complete, and the Deserving were taking their place. Those left above ground, the hundreds of tired, frightened peasants who had hoped to earn a humble seat in the chambers beneath the earth, where they could grovel and serve and breathe... they heard their doom pronounced. Their place was here, the final surface-graves closest to the doors, not to be filled with the slain Enemy as promised, but instead

by the weakest of loyal Despair. Screams of fear and protest, and the booming voice of the Master, calling out the Mage Command to Stay them. Their bodies spell-stopped, the mouths of the chosen were free to scream, to beg, to gag as the great Makine seized them, cored the earth, and buried them head-down and alive. He recalled with lustful fondness one man, whose calf was close enough as he kicked and squirmed and the earth-moving Makine filled in his grave. One huge, blissful bite, full of flesh and tendon and blood, and then the rock-setting Makine smashed down his marker, tamping the last foot of dirt onto the victim who by then had earth in his throat. One huge, inadequate bite, tinged with screaming nerve-juice trying to report agony and instead sluicing with a sweet tang around the edge of his tongue. And he saw the Master close the door to the sacred Tombs, while he and the pack howled their madness from beyond the Inner Band. That taste, one bite in the last twenty centuries... and the pack had never dared cross the Band since, though the Makine were now still and rusting, their final orders executed. Now, the chance for another bite...

The ghoul leader snaps back from his red reverie to the sounds of agony and howling, and the chant of power from the lips of the meat-man. The fourth utterance of words on the Plains, and the first the ghouls have heard since that night of feast, is a song with victory and death in it. The leader's eyes sting with a flash of blue fire in the night, and the closest ghoul—less enamored of memory, perhaps less sane than the leader—explodes with a charred chest and a broken limb, going down like a tombstone felled by a quake. A Master! The pack yowls in fear, cowers back and waits for a merciless doom to come for them—but no, his magic is the color of the Enemy, and his right arm bears a wound now, hacked by his fallen foe. Yet the ghouls move in only to gnaw the dying pack-mate—it is the law of hunger, and cannot be overruled—even the leader falls prey to it.

When he regains his limited control, spitting out foul shreds of damp artery and dry muscle from a former ally, he looks about and sees the meat-man is nowhere in sight. Howling in fury he falls upon his pack, swinging his terrible arms and wounding several of them; one backs too slowly and is disemboweled by his blow, which spawns another feeding-frenzy, but this time more quickly broken up. Pounding each of them by turns into submission, the ghoul leads them after the sharp scent of blood. East—the man has moved beyond them, past the larger stones, more intact and less weathered, closer to the forbidden Band. With a cry of aching emptiness, the leader scrambles after the bag of breathing flesh; the ward must be kept, the enemy eaten, the hunger served. The leader knows it not, but this is why he was created, crafted to survive and left on the surface these centuries ago.

They pursue with speed and soon the leader sees the cloth rustling ahead, no longer moving but awaiting him. This is more to his liking, and he ambles quickly in to swipe with his longer arm—and recoil, as the claws break on stone beneath the cloth. Ripping away the disguise of cloak-on-tombstone is enough to confuse, then enrage the ghouls for nearly a half-minute. There is fresh blood on the cloth! He eats a portion of the wool while he ignores his injured arm, then mounts the stone and sniffs. North now, he has turned...

A quarter of a furious hour later, the ghoul pack has been led to four smears of fresh blood on stone, howling with frustration and moving, unaware of their direction, in a lazy circle. Suddenly they come upon the body of their slain and torn pack-mates; already hard to recognize, none of them note that extra pieces have been hacked hastily free. But when the leader sniffs the air, the scents are suddenly too faint and confused to give him guidance. He screams with rage, and his pack imitates him, but there is no clear direction. Dawn is approaching—already their eyes begin to hurt, and their bodies shrink seeking instinctively for cover. The leader pummels them into continuing the hunt, and at last, he smells fresh foot-track: not as sweet as blood, but carrying a salty musk that promises treasure like a golden vein in rock. He is back to east, and has gained away from the hunt.

They howl and run and howl again, and soon by the stabbing light of dawn ahead they see the Inner Band. Three wide avenues of stone markers converge to a central plaza demarked only by a meter-wide circle of solid bronze set into the soil and incised with eroded symbols. It circumscribes a district nearly a half-league across, though no ghoul could comprehend that size, or even the shape. From the northeast and southeast, the other two broad paths of tombstones march to join with the circle, completing the colossal shape of nameless evil and built with the bodies of scores of thousands now buried and marked. Within the bronze border, the landscape is littered with iron frames and off-sized boxes the height of small buildings, remains of the mighty Makine the Masters built to shape the land and further their work. At the epicenter of the Band, just coming into view for normal eyes, is the low stone-mounded structure that forms the entrance to the Tombs. And the living man, their Enemy and meal, is already there.

The ghouls feel nothing so pale as a need for vengeance—the hunger beyond madness drives them, yet even the law of hunger cannot force their steps beyond the Inner Band. Helpless and writhing with the aching pain of satiation beyond reach, they watch and howl and scream as he calmly examines the portal, looking closely at the incised marks upon it as if there were a purpose to doing so, and finally gesturing with both arms. If the man speaks again, it is too far for the ghouls to hear—but the grinding of stone is loud enough to be dimly perceived, and the earth itself vibrates slightly. He is within; he descends the stair—he will meet the Master—the portal closes behind him.

And the ghouls, even as they shrink from the rising sun to shelter behind the stones, scream as one at the scent of meat cut off. They will cower in the shadows all day, unsleeping, insane, unfed, for whatever stretch of time exists between this moment and the next scent. Even their leader truly comprehends no thought beyond the slicing pain of his hunger denied, ever-growing but now seemingly doubled by his failure. He catches sight of the bald, hooked-backed one, squinting at him with pained, near-shut eyes, and again he scents the chance of another fight. But leadership, and life, and victory are all straws to be swept from sight compared to the hunger. The hunger ever-growing, ever-driving, and now denied.

12th Raccoon 1995 ADR

My Dearest Kia,

Snow! After three days I can hardly incorporate this wonder, and I hope you have the chance one day to see it. There is snow everywhere here in Shilar, coating the ground and painted atop every roof of this wonderful fortress-city. With hand on my heart, I swear to you, they must shovel it from the streets. Enormous piles of snow are gathered on corners, there immediately taken over by the children, who become Dwarves and tunnel out parapets, escape hatches, and storerooms for frozen projectiles in a war never won, with their temporary enemy across the alley. I have been struck off my feet laughing, and defended my honor in retaliation, with mixed success. What Hopelord could cast a spell so large, to enchant a nation with flakes outnumbering the grains of wheat in a harvest, bringing a chill that enlivens, a nuisance stuffed with joy? I have become thoughtful, lying in the snow—yes! Upon a bank of snow thicker than a mattress, it is beyond credit.

I write you from the capital Cil-Cilurion where I have been dragged next in my rounds of the kingdoms of Man. My apologies for the long delay in corresponding. No stop along the route from Conar was endowed with the wondrous gates I have been allowed to use for my messages (and once, one blessed day, to get married!). I spent a very pleasant evening in the tiny city of Trainertown. I gather it was formerly a trading post of some importance but now fallen into near-abandonment with the curse of the Percentalion to its south. Yet here is where the famous

Kingdom Chronicle is composed and copied, and by good fortune I met its author, Sage Valenthur. His young apprentice, Anteris, was truly sent by Hope when I felt low and lonely in your absence. So earnest, dedicated and above all young! I saw in his face the same studious purpose and lively mind that my dear friend Solemn Judgement had, but Anteris acts his age. He laughs, he becomes excited and gestures wildly, he is amazed by tales of the ancient days. Already he has some marvelous ideas about his course of study within the Guild, and I have encouraged him. How I wish that Solemn, who is close of an age with this lad, could find that same delight in books alone, and enjoy his well-earned accolades without rushing into ever-greater dangers. The last I heard, young Judgement was headed into the wildlands, in the dead of winter, to discover one last clue of hidden lore he claims will be of use for all the Children of Hope. Even without the cold I shiver for his sake.

Shilar is one of the ancient kingdoms established after the Second War of Liberation, and I hoped for a quick furlough to visit you. Yet even here I found, to my frustration, that the royal gates in the palace have been unused for so long that no one dares ask the rules of their function. Outrageous! Here a major center of Hope, nearly threescore thousand living in Cil-Cilurion alone, but they rely on horseback and boat to carry their messages! This letter, I am told, will reach you in roundabout a month, by which time I could hope (ever I hope!) my mission would be concluded. But I promised I would try not to fret you. The Heroes grant this reaches you sooner, but best of all that I arrive before it!

I entered a snow-capped land to see a nation in mourning at the loss of its king, and have stayed long enough to watch it burst into joy with the recovery of its prince. What a horrible shock, each cottage and inn our carriage passed was striped with white on top, but draped in black cloth over each window and door. I'm sure you can immediately understand that, though mortals, the Shilarian nobility pride themselves on their capacity to read the stars. No one dared whisper the blasphemy, "how could our king not have known?" Thus no one said anything, at any post-stop or tavern, until we had nearly reached the capital.

Then the wild news, rejoicing, spontaneous song and sudden embraces from strangers, as riders pell-mell spread the word that Prince Gareth had been found. I heard of his incognito departure that night in Trainertown, when rumor insisted he had fled to Mendel. I was shamed, my love, to feel relief that our nation was not caught in this tragic net.

The coach carrying me with my chaperone, the humorless and dutiful Sir Carredin, arrived in the city to the constant ring of bells, barely ahead of the rescue procession returning from beyond the great river. Our delegation at the palace was swept aside by the returning hero; I saw him across the outer bailey, with his Barons and personal squire, addressing all and sundry whether knight or nightwatch, and declaiming an honest joy to be back home. Prince Gareth wore a black sash of mourning and always held himself in admirable restraint for one so young (I thought I had met the only youth with this quality). Naturally, my opportunity to report to him must await on important affairs of state, but we have been housed in regal fashion here in the castle and I can certainly have few complaints.

Two blessings came my way at once, though I must beg your forgiveness in the first case for calling it such. The fighting nobility here, called Knights of the Sword, have arrogated to themselves all of Prince Gareth's attention with issues of war. Indeed the rumor runs about that the new uncrowned king embraces this role, and has some incredible scheme in mind to mobilize his feudal levy for the first time in centuries. They say he intends war against the Bordbeyonds in retaliation for his capture, but I dread such a prospect and pray it is not so. At any event, he has been closeted with them in council at all hours for the first days since his return, to the great frustration of his court advisors (who call themselves Knights of the Quill).

As part of the warriors' ascendance they have declared a tournament to celebrate the new king's return and at which, it is said, a great announcement shall be made. Now to the blessing, and again I beg your forgiveness for such unworthy thoughts. Sir Carredin, my hounding escort, has been carried off with enthusiasm for this joust, and has actually left my side for hours at a time! He clearly intends to enter and compete. I have been free to explore the castle seeking knowledge of this wonderful, chivalrous and honor-laden people, asking after their understanding of astrology and of the strange Bordbeyonds who are our mutual neighbors.

In such peregrinations, my second blessing in the acquaintance of a true friend. Everyone in the palace assumes that an immortal from Mendel on king's business should talk only to nobility. I had a torturer's job to get more than a quick answer from any of the common folk before a hasty bob and retreat. But on the second day here the Baron Kalney came to introduce himself and offer his services, which have been hero-sent. He is with the office of the Royal Coroner—deputed to investigate deaths attended by violence or suspicion of wrongdoing—and is one of the Quill Knight faction. He too has been cooling his joints awaiting audience with His Majesty, and we have become fast friends.

Kalney is so kind and patient, listening to my endless complaints and finding tea to brew in this ale-mad company. He willingly heard with horror the tale of my deputation, and earnestly agreed to seek to move my audience forward, even above his own if his influence can count for anything. His Elvish is charming and halting, but shows his erudition in a land that worships prowess with the lance above the pen. Still, it's clear that this palace and the new king's administration would not run a day without the efforts of such scribes, these book-learned men and scholarly types collecting taxes, keeping accounts, recording and paying as others train to fight. Shilar in his wisdom accorded them equal status in the law even to the noble ranks, though the custom seems strongly bent the other way.

And so you have my full tale of ongoing woe, waiting on the young king and keeping warm with thoughts of home and hearth. And how are you, madam? I understand you married recently, have you seen your husband! A poor joke, my wife; I ache with the need for this mission to end, that I may return home to the south (by the moment, the constant cold has worn away some of the enchantment I feel at the sight of so much snow). A part of me grows rebellious, so far from Conar and recently out from under the watchful eye of my noble jailor. I wonder if I might do something unlawful soon, and simply head south on my own. I while the hours in such fond imaginings, an act of the adventurer others take me to be. Meanwhile my good friend Solemn Judgement, if he lives, is no doubt all alone and facing real trials in his quest for lore that will bring him unknown rewards. I pray for him, and ask that you will also pray for such a worthy young man. Not happiness, for I fear even he does not wish that, but safety and continued life. The Heroes will guide the rest. May they bring me back to you soon as well.

Yours,

Cedrith

Post-Script: I have decided! So much has happened and now the time is short but I append this note to let you know. I shall also need your prayers, beloved.

In brief: I have been granted audience with the young king, the blasted tourney has happened, and my escort Sir Carredin is injured. In his convalescence, he can of course keep no eye on me, and I have determined in fact to escape this durance of diplomacy, with the willing and generous help of Baron Kalney.

I shall tell you all when I arrive in the land of time-proper, but briefly (in hopes this reaches you sooner than I). Prince Gareth is the soul of leadership, remarkably charismatic and impressive beyond his years, touched by grief and the responsibility to rule well. He acts as a man who owes his fellow Children of Hope a debt, and I have no doubt but that his rule will be sparkling with achievements. He greeted me warmly and heard the awful tale (may I never have to repeat it!) from start to finish without interruption. He seemed especially affected by the fate of my dear friend Natasha; I could almost credit he had been there with her, to see his grief and shock.

It was clear he gave my embassy the highest credence and wanted to show me any honor he could. I said a few words to indicate that I only wished to do my job well and be back to my bride as soon as I might. He looked on me then for a long moment, and shook my hand before giving me a traditional send-off among the Bordbeyonds wishing me first sight of the enemy. But then he leaned in and said as clearly as I've ever heard a word spoken "you have my leave to go". I bowed and thanked him, departing the royal presence thinking it was merely the audience he was referring to. But the thought stole over me later, the King of Shilar spoke with deliberate meaning. And after all, he is a king! I am certainly bound to obey a monarch, crown or no, and the fact that it happens to accord with my fondest wish is of no account.

So I have decided. I shall leave Cil-Cilurion tonight, and head south toward you, beloved, my home and my heart. I know the general area of our new house bequeathed by your aunt, and Baron Kalney is a willing accomplice in my escape. As Carredin convalesces, I shall be spirited forth with a merchant—bundled in a carpet no less!—and go with him until out of the capital district. From then, I have a few directions to the southern fords where I am told the Rom are often in traffic, and I may reliably go with them a while. Traveling with the Gypsies! What fantasist composes this epic fairy tale? But I will risk everything to be with you again, my love. I am done with kings and orders now, I strike out on my own as others have, to my shame longer and further before this. Fear not, nothing will keep me from you, for I feel the hand of purpose on my heart since Gareth spoke to me.

In Haste, with love, C.

⊕⊕⊕

The reappearance of the Great Road south from Trainertown caused a sensation lasting almost three days. The City Council went into immediate session, in the dead of winter no less, and debated everything from declaring a holiday to evacuating the town. The foresighted preacher Alaetar, when summoned, solemnly declared the Hand of Destiny was at work, and as usual no one could argue with that. People at market even whispered they should perhaps elect a mayor.

In the end it was decided to dispatch riders to Shilar and Conar with the news and a request for instructions; two men were detailed to stand guard at the old limen-post, not just at the gate, to watch for any sign of life. After the smith's boy Forgisson was caught ten rods down the road and dragged home under protest, a unanimous edict was passed forbidding citizens from straying beyond the south walls until further notice.

That last, the children ignored completely. Every day the race was run just as before, and the guards had only weapons to stop the human tide, which they would rather have swallowed than used. The gaggle of feet and voices plowed past their bellowed orders and half-gestures, and a great many spears were thrown to the ground in anger, parental notices threatened, punishments promised, but the children never paid the slightest heed. Now they ran to the post as before, declared a winner, and then dropped to their hands and knees to feel the great solid stones of the road for a few moments.

Looking south, they panted clouds of mist into the freezing air and felt the touch of wonder, to see a bit of what they had always dreamed of, the days of legend when all was well to the south that even their grandparents had only told tales about. To either side the land was still flat and lacking, a pallet for the curse, but slicing it like a death-blow was the road, as tangible as ancient, a stroke of Hope from the centuries past matching the highway running east and west through the city. Trainertown was once again the intersection of three roads built by the heroes of old.

Only then could the guards, with diligent shouting and herding motions, at last prevail to get the children back into the city and save their jobs. The Council never officially heard a thing.

Anteris spent the rest of each short winter day atop the wall with those few veterans not pressed into guard duty by Trainertown's state of alert. Conversation was thinner like the company, as they mostly smoked, or drank, and watched the road. Tales of great deeds, suited to hot summer days when nothing was truly happening, faded now in the shadow of expected legend. Alaetar had constantly preached his message of fate, Anteris and the veterans could feel it pulsing to warm the blood. The Hand of Destiny would come.

Late of an evening in mid-Raccoon, Anteris was again first to see them. Many of the children were still hanging about within the gates arguing what to do next, and quickly everyone fell silent to see the shapes advancing in the gloam of twilight up the south-reaching road. Before there had been cheers and wild rejoicing, when the adventurers' return was unexpected and formed a deed in itself. Now, Anteris could sense no matter how hard it had been, no matter what role they played in the miracle of the road, the party before him had only done what was expected of them. He remembered conversing with the young Woodsman before he left, how human he was and how decently he spoke. Now that slender form in front was a hero, beyond the need for speech with a mere scribe's assistant.

Then too, the shape of the Hand was horribly changed.

"Where is the halfling?" he breathed, and Calper in answer just clasped a hand to his shoulder.

Treaman could feel the solemn quiet of the city jabbing his ribs like the warning of a chaos-storm. Heads along the walls, staring children packed into the gate area. No words, cheers, shouts of welcome. Even the guards seemed tense; perhaps afraid, or the way a crowd stood silent in a church. The Woodsman stopped, halting the group behind him, and stared back down the road now disappearing into the swelling darkness.

Mhoral spoke from within his helm. "Cold comfort. Am I right?" He turned looking down for an expected rejoinder. Finding no one there, the Elf gave a quiet choke.

Braja gaped at the walls and people all around, and Treaman started with fear when he saw the tent bag on his back.

"We don't tell them about the Sword," he said looking at Haltar.

The leader considered with a rare narrowed brow. "Our fame is assured."

"Tell them we found Oncario. Say the road reaches it if you want." Treaman urged. "Say anything, but not the Sword." He didn't know why he should feel so desperate, but something inside assailed him with misgivings.

"Remember what happened back there. The leaders, they'll take it."

"Of course they will," Mhoral said, "that's the point. Treaman, this is not our responsibility anymore. We turn it over."

"And what will happen!" Treaman shouted, while the city waited and the freezing cold of a winter's night did not.

"Who do we give it to?" he panted looking at all of them in turn. "That board of elders, or whatever they call it? Do you remember how they argued, which way to give us credit for the dragon's treasure? Half a day!"

He paced to Haltar, who would make the final decision. "Perhaps the sage, Valenthur? There's a friend indeed! He'd throw us in gaol, frame it on a wall and study the decoration!"

Haltar spoke down to his guide. "What would you have us do, Treaman, smuggle it forever? Try to use it? Against that demon-thing?"

"Wait. One day," Treaman urged him. "Tell them everything else, and look at their faces. If you see anyone with a stronger will than Vuthienne of Oncario, we'll show it."

Mhoral chuckled. "Perhaps ask for someone nine feet tall while you're about it. There will be no heroes found in this hamlet, Treaman. Why not alert the king of Conar, then?"

Treaman spun to face the Elf, and his first thought was that by now Bildon would have already made fun of what he'd said. He bit his lip for lack of his friend's wit. "One day," he said quietly, "we'll all decide together but look around you and think about it for one more day. Please."

Linya put one hand on his back in comfort. "One day," she said in agreement.

Mhoral shrugged as he always did when the vote went against him. "One day, fine. Tomorrow, we'll talk sense."

Haltar grinned, then stepped over to Braja. Thumping the tent bag he said clearly, "Bright sword, we tell no one." He raised a shushing finger, and Braja broke out into a horrid, cheek-holed grin and nodded. Then the party turned to enter the city.

Treaman spotted the youth in white atop the wall and waved to him. The boy seemed surprised and returned it with delight. Treaman saw him descend the steps as the group was accosted by a swelling crowd of townsfolk just inside the gates. No one spoke to the adventurers, but everyone buzzed among themselves. Braja drew gasps of fear and astonishment, and Treaman heard the people speak of the Nubian quite frankly.

"Black as pitch, is he a prisoner?"

"He must be, look at his wounds."

"I wonder why he isn't tied."

"Perhaps the sorceress…"

Haltar stepped up and threw back his cloak, revealing many unhealed wounds. Mhoral raised his visor and his white scars stood out in the lamplight enough to draw screams.

"We have returned," Haltar said gravely, making the obvious sound like a revelation. "The road of ancient days is restored, and we bring news of the lost city Oncario."

Gasps and exclamations broke from the crowd, drowned by a young woman's squeal of pure hysteria. Hurtling through the parting throng, Marindya flung herself bodily into Haltar; though caught by surprise, the foot-knight yielded but half a step from the impact and belatedly raised an embracing arm to return the death grip she had around his neck and head. If the town elders had not arrived to demand his attention, Haltar's former lover might have stripped them down right there in the street.

“Welcome back, brave adventurers,” said a councillor in a voice that fell far short of the occasion. Treaman saw Alaetar striding up and his heart dropped at the unblinking desire in the preacher’s eyes. Haltar, still holding Marindya casually off the ground with one arm, faced the delegation with his usual aplomb.

“We are very glad to be back, and we have much news,” here he glanced quickly at Treaman, “of great importance to share. First, my band requires rest and time to heal.”

“How much time?” Alaetar broke in. “Your opportunity lies before you,” pointing his arm south like a living scarecrow.

“We know the way, holy father,” Haltar said, returning his glare in a voice colder than the night. “In fact, we created it. And we will travel that road again, when we are ready.”

The stare-down commenced, between the holy man and the harlot-holder; across the south gate square one could have heard snowflakes hit the ground. Treaman realized he was holding his breath. Then he actually heard them falling.

“Snow,” he announced as everyone exclaimed, the youngest with delight.

Now the celebration at last began, children dancing in the falling flurries, grown-ups chatting about wonders, all breaking into smaller groups and moving off in the white-flecked evening breeze. Haltar signaled the way to the inn, and Fairnum led them with a smile as wide as his neck.

Treaman sidled up to Haltar as he finally let Marindya down, and murmured, “Make sure you unload your pack alone. I put everything from Oncario there.”

Haltar turned to look at Treaman while walking, a rising eyebrow and a growing smile leading to the heartiest, fullest laughter that the Woodsman had ever heard. Haltar’s laugh was infectious, full of relief and the promise of deaths left in memory. Treaman started chuckling too, and Linya and Mhoral joined without understanding the joke. Haltar clapped Treaman's back in thanks and pointed to him in comradely fashion as they went.

Two days after the enemy mage entered the forbidden tomb, the leader of the ghouls suffers through a sunny morning like all his fellows, as with all sunny days for the last thirty centuries. Whimpering and groveling with the dawn, he screams face-down into the earth, clawing and scrabbling with his head to get another finger's breadth deeper under the frosty loam. By midmorning, he is incapacitated except for the occasional flinch, and a periodic crawl to stay in the shrinking shade of a tombstone. Dimly, through the haze of pain stabbing into his closed eyes, he recalls days when the digging brought rewards, for a few scant decades after the portal had closed and the Makine ceased to run, there were a few bites that could be scavenged from this earth. Dead and tasteless corpse-flesh, it did not answer the law of hunger, but it did distract from the pain of day for a time. Now, though, the nose rarely catches even the barest hint of... richness, of otherness in the hard soil. Today is not one of those days, and so he like the others writhes and works his torn and broken face down into the tundra, trying to block out every crevice where the light can slice in and form agony in his spine.

The leader knows nothing of history, or of luck. That after many centuries of sleeping lore, the War of the Corpses is begun anew. That the immortal master of the ghouls, able to scry the entire world at will, was at this moment not within his Tomb, not paying attention to it, but hundreds of leagues away, celebrating and distracted while his fortress was plundered. That his foe, the grey-clad meat-mage, had combined persistence, scholarship, an inspired guess and no small amount of good fortune to locate this hidden bastion. That he had miscalculated about food, about the cover of night, about the existence of the ghouls themselves, but managed to survive them all and is now returned. Ghouls are ignorant of all such things.

The pack leader is in agony, and cannot raise his head to see Solemn Judgement emerging from that unspeakable portal with eyes like silver orbs on fire in broad winter daylight. Ghouls cannot bear more than moonshine, but the Man in Grey is hardly blinking and filled with knowledge that might have driven a born Child of Hope insane. The flaming gaze of the intruder would have shown him that luck, at least, was no longer part of the equation.

The ghoul does not hear as the stone portal grinds closed again, nor smell when the fire-eyed intruder passes carefully downwind with boots in hand. His preternatural sense for life cannot penetrate the clangor of daylight to warn him. Quiet and brave indeed is the Man in Grey. But not lucky, not anymore. The sun had been even brighter yesterday, the weather warmer, the sky clear, though the ghoul neither knew nor cared at the time. Still, if not for the clouds that forenoon, and the snow that followed, the meat-mage might have gotten clean away.

By the hour beyond noon today, the clouds gather in strength, a thickness that means business, and the pain dims enough to be bearable. For the law of hunger to reassert its primacy. And when the leader of the ghouls, first among the pack to raise his head, climbs a marker to scan the area, it has already been snowing for ten minutes. Enough to further obscure the day, making it nearly twilit again, easing the light-pain; though his vision is hardly full, the ghoul can easily see up close. And in the snow ahead, he spots the faint impression of bare footprints, headed west.

He drops on them now as if pouncing on their maker, and sniffing furiously, catches the familiar scent. With every instinct, he yearns to rear back and howl, summoning the pack and starting the feast-hunt. Yet in mid-rise, an unnamed impulse checks him. The face of the ghoul leader is marked by an unfamiliar emotion—the atavistic greed of an animal, or a lust for revenge worthy of the higher being he once was. Thus he throttles his instinct, crouches low and lopes off after the intruder by himself. The law of hunger drives him, and he intends to feast alone.

Within a half-hour, the snow is deep enough that the old footprints are starting to fill, but never enough to erase them—and they are boot-tracks now. The ghoul pounds on, using his arms at every other pace to propel him even faster along the ground and over fallen stones. Then, as evening draws on and the last light dims ahead of him, his vision improves and he sees ahead, a tiny stone-hued shape that flees. At this, his rage overcomes him and he howls, long and rough and ripping, into the falling night. The pack will hear and follow, too late, and he will be fed and victorious and leader forever.

The vast majority of the Percentalion, under the curse of chaos, looks depressingly the same. In all directions cracked blasted earth, tiny clutches of anything growing, hardly any movement, barely any change in height. Sometimes a rock, as here, perhaps a trio of reaver birds overhead. But the sun's position tells nothing, and if the weather is banked in cloud, as today, then day tells you nothing more than night.

And the empty land is very quiet, most everywhere and everywhen. Except here, now, where the sudden clamor of torn existence brings Kog and its twin to being, furiously eating each other accompanied by a circle of howling helldogs. All the titanic struggle—ripping tendons and snapped bones, howls of agony and triumph—all are simply there. The land quakes enough to knock the hounds of hell from their feet. In the loose circle between them, nearly eight tons of roiling flesh make war.

It is an attempt at murder by meal. Each leviathan tears off limbs and swallows them, grows new heads to bite down patches of flesh the size of calf-hocks. If they feel agony, the two demons must grow new mouths to scream their pain or anger. Hogsheads of ichor slosh their battle-site, soaking the hardpack into slick, muddy clay where only deep-clawed feet can find any purchase.

The son unknowing, the two-eyed Kog who moves just a little faster than his unknown sire, he brought them here across more than distance. As the monstrous struggle wears on, he gains slightly in the war to consume. Each limb or fleshy shank he can swallow adds immediately to his own bulk; the slices he loses are every bit as large, just as painful, but not quite as frequent. He grows, he bears down, he begins to triumph.

But he is not aware. Despite both eyes, the demon-born cannot see his doom, until the other speaks in his mind.

{*"Son."*}

{*"Imposter!"*}

{*"Son of my loin, birthed on this plane."*}

{*"Never!"*}

In fury, the larger demon bites his foe at the joint between its three legs, snapping through bone and chewing off the inner place where the seed-organ is tucked away. Kog howls in gleeful agony, but does not retaliate at once, instead continuing to speak without words.

{*"Well and truly eaten, my son! And where are yours?"*}

The demon atop the pile starts and nearly chokes on his food. He attempts to create the needed organ, and fails. For the first time a look nearer to panic crosses his features.

{*"Cark you! I have made no son, and you are an imposter, now mine to consume."*}

{*"Indeed? And what of my eye?"*}

{*"More proof! Kog is perfect, never defea-"*}

The larger, newer demon staggers back then, his chewing mouths drawn back into his body as his mind runs up against the knowledge of history he shares with his foe. There was Areghel. A fight long ago. An eye taken from him.

{*"I can never replace it, yet still it is far from me. You can feel it too. My son."*} The wounded, one-eyed demon grins hugely at its thunderstruck offspring, and delicately pulls off one of his legs to eat, smacking and savoring the food now that the meal is in its final course. Moving to the tail, Kog rips it out along with a few links of backbone, delighting in the pain that too late arouses its child to attack again. Crunching the vertebrae and slurping down the spiked end, Kog has now reversed the size difference; as its child rushes in with four limbs thrashing, Kog catches him in a final, for once fatherly embrace. Mouths appear everywhere their bodies touch, and feast.

Kog saves the son's eyes for last, that he may see his defeat to the end.

Now the hell-born lord of the Percentalion, drenched in fluid and bearing the strings of uneaten ligaments anywhere it had created a mouth, rears back and laughs at the triumph of this scheme. Kog is nearer ten feet tall, and weighs as much as a stone-loaded sledge. The dogs, once again sure who to worship, add their bone-chilling howls to the horrific din.

Kog's good mood lasts some time; it is certainly growing dark before boredom sets in. The points of light, it recalls, and the lost Eye, and of course—the mortals! Bearing the sword, they dared to defy the king of this land. Burn the rest of them. But when Kog extends its senses to locate the offenders, the recoil of newly created Law is stunning. They are gone! Beyond his easy reach, fled into the orderly lands, and now, an ancient stain of Areghel's day, brought back to insult the lord of chaos.

How much time has passed? Kog briefly contemplates, and begins to chuckle with admiring fury at the dead son's gambit. Through time! Several mortal days lost, and now the sword has escaped its grasp for the moment.

But no! Nothing may ever interfere with the will of Kog. Completely forgetting the stick, the crown, even its own Eye, Kog roars in anger and sends out another summons. Every chaotic thing is levied, an army not seen since the Second Age. In moments, Kog and the helldogs are at the Road, on its eastern side. The earth demon rages to see that straight, reliable line drawn across the kingdom it, by rights, should rule. Blasting it with waves of hellfire, Kog smolders at the utter failure; the stones remain unmoved, grass along its edges unburned. Kog cannot even approach closely without feeling the stinging needles of Law in the ground below its feet.

While awaiting the levy's approach, Kog shouts in rage and blasts new holes in the lifeless turf. Once the army of chaos is assembled, Kog will lead them out using this accursed path as a guide. The weak and puny kingdoms of mortals have no magic or numbers to resist the tide of destruction Kog brings. On a whim Kog sends its thought after the other points of pain and interest. The Eye, with a mortal woman, who curiously can resist the summons for now; perhaps because she wields the stick, and perhaps because she has sacrificed her sanity to avoid his commands. No matter, Wolga Vrule and his army of undeath approaches; he will no doubt take possession, and try to use both to his advantage. The liche's lore is strong, and he will mistake his power to mask the Eye from its master. So then—all will be well with Kog's vassal, who like the son shall have no idea his weakness until it is too late.

And the crown is safe, unreachable to Kog and undiscoverable to the mortals. Naught else matters; this is an excellent time, therefore, to pursue revenge. As whims go, Kog has always liked that one.

⊕⊕⊕

Anteris walked on air for nearly a week after the night of Sage Cedrith's visit. Having the matter settled now, and the immense relief of being allowed to study as he wished, gave him a steady thrum of excitement and consequence he had only ever felt from reading of heroes. Valenthur too, now that he had given in, seemed to take matters with a better humor, and Anteris hopped to every chore he could think of to show his gratitude. His master's constant kindness and concern were always spiced now with the vivacity and talk he once reserved for company. Anteris got the sneaking feeling he was considered an adult, or nearly.

The return of the heroes had set his mind aflame, and he eagerly researched the Kingdom Chronicle for mention of other worthy deeds in more recent times. Valenthur indulged him; though the topic was not to his liking, yet the writing was often his own.

In fact, Valenthur was better than his word, posting the messages Cedrith had written to request the tomes, and finding a few in the library which had a bearing on tales of older times. Anteris left off the nightly races, talking with the veterans, or even the ghost-parades of the gang; candlewax melted on his account now when the sun set early and erudition beckoned. On the rarer occasions he did leave their quarters, Anteris glided over the slippery avenues with winged feet all the faster for their unaccustomed burst of freedom.

In one afternoon, Anteris went from walking on air to stepping on eggs.

Tea-guesting on Conar's Day was becoming the special preserve of the holy man Alaetar. Anteris returned with sweet rolls from the bakery to find him already with his host, and furious.

"Words cannot contain the outrage!" he fumed, eyes always imposing now alight with their own fire.

"They would not heed you?" Valenthur asked, his too-shocked face betraying that he was more pleased than the cat munching on fish behind them.

"They threw me out! Me, their protector and advocate, bodily hoisted like some drunkard in the tavern below. Cowardice! Impiety! They refuse to take their place as the fist of providence; our world crumbles for it."

"Good Myster Alaetar, holy sir," Valenthur purred, "try to calm yourself. Here are the pastries, sit and take tea, tell me all."

Anteris hastened to set the sweetbreads next to the ever-present apples and poured tea for the two. Valenthur, in a mood as high and bright as to make Anteris nervous, generously gestured that he should take a place at the table with the grown men. Anteris scraped his chair too loud, rattled his teacup on the first attempt, and did not dare reach across the table for a roll.

Alaetar sat without touching a crumb or drop, but stewed with full breaths for several moments. Something of his anger left him briefly, and he sagged with a hand to his brow, murmuring, "A catastrophe, the future is all black and fire now."

"Tell me everything," Valenthur suggested. "Then I can see about summoning the guard, and a council member to arrest these vandals."

Anteris felt the first crack in the shell of his good fortune: his happy course of study, his master's good mood, none of that weighed a thing in his heart, versus the future of this band. A small voice urged him to speak, but he lacked the courage yet.

"I went to see them immediately following service." Alaetar stared as he always did, at but also through both his listeners, oblivious to the chagrin on their faces that they had not attended.

"It was clear, as I entered to accost them in their rooms, that they were deep in some scheme whose purpose I could not make out. Perhaps one of them said 'demon' and another spoke of a sword.

They stared at me like a stranger. I asked them why they had not thought to take the Hopelord's blessing before setting out, and they kept staring like images in a painting. At last the sorceress started up and said 'It's Conar's Day'. They had no idea!"

"Shame, shame," Valenthur clucked. "And drinking already, no doubt."

"Eh?" Alaetar had not considered this crime, but now it stoked him back to former levels. "Why yes! Tankards across the table, and bits of food, as if they had not so much as left the room in days. And when I demanded to know their plans, nothing but a coward's silence. The big one, with his mocking grin, stretches out his legs and tells me, 'maybe not when, holy sir, but if.' Then 'If!' says I, 'What man chooses whether to play his part in destiny?' And of course they had no answer for that."

The little voice inside Anteris nudged him on the nerve that controlled his mouth, and he spoke. "They had grievous wounds, holy sir. And, and perhaps were planning how to face—"

Anteris' small burst of courage drained away as the preacher from Shilar shifted his gaze across the table.

"Wounds, lad? I myself have succoured their injuries, and would do so again at once, if asked. But nothing have I seen of them in days, nor—"

"Nor anyone else," Valenthur broke in acidly. "Much to our benefit, I may say; the tavern has been quiet, Fairnum tells me, no one wishes to celebrate with those slayers upstairs in their dark conference. Excepting wretched Marindya, poor ruined maiden."

Here Valenthur paused to gauge if his arrow had caused further shock with his ally Alaetar. The preacher was glowering and silent, his eyes looking through walls and into the Percentalion itself. "And the council," the scribe resumed, "I hear from them, had a very unsatisfactory report; that young woodsman did most of the talking, full of stuff and nonsense, some claptrap about meeting with a demon."

"Master, I believe—"

"And no treasure!" Valenthur crested on. "One small cask of gems to declare, bah! Mark my words, they are hiding something."

"The heroes would never lie!" Anteris blurted out the words like a child; his voice cracked, doubling his embarrassment. But when he met Valenthur's eyes, and saw the face of a man who has been called a liar, he knew something beneath his feet was irretrievably broken.

"You cannot be serious, my son. Vandals, exposed now as nothing more than cowards and drunkards. Mark me, I knew them from the start."

"They have risked their lives! The dragon of Maladon, the road returned!"

"Loot, and revelry, bawdiness and dissolution!" Valenthur thundered. "I forbid you to speak of these criminals again, much less to use such a word to describe them. 'Heroes'! Anteris, when you scribe the history of these kingdoms you must exercise a proper judgment, a sober discernment, about persons and deeds. And no book of history need ever mention such adventurers!"

Anteris was sick in his gut, but the voice that was once small and whispering now stood and shouted through him.

"One of their number has died! To question their courage or deeds could only be the act of a fool or a coward."

In the deafening silence that followed, the master of the house rose from his chair, and silently turned to stalk from the room. All the lovely tea-things in their neat places around the table might as well have been crushed to powder.

"Heroes." Alaetar spoke again, and Anteris felt his blood freeze at the word so seldom spoken here. "Heroes are those who do their job, young scribe, mark that. They are known by their deeds. By their respect for what the signs of heaven say. I have tried to tell them… a sore stroke this, a black day ahead."

"Holy sir," Anteris stammered as the preacher rose to go. "Please sir, tell me, did you hear them say they would not return?"

"To my face, lad!"

"Sir!" Anteris could hear his desperation as Alaetar reached the outer door. "Did they say no to you directly, please, tell me. However cruel, whatever you think of them. I must know." He panted awhile in Alaetar's shadow, trying to retrieve enough fragments of his former happiness to cobble together the demeanor of an adult. Forcing a sickly smile, he said "It is a part of my researches."

Alaetar gave a small start of recollection then, and placed a hand on his shoulder, trying to be kind.

"Ah that! Worry not, young scribe; these, these adventurers will form no part of any tale that you should tell. They have turned aside from the signs in the sky—"

"Like the red star?" Anteris could see the shock then, and added "not everyone sees it, sir. But I can tell it is moving."

Alaetar looked down on him with more respect then, as if noticing an individual person instead of a place where starlight fell to earth.

"It is indeed moving, Anteris. And before it passes, or strikes the earth, before then a great blow for Hope must be dealt. I had believed, had hoped. But it is not to be." He looked like a man making a great decision with his words; Anteris felt a chill run completely down his spine at the thought.

"Please sir. I must know."

Alaetar drew a deep breath. "I braced them about their mission, young man. There can be no doubt, I told them again of their destiny and exhorted them to return at once. They sat and said nothing; except for their stares it was as if I had not spoken. I urged them again, and suddenly they all spoke at once. They said no."

Anteris held his breath to keep his heart from escaping. After a moment, Alaetar grumbled an addendum. "Most of them."

"Most, sir?"

"The young Woodsman, he started to say something. But the Elf, he said no. The mage, she might not have said anything. And that enormous black savage he never seemed to talk. So the leader spoke for them, and refused me."

"He refused you sir? Directly?"

Alaetar seemed impatient of this precision, and his face grimaced with the needless effort to remember.

"He said no. Or rather, he said the same thing. 'Not without a Stealthic'. I think that was the word. And the rest, the sorceress and the Elf, they at once agreed. I became somewhat angry then," the preacher continued, "and before I know what, that great bear of a black giant had seized me by the collar and hauled me from the room, like a sack, like a crate. He set me down outside the door, said 'not same', then slammed it in my face!"

Back in an angry mood, Alaetar opened the door to the outer stairway, and Anteris could see the sun had already set. Stepping outside with the preacher, Anteris instinctively looked to the eastern sky, as did Alaetar. There, the red flash seemed larger and more alive than ever before, a lantern presaging a storm, or a great evil eye of Despair, invading the heavens for the first time in history. Anteris nearly cried out when he saw it; he could not doubt that tonight, or perhaps tomorrow, it would explode, or strike the city, or carve a titanic rent in the sky beyond repair.

The sound of Alaetar's boots descending stirred Anteris from his trance.

"Alaetar, where are you going?"

Not turning back, the preacher responded, "To do what I can." And without further comment he strode out of sight toward the south gate.

The night air was chill and the nearby city was empty. Anteris could feel behind him another void in the rooms he shared with his mentor. The rift he had made stabbed him deeply, and the tears came. But the scribe did not go back inside, to warmth and apologies, books, bed and shame. He thought about adults, and Stealthics, and angrily dried his face as he watched the red star until it had moved as far across the sky as the town clock-hand did when it measured a minute. Then Anteris descended the stair, and headed for the tavern do what he could.

At the end of the day, on the border of the Plains of Ranebruh and near the edge of insanity, the grey traveler staggers across a small frozen stream and then turns at bay to face the leader of the ghouls. Parted by less than two lengths of ice underfoot they stand a moment, staff and claw in readiness. The man's breath is clouded and forced, from the last two leagues' retreat in greater and greater haste: he can run no further and still have strength to fight. The ghoul's breath makes no sign, leaving his lungs as cold as it went in: the creature needs no sustenance or comfort from the air, and its only purpose in the act is for its howl, which the leader again unleashes now as he nerves himself up for the attack.

The answering chorus is not distant enough to offer the slightest comfort. The man in grey glances quickly back to the forest, just a half-league off now, and faces his foe with a look both grim and fey, without remorse for what could have been. The leader of the ghouls can well afford to wait, yet the meat-man's warm breath is close, a constant reminder of what he can have, and all to himself if he acts soon. Confident and merciless and starving, he lopes in low across the ice, and the man with the staff steps in to meet him.

The sage swings his quarterstaff overhead and begins the invocation, but he has not reckoned with the unearthly reach of his foe. Feinting with his left claw at the man's groin, the ghoul causes him to stoop awkwardly, bringing his staff forward without force, in advance of the miracle. Now the ghoul lashes with his right, seizing the staff and wrenching it nearly loose. The traveler, in desperation and off-balance, throws all his weight on the weapon and drives it down, into and through the layer of ice beneath them. With a crack, they both fall two feet into the ice-gash, soaked to the thighs with frigid water. As the man struggles to retain his footing, the ghoul returns with his left past the guard and slices through the jerkin at the right shoulder, cutting at the joint deep enough to expose bone. Staggering back, the grey man falls to the bank among a small stand of frozen reeds, losing his staff as the ghoul pounces in for the kill.

Judgement has taken three more wounds before he can think, two scratches on his side and chest and the merest nibble on his wounded shoulder. They burn like acid and the blood steams loose with every movement. Convulsively he flings out and around, throwing the lighter opponent over even as they both twist and thresh among the bracken. His calves are threatening to cramp from the river's water, and he is wet all over now from the slush of the shallows. Gasping for breath and gargling back his screams, he finds himself atop the creature, holding it face-down for the moment with his left side, and using his unwounded arm as a bar across the shoulders and neck, to keep him pinned. Scrabbling blindly with his wounded right arm for anything nearby he can use as a weapon, his face is dangerously close to the ghoul's mouth as the monster strains to rise or turn far enough to bite his neck. The breath of the monster reeks of rot and illness, and Judgement grimaces from nausea as he strains to stay atop him. The howls of the pack are constant now, they can smell the blood and will soon be in sight.

Daylight dies and his last chance is expiring with it. He cannot look away from his foe, he must concentrate to keep him down and dares not shift position to give him a chance at escape. His right hand closes on a knot of something on the creature's waist, and without thinking he pulls. Firey blood explodes from his right shoulder and the Man in Grey cries out, but he pulls harder and feels the rope come closer with a sickening sound of tearing meat. The ghoul roars as well, champing with his mouth as he lunges to turn towards the living flesh so intimately near; the teeth are shearing through the fabric of his cloak now, the beast is gaining leverage by the moment. Judgement feels the rope catch and stop, and cannot imagine how it may be caught or where it is from. He can see beneath the flowing blood of his right shoulder there is a ball of white bone, pushing further up beyond his skin as he continues to strain.

The pack howls, nearer and nearer. With each pump of his heart, more of Judgement's blood and warmth is escaping. With a tremendous effort and a rising scream, Judgement wraps his bloody right hand around the meat-scrapped length of rope and pulls. For a hanging moment, there is no movement at either end of the wounded arm. Then a loud pop, and all is darkness for a time.

The ghoul pack is rapidly losing control, so close to its feast denied. Across the tiny frozen stream they come pounding and screaming, to the patch of broken ice where a few stop to bite off the blood-stained edges. Up the opposite bank and into the frozen marshy shore they jostle and growl, right up to the broken body on the ground. Their former leader lies there, twitching and champing reflexively in two pieces, split at the waist and torn from the inside out. Already dead and just moving with the remnants of orders its brain had given minutes ago, the claws and feet and face still try to rend, to destroy and eat the foe. Now, he is nothing but fodder to be served up, a momentary proof for the law of hunger. Wordlessly, the pack falls on him and takes their bites, leaving only the stilled and mangled remnants of something once vaguely humanoid on the churned snowy ground.

Now the loss of control begins to manifest. The smell of the meat-man is again dulled, and though several of the pack circle the area with faces to the ground, no trace of his scent comes. The waning light of the winter day, less than a half-hour to a cloudy dusk, still hurts enough to make them flinch, but though they strain to see, no human track marks the snows. Some bay and make for the woods a few paces, before turning back with no sign to guide them. Others return to the ice-hole, prowling there waiting for him to surface: but he never will. They crowd each other and scuffles break out. There is no longer a leader for this pack, except in the small bits that lie on the snow and in the gullets of the former followers. Lacking direction, they resort in turn to howling, until twoscore throats are keening their fury and loss to the growing night.

Long moments pass this way, as the furor grows towards frenzy. They scream in disjointed chorus, and pound the ground until it seems the bank is heaving and quivering with fear of the pack. Fights break out in earnest, and with no let-up in the howling three more are slain and eaten in service to the law. The noise has long grown past the point where it could have seemed no greater, and darkness has fallen in full, when another sound is born on the Plains of Ranebruh. It is far-off and too quiet to be immediately heard, but too steady and tuneful to be completely drowned. Soon enough ghouls stop their dreadful caterwaul that the character of this new sound can be made out. It is a battle horn, from a hill by the eaves of the forest to the west.

The snow has stopped, in places the cloud cover is breaking to show stars. The ghouls have all quieted now, though it may seem the ground beneath them still shivers a bit in fear. The horn sounds again and yet again, and as Unal breaks into an open space between the clouds, the ghouls can clearly see a mounted man, the length of a lance, the glint of armor. As one, they gather and lope off in his direction, and having put away his horn he seems content to let them come. Honor, like hunger, can substitute for leadership and strategy.

The tracked-up ground by the stream bank is quiet once again, for several long moments after the invaders have left. Only the dead remain, and even the stream beneath the hole flows too slowly to make a sound. Suddenly the land on the west bank heaves and splits, and up from the earthy snow rises a grimy, blood-spattered spectre, covered in icy mud and spitting a hollow reed from his mouth as he chatters and groans. Hugging himself tightly with both arms, the Man in Grey staggers toward the ice-hole, falls to his knees and checks the distance to the ghoul pack as well as the gentle breeze. It blows toward him from the forest. He peels back a sheet of the ghoul leader's skin from his right shoulder, and it comes free with a sticky tearing sound; even as he starts to scream, the man throws himself face-first half into the hole, dunking his wound to cleanse it and his mouth to stifle it.

Five long counts later, he heaves back and lays on the floe, shivering now hard enough that the back of his head bounces on the ice. Staggering to his feet, he endeavors to replace the ghastly dressing, but his good hand shakes too hard to do the job. His entire body quivering, the man attempts to speak the words of healing, and again his chattering jaw will not cooperate. He sinks to his knees, his face a blank slate of pain and chill, and the growing need to sleep. His shoulders sag a moment, and he leans towards the ground; but snapping back he reaches to his pouch and scrabbles there desperately.

On the distant hill, the howls of the pack include pain as well as rage; the mounted knight charges and turns, charges and turns, and at each pass ghouls are speared in silhouette against the starry sky. In the moonlight the Man in Grey can make out the symbol on the knight's shield, a rampant hawk symbol of Ganelake the local lord.

Leaderless and of no courage, the ghouls invariably shrink back from the destrier's speed, and their claws cannot break the guard of his lance and momentum. Suddenly the largest, the one with the hook in his back, lets the knight pass and leaps instead at the flanks of the horse, sinking in claws and teeth. The piteous whinny of the mount cuts the air, and the knight reaches too late to slam down with his shield, snapping the neck of his foe even as his horse founders beneath him. Now the chopping blade of the knight is all that can be seen, for a time, killing two more before he too is swarmed under the pack.

The man by the stream finds his breath is coming harder and heavier, producing ever-smaller clouds of mist as his hand continues its search. His lungs are cooling, coming to match the temperature of the night, of the ghouls, of the state of death. At last he turns the pouch inside out, and from the scatter of small objects on the snow he seizes a small stone, inscribed with a symbol on both its flat sides. His breath now comes in huge gasps, yet he takes a moment to focus his effort, before crying out the single word that activates the magic. As it begins to feebly glow with warmth, the man hesitates one moment more, and then deliberately puts the stone in his mouth and swallows.

His agonized cry is drowned over the distance by the victorious howl of the ghoul-pack. The Man in Grey falls to the ground and slowly masters his screams, bringing them to gasps as the breath of his lungs produces larger and slower clouds for the night to eat. Soon his shivering also begins to fade; more pain will come, of course, but the stone will be easier to pass once it has broken. In a few minutes, the man has mastered his body enough to speak the miracle of healing; he begins to scavenge the bank, picking up varied items to survive at least the night. And a few yards away nearly hidden by the bracken of the bank, the man locates his iron-shod staff.

In half an hour, the surviving ghouls on the hillock have finished their feast and begun to agitate among themselves for more. The horse's track is fresh here, and they begin to move off towards the woods, the Snowdon Hills, and the world of men. There is a hamlet, just the other side of the trees. Ganelake had been its protector.

None of the ghouls look back once the romp is underway; through breaks in the cloud it would have been just possible to see a lone figure toiling to weave a grim snow-rake from reeds and sticks and studding it with ghoul flesh. The man ties it behind his back by a leather cord, and as he begins to walk it drags behind him, obliterating his track and leaving shreds of undead scent in his wake. That will do for the nights, times of wind-shift and retreat: but in the day, and downwind, there will be chances to attack. The face of the man in grey is hard set now, for vengeance. He pursues the pack into the Snowdon Hills.

Late night in Raccoon, and the outer gate guards on the river-bridge of Oncario might as well be blind. Aral a sliver, half of Unal, plenty of clouds to boot; and what fool stands his post without a heat-brazier in the onset of winter? The glow of the charcoal guarantees that Pekar and Camus can barely see a rod out into the plaza, as they rewarm their hands and jokes alike.

The first sight of the incoming group occasions no particular alarm. True, the dimly-visible shadows are on a different road than the charcoaling party that set out in the morning. And they are not due back until the morrow. As the shapes come closer, the guards make out other signs that perhaps all is not well. No one is singing or talking, for one thing, though there is a solitary crack of laughter. None are wheeling the colliers' hand-wagons, and there are too many horses among the group. Also, they move far too slowly, even for men who are perhaps dead tired.

And too late, the guards at the river-bridge realize that the visitors number not ten or fifteen, but hundreds.

Camus stands his ground with the spear while Pekar reaches for the alarm-horn. But when the first rank of invaders shambles in view, the only sound is that of the pole dropping to the brick, and boots in desperate flight. Pekar is pulled from the mouthpiece by a grip that feels like bone; by the time he has been dragged around to face his assailant, to see a toothy skull and pupils on the end of stems in empty sockets, his wind has been crushed, life already fleeing his frame.

Barithul at the inner gate hears no horn, then, and is not even watching at the window to witness Camus in retreat. Truth to tell, he is considering a short nap, alongside his partner Mag, who had a late night. But when he dimly hears an unfamiliar voice echoing "*Stay!*", his curiosity gets the better of him. There, at the top of the bridge-span, stands Camus, facing town but coming no closer. Barithul calls to his partner, who snores on and even ignores a judicious kick.

He returns to scan the curious scene by shreds of cloudy moonlight. Two men are approaching Camus now, one about Pekar's height and another as thin and tall as a scarecrow on a stick not yet set in the ground. There is a dreamlike quality to the play he watches; it is odder than three feet, to be sure, but there can be little of urgency here, since they all move so slowly. The pair catch up to Camus, who evidently knows the stranger. The tall man pats Camus on the chest and seems to draw something from his tunic. A friend, then surely. Ah, it is drink, a flagon of some sort, for Barithul can make out the tall man's hand dripping now and Camus nearly falls to the ground. He chuckles at this comedy, and reflects it better to let Mag sleep indeed.

The two river-guards leave the stranger behind and approach the inner gate. Perhaps it's another traveler from the world outside, with a deputation to the Primara. Or someone with news of the escaped robbers, those the guards were alerted to arrest on sight and search for the ancient artefact they stole. It is almost impossible to make out faces in the clouded half-moon, but Barithul can see Camus' beard and bald head. As they arrive at the gate, they have given no word, but after two long moments, Pekar raises his hand in a friendly way and Barithul affirms it must be alright. He turns the wheel and throws the lever to engage the marvelous *automakoi* of the gateworks before returning to the window for a few barbs about his fellows' inebriation.

At that moment, Unal breaks free overhead, casting a slant of moonlight across the bridge. Barithul can see that Camus' tunic is covered in red, Pekar's head hanging too far to one side. Across the span comes the clatter of horse's hooves, the slowest and most terrifying cavalry charge since the Third Age. The undead are inside before his mind can even grasp what has occurred. Only that awful sight and his scream precede the moment Barithul's mind is stilled.

Such cries are scarce at first, and even late at night Oncario is crowded with other noises. Between the chuffing of forge-ovens, sailing thinly above the clamor of late-night commerce, there are discordant shouts of unrhythmic terror starting from near the western gate and spreading as spilled blood does. Brick haulers and late-returning miners encounter familiar faces with unrecognizable wounds, shuffling toward them in the darkened streets. Naturally, their first instinct is to help; only when it is too late do they kick and shriek and try to break free, under the claws and bites and ill-handled weapons. There is an indigo mist rolling in the streets now, causing the living to freeze and the dead to rise. Barithul shuffles into the newly-formed van of Oncario's undead traitors, two spears through his chest seeming to cause him no undue pain. Mag beside him looks strangely less sleepy than usual. In the market stalls, Pekar's crooked head and the fist-sized hole in Camus' chest cause a wave of terror on their own. But the guardsmen, as ever, are only following orders as they seize the charwomen and girls minding the carts, and rip their limbs or snap their backs. The young feminine corpses dropped to the bricks are only motionless for a few moments. The undead army swells.

As the gaunts come to outnumber the living, the sounds of Oncario's industry start to scream in death as well as its people. Shops with forges and water-wheels make more noise as their doors are flung wide and windows shattered. Fires break out, flame and steam and the rising grind of torn gears remind the ear of shouts and shrieks. The undead pour into each shop, home and foundry; a few victims exit at a sprint but are quickly whelmed and converted to a less mortal pace. Behind the wave of undead as it moves on, the buildings puff smoke or steam that rises in intensity, then crests, fails, gasps and ceases. Nearly twenty thousand bodies are moving through Oncario, yet almost all the windows are black and lightless.

At every new district, the tall one totters and capers, pointing and invoking with slurred speech and undisguised delight. The *miasma* appears at his call and multiplies his enemies' fear, recruits his own strength as the dead join him and the living witness in anguish. A few soldiers try to hold their lines using bows and spears, but it is hopeless. Seeing one's foe take an arrow in the eye and continue to close grips is unnerving. Recognizing him as the neighbor whose Darksebb gift you have stored in your home is beyond answer. Men who laughed at the assaults of grinaki or beasts of the pine barrens, weep now as death wraps cold familiar fingers around their throats.

The skeletal one dances into a dark lane searching for new victims. His attention is arrested by the cries of a survivor. A short wiry man in a leather apron backs away from one of his minions, a female.

"No, Jaya, no!"

The woman reaching for the wiry man was not unattractive, to judge from the curve of her left breast. But her erstwhile lover can only stare at her right, cloven by a halberd and still slowly bleeding.

The man draws something from his apron pocket, thumbing and clicking in panic as he jibbers out mangled syllables like Wolga Vrule's. The liche is amused, then amazed at a huge retort from the alley. With a flash from the wiry man's hand, the woman's face blows completely off her skull. Even so, she bears into him and pins him to the wall, screaming and struggling.

Vrule is intrigued. With a thought, he stills the woman, who ceases to strangle the man and stands dripping on him until the liche arrives. The touch of the master's hand, the steam and scarring follows, and then another revenant joins Vrule's army, taking some gaunts with him down the steps to plunder this unexpected armory of Hope.

In two hours, all the common quarters of Oncario bear the shade of night and the temperature of winter. Gaunts and skeletons by the thousands crowd into the palace grounds, bearing down the doors, the purple mist routing a few more, the last corpses converted to undeath. The bodyguard still loyal to the Primara retreats, up the tower stairs, battled back across the brick bridge to the other tower, and falls to defeat in a pile of flesh at the last, most secure chamber of the city. One survivor only, by Vrule's orders, tall and beautiful and shocked beyond description, is dragged back down and stands tied by her former guards to a column in the main chamber, there to watch the new lord of the city take his seat.

Vrule, already glad to giggling, is transported with joy to discover the Scepter of Law. The merest touch brings a crackle of lightning-energy that would char the skin, if that hand had blood or muscle or warmth still within it. The pain, however, is great and the liche delights in this, as he misses the occasion of most physical sensations in these latter centuries. Immediately next to the Scepter, on a velvet pillow lies the Eye of Kog, and at this sight Vrule is so surprised that he sits back in the throne. After several moments spent gasping in surprise, the skull atop his neck swivels to regard his beauteous prisoner.

"And ware ded uu akwiyer sush uh treyzur, muh deehr?"

Vuthienne, descended of Hope's nobility, knows enough to master her terror and give no hint in her face that she understands him. The liche kindly repeats his words slowly, descending to approach her with a tender bone-built hand outstretched. When he is near enough to breathe on her, when his lightest touch brings agony and steam, still she tells him nothing. Vrule looks to her critically, then glances over to his two existing revenants, and shrugs with a generous air to return to the prizes by the throne.

Focusing his energy and gathering strength, Vrule seems to draw the various wisps of *miasma* to himself. With a great shout, he seizes the rod in one hand, the gem in the other, and slams the red atop the silver to hold them together while bolts of argent light burst forth and crimson reflections strike all the walls. Small shreds of Vrule's remaining clothes and skin tatter off and arc to the floor; purple mist congeals around the two dissimilar artefacts and Vrule's cry of pain is tinged with triumph.

It is finished; he sags against the throne in an exhaustion not felt since the Second Age. In his left arm, the scepter now rests in the elbow crook that a rightful ruler uses, still spitting and sparking in muted yet constant complaint of its seizure. Set atop it, the Eye of Kog throws its own light, reflecting no glow or flame except perhaps the glint of hell, made not quite so distant by its presence. Vrule looks long and lovingly at his work, savoring the outrage of Despair to make use of Hope's own tools. Running a rock-solid tongue over bloodless lips and teeth, he is at first a bit hesitant to test its powers.

"I appear to have succeeded beyond my wildest expectations." Vrule ends on a high note of wicked jubilation, and again leaps up to caper drunkenly about the dais.

"Ah, how I have missed the sound of an intelligent voice," he declaims heartily, and then laughs again. "Now, my dear, there can be no question of misunderstanding between us. I shall return shortly to question you again. Please believe that I shall learn everything I desire. Resist me if you wish—I enjoy interrogations of both kinds. But first, I simply must set this city to order. You know, guards posted, the country scouted out; as a former ruler, you must appreciate the difficulty of mounting a large expedition."

He strides to the archways then, contemplating the decoration as he strokes his chin. He speaks to himself again, by long habit.

"Yes. A pretty problem. We shall try the land path first. And assuming failure… we shall need a volunteer." Vrule turns back to regard his breathing captive with an intensity which by itself brings her to tears.

At that moment, the still night over the mute city is punctuated by a long, lonely howl from the pine barrens. Vrule tilts his head an instant and then ignores it. But the woman gasps and straightens at the sound.

No one is alive or listening by the outer bridge, at that moment. It would take sharp eyes to see the misty, vaguely feminine shape gliding by inches across the span, and even sharper ears to hear the sound of her high-pitched wailing. A last straggler enters the corpse known as Oncario through the gaping mouth of its western gate. Smoke rises into the moonset-sky like the aftermath of life.

⊕⊕⊕

Snowfall

The night of Barden's doom was snowbound and icy-clear, a night of the twin full moons that shone near as bright as the sun. The glint of ice from coated branches, frosted roofs and the nearby stream was sharper than on a cloudy day, and men's breath rose in puffs that spoke of the crisp, chill air. Three days in a row it had snowed, over a foot lay everywhere, with waist-high drifts in the corners and nooks. The cold had bitten down, crusting and frosting the surface of the world. Near midnight in late-Raccoon, and already the grip of winter held the country fast. At the village's edge, men paced like sentries, huddled with blankets on their backs and hand-cloths about their heads, and holding picks, bill-hooks and sickles: they walked to keep warm, and talked to keep awake as they scanned the hills on all sides, and waited for the doom to come. The youngest man, Jedden, paused by the smithy and looked to the sky once more, searching the brilliant orbs of Aral and Unal above as if they were speaking to him.

"I've always thought the double-twins were beautiful, no matter the season," he said to no one in particular. "Once in six months, but almost never when the sky is so clear... might feel the moonbreeze tonight."

"And you wan' know what I hates about them, this time?"

Two other watchers had approached unheard by the young man, and the tallest of them, the smith spoke.

"I bet I don't, Cree," returned Jedden, but they both listened anyway.

"That they'll like be the last uns I ever see."

"See? You were right, Jedden. Pay yourself a silver!" this from little Pad, who always fancied himself too much a wit, but was more welcome on a night when sleep and cold threatened.

"Cree, don't talk like a fool!" Jedden hissed with more heat than he could afford. "We've no way of knowing—"

"We know, as right!" Cree spat, in no mood for sass from the young woodcutter. "All our lives, we've lived here, and how many of *them* has anyone ever reported? I did seen spoor and track twice, in thirty years. My uncle claimed he sar three together, scrabbling at the earth and fighting 'mong themselves. But that was thirteen years ago, 1985, a year ah Conar; and away to the other side of the hills, almost to Ranebruh."

Pad's smile faded on that dread word, and he made the sign to avert Despair. The three stood in silence for a time then, watching the hills—Jedden rubbed his arms quietly, hoping the others wouldn't see. The moons looked gigantically down; he thought he could almost hear them say, *'We have seen Ranebruh, mortal. We know where the doom has slept these last twenty centuries.'*

Then he ventured, "And now... we hear them."

Cree spat again, directly on top of his first effort, which had already frozen. "Hear! Aye, we hear—now, it's every night, *every night*, and a'most every day. We've seen tracks roving in the woods north-a-way, boilin' with the undead. And they've attacked the hunters twice a'ready. Men and women are dead, Jedden—soon, the rest of us. Could never move our families out in this weather, not 'til spring."

"Aye, and those poor Halflings, stuck here on their way back to the Woods," put in Pad. "They're staying over in my barn and making the best of it—the father knows something's up, but I didn't want to say much with his little girl there: she's probably eight or nine—my cat's bigger!"

That elicited a chuckle from the group—the size of the Halfling people never ceased to amuse the larger races. "But come now, good smith, it cannot be as bad as that," insisted the little thatcher. "We have the brave knight of Shilar, Sir Ganelake, out there now—"

"He's dead," said Cree, and the others gasped in response as if slapped in the face.

"Dead! Are you mad? Jedden cried. "We saw him only four days ago, riding off to the hills." And he pointed for emphasis directly north beneath Aral's face as she shone from the clear sky strong enough to highlight the prints of his horse, headed straight as an arrow into the wildlands. The perfect cold and breezeless days had preserved the track in the crusted snow, like a memorial it seemed to Jedden as he heard the smith's shocking claim echo in his mind.

"He was large as life and armed for war!" Pad almost shouted in agreement. Even a week later, both men carried an echo of the astonished gaze they'd had in their eyes when the local knight had passed through for a spot of winter hunting. Among humans, the impression made by a noble was always strong—and few men cut a more dashing figure than a mailed knight of Shilar.

"Sir Ganelake's a landed knight, one of Shilar's best," Jedden practically panted.

"He can set it to rights," added Pad.

"He's dead," Cree intoned again, with pessimistic calm.

In a tick of icy silence, the smith looked down first the woodcutter, then the little thatcher before continuing. "Gone four days, and he took no food with him. Ya both sar, but ya din't *see*. Ya were there—I tole him, he asked me how many we had tale of, and I tole him at least sixty. I was a'hope not be taken for a liar, it could be two hundred a' them blasted horrors slavering out there. And *Sir* Ganelake," Cree added with rebellious emphasis, "the lord *knight*, he says 'So, six at most, then'. And off he rides, lance and sword and shield and suit of tin. Six! WE might have fought six, if they came not all at once. He's in their bellies by now, the arrogant bastard."

Jedden kicked the snow, breaking loose a diamond-shaped clod that rolled and skidded thirty yards down the crusted slope and almost onto the frozen stream. The moons bore down in white light and whispered to him, *'The dead, too, we have seen, those slain and those lost in nights as cold as these. Why should armor and noble birth survive, on the Plains of Ranebruh?'*

"We don't know he's dead, he could... and we know they can be killed at any rate."

But the smith stubbornly shook his head to this last. "We only know they *ken* die—hell a'bornin' man, they're the undead! What difference. We've seen them dead, aye, one or two when we go out to search for 'er lost hunters b'day. But we don't know why—for all we can say, they sometimes kill each other, is all."

"I wonder, what do they eat?" Pad quietly put in.

"Us, o'course!" Cree fired back, some anger mixed with grim jest.

"No, but, they haven't—they only took away Kalber there, the hunter, as far as we know—the rest we, got back and burned proper—and we're the only village for leagues about. It's the middle of winter... do you suppose they eat, eat each other too?"

"We can only hope," murmured Jedden, staring again at the hoof-track as if he could will the knight back to their side. "Yet the wounds on the bodies we saw—not tears or claws, but blunt and... with burning. And not enough—"Jedden's voice sank as he shivered. "Cree's right, there are still scores of them left, maybe." And the crystal, frigid midnight said nothing to this, but only nodded in his mind.

"Perhaps at least they finished that evil stranger."

"The grey one? Aye, that was an ill day, when he came through us." Cree nodded. "What a specter—I'd almost rather as have the ghouls."

To finally mention the doom's name sent a shiver up Jedden's back, and he looked sharply at Cree as if the man had let out a secret.

"He's been out there—what, three weeks, longer than Sir Ganelake?" asked Pad.

"He's dead too, 'suredly." Cree was becoming more definite all the time, morosely satisfied to be winning every point.

"Yet, what did Gelia say about him?" Pad demurred, "She said he was quiet, no trouble, just seeking lore."

"Innocent enough, I'm sure!" Cree finished triumphantly. "Can never tell what a man intends, just by what he says now, can ya woodcutter?"

But Jedden was listening again to the moonlit night, surrounding him like the cold. *'Our intent is as clear as the stars—next winter, we will burn down on an empty, gutted stand of man-homes. And we will care no more than we do now, mortal.'*

Pad, meanwhile, had lost the last of his good humor with the warmth of his breath. Somewhat crossly, he swore and said "Enough of this talk, then. We'll make it through this night, Cree, as we have the others. Those... we can stay them, if they even come, we have our weapons, and there's our torches too. And the Heroes protect us, we'll make it."

But having won his argument, Cree was in no mood for further guff. He shoved Pad with his free arm so hard the smaller man skidded away three feet on the icy path, fighting for balance. "Never mind your lousy heroes, what have they ever done for ya, er me, er any Bardener? If'a had to ask Mickhel for his blessing before I bent a shoe, you'd still be waitin' for the set on that mule a'yers, Pad! An'

Shilar protect us from the bad omens inna' stars, and Conar watch over our council er we won't be able to judge the boundaries right, er-"

"That's enough, shut your mouth, you unbeliever!" Pad shouted as he slipped and half-stepped in Cree's direction. It was clear he wanted to fight and had his club up high, but was lacking a foot of reach.

"These are *ghouls*, boy!" the smith shouted, heedless of the noise. "The undead are comin' and it'll be a matter of fighting, not prayin'!" Jedden knew, in a corner of his mind, that he should stop the fight, but he had become so rapt by the conversation of the frozen moons that he didn't dare add to the wrack. If he could only hear; perhaps there was a secret to their survival, and the shining orbs might tell...

Pad finally got his purchase, lurched in and swung. Cree saw it coming and didn't have to step. The smith jerked his hammer up and blocked the club, then on the backhand cuffed the thatcher across the mouth with his gauntlet, sending him skidding back and down to the ice.

Pad rolled to his stomach, coughed, and slowly stood. Even distracted as he was, Jedden could see between the thatcher's feet the crimson blotch and the line of red from his lower lip. Though it hadn't seemed possible, he felt a chill even deeper than the night.

"Ya little fool," hissed Cree in horror mixed with disgust, "why'd ya come on me like at? Ghouls ken smell blood from a league away. Jedden, ya dolt, wake up and help me cover it."

His former good humor completely drained away, Pad covered his lips with his free hand, while the smith moved in to press some caked snow on top of hand and mouth together. Jedden strained his ears to the utmost, and just thought he could hear the night say, *'Too late, for all the living.'* He prayed then, as the others stood stock-still, prayed to every hero he could name. To Shilar, that the signs of the night stars might be favorable: he saw the constellation Spirit Circle above but never knew its meaning. To Aballe, wife of Ekhonon and arbiter of disputes, that the town in justice might survive this unprovoked assault. And to Astor, the Prince of Peril and first lord of clever ways, that he would be with them in their danger and show them a way through it.

Away to the north, over the first crest of the hill, came a long, ragged cry as if shouted through a moldy cloth. The first was joined by another, and then three more, and more, until the sound reverberated across the vale. It was the trumpet call of hell, the hunting-cry of the ghouls from the Plains of Ranebruh, gone so long as to be thought a myth by common folk, now somehow aroused and across the Snowdon Hills to plague the lands of men. From the crest of the hills, still more than a mile away yet clearly visible under the twin full moons, came a shambling figure, directly back-tracking the path of the horse-hooves in the snow. As it came on, figures also emerged to either side, taking every third pace on all fours and stopping in alternation to howl their hunger down upon those who could still bleed. Jedden saw eleven figures, and when no more appeared, he wondered dimly through his terror if some of Barden might survive, at least the night. Then he saw the creature at the back waving what seemed an extra-long arm, and realized that as he raised it to his mouth he was taking bites from the limb as he came. And the bottom half of this limb was coated in torn chain mail. Then in the full sight of his fellows and the moons, Jedden fell to his knees and heaved out a gush of bile that stained the snow an ochre-yellow he could see by the twin moon-light.

By then, the cry had gone up along the village front and men were running to the north side, a serried picket of torches and tools, in no particular order. The shuffling, errant progress of the ghoul pack seemed to take an eternity, and the fear of them grew as the villagers could see them stop to sniff the air regularly.

Suddenly one of the watchers shouted "Look!" and pointed up the hill, back to the tree-line as another figure emerged. Whereas the creatures of Barden's doom were irregular, bent and coarse in every way, this lone silhouette was straight-backed, and walked with a regular pace like the click of a clock. The distant figure bore a staff and a broad-brimmed hat, and his ashen hue looked like it would stand up to sunlight.

"It's the grey stranger!" cried Pad around his makeshift bandage.

"Curse him, has he come to watch?" Cree ground out.

Once or twice, a ghoul turned back towards the following figure, cowering up with its irregular gait as if testing or asking permission. Without breaking pace, the stranger whirled his staff each time and clipped the laggard, sending it scuttling down the hillside to the relative safety of its brethren and far ahead of the man in grey for the moment. Now the pack mates had reached the borders of the stream and were testing the ice, still howling and clawing the crust underfoot in practice for softer targets very soon now.

The men of the village moaned in fear, and the moonlight clearly showed rakes and hoes shaking in the hands of most. "He's leading them—he's a necromancer, curse him!" Cree hissed "We let him through ahr fingers, and now he's roused this pack to murder the knight en us all!"

One of the men had a small bow for hunting rabbits, and he took aim to try and hit the Man in Grey. The shaft arced and fell, across the brook and halfway up the hill, but not close to the man. If he noticed he showed no sign but came steadily on in the wake of the pack: and now the ghouls had reached the near edge of the bank and were scrambling up the rise to feast.

Jedden could see their eyes now, unblinking, enormous orbs full to their rims with the palest yellow. Each of the corpse-eaters had a face like the night, dark and frozen, punctuated by full moons above that shed their own light without pity. The men now began to waver and fall back, as the glare of those eyes and the stench of graves long ago mouth-robbed stole over them. One man—either braver than the rest or else the earliest to lose his mind—screamed as he sprang forward to drive his home-made spear directly into the thigh of an advancing ghoul. It took the shaft without pain or altering its stance, but merely gripped the haft in both its clawed hands and pulled the man closer, driving the spear further through its own leg to get his clenched hands within reach. Grasping the nearest wrist, the ghoul released the spear and sank his teeth into the forearm, heedless of anything in the world except that at last it was eating. The man's scream rose to a singing pitch and he went down. Then the chaos overwhelmed them all.

Jedden experienced a moment of blackness, devoid of all sensation except screams and chill, before he realized that his eyes were closed. He wondered vaguely if he had started to run, and hoped he would find it true. But he opened his eyes, staring down at his boots, and saw his feet encased in crust, holding the exact spot they occupied when he started listening to the night. Only now there were more shadows, cast by the ragged light of buildings on fire. And as one shadow fell across his feet, his nostrils took in the stench of the long-dead, an odor that made the vomit in his mouth seem sugary. He raised his eyes without willing to, and saw the ghoul rise up and lunge for him with widespread talons.

He did not remember lifting his wood-axe, much less swinging it in such a deadly arc. The creature's arm came down directly in its path, and the heavy blade chopped it like a sapling, severing at the elbow and sending the lower arm gyring on and into the side of his head. At the same moment, the rest of the creature slammed into his side, and Jedden was amazed to feel how light the thing was. He stumbled back a step but would not have fallen, except that his boots were wedged in the crust and tripped him. The ghoul remained latched to him by its remaining claw as they went down, and Jedden saw its jaws sink into his jacket directly above his heart. Ignoring its amputation the beast pulled back its head, ripping the wool like parchment and exposing his naked flesh, where the woodcutter could see his heart pounding in panic with only the skin between it and the ghoul's next bite.

Frantically, he rolled over, and though the creature came with him, it was unable for a moment to bite again. Jedden had a whirling view of images—Pad's body sprawled face-down with a ghoul worrying his arm, the Man in Grey approaching a villager as he grappled with another of the pack, the thatcher's barn door wide open and a ghoul entering backlit by the fires, to the sound of high-pitched screams within. His foe felt like a rope woven of snakes, tightly coiled beneath its skin and with muscles and tendons constantly moving in differing directions. Jedden kicked it off momentarily, and the creature came up facing another of the pack, which had just fallen on its severed arm. Evidently amputations were fair game in the lust for food—as the big intruder sunk his teeth into the bloodless, stringy prize, its former owner howled in rage and hurled itself on the thief, bringing both of them down and tumbling in the crust.

Jedden staggered up and was halfway to the barn door before he realized he'd dropped his axe. Fear froze his legs, and his momentum carried him down to the ground again, skidding half-through the aperture and tearing his naked chest on the ice of the lintel. Within, he saw the ghoul raising its head from the ravaged chest of the halfling woman, its mouth full of vital organs and a look like ecstasy in its eyes. The father lay sprawled against a post, his head bleeding from the back and one hand missing at the wrist. Between them, in easy reach of the monster, stood the little girl, not an inch over two feet tall yet and spattered with blood, completely in shock.

Jedden started to weep, then froze to hear the tread of booted feet behind him. He saw the firelit shadow of a broad-brimmed hat against the barn wall, and felt the edge of a woolen cape brushing his shoulders as the thigh-high charcoal leather boots stepped over his body. The ghoul, evidently preferring the most freshly-dead meat it could get and unwilling to wait even a moment to get it, looked at the intruder but moved directly for the girl. Jedden saw the staff's heel, flaring silver, leave the ground as the man in grey called out in a language unknown to him, *"Calem toxis bellatara victorum!"* The staff came ringing down on the back of the creature's head, and it exploded with blue fire, to collapse at once into the hay, with its longest talon just touching the girl's naked foot. On the same level, and between the grey stranger's boots, Jedden could see that even as it writhed in its final moments, the creature was desperately chewing and trying to swallow.

As the halfling girl stared up at the man in grey, he whirled and stepped out of the barn again. Jedden scrambled to his feet and turned, in time to see him assail another ghoul with equally effective results. As the creature went down with a fire-marked crush in its ribs, Jedden grabbed a plank of wood and charged out into the melee.

Incredibly, more than half the ghouls were down, though in two cases it was their former pack-mates who tore at them and finished them off. Torches and repeated blows from the villagers had killed one, or perhaps two: the man in grey had destroyed four on his own. The bodies of slain villagers were everywhere, and the heedless way the ghouls fell on the downed had been the best chance of victory for the others.

At the last a lone survivor retreated from the edge of the village towards the stream, and no one among the village defenders had the heart to pursue. But the grey stranger, seemingly unaffected by his journey or the fighting, jogged out after it, stopping only to grab the body of a slain villager and roughly sling it down the slope.

The bright smear of blood it left on the crust as it skidded brought the beast around as surely as if it had been roped: coming between the monster and the food it craved, the grey man planted his staff in the snow and clutched a pendant hanging around his neck. The ghoul came loping on, then barreling in, intending to duck past the stranger and into his meal. But with an arcane shout the defender thrust out his hand and showed the ghoul the Hope-symbol he had covered, now glowing brightly blue against the white of the frozen stream. The azure light boiled for an instant, then shot forth to strike the moving ghoul full in the chest and in both eyes: as it howled in hunger, its body crumbled into moldy embers.

The end of the final attacker brought little abatement to the noise on all sides. Villagers screamed in agony from the razor-sharp teeth and infested talons of the ghouls, three buildings were on fire and the village was still up in arms. Through it all, Jedden could hear the tiny wailing chant of the halfling girl in the barn at his back. The man in grey approached the nearest wounded villager, who was clutching at his shredded thigh and trying to keep the pieces in as the blood welled past both his hands. When the man saw the stranger approach, he tried to scuttle back despite his wounds—but the grey man knelt and looked closely at the leg, then tented one hand over the wound and muttered something low and powerful. The man kept scuttling back, but when he took his hands away to move faster, the wound was no longer bleeding. Without pause, the man in grey stood and moved to another, and then a third—after pausing by a fourth man whose chest was torn to the bones of his ribs, the Man in Grey only shook his head and moved on. And three steps later, without the slightest warning he fell to the ground unconscious.

Jedden surveyed the wrack of Barden, and saw Cree to one side, trying to clear the stringy gobbets of ghoul from the peen-end of his hammer. After several frenzied attempts, the smith suddenly flung it in revulsion high and away from him: they both watched as it hit the frozen stream and broke through. "Get another one, come a'thaw," the smith muttered, and then turned to drag a corpse towards the flames. Jedden started to help, but heard the muttered voice of the halfling girl in the barn behind him. Limping over to look in, he saw her standing rooted to the spot where she had been saved, as if she hadn't so much as blinked since.

"Here now, girl," Jedden tried, his heart feeling lower than Cree's hammer as he saw the orphan there. He began to lead her away, and just to make converse, said "So then, what's your name?"

But the halfling girl only repeated the same word over and again. "Bellatara, bellatara, bellatara..."

With a second leg broken, the hut-sized mantis could no longer stand. Plumes of snow as it fell obscured even its own carapace a few moments, and the threshing of a half-dozen limbs still obstructed the path of the man in black. He circled to one side, but the creature continued to snap and reach out from its back, forcing him to stay and block the attacks with his open hands. In Pol's gaze, survival and mercy aligned; with a cry, the assailant leapt between the scissoring limbs and struck once with his foot at the joint between neck and head. Another snap, too tenor and hollow for the width of the target, and the monster's flails became faster yet aimless. They slowed and stopped, allowing the lone traveler to move on through the enormous pine forest.

He wended his way generally south, taking trails where available with less snow drifted on them. Even so, his feet were red-white with the chill. Stopping a moment to scout the terrain, Pol snapped fingers to create a patch of magic fire on the flurried earth. It burned for a short space without fuel, as he rubbed his feet dry and stood close enough to feel the heat. The pain of returning circulation was almost as bad as bleeding, but there was nothing there. The man in black had found food, taken rest, and recovered his inner balance. Warmth was needful for his feet; he shut out the pain as if slamming a gate.

Pol was no outdoorsman, but eventually sensed the nearby water and drifted to the bank of a mighty river. No doubt, this was no longer the Percentalion; Pol could sense remnants of order and nature here, though there was a stain across the land. The looming peak of Skysword dominated the horizon, so this river could not be the Sweeping, bordering the land of his childhood in Mendel; he must be near the center. The floe was frozen over, to the opposite bank. Pol would have thought the current too strong for that despite the bitter cold.

Traveling near the banks with occasional glimpses of the ice, he came across an old kiln, burned out yet containing new-made charcoal. Noting the irony he filled a sack with the blackened bricks; there were men nearby, but what had happened to them? The pine barrens gave him clues of previous occupation—tracks, more kilns, trees clumped together to look almost planted—yet now as he moved there was an unaccustomed silence to the forest, with neither bird nor beast to break the gloom. By night's small charcoal flame, Pol heard the distant howl of a lone wolf, which seemed to his ear filled with despair, perhaps the loss of its mate.

The following day, Pol came to the brick road-junction within sight of the river bridge and the magnificent, abandoned city of dark red walls with Skysword behind it. He stood there in the lonely, windswept piazza and contemplated the barred portcullis of the outer wall, the empty parapets and their upper-level bridges, and the ominous sign of thin, curling trails of black smoke that still drifted above the roofs.

Pol looked about him too, at the five arches of metal set into solid brick walls between the incoming roads. Was this perhaps Reghalion, he wondered. The large city seemingly placed against base of the mountain, with gates outside; the ancient tales confirmed these facts, though nothing was said about a river or bridge. Yet when he looked back to those walls, Pol saw not one sign of life. And rational though he had always trained to remain, the word that invaded his mind was "haunted".

He resolved to wait. More signs of recent occupation, handwagon tracks and the outer buildings with cleared snow before their doors, indicated there might yet be inhabitants of this foef. Exploring the area nearby, Pol found a side-path leading to the river just north of the city-island, with ice all between the shores. Nearby, he heard gabbling and curses; moving closer in a low crouch brought him to a strange sight, a band of pygmy-garruk at the edge of a deep cleft in the ground.

Moving silently downwind to a small copse of coppiced beech, he observed them. In no way could this tribe, or an endless horde of the same, have built the things he'd seen. They even looked a bit frightened of each other, as they beat skin-drums, shook tiny weapons and dragged the carcass of a slain wolf nearer to the edge of the earth-gash. It looked unnatural and reeked of sulphurous steam; twice the wolf's pall-bearers lost their nerve and fled, each time harangued back into duty by a beaded-chieftain of some stripe. Pulling the corpse to the very edge, the others fell back leaving their leader in a palsy of excitement, as he gibbered and gestured by turns in all directions. Finally he kicked at the wolf body, nudging it over the lip and down. Everyone waited then for several long seconds, until a distant hiss and spurt of hell-steam signaled the start of a combined celebration and rout from the tribe, who fled trailing tones of tinny triumph into the barrens.

Pol emerged from his coven and strode to the opposite edge of the crevice, barely a man's length across but suggesting there was no bottom to it. Vainly attempting to pierce its depth with his eyes, he shortly became ill and dizzy from the constant vapors, and fell back no wiser than before. But Pol's sense of trouble, of wrongness and the stain of Despair only increased. He found a safe spot of flat rock, raised enough to see the frozen river and the city, yet shielded from casual view by trees, and settled in to meditate.

With every cycle of slowing breath, Pol felt his muscles, long tensed by the struggle to survive, lengthening and shedding the distractions of pain. It became unimportant to see the sun, and later the stars, to hear the crack of ice or the gentle patter of tiny hail-like flakes on the stone. Pol catalogued the smell of pine needles and river-marsh and the elusive hint of charcoal; all filed away, and attended to no more. The little air he still took in barely moved past his nose and lungs; the comfort of his body-pose was one he could sustain indefinitely.

Never before had Pol mastered the trance-state long enough to detach from his own body. But now his spirit soared.

Rising toward a starry-sky, he saw it all at once. The space between this brick city and the capital, still further in beyond the woods. The swirling energy of the spells that surrounded the base of the mountain, the unthinkable weight and substance of that spire itself, the touch of the heroic hands that raised it. Pol knew, though unable to trace the logic of the thought, that he would climb the slope of Skysword someday. He hungered to, felt it was not simply a challenge but a duty, as if passed on from others he had never met.

Pol looked to the sky and heard the tones of the planets, the chords they struck from their various positions, music repeated precisely only once an epoch. The south-sailing moons created a shimmer like enormous cymbals beneath the heavenly notes, waxing in volume and filling him with energy tinged by panic. He noted the huge red star, moving down and nearly passing him in fire. With his left hand he reached out and gently touched its surface, feeling the dimmest echo of its heat, the smoothness of its hull, the flicker of emotions its crew had once felt on the last course they set before their deaths. Again, there was so much he did not understand, but Pol did not tarry to puzzle over it.

By the shine of the cymbal-moons, Pol saw an enormous mass of moving beings far off north, and brought the view closer. Distance required only thought to conquer, and in a moment he beheld the vast army of Despair, moving toward the edge of this domain. A straight path to one side of the myriad clove the chaos-land, and near its south-most end, closer to Pol's body than this nightmarish host, a star-bright point of Law slowly moved even closer.

Returning to the stony plain, Pol made out another point of heaven, somewhere within the brick city, this one coterminous with a crimson spark of potent evil. There was much movement within the city, but he could see no life. The third gleam of order and Hope—for Pol sensed there would be three of them—lay further on, further in, at the true capital. Pol knew, again, without knowing how, that he must see all three of these things before he could fully understand.

Before he could reach the center.

Pol's spirit sensed no immediate danger in the vicinity of his body, but his instinct prompted him to return rather than risk further separation. The body would still be important some time yet. The spirit-world turned from day to night seemingly at the direction of his mind, and he could not be sure how much time had passed. He eased back into his frame and took care not to return to consciousness too quickly. Dawn had indeed passed by the time his breathing returned to a visible level. But for several moments it seemed to Pol still dusk of the night before. An iron wall of clouds had battened down the entire sky, and snow was already piling over the level of his crossed legs.

The gradual return of feeling to his limbs brought increasing numbers of reports to his brain. The trend was unanimous, his body was freezing. Pol cleared back a space from his knees and summoned flame, once and then again, to beat back the worst of the chill. Marveling at the puckers on his skin from such a long interval of neglect, he began to melt fallen flakes to warm them before drinking.

By the time the complaints of the flesh retreated, the storm had fully moved in. At a guess, Pol headed toward the river to seek shelter. Something told him to keep the city in sight. At the frozen water's edge stood a thick cluster of bracken between the arching roots of a cypress half-in the water below. An hour's labor packing the drifting sheets of snow to his purpose created a thorn-studded wall from trunk to root-stump, and Pol settled into its lee to wait out the fury of winter.

The wind gusted at times hard enough to snap branches the width of a waist and send them skittering across the floes. Snow knifed in shards creating mounds in moments, and quickly blowing away again to reform elsewhere. The cold became quite intense and the wind cracked and boomed, once or twice with lightning in it and a freezing slap so loud it shattered the ice. But the crevices there quickly refilled and refroze, at the outer edge of Pol's vision in this blizzard that felt to him as if it hated the world.

The trance state was harder to achieve among this cacophony, but Pol knew how to settle his breathing, to not waste his energies as he waited and thought about this land, its curse, its center and why one point of light had been moving. The bracken bore a kind of hard chalky berry that bloomed best in the middle of winter. The Elves who raised him called them Hardhopes, since the birds and squirrels hated the taste and ate them only as a last resort. They succored him sourly now, as he remained seated and tried not to rouse but also not to sleep.

Pol stayed where he was through the heart of the storm, and saw the point of Law as it passed, its magic showing to his spirit like a lantern across the ice, crawling forward with a few shadows against the storm, who persevered through stumbles, cracking ice, winter lightning and howling winds to reach the base of the island. Pol rose to follow them, and though no creature could leave a visible track he sensed the Sword, and found a cave leading up into the haunted city. A step closer to the center. For surely, surely there was something there.

In the aftermath of Barden's doom, Gelia had taken over direction, and her requests for assistance were always honored. That was the only reason the Man in Grey still lived. She had emerged from her barricaded hut on the edge of town to call for wrappings and warm water, and was seeking among the bodies for more wounded when she caught sight of Cree, about to drive a dropped hayfork into the prone stranger's back. Her call did not stop him, but the eyes of the rest of the villagers did, though he did not like it.

"Finish him now, before he wakes!" he cried with his weapon still poised. But Gelia never hesitated, stepping in to take his arms and stand under the wanted blow. And that gave Jedden time to become the head man of Barden.

"He saved us, Cree, I saw him."

"He's a necromancer, drove them onto us, ye sar that, idn't ye?"

"I saw, but—he must have been chasing them."

"Chasing? One man on foot chasing the batch as did for 'er knight on horseback?" Cree's voice rose in the heat of his anger, but the gathering of villagers was taking the steam from his spirit. In Barden, respect went to the man who was right.

"He has magic, that's what burned the dead ones we saw before. He saved us—he saved the halfling girl, I saw it with my own eyes." Jedden gestured to Melessa, Pad's wife when the night began, who cradled the little halfling in her arms like a human baby, now finally asleep.

Cree chewed his lips in sheer frustration, but Gelia wasn't waiting for him to agree.

"He goes into the barn, with the others. Gently with him now, he's probably in casting shock—spent too much of his spirit at once, and no wonder with the trek he's been on. Who's knows what he's seen..." she trailed into muttering but kept her body moving, assisting a man with a lacerated foot to hobble after the three others hauling the grey stranger into the makeshift hospital. Jedden walked behind, having picked up the man's hat—Cree, after crossing eyes with the woodcutter, stooped quickly and came up with the staff, now just iron-shod once more. The two of them followed the procession, well lit by the glow from the houses still on fire.

Jedden told off all but three to fight the fires, and they went; one stopped by to hand him back his lost axe. Jedden stowed it in the barn before returning to help. "Not the creek, don't bother!" he cried to the forming line. Kicking at the crust beneath him, he said "Just use snow." And so they clustered closer to the buildings, using buckets and shovels and even bare arms to mound the winter harvest around the burning buildings. Jedden gave up on three at once—no one questioned his decision, since his own cottage was one—and focused on saving the thatcher's barn and the rest.

In less than an hour's hard work, with a few children pitching in taking turns in the bitter chill of midnight, the work was down to watching the piled embers for drifting sparks. The bodies, too, were taken care of, with the seven dead villagers and two halflings incinerated together on a pyre of true firewood, while the bodies of the ghouls they threw into Jedden's house to burn. The village folk shared grim jests with him on this, clapping his back as they brought him their respect and shared some of their relief to have survived.

Jedden found the strength to offer comfort to those who had lost a man. Melessa seemed to bear up very well with the orphan in her care, and Jedden saw fit to leave this matter to rest for now. He returned with rapidly-tiring steps to the barn to check on the wounded and Gelia. There was still no hint of dawn in the sky, but Aral had exited to the south and Unal, nearing its moonset, seemed to be winking wickedly at him. A night no sooner done than good, he thought.

Inside the barn, Gelia worked by candle among the nine hurt men, laying back on hay piles or between the stalls where Pad's mule placidly munched away. The grey stranger was stretched on a blanket on the floor; his hands were folded as if a corpse. Even unconscious he lay apart from the others. Jedden walked over to where Gelia was tending to the barley farmer, who had a nasty set of claw-marks down both arms. He was hissing in pain, but the healer had stanched the worst of his bleeding with moss-poultices.

"So, Trowden, how are you holding up?" Jedden had not addressed the healer, and began to realize that he seldom spoke to her the past two years. She looked up at him in the candlelight now, though, and he hardly minded what the farmer said in response. He only heard clearly again when Gelia agreed, saying "Yes, he'll be sore for some time but I see no sign of infection."

Rising, the healer moved to another pallet and the woodcutter went along. "Here's the one that worries me," she murmured, pointing to Cree's nephew Fal, who tossed in fevered half-sleep as they stood over him, a ragged bite on his shoulder bleeding out around the bandage. "I don't think he'll ever be able to raise his arm over his head again," she said, and her eyes seemed to say more. Jedden looked at the bandages, and saw the tinge of dirt-yellow along with the red. "I hear the bite of a ghoul makes another," he said cautiously. "Can you cure him?"

Gelia shook her head slowly. "I don't have the skill," and again Jedden sensed there was more to her thought than what she said. She took a half-glance to one side, and Jedden saw her intent—the man on the floor behind them.

"I shall wake him," he said, but the healer shook her head.

"It's dangerous now, he was beyond exhaustion. I don't know how..." she shook her head again, and as he gazed on her, Jedden realized the source of his reluctance around Gelia. It was her beauty, and his ankle that abashed him so much. The first he hadn't truly seen until now, but the other he had never forgotten.

Only three years ago, and his father was still alive the day he chopped his axe through a log and into his own foot. The healer had fixed him up so well he hardly limped, but Jedden was still mortified to have been so weak and helpless in front of her. Now, her strange looks and silences mystified the woodcutter: before tonight, he would have recalled the energy he had spent just arguing with Cree a night to remember. Since then, he'd fought a battle, and won another: now the village healer, ten years and more his senior, was conversing with him alone, a council of leadership.

"It is in my mind," she said with a formal, quiet tone, "that whatever befalls young Fal will be... resolved in two days. Surely we were on Shilar's watch tonight— by rights this should have been the end of us. But now, either way we'll be ready."

"Ready for what?"

"To leave the village," Gelia's reply was still quiet but firm, and her gaze spoke of more, "if you should lead us away."

"To leave..." Jedden realized the burden fell to him—of course they would all take counsel and vote, but his word now would weigh more than double any other man's. And the healer was as much as telling him she would back his word, which in the village of Barden was a decision as good as made.

Jedden stammered for breath and words. "We need to know... if there are any more."

"No more," spoke a tight voice behind them, and they both whirled to see the man in grey with eyes alight, watching them. As Gelia rose to attend him, Jedden again followed, but his steps were slow and he stopped a full pace away. The stranger made his hackles stand, despite his deeds, more surely now than when he had first seen him a week ago.

The grey man tried to rise, and got nowhere at once: falling back to the blanket, he murmured, "the man in green, his arms... blood on his arms..." Gelia knelt beside him and placed her hand on his head, not only to comfort him but also to hold him down. "Trowden will be fine, sirrah, you just rest now." The stranger's mien was haggard, thinner even than Jedden remembered, the flesh of his face straining to lay on the floor alongside the back of his head. But the eyes—the woodcutter could not stand more than a glance across the gaze of those silver flints. They seemed to reflect shreds and bits of what he had seen. He spoke to the man in grey, and realized only later that he did so as the head man of Barden.

"Sir, can you say for certain—no more of them?"

"Aye, this pack was the last. The last of those... awoken."

"So—there are more."

The man in grey contemplated Jedden for a short while, and he looked at Gelia instead as if she might take up the duty of returning his gaze. Finally, he said only, "Hundreds more, further east on the Plains. But they sleep, as they have for centuries. This pack has been destroyed."

"The Plains of Ranebruh? That's a barren land, I've always heard, flat, rocky and windswept, without life."

The corner of the stranger's mouth may have flicked just a hair. "Aye. There is no life on Ranebruh. Only cold wind, and death... and the Tombs Thanazun."

Jedden looked to Gelia but she shook her head; the name chilled him though he had never heard it before. "You deserve rest, sir, and we owe you our lives. But I must trouble you with more questions. First, however, my apology. I treated you as an enemy, when you first arrived." Jedden bent over to put his outthrust hand within the stranger's reach.

He looked, but did not take it, saying only, "You owe me nothing. I was the one who woke them."

On this, Jedden straightened up as if struck. "You? But—why?"

"I sought knowledge. I am a sage."

"A sage! You are far from your books, sir," Jedden snapped before he could stop himself.

Gelia leaned in towards the stranger and said only, "Did you find it? The lore you were seeking?"

The man in grey gazed at her briefly before nodding once and slightly. Then he looked back to Jedden, saying, "Ask your questions."

Jedden composed himself a moment. "How do you know there are no others, awake?"

"I know what I saw. I moved north by east across the Plains and encountered none for two days. Then the *kemetaria*." He paused as Gelia gasped and sat back. "Verily, there are packs of ghouls to all sides, but as I left no trace of human scent, they shall not follow as these did the horseman. Thousands of the mortal dead are buried there outside the underground fortress, known as the Tombs Thanazun."

"For which you sought?"

"Aye."

"And for which seven villagers of Barden perished," Jedden said with heat, "and in defence of whom Sir Ganelake has died."

So taken with anger, Jedden actually locked eyes with the man in grey; after a moment, the stranger nodded once and slightly. Jedden noted the man's clear skin, the unmarked brow contrasting with his hair, not decrepit but grey as if by magic. With a shock, the woodcutter realized that the two of them were of an age. There was only silence for a time.

"It is in my mind," Jedden resumed using a leader's tone, "that your actions were not meant to bring harm to us, and you have risked your life to make recompense. I will not judge. You bring us news that all these centuries there are buried bodies on the Plains beyond the hills, and that is serious reason to consider flight to my mind. But tell me, sir, what are these foul creatures, these ghouls? Must we fear them in the future, or are they as you say, 'asleep'?"

Now the Man in Grey could lever himself up on an elbow, and Jedden sat on a bale to listen while Gelia took the floor between them. The candle began to gutter as he spoke, and Jedden felt as he did as a child, when someone told ghost-tales around the fire.

"The legends do not agree, whether they are truly undead or simply a degraded race. They are often described as 'immortal' but some in the Guild argue they regenerate as other beings do, and had so little contact over the centuries that they but seemed unliving. We have noted now," he said with some irony, "that they have not—the physical means nor genders to give birth, and so I tend to think they are unaging."

"How did you survive them? And why not Sir Ganelake?"

"The knight slew over twenty of them on his own. I saw him fighting across the tundra but could not reach him before... he lost because he fought," the stranger said in a cold tone, and stopped for a time as if the statement needed no explanation. "The ghouls can be slain, or at least destroyed, through blows or fire. But they are so heedless of their safety, and hunt in packs, that this aside from their repulsive scent and demeanor, is too much for any single warrior. He fought with great distinction and never seemed to consider retreat, but eventually both he and his horse were bleeding, and then there could be no escape from them." The stranger halted a while and turned his head aside. "It is their hunger, that is the key."

"I don't understand," said Jedden.

"I cannot completely explain it," the man admitted, "but they seem to have a limitless ability to suffer hunger. Ghouls can go without food completely, but they ache with the need to eat. And their hunger grows with each day, each year, without end. I knew all the lore agreed on this point, and the scenting of blood, so I reasoned they did not eat each other."

"But were you never wounded?" Gelia asked, and patted the stranger down to check. Feeling bandages beneath his clothes, she began to work them back, but the Man in Grey stayed her hand and pulled open his clothes after some struggle. A vague echo of the horrible stench arose and Jedden saw a half-dozen places where the Man in Grey had been cut or clawed. On each one, he had strapped a piece of ghoul flesh over the wound. The woodcutter stifled an urge to vomit again, and the stranger began to remove the unearthly dressings that served as a disguise. "I avoided them when I could—their vision is remarkably poor, except on moonlit nights—and fought when I had the advantage. I was able to salvage the materials I needed to confuse the scent. It was enough for me to complete my researches. But when the knight came, they had a track to follow, and could sense other living beings in your direction. So they came off the plains, and I followed them."

"Your spells," Jedden continued, "you slew them with fire on your staff, and your holy symbol destroys them. Are they undead, then?"

The man in grey contemplated this awhile before answering slowly, "I do not know. I believe... the thanes of Despair who saw fit to inter themselves below the earth," as Gelia and Jedden both shuddered, "evidently had servants to tend their tombs beyond their own deaths. It may be that these slaves degenerated over the years, and practiced eating human flesh to survive. That combined with the considerable unholy power locked into that cursed place, may have wrought a change in them. The sons of Despair worship undeath, and their servants may have... hungered to achieve their state. Mayhap the ghouls *believe* they are truly undead, and through years of such belief have come to imitate them in some respects. At all events, it is true that the power to harm undead creations does affect them, another stroke of fortune for me."

"Did you... did you go down there?" Gelia asked in a whisper. The man in grey for response looked her in the eye for a wordless moment, and she cringed back against Jedden in fear. Feeling his leg and knee, she wrapped an arm around his calf and rested her hand on his foot, on the boot atop the old scar. Her touch sent a thrill up his frame, even as he feared the man's words. The woodcutter instinctively placed a protective hand down on her shoulder, and wondered that he should be able to comfort this full-grown woman, who always seemed confident and mature to his fumbling, foot-cutting fool. Things change rapidly, he reflected.

He said to the man in grey, "I thank you again, stranger—for all your tale is beyond belief, it is in my heart that you are a worthy man. You may rest here as long as you wish and safe travels to you when you choose to leave us."

The Man in Grey nodded once and slightly, leaned back to close his eyes, and appeared to fall almost instantly asleep. A while passed as they watched him and wondered. Then Jedden felt the healer playfully removing his boot before he could stop her. Tracing the very light scar atop his foot that she knew would be there, she looked up at him from her knees.

"I knew a boy, once, who cut his foot exactly as you have."

"He was a fool," Jedden said quickly, "and he may still be."

The healer shook her head as she slipped his boot back on. "Perhaps. But he is grown now. And I must say, I do good work."

Jedden helped Gelia to her feet and their eyes came close for an instant. He was now heedless of the bitter cold, except for his frozen tongue that needed an act of will to unlock it, even for a formal speech.

"It is in my mind that our village is safe at least for now and that we should not move away." Gelia nodded at once to this but kept her gaze on the new head-man of Barden. Jedden thought her eyes were like bright, twin orbs of the sky, and he wanted to listen to hear their secrets.

"Many have lost family," she said and he nodded moving ahead of her intent.

"I think Melessa and the halfling child will need shelter most. I could take them in with me," he said cautiously. "Or rather, I could move in with them, as my cabin has become a pyre this night."

She giggled at this and moved away to retrieve her things. "She needs a child, and seems quite attached to the little babe. Fortune has given her the motherhood that nature could not," Gelia said with meaning. And once again Jedden stared into those orbs, wondering at eternal secrets.

"I could offer to live with her as a brother," he said carefully. "It is in my heart that this arrangement would be the best for the future. Of the village, of course."

"For the village, yes of course," was the healer's reply. And then she winked so deliberately at him the he could not see anything other than mischief in it. But he laughed, for he saw no harm in that.

The next morning, Fal's diseased scratches were completely cleansed and healed, as if by magic. And the only men still in the barn were those who would live in Barden the rest of their lives.

⊕⊕⊕

The room's single tallow candle drew low enough to gutter in its cup. Treaman reached across the table for another but Mhoral stopped him.

"Let it go, Treaman. We know where everything is."

"And what we all look like," Haltar added companionably.

"Good news with the bad, there." Linya spoke unexpectedly, and everyone laughed, mainly from surprise. Treaman looked to where the mage's silhouette hinted at her beautiful face, and recalled the rest of her even better in the widening darkness.

A last flicker, the hiss of extinguishment. Treaman reluctantly set down his tinder-box, a single wooden click into a long moment of silence. Truly, he thought as his heart sank back down to its accustomed resting place these last few days, the dark was right for them now. Nothing to see, no way forward.

The party always slept when the light went out, before this. But no one headed toward the bunks here in Fairnum's upstairs rooms, moved off to eat or smoke. No one left to relieve themselves, or get more drinks, or to re-enter the Percentalion carrying one miracle treasure in search of two more and an unknown man to wield them. To fight a demon beyond their power, and throw their lives after Bildon's in an insane gamble without a shred of hope to sustain it.

Braja leaned against the wall near the door, his massive frame a blacker black, suggesting ease and patience while the night covered the rent in his cheek.

He had all the time in the world, because despite his constant improvement in the common tongue the southern warrior showed no interest in arguing the party's course. After trying everything else, they had asked Braja several times to vote, in the past dozen-odd hours of fruitless argument. Always the hulking Nubian merely shook his head, shrugged, and pointed to Haltar. Leader.

Treaman's ballot always stood alone. He faced the darkness at the middle of the table, flogging his brain for a new argument, a brilliant point that would convince them of a course he could not even describe. The young Woodsman still felt Bildon's loss as keenly, carried anger as well as terror for the demon who had burned him. He knew the feel of the Sword of Air, remembered the helldogs' howl and the distant gentle scent of the flowers in the glade where he had his vision of Helmon and Areghel. Treaman knew as surely as he breathed or Hallah slept, that the curse over the land must be broken, order and the kingdom restored.

But he had no idea, none at all, how they could re-enter the chaos realm and survive. That he must try made no difference: all the facts were piled against going. The others only waited in deference to him, to tell the town about the Sword of Air: one day had turned to five and still it lay under wraps beneath the barrel of riddy in the corner.

"We were never attacked, while we were on the road." Treaman knew the voice for his own in the darkness, a lifeless tone repeating itself the dozenth time.

"On the road, yes," Haltar agreed equably. "Of course it's hardly proof, but I would be willing to believe that." The party leader was quietly declaring his readiness to risk the group that far. He had affirmed this before.

"And from the end of the road," Linya continued, "you think it might be… not very far to Oncario."

Treaman nodded invisibly, and the tears started. When Mhoral laid a hand on his arm he nearly jumped out of his skin. Forgot, with even one window open for starlight's shreds, the Elf could still see.

"But you can't know. That thing out there, it wants the Sword, it found us the first time."

Treaman could nod and weep, but he could think of nothing else to say.

"And then," Mhoral continued, announcing the verdict. "The city. Oncario. The Primara will be on guard, and the only way to Reghalion must lie through there."

Treaman snuffed hard, and popped the table with his fist speaking too loud. "I know! We must have a Stealthic. Bildon's dead, and I have to avenge him. Without him."

"Someone to get us quietly through the streets," Mhoral nodded and spoke as if everyone agreed now. Treaman wasn't sure he was wrong. "To pilfer that cursed gem, retrieve the scepter, pick the mechanism by the opposite gate, get us through and on to Reghalion. Without Bildon, we simply can't, whether one demon chases us, or two. So we shall reveal the Sword to the authorities. In the morning. They'll send an army, I'm sure of it. And if—"

When the door to the room rattled open even Braja was caught by surprise.

⊕ ⊕ ⊕

Anteris was not surprised to find his feet had carried him to Fairnum's Tavern. The main room had several patrons, all residents, and this was no great challenge to his confidence, though it was the first time he'd ever entered the drinking place without Valenthur. After a few moments standing there stupidly and gathering gazes, he tried to assume a businesslike face and crossed to the stairs like someone with every right to be there. Like an adult. It wasn't until he'd reached the bottom step that he knew for a fact his courage was completely drained. He regarded the tread as if it were made of serpents. Climb to their room? Speak to the heroes of destiny? Surely it would be easier to change into a bird and fly to Novar for the winter.

It was no inner resolve or any shred of a plan that pushed Anteris onward. But the sound of voices from above, tantalizing word-parts from the direction where the Heroes lived drew him up, without thinking about the stairs, or the noise or what he might say. Those who had faced death were speaking, no doubt of history, and the scribe felt as if his ears were tugging him along, to get close enough to hear more.

"… not very far to Oncario… must have a Stealthic… on to Reghalion... demon chases us… reveal the Sword…"

Anteris shivered by the door, hugged himself and started praying to Rallantan, hero of his order. Sorrow for their lost companion, that explained the delay. These heroes were strangers to Trainertown, ignorant of even its most famous secrets. Anteris saw with clarity how he could help; his first instinct was to write a note to tell them.

Then his mind moved to other words, about a weapon, of cities and monsters. These things of which he had only read, the heroes within had been there first hand. His life's work, would he forever just study it in books? The image of Rallantan flashed before his eyes, the lore-master whose actions at the Battle of the Razor were the greatest contribution to Hope's victory. He was there, he took the risk. And Forge would go without him, unless…

Someone's hand clicked the latch, pushed the door open, and before he knew it Anteris was standing in the darkened room.

⊕⊕⊕

Treaman snapped to at the intrusion, alarmed that someone could have approached the door unheard. Bildon would never have missed it. Haltar stood as Braja instinctively grabbed the human-shape by its neck; the vigor of its wriggling revealed the intruder was young.

A small point of light appeared above the table, returning vision to the room.

"Who is this?" Haltar demanded, and Braja turned to eject him.

"Wait!" Treaman cried, "I know him, the scribe's assistant. Anteris, isn't it?"

Braja looked to Haltar who shrugged, then set the boy back down without an ounce of strain and patted him twice atop the head. The boy looked breathless and almost faint, staring at Braja, Haltar and the light in alternation.

"Anteris?" Treaman repeated to gain his attention. "What is it you wanted?"

"Masters, I—" Anteris gasped under the attention of so many great persons at one time. He wanted to speak to each of them; to ask the Nubian of his homeland, the mage of her lore, and the Elf about the Moments his life had seen. Anteris could form a perfect picture of a future day, when he was already accepted by this group, at his ease among them. But starting where he stood now…

From no place he could name, his mind brought out a thought of the wise and kindly Elf Cedrith, who dared to speak for him and gave him his present course, permission to study and the encouragement to do so. Anteris groped for that courage and drew breath while they all waited.

"I know what you need. I can bring your Stealthic."

That got them all to straighten up; his equal treatment began, and curiously Anteris felt a bit less afraid than before. He paused a moment, and added a word completely beyond the courage of any mere boy.

"But only if you take me with you as well."

Treaman felt a stab of fear at the youth's words so strong that Hallah woke up. How dull of brain, he thought, not to have asked around about it. But this absurd demand, and no doubt the one Anteris spoke of would also be young; Treaman did not know if he could pay the guilt-price before him, two more lives for a chance at vengeance.

Haltar handled the interrogation while the Woodsman thought furiously how to react.

"Lad it's a brave offer, but trust me when I say you have no idea what you're asking."

"I shall stay out of your way, and only observe."

"Observe!" Mhoral laughed, "perhaps you'll bring a chair to sit in, when we meet Kog and the dogs of hell!"

"Just tell us the Stealthic's name, and we'll—"

"No," Anteris was panting for breath, but held his ground. "You're strangers here; ask for a week and you'll never find him."

"We will not drag a child into danger!" Haltar thundered.

"No hero would!" Anteris shot back in a shout that cracked. Another deep breath. "But if you think us young, ask what parent would willingly give you the name you seek?"

They took that in a moment, and Treaman felt the beginnings of something deep in his gut, that pointed upward for the first time in days.

The young scribe planted his arms akimbo, though he looked ridiculous. "He is my friend. It's both of us, or neither. Those are my terms."

Haltar's face sprouted a tiny version of his crooked, murder-meaning grin. "You have pith, lad. But it is absolutely—"

"Anteris," Treaman interrupted, standing, "would you be willing to feed Hallah, she's hungry." As every eye pivoted to him, Treaman gestured once toward the barrel and fiddled in his pack for some note-sheets. The scribe hesitated only a moment before moving to the corner and uncapping the tub of salted fish. The little dragon squalled in tinny delight, flapped twice and glided over to reach directly into the treasure-bin. Mhoral as usual fell back a half-step; Linya was stunned, Haltar incredulous, to be thus interrupted.

Treaman doubled down. Having found the notes, he raised his gaze to Haltar's and casually added, "Bring over that wrapped bundle as well, will you? There's something you need to see."

"What are you doing?" Mhoral hissed.

As he answered, Treaman didn't take his eyes away from where the real struggle lay.

"Nothing, really. In a few hours, you were going to tell everyone."

Haltar's grin had grown into something quite lethal now, and he leaned down to whisper with emphasis.

"That *boy* is not a member of this party."

Treaman assessed the chances of having his jaw cuffed off and decided that compared to the sickness of his spirit these last few days, the pain would probably be less. Something was happening deep inside him, and the upward movement continued.

"You haven't been paying close attention, fearless leader. Either he *is* a member, or we don't have a party."

Treaman could see in Haltar's eyes, the foot-knight had never considered the point. Until this instant, neither had he.

Anteris laid the bundle on the table beneath the magic light, and Treaman gestured that he should open it. Everyone watched the youth's hanging mouth at first sight of the artefact. He reached out to lightly trace some of the silver filigree, the slopes of Skysword on the scabbard.

"Don't draw it," Linya warned, "it can really sting."

Anteris looked up at them with awe at the implications.

"It is one of the Tridium," he whispered, "no one will believe I've seen it."

"The Scepter of Law," Treaman replied, "is in Oncario. And the crown, the Order Brow, we don't know. Nor how to get to Reghalion from there."

"By the gates," Anteris responded at once, as with common knowledge.

"What? No, they aren't real." Mhoral was adamant, but Treaman noted he was arguing. With an equal.

"The gates have never lost their power of operation, it cannot be."

"We passed them, in the plaza before the river, just arches of stone."

Anteris started to answer, then smiled with knowing. "Those are the arrival gates, sir. Oncario has two sets as an added protection for the capital. To leave Oncario for Reghalion or any of the outer kingdoms, you must use the exit gates in the throne room."

Treaman chuckled, but kept looking over to Haltar, who held his gaze companionably as before. Here was the greatest puzzle of all, the secret of what lay in this warrior's heart. They would go nowhere without him. But what did Haltar want?

"In the throne room," Mhoral wondered aloud. "So, we could avoid the surrounding woods?"

Anteris could hardly believe how little the others knew of such things. He spoke with renewed hope of his own usefulness.

"They are impassable, set with spells by Areghel at the foundation of the kingdom."

"But the Primara," Linya said, "she told of sending Januelus to search across the eastern gate, into those woods."

In the silence everyone looked at Anteris, who felt a shock at the attention. It wouldn't do to start his new life on a lie. "I don't know who this person is," he confessed. "But the ancient sources are clear."

"They must have forgotten," Haltar said slowly. It seemed to Anteris that the strapping knight looked down on him with a more calculating eye.

"Tell me, sirrah," Haltar asked from across the table. "your Stealthic friend, has he any experience?"

Anteris gulped before answering. "He's the finest talent in this country. No one better."

"As I thought. Brave enough, I suppose?"

Again, he knew better than to lie with so much at stake. "Practically suicidal, sir."

To either side, the lovely sorceress sighed while the Elf laughed bitterly.

"Good enough with locks and his hands?" Haltar pursued.

From a side pocket, Anteris drew out his favorite quill, demonstrating that he had glued it by a rawhide thong tied to the waist of his pants.

"Otherwise he keeps taking it. Only for fun."

Now the Elf groaned and sat heavily. "Just what I needed. Another one." No one laughed. Instead the others took their seats again, leaving Anteris standing at the table and the great Nubian by the door. They sat still and quiet, yet Anteris had the feeling they forgot he was in the room.

Treaman looked across the way at Haltar, and Anteris watched as the knight returned his stare. The young, hardened Woodsman did not flinch, seemed almost tense enough to draw a weapon. The knight for his part never seemed upset at all, cocking his head like someone with a strong hand of cards considering whether to raise the bet.

Finally the Woodsman spoke. "I'm going. With just Anteris and his friend if I have to. The Sword with me."

Anteris tingled with the compliment, and felt ice in his spine a moment later.

"Can we do it?" Linya asked. "Do we have a chance?"

Treaman snorted. "Did we ever? But it's what we have to do."

The Elf looked first to Treaman, then Haltar. Braja unfolded his arms and stood up ready. Hallah flew back to Treaman's shoulders and curled there, looking steadily at Anteris.

At last, Haltar shrugged and laughed; some unspoken matter was settled.

Anteris asked, "When, when do we leave then?"

The foot-knight pointed across the table with finality.

"Ask our leader."

The room fell completely silent then, as every head swiveled to regard the young Woodsman, who returned Haltar's gaze with a single nod.

"You still direct us in combat," Treaman offered. Haltar shrugged as if acknowledging an obvious fact. Now Mhoral and Linya's mouths were open.

Braja stepped across to the table with a puzzled brow.

"Who is leader?"

"When we fight, Haltar," Treaman responded. "For where we go and when," he pointed back to himself.

"And this one," Braja said with an enormous hand on Anteris' shoulder. "Same?"

"Equal," Treaman agreed with a grin. "And one more, when we leave. At dawn."

⊕⊕⊕

The light-bridge had not appeared in nearly a fortnight.

Renan stood his watch like the others and the secret visions that came only to him continued as before. The cloud of dark mist that had consumed Hollinsfen moved now to hover over Oncario, and he dreaded the result for the twoscore thousand who had lived there. Other glimpses of the barren land showed mainly emptiness, an eerie lack of life, a world scraped free of the monstrous creatures and roving bands that had formerly been everywhere. Stathos and Maladon, other villages remained unmolested, for which he gave thanks. But where had the creatures gone?

Once he saw the red star as if up close, dripping flame and frightfully even and round, hanging over a stone roadway made straight as an arrow, shedding its crimson light like spilled blood on a small town with too few persons—Trainertown, he guessed.

And to the south, it was as if Renan's gaze could take him nowhere except to the female Elven Preacher, with her adventuring band in the Southern Empire. Every time, he felt trouble in his soul; this was far beyond the ambit of the Chosen Wanderers, and she was hardly ever in direct danger. Yet Renan took a strange comfort, like a soothing bath, to see her dickering in the market, laughing with her friends, praying—especially then, he admitted, for her beauty stood out to him enough to light the night. Though the visions never carried sound, he sensed her honest nature, courage in fighting, her prowess with spear and shield and the piety behind the miracles she summoned.

Was she somehow important to the fate of the Order, though dwelling hundreds of leagues to the south? Perhaps, Renan mused, this was just an example to him, of how far the brothers should range to seek fulfillment of their vows. Yet surely, despite this unnerving drought of calls, there was work aplenty here. Renan sensed in his prayers that a time of testing lay ahead for them all. The vow of chastity, at least, he had no desire to test.

Every time he served a turn in the Farsight Chamber and the bridge of light did not appear, he left feeling unworthy. Renan saw the same feeling in the eyes of all he met when he left the tower. Across the keep was a sense of heightened doom; incredibly, the members seemed more watchful than ever. Prayers sounded more diligent, and several knights fasted during meals. Renan did not know whether to approve of this, since readiness was all. Then he realized, he was not touching his own meal. Dutifully putting bread in his mouth, he noticed others doing the same, and it was all he could do to swallow.

The knights were following his lead everywhere it seemed. Since the funeral for Gaheris, Renan had become nervous about risking injury in practice. Wooden swords and buffered lances could still break a limb, and breakaway spears were out of the question with the shortage of wood. Renan appeared in the tilts with his sword wrapped in cloth, saluted his practice foe and hove to. By the next day all the Order was doing the same. Renan worried that the new leader, whenever Dunedin saw fit to send him, would find all the customs against his liking.

The cold of winter closed in around the keep, and every breath added to the wall of mist below the outer bailey. Whenever Renan saw Niles he nodded to him tightly as his mind returned to ponder the Brotherhood's loss. He was now a squire, no man would gainsay another's choice. If Niles ever stood again with the knights he would be welcomed, though there was no precedent Renan knew of.

Yet he was the newest in the Order. Renan took to the library and plumbed the chronicles, looking for mentions in the histories. The books only gave isolated statements of what this or that brother had done, not a neat rule or its exceptions. Praying for solace, Renan realized this was its own answer: the Chosen Wanderers were no guild of debaters, arguing for points before a teacher. Men led by example, keeping to the dictates of the Order by their free will, and deepening the customs with their sincere desire. Renan's hope for the recovery of his comrade and friend could not be wrong.

Niles had dutifully groomed and exercised Harbinger as the main part of his duties, and the mount was a bit readier to tolerate his hand and brush, provided the squire came armed with feed. Renan observed how they were together, a mix of cautious acquaintance and tussle: it was rare for a warhorse to outlive his rider, and few ever turned to a new master. Renan knew his plan relied on that rare chance, and time would have helped. But despite the quiet of the tower, he felt the hours were short.

"Squire Niles," he called from the paddock, "how is this horse for exercise?"

"Well enough, Sir Renan. No mare will resist this handsome fellow." Niles thought, as anyone would, that the stallion's future lay in the line of horses to come. Renan opened the paddock door and gestured them out on the rope-lead.

"Let us see if he still canters. With a rider."

The squire in shock came up so short that the stallion did the same. Renan laughed into the bitter cold, pleased at this connection.

"Sir," Niles pleaded, "you mustn't, he won't, I cannot."

"Up, Squire," Renan pronounced the verdict. "We are alone now, no one else to witness if you fail."

The implied insult to his courage was an added sting, and Niles stiffly moved out to the center of the ring, searching the ground as if for the softest patch of frosty turf on which to land when thrown. Saddle, reins, girth they both ignored; either Harbinger would accept him on his back or not, the rest was just decoration. Renan watched with tight breath as Niles turned and slowed the warhorse, laid one hand on his shoulder and stood with his head bent in prayer. Renan joined him from the side in those thoughts, surely the same. *Let events benefit the Order, whatever befalls me.*

With a last long look into the stallion's eyes, Niles slipped up and across his back.

Habits took over, for horse and rider. At once Harbinger neighed strongly and reared close to vertical; Niles squeezed his knees and leaned forward to embrace the neck, waiting out the move. The centaur held an upright pose as its twin heads communed. Harbinger returned to earth, and there was no tell-tale back-kick or twist, the stallion simply stood with chest out and head half-turned in challenge. Niles returned to upright and sat still, not even hauling the lead rope tight which would have been a useless gesture.

With one hand he slapped the shoulder in affirmation and called out the horse's name in praise. One gentle touch of his heels, to suggest a walk, resulted in a spirited trot around the ring, and with Harbinger's land-eating stride the arena suddenly seemed as small as a tub. One turn, one return, and then Niles slid off smoothly and stepped away to avoid any last-moment nip of regret. Harbinger looked him in the eye a long moment, snorted in challenge, and then nodded his head as he did to demand food. Renan tossed over an apple which disappeared with barely a crunch. The two men looked at each other and slowly grinned. Niles was still tight with regret and there were bright tears in his eyes. Renan caught the disease, but left the paddock with his heart full of hope.

That next morning, on Renan's watch, the bridge of light returned.

When Renan beheld the monster climbing from one of Delvehold's smoking shafts, his heart quailed a moment. Not simply the staggering size of the beast, but the knowledge that at least a dozen of the Dwarven miners living below must have died hit him like a first blow of combat. Renan struggled for breath and gazed at a thing as tall as a pine and made of solid, shiny coal, until the desire to avenge the dead and save the others infused him.

He reached toward Quester's bridle, then stopped with a sudden reckless thought. Renan called for the duty-squire and headed down the ramp without waiting for him to arrive. Niles was up and praying in the chapel.

"Master?" he asked rising from the pew, and Renan was struck by the use of a title he had not heard since his arrival.

"Arm and mount, the bridge calls us."

Shock and horror crossed his comrade's face.

"I cannot."

"There is no time to argue."

"Each knight shall answer the summons of the light when called; let no peril dissuade him to seek a substitute."

Renan stepped in and spoke quietly, giving word for word from the oaths they both had sworn. *"Let no squire of the Order refuse to obey the lawful command of a knight."*

"Not for fighting!"

"For whatever may be required. Your armor, and your horse, require exercise, Squire Niles. I shall attack, and you stand by to support me."

"Stand by?" He seemed thunderstruck, and indeed Renan knew he was as close to breaking the rules as ever. Two on the bridge? He couldn't tell what would happen. But he knew the Order needed every arm.

"The thing looks to be made of solid rock."

Their eyes met, and a grin grew on Niles' face.

"Sooth, Master, you will likely need another lance."

"Assuredly, squire. Come to the tower."

Back in the Farsight Chamber, Renan checked Quester's girth and twitched his gauntlets snug to his hands. The thing in Delvehold was still emerging from the mine, as if too big for the entrance. It had more than three legs, and its head and forebody was vaguely ursine. Even the teeth were ebon, and except for the glints of sunlight off its edges it would have seemed a thick, hanging smoke, rather than a living thing. The bridge remained bright and strong, but Renan felt the urge to go and had to pray to hold his place another few minutes.

Then came the sound of hoofbeats on the ramp, and the duty-squire fell back in fear as Niles, armed at all points, led up Harbinger in full mail and with three lances strapped to the saddle-socket. Niles could never have done the job alone; looking to one side of the wide chamber window Renan could see more than a half-dozen members of the Order in the courtyard looking up and murmuring to each other. No secrets.

When Niles saw the coalhemoth, he gulped hard and uttered a prayer to Dunedin, for victory and the safety of those in danger there. Renan mounted and brought Quester alongside—the two warhorses jostled each other a bit, each one eager to be the first down the bridge.

"Are you ready to assist me, Squire?"

"To the death, Master," Niles replied, his old spirit as awakened as it was with his horse.

"I am privileged to have you with me," Renan said sincerely, and the two men clasped arms, lowered their visors and spurred down the bridge of light.

The duty-squire saw only their approach to the monster, and cried out as the difference in size became apparent. The bridge of light faded when they reached the land, removing his view; he could only wait, and pray, for their return. It was nearly noon before the bell tolled and the bridge once again stretched out before the Farsight Chamber. The squire saw two armored forms, their armor declaring them like the Ebon Baron of legend, returning up the span. In Delvehold, the miners on all sides tended an enormous flame which spat geysers of smoke into the sky with no sign of slowing. Between the two men, there was not enough wood in their hands to mend a broken chair.

"Sad about the lances," one remarked as they arrived and dismounted. The soot and scorch covering even their insignia left the squire still in doubt as to which was speaking.

"Nothing unexpected, Master, when you are in the lists." So the second speaker must be the squire. "I should not have let you charge the third time."

"But with the swords, cracks and also sparks. Who would have thought the beast so flammable."

"Hope was with us this day, as we fought."

"My Hope rode at my side before the fight began."

Seeing to their steeds' watering and uncinching, the brothers allowed the duty-squire to lead the winded stallions back down the ramp as Sir Broders ascended to congratulate them and take the next place. Renan endured the looks of wonder and worry from the Wanderers in the bailey, and he did not blame their misgivings. But Renan was learning to trust his heart again: the Order would not survive with each man off on a lonely path, awaiting his lonely doom. Like his visions, which carried to Trainertown and to Argens, the connection to Hope was what made it strong. He had never hesitated to offer his aid; now he had learned to call on it.

Somewhere deep in his mind he thought he heard a chuckle.

⊕ ⊕ ⊕

A mother and daughter started home from market through the main plaza of Cil-Cilurion. To one side, before the lovely manse of the local Healers Guild, there stood a newly planted tree.

"Come dear, we've all the things we need from the sellers. Time for home."

"Mother, didn't you say the Great Healer of the Tree was a woman?"

"Um-hmm, yes dear."

"Then why did they put a statue of a man there?"

"Ehm—what? Oh... no dear, that's not a statue, it... it's an old man. At least, I think—no, there, he is moving, do you see?"

"What is he doing, mother?"

"I don't know, dear. Come along."

"Why is he dressed like a statue, mother?"

"His clothing is grey, that is all."

"Is he going to stand there forever, until the statue is finished?"

"Enough silly prattle. There is no statue—come home."

The woman at that moment saw an acquaintance and stopped a while to chat. Upon saying goodbye, she looked down to see her daughter was gone. Frantically, she scanned about the crowded square, her heart rising in her throat. But when after a timeless second she located her beloved, her heart jumped an inch higher. She had not noticed, the Man in Grey was armed for war, his hauberk tanned to suit the stone of his jerkin, and his staff, shod in thick iron, matched more than the road. Even as the mother fought the terror to act, the little girl said something to the statue-man, and he reached one gauntleted hand to rest briefly on her shoulder.

"Annekah! Daughter, come here this instant!" the mother shrieked, her feet rooted to the spot. The man's hand dropped away at once, though he did not face the verbal assault. The little girl turned to go automatically, but stepped back to bob a quick curtsy before continuing. As she reached up to take her mother's hand, the girls saw the slap coming and easily evaded it. Now at last the mother's tears began to flow, and she drew the child of her loins into herself with both arms.

"What is wrong, mother? I saw the statue-man fall to his knees and I thought he might be hurt."

"Never, never, *never* approach a stranger like that again! I have told you time after time—"

"But he did nothing, mother. And he is not old, I saw his face up close and his skin is smooth."

"Listen to me. He is a warrior, do you hear? See his weapon and his armor? Men like that are *dangerous*, you must never go near one again. Promise me!"

"He is no warrior, mother. I asked him if he knew the Lady of the Tree, and he nodded. Then I asked him what she was like, and he just looked at me. Mother, his eyes are like silver."

"I don't want to hear anymore. Come with me this instant! If you ever frighten me like this again, I swear—"

"But don't you want to hear what he said?"

"No."

"He said, after he looked at me, he said that She was just like me."

"What nonsense. The man is deranged, dear, and you are never to speak—"

"He said that I was kind and brave, and thought of everyone as a friend."

"True enough, my dear darling girl, you are unspoiled—though he forgot to add that you are also headstrong and foolish, and do not know the proper response to danger. Strange words, for a warrior..."

"He is no warrior, mother. He is the gardener."

"A gardener with arms and armor? Speak no more foolishness, girl!"

"It's true, mother! He is caring for the tree, I saw, the soil where he stood was wet."

"Not another word, off home with you straight."

In another hour, the Healer's Square had but one occupant, and in another hour, none at all. But over a branch of the sapling tree hung a small, unpainted figure of a woman in robes and bound by silver thread. The work of a smith, or a jeweler, it bore a passable resemblance to Guildmistress Natasha Ioki, for whose sacrifice this tree and others like it all over the Lands had been planted this month. By dusk, the soil had dried. After several years, barring fire or other accident, the branch on which the figurine hangs will be too clouded with leaves to see. But for decades thereafter, a remarkable woman who was once a little girl will carry with her a memory of the day which changed her life, and who would change in turn the lives of those around her. And in that way, she will prove the words of the statue-man, and of her mother, to have been true.

Kog is already angry, having to wait so long for the army to assemble. The latest arrivals, running as hard and panting as fearfully as the rest, become meals for the waiting horde after their master takes the juiciest bits for himself. Yowls of those torn apart crest the chuffs and brays of the feasting victors in a never-ending crescendo of cacophony. Kog's nostrils wrinkle with pleasure at the smell of ichor. Only mortal blood has a sweeter scent, and its taste is of course beyond compare.

Kog is also furious, to be forced to choose a northern path. The horde's gathering spot lies just south of the ancient road's current terminus, an offensive symmetry bisecting the way. Surveying the levee while absently chewing a few more garruk limbs, the lord of chaos decides on a whim to take the right-hand side, but growls continuously leading the wave of Despairing flesh towards the realm's northern border, where the speck of law, the stolen Sword, pricks at the senses.

Time probably passes as they march, endless ranks of things wolfish, ape-like and insectoid, over the shattered barren ground with the thrust of order to their left.

Kog tests the barrier every so often, throwing that enormous mass against the invisible, intangible sheet just beyond the edging stones. There is no flash, no flame, no backwards fling; the former lord of the Percentalion simply stops midstride, and roars to shatter marble but can step no further. Kog's minions, either heedless of this example or eager to please their master, also throw themselves westward at the road almost constantly. The mantis-huts are not strong enough, the snake-stags not fast enough, the helldogs' fangs not sharp enough to do any better. Overhead, a thundercloud of dung-brown reaver birds wheels above the road on both sides and nearly to the horizon. Kog notices this and snarls; the limits of the enemy's magic are beyond its abilities, for height Kog cannot abide.

The Earth Demon stores all this anger on the march, a rolling tantrum of imagined injustice from a child nearly ten feet tall, to vent upon the cities of Men. Kog fondly imagines the horrors to be visited on those who survive this army's initial onslaught. First, of course, Kog will secure the Sword and complete the annihilation of those scum who escaped with it. That power alone brought back the road, clearly; with the blade shattered, the ancient way will become nothing more than stones and straightness, both of which can be corrected. Later, Kog may hunt the survivors a few days before returning south. Perhaps another son, or several…

But no sooner does the mood improve to murderous, than Kog catches sight of a lone man ahead, walking the road south. Though stained by law and Hope to the point of disgust, yet the tall thin human is alone and unarmored, his walking stick not a mage's staff. No armor, no hat, indeed barely a cloak, one small mace at his belt and sandals on his feet. A moment's work for some of Kog's followers—yet on the road he is safe, and more, he stops to glare with righteous disapproval on the glory of Kog's army. It is too much, and the lord of hell bares all three mouths to shout a fury with flame in it, directly at this blasphemous mote of insolence.

The hellfire flaring up scorches the air itself to smoke, washing low to the ground it turns the exhausted soil to glass. But at the level of the man standing on the road it simply stops, ending though the energy behind it is like an ocean wave. Kog sees the results of this first attempt, and the anger within becomes nearly apoplectic. The loyal helldogs have seen this rarely, and know to cower and back away. Other creatures, too eager to eat human flesh without their master's will, charge ahead into the barrier of law, falling back at Kog's feet, and shortly after are crushed by them. As the demon stamps these followers to pulp, the human sweeps his gaze—an equal mix of shock and outrage—across the myriad of hell covering the eastward plain. He is appalled, yet not surprised; a preacher, Kog thinks, one of the star-seers among the enemy, who knew the doom was coming.

This human is older, bony-thin, and Kog imagines he would make tough eating. Plus the taint of Hope is a stench which the invisible barrier does nothing to quell. Chewing him will be painful and sour; Kog relishes the thought, the rare chance to feel again that disquiet others can so rarely inflict. Yet the demon has no opportunity so long as the human remains on the pavement.

Tiny and alone, yet this one alternates between kneeling in fervid prayer and standing to shout his disgust at the horde. There is a hardness about him, the demon notes, and a sudden thought strikes, of a comparison between this one and Kog's erstwhile vassal Wolga Vrule. *They should meet!* the demon thinks and hilarity replaces anger. The human's reaction is puzzlement and outrage, which only fuels Kog's laughter. Kog signals the army to move on, and they pass jeering before the mortal's eye while he watches in impotence. He shouts, curses, gestures to the skies, but any sound from him is crested by Kog's manic glee.

Yet that laughter dries like water-drops in a hot wind, when the human deliberately steps off the stones of the road and onto the unprotected Percentalion.

On the opposite side from Kog and the hell-horde.

Every sound of chaos, each bark and chitter and screech dies away as the monstrous throng halts, looking to its master for an answer. Kog stares with three open mouths, as the human marches some hundred paces away, then turns, draws his mace and beckons to the lord of hell.

For a moment Kog forgets, throwing its frame against the barrier. Now the human does not laugh, but smiles grimly, mouthing more words still drowned by the resumption of clamor behind the demon.

After another tantrum—Kog knows only that several more torn body parts are on the plain than before, and the sun is now gone from the sky—Kog finally realizes what must be done. Extruding four muscular limbs with hand-bones shaped like shovels, the demon begins to dig. Beneath the road itself, nearly as deep down as the reaver-birds above, but at an altitude much more to Kog's liking.

The work moves quickly, as measured by the ruler of Kog's patience, and it is still dark when the ground west of the road erupts nearly at the human's feet. Kog admires the doomed one a moment, standing defiant with mace in both arms, his face an etch of tension and hatred.

"Demon beast! Your throne will elude you, as in the ancient days."

"You recognize me, mortal, it is pleasing and only proper. Pray tell, what hero survives this side of the Swords, to repeat the victory you tell of? Is it you, perhaps?"

The rail-thin human crooks a grin to one side now, never hesitating and speaking in a bell-clear tone as he rejoins. "My place in destiny is clear, Kog."

Such is the purity of the preacher's spirit that the lord of hell flinches from the sound of that name, an impressive feat promising more pain to be experienced soon. Kog's need for such amusement is great now, showing in wide grins from two mouths, while the central maw alone speaks.

"Ah destiny, your precious stars and the puzzle-signs from the puny Heroes you claim to see in them. What say you, preacher, to tonight's omen, then?" Kog points with one shovel-arm at the glowing red ball bearing in from the east, which has grown to twice the size of a star and does not twinkle, but seems instead to ripple as with flame.

"I see the end of fear, the heroes cleansing our day of uncertainty."

"Your kingdoms fall, mortal! See the legion I bring to your cities, what strength have they to resist it? The fire of hell reaches unto heaven."

"Hell's fire is the only thing that falls, demon. Before the fortnight is out, that flame will be borne to earth, signaling the end of this evil, and your doom as well, Kog."

Again the demon flinches, and decides this particular pain grows tiresome. He raises his arms to strike while bidding farewell to his foe.

"A day that can never come, and in any event one you shall never see, preacher. Join now with my other victims, sink into obscurity among the numberless fools who thought to oppose me. You have afforded some amusement, but in an hour I shall recall you no more."

Laughing, he strikes with four arms at once, each now tipped with blade-like claws and massive as timber.

But the preacher shouts "*Innocens defendar!*" and mystic aura flares to all sides of his frame, deflecting the snake-like arms in mid-strike. Again and again the demon batters the protective sheath, but though the preacher staggers and cries out within, he remains unharmed.

Truly, this level of holy power has not been wielded in several centuries. Kog's fascination overwhelms the anger for a timeless time, and the sun is not quite drowning out the red star with its dawn before the preacher at last falls to his knees. His protective shield, renewed many times by the Ancient cry, still holds, though his nose and ears drip blood to the hardened earth below. His end nears at last, and the lord of hell graciously allows him a moment to catch breath while savoring the victory.

"Will, perhaps you recall me now, demon?"

"No," Kog answers truthfully. "You are nameless and without deed."

"Then… allow me, to assist your vagrant memory. I am Alaetar." The human draws one large breath and shouts again with both hands held to the sky above. His voice is larger than it has ever been, borne from a throat at the end heroic.

"Heu, thybolda Aralun victoris!"

Too late, Kog recalls that for worshippers of Hope, a miracle works best under the light of Solar.

From that morning sky arcs an enormous swath of purest lightning, ripping down Kog's head and side. The flash of light blinds every being with eyes for a league around. The preacher falls back on his knees, his shield no longer standing now that he has struck an offensive blow.

The furor fades to reveal a sparking, oozing gash along one side of Kog's main face, a flesh-trench deeper than a human arm. Kog staggers and stumbles, without three legs would have fallen. Its one eye blinks endlessly, recovering only shreds of sight for several minutes though the prostrate foe can take no advantage. The central face registers, not pain, but astonishment for the first time since the demon's return to this world. The wounds inflicted by the son were less agonizing.

And this one, at least, will not vanish. Kog sends its other faces away, reforms the arms replacing one shredded by the blast. The flesh of the torso ripples as the wound there submerges and disappears. But on that face, one cheek is deeply gouged; the bleeding and sorcerous sparking slows but does not stop. Kog steadies, probes the wound with one talon, screams in agony and surprise, and licks the fluid back into its mouth.

"As you wish, human. I shall indeed remember you now."

Then Kog opens its mouth and there is only flame.

The sun is well up, the red star just a faded spot of blood beneath it in the eastern sky when Kog's fire ceases. A lake of black glass, boasting one small bump with the molten head of a mace. There is nothing left to eat here, and the fury is back, renewed and untamable. Diving into the tunnel, the monster emerges on the eastern side to devour a helldog and some ape-men instead, before turning north to wreak vengeance on the nearest Children of Hope in that direction.

Kog's face still gapes with that gash of heaven, the pain so constant as to cure the demon, for a time, of the need to feel new things, or to examine old plans.

The lord of hell does not bother to check again for the added sting of the Sword. Trainertown is ahead to the north, Kog only needs to reach it for satisfaction to return. None of that army marching behind the hell-king dares to whine, or point, much less speak of what they have seen. Thus the demon does not notice, as of yet, that the stab of pain represented by the Sword of Air has now moved south of the horde.

⊕⊕⊕

Chancellor Odric opened the Council doors and gasped at the changes. Winter sunlight slashed through every upper-story window with the heavy curtains drawn back, illuminating the freshly polished metal fixtures and burnished wood of the open-square table. It was cold, to match the light—the window behind the king's throne stood open, increasing the sudden sense that Odric had stepped outside.

But most astounding and new of all, the room was already occupied.

Gareth sat diligently writing something on a parchment already covered in cross-outs. His personal squire Hobsel stood behind him and the scritch of the quill was clearly audible.

"Your Majesty," Odric began, but stopped when he saw no interruption to the young man's writing. He repeated himself more loudly; Gareth snapped in surprise to see him, hastily hiding the sheet behind his chair. Odric's heart fell when he realized, Gareth was still unused to his new title.

"Chancellor. My apologies, I was rather lost in thought."

"Majesty, your council awaits."

The king rose at once, showing no recollection of his place. "Send them in, of course."

"Majesty," Odric hesitated, "if I may, it would be customary to announce, that is, before the Council begins business, any changes you might wish—"

"Odric," Gareth interrupted urgently. "Do not leave me."

The Chancellor was stunned at the sheer honesty behind the plea.

"Majesty, have no concern for my comfort."

"Please, Odric. You are all I have left of him."

The Chancellor had to turn away a moment, to wipe an unmanly tear. Gareth's composure, throughout these harrowing days of acclamation and feast had remained unbroken. No crowd or demonstration subdued his quiet grace, though indeed it seemed a sadder flavor of charm, as befit his heavy loss. Odric had been unsure if he would continue in the office, and even thought of consulting Kalentire for an oracle of his future. He hoped to stay, was prepared to retire. But the Chancellor had never expected such a touching affirmation. Bowing low before the man, now more than ever his King, he turned to admit the council.

Gareth remained standing to show honor to Barons, High Preachers, Magisters alike as they found their seats. Another custom changed, then. Last to arrive on Odric's arm came the elderly High Seer Kalentire, who glared at the new king before gesturing his escort to a chair somewhat further away from the western throne. Odric had heard whispers, that the Reverend Myster was upset not to preside over a coronation already.

And indeed there was a delicate, weaving dance to the seating order that no mortal mind could trace in its complexity. Quill-Knights boldly took seats a bit higher within their social rank than before. The effect was not marked, as the choicest chairs were still stuffed with the landholding lords of the Shield: the Baron of Hirion, taking advantage of the empty seat on his right, now sat closer to the king than ever.

The youth took the scepter first used by Shilar in the crook of his arm and spoke.

"I thank you, milords and ladies, for coming at my request." Thus with his first words Gareth brought puzzlement to his inaugural Council of the Talking Stick. All were summoned here, doing their feudal duty to attend. After a moment, he clarified. "It is in my mind to ask—is it your will that I should lead this assembly, in light of the fact that my coronation is still—"

"Long live King Gareth!" the shout from the far side of the table broke all custom, yet it reached throughout the chamber in an instant, matching the sunlight as the nobility affirmed their desire to be ruled by the son of Genel Shilarion XXXI. Swords and gloves fell to the carpet in a muted rain of loyalty. Gareth bowed somberly, and from behind him Squire Hobsel smothered a smile before scrambling to help return them to their owners.

"Then let us attend to several important matters, once the Reverend Myster has led us in prayer."

The High Seer's face broke into surprise, then a glower as he stood. "And why, milord," he grated, "should this among all your father's customs continue?" Silence across the chamber: he alone of the Council had not cheered the new king.

Gareth rose to face the effrontery but spoke in the voice of a breeze. "Because at no time in our nation's history have we needed the guidance of the Star Seer more."

Holding the king's gaze, Kalentire took the scepter Odric brought him, and intoned the prayer as before. The sunlight and breeze in the chamber were already so strong Odric could not be sure if his prayer brought any miracle with it. But it also seemed to him the High Seer's heart was not fully in the ritual.

Everyone sat and King Gareth II took the scepter again to speak.

"Milords, the Bordbeyonds are coming and we must be ready."

The Quill Knight faction gasped in surprise; the Chief Sage, Treasury lords and Coroner's men were not privy to the councils of war. Yet Gareth did not enlarge on his meaning, but held out the scepter instead for the Baron Hirion; Odric noted the chief vassal among his Shield Knights was not as happy as the prospect of war suggested.

"We shall escort the half-elves… the Shepherds, from the fords to the capital, in three days' time. The bridge which His Majesty commanded be reinforced, is now wide enough to take two riders abreast, and shortly four."

"How many are coming?" a knight from the southern foefs dared to ask.

Hirion sneered above a stiff jaw. "As many as they can bring." At this, the room broke into unaccustomed whispers and half-shouts, disbelief and fear vying to darken the daylight.

Gareth held his calm and reached to take the Talking Stick, so close to Hirion that Odric needn't stir. Everyone quieted to hear him.

"This is well done indeed, milord Baron. I praise you for obeying me though I have told you nearly as little as anyone else here. That ends now."

"Milords and ladies, the Bordbeyonds are our allies as they have always been. However strange we may find their customs, we band together now to fulfill a common destiny under the stars of heaven, now at the ending of an age."

Odric found he was barely breathing, and only the breeze stirred when his king took pause.

"They will meet our army here near Cil-Cilurion. From there we shall follow the sky-signs. I demand the feudal obligation of no knight, as a king should know the threat and his enemy in greater detail than I can claim."

He gestured then with an open palm for questions, and still Odric did not need to shuttle the scepter, as by custom these were allowed.

"The red star, Majesty?"

"Sooth, Sir Tustic, as the Bordbeyonds themselves foresaw, it divides the sky and grows larger."

"But Majesty, it leads not east, but west."

"Elaborate, good knight, what is in your heart?"

"How if it is an evil omen, leading us away from the borders we must guard?"

Gareth nodded, his gentle smile undisturbed. "And so every one of us must search the heart to find the proper course. I will not command this. But think you, milords and ladies; if that crimson star is from Despair, how be it that they have stormed heaven itself, yet stoop only now to ruin us? And if any people have the right to stay on guard for eastern attack, how may we of Shilar gainsay the Bordbeyonds, our brothers?"

"Brothers!" the cry came from several throats at once.

"Aye brothers," Gareth returned now rising, "and more, my brothers and sisters, since I intend to wed their princess."

This brought gasps from the Shield Knights, who were not as close to the betrothal as the clerks and scribes busily arranging the ritual. Gareth pressed on, walking between the open sides of the square table to address the gathering more closely, turning left and right as he spoke.

"It was to complete my proposal, in accordance with our code of honor, that I left my home and father. It was because of my deed that my noble sire lost his life. And in trying to prove worthy of Sidrathay the Combatted, and again to uphold Shilarian honor, more men died among the Shepherds."

"Do not follow me, nobles of Shilar, in the vain hope that I am beyond error. Mistakes trail my every step and they are soaked in blood. If you think as I do, that heaven can only point us in the right direction, then follow the sign with me and come prepared to do whatever Hope may require."

"Will your Majesty consent to wed before the army departs?"

"My consent, milord, will not be at issue, but rather hers."

Everyone began shouting, many stood, and Odric knew he needed to act. Stepping behind the king, he thumped his long staff of office on the floor hard enough to nearly chip the stone.

"Nobles of Shilar! Your king holds the Talking Stick; say now, who will disgrace him to yell like a commoner in his presence."

They sat at once like chastened students, and Gareth turned to smile at him in gratitude. Odric's blood pumped hot, to think that in Genel's day there had never been such an outburst. But then, there may never have been such events to ponder.

"I shall ask Sidrathay the Combatted to marry me, milords and ladies, with my hands clasped and knee upon the ground, as our customs prescribe."

In a flash, Odric remembered the crossed-out paper and knew it was the love-poem. With all that weighed on the new king's mind, Gareth was trying, as they all had in their day, to express his love on paper. His heart surged with sympathy for the youth. Odric's wife Nera had laughed when he read his out loud, fumbling and stuttering, but she had said yes, which was all that mattered.

"Surely your Majesty cannot think she will refuse you."

"I can hope, milady, ever I hope. After all, she did marry me once before." Odric saw his gentle smile on this private joke suffuse the room; though hardly anyone understood their king, yet they accepted his word, and this was loyalty no coin could sway, no blade guarantee.

"But this is only to the proposal, not the ceremony. It is in my heart to ask the Council—should the marriage be postponed, in light of the tragic losses our kingdom has so recently suffered?"

A space of silence, then Baron Hirion raised a hand and Odric brought the scepter.

"Majesty, though we had no body, we did in sooth inter the king your father with all pomp and great honor. By the Sweeping's shores the fires burned through a day and a night. The kingdom was draped in ebon until your return."

"And I thank you, Baron, for the great honor you did him in my absence. But I think also of the Guildmistress Natasha Ioki, the great Healer of all Hope who has also been lost to us."

The council members again exchanged looks of confusion, which Odric shared. He recalled vaguely the tale of how the prince had suffered a broken leg years ago, healed by the woman, then an itinerant, who later rose in Conar to lead her Guild. Gareth noted this and spoke on.

"Can it be, milords and ladies, that the urgency of this matter lies beyond your hearing? The Healers Guildmistress is beloved not just of Conar but all the Lands, among the common folk more than any. Have you not seen, in so many places around the city, the black draping has been only pulled back, not removed? This is in tribute to our great loss as a whole people."

"Majesty," the Baron once again spoke, with caution, "Sooth, this custom is not lost to us. We have directed the planting of yon tree in our central square, and the further days of mourning were set aside by thy decree and our unanimous approval. Shalt obtain a new Guildmistress or master in Conar soon, certes. Tis plain ye are troubled, to celebrate in the shadow of such loss; thy noble mind marches on paths that lie in parallel, to dwell on thy father and the Healer Natasha. I urge thee, shake off this path of death for the sake of the nation."

"The Guildmistress is not dead, milord Baron."

"Nay, but gone from us forever as if finally dead. She affects us no longer, sooth my king. An' it doth pain us, Majesty, to see thee in such pain. Ye have summoned our array and that of the half-el, em, of the Bordbeyonds, for a great enterprise. Ye are plighted to marry, or nearly! Wouldst fain ye bring thy mind and heart back to matters we can touch, those we can succor here and now."

"Should we milord? I wonder, should we give up on any of our kind. I have heard tell of what transpired in that distant Hopeward, from one of our immortal brethren of Mendel who did survive the quest. Tis a tale to chill the spine, councillors, an' I would not willingly ask the noble sage to repeat it."

"Despair in sooth hath been loosed again upon the Lands of Hope, bringing hell's fury and the curse of undeath in its wake. Certes these challenges and mayhap worse lie before us. We fight them not merely with blade and spell and miracle, not only with our lives, but with our love of life. We must show we defend the right to live on, free and in Hope; for every child knows the tales of Despair's ravages in the days of legend, and all of us have dwelt, in weak moments, on the horror of facing a familiar, undead face. Mayhap even those who have died require our protection."

At this strange speech Odric found himself thinking of his beloved Nera, dead these past fourteen years.

The silence was marked by a curious look on the face of one councillor. The Lady Blenia was young indeed, and Odric knew she had never spoken in council nor even raised her hand for the Talking Stick. But Gareth attended to her strange mien at once, and gestured for the Chancellor to bring it to her unbidden. She swallowed hard and stood, holding the rod with both hands.

"Majesty, your words oddly reminded me of a report I have had on my desk just these past few days from the northern reaches. Ye may not have heard of the death of Sir Ganelake—"

Odric saw a wave of shock cross the King's face.

"Sir Ganelake has died? This is sore news, milady, as every sword is needful and he was host to me not three months ago."

"I cannot track the news to its source, Majesty, forgive me but the letters I have come from common folk unversed in letters. Then too the tale they tell is most extraordinary. It seems, or at least it is so claimed, that someone has discovered a ritual of sorts, in just the vein that your Majesty did describe. A miracle with the power… that can protect the dead against raising."

"Art thou certain, milady? Please enlarge on this as ye are able." So saying Gareth returned to his throne and gave Blenia his complete attention.

"Majesty, nothing is certain here, I should apologize to waste your time with rumors. But the report I have affirms that Ganelake is dead—"

"Tis true, Majesty," interrupted a lord from the Coroner's office, Kalney. "The good knight was slain by monstrous creatures in the region of Ranebruh, beyond our kingdom's borders. I have just returned from there and viewed the, the remains. The locals claim to have fought… well, to have encountered ghouls, Majesty."

Sussurations of alarm circled the room as Kalney returned the scepter to Blenia. Gareth remained fixed on the speakers as if he were hearing a sentence in court.

"As I say, Majesty, this attack occurred during the time of your captivity among the savages."

"They are the Bordbeyonds, milady, and you might do well to recall the proper honor due a people I intend to join in matrimony."

"Majesty, a thousand pardons!"

Odric could see on her young face the anguish born of dwindling ignorance, and wondered how far such prejudice was still spread among their people. Blenia seemed nearly fainting with humiliation, but Gareth smiled as if she had mispronounced an Ancient word, and gestured for her to continue.

"At all events, as Baron Kalney can affirm there were found traces of several such monsters, and legends tell the ghouls were created by Despair to guard their horrid burial grounds. Here is where the reports become confused; mayhap a solitary hermit, or some said a sailor far inland, others insisted a soldier or holy man, and it may be there were more than one person. But some Man in Grey, of whom we have no name, returned with these ghouls, claiming to have recovered the knowledge, which he carries in writing, of a ritual used to shield the bodies of those who have died, protecting them from the curse of necromancy. Wherever the remains lie, or even when the ashes have risen to heaven, the proper words and other accoutrements, together with the strength of the caster's spirit, can suffice to make the dead immune to raising, or so they say he claimed."

In the ensuing silence, Odric could see Gareth's steady stare at his young councillor was increasing her agitation.

"We wanted to wait, Majesty, until we had a fuller record."

"Wait no longer, milady. We must find the Man in Grey, at once."

"Majesty? He is by all accounts a landless itinerant, last seen in a tiny hamlet more than a week ago. Quite possibly a criminal. He moves through our kingdom afoot at no man's pleasure."

"Take horse, then, milady. You and the Baron Kalney have my leave to withdraw and seek him at once."

"To arrest him, Majesty?"

"To beg of him, the privilege of an audience. Use any inducement short of force, milord, but bring this man back to me before your bodies rest again on down."

To the bubble of more unaccustomed whispers, Baron Kalney rose to offer the Lady Blenia his arm, and they both bowed before leaving the chamber. Odric surveyed the wrack of noble converse in their wake, and reflected how difficult the new reign would be with this for a debut. On hearing the talk, the king's face fell for the first time in Odric's memory. He turned to Hobsel, who advanced to put a hand on his liege's shoulder in support. For a mere squire with his knight in public, this would be a step too far. Yet these two held something dearer than the code of their fathers.

Kalentire rose to ask for the scepter.

"Majesty, what boots this sudden expedition? Why dispatch Blenia and Kalney, with guards no doubt, when you meant to gather your forces for this… adventure?" The elderly preacher could not prevent a sneer, but Odric detected the honest doubt in his tone.

"Why, High Seer? So that the battle I fear is coming, and the victory I hope to win shall have meaning."

"I do not understand."

"Aye," the king responded, and sighed. "Milords and ladies, I beg you to think now, and attend to me. Try to ignore my age, my past if those impede you; for surely these are not my thoughts. I have asked you to follow me to war, and be certes that war lies ahead for us. Of the enemy I know nothing, except that it is of Despair. We go to battle as our blessed ancestors did, and each one who comes may indeed die."

"Dost hear, nobles? This is not some tourney with buffered lances, nor a senseless skirmish with imagined enemies, which I know some here did long for. If I aspired to knock down ten knights and lose only six, I would stay at home. We must not simply win. We must bring Hope, as the heroes before us did. No lesser ambition will suffice."

Gareth took a breath before concluding. "And Hope is what this lone explorer, this Man in Grey, has in his hand."

"Majesty," stammered Kalentire, "we know naught of the truth of this. More than like, the wanderer has nothing, and we are hearing only rumors of his delusion. Protect the dead from necromancy? How did the Heroes not give us this cure, if it were real? And what possible use? Assuredly, 'twill serve sentiment to protect the chosen few, those among the noble classes—"

"But that's a cavil, eh? Merely a symbol? Milords can you walk with my thought a while further? Suppose then, that this ritual is effective, and we deploy it at every funeral and pyre across the land."

"All of Shilar!"

"All of Hope! From the Sea to the Swords, if every healer with the strength campaigns to protect not dozens but thousands, scores of thousands of our revered dead."

"Thousands!" "Majesty, the waste!" "—the time lost"

"There have been no undead reported, Majesty, in time immemorial."

"Indeed, my good Baron of Hirion? No ghosts walk the lonely castle keeps, no ghouls attacked our northern village? There were not scores of undead warriors locked in the very Hopeward where our revered Guildmistress today lies trapped?"

"Stories, my king, nothing but tales, all of these!"

"Tales, yes good Hirion. The most powerful weapons ever devised by Hope or Despair. The history of our victories. The deeds of the Heroes themselves. And our people believe them. They believe them all. And I intend to tell a new tale, a true one that changes the lives of all the Children of Hope."

Kalentire spoke in wonder. "The undead were creations of the elder age, and I know your Majesty has heard of one, the first necromancer now rumored to be escaped from that Hopeward in which he was interned. You believe this? You fear the plague of undeath will return?"

"Aye, Reverend Myster. And he with his allies would be west of us now. I credit the tale I have heard," here Gareth's gentle smile returned to its normal place. "I know not if the knights of Shilar and the Shepherds will face him, or mayhap something worse. But face it we must."

Slowly, the High Seer nodded and sat, his face that of a changed man.

"My king," asked a lord of the Treasury, "if this miracle is true, and we do as you say, will not the nomads across the river have cause to resent us?"

Gareth drew breath to answer, but the squire stepped forward and held out one hand for the scepter. Councilors gasped in shock and the Baron of Hirion pounded the table with his fist. But the king held up one hand for silence and gave it over. The squire with the strange feathered pelt over one shoulder stood straight before the council.

"Perhaps," the Baron muttered, "we shall hear from the servants next."

"The Bordbeyonds are a proud people," the squire began, "used to surviving on their own efforts. They bury their dead as properly as we, with fire, and thus fear mainly the return of ghosts instead of earthly corpses. They speak of these things little, as they do of most things. But their children shiver at night from more than the cold of winter."

"And you know this, good squire," Baron Hirion interjected, "from your extensive time spent among them?"

"He spent, time enough milord Baron." Gareth took back the scepter as Hobsel retreated. "But I wonder much how any could have doubted, since these people are Children of Hope, that they would suffer our fears. And I wonder also how they might resent our discovery, since we shall of course give it to them as well."

Odric heard the collective intake of breath from all sides of the table, as Shilar's nobles were struck with what their king meant by this alliance. Odric thought only of his dear Nera, many years since interred in ashes by the customs; he hoped she was still happy wherever her spirit dwelt. And he felt a hunger then, to know of this ritual.

In the profound silence that followed, Odric could see a few tears among the council. Even the Baron Hirion, who raised his hand to ask a final question, seemed somewhat subdued.

"And if it works not, Majesty? If the ritual be false, or the grey man a villain, what then."

"Then, my good Baron, there will be other dreams, tales we hear of that speak to us of Hope. And we will fight to defend them, and risk our lives to bring them here. We will chase them all, or I am not the king."

On behalf of the council, the several Barons rose then to wish the King well in his impending betrothal, and better in his wedding. They then departed to prepare for war.

Treaman led his band out the southern gate before first light. Seven pairs of boots on the wide slabs of the ancient way sounded like an army to the Woodsman, easily drowning out the startled complaints of the guards who lagged their headcount until the group was already rods beyond the limen posts. Couldn't break the law to keep it.

The two youths, Anteris and Forge, trailed in the rear; by noon, Treaman felt burdened as if he were carrying them both. Their unsettled gaits, the whispers and stares, everything about the boys screamed their inexperience. When the town walls disappeared behind them, the scribe sobbed, and his friend's laughter was strained, the back-pats too hard. But they were game youths, both of them, stumping along as Treaman set a hard pace with no complaint or plea for rest.

With the party veterans, it was a different story.

Haltar ambled along in front, with a carefree gait and often whistling. Linya's face was so drawn with worry it appeared she was ill; every time Anteris or Forge spoke it seemed to make her flinch. Mhoral said not one word the entire morning, and barely looked at Treaman.

Clearly the Elf was furious and feared the worst. Only Braja, and Hallah on his shoulders, appeared unfazed by the new additions.

Forge kept drifting east, then west away from the highway as if testing the limits of the Percentalion's chaos. Or the party's patience.

"Stay on the road," Treaman ordered tersely, and the young Stealthic drifted diagonally back as if it were his own decision. Perhaps he wished to prove his courage, which would be typical, and very bad news.

"How far can you go," he asked, "before, well you know, you lose sight?"

No one else spoke. "It varies, as you might expect," Treaman said, adding, "on another day, you might already have gone too far."

Forge snapped a look of suspicion on the Woodsman, then grinned and nodded. Everything was a game; the similarity to Bildon in that one instant was so marked, Treaman felt a wave of panic.

They stopped around mid-day to rest their packs on the stones and eat. Treaman did some careful scouting around, and felt the increased cold even a few feet beyond the road's edge. There was no telling what nature was like in a land falling into chaos, but he sensed a bitter winter, as bad as those he lived through in Novar. Back on the road, the breeze was milder, more like a crisp fall afternoon, and even the sunshine seemed more hale.

"You say the road stops after another day?" Forge asked no one in particular.

Haltar shrugged, "It did when we came north. Who knows?"

"The Ancient Way stretched from Trainertown to the under-capital Oncario," Anteris said, not realizing as he gazed ahead that everyone was listening. "That's why our city stands where it does, and saw double the trade in the early days."

Linya asked, "But it continues from Oncario to Reghalion, yes?"

He shook his head at once. "Not in the records. That is," the scribe now noticed he had the party's attention and faltered, "there could well be a road, into the foothills and Tallwoods surrounding Skysword. But in the chronicles, that is, there is only mention of the gate."

"A gate?" Mhoral asked, curious in spite of his anger-fast. "Between Oncario and Reghalion? Who would build a gate for such a short distance of travel?"

Anteris dropped down to flip open his pack and remove a wide-spined tome, which he opened to thumb through the handwritten entries. The youth acted in every way as if the Elf's question was a task assigned to a student. The group sat by in dumb wonder for a long time, as Treaman added this to the list of crimes he was personally responsible for. Theft from the Sages Guild, kidnapping, and soon…

Anteris closed the book on his lap and crossed his hands atop it. He considered a moment and then declaimed.

"The records speak of the gate in use specifically between Oncario and Reghalion several times, as late as 1565 ADR. There is one brief mention almost a century earlier of a disturbance of some kind in the eastern mines, so one could infer a road—"

"But no foot traffic between the cities," Forge finished for him. He turned to smile indulgently at the others. "He'll tell the history until Darksebb if you don't turn the crank."

"So," Haltar drawled as if it couldn't matter less, "we'll have to get through the throne room and use the arches we saw in there."

"We were headed through anyway," Treaman replied, "we have to get the scepter before we move on."

"Certainly," Mhoral growled, "I'm sure the Primara will be delighted to give it over, and her red gem to boot, before we traipse on to waltz with the ghosts in the capital."

In response, Treaman just shouldered his pack to continue.

"You can turn back now and be drinking in the inn before sundown." It was by far the most mean-spirited thing he'd ever said to the Elf, and Treaman's spirit burned and roiled in his gut as he stomped off south.

It was Forge's cry that warned him: the Woodsman went flat to the earth as a low-humming sound buzzed above where his neck would have been. Hallah screeched and flapped up as he fell, and Treaman saw ahead of him a whirling angle of flat wood, Mhoral's bent club now flying and gyring up to turn about and return.

Everyone else cleared to either side of the stone road, as Treaman stood and slowly wheeled to keep the wooden foil in sight. Down the avenue it sliced with its low hum, back to Mhoral's hand as he caught it by one end, instantly ready to wield as the club Treaman had known it for till now. His visor was down, his breathing visible beneath the leather surcoat.

{*"Elf-man hurt Treee-man. Hallah will bite him."*}

"No Hallah, stay back," Treaman said quietly, and now Mhoral's helm pivoted to scan the skies. Treaman rotated his spear in one hand and waited; when Mhoral looked back, the Woodsman deliberately took it up high a moment, then cast it down to quiver in the broken earth beyond the ancient road.

"To stay safe behind walls while others fight," Mhoral cried, "is a settled thing."

Treaman could feel the anger though he did not understand such strange words.

"I was wrong to question your courage, Mhoral. Haltar is better suited to bear up with your pestering."

"You have no plan! Admit here before us all, you don't know how we will gain the city, recover the Tridium—by the Swords, we don't even know where the crown is—and no heir besides! You've told us nothing."

Treaman cocked his head in acknowledgement, then barked a laugh. "Neither did Haltar. So where is your complaint, Mhoral? Why so concerned now to know—"

"Because this time we cannot fail!" The Elf bellowed from within his helm. He holstered his weapon, advanced to Treaman and raised the visor. "That thing is lord of this domain. Bildon was, you, I, we all miss him Treaman. But the desire for revenge does not provide the means."

"I know, Mhoral. I know." Treaman reached up to grip his shoulder, and suddenly the two embraced. "I just have to have faith."

And there it was, the words themselves quietly spoken. Treaman realized it was all he would ever have, more than likely.

"Come on, everyone, the noon nap is over." Treaman held up his arm for Hallah, who landed and hissed at Mhoral for an absurdly long time. Even he laughed. Then the pounding rhythm of Treaman's fast pace devoured all conversation.

As night fell, Anteris grit his teeth and wondered how much longer he could keep marching. He glanced over to Forge, who grinned and rolled his arms like he was on a stroll but occasionally mopped a sleeve across his forehead and chuffed a sigh as he shifted his pack. Since the near-fight between the Woodsman and the Pious Warrior there had been no conversation, nor any stops, just jerky and water passed around as they continued to walk.

Anteris felt sure he and Forge were being tested. And he was increasingly certain that soon now, he would fail. Both feet felt cut, his thighs burning, and his last easy breath seemed a year ago in his memory. Sprints, fast runs and turns were always so easy for him, but this marching pace devoured his energy. It wasn't even heroic, to walk and walk with nothing to see as the sun fell and set, nothing to look forward to. His morale dripped away with the light. Another few steps, and then surely he would fall.

Anteris came to after a timeless stretch and wondered if he had actually fallen asleep while hiking. It was full dark; looking around behind him he could see a growing light in the north, the moons about to rise. They had been walking almost without a break for more than six hours. He looked at Forge next to him. The son of the smith was gritting his jaw, grin gone at last; Anteris realized Forge had an arm under his own, helping to prop him up as they walked together. Last legs, four of them…

Then the moons rose, and the horror began.

Light from Aral and Unal, both waxing now in late Raccoon, poured through the land and revealed a myriad of hellish creatures ahead, to their left by the ancient road. Everyone stopped as the helpless rabbits do, hoping their stillness would suffice to hide them in plain sight. Anteris saw thousands of monstrous beings gibbering in the moonlight, writhing and jostling and occasionally killing each other. The hell-horde held its place, a sea of chaos surging against some invisible dam, wanting to move on and destroy but unable.

No one spoke for what seemed an hour.

"Mage's mind, we are doomed," Linya gasped.

Haltar studied them a moment. "Why don't they attack? Can they not see us?"

"We need to pull back," Mhoral advised evenly.

"The road!" Treaman cried, then dropped his voice to a whisper. "They cannot enter it, we were right."

"You seriously mean to risk—"

But Mhoral never finished his diatribe, as Forge dropped his pack and jogged off the stones to the east, directly in front of the horde.

"Forge, come back!" Anteris was among those shouting, but the young Stealthic waved a hand as if to say "just a moment". Several rods away, things with wings the size of horses screeched and flapped up to approach him. Forge bent his knees and gauged their attack, and long after he needed to go, finally ran back diving onto the stones as the cawing, hook-beaked tiger-things swooped down. Two pulled up in time, a third soundlessly slammed into what seemed a wall of glass at the road's border where Forge had just come in.

Limbs splayed, one broken, a few feathers come loose, the feline raptor tumbled to the broken earth not seven feet away, and floundered in a half-circle on two remaining legs until its mates and a few ape-men descended to devour it. Linya fell back into Anteris' arms as everyone scrambled off the road to the opposite side. Even the spattering blood of the dying beast did not touch the stones of the ancient way.

When they could tear their eyes from the horrid scene, Haltar reached over and pulled Forge up by the collar to his eye-level with his feet dangling four inches off the ground.

"This party will not tolerate idiots. Your share will be paid to your family if you die while doing as we need. Take another risk like that, do anything without express orders, and I will throw you off the road right now. On the wrong side."

"It's safe to move on," Forge replied. "You are welcome."

"Heroes above," Anteris cried, "look! It's Alaetar."

He pointed at the lone preacher standing a few hundred paces away on the west side. The nightmarish absurdity of the scene made Anteris doubt he was still awake. With thousands of monsters not a furlong away, the thin preacher held his mace in one hand—did he intend to do battle with this army?—and furiously waved the party onward, in the way one would to folks late for a church service.

Treaman looked at the preacher, then back at hell's myriad, and finally to the group.

“Let’s go. Quickly and quietly, and stay on the road whatever you do.”

“You’re serious.”

“As death, Mhoral. Now stay quiet and follow me.”

They stole back onto the stones and hugged the right-most ones as they crept past the feast-scene. One of the ape-men bared a bloody maw at the group and lunged toward them; it was impossible not to react defensively, but he slammed into the same barrier the flying tiger had. The party continued, weapons out and stepping toes-first in a ridiculous attempt to make less noise while the horde to their left watched them in rapt attention and disquiet.

Anteris was still too stunned to feel afraid. Before moonrise, he had wanted nothing so badly in his life as to stop walking, and would happily have slept on the stones to avoid another moment awake. Now his entire frame began to pulse with terror, and he could not imagine stopping, or ever sleeping again. All the time, though the gibbering, flapping myriad to his left demanded his view, Anteris looked to his right, as the party came slowly level with where Alaetar still stood. He felt his spirit drop well below his stomach, and seeing the quiet, almost calm determination on the preacher’s moonlit face brought tears to his eyes. He thought of how the dour Shilarian had patiently answered questions, broken up fights, kept all the children company. Nothing made sense any more.

Anteris was off the road and walking toward him before he knew what he was doing.

“Anteris!” the cries behind him only impelled the youth to run, and Alaetar’s waving arm did not slow him. Anteris ran to the seer as the hellbeasts had lunged toward the party, reaching out with both arms to embrace and nearly tackle the man, who staggered a step and then stiffly returned the affection with his free hand.

"There lad, never fear, go with the others. I don't know how you came to be with them—"

"I am going," Anteris sobbed, "to do what I can."

"Aye, then. Go, and may Shilar watch over you, lad."

"But you, Alaetar. You must come with us."

"I have work here, Anteris. You must go with the Hand of Destiny, help to point them on their way. Remember the prophecy. The Tridium, the heir, all of it. Heroes go with you."

"Alaetar, please."

"Go, lad, go now and help them." Alaetar looked down on the scribe and tried his first full smile, and his first lie. "I shall catch up to you soon." Neither one fit his face, and Anteris was swept under a wave of tears. The preacher turned him by the shoulder and pushed him gently back towards the party and the legion of hell. Anteris kept walking, knowing that if he looked back he would never move again. No one spoke when he regained the ancient stones and joined the march; after a time their pace picked up, never relaxed but a bit faster. When a hut-mantis dashed in to try again for their deaths and staggered back, Forge even laughed at it tauntingly. It sounded to Anteris as if the earth below their feet was growling and rumbling, here at the center of the army to their left.

Slowly, the chittering, grinding horde faded into the distance behind them, and the night scene ahead under the twin moons was as flat and barren as before. No one asked about stopping, but the pace was a crawl compared to the clip they had managed before dark. The red star overhead was twice the size it had ever been, moving so as to cross the moons' path tonight, or perhaps the next.

Treaman finally announced a halt, and the group simply sat, leaning against their packs to rest without bothering for the tent. Anteris looked north and thought he saw flashes of red and argent, like two shimmers of distant heat-lightning. Something inside him felt a stab of horror, and the tears began again. The heroic life of an adventurer, it seemed to Anteris, was not quite what he had read in books.

Not even two days with his guest, and Guildmaster Frakes was already eager to be rid of him.

It seemed such a simple matter, at first; a stranger to the town of Connor offered a newly-unearthed ritual from Hope's past, in return only for the paper and ink to scribe the copy out and to be allowed within the Guild's protective circle for the duration. True, the messenger looked as strange as his lore: an incantation to protect only those already dead, borne by one who seemed drained of life himself. It was not until after Frakes had lowered the circle's barrier to admit the interloper, that he noted the steel in his eye and arm to match his wardrobe. From then on, for every moment the Guildmaster was present for the next forty hours, he felt trouble in his soul.

It was nothing obvious, no matter for complaint or grudge that the learned man could place his finger upon. The stranger had taken up station at a small desk on one edge of the circle, and immediately begun his laborious work, scribing not only the ritual itself but also a compendium of facts relating to its history and discovery. Tedious opus, no doubt, and even more tedious the introduction, from one so grim and serious. This tome was doomed to the back shelves in the Guildmaster's mind, but no lore should ever be turned away no matter how useless.

The stranger gave his name, and quiet thanks, and once seated set straight away to copying, fresh off the road from Cil-Cilurion and without so much as a drink of ale. Indeed, the stranger had taken the promise of hospitality at its minimum value, asking for neither food nor any drink except one cup of water that day. Half in guilt, Frakes ordered his acolyte to bring the slate-hued fellow a plate of dinner, an hour past dusk. Rising for the first time, the stranger greeted the boy as if he were an ambassador from the Elves, took the plate with gravity and laid it on the floor next to his chair. One bite, perhaps three, and no more; back to his work.

Hour after hour this continued, and here was the chief part of the Guildmaster's grievance, if truth were known to him. For how can one take ease in the presence of labor? The Healers Circle was not overly large, and even with the Man in Grey to one side, it seemed crowded: Frakes was used to having this space inviolate to himself, and had not anticipated the slow, rising frenzy that stole upon him to share it with anyone. Leisure reading, tea, even the chance of a short nap, all were spoiled by this merciless drone, scratching and dipping his quill without cessation.

Damned if he were to record the monthly accounts a week early, just for something to do, Frakes eventually excused himself with ill grace, to take a walk. At the last moment, realizing his guest would be marooned within the magic circle until his return, he turned back to ask if there was anything the man needed. The grey stranger only shook his head, once, and never stopped writing for a moment.

The blazes with him then! The Healers Guildmaster took extra pains then to make all social rounds he could think of, and was in no hurry to leave any friend upon whom he called. Several hours later, a bit saddened to notice how few had been eager to see him (a man of his station, to think!), he returned to the Guild and passed through the main chamber on his way upstairs, drawn by simple courtesy to check on his guest before retiring.

Thinking without doubt to find him asleep, Frakes was stunned to see the man still working, a pale shadow among darker ones by the light of a single candle within the circle. The unpleasant prospect of having to chaperone this man later into—or even through—the evening was too much to bear.

"See here, sirrah, 'tis late enough and you may with great honor withdraw now. Our chambers adjoining the Circle Room are, I think, quite adequate."

"You do me too much honor, Guildmaster Frakes. I desire nothing but to continue, with thanks."

"You joke, sir! Surely, you will sleep?"

"Certes, I shall milord, and far too soon for my taste, for I am weak and ineffectual at real work. Yet this floor shall serve me better than the berm of the road has done, these three nights past."

"And is there nothing you require, then, Goodman? Some food or drink, another blanket..."

"Might I have a book?"

"A book, you say?"

"Aye milord, a book if you would be so generous. My hand begins to cramp, and I would not be unoccupied."

"Well—what, ahm, what subject would you..."

"Nearly any subject, milord, will do. I am close upon complete illiteracy."

At this, the Guildmaster gave the stranger his hardest look, determined to unearth the insolent jest for once and all. Three long moments he stared into the granite points of the Man in Grey, and marked not one trace of the humor he expected. What he did see, he never saw fit to tell another living soul. But he withdrew, and with a slightly shaking hand pulled down a musty tome entitled *Legal Practice in Seventh Century Shilar*, a work infamous among his circle of morning acolytes as both the heaviest and least accessible work in his small collection. Often lobbed at one of his nodding students, Frakes had once even threatened to assign part of it, to frighten the youngsters back into attention. Triggering the circle down, he handed it to the stranger with mock grace. As the adventurer scanned its title, Frakes saw for the first time something like an emotion come over the man's face.

"A worthy subject, milord, and I am now more in your debt."

"In my debt, sirrah? Do, do you mean you have actually—"

"Nay, sir, I have only read of Shilarian law in the second millennium. With this, I can amplify my understanding significantly."

Not knowing whether to laugh or shout in rage, the Guildmaster barked the circle back up, spun on his heel and stomped upstairs, leaving the guest imprisoned to enjoy his witticism alone.

But Frakes was haunted by dreams of being watched; he slept ill and was late in arising the next day. He hustled down, certain that his morning students would have assumed him out (disrespectful children), and fled for the day. But they were gathered in a line on the floor, notebooks out and listening with rapt attention, to the Man in Grey.

"And so it is that the law of a civilized nation must create greater protections for its own citizens, who sacrifice on its behalf, than for strangers, aliens or enemies. This has always been so."

"But if you kill someone, he is a dead man, isn't he?" This from the wheelright's son, one of Frakes' most surly and insolent students.

"Aye, that is very well thought of, young sir; your mind ranges far and fast. But is the dead man always murdered? 'Twas as I have told you—see, read here...". Thumbing through the tome on his desk, the stranger lifted the old Shilarian legal text to a page very near the end, and held it up close for the class to read.

Crouching forward to the edge of the Circle barrier, the student murmured aloud, "... and so the court released Sir Palanton upon his own rekognzzz—"

"—recognizance. It means he is free so long as he returns for trial upon his honor."

"—recognizance, in view of his distinguished service in defence of the land prior to this dispute."

"So you see, the law is bound to give greater consideration and honor to those who support it. This is only natural—but here I see that your tutor is arrived, and so the lessons may begin in earnest."

The Guildmaster was momentarily taken aback by the sudden shift of attention—truth to tell, he was becoming interested—and felt a simultaneous rush of fear and shame as the students looked at him, and their faces fell a little. The guest behind the barrier had immediately closed the tome and returned to his copying, as if no one else were there. Frakes' temper, which in truth had been fraying for almost a day, now began to shred.

"The students are dismissed."

"Master Frakes, may we stay? I would like to ask the man—"

"You may not. Leave the room, I am about to lower the Circle and excuse this man from the Guild."

For several seconds then, the only sounds were the shuffling of feet and the constant, damned scratching of the quill. As soon as the door had closed upon the last retreating student, Frakes lowered the Circle.

"And now, sirrah, enough. Your constant imposition was hard when it was confined to this quackery of a ritual and your personal eccentricities, but when you move so far as to subvert the children of this town—"

"I have finished the work, Guildmaster."

Frakes swallowed the rest of his lecture despite himself. Finished? That roughbound fair-copy was forty pages if it was a paragraph— and the stranger was either a lucky browser or had read the dullest legal tome on his shelves as well! Risking another glance into those steel orbs, Frakes searched for signs of fatigue, and saw only determination, a wall of will. But his awe could build no bridge to his courtesy.

"Ah good. We can use it to bookend one of the back shelves, and keep a useful work from the damp. The Circle is down, sirrah, you may leave."

Wordlessly and with no outward sign of response to the insults offered, the Man in Grey put on his cloak, stowed his gear, and withdrew from the Circle. As Frakes entered and raised it to nearly click the man's heels, the stranger carefully replaced the legal tome; turning, he bowed to the Guildmaster with straightened knee, a gesture his host took as an insult. When he turned to go, the Guildmaster, still feeling behind in the scoring of points, could not resist a final barb.

"I'll thank you not to return to this Circle, nor even this town. Good riddance to you and your worthless find, sirrah."

At that, the Man in Grey stopped with one hand on the knob, and turning strode back towards the Guildmaster of Connor. There was an iron fire combusting in his eyes now, and as he shifted the staff in his hands it flared with silver—how did he *do* that? He took only three steps, to reach the Circle, yet the Guildmaster safe at its center shrunk back as if being attacked. Halting at its edge (thank all Hope, thought Frakes, it holds against this revenant), he spoke with a quiet, contained fury that belied the stone of his visage.

"Do not equate the value of the message with the worth of the bearer, Guildmaster. Mine own qualities are not at issue here, dispense with me as ye have, as ye wish. But keep the word I bring ye in more respect."

"Or else what. Do you threaten me, sirrah, an' I shall summon the guard at once."

"Fool! The threat is to ye and all ye hold dear; in thy family, in this town, upon this continent. The War of the Corpses begins anew."

"What? What 'war', there was never any—"

"Aye, the first battle was lost to Hope, and now is found. And what the learned and magnificent Exeter Polanquan had discovered is again brought into the light. That ritual, lying there on your desk, holds the key to protecting the bodies of the dead from the ravages of necromancy. With a miracle of Revival, which surely ye have mastered, and that bit of granite there on your desk, or any other common and pure element of earth, ye may employ the ritual to protect a corpse, or perhaps several. With more preachers, ye may shelter a dozen, or a hundred—"

"What arrant nonsense is this. What possible use, to those already dead..."

"Think, man! Your students each morning do no less, think! Each body permanently denied to the use of liches, vampires, and demons is another small weapon struck from their hands. The Corpse War is begun, whether we fight it or not."

"Do you, are you seriously suggesting that we should try to protect every corpse that has ever been buried? You are mad, and your ritual could never work, not to so worthless a purpose. What you propose could never, never, never be done."

"Nay. Not from behind closed doors and the safety of warding circles, certes."

In silence the Man in Grey turned to go. At the door, he spoke once again without turning.

"But mayhap, in another twenty centuries, there will be a Guildmaster who shall read, and understand, and begin."

In silence left the Man in Grey. It was only several moments later that Guildmaster Frakes recalled, he had not yet willed the Circle down, as was his habit when alone. Doing so, he began to rummage among his effects as if he had some purpose standing here. The fair-copied book seemed to move to be near his hand whatever he thought to do, and for sheer stubbornness he refused to touch it. Summoning his acolyte, Frakes ordered him to take it to the rear shelves well beyond his sight.

Then a commotion from outside drew his attention, and Frakes could not resist his curiousity.

Beyond the Guild door, the main street of Connor was unwonted busy, with two processions approaching town from the north. To one side of the thoroughfare, a caravan of Gypsies pulled to and allowed a troop of Shilarian retainers past, with two court-lords in their midst. Folk were gathered from all sides to witness this unusual occurrence; knights had been riding through Connor to the north for days now, on news of the young king's return and rumors of war. Now south?

Frakes looked that way and there, already at some distance was the Man in Grey. One of the riders called out to him and the Guildmaster straightened in the presence of the nobility.

"Healer, have you seen a man, broad hat and staff, all in grey?"

His heart surging in his chest, Frakes pointed down the southern street. "Not three furlongs off, milord. Hurry, you can overtake him."

The lady cried out in relief and the horse-troop spurred to a trot scattering foot traffic to either side as they dashed out of immediate sight. Frakes felt a savage sense of satisfaction, no doubt this villain was wanted and would now receive his due at the hands of the law.

The Rom elder had to address him three times before he heard her words.

"Guildmaster Frakes, of Connor?"

"What is it Gypsy, I am quite busy." Frakes was intent on the wished-for moment the guards would bring their prisoner back into his view. Perhaps he could have the last word with the insolent churl. Perhaps there was a reward.

"Guildmaster, we bring news from the capital."

Sparing a glance, Frakes saw the usual array of vagrant entertainers; the chest-naked man with his feats of strength, the jugglers, dancing women, fine horses all about, and several covered wagons which served as their houses. Any other day he might have taken leisure to visit their evening show. But today, he wanted only one act performed and it was about to start; he could hear the slow return of hooves on the cobbles.

"Out with it, and begone."

"Your mother has died."

Frakes snapped down to look the elderly woman in the eyes, and suddenly felt the cold of the winter morning pour into his soul by way of his hanging jaw. Nothing moved, except a slight creak from a long box on the side of the lead wagon. Absurdly, its lid moved up and a single face—an Elf, evidently hiding for some reason—peeked out. Frakes could not take in any sense from this, nor from the morning sun behind him, nor the slight clean breeze.

His mother's illness was the sort that resisted all miracles of healing. Frakes had visited her monthly for years, invoking it scores of times to stave back the disease's progress, but ever as he returned she was worse. Finally he stopped coming, with her consent given unasked. And Frakes knew himself to be a peevish, vain, short-tempered blight upon his own town. No rank, no accomplishments in his career mattered compared to the inevitability of his loss and his cowardice in its face.

The returning horses were at a walk now; the Man in Grey rode behind the court lord and strangely his hands were unbound, his staff on his back instead of taken from him. One hoof cracked a frozen puddle and Frakes felt the painful fracture within his chest. Mouth still agape he stared at the Man in Grey, who returned his gaze in stolid ignorance, unchanged though he now moved north instead of south.

Whatever else the Rom elder said to him Frakes did not hear. Turning slowly he walked back into the Guild. The tamboor player, fire-breather and their immortal stowaway looked on in wonderment as the door gently closed behind him.

Inside, Frakes found his steps had carried him back to his desk. As the grief of his loss broke through the walls of pride he had so carefully erected, tears evacuated the fortress and fled his face. A moment later, Frakes realized he had picked up the granite stone, and slowly his grief ebbed.

"Guildmaster? May I help you somehow?"

Frakes looked on the youth who served him, and when he spoke it was in a far gentler and less imperious tone than ever before.

"Yes, lad, my thanks. Will you tell the hostler I shall need a horse, as soon as he can make one available. I shall be gone some time, to the capital. For a funeral. And lad, there's that book, the one I just gave you. Bring it me, would you? I have—I have some work to do."

⊕ ⊕ ⊕

Another such wedding, Tossa wanted no part of. His nation would not survive it, for one thing.

The Bordbeyonds rode into the city under escort, and Cil-Cilurion buzzed like a hive the entire time. Tossa joined the honor-guard near the front, and guided them down the main way to center-city past the largest throng he had ever seen, virtually a census of the capital. The sight of twenty-score riders in their ancient, piecework armor, adorned in strange furs and feathered bands, and row upon row of visored helms was striking. But the silence was by far the most strange, and it spread to all the crowd nearby until they had passed. Not one of the nomads spoke, it seemed, through the hours of their passage as the Baron Hirion, in full armor and plumed in blue, led them all to church.

The cathedral to Shilar lay open to the elements, every window thrown out and the doors on all sides tied back to afford their sky-loving guests a view from the porticos. Tossa jumped down and went in first, to see Gareth standing with the High Seer by the Foresight Dais. At the foot of the entrance steps, the leather-helmed warrior with the long black braid dismounted, and took a prisoner's pace as she ascended escorted by a Shilarian squire who wore no family crest but did not escape her brother's recognition. Tossa grinned at her before hastening to join the royal groom.

Within, Shilar's nobility sat bundled and shivering in the pews while the elderly Kalentire, quaking even beneath his ermine, could hardly speak the words. Tossa overheard some of the eldest in the crowd, calling it a much briefer incantation than his father's wedding had heard.

Commoners eager to see the uncrowned king and his bride squeezed as close as they dared to the mounted foreigners outside, jostling and cursing and alarming the plains horses. The noise rose to echo in the soaring rafters. Tossa could tell no one was able to hear what Gareth said from one knee.

Standing nearby the squire heard every word, from the King, the High Seer, the Combatted, and his sister. He dearly wished he had not.

Gareth's words were pure poetry; though Tossa had helped proof the poem, the King's vow and testament of love came from his heart and seemed to the squire completely extemporaneous. But the groom's voice, couching these brilliant words, was a disaster of teenaged nerves and self-doubt. Stutters, cracks, coughs and squeaks accompanied every moment Gareth spent on one knee: Tossa closed his eyes in gratitude when the King stopped speaking, for now every mouth hushed its fellows, to hear the nomad princess respond by reading his poem.

Sidrathay's speech was a like-for-like catastrophe, in reverse of her intended's. Her voice in reading the poem rang clean and pure in the chamber despite the helm, with measured calm and the confidence that comes of not caring about the result. Shilarians eager for the first words of their new queen leaned in and paid the closest attention to a brand of verbal butchery unheard even from the mouths of infants. Each syllable was hacked and distorted. Every mistake that a student of letters could make on their first day in school, Sidrathay committed as if doling out a merciless lesson in how not to read. No two consonants could be pronounced together, without a small "uh" or "eh" between them as the Bordbeyond princess wrestled to give each letter the sound she had learned. And no consideration of poetry or flow held the slightest interest as she turned time and again to Thula to demand the proper sound of every fourth word. Always the most embarrassing word: "beauty", "embrace", "entwine".

Tossa marked his lord's face, a mask of patience and chivalric composure as he heard each crystal phrase broken in two, dropped to the stones, and ground to powder beneath her boot. Not a lord in the hall believed the King knew the first thing about a love-poem, and they would never learn otherwise from his mouth.

Lurching at last to a halt, Sidrathay held out the scroll for Thula, or Gareth or Kalentire to take: politely rebuffed, she folded it to stuff in her weapon-belt and stood with arms akimbo.

"And now, Diamemne? Are we a husband and wife yet?"

"Nearly, Sidrathay," Gareth said rising to take her hands in his. Raising her visor, he leaned in and administered the most courteous, gentle and cherished kiss that Tossa had ever seen. Their first, but the King was driven by his spirit and it smoothed every obstacle. The chapel sighed, and the crowd without as well. Tossa could see as the pair parted, the bride was well impressed.

"And now," she said flatly, "we must lie together and couple."

Strong knights choked, ladies gasped, and the crowd outside, when the sense of it trickled that far, began to cheer and hoot. Gareth's face broke into his accustomed grin just as the sun peeked through a break in the winter clouds overhead.

"As for that beloved, it is indeed customary, but perhaps not quite so urgent."

Sidrathay pulled off her helm, ignoring the strong reaction the sight of her face brought, and spoke with her usual directness. "We should couple, it is the custom, and then we may ride to war while there is still light."

It was impossible to hear this frank and earthy discourse with a straight face. Tossa noticed the chuckles finally rippling through the nobility now, as if the commoners outside had the right idea first.

Sidrathay turned to Thula with hands spread. "Or did I get this wrong? Perhaps you must strike me again." Tossa saw his sister quite ready to do her part in this.

"Consider, beloved," Gareth said while interposing with a chuckle. "Not simply when, but ahm, also the question of where. If we retire now, sooth and it will be to the palace, where the beds are of thickest down and the coverlets heavy and soft. I can have the windows opened and for the rest, I feel confident you will not be displeased."

Mouths agape all over the chapel, and poor Kalentire looked as if the King proposed they strip right here before the dais.

"But think you," Gareth continued, fully in love and no more embarrassed than if they were all alone. "If we ride now, evening will find us on the road, and then we would come to each other beneath the stars, with but a blanket or two for our bed. The cold of winter will drive us, mayhap as fast as our—"

"It is well indeed. Let us ride then, Diamemne. Perhaps on our return we may see this large bed you speak of. Unless it is forbidden that we couple more than once."

"It is not forbidden, Sidrathay. And it is very well indeed."

Gareth led his bride forth and Tossa fell in with his sister just behind them.

"You did your best," he offered to her glowering face and stiff stride.

"She did her worst on purpose," Thula ground out between her teeth. "I swear, this war will be a relief compared to one more day with that arrogant block of snow. It comes of being an only child, I vow."

"How fortunate for her, that she had so patient a tutor."

Her punch was affectionate and the siblings hugged as they continued walking.

"So," Tossa managed carefully, "which of us will be Hobsel Parry from now on?"

Thula, once Hillel Parry, looked to him in shock, then managed, "Let's just see that we neither get killed first."

Tossa could only nod to that.

On the front steps the cheers were deafening, but carried a tinge of riot. The Shilarian commoners pressed up, causing even more confusion among the Bordbeyonds and their mounts. Some dandy had started that naughty song about the first night of a wedding which everyone knew to either try the verses or laugh at the chorus. But in many places there were elbows being thrown, and now some fists, and the sound of curses and insults between the two peoples.

Gareth's upraised arms stemmed but did not quiet the clamor. Baron Hirion gestured for his men to restore order but they were outnumbered two thousand to one. On an impulse, the King reached to draw his bride to him and kissed her again. This produced a thunderous cheer and a momentary attention which he could use to his advantage.

"My people, I rejoice that you were here this day to celebrate my good fortune." He kissed her hand and another cheer hammered the walls all around. "The Children of Hope must ride in this hour to the west, and face what adventure may come there. Pray, my people, that Shilar will guide us to do as we must. And give us leave to go now, while the signs of heaven beckon."

The crowd began to back away from the horsemen, all fighting now quenched and the crisis averted. Gareth spoke with his barons as already the vanguard and wagons started moving toward the Ancient Waygate, at a pace the knights could easily overtake along the road toward Conar. Tossa began to think of the armoring and his other squirely duties when suddenly Gareth addressed them both in a private tone.

"Thula," he said with a hand on her shoulder, "my thanks for all you've done, I know it could not have been easy."

"It did not sound like it!" Tossa jibed, earning him a blow to the stomach and too short a breath to interrupt further.

"Thula, Tossa, hear me. Sir Ganelake of the northern foefdom has been slain. By ghouls."

Tossa watched his sister's shock at the ghastly news.

"This is now a dangerous frontier and Sir Ganelake was a widower without issue. Decide which of you will ascend to take his place."

"But Gareth," Thula blurted, "Your Majesty, I mean—but we are riding with you."

He shook his head. "We have only scattered word that the threat is averted. If we leave the good folk of those villages exposed to further attack, what point in our grand expedition to the west? One of you will stay behind. A vassal in my closest trust, I must have that."

He stood back a step and smiled gently. "And I hope a happy resolution to the question of inheritance."

Tossa stared at his sister and felt the weight of their choice crash upon them. A knight, at seventeen! It was indeed an awful gift. He barely heard the frantic shout of the Quill Knight who had worked his way to the steps.

"Majesty! Your Majesty!" It was the Coroner, Baron Kalney looking rather unkempt and breathless. He approached the cathedral steps and fell to one knee.

"My king, we have found the Man in Grey."

Instantly, Gareth was all eyes for the man before him. He raised Kalney up, saying only, "Where?"

"We brought him to the main throne room, Majesty. The servants told us of your wedding, may I congr—"

"This was well done indeed, my good Baron, please attend me. Sidrathay, please marshal your force and follow the Baron Hirion as soon as the columns are ready. I shall catch you up before mid-afternoon."

"And tonight," Sidrathay said with the hint of a smile, "we shall couple."

"Assuredly, milady, if it be your will we shall." Sidrathay replaced her helm and moved to remount.

"Tossa, Thula, with me." The quartet plus Baron Kalney took horse and headed to the castle.

⊕⊕⊕

All through the bailey and down the central corridor no one spoke, as pages fled by and courtiers dodged while bowing. Thula was thinking hard, Tossa could see, and hardly noticed her familiar environment again, the court she had known for years while he was living on the still, lonely Plains.

"What is it like?" He asked her quietly and she started. "The foef of Ganelake, you were there. With him."

"Oh," she said. "It's lovely. Forests everywhere. Large and lonely."

Tossa had hoped something in his sister's words would tip her preference. He could not abide leaving Gareth to risk his life in war. But neither could he condemn his sister to the remote frontier, possibly to face ghouls.

The king pressed ahead down the carpeted hallway, speaking in low tones with Baron Kalney. Tossa could hardly understand the urgency in Gareth's manner now, but his loyalty was long ago a settled thing. He would follow him anywhere. He would stay behind if asked.

The main audience hall seemed nearly dark by comparison to the punctured cathedral and the open air. As always, day or night, courtiers and officials swirled in groups and pools, this time staring to the far wall. Gareth plunged into the human tide, which splashed away on both hands as he crossed the marble floor with Tossa and Thula in his wake.

There, beneath the parting depths of nobles and servants, stood a human-shaped stone inspecting the jeweled skies of the ceiling and surrounded by a detail of guards.

The Lady Blenia turned and deeply curtsied on their arrival. Tossa laid a hand on Thula's arm, and they hung back. The guest moved to bow over his straight leg in a fashion Tossa had never seen.

Gareth first raised Blenia up and turned with her to Kalney. "My thanks to you both, for your good service. Retire now and refresh yourselves, doubt not that I will reward you properly if it is in my power."

With a gesture he dismissed the guards as well; the retainers looked askance at the grey man's staff, but Gareth's smile disarmed all objections. As the guards went, so flowed the courtiers and servants, and the throne room rapidly drained. Tossa and Thula fell back a few steps, but drifted behind the throne to watch. Baron Kalney also lingered, after whispering urgently to a page who fled.

Gareth and the stranger regarded each other for a moment after the doors closed out the world, and sealed in the echoes of any noise thereafter. Tossa saw them in profile: the coiffed, handsome prince in azure and silver to one side, fresh from his wedding vows and smiling kindly; the grim, road-weathered Man in Grey to the other, perhaps still keeping some dreadful oath and either unwilling or unable to bend his face for any show of emotion.

Tossa was shocked when the stranger spoke first.

"Majesty, may I offer my condolences on the loss of your father."

The king held his breath a moment. "My thanks, stranger. May I know your name, and ask whether you are one of my subjects?"

"My name is Solemn Judgement, Majesty, and I have no country in this land to which my father brought me."

"No country, sir? I can gain no idea what you may mean by this. Are you of the Rom, then, a wanderer?"

"A wanderer, certes, milord, but only briefly among the Rom. I traveled here across the water, from the west. Though I have come to believe that the ocean of my land begins in a different place from where the waters of your world wash upon the coast of Conar."

"You speak of marvelous strange things, sir. Yet I feel desirous to accept you at your word, for I mark you to be a man of honor."

The stranger at this let out a long sigh, and may have relaxed the set of his shoulders a bit. He bowed again to the king, who continued.

"I perceive to look on you closely that you are hardly of the age that your, well that the first sight of you argues. Where is your father then?"

"He too has died, milord king, in bringing me to Hope."

Echoes of "hope", then silence stretched between the two; Tossa sensed, as Gareth gazed on this unnerving stranger, that the king felt a kinship with the commoner. Nothing new there, he reflected: Gareth charmed everyone he met because he so stubbornly believed the best of them. Yet these two youths who each lost a father had come to an empty throne room by very different paths, he'd wager.

And then too, Tossa recalled, he'd also lost his father too soon, and Thula's. Was this a curse of the present age? Would those barely more than children have to decide the fate of the Lands of Hope?

"Well, Solemn Judgement, I offer you sympathies, as you so graciously did to me. How, if I may ask, did you come into my kingdom?"

The grey stranger shifted his stance and paused. "Sooth, milord, I walked."

"All the way from Conar! The Ancient Way would take a man five weeks on foot."

"Three weeks, majesty, by boat to Mendel."

"What! Mendel?"

"Overland to the capital, and then…" the Man in Grey stopped short, eyes a bit wider and evidently searching for words. He lurched ahead. "By the ferry into Shilar. And most recently, I have searched beyond your customary borders. On the Plains of Ranebruh."

"But this is extraordinary, sir. I thought I had undertaken a great expedition when I traveled mounted among the Bordbeyonds, but—"

"Majesty," the stranger interrupted heavily, "is there perhaps some reason you wished my presence?"

Gareth looked upon this interruption with his usual gentle smile. "Why Solemn Judgement, is there somewhere else you must be at present? I do not keep you against your will, and if that were your understanding I apologize. But to come to the point, as you wish; I hear you have uncovered a great and miraculous lore, sir, and I would hear of it, and have it if I can."

At this, Judgement looked about him uncertainly. "My lore, majesty? What do you know of this?"

Chuckling quietly at this interrogation, Gareth explained. "My reports are that you have discovered a ritual that can protect the dead of Hope from raising. And I hear too, that such protection is now sorely needed."

Like a dawn, emotions lit the face of the Man in Grey and he stepped toward the king in his fervor. Tossa saw at once two decades shed from his frame, as he became someone as young as he, discomposed, touched by doubt and eagerness.

"Certes, thou dost understand!" He drew forth a small book with rawhide binding, holding it with great reverence. "It was in my heart to bespeak the healers wherever I might find them, and there leave a copy."

Gareth looked on the book, putting both hands to his mouth for a moment. "You sir—let me be certain I understand you—you have journeyed a circuit of the northern kingdoms, and then into the wild lands beyond our borders, finding the key to this ritual and copying it into a book. At some risk to yourself, without doubt! And now you intend to travel back across every city in the Lands, showing or teaching this lore—"

"Leaving a copy, only milord. The teaching is not an easy one, to some minds I trow."

"A copy, very well then. On your own you think to do this!" He chuckled again in such good nature that no one could find it an offence. "Solemn Judgement, may I see this book, will you allow me?"

With a deep bow and just an instant's hesitation, the Man in Grey handed it over. Gareth flipped it open and read awhile in silence.

The king looked up at the end and spoke. "Solemn Judgement, is it your will to continue your peregrinations, making copies and walking between every town in my kingdom?"

"Certes milord, aught else may I desire? The War of the Corpses has begun, and 'tis mine own fault, for I did release this plague upon the Children of Hope."

"You?" The king was stunned. "You were there, in the Hopeward with Natasha?"

"She was my teacher majesty."

"And I see she taught you well enough to endure distance, and men's displeasure I might guess, and not least of all the ghouls."

The Man in Grey took no note of these compliments, saying only, "By my hand is she left there, and the liche Wolga Vrule now free. And also the demon Kog, since the Eye rests again within the lands. I made the choice which led to their escape."

"Yours is a hard telling, Goodman, far harder than the account from the Elvish sage with whom I spoke."

"Sage Fellareon! Majesty, you have seen him, he is well? Is he here?"

Gareth looked to Kalney, who hung his head in chagrin.

"Alas, majesty, on his request I assisted Sage Cedrith to leave Cil-Cilurion not three days ago. We had thought your blessing—"

"You had it, my good Baron. But Goodman Judgement, I regret I cannot bring you together with your friend. How strange that you both should have been so close to meeting."

"It is our habit, I trow majesty. But may I, please, may I write to him?"

"Of course! I shall house you here in the palace with every convenience, you may rest as long as you wish, and letters you write will be posted at once."

"And my book, milord? Will you send copies to other Healers in your kingdom?"

"To every Healer in my kingdom, sir, and they shall arrive—in somewhat inferior penmanship to yours, I avow—but with the king's seal upon each one and my express command that it be read and attended to with all speed. And more," Gareth continued, "I shall send this lore to every kingdom in the Lands of Hope. And as soon as we are able, I shall extend an expedition to the Plains of Ranebruh. There my healers shall cast your ritual even upon the dead of our ancient enemies, that they too will rest, and undeath will not curse them."

The Man in Grey drew a shaky breath, and nodded his head.

"This will be well done indeed, majesty."

"It is you, Solemn Judgement, who have done well among us here. And by my advice, you will consider your work well done, and take your leisure as my guest."

At once, Tossa saw the stranger straighten, and the years come back upon him. "Your majesty is entirely too kind to a vagrant alien," the Man in Grey said stiffly. "I must leave at once. For the Percentalion."

Gareth looked truly pained at the stranger's eagerness to refuse his hospitality. The Man in Grey looked to the gold-incised arch to one side, then again at the gem-stars overhead.

"Yet will you not stay? I must ride within the hour but you would please me to tarry and rest after your exertions."

"I must seek the center, it was ordained to me. In a letter. The tale of it is long and I would not for the world detain you, majesty. But I feel I must seek out my foes at once."

"By yourself? A demon and a liche, what manner of king would allow such risk? Come with me, if you must, within my host and those of the Bordbeyonds, to take what adventure may come to us."

Judgement tilted his head as if in suspicion.

"By your majesty's great favor, I am relieved for a time of the burden to dispense this ritual. Would it please your majesty, to extend a second, even greater gift upon me?"

"Anything within my power."

"I beg that I may use the ancient gate, to reach the center in Reghalion."

Tossa heard Thula gasp, as they both stared at the golden arch. No one he knew had ever seen it used, and many believed it was a fable. Gareth turned to Baron Kalney with the question.

"Majesty, I have no knowledge of the gate's use, only that its power must be invoked from this side before any may travel it in either direction. If it still functions, that is."

"It does, it must!" Judgement removed his hat as he pled.

"Who would know the proper invocation?"

"Surely it would be the High Seer if anyone, milord. Shall I bring him?"

"At once, my good Baron." Gareth turned back as Kalney retreated. "But Goodman, you would be alone, in the center of the chaos land, in a city rumored to be haunted."

"You ride to war, milord."

"In the midst of my host! And because I feel I must."

"Just so."

"But are you not afraid, sir?"

The Man in Grey shook his head, not in denial but impatience. "What of fear, majesty? Can a man follow it? Nay, for fear never leads one anywhere."

The king smiled at such an answer. "What, then?"

"Duty," Judgement answered. "My father gave me a task, to learn, to stand. To do what I could. I follow him."

They stood awhile in silence then, and the king nodded.

"You are a singularly fortunate man, Solemn Judgement. You surely must have been, to come through half such trials as I have already heard tell. But you are favored too, in having such a father. I must try to live up to mine, though my way is not as clear, I think, as yours."

The doors opened again to admit the Baron, and the High Seer, each in the company of pages carrying some portion of their armor. At the sight of the Quill Knight and the septuagenarian High Seer in chainmail shirts, Gareth cried aloud in surprise.

"Milords! Do you both mean to accompany me then?"

The Baron laughed. "I did rather well in tourneys, majesty, in my youth. I admit it has been some time, but I will not leave you now."

Kalentire looked down his thin nose at the king and said only "Your majesty summoned me." Each piece of armor his attendant strapped on seemed it might crumble his spare frame to the ground, yet he hung on doggedly.

"My very good High Seer, you honor me. Can you activate the magic of this gate?"

Kalentire's eyes flared wide with surprise. "For you, majesty?"

"For this, this fellow here. He wishes to enter Reghalion."

Now the High Seer was agog, and for a short space could make no words though his mouth lay open.

Tossa felt a charge of the same fear and stepped forward. "The capital is haunted! The ghosts of the ancient court are said to be everywhere."

The Man in Grey showed no response, but Kalentire huffed with impatience. "In fact," he snapped, "the gate does not lead to Reghalion but to the under-capital, Oncario. Whether it is occupied or no, who can say? But rest assured there will be no undead there."

"Why was this done, High Seer?"

"For safety's sake, according to our histories, majesty. The visitor to Reghalion comes first to a space beyond the walls of Oncario, and then must travel within that city to use the gates set in its throne room, as it is here. Only from there can one access Reghalion."

"What of the gates here?"

"But one, milord king. Shilar in his foresight saw that little traffic would use it, thus the form of safeguard he chose was the invocation, which includes the name of the destination. No one may travel here, to this throne room, without a similar incantation to allow entry."

"All this time," Gareth mused, "these centuries we could have kept contact with our sister kingdoms. And it took this man here," gesturing to Judgement, "to awaken the habit. Goodman, I am again in your debt."

"Mind you," Kalentire interposed, "there can be no telling what condition you will find Oncario, nor even if the gate still works. If the destination has been destroyed, it would likely mean death."

Tossa looked to Judgement, who again held his face as if someone else were the subject of conversation.

"Please High Seer, if you would be so kind as to open the gate to Oncario."

With a shrug the elderly Preacher moved to the archway. Thula and Tossa came up together near the king as he held out his hand for Solemn Judgement to grip.

"I hope we may meet again, sir."

"As your majesty pleases; and may Hope watch over you in turn."

"The north, the ghouls!" Thula breathed.

"The dead still sleep," Judgement responded. "More ghouls there may be, but those I awakened have been destroyed."

Behind them the room rang with Kalentire's voice calling out Ancient words concluding with the name of Areghel, and a golden glow threw shadows across the floor. They turned to see the elderly preacher huff with triumph, then lean briefly against Baron Kalney as he caught his breath. Kalentire turned to face his king even as the dogged page strapped on another armor piece, looking ever more fierce though the helmet over his gaunt head rattled with the motion.

"Time enough yet to deal with any others," Gareth said, "as I have devised. But first, we ride to war in the west. Fare thee well, Solemn Judgement. May the duty you follow serve you in what lies ahead."

At the glowing gate, the Man in Grey turned back and bowed a final time.

"I shall remember my father's face," he said. "And for the rest, let it come."

He stepped into the archway and out of sight.

⊕⊕⊕

Since leaving Trainertown Anteris had abandoned his dream, to chronicle the deeds of heroes. Nearly every waking moment, a mind-numbing monotony pressed between his loneliness, confusion and fear tramping along behind the group. But as the aches of his exertions took an accustomed place, the scribe recovered more of himself. Always inclined to look on the bright side, he reflected that after leaving the mob of hell-beasts behind two nights ago, he had not thought again about his own death. The risk of that had sprung hard off the paper of an imagined deed and become a very real, if occasional, jolt to his nerves. But now it was a memory.

They had reached the terminus of the ancient road early morning that day, and stopped to consider their options. Treaman ranged about checking for any signs while Haltar and Mhoral argued, which seemed to be their pastime. The mage Linya raised both arms to cast a spell of detection on the ground, and Forge stood near Anteris to watch the waves of color spread before her like lantern light as she turned this way and that murmuring nonsense syllables in a low tone.

She never said what she was looking for, and Anteris could see no sign of anything different under those waves of unearthly illumination. But she kept it up so long that her breathing became labored. Forge stepped in to offer his hand under her elbow, just as the spell ceased, and she thanked him. Forge was the perfect gentleman as he guided her back to sit, and never tried to make conversation with the mage. Anteris wondered how his friend's work in the grimy smoke of a smithy could confer such maturity. Maybe he really was still a child.

The cold closed in here, as if there had been invisible walls along the road holding in some warmth, or shelter from the wind till it ended. They had marched south yet weather grew colder. Anteris hopped from foot to foot as he waited: the short hike to this point had shed the morning pains, and he knew moving again would bring some warmth.

Treaman returned, consulted briefly with the other veterans, then turned to Anteris, Forge and Braja.

"I believe Oncario is not far. In a sane world, it lies just west of south. Right, scribe?"

"Yes sir, the maps would have put it in that direction, though how far I do not know."

"Nothing much we can do about that. Follow close, don't stray," the Woodsman threw a dirty look at Forge, "and stop whenever I tell you."

The giant black warrior nodded, evidently taking in most of the instructions, and said "In Oncario all burn. Warmer." Everyone laughed at that and hitched up their packs again.

The rest of the day was a process of constant wearing-down, from tired through exhausted and on towards agony. Anteris realized Treaman had not been testing them earlier; he was setting a pace even the veterans found taxing, driven near to panic. Yet the terrain was flat and lifeless, boredom as big an enemy as exertion. Anteris grinned, recalling his dream of being the historian for this brave band. To witness their heroism first hand, to record their deeds in words, had been a forbidden goal all through last summer after their first return and down to today.

And what words! He remembered now the gaudy descriptions he had in mind, the timeless phrases he'd seen written for the heroes of old. Words like Haltar had used, that first night by the fire outside the south gates. Somehow "marching to death" had not been among them. Anteris doubted he would have anything to write about, if the group returned at all. He imagined the choice, between malaise and massacre, and grinned again.

Distracted by the burden of keeping up, Anteris' mind was slow to reason why Treaman was marching so hard. In dribs and pieces, he realized, it must be about the army they had passed. Every monster in the kingdom, perhaps, responding to the call. And headed where? Increasingly frantic, his mind hunted for another excuse, a different reason, but ineluctably his thoughts were dragged to think of Trainertown.

That fell legion of hell was headed along the new ancient way, to his home.

The world around him provided no distraction for this horror. The sight of Haltar and Mhoral just ahead was simply a marker in the rhythm of the march—don't let their backs get too far away. The land and sky were two giant slabs of uncolored oppression, and the weather closed in, cold and still humid somehow. It wouldn't do to think on his remaining strength, or the next stop. Anteris staggered along, desperately looking around for any new thing to relieve his mind. Nothing, never anything.

So he began to think of Calper, and Forge's father, Marindya and the others, attacked by hell's horde. And fire, consuming flames that licked in time to his pace and ate the market, the church. The library. It couldn't be. It couldn't be anything else.

When the others stopped before the scaly river, Anteris nearly fell.

⊕⊕⊕

Treaman was pressing the pace as never before, hoping the massive horde now to the north of them had emptied the lands hereabouts for long enough to make the pine barrens. Where that monstrous band was headed, why Alaetar was there, what would happen to Trainertown; none of that mattered. It couldn't, not for now. He would think about it later.

The road had probably cut the time to the city of brick in half, and he hoped by more. The Woodsman only paused when he thought he detected a sign of change, and pretended they were rest stops so the others wouldn't worry. He was surprised either of the boys were still able to keep up: tonight, he would have Linya check their feet and use a salve if needed. He strained to see the line of the pine barrens ahead.

Instead, he halted at the view of a brownish, black-streaked stream moving slowly across the party's path. Many creeks that size would be frozen over by now, but this one flowed steadily. The party halted behind him with oaths and questions at the sight; the scribe, obviously exhausted, almost lost his footing.

After a moment, Treaman thought his eyes were playing tricks. The stream was not just moving, but slightly undulating; its surface seemed rounded, in a way even slushy water could never be. And the texture of the half-frozen ice resembled scales, absurdly.

"Treaman, what is that?" Mhoral demanded.

"I have no idea," the Woodsman responded, looking up and downstream to see an arrow-straight course either way.

"En—surr, su-punt" the scribe gasped.

"What?" Forge asked him, but Anteris just held up one hand for mercy. The young Stealthic clucked with impatience and turned to approach the banks, evading his friend's clutching hand.

"Forge, stay back." Treaman was annoyed again at the boy's headstrong nature, and felt a sharp pang of remembrance.

The youth stayed on the balls of his feet as if he expected something to leap through the scummy surface while he approached. In less time than could be told, the stream began to shrink in size, narrowing and dropping its level. Forge turned back to wave the party on, then leaped to one side as a quartet of fangs as long as arms snapped on the spot where his head used to be.

The stream was large and fat again, rolling onward without interruption as Forge scrambled to his feet and trotted to the party with his head looking back. Treaman was sure his eyes were mistaken; the head of something reptilian, and perhaps a tapered end. But the stream flowed on now, returned to its previous size and undisturbed by whatever the Woodsman thought he saw.

"A head! Some monster in the water."

"How quickly it struck, how did it know?"

"You. Moron, come over here." This last from Haltar who spoke without heat but wearing that perilous grin Treaman knew. Several times now he had worn that smile and not slain anyone, but the Woodsman knew the odds could not hold forever.

The Stealthic marched over, matching smile for smile. Haltar gently turned the youth around and pointed to the river. "Take one step." Forge did so, giving Haltar ample room to plant the side of his boot emphatically across the buttocks. Forge left the ground and pitched headlong into the battered frozen earth. Scrambling up he drew his long knife and turned back to face Haltar, who did not bother to arm.

"One more time, without orders. And I will throw you in." And he held up a single finger while giving his deathly stare of intent. Forge bit his bloody lip, nodded, and resheathed his weapon.

"But what is that thing?" He cried in complaint.

Anteris had at last caught his breath.

"Encircling Serpent."

In the quiet, Treaman could hear the deep low shushh of the creature as it flowed past a few rods behind them.

"I don't understand," he said to Anteris. "That is one creature?"

The scribe nodded unhappily. "As in the legends. Of the earliest days."

"Sounds vaguely familiar," Linya murmured, but Haltar shook his head and shrugged.

"It was before the Battle of the Razor," Anteris said, "when the outer kingdoms were still being established, and Despair created or summoned all manner of monsters to plague the people. Gelissar's

Tower, they say, was somewhere in the Percentalion, and she gained favor with Khoirah the Betrayer—"

"Favor!" Forge snorted, "we know what that means."

Treaman saw Anteris blush, then he glanced at Linya before he could stop himself. She looked back and he felt the heat flush through his head and neck.

"By means of his sorcery, Khoirah summoned a mighty serpent from the world below, which seized its tail in the mouth and constantly circled her keep whenever Gelissar was absent. Its size and ferocious fangs kept away all intruders, for by magic the head—"

"I can guess," Forge broke in. "The head will always be coming past whenever one tries to cross."

"Ridiculous." Mhoral said, "where do Men come up with these dream tales?"

In the silence everyone looked at the evidence of their eyes and compared it to Mhoral's strident admonition. Treaman had to laugh, for the Elf came up as short as always. Bildon would have loved it.

"We hike around," Haltar said, " we don't need whatever the thing is guarding."

On a guess, Treaman turned right—upstream—and started the march. Every hundred steps he signaled for a stop and scrutinized the colossal body flowing by unchanged. After a quarter-hour he could make out no alteration, and his spirits were under assault. The delay, the frustration were herding him toward frenzy. But the unthinkable size, the mass of flesh represented by this monster appalled him to shaking. The banks remained straight— did it encircle the entire world?

The others must have felt it too. Forge picked up a clod of earth and flung it at the creature, where it broke in pieces and caused no change. Braja strung his bow; Treaman nodded at him, and the Nubian drew and fired a thick shaft that buried itself in the snake-stream almost to the feathers. The river of reptile flowed on uncaring.

None of it made sense, the level of sorcery involved. Treaman knew he had to do something; though he was leagues away by now, he felt as if the army of hell could return any moment. And to keep marching aside of their goal could only bring on the chaos-change sooner or later.

He prayed, too embarrassed to kneel in front of the others but with eyes closed and hands together. This snake, this land's curse, all of it was an affront to nature. Surely Helmon would help?

No answer came walking up to strike him over the head, so Treaman drew his pioneer sword and slowly advanced on the river. Toes-first he took one step at a time as if the thing might hear him; his eyes felt dry from the effort not to blink, not to miss it.

He nearly missed it.

The slightest tapering in the size and height of the stream, before he could even be sure, and the Woodsman felt a rush of movement from overhead, caught the edge of carrion-breath and a larger, closer hiss. Dropping back and half-rolling, he held his blade blindly overhead, and felt an impact like a runaway wagon crash into his arm, wrenching him painfully the wrong way and nearly jerking Gutter from his grip.

The others shouted as he kept rolling away, and he caught just a glimpse of a thinner stream, a bone-white rattle the size of a barrel. One more roll further away and Treaman sat up to confront the river again, unchanged and thick as before.

Treaman rubbed his arm as he sat there and thought. A few minutes later, he rose and walked back to the party.

"Are you alright," Linya asked, "are you hurt?"

"Which of us," Treaman demanded, "is the fastest?"

Immediately, Forge said "He is." Everyone stared at Anteris.

⊕⊕⊕

They all looked his way when Forge spoke and Anteris nearly stumbled back. He felt urgently as if he needed to urinate, and the anguish of imagining that gave him the strength he needed to clench, and stay upright, and nod his head.

"A little. Forge is quicker though, dodges better."

The Woodsman nodded, then looked around the group with a kind of intensity Anteris had not seen before this trip.

"Right. Here's what we will do."

A few minutes later, everyone was lined up two paces shy of the spot where Treaman's body had vaguely marked the broken earth. It had taken more courage than Anteris thought he owned to approach this spot, even with the others nearby. Glancing down the line, he realized Forge was having trouble holding back, his legs twitching with the need to go even closer, to risk his life for some reason, or any reason. Anteris felt for the first time a wave of fear, not for himself, but that he might lose his best friend.

Treaman looked at everyone, last to him, and nodded.

Anteris thought about the bell ringing the end of the day back home, and suddenly his feet had wings.

Sprinting at a slight diagonal, he crossed the spot where Treaman had fallen and ran downstream just a few feet beyond the line. It was all he could do not to look back; Anteris' back muscles clenched as if the snake's tongue were licking the length of his spine. Not once did his heels touch the ground as he danced away from death.

A heavy thunk, the flare of fire, shouts from the group behind him. He heard a hiss from an enormous mouth, from the side of his eye could see he was not quite moving as fast as the stream. Anteris took two more steps on a slant away from the snake and dove as if there were water ahead to catch his body.

The hardscrabble, frozen earth that stopped his hands, chin, and chest were a bloodier welcome. But Anteris continued to roll and scramble away. Two seconds later, he confirmed that he was not in fact being eaten, and rolled over to look back. The body of the snake continued past, the party stood right where he had left them. Anteris rose and returned to the group.

Linya stepped over and inspected his scrapes. Anteris was too dazzled and breathless to speak, and it never occurred to him to try and act tough. Her face seemed to give a judgment, but when she caught his eye, the mage changed her mind about something, and drew out a small vial of salve to put on his seeping cuts. Behind her Forge smirked, and Anteris was fairly sure he had no idea what was happening. But the thick syrup faded into his scrapes and the bleeding stopped at once. When Linya put one hand out to smear more on his chest Anteris believed he might faint. Here was woman, and magic and kindness to boot. He had to bite his lip or say something idiotic.

Mercifully, it ended. Treaman drew his sword, and turned to Forge to say, "Now the second part. Your turn."

Forge stepped right to the edge of the mark, cackling under his breath. Haltar drew his wonderful longsword, Braja took up Treaman's spear. They stood a half-step behind Forge and waited.

The young Stealthic rocked back and forth several times, then suddenly jogged four steps directly across the line.

There! A metal spear embedded in the body, a scar of fire from a mystic bolt. Just another two seconds' warning, but the warriors were ready. The Elf had already begun to sing, and his bent wooden weapon sailed in as the others crossed the line. The snake-head lunging forward now met an onslaught of blades coming between it and its intended prey, as the Stealthic stood up and also slashed with his shortsword, in defiance of the plan.

The wooden foil and the spear in Braja's hand both bounced away. But Treaman expertly thrust his saw-backed blade right into the creature's mouth again; it spouted bloody specks even as the force of its strike knocked him back to the ground. Another bolt of fire slammed just next to one of its eyes, burning and flaring wildly. And the strapping warrior Haltar slashed twice in less time than it took to tell, gashing a deep "X" in dark crimson across the monster's neck.

The Encircling Serpent hissed like a pond full of steam, thrashing its head back and away to the height of a house. The tail moved on, rapidly fading from view; a trench in the barren earth lay open.

"Run! Through!" Treaman shouted and everyone lurched forward. Again, Anteris did not dare look back. He slowed when he realized he could not hear the sound of anything human behind him, just the distant hissing of the beast. There was nearly a furlong between him and the party, and the scribe felt another chill of fear to think he could have been lost in the change at such a distance.

As he walked back to the group, he could see the body of the snake already reformed behind them, flowing on as placidly as if nothing had happened. But his companions; Anteris could see stares from all except the helm of the Elf, and of course Forge who was grinning in pride.

"I told you," he crowed, "fast as the sunrise."

"He vaulted that trench," Haltar said quietly, "in a single bound. Twenty feet if it's an inch."

Treaman nodded and also grinned, clapping him on the shoulder.

"Fast then, alright. Here's hoping you don't have to run like that again, Anteris."

Mhoral and Linya distributed the extra packs they'd run with, everyone tightened straps and kept on. Throughout the day as it grew colder, Anteris thought he caught sight of the others glancing sidelong at him, something a bit changed in their attitude. He reflected that the tale he told held true, and there was some use in that. It was too cloudy to see when evening came, but the bulk of great pine trees surrounded them as they pitched the tent and huddled by a small fire for sleep.

Treaman had noticed the others looking sidelong at him, something a bit changed in their attitude. After all, his battle-plan had worked, that titanic serpent evaded with no one badly hurt. If they needed to face it again, they might have to think of another way past: the scribe said Astor had vaulted it with a wooden lance.

Three days out, two of them beyond the protection of the ancient way, they reached the pine barrens outside Oncario: all still alive by the Heroes' grace. Treaman heard an inner voice now that sounded like Hallah, one that believed in what he could do.

When they came across a kiln—strangely cold and unloaded for several days—he gave instructions for setting up the camp as usual, and found that even Mhoral simply did as he was told. Treaman used some of the bricks to build a small, almost smokeless fire inside the tent that acted like a brazier against the increasing cold.

It must have been pure chance, that his bedroll wound up next to Linya's. When he saw her lying there, Treaman decided to take an extra turn around the outside of the tent. He noted the weather closing in; snow soon, maybe a lot, though the wind was still too high for much accumulation. The moons should both be waxing, unless of course he had somehow led them through time, as happened the last trip here. Where was Januelus? Treaman knew they'd be greatly outnumbered by the Primara and her guards, and beyond getting them into the city by the river-cave, he had no plan. But first things first.

He returned to the tent and heard Haltar's snore like a soothing balm. Quietly disarming he slipped into his bedroll next to Linya's sleeping form. Her blanket was half-off her from turning; with his heart pounding Treaman extended his to lay just atop her shoulder, a tent within a tent. Sensing the added warmth, the mage rolled back and smoothly put her arm across his chest.

Treaman knew if he couldn't force his lungs to breathe she would awaken. Ah well, he thought, who really needs to sleep. Wrestling with his desire should take until morning anyway. He looked carefully on her fine chiseled chin and nose, recalling the depth of her eyes and how her intent showed in the lips when awake. Her eyes closed, he could look on her steadily now, the lips barely parted and her breath warming his heart.

{*"Treeeaman and magic-lady will make a baby now."*}

"No Hallah," he whispered. "She, she is tired."

There was a long silence as his dragon settled herself down on his abdomen and lay still.

{*"Later then."*}

The Woodsman bit his lip hard to avoid laughing out loud. He gently put one hand atop Linya's arm, as his gaze naturally turned to the charcoal-fire nearby, winking at him like a red eye, reading his least-worthy thoughts and warning of unknown dangers.

And then it was morning.

Treaman only knew it by his inner sense as he awoke, for the light hardly increased with the unseen sun. A few wet frozen beads came in through the smoke-hole to spit and hiss on the dying fire; their patter on the canvas sides rose higher and lower in sound and frequency. He rose to open the front flap, spilling enough snow into the tent to crest his boots.

"Everyone up," he ordered urgently, "we're leaving now while we can."

They all exclaimed and began to rise; Forge dawdled so long, the tent was practically pulled from under him when Braja and Mhoral broke it down. Snow in tiny rounded crystals was piled to the knees even here deep in the woods, and the wind was still too high. Treaman sensed it was nearly mid-morning, though there was no more light than dusk. He had to find the river-bank quickly.

Their course through the barrens was now a bit east of south, a zig-zag compared to the first leg of the journey. The trees never quite aligned in rows, yet still left long avenues of sight in places. Treaman pictured the band crawling like ants on the back of some colossal tree-furred creature. In places the lower branches bent to the ground, resembling fallen warriors struggling to stay up in battle against these elements.

The snow of tiny beads came down thicker with every half-hour. By the time pines gave way to cypress it drifted nearly thigh deep everywhere. Several times they started at the sound of an explosion ahead, deep and powerful yet strangely muted by the wind. Treaman found a place to rest in the lee of a large spreading cypress, where the ground was oddly still bare; the party had to climb up into the snow like a staircase when they resumed the march.

Without preamble they broke into the open, stepping onto the ice of the Cario. Several slipped and fell at once, as the beady snow did nothing to increase traction. The other bank lay in mist, the river here iced all the way across. Roiling cloud cover overhead looked muscular and dark, Treaman felt he could reach up to touch them perhaps from a treetop. The island was not in sight to the south, and the wind slammed in from the opposite direction, where the surface was either thinner ice or still unfrozen. Every instinct Treaman had shouted at him to stay off this surface, but he had no choice.

"Rope together," he yelled to the others, his voice barely carrying against the howling wind. Snow-spheres pelted into them without cover now; Treaman broke out their sleeping blankets to tie under the waist-ropes as added warmth, cutting corners off to wrap their hands and faces against the biting wind. Everything hung encrusted with snow-beads before they set out.

Progress was worse than a crawl. Companions fell constantly, and sometimes the wind grabbed on and sent one or more linked bodies skating several feet downstream. Mhoral caught Forge eating snow and cuffed him behind the head. The ice was often clear as crystal beneath; Treaman cried out to see the claws and open mouth of a hathlagor just inches below the surface, caught in frigid amber until spring, if it managed to survive.

A searing flash of lightning struck the ice over by the cliffs, followed by a deafening pound of winter-thunder as blocks the size of horses flew up and crashed back onto the river. More ice broke as the party staggered from a minor quake even though the blast was hundreds of steps away. Treaman heard immensely deep, powerful cracking sounds from that direction.

"Run! For your lives!"

The party scampered and slid headlong downstream, those still up taking turns pulling the fallen through drifted snowfall along the slick surface. It was hopeless, their progress slower than walking on land. But the cracks rose in tenor and diminished in sound, as the danger evidently passed.

Mhoral shouted something at Treaman, but refused to lift his helm. All that could be heard was "impossible". Treaman nodded to him because he didn't have the strength for anything else. Peering south, he could not make out the island: in rising desperation and fearing he would miss it on the left, he led the party at a diagonal towards river-center, constantly straining through the storm to see if the surface held.

A tap on his shoulder from Haltar got him to turn his head.

"Might miss—too far across!"

Treaman nodded. "We'll see the lights!" he bellowed back "Hear the forges!" Haltar shrugged, but continued alongside him; even a glimpse of his face through the blanket showed that same lack of concern. Treaman wished he could master such uncaring, probably the source of Haltar's courage.

The march had gone on too long, cold seeping past his toes and fingers when another arc of lightning blasted into the river behind them, closer than the last. Forge had to grab Anteris and dive to one side to avoid a gyring chunk of ice; Linya and Mhoral fell by consequence, and the party scrambled away mainly on hands and knees, winding up completely soaked in icy particles and still battered by stronger winds than Treaman had felt in years. All blasting down from the north, coming off the unfrozen river behind them, wedged beneath the low-hanging clouds and funneled by the river-banks; they were out in the open yet Treaman felt boxed into a trap. His wet clothes were stiff and frozen a few moments later, and he already could not feel his hands.

Worse, he made out a looming cliff ahead, a wall of darker misty menace in the snow-blinding storm. No lights, no smoke or sound above: they must have missed the island and made the far bank, just as Haltar claimed. Treaman felt the last energy leaking from his knees to realize his error. There was no way to correct it now; they had to find shelter or perish from cold or crushing.

He prayed to Helmon, not fearing to speak aloud in the rushing gale. "Shelter, please; don't let more die on my account."

He opened his eyes facing the cliff, and immediately saw a darker blotch down by the water level.

"Cave!" he screamed to the others; no one seemed to hear him, but when he tugged hard on the rope Haltar moved a step. Treaman used the knot-end to whip Mhoral across the helm and get his attention: Linya clung to the Woodsman's waist like a child, and Braja herded the two boys, almost carrying them under his arms and looming to monster-height himself through the blizzard. They trudged in the direction Treaman tugged.

Another blast of lightning, this time striking a section of cliff just behind and further away but still far too close for comfort. Treaman looked up in horror, as the entire white-face of the steep bank began to slide down, hundreds of feet wide and more than a man deep, tons upon uncountable tons of snow starting to fall downhill and spill onto the river.

Screaming, he tugged and trotted, hugging Linya hard and closer than he would have dared on any other day. Her legs went limp with the feet dragging across the ice, then flinched into life for a step or two as she gasped and choked. Her distress infused him with an energy he had not known before. And up ahead—yes, it was a cave, large enough no one would have to stoop to enter, promising life. A last look up and around at the oncoming avalanche, and Treaman realized the good and bad news at the same time.

The cliff-snow hurtling their way was indeed from the opposite bank; this was actually the island after all.

But the mass of frozen death was not diminishing nor slowing as it came on; the base of the island would be engulfed in seconds.

Haltar surged ahead first with Mhoral, and now turned to yank Treaman and Linya forward into the lee of the cave mouth. Already the wash of snow-spheres was crossing the entrance, and the rope to Braja and the boys went taut. Everyone seized the rope, except Linya who fell across it perhaps unconscious. The combined weight and pull was enough: as the cave-mouth filled to over halfway the massive form of the Nubian and his twin load plowed through to lie on the stone shivering with a cold he no doubt had never encountered.

Seconds later they were sealed in.

"Fire, we must have heat," Treaman mumbled, tearing off his face rag and digging with stone fingers after his tinder. Linya, who could have summoned mystic flame without so much as speaking, lay disturbingly still on the slick stone floor. Immediately, Treaman noticed the smell was horrendous. Bats. But nothing for it now.

He laid out several strips of former face and hand coverings, drier side up, plus most of his precious remaining tinder. Mhoral fumbled out a vial of oil for torches, and Treaman simply broke it on top of the pile. If the flare of fire didn't revive Linya, or if its light failed to reveal anything more durably flammable, the shelter of the cave would not save them. Already the muffled sounds of the storm without indicated they were entombed by yards of snow.

Two strikes and the oil-fire flared more than halfway to the ceiling. Everyone except Linya and Braja stepped back, then grunted in pleasure at the brief heat. Treaman hesitated a second over Linya's still form, then with a curse he put aside his prim reservations and tried to save a friend. Dropping to his knees, he drew her body to him and vigorously rubbed her core, slipping off things that were soaking wet and passing his hands over every part of her skin where the frictive heat would do some good. Anteris and Forge turned to do the same to Braja, who was conscious with chattering teeth. In the few seconds of light that remained in the fierce flames, Treaman looked hungrily around the cave area.

When the tears came, it may have been because he heard Linya gasping. Or perhaps it was the sight of something back on one side, a little hand-worked alcove in the stone, where someone had placed several pairs of leather boots, a small wooden box, other items of clothing. And a large stack of charcoal bricks.

By the embers of the fire, Anteris huddled beneath a blanket he shared with Forge and tried to hide his tears. Next to him, his friend lay closer to the coals, shivering like someone being shaken for information. Both Forge's hands were cracked open and red-white with exposure. Linya, the mage had awakened but was blinded: Treaman told her it was temporary, though Anteris saw uncertainty in his face. And even a healing salve did nothing for Forge's hands—he could not bear the slightest touch without crying out.

The mage-light when summoned created a storm of bats, so Linya had quickly doused it. The party huddled in the entranceway, the storm outside still raging and snow already walling over the cave mouth Braja had dragged them through less than an hour ago. Anteris thought of the tales of ancient tombs in the days of Despair, bodies plunged beneath the surface or even buried alive, and began to pant with the closeness, the stuffy darkness, the ageless fear of the time when a body survives the death of thought, and love and Hope. Tears were a compromise for him; Anteris would rather wail in terror.

In the shadows by the entrance, Braja stood and periodically thrust his spear into the snow covering the top, working and widening a tunnel for fresh air. It continually refilled and closed off, but he seemed happy to have something to do. Anteris heard Haltar speak from the other side of darkness, a few feet away from where he lay on the floor beyond the fire.

"Are the boys asleep?"

He froze at Haltar's words, even forgetting to cry for the moment.

"Yes, it sounds it," Treaman replied, followed by a heavy sigh. "Poor youths, they've been game, but I don't know what we can do for the Stealthic now. I admit, I've never seen frost-cracks like those. It could be weeks, and that's provided we keep him warm."

"Well this is coming along wonderfully," Mhoral muttered. "A mage who cannot see, and a Stealthic without his hands."

"Mhoral, you can't—" but Haltar interrupted Treaman.

"Perhaps you could make more use of your vision, Elf, to tell what's around us, and somewhat less of your mouth alone."

"Our former leader forgets, I can see outdoors in the darkness, not within."

"Not to worry," Haltar responded cheerfully. "If you go outside now, you will still be more use to us than usual."

"I saw briefly," Treaman continued, "when Linya cast the light, for a moment. The cave continues into the island, and I'm fairly sure there's a passage on the right that ascended. Maybe even worked stone. We'll rest and look at that next."

"In the morning?" Linya asked.

"Who can tell?" Mhoral quipped. "I know my opinion is never welcome, but I would say at the least we've earned a rest before any further moves."

"I agree," Treaman replied.

"You do? Then I must be asleep and dreaming already."

"Do you always talk this much in your sleep?"

"Where else can I win the argument."

A round of chuckles, some turning and shifting, then quiet. Anteris lay back and thought what the others left unsaid. With the scribe, not even a loss of ability, just a dead weight not worth mentioning. What madness had overcome him, to insist on being here? The loss of his life, he tried to think, was acceptable; Anteris still knew in his heart that the Hand of Destiny must succeed. Or else, Alaetar… he brushed past the thought and moved on. Somehow, he must prove his worth, find a way to help.

Sleep stayed far away as he racked his brain. In the city above they sought the scepter and a way onward. Anteris knew the proper passwords for the gate, and the general location. The palace of Oncario would be laid out in similar fashion to that of Reghalion, so he resolved to memorize whatever he could there. But any of them would. His thoughts stirred and roiled without further result.

Braja came back from the entrance to lie down and soon there were sounds of snoring from two, to punctuate the darkness and cover any moment of peace or rest. Anteris lay next to Forge, whose chills had subsided a little and now wheezed in the sleep of utter exhaustion that conquers even pain. The scribe tried to imagine that resting was as good as sleep. It wouldn't do to be useless and tired when the party rose again.

Still he must have drifted off eventually, for he had a most vivid dream.

Like all rare vivid dreams it had the quality of life itself— small sounds such as the snow stirring at the entrance; the texture of cold fresh air accompanying the vision of Areghel coming through the snowbank to stand with them in the cave; and the specific shade of color in the golden glow of light surrounding this dream-figure, in the royal garb of all-black denoting an unascended heir to the throne in Reghalion. Anteris was frozen in awe, unable to participate in this dream as he would wish. He could only lie there barely breathing, as the dream-figure glided silently into the cave on bare feet undamaged by mortal cold, to regard the sleepers.

He could not shake the sense of reality that clung to his dream. Anteris could even hear the snores of Haltar and Braja, feel a little heat from the ember-side, more cold from the rush of outside air on the other. The man in black robes looked around the group before him, then something over by their packs seemed to draw his attention. He stood a moment with palms upraised and eyes closed; his golden aura of light brightened and an answering glow came to him from the tent bag. Anteris did not dare breathe in the presence of this miracle. But what could the heroes mean by the vision?

The man dropped his hands and stood awhile in thought. Anteris closed his dream-eyes and prayed to Areghel, that he would send Telhol to heal Forge's hands. He never prayed harder, for his own future, for permission from Valenthur to study, for any childish desire as he did now for his friend.

The dream seemed to go on forever as vivid ones had for him in the past. Anteris looked out again and gasped to see the man in black stooping close over his body to look at Forge asleep. Drawing back the blanket, he observed the young Stealthic's ruined hands, and lay his own palm across them, for once not making them twitch with pain at the contact. But of course, Anteris reflected, this was a dream. He hardly dared hope that his prayers were being answered, but as the man in black crouched over him the youth saw on his chest and neck the scars of horrific wounds, now healed. And when the man arose Anteris saw that his friend's shivering had stopped completely.

The dream figure moved on into the cave, turning slightly right after perhaps twenty paces. The bats did not stir at his passing, and the aura's reflection rose as it faded from sight. Feeling a sense of peace unlike any moment before he set out from home, Anteris settled back, thankful the heroes had sent this strange vision to comfort him. Surely it meant that Forge would recover eventually, and that Treaman's guess about their future path was correct. Anteris settled back for sleep feeling calm at last.

But he sat bolt upright, when he realized the man-sized hole in the snowbank was still there.

"Forge, wake up," he whispered, nudging then digging in his elbow until the sleeper reacted.

"Leave me be awhile, I'm tired," he said shoving Anteris away.

The scribe leaned over to speak in an ear. "Check your hands."

The Stealthic lay still another few moments, then sat up wide awake, staring at his unbroken palms with an open jaw.

"What, what did you do?"

"Ssh. Come on, get up and stay quiet."

"Why, what happened?"

"We're going to make ourselves useful."

The others were deeply out, even the light-sleeping Woodsman. The breeze from the dark snow hole at the entrance was icy; darkness had fallen outside. Each took up his own gear and a few lighter items of common kit. Anteris looked to Treaman's form and saw two jewels reflected in the coal-fire. Rummaging in the Woodsman's pack, he pulled out some fish and gently fed the tiny dragon who gulped them down and settled back for sleep. Forge drew his dagger and stabbed a coal from the firepit, blowing on it to produce some illumination. Anteris groped along the right-hand wall until he came to the crevice. Then Forge took the lead, still shaking his head and flexing his fingers.

The passage was very narrow but clearly had been used, with sharp projections chiseled off and flattened underfoot. Anteris noted that Braja would need to duck in several spots, but everyone could make it. He whispered to Forge about his dream, and Forge in response used curse words normally reserved for contempt and disbelief but which echoed in the passage with a tinge of awe.

The way rose steadily for what seemed a long time, then opened into a flat space much larger than the cave. Forge blew on his coal until it flamed like a small torch, but the light did not reach the far wall. The interior sides were smoothed, looking circular; the floor was flat and the ceiling very high. In the fast-fading light Anteris caught glimpses of letters and numbers incised on the walls, in the numerals of Despair.

He gripped Forge's arm so tightly his friend cried out.

"What!"

"We need more light," Anteris whispered.

"Right, I'll think of something," Forge responded and stepped closer to the center to drop his pack and rummage. Anteris had to follow; he felt a groove cut into the stone beneath his boot, running in the same direction.

"Hah!" Forge exclaimed, "right here, rubble of something and some of it is wood." He assembled bits and chunks by feel and then used the coal with some paper from Anteris' notebook to get them burning.

The light confirmed everything Anteris feared.

Both boys looked around, at the four diagonal channels leading toward the center where they stood, in a place that held the crumbling remains of something rectangular. Lining the walls were square incisions three feet or more across, numbered and sealed with mortar, stretching up out of sight.

"What is it?" Forge asked again.

"A tomb," he whispered back, his throat tight with fear.

"What is a tomb?"

"In the walls, behind the numbers. Dead people."

Now Forge gulped as well, looking around for movement. "You mean, buried here? Like in the tales? Astor's loins, there are hundreds of them. But Oncario was built by the Children of Hope!"

"Yes, directly on top of the fortress from the earliest days of Kog's rule. Areghel destroyed that place and put his under-capital atop it."

There was a long silence as the flames flickered down. Anteris could see that parts of the stone block, and most of the channels, were thickly stained. Dragged here, sacrificed, perhaps laced with preparations to rise again when summoned; the gorge of panic threatened to overwhelm him. What hero could fix this great, savage wrong?

Forge, still shaken, recovered some of his practicality. "I suppose we can tell the others now, save them some trouble coming this way."

Anteris remembered with a jolt, his vision had led them here. "There must be something. Let's look around."

"Here? What for?" But Forge dutifully scavenged up a few wooden rods and part of his tunic to make a torch.

They saw it almost immediately. Up the far side of the chamber, one without numbered squares, a series of spikes had been hammered into the wall, offset in such a way that made them useful for climbing.

"Balls of Khoirah!" Forge exclaimed, "how did you know?" Before Anteris could answer he found himself handed the torch and Forge was already above his head.

"Get back here!"

"Amazing, these spikes don't look rusted, must be steel. I can probably get to the top."

"They're not part of, of this place, not put here by Despair. More recently."

"So this is the way up into the city."

"Get down."

"Come on." Forge's feet disappeared beyond the range of the weak torch.

Puffing in frustration, Anteris set it down and started up after him. The spikes were indeed thick and strong, never shifting an inch under his weight. Anteris went carefully, but felt the vertigo almost at once, as only the smoldering light of the altar-fire below was visible. The higher he got, Anteris still could not resist peeking back down at it. Gradually his vision became unreal, showing him nothing related to the spikes, or his altitude. He might have been one rung high or a hundred, but all he saw was a blotch of red looking up at him unblinking and perilous.

His groping hands touched something made of wood and Anteris stepped onto a ledge, his fingers making out a portal of some kind, slightly open and with a section near his waist broken through, right where the lock and latch would have been. He pushed and it gave, pivoting to allow him into the smell of perfume and the feel of a plush carpet beneath his boots.

"Forge!" he whispered, regretting it at once.

"Just a moment," came the answering whisper, then a scratch and a candle's light showed the bedroom of a queen.

The scribe and the smith gawked at silk and crystal, brass fittings, a deep wardrobe, tall doorway to one side and the enormous tented bed with sheets deeply dissheveled. Forge chuckled to see items of men's clothing laying over a shelf and a stool, a garb of much rougher weave than the dresses hanging nearby. One pillow, fallen beneath the bed, was deeply gashed and barely hanging together, its down leaking out. They looked on that awhile in silence.

"So where are we," Forge asked, lighting a second candle from the first, "aside from milady's chambers."

Anteris thought hard. "Treaman said her lover had a secret way into the city to visit her. This is certainly the palace, and if the Primara's bedroom, then we're in one of the two innermost towers. We should go back and report now."

"You wanted to be useful," Forge quipped, heading to the chamber door to listen. After hearing nothing, he tested it and found it unlocked.

"Why is there no sound?" Anteris whispered.

"And why is the Primara not in her bed?"

"Hold, Forge, what did you do to that secret door?"

"Me! Do you think you would not have heard that?" He grinned back, "Perhaps it was your vision-man."

The door let out into a straight corridor with no apertures, light or occupants. They passed a left turn, then another, coming to a second door, also unlocked that led to a small study or audience chamber and circular stairs leading up.

"Still no one, no guards?" Forge was incredulous. Anteris was even more frightened: the party had told of a city full of people, noisy at all hours. He gestured up and they explored this second tower, passing landings with alternate staircases, chambers, and occasional windows showing the night beyond the city.

At the topmost chamber an archway revealed a brick bridge leading back to the tower above the place they had entered the city. It was wide enough for three to walk abreast and had brick railings on either side, but with no underpinnings it seemed impossible it could hold any weight for the hundred steps or more of its length. Carefully stepping out first, Forge shivered from the cold and confirmed it was safe. Anteris followed, and felt a stab of height between his legs, to be higher off the ground than even the bell-tower of Trainertown. The storm had passed but the sky was still clouded. To the east ahead a strange reddish haze suffused the heavens, which could only be a pre-dawn glow but did not look like that at all. To the left, the northern view was a black shapeless void full of falling. South, Anteris strained to make out any movement from the palace courtyard below. Perhaps there were some guards there, a few, every so often he thought he caught a hint of movement.

"Blood," Forge said quietly, bringing Anteris in from his attempt to see far away and focus on their immediate surroundings. The flickering candles, shaded by their hands, cast only small spots of light and they had to crouch to see the bricks nearby. But there was no question; blood was spattered on the rails and bridge as if someone had gathered it in pots to hurl in all directions. Crimson prints continued from this spot onward, and more patches of blood as they went along. Anteris realized with all the storm they had survived, there was not one flake of snow on the bridge itself.

The chamber on top of the opposite tower was also bereft of humanity, except for further signs that several people had died here. It was a private study of some kind, with wealthy relics of art in glass cases to all sides and coin-filled chests lying open to view. A few things were tipped over, broken or chopped.

"Cark me," Forge whispered. "What is this place?"

"The treasury," Anteris said. "Safest room in the city, high above the ground to discomfit Hope's ancient enemies. But where is everyone?"

Forge pointed to an open case, long and velvet lined, deeply dented where something about the shape of a mace had rested. "The scepter we were sent to find, maybe, it's not here."

"The Primara must still have it. Perhaps she dared to take and use it, unlike her ancestors, which is why the city lands began to grow."

Forge shrugged. "So we'll have to get it from her somehow. Not my job, I'm sure." He turned to face Anteris in the twin candlelight. "We need to find the people."

"We need to report back to Treaman," Anteris responded, as the nervous energy of his vision was long drained and fear flowed in to take its place.

"No way out of here, looks like. We'll have to retrace our steps."

Anteris was increasingly sure, crossing the bridge again, that the courtyard and city below held movement. Checking the clouds overhead he called to Forge to wait, and they stood there shivering a long minute while the Stealthic grumbled at the delay.

A break in the overcast brought the light of Unal, nearly full, to bear on the city below. Tall towers and narrow streets, lower bridges and balconies dotting the view, banners and chimneys and building after building, a city far larger than Anteris ever thought to see in person.

And Anteris saw them. People, in the courtyard and at the outer bailey, and some even in the streets beyond. Scores of bodies, shuffling slowly along in aimless patterns, without purpose, without speed. And in several cases, without limbs.

"Heroes protect us," he breathed. He jumped when for once Forge gripped his arm.

"Alright," he croaked, "I agree with you, time to tell the others."

But then a single voice echoed through the darkness of the courtyard and neither one could move.

"So you see, Primara," the haughty, confident tone sounded like a crime committed on its own. "This business of truly ruling a city has its cares. But the patrol I have set over the entrance gates will be sufficient to detain any intruders."

Anteris made out a spot of red light glowing and moving across the bailey towards the front palace door. In its wake were several forms, the first one tall and thin, followed by one that made irregular progress, as if limping or being pushed along. In the wake of this procession every creature in the courtyard was pulled to follow, as iron trails a magnet. Those further back eventually lost the trace and returned to wandering, but at least threescore beings disappeared from view as the leader entered the palace below.

"Come along now, let us return to the comfort of your audience hall and discuss again the use of the exit gates."

The two boys, feet released from prison by the disappearance of that apparition, fled on to the upper tower chamber and down stairs as quickly as they could move. Candles out, they stumbled ahead on moonlight through the outer windows and the occasional reflected glow from that reddish dawn that never came.

And they went wrong in their haste, coming out on a glass-floored promenade above the audience hall, feebly lit by a few wall-torches and already filling with the undead from the double-doored arch leading to the front entrance.

Near the center of the room, the man in black from Anteris' vision sat cross-legged on the floor, eyes closed and hands at rest on his knees.

Despite his terror, Anteris could not help but feel that he was again dreaming, easily the worst nightmare of his young life. That the emblem of his hopes should have led them so far astray; that he should now sit awaiting destruction rather than save them; that his own rash actions in coming here had doomed his best friend along with himself. Surely one could only awaken now; or if he died soon, Anteris thought strangely, he might test that notion about dying in dream. He watched the undead lumber toward the man in black and wondered, how he might tell if his own end were a real or dreaming one.

The evil voice echoed in the hallway without, and at last the sitting man opened his eyes. Taking in the scene without haste, he rose and again raised his arms to either side, casting some kind of spell. At once, an archway to the side of the chamber began to glow with golden light, and the man moved toward it. Three gaunts that managed to shuffle into his path were destroyed, each with a single well-placed punch; the man in black did not even break stride. He reached the arch just as the looming owner of the voice and red-gemmed scepter entered with its prisoner. As the master of the undead cried out in shock, the man in black spoke the Ancient passwords in a confident tone—words Anteris knew from his books—and stepped through, abandoning the scribe and disappearing back to the land of dreams.

Screaming in panic, the tall skeletal monster loped across the audience hall, scattering benches and minions to reach the archway. The glow faded just as it arrived, to pound the stone wall in fury.

Anteris hid behind the rail of the promenade, not daring to move lest he attract the attention of the bony horror below. It turned now and gestured to its minions that the woman—evidently still a living creature, and a prisoner—be brought and tied to a pillar near the throne, where it took a seat. The skeletal giant regarded her a long time; Anteris could hear a tiny sparking sound, which he realized came from the scepter where it touched the monster's hand. A small voice in the back of his head murmured that he had found the Scepter of Law, though no record spoke of the enormous red gem at its top.

The enthroned monster spoke again, and Anteris shivered at the sound.

"Your lover, milady, seems to have abandoned you."

The tall long-haired queenly prisoner sagged against her binding ropes in torn dress, seemingly already the target of some torture. But she straightened her back again with effort and pulled together enough strength in her face to show only haughty hatred to her captor. If the man in black was intimate with her, she showed no sign, and after a moment a small grim grin overtook her mouth.

"I offer my condolences, and should you in time wish to open your heart again, I hope you will consider my sincere affections for you in a better light." The skull-faced monster sat back and laughed at this joke; Anteris clamped one hand over his mouth to contain the scream he felt.

"For now, at any rate, it is just the two of us," it continued. "And while I hate to interrupt my own courting, I must know the secret we have just seen on display here." It stood and moved down the steps to where she shrank back against the pillar. "Tell me, Primara, the words used to escape this city and reach Reghalion."

Again the woman straightened with resolve. "I do not know them," she replied in a strong voice. "Our ancestors forgot, the words were not passed down. But if I knew them, I still would not tell you."

"Oh but you would," her captor said with quiet conviction. "You must understand, dear Vuthienne—it is permitted, I hope, that in my sincere courtship I may use your name? I have been here so very, very long; and while I suppose I shouldn't boast of previous lovers, still we can be open with each other, yes? I have had many, I will tell you, some nearly as beauteous as you, and few less willing either. At first. So I have mastered certain arts of persuasion that I doubt very highly you've ever encountered. They have nothing to do with the more… fleshly approaches you may be used to." Here the creature thrust forward his midsection against her hip, causing a yip of fear. "Yes, I rather imagine you will be quite, overcome at my seduction technique and I have no fear to reveal that fact to you."

It sidled in, using the red-tipped scepter to trace suggestive lines across her body beneath the silken gown, as if already in the act of climaxing his victim. The skull-face leaned near her ear, yet still spoke audibly in the echoing chamber where witnesses to its love-making shuffled dully in random directions.

"Why, I recall one such as you, tall and proud, so well-shaped. To begin with. A close follower of Aballe, I believe, when she was captured still betrothed to some strapping, breathing swain or other. Shall I tell you how I, quite literally, won her heart?" It paused a moment to take eye-contact with the woman, then leaned even closer and whispered lasciviously in her ear. Anteris saw her face crumble into shock, she cried as if he had stabbed her, then fainted so hard and suddenly that only her restraints kept her body from the marble floor. Peals of horrible laughter rebounded from the high walls and ceiling of the audience chamber.

Anteris never noted that Forge had stood up.

A small brass something sailed errorlessly through the chamber to strike the monster square on the skull.

"Up here, you carker!" Forge shouted, pushing Anteris completely out of sight behind the railing.

"What ar—" Anteris found his voice could not work as he slumped there. Forge stooped to take the other candle-holder, and threw it as well.

He turned slightly in Anteris' direction and muttered. "My job. I'll draw them off, you free the woman."

Anteris heard the awful voice from below and behind him. "Get that one!" Bodies shuffled in their direction and up the nearest staircase from the hallway floor. Forge signalled a farewell behind his back as he waved his other arm, shouted more curses, and fled along the promenade to take a turning out of the hall on this upper level and into the unknown palace. Anteris did not breathe as a half-dozen of the undead—guards in life, bearing spears and shields—shuffled up and past his position to pursue the one moving.

The monster in charge did not follow. Anteris felt his heart drop, to know the plan had already failed.

A stinging slap of leather on flesh brought him up to peek again despite the danger. The monster had used one hand on the lady's face, to revive her, and her eyes rolled around to focus on her captor once more. Now that haughty determination had fled her face, and she was a beautiful, helpless victim in the clutches of pure evil.

"No more games. First your lover, then a vagrant boy can also come and go to your palace at need? How do they escape my patrols, tell me at once."

Anteris just began to hope that Forge could escape, that he might gain a chance to warn the others, when he heard a commotion below him, the shouts of familiar voices. And his heart turned to ash within, to know he had completely failed. Looking down, he saw Haltar and Braja charging forward, Mhoral guiding Linya near a pillar's shelter, Treaman circling to one flank with his sword held low.

"What!" cried the skeleton in disbelief, "are your walls all fallen, milady, that anyone can come and go as they please? No matter, we shall amuse ourselves awhile and then return to the previous conversation."

Anteris could see everything, would remember everything, would never write a word of anything. Braja screamed in fear but still thrust his long spear into the torso of the monster, where it stuck and did no harm. The skeletal foe, as tall as the Nubian, blasted an ebony bolt that threw him on his back to lie unmoving. Haltar cut down body after body, almost one at each stroke, until the wave of unliving flesh simply pulled him down and out of sight.

Mhoral's song foundered and died under the same choking hold that Anteris felt around his own neck; Linya cried out when she lost contact with Mhoral's hand, shouted a word and set the area before her aflame, which destroyed two of her foes. But they both drowned in undead limbs as well.

Treaman had nearly reached the pillar before the lord of the undead noticed him. Seizing the Woodsman by the collar it hefted him easily off the ground, holding him there and laughing as a part of Treaman's collar flapped off into the rafters. It waited as the Woodsman gamely swung his blade to no harm, then tossed him to one side and watched as its gaunts and skeletons also smothered him beneath a wall of corpse-flesh.

And Anteris only knelt there, doing nothing and helping no one. Because he was worthless dead weight, and only a child. No one would need to read the histories anymore.

⊕ ⊕ ⊕

Dawn of the third day out from Shilar didn't reach the entire sky. Thula staggered out of the tent she shared with Tossa at the sound of the summons-horn, but her eyes still reported night when she faced west. The dawn-glow behind her diluted, as the roiling clouds were nearly black ahead. The reddish streak against the dirty white heavens to the south was larger and more ominous than seeing the red star. Something above them was already wounded and bleeding.

Tossa came to stand behind her as they each struggled to fit on armor, and both stared at the land ahead.

"Birds," he said at last, "it's an enormous flock of birds."

"That's not possible," she breathed. But they both hastened to finish arming.

The rush to march from Shilar had left certain important details unsettled. Thula had been Gareth's squire for years, but Tossa served in the most recent weeks. Both came, on the grey stranger's assurance that the keep of Ganelake was unthreatened, and they had adopted a sibling rivalry, racing to see who could be first each night. But ever since that first evening on the road, Tossa won every morning. Thula could not make her feet move quickly to the tent where Sidrathay slept with her king.

Tossa entered after rustling the entrance flap and calling out for permission; in moments, the Half-Elven princess emerged with her helm off and hair unbraided. Tossa caught her breath at the sight, so unaccustomed feminine. Even that face seemed gentler now, still proud and tall but more willing to be seen. She noticed Thula standing there and after a moment returned the squire's bow.

"Knight of Shilar," she said though Thula had not been formally raised to the rank, "will you consent to arm me this day?" Her gaze actually dropped from contact, for the first time in Thula's acquaintance. "Not my armor, I am no settled woman. It is, my hair you see."

With a churning gut and tingling hands, Thula turned the princess away and began to gather the waist-long strands into a weave. The act of touching and arranging in such prolonged fashion created a mundane magic of its own, and the two women relaxed a bit, even in the shadow of combat. Not believing herself, Thula even felt a little reluctance to finish. Sidrathay strode off without turning, even to speak to Gareth within. But she spun back at thirty paces, to salute in the Bordbeyond fashion with a fist upraised.

"First to see the enemy." Thula returned it and something nameless was settled between them.

Gareth emerged with Tossa armed at all points, and Thula made a great show of inspecting the work for flaws while her brother sighed. Gareth signaled the barons to mount and ride, then turned for a final word to them both.

"It pains me to stand on ceremony, but you have neither yet been knighted." The siblings both started to protest but he cut them off with a sudden hand and tense face. "I instruct you to remain in the rearguard with the remounts and baggage. Stave off any threats that may break through, and bring up new mounts if any of us should be unhorsed."

Direct orders from a lord had the code of chivalry stamped all over them. Thula and Tossa bowed stiffly to the king of Shilar. He embraced them both fervently then spun to take horse, drop his visor, gain a lance from Tossa, and ride off to the van of battle.

The two took turns sulking aloud as they rode the ancient way east at the head of the baggage train. Then came sight of the pillar of smoke ahead, rising to join the writhing dark-feathered cloud above. Trainertown was already in plunder, the area around its walls boiling with a menagerie of chaos headed by a three-legged monster standing ten feet tall and pulling down sections of its wall as a cruel child yanks books from a shelf. From the right flank where Gareth stood on the road with a small bodyguard including the Quill knight and High Seer, a trumpet blast signaled the advance.

Thula moaned aloud as she looked over the mass of polyglot flesh before the knights, jostling and entwining with each other as it turned to meet their charge. Where was the neat symmetry of the lists? She could only imagine war as an enormous tournament where many charged, yet all would wait their turn to strike. And there were no judges here, either, to stop the fray at first blood.

She watched as the armored line cantered home and the lances came down to bear almost as one. Just before the shock of contact, Thula belatedly recalled to find the Bordbeyonds; in the battle planning, they were to take the southern flank on the left. But when she glanced that way, she saw only the pennons of Shilarian foefs. And not nearly enough to match the roiling line of hell across from it.

No time to imagine; the rolling crescendo of metal and wood on bone and horn dwarfed the loudest drum or crash of tree she had ever heard. With wide eyes she saw the impact, even as the line of remounts jerked and whinnied in sympathy with their fellows in the battle. Gareth's wedge of knights plowed into chaos and furrowed them to either side. Hirion's battle did just as well, and against larger, insectoid foes; his lance already broken, he was hewing now to either side with a two-handed axe hefted in just one.

Something inside Thula awoke, not instead of the horror and revulsion, but alongside it, welded in like a hilt to its pommel there was a thrill that was nothing like her childhood, here at its ending, but which grew from there, a root that flowered now.

Tossa sensed it. "You always wanted this," he said and she nodded without looking to him. "To be like a man?"

"To be just like a knight," she replied, though neither of them needed the affirmation of a thousand hours of childhood talk and dreaming. Thula thought about the tales of those years, of the first Gareth and the squire Counsel Broders who gave her life in armor. All the giants were supposed to be dead, but she had fought them with her own arms already. Now this gigantic menace bore down on her king, too unsure of his own strength to risk his friends in battle.

The city smoked more thickly as licks of flame appeared over the town-center. The great Earth Demon roared and lashed with ever-changing arms, calling to the cloud of carrion birds overhead who screeched, wheeled and plummeted to the attack. Thula quailed to think of the demon's power. But from near where Gareth sat, the thin elderly High Seer gestured and called, summoning a blazing wide bolt of power-light from beyond the clouds, which seared through the bird-pack, scattering hundreds of them and routing thousands more before slamming into the pack of creatures immediately before the King. Staring into the triple-width lightning bolt, Thula lost sight for a minute, long enough to worry it was permanent. Distant cheers of the knights and Kog's basso roar of anger let her know how well the miracle had struck.

But when her vision cleared, Thula could no longer see Kalentire in the press of battle.

Kog recalled some of his more man-like minions from inside the town walls, to reinforce the battle line. Though sitting horsed and at ease, the siblings tensed as the charge of Shilar slowed, stopped and by inches reversed itself. More than half the knights had no lances now. So—knights who cannot advance cannot win, the charge was not enough. Gareth did not signal a retreat, but steadily they fought backwards, riskier and costlier for ground of no importance and drawing the whole strength of the enemy upon him. For surely no one in the city was still resisting, its white stone walls already holed as broken teeth in a bar brawl.

Kog advanced on Gareth directly, roaring and laughing in turn, growing new mouths it seemed for the purpose of taunt while the first spouted flame. So massive and strong, all marks of lance and edge disappeared from his frame in seconds, save only the long burned scar down one cheek and the horrid sore where he lacked one eye. At four furlongs' distance, Thula shivered and went so rigid her horse started. Closer, he came and closer, pulling down knight and horse together or stomping even his own creatures underfoot in his impatience.

Gareth seemed to be waiting on his doom, the field clear between himself and the monster, only gesturing to one side as a signal. A knight behind him raised a pennon with the watching eye; maybe Gareth was declaring his love here at the end.

There was no flash or other preamble. To the south along and behind the right flank of hell, the Bordbeyonds were simply there.

Thula and Tossa both hooted and crowed as the lighter, faster horsemen slammed into the startled ranks of hell, who were unable to form proper line abreast before contact and suffered immensely. Sidrathay was clearly visible in their ranks, hewing and checking her horse with skill, and Thula had to admit, what she had always felt of the plains princess was jealousy. Not of Gareth—or not only of that—but here, now, that his lover could fight for him.

It was too much. Drawing her knife she cut a stallion out of the tether-line and said, "Lord Kalentire has lost his mount."

"Kalentire has lost his life!" Tossa yelled after her, "come back here."

She pressed on, ignoring the hoofbeats and cries behind her, ignoring her king's commands, abandoning the code to join her battle-sister and the one she loved in combat, whatever came, whenever it came. The line of knights was falling back at last, hell's hordes still too much for them even after the great gambit played its force. Kog was too enraged to care what transpired around him now, shedding great waves of fire in all directions and no doubt hurting his own more than his foe. Thula's training took hold.

To the right of Gareth, a space made by a knight's fall—that must be filled. The King with sword and shield held his ground before the leviathan, who swept in with an arm the size of a tree trunk. Interpose, reach the spot, create time for Gareth's counter.

Thula felt the impact that turned her shield to strips of bent metal, heard the snap of her horse's spine, and the pinning pressure of its body against her left leg. Lying in the eye of battle, yet curiously the only sound she could hear was the cry of her mount, so human and piteous as it flailed atop her. Knightly duty; never hasten death for oneself, but a loyal animal should not suffer. Through blinding tears, Thula raised her blade and brought it down hard, then lay back waiting to join horse and king together.

The bell's toll sounded very appropriate in her ears.

No knight of the Order knew why one brother had kept the vigil for a fortnight by himself. They acceded to Renan's wish, but even he could not explain his actions.

After the victory he won alongside his squire, Renan volunteered to stay on another shift out of sheer exhilaration. So much had been restored to him then, and he could see that Niles understood it as well. He wanted nothing more than the night, and the incredible vision-view of the Farsight Chamber, to sustain him. When Jeceb announced himself to ask if he would eat, Renan realized by the rising sun it had been many hours.

He took a meal there in the chamber, and the next morning another; gradually his spirit quieted from the elixir of triumph, but a reluctance to leave only grew stronger. He let it be known then that his vigil would continue until he felt tired. Renan slept, a little, over the succeeding days, but true exhaustion never overtook him. He watched, prayed, and waited thinking every moment, the next time the bridge of light should appear he must be the one to answer.

This feeling itself was a cause of mystery. Renan's prayers brought no guidance, but visions he still had aplenty. Some were strange; a gathering storm from the northeast which pounded snow across the northern kingdoms and into this land, after which Oncario lay cold and quiet as never before; a line of brightness on the kingdom crossing his view leading to Trainertown and the other nations; just beyond that mark, tracing its course, a cloud of chaos from which he could perceive nothing. Once he saw lights and fire in the Bay of Mendel south of the Percentalion, two large fleets of ships in night combat near the rock-spiked islands.

Mostly his visions showed him the fair Elven preacher far away to the south beyond the Great Cleft in Argens, questing in remote places with her companions, acting to protect them in combat, healing minor hurts afterwards. She also took the lead in counsels both among her group and with others they met. A judge of sorts, he realized, gifted with intelligence and discernment. Was she to be an example? Or perhaps the new leader of the Order? It had been nearly two centuries since the Wanderers admitted a woman to the ranks.

Renan concluded the answer was far simpler than that. He was in love.

It meant the end of his time with the Wanderers; indeed, there were no recorded instances of resignation or ejection from the sacred brotherhood. But marriage and family were forbidden, and for sound reasons. Here was surely the meaning of that ambiguous oracle Niles had delivered when he first entered the keep, that Renan was destined both to his vows and to marriage.

He gazed on the preacher and reflected that herein was likely the real cause of his pious vigil. The attempt to repent of his heart's misdeeds and prove worthy by keeping watch here, he realized with rising frenzy, was the same as setting the town drunk to guard the wine. Only here in the chamber did his visions emerge from memory to show her anew, where he would admire her again as if for the first time. He never knew her name.

Such unhappy thoughts, and the resolution they brought to renew his duty, were plenty to keep him awake almost like an Elf. Day out and night in the bridge did not return, but Renan never again doubted it would come, and knew he must be ready. He began to imagine, to fondly wish, that the light this time would bring the long-awaited new leader to the keep, one who could return the vigor of the Order.

The next day he heard the sounds of the lists. From the side-balcony used to call down messages, Renan saw the other knights practicing with unwonted fervor, exercising and keeping in readiness. The quiet time of the last week had been good for healing wounds, bringing back eagerness and the appetite for risk. Some of the brothers caught sight of him up there and hailed. The next day, the entire Order was out and practicing in the yards: Renan realized they were awaiting his appearance, his friendly wave, as a new part of their routine. He could not name this fresh excitement, and knew better than to speak of it. Something was coming; perhaps the Order's end, perhaps its greatest victory. Perhaps both.

Just after sunset on the evening of his fifteenth day, near the end of Raccoon, Renan knelt in prayer. The Farsight Chamber was tinted red with the looming light of the red star, sweeping now slightly south and drawing so low and large as to inspire terror with every glance. It moved nearly as fast as Aral the lower moon would when it rose later on, a night of the double-twin moons tonight. Having studied and prayed about the red star without success, Renan just watched it, ticking with a breath-stealing slowness across the lower heavens and sure to strike the Lands this night, or the next.

The white flare of the bridge, after all this time, made him cry out and Quester rear. Renan scrambled to his feet, reaching for gauntlets and a lance, while staring down the long glowing span to his doom.

An open empty plaza of brick, outside the city of Oncario. To all seeming, the spot at the bulls-eye of where the red star would fall.

It was just, he reflected as he flexed his hands within the metal plates, shifted his hauberk and settled the helmet into notches on his cuirass. *Only victory or blood can dispel shame.* His visions of lands outside the Order's ambit were signs of his unfitness to serve. Empty victories weighed nothing against the distraction of his heart, to love a woman however worthy. So the bridge led him to a fiery execution, he could be content so long as a leader came back on the bridge of light to forge straight what he had bent.

Renan hesitated to take Quester, knowing what would happen. He thought of Niles, how hard it had been to lose his horse, how sad he must be even now to ride another, however well. Perhaps even that had been poorly done. The Order could ride together at need, as the two of them had proven, but surely no other brother need die for his shame tonight. Renan swung into the saddle as the bell's toll brought the sound of running feet on the ramp below. He had no words of goodbye to share with anyone, any more now than at Farivaine's funeral. Let his deeds speak the best of an imperfect life tonight, at its end. He spurred his horse down the bridge resolved to act a Wanderer.

He arrived on the ground to stillness and cold, the only sounds his stallion's hooves on the brick of the plaza. To all sides, five roads and five arch-inscribed walls surrounded him. At first he thought himself alone. The red star above was half the size of Aral, and as he looked up Renan felt his insides turn to liquid. Such a gruesome death, but perhaps a clean one. He addressed himself to prayer, asking Dunedin and all the heroes to forgive his shortcomings and to heal the Wanderers now that a blight would be removed from the Order.

Movement caught his eye and with a shock Renan realized there were a dozen persons aimlessly huddled and shuffling on the bridge-side of the plaza. A rescue mission then; he quietly cursed to realize how close he had come to another mistake. Spurring forward from the base of the bridge, he called to them.

"Children of Hope! This way, I can take you to—"

At first, Renan dismissed the eerie look of these townsfolk, an effect of the reddish tinge hanging over the world. But Aral was rising even as he spoke, and Renan saw that some of those turning and advancing his way bore horrible wounds. A dragging ankle, crushed hand, neck askew. Almost as one they advanced on the knight; behind him the bridge of light disappeared.

No rescue for anyone, therefore, but the undead had returned to the Lands and he was chosen to resist them.

He dropped his visor and brought lance to bear. Quester was tensed and snorting at the charnel smell, but Renan held him back. These gaunts were living persons just a week ago, under his care as a Wanderer. Was his every act bound to form a betrayal of his oaths?

He called out again at the mob, to fall back, to wait, to no avail. They swarmed slowly upon him in a half-circle as a lasso tightens on the throat. With less than four feet between them, Renan spurred Quester and plowed slowly through the ranks, spearing one randomly and using his shield edge to scrape away several more, reaching to pull him down. Two gaunts and a skeletal garruk hung grimly to his legs and tack, preventing him from breaking clean away for a second pass. Hammering down with his lance-butt, Renan dropped one on the right, giving Quester freedom to turn left and gyre free of the others by trampling in a circle. Both horse and rider were crying out now, and Renan's heart froze when he saw one among the undead group coming on faster than the others, not stepping but flying or sliding over the ground more quickly than he could trot. His spine tried to stand apart from his body at the sight.

Now free of corpses, Renan spurred Quester to one edge of the plaza, turning sharply and this time bringing his point to bear with determination. At a full gallop he aimed for the leader, who made no effort to dodge or step aside. The lance bore into his chest directly; Renan felt the contact, a slight sting in his leg and then was through on the other side of the plaza. His lance could not have missed the foe, yet the thing was turning to advance again, completely unharmed. Quester was unable to stand still and quivered as if covered in flies. Looking down, Renan could see the clear mark of a single hand burned in white scars across the stallion's shoulder.

All decisions now were likely bad ones. Renan hefted and threw his lance to impale and bowl down a slow-moving gaunt, then dismounted drawing his blade. Unconsciously, he maneuvered to keep the gliding cloak on the other side of the undead pack. Hewing furiously and slamming with his shield for room to swing, Renan brought down four, six, seven, chopped to the brick and severed bodily, unable to rise again. But the press of those remaining was too much; his arms and legs were restrained by body parts piled around his feet while corpses reached to hold his arms, clawed ineffectually at his armor's hinges, and dragged him toward the ground where he would be helpless. Two still bore weapons and clumsily but powerfully drove them in, wounding his leg and side. Behind them, the undead horror shouldered closer, raising its one remaining hand to touch the living and draw forth that spark of life.

Renan went down, and discipline kicked in. The knight was pinned, but Quester was as well trained as his master. Storming down with hooves flashing and a vicious bite, the warhorse dispelled all strangers, felling two more gaunts and bearing their leader back several steps with the sheer force of body. Stamping in a fear-driven fury, Quester rolled his eyes and stood directly over his rider's body, daring one or a hundred to approach unbidden. Renan lay in shock on the bricks, slathered in chops of cold flesh and bleeding hard. Nearly all of them, he had given a good enough accounting. With fortune, he had delayed these horrors long enough for them to be destroyed when the red star fell.

To one side, a golden glow competed with silver moon and crimson star to throw its light across the plaza. Renan saw a misty figure step through the false arch, bearing a staff and dressed all in grey.

More failure! Here was the poor soul the Tower wanted to be saved, arriving by the mystic gates unused in living memory. Yet Renan's hesitation and diffidence had doomed him in his moment of need.

Before an innocent life, mine and my steed's—for without their succor, there is no Order. With a groan Renan attempted to rise, but the loss of blood made his head swim and the remaining undead were already turning to destroy the interloper.

When he could focus again he saw the grey man facing off against two skeletal beings, plus a gaunt and the horror that did not walk. Bearing his staff in both hands, he brandished it with expert flourishes that showed martial practice, felling first one, then another foe with mighty sweeps while it flared with silver magic. Renan could not credit his eyes, as the warrior, though of common rank by his strange dress and weapon, showed no fear nor even surprise to be in combat with undeath.

The fellow stepped back at a slant before the gaunt, merely to interpose it between the reaching horror and himself. Two sharp blows, and then a third, beating past the creature's weapon and crushing its skull, left him alone at last. Renan could do nothing but watch. The grey man planted his staff with one hand while the other took up his holy symbol on a chain around his neck. With a strange longer bottom arm it fit well in his fist as he held it out before the creature who glided in, arm outstretched. The mortal shouted in the Ancient tongue:

"Areghel permam toxis calem bellatara victorum!"

A mighty blast of blue fire sprang from him to strike the creature, stopping its advance, throwing it back and filling it to the edge with azure energy until the thing fell into a moldy pile on the bricks. It was over, and between them they had defeated nearly a score of the undead.

The grey man strode closer, staff ringing on the stone, and Quester threw his head in defiance. Renan was reconciled to his own death, but not that his warhorse would cause another's.

"Stranger, stay back! You cannot—"

"Be at peace, Sir Renan," the grey man replied. Laying down his staff he held out one hand to the stallion, saying "Easy, Quester."

Whether from his wounds or long watch, Renan felt stupid, unable to make his mind work. How did this one know their names? The horse started to bite at the gauntlet before him, then sniffed and calmed somewhat. The stranger ran one hand lightly down the neck, careful not to abuse the privilege as he came closer and knelt by the knight's side beneath. Checking his injuries, the man spoke again in the tongue of power saying *"Intacta volar."*

Renan felt the wounds close at once and drew a deep breath at the miracle. The grey man stood up and rustled in the second saddlebag, where Renan always kept treats, drawing out an apple for Quester before retrieving his staff. Turning and bowing in an odd fashion, he spoke again.

"Well met, knight of Altrindur. I see by your tabard you have joined the Order of the Wanderers, my congratulations."

Gazing on those grey eyes in the moonlight, the memory finally stole back into Renan's mind.

"You. The boy from the stables."

"Once, Sir Renan. Long ago now, it seems, in Conar where I studied."

"Indeed!" Renan managed now to gain his feet and leaned on his horse a moment. "And did my groom, then, teach you ancient miracles?"

The grey-haired youth shook his head. "I have had many teachers, milord."

"And I come to believe, young… Judgement, was it, that you shall teach me now. How came you here, pray tell?"

"From Shilar, sir, but it would appear I have lost time in doing so." He studied the sky a long moment, as if the red star did not hang before them. Renan could make out its disk clearly, and fancied he saw the lick of flames around it. If he was not meant to die here, where was the bridge of light?

At last the youth continued. "I set out somewhat past noon of the Twenty-Fourth. By the twin full moons above, I have lost close to three days. Mayhap the chaos over this land changes more than is known."

"We should seek shelter, before that dread sky-sphere lands atop us."

"As for that," Judgement replied cooly, "I am for Reghalion." He pointed down the way that crossed the bridge into Oncario.

"But the city may have more undead there."

"Certes, it will. I know their look, as I know their author." The youth appeared to chew his lip, and the rest came out with force. "Sooth, 'twas I who released him."

"You! A stable-boy, claiming guilt for—" Renan could not frame the words in ignorance of the full story he sensed was there. "Heroes bless you, boy, if you persist."

Judgement stood awhile gripping and regripping his staff before continuing.

"My blame is mine, milord. Seek not to arrest me, for I am bound to find that horror now loose on the earth, and defeat him or perish in the attempt. Doubt my chances if ye like! For myself I would not bet much, but there is no life for the coward, only a different flavor of undeath. I shall go, and not seek the aid of the heroes, either. I have seen their help, and it comes too lightly and too late for my taste."

Renan was so stunned at the blasphemy he could not respond. Had Dunedin, also, just strung him along with promises? Were the heroes truly powerless?

"Yet be not that quick, milord, to scorn the efforts of those not born to the noble class. You indeed have met your obligations and I feel sure have borne your duties honorably. Many of your rank in the

City of Wonders did less well, by my lights, seeking crude revenge on a knight acting in defence of his love."

"Pron Dedicar! Do you have word of him?"

Judgement nodded. "Free now, and pursuing his penance-years in the north."

"It is well. None of that, the marriage pact, the dreadful sanctuary watch, was of my choosing."

"Certes. And so fare thee well, Sir Renan."

"Then you will not return with me? We can offer you shelter for a time, a safe place away from these undead."

"Sooth, milord, safety is not what I need right now, but the center and mayhap some small part to play in the destiny that hangs above us."

Renan looked in wonder on the slender, hard youth and felt his heart stir within him. No doubt the bridge would never return for him. Was his path onward then, with the Man in Grey?

"I had hoped to find the Order's new leader on this quest, one who could guide the brotherhood forward in our time of trouble."

The Man in Grey gave just a fractional shrug of his shoulders, and said "Do so, then."

He stepped forward and stroked Quester as he continued. "I know nothing of commanding others, milord. My course is set and if others oppose, or decry or carp, I cannot help it. But a great evil is unleashed upon this land, and if you would be guided by my advice you would take up arms against it howsoever you may. I shall seek the liche Wolga Vrule, be he in Oncario or already at the base of Skysword or at the furthest reaches of this land. I shall do my best with him as I can. But Kog the Earth Demon too is loose in the Percentalion." Again he hesitated before forcing himself to continue. "The king of Shilar rides with all his knights to the aid of the Percentalion and may be already in combat. Kog will show no mercy, spare no effort if he comes against the world of men. Every blade should be raised in our defence now."

"We ride out separately, by custom."

"You will do as you think best, milord. But I can tarry no longer, and so fare thee well."

"You saved my life."

"We fought together, milord, certes I would have had rough treatment at the hands of all these undead alone. Together, I warrant, shall always be our best hope."

Renan smiled, looking up at the star as Judgement did a final time, two men bidding doom defiance. He mounted in the grip of a deeper faith than he had ever known: almost at his summons, it seemed, the bridge of light appeared. Boarding it, Renan looked back to see the Man in Grey salute a final time before crossing the bridge into Oncario.

Renan moved to a canter and full gallop along the light-bridge; in moments, the sun rose on his right from a strange magic never experienced in the annals of the Order. Hours passed though he felt only moments; Renan arrived back in the Tower, hauling hard on the reins to check Quester and dismounting while still in motion. Running to the balcony, he saw Jeceb already approaching the tower in response to the bell's toll.

"Milord! You are well, praise the heroes."

"Ring the bell again," Renan ordered, and Jeceb stopped cold in shock before running to the lower level to yank the thick bell-rope for an alarm.

In moments, every brother and squire was in the courtyard below, standing silently and awaiting orders. Renan never gave the question of leadership a moment of his worry. The words of the Man in Grey still burned in his heart, and now his only question was of the deed before them. The others had to know; he would need to speak. And now, at long last, he could.

"Brethren of the Order, squires and knights together, our test is arrived. Every man arm and mount, and take station along the ramp. For an army of hell marches across our beloved land, to threaten all the kingdoms of Hope. Kog has returned, and we shall do our part to obstruct his intention."

"Let no one remain behind today; bring every lance, wear all armor. Let every man say *'If I can stand, I can stand my watch'*. We are a brotherhood, and shall respond to the present threat with suitable force. Tonight, our watch is for the world."

The echoes of his speech still resounded in the stone-made keep when the flare of light emanated from the tower again, with the toll of the summons bell. Every face showed awe, Renan could see they held him accountable for this miracle, as if the Tower were his own apartment for longer than these past two weeks.

Niles shouted *"When the bell tolls for me, I tarry not"*, and as one the brethren split to their chambers to arm, mount and return. Squires readied the horses and snatched up equipment. Knights took station close to the front, but Renan could see them all. Pallus was there in line, his twisted arm holding a mace instead of a lance. And Niles, ready first of all, sat astride Harbinger in the Farsight Chamber, rejoining the knights for at least one last battle.

Together they saw down the span of light, to the burning city and the faltering pennons of Hope. Renan signaled the charge. The Order of the Chosen Wanderers filed down the bridge as one, and for the first time in the annals the keep lay empty behind them.

⊕⊕⊕

There was no festival known to the settled folk of Roamsedge two days before new year, when the gypsies approached the fortress in the dusking light. Yet the tambours and the singing, the cheers and horse-vaults rang from their caravan continuously as the group paused at the crossroads outside town. Every day that the Rom survive, for them, was cause for celebration.

Several folk passed the caravan, some hastening to tell the news of entertainers coming. The Rom dressed too lightly for winter, and sang too loudly for evening. Most shocking to the Elves of Mendel, the Gypsies acted as if there were no tomorrow, forming a ripple of mortality in the land of time-proper. Amid their colorful hubbub, hardly any of the passersby noticed two quiet, well-dressed Elves in their midst. But the hosts knew well their guests, and would not let them off without a final well-wishing.

"We hope, Sage Fellareon, that you and your wife have had no cause for complaint in your time with our rough folk?"

The husband spoke first. "Not at all, madam Valeria—the company of your delightful band is most welcome, after some of the things I have seen from my time in the kingdom of Men."

"Aye, this you told during last evening's story-round. Auch! Such a fate, to travel beyond the world and there to meet an ancient horror."

"As if today's were not enough!" yelled the young horseman Crass, just then cantering past. His comment brought a roar of approval from all within hearing, who agreed, and a second roar from those beyond earshot of the original remark, but who nonetheless agreed on general principles.

"Aye, and to recover this knowledge at such a sacrifice." Valeria remarked. "'Twas too great a price to pay, say I, and there will be ill omen for it, mark me."

"Yes," agreed Cedrith heavily, "the loss of the Guildmistress Natasha was beyond all description. Yet describe it I have had to do, so many times to the various Guilds and authorities of the kingdoms. And now perhaps the final time, perhaps fittingly, to you her people."

"Guildmistress Natasha!" came the baritone shout of the fire-breather. He stomped up to the trio in mock anger, puffing out his oiled and naked chest against the chill of the ebbing year. The Elven couple knew what was coming, as it had come a half dozen times before in their brief stay; yet instinctively they shrank together even as they smiled.

"*Fwaugh!*" yelled the Rom, and with his awful cry came the burst of flame for which he was renowned among the band. Even the tambour dancers paused a moment, to hear the jest. "See to it, *gaje*, when you tell the tale, that you give Natasha her highest honor—she was a Rom!"

"Enough, Geltar, you insult our guests, you with your loutish grammar and the manners of a goat in heat. Begone with you!" Valeria slapped the muscleman with mock force—she was near to seven decades, he in his prime, yet it was always the same. He flipped backwards as if struck by an ocean wave, this time knocking the jugglers into each other and collapsing in a heap of limbs and pins. There was much to celebrate at this tumult.

The elven sage considered before replying. "I shall do my best to give all due honor to Natasha in my accounts. But that shall not be done tonight. We are fairly near home at last, as my bride tells me; I am indebted to you for the grand hospitality shown while we traveled together today, yet I am eager to see, for the first time, the comforts of our wheel-less house."

"Yes, you *gaje* are a queer lot," said Valeria, and it was hard to tell, in the waning light, if humor lit her handsome lined face. "Recall your promise to us, Sage of the Elves, not to reveal in any way how the Rom were able to cross the River Sweeping."

Cedrith smiled, raised his hand and repeated his vow, "*Promissar.*"

The Gypsy band at last began to veer away, north by east towards Roamsedge; the horseman performed another flip-a-canter to salute the guests, and one of the tambour dancers ran up to kiss the Sage, just for fun, to embarrass a new husband and annoy his new wife. The sounds and the sight of them faded, down the road and toward the town, but the palpable sense of their raucous emotion remained like the afterglow of sunset. The couple stood for a time, hand in hand, watching them fade from sight and sound, before turning back to stand again and contemplate the road to their cottage.

"Come, Cedrith," said the wife. "You've been kept from your new home too long. And away from me too long."

He turned to take her face in his hands and kiss her, for the hundredth time in the two days. "You always say that, dear Kia."

"And it is always true. There's a stew once-cooked and set aside, with bread and cheese, only waiting for a half-hour's fire to warm it. And I did not come a league down the road, spend a cold night on hard ground to return and find a block of ice."

"Nor would I have it so, not if the fate of the lands depended upon it! By the Stars, but I am empty inside."

The two turned arm in arm to move up the smaller road, around gentle turns and past quiet copses of elder trees that were beautiful even in the heart of winter under the stars.

"You speak of more than hunger," she offered quietly.

Cedrith looked on his wife with a sad smile, and kissed her yet again. "What day have I reached yet, love?"

"At six kisses a day apart," she pretended to calculate on her fingers, "you may have reached midsummer. Six months to go, if you insist that a half-dozen kisses a day is enough."

"My debt is indeed great!" he cried and paid her a little more. "Hunger, aye, 'tis as if... as if I have lost more than a great life, indeed I feel we have all suffered this death, most of us blissfully unknowing, the loss of part of all our lives. I think only a prolonged spell of home can cure the ill in me. Yes, some dinner, perhaps, and a warm fire, and of course I must marvel at the details of your housekeeping."

"A nest of spiders, after such an absence!"

"I am serious, my love, I have every confidence—and then tomorrow perhaps will be time enough to write. I feel I can never answer this obligation, my dear— what happened in the City of Wonders was simply too, too *large* to be held by pen and paper. But I have a duty to the Guild, and I am urged to it: the 'adventure' must be chronicled. Why, even Solemn Judgement wrote of it as a need. My thanks, Kia, for bringing me his letter from Shilar. It was such a blessing to know that a few days ago, at least, he was still well."

"What else does that poor man have to say?"

"What! I know not if he is poor, Kia, though I admit he prefers to pay in silver, rather than gold."

"Away with you! You know what I mean, he is all alone and friendless."

"He has a friend in me, or at least I am determined that it shall be so. He urges me, at any rate, to publish our story formally for the Guild, and I half believe I can do a fair job of it, in time. I shall write back and invite him to visit with us, of course."

"Of course, and he shall come too, when the snow falls in Salamander. What would such a man do inside a home, I wonder."

"I am so fortunate, my dear darling Kia, to have such a home, and a helpmeet who shares my vocation to study and write. How much further?"

For answer, Kia held up one finger in the clear moonlight, and led her husband around a final turn in the road.

"By the Moment," Cedrith breathed.

The couple stood at the curved end of a lovely path, hidden until just now, where the lightly wooded land thickened into a small copse. The turn in the road brought a perfectly-situated, small but stunning cottage into view. The half-stone construction was artfully uneven, designed to match the contours of the enormous timbers used on the upper storey. Cedrith and Kia took it in for several minutes, standing together for the first time before that most precious of all elven possessions, their own home. Not new built, but preserved and passed along in the vein of time-proper.

"Stars eternal," he whispered, slowly stealing forward as if frightened the vision would pop and disappear. Swallowing hard, he turned to embrace his wife with gentle passion, and the night chill retreated from the loving pair.

"My dear, your lavish descriptions did not do justice to this place," Cedrith managed upon finding his voice. He leaned back to see her smiling face while holding her waist in close. "It is beyond doubt the most wonderful home in the kingdom, in the Lands. I am happy beyond the worth of mortal life." Cedrith cupped her face and resumed payment on his debt, coming up to early autumn standing there on the front stoop.

"Truly love, it was the moment," his wife responded. "For my mother's sister, may Hope preserve her, to be so generous in her final days."

"I wrote to your mother as soon as I heard the news, dearest. So long ago it seems! Such a strange illness, and she less than four hundred. I am struck with wonder when I think of it, and a little fear as well. Did I wish this ill upon your family?"

"Of course not, dearest: it was her time, and none of us can fully understand the coming of another's moment. But of course mother had spoken to her of your suit, and she being childless herself, bequeathed it to me on her death."

"Free and clear, a house of our own." Cedrith said in wonder, "I would never have thought it possible, to have either a home or a wife so far beyond my station. Riarden's Rest, after the great storm-felled oak that went into her. And Kia Weitherton; it is too much to have hoped for."

"Then let us go in, husband. And may this first stay here be a long one, with no news of summons, or hopping across the Lands, of demons and magic."

"Your words are my wish, dearest Kia."

"And all for what? To make an awful trade in human life? No, let others keep this adventuring path, Cedrith; just you be certain to come home to me, if you should ever leave again."

"Yes, my dear, let it be as you say."

"And be not so long away next time."

"Peace, prithee! A truce, or else I surrender for only some food. Let us go in."

She looked up at the liche on her throne and realized, soon would be the right time to die. Across the audience hall shuffled dozens of gaunts and skeletons, most of them her former subjects. The night outside the high orison windows had turned red instead of black, and Vuthienne had no idea if any of them would live through this night. For herself she held no hope nor wanted any, and close to none for the adventurers now bound to columns around her as she was. Drawn back into a trap she had helped set, with her pride and ambition.

Such an old story, she thought as she sagged against the column where her wrists, but not her feet, had been bound with rope by the undead minions of Wolga Vrule. Evil comes not only in cruelty, or lust or hatred as with him, but with too great a desire to do good, too much pride in one's own part to play. Vuthienne saw everything in her chamber, even as she mimicked the helpless captive, and prepared to play her own part now.

Since the Scepter and Eye had been taken from her, the constant pain of the one and the battering power of the other were gone. The Primara's original clarity of mind had come home to her, with biting sorrow and stabs of regret she now noted the situation perfectly. She saw that the massive black warrior was not dead there on the brick-laid floor, but gravely wounded; the mage's sight had indeed returned, too late now that Vrule had ordered her eyes bound with cloth in addition to her hands. The others not badly hurt, though the big warrior was furious to frenzy when the undead prised the longsword from his hands. Vuthienne had seen that kind of rage before, was counting on it.

Yet the young Woodsman; why hadn't she seen it earlier, probably like most women too busy admiring the strapping fighter who took the lead and spoke more often. But the weathered youth with the dragon pet; he too was alert to every sound, took in the meaning of whatever was said. They made eye contact several times since they had all been bound to columns by the undead. Vuthienne knew, the one named Treaman could be counted on. When her time came, he would act.

She noted the boy up on the balcony, hiding as he should since his companion had shouted to lead some of the others out. She could sense Vrule was focused elsewhere, on his scheme of power and vengeance, not paying heed to minor details. His arrogance was leading him close to where she had been. He did not know about Januelus. He carried his scepter loosely, probably to lessen the shocking pain its every touch gave him as it had given her, indeed worse than her pain, she hoped.

And he failed to see, did Wolga Vrule, that the young Woodsman bound to a nearby pillar no longer had a knife in his belt. Hands tightly tied back, he glanced to a spot behind where she stood, and slightly nodded. When she moved her arms a bit, she felt resistance;

the blade he threw had stuck into the mortar between the pillar's bricks, near her binding rope.

Vuthienne had no illusions. She must continue to cringe and gasp whenever Vrule faced her—no difficult feat, when he breathed such abominations in her ear—she must draw him on until she saw Januelus, and then her part well played would mean her life was over, the others perhaps continuing a while. It was the leader's job, the Primara's responsibility, to make good and not spare herself.

Vrule opened his eyes, evidently from communing with his minions and turned to her with the suggestion of a smile on his skull-hugging lips. Time to pay attention.

"As I mentioned before, Primara, truly ruling a city is onerous work. Even now I must take leave of you momentarily, to ascertain what has become of my patrol at the gates."

Vuthienne tried to look exhausted, played out even as her heart rose to think of Januelus. She had not heard his call yet this evening and hoped only that he still survived, would live on after her mistake was partly paid.

"But I shall not leave you destitute of… entertainment. My thralls have at last captured that skulking urchin who left us so abruptly an hour ago. One of your subjects, no doubt, though perhaps unknown to you. I shall see him properly esconced before my inspection tour. Ah, here he is now."

Vuthienne saw the prisoner dragged in cursing and struggling, and her heart turned to ash within her.

When Anteris, huddling behind the rail of the upstairs balustrade, heard that ancient voice in conversation, he lost his breath. When he got the news Forge had been captured, he had to cover his mouth with his hands or he would have been discovered too. But at the sound of shouting and grappling he peeked over the rail and looked down into the sparsely-lit audience hall.

It was not Forge. The man was too tall, and wore a chain shirt beneath his tunic. Four gaunts were barely enough to restrain him and his boots were already torn to shreds, barely hanging on his ankles as they slowly dragged him to a pillar and bound him with chains at the liche's order.

It must be the timber-man, Januelus, that Treaman had spoken of. A skeleton nearby placed a two-bladed ax on a table with the party's other weapons. Anteris saw the backpacks scattered where each member had fallen; when his eyes lit on the tent bag he felt a charge run through him. It lay half-way across the floor, littered with broken furniture and studded with the shambling undead not under direct orders at the moment. On the opposite wall beyond the prisoners and the lord of undeath, was the archway the heir had used, the way to Reghalion.

Anteris saw the scepter as well, hanging casually in the liche's arm as he contemplated his newest prisoner. Two of the three artefacts in the Tridium, within a few steps of each other. His blood raced from heart to head and Anteris felt as winded as he would from his daily race in Trainertown. He looked at Treaman, who caught his eye and gave him a look filled with consequence, along with a tiny nod that said "be ready".

Ready, for what? The heroes had failed, most likely none of them would escape alive. The strength of Haltar, Linya's lore, none of it had mattered versus the power of Despair summoned from centuries past. What could Treaman possibly expect from a scribe's assistant in this horrid place, all by himself?

As the interrogation began, Anteris sank behind the railing again and tried to get his wits about him.

"Such a strapping fellow, not like a street urchin at all. Tell me Primara, do you know this subject of yours? Or is he perhaps one of the merry band of mercenaries we have with us as well?"

"He is—one of my own, liche. A forester."

"Ah, and I see from the sad state of your shoes that you have been long in the woods, sirrah. Was it you perhaps, who drew my patrol's attention so far from their duty to report? Hah! Did you cut them all down with this doughty ax, then? Nothing? Never mind, when I return we shall see what little you know. Then most likely I shall recruit you."

A slight rustle of wings, and Anteris was startled to see Hallah stoop from the high rafters to cling to his shoulders. All the horror of this evening could not quite dispel the delight and wonder he felt at the sight of Treaman's pet, who had never trusted him this far before. The tiny dragon weighed a little less than Folio, but had sharper claws which dug straight through his jerkin. Anteris looked into her jewel-eyes and thought he saw a message, from Treaman or the heroes, that he should do something.

Forge had not hesitated to act, may the Heroes protect him wherever he had got to. How could it hurt to explore this area a bit? It took all his courage, but Anteris slowly turned onto his hands and knees with the tiny dragon on his back, and crept along the glass-floored balcony, to the spot where the stairs led down to the left into the audience hall, and the corridor across from it plunged further into the palace. That was the way Forge had run, and those horrid creatures after him; how long ago? It seemed half a day, but when Anteris checked the night-sky through the windows in the domed ceiling above he saw only a wicked red light.

Again the voice from below.

"Ah, my loyal tinker arrives, bearing the rest of his treasures."

Anteris risked another glance, and his horror renewed as this undead thing, arms loaded with odd-shaped items and wearing a blood-stained leather work apron, did not walk but instead glided across the floor to stop before its master. The liche, still with his back to the spot where Anteris hunched, looked quickly over the armload and waved his hand in dismissal.

"Drek, no doubt toys for your idle hours, but worry not, tinker, you shall need no more leisure to occupy your mind. The great stores of powder you so graciously assembled for me is safely kept below this level, and it shall be most useful when the time comes to build once again the mighty *Makine*. Put this up there, out of the way, and then return to watch our guests. Go."

The workman-thing skated across the floor towards the stairs where Anteris huddled. The boy scuttled back as fast as he dared, sure that he would need to rise and flee soon, but hoping the liche would leave the room first. Maybe he could find Forge somewhere.

The doors to the audience hall closed behind the lord of undeath, who took many, but not nearly enough, of the gaunts and skeletons in his wake. Anteris felt his heart gripped with ice, to see the undead thing glide to the top step and slowly turn. Away from him, to a set of tables on the far side of the balustrade.

Anteris lay low and froze. There came a clatter of things hard, soft, partly hollow. The leather-clad corpse stood there a moment, as if contemplating its work, then spun and glided back to the stairs, within ten steps of Anteris' half-shadowed hiding place. Down the stairs, out of sight.

Do something, he thought, and Hallah seemed to wordlessly agree. Anteris crawled to the edge of the stairs again, looked down to see no one in view, then across to the table.

There were no weapons of any kind, and Anteris' heart fell. Several small, intricate devices with gears and catches, which reminded him of the workings of the clock tower back in Trainertown but on a much smaller scale. Perhaps they were tools of some kind, or the toys a monarch would give his child. There were dozens of small capped cylinders of thick paper, filled with a powdery substance like flour or sugar. And small, half-shaped beads about the same shape as the top of Anteris' thumb, but made of a dark, glitter-specked metal. Finally there was a crafted item with three long metal tubes set into a beautifully carved wooden stock, and studded with small catches and slides in a way he could not understand at all.

"Anteris." From below Treaman's voice was quiet but carried. Anteris half-stood and peered over the railing to where the prisoners were tied against their columns. The newest one, the timber-man looked up and around with surprise as well. Anteris waved meekly and pointed to Hallah to assure Treaman all was well.

"Can he free us?" the timber-man asked.

"No," said the Primara and Treaman at the same moment.

"Not yet, but stand ready," the Woodsman added. He jerked his head towards the floor where the tent-bag lay. "We just have to find a way through that gate."

In the heavy silence, Anteris tried twice to speak but failed. The undead in the chamber all ignored the conversation but that only made it harder to speak. Finally swallowing hard, he whispered a bit too loud.

"Just say the words. I know them."

The party kept speaking, but Anteris sagged back down too stunned to answer, as on his left the ghost entered.

"You do?" Treaman cried with surprise. "Anteris, the words, what are they?" There was no answer, and Treaman sagged in defeat. Too much needed doing, too little to do it with. This undead master, the entire town enslaved to necromancy, he had never imagined these obstacles when the party had followed the boys' trail up from underground. It was the worst memory of the tales of ancient days, and made him feel a child again to face it awake. Even freed, he knew that combat held no hope of victory.

But Vuthienne, she had some kind of plan, he could sense it, the fire in her eyes gave him dread even as the red light outside the high windows grew into a bloody dawn, hours early. Treaman felt like a knife was slowly sliding up and down his spine, and realized it was a high, keening sound he heard, as of something distant but approaching.

"Primara," Januelus said, "I came over the walls as soon as the plaza was clear of undeath. Something, someone had destroyed the entire patrol, I did not see. But there were too many, in the streets, I could not fight them. They are, these were my people, Vuthienne." Treaman could see the tears streaking Januelus' face; his companions began to look away, a bit embarrassed.

"I understand Januelus. This is my fault, and you tried to help me but I wanted too much. When the time comes, do your best to get away."

"No! All of us, Vuthienne, or none."

Treaman heard a very low rolling sound behind him, stopping and resuming several times.

"Januelus," he said carefully, "I'm sorry we couldn't help you as I promised."

The timber-man kept his eyes on his lover and shook his head. "You did your best, my friend. None of us could have known the curse that would overtake this city. But why is he here, what does this horrid creature want?"

Now one of the undead was behind Treaman's pillar, and the rolling sound stopped. Something was placed in Treaman's hand, with fingers warmer than death, and his wrists were cut free while a warning grip held his arm in place.

"Keep pretending until I get the others loose." It was Forge's whisper. "I brought you a little present." Now the sound of wood sliding on brick; Treaman looked down to see a cask, perhaps twice the size of the one Bildon had thrown in the fire, with a small rope emerging from its top about a foot long. The thing in Treaman's hand was his tinder-light, rummaged from the Woodsman's pack.

"There must be forty more barrels on the level below. That fire-powder you told us about. The rope is soaked in oil, probably turn the whole palace into rubble."

"Well done, boy. What about the others?"

"I'll do what I can, but have to keep out—oops, time to go."

The gliding undead chief had turned in Treaman's direction and moved to investigate. Treaman caught Haltar and Mhoral's eyes and briefly flashed his arm was free, nodding to indicate their turn was coming.

Still, what could they do, if free, rearmed and able to attack with surprise? What magic or weapon would suffice to harm this thing? And Januelus was bound with chains, not rope. Treaman looked back to the stairs, and thought he saw a misty something at the top, very hard to spot in the dim light but shaped like a woman in rags.

{*"Hallah, is the boy in white alright, are you with him?"*}

{*"Hallah here, but no boy. Is man now."*}

The Woodsman threw his thought towards Hallah with his eyes closed and immediately saw what she did. The misty female shape facing their way, hands to her mouth in horror, then backing off and moving down the stairs out of view. Treaman felt a wave of sorrow, salted with fear of course, but some kind of overpowering regret and a sense that this spirit, at least, was not truly evil.

He opened his eyes and barely made out the spirit as she wavered slowly down the stairs, moving through overturned chairs and even the gaunts in her path. He could see her mouth open to scream, but at this distance he could detect no sound over the high drone now quite audible to everyone, making it harder to talk and hear.

"The main thing is to get through the portal," Treaman managed, afraid to speak so loud in the presence of the undead. But they paid no attention. "When we are all free, and the moment comes, get to that arch."

"What if it isn't open?" Mhoral asked, on cue.

Treaman looked up to the balcony level and put his hope into the scales. "It will be."

"He's coming back," Haltar said calmly, as if Wolga Vrule were late to refill their goblets.

The gliding workman returned to the center of the room, without Forge. Small blessings, thought Treaman, as he tensed his arms and gauged the distance to the throne, to the back of Januelus' pillar, the arch, and the tent bag.

Anteris still heard Treaman and the others talking, beneath the rising whine ringing around the room, the ceiling, the world. But he could not have answered for his life. Frozen with fear, he watched the ghost enter the balcony from the hallway Forge had run down, what seemed like days ago.

It was a young woman, from the look of her, in torn clothes and her face molded into permanent horror that varied only in intensity. Unlike the leather-clad glider—a revenant, Anteris' memory suggested—here was a ghost, the sort Forge and the others had tried so often to mock, not believing while safely back home. She might have been as young as he was, from the look and size.

His breathing was already short; it stopped completely when she turned his way.

The figure swept slowly in, peering at him crouched there by the table as if he was as hard to see as she was to mortals. Anteris could think of nothing to do, nowhere to run.

"Please," he begged quietly, "please."

Convulsed by something down in her middle, the girl writhed back and forth, finally leaning nearly on top of the scribe to open her mouth and scream with all her might. It was the dimmest, most muffled echo of a young girl in agony. But she was so close to him, Anteris heard it all the same.

It was as if every inch of him went cold, touched by the air of the world beyond death. Anteris lay back, shuddering and warding uselessly with his hands, eyes wide to see every detail. The girl screamed so long and faintly, the scribe felt drawn to witness whatever horror had kept her from a restful death.

Without warning, she drew back from him, looked again and put her ghostly hands to her face. It was the look of someone who realized a mistake, who said "no, not yet". Swishing smoothly backward, the figure turned to look down the stairs, then back at Anteris in a mute appeal of need or sorrow. She moved on, out of sight.

Anteris could not even think, much less move, until he felt Hallah's claws in his shoulders again. The little dragon, incredibly, was settling in for sleep, completely unaware of the attack or else unaffected.

That broke the spell a bit, and Anteris began to get back up.

He hit his head hard on the underside of the table; it seemed lower than before. When he used his hands to scrabble from beneath it, they were larger than he remembered. And when Anteris stood, he felt such a shock he nearly wet himself. His clothing was too short in the sleeve and leg, hair much longer than before. Sensing a slight itch on his face, he felt with his hands the hundred points of new whiskers.

Anteris almost fainted, as his mind scrambled to recall the lore he had read of ghosts. From sheer fear, they pulled their victims through life, aging them until quite plainly they were scared to death. With a single scream, that thing had taken Anteris' childhood from him.

Vuthienne flinched when the chamber doors banged open, and she read the fire in Vrule's eyes as he tottered at maximum pace across the floor with his uneven, skeletal feet. She knew she must draw that anger on herself, without giving away her plan. Januelus stared only at her, pleading with very different eyes for a chance, for love, and life with her. But she must play her part.

Accompanied by several of the mob of undead he had taken with him, Vrule paced before his prisoners muttering to himself in a foul tone. He looked up once or twice at the orison windows, now so deeply red as to appear painted, and scowled at the need to raise his voice, though too impatient to discern the reason why.

"You!" he cried, spinning to face Januelus, "was it your doing, that my patrol was destroyed? It hardly seems possible for any man, certainly not to destroy my revenant. Still and all, you seem well suited to serve as a partial replacement." He raised one misshapen hand toward the timber-man's face even as the prisoner strained against his chains to no avail.

"Vrule, stop!" Vuthienne screamed, a bit too high and hasty. The liche halted his hand but only tilted his head instead of turning back to face her.

"Primara, you have some interest in this fellow? Does your lover in black who fled through the gate know of your unseemly affection?"

"I, I care for all my subjects." The monster cackled with the interpretation he chose, and she allowed him, forging ahead. "Free him, let him go, and I can tell you where worthy followers aplenty lie awaiting your call."

Now she had earned his attention; Vrule turned to face her and his eyes still gleamed wetly with need and restrained anger.

"Primara, no!" Januelus cried.

"You recall no doubt, liche, that our city was built atop one of yours." She could not hesitate now, to save her lover's life whatever the cost.

Vrule nearly smiled and took two steps in her direction. "Do you mean…"

She nodded to him. "Free him, and these others, who mean nothing to you, and I shall tell you how to reach the tomb."

Vrule put one hand to his chin in contemplation. "Then they followed my instructions those many ages ago, how fortunate. Oh, I can almost sense the power in them, not recruits but volunteers! You have no conception—well then, how could you—but the increased power and volition of the Children of Despair, to serve my needs. Revenants and Wraps, mayhap even new forms that evolved since the days of my early experiments. Show me these, Primara, tell me the way to my children."

"And the others you will free."

Vrule seemed surprised. "Oh, nonsense, these will also serve, in more minor roles of course. I've already learned to expect the unexpected in this chaos-land."

Vuthienne felt the time drawing near now. She shook her head in defiance only half-feigned. "I shall never tell you. Without my word, you won't find the passage."

"My dear, of course I shall. You know I have eternity to seek the answer, and as I said, the process is almost as pleasurable to me as the answer. Tell me now, and I promise to close their minds, as I have those of your subjects. Their bodies, I assure you, belong to me.

As does yours. But you can spare them, and yourself, the torment that comes with awareness of their servitude, the crime of helping convert others to the cause with their touch."

Vrule was very close now, and it was not hard for Vuthienne to act terrified. She kept her emotions in check, though barely, and gauged if she could get him one step closer to any advantage. Her arms had worked the ropes against Treaman's knife until it was quite nearly cut; she didn't dare complete the job since the liche stayed so near her.

But a misty shape behind the liche's shoulder distracted her attention, and then his. A ghostly form, the young woman from the stair, gestured to Vrule as he turned halfway from Vuthienne to regard her, first with curiousity and then growing glee. The half-seen shape wavered and twisted, her mouth leaning in to scream at Wolga Vrule, who leaned back on instinct.

Vuthienne heard nothing, over that dull rising whine around the palace, so long a part of the background she forgot she and Vrule had been nearly shouting. The liche also was evidently unaffected by the ghostly wail, a growing smile and chuckle spreading across his ghastly features.

"Ah, my dear! But this is the mother of our ally's child, of course! And you followed me all this way from the village, did you? Hoping for revenge, no doubt. Poor thing, I cannot hear your scream above this infernal clamor; try again. No, not a sound I'm afraid."

Peals of the liche's laughter crested the droning din. The liche capered clumsily at a joke only he understood. "Truly, that is the most pathetic story I've seen in centuries, aside from my own of course. Scream away, wretch, my body is four thousand years old and quite immune to another few decades I assure you. Stay on your plane and I may allow you to frighten a few prisoners one day." He turned away speaking to himself, "A kind of ethereal court jester."

Stopping within arm's reach of her lover, Vrule looked back to fix her with his fiercest glare. "Now then, Primara, choose the form of this strapping swain. Tell me the location of the tomb, or—"

"Or nothing, you undead carker," cried Treaman to her shock.

"Silence, stripling, your betters are discussing matters beyond your understanding."

"Really?" cried the Woodsman, with more confidence than he should have. "I suggest you put your hand down, skinny one, and understand this."

Vuthienne kept her eyes on the liche, as his face turned in the Woodsman's direction, and changed from annoyance to shock and the first moment of indecision she had seen. This was worth the delay, so she held back her plan and looked as well.

She saw it all. The slender adventurer free of his bonds. The mien of outright defiance overcoming his fear. The keg of prime blasting powder at his feet.

And the lighted tinder-wick in his hand, not two feet from the fuse.

Anteris knelt by the railing, hunching even lower now than before to stay covered, and watched the standoff below. Treaman called out to stay Wolga Vrule, and now Hallah left his shoulders to return to her master, circling down to further the tumult of curse and demand. He knew he had to be ready, to answer when Treaman called; surely the threat to light the powder was merely a bluff, but beyond that he could not imagine what the plan might be.

Almost directly below him and behind the liche's back, Forge was sneaking in to cut Mhoral, Linya and then Haltar loose. He only had time to press the longsword into the warrior's hand before the revenant noticed him again and moved that way, forcing the Stealthic's retreat. The other undead were much slower, and only reacted to the living if one came within arm's reach; Forge evaded them with ease and still managed to move quietly. The others had the sense to stand still and not draw attention until the time came. Linya pulled off her head covering and adjusted the bronze headband. Then, they waited as he did above them.

The argument, or perhaps negotiation, was hard to make out above the din of the night, a crimson storm of a kind Anteris had never experienced nor read about. He flexed his larger, stronger hands, and ripped out the seams of his pants to accommodate the legs of an adult. He felt strange as he thought about it, to be the size and age of a man chilled him like a column of ice where his spine should be. But he moved just as before, breathed as he always had; Anteris knew, without knowing how, that if he had to run he would be even faster than before. He wondered if his voice was deeper now.

The noise and shouting almost drowned out the sound of boots coming from the hallway behind him. Anteris drew back as the Man in Grey entered the audience chamber. With his strange attire and iron-shod staff he seemed another apparition, the many shades of grey from hair to heel defying the reddish glare pouring through the windows. Anteris made no sound or movement, yet somehow the intruder sensed him at once. The scribe, still not sure if this was a Minion of Hope or a servant of the enemy, put one finger to his lips. The Man in Grey nodded, then stepped over to him by the table.

"Who are you?" Anteris asked, with mouth more than voice.

"I am named Solemn Judgement," he returned in a quiet timbre that carried against the noise. The name jolted Anteris' memory, the tale told by Sage Cedrith in what seemed another world.

"You! The survivor of the Hopeward, can you help us, will you save us?"

The grey man raised an eyebrow at this salutation, but when he turned to see down into the chamber, his face hardened and he nodded fiercely.

“Aye, sir, I shall make all poor efforts I can to repair that great wrong, and stop yon evil.” He turned to go at once, but noticed the table near them and paused. Anteris could not believe his eyes, as the Man in Grey seemed to make good sense of the motley assortment in front of him.

Seizing several handfuls of the capped paper cylinders and dark metal beads, he stuffed them in a front pouch but saved out three of each. Taking up the wood-metal tool with what seemed a familiar hand, the stranger examined it a moment, then pushed two studs and broke the item open, so that the three metal tubes dangled down at an angle to the wooden end, which he grasped as a handle.

Quicker than could be told, he inserted a metal piece into each tube, followed by one of the paper cylinders. Then he snapped the tri-tube arrangement back in its original position where it stuck with a click. Showing remarkable ease, he thrust the entire tool into his belt and moved to the head of the stairs. He bowed to Anteris and strode down. Anteris clung to the rail, sure that he had sent the mad stranger to his doom, but ready to do what he could when Treaman called.

A part of Treaman’s mind was amazed at how clearly he spoke, how firmly he stood against this horror. The suggestion that he really should drop the wick, or back away, or run now, was not loud but it was persistent. If he had been less sure of his own death, perhaps he would have faltered. Now, though, he was starting to understand how Bildon must have felt, at the very end.

“Put your hands down, you fatherless scum,” he ordered calmly, “and step away from him.”

The liche lowered one hand slightly but stayed where he was. “Mortal, you cannot be serious. You will die.”

"Everybody dies!" Treaman bellowed. "The only questions are when, and how well. A friend taught me that. And I can answer both questions right now, for all of us."

The liche cocked his head, and Treaman recognized his attempt at a poker face. If Haltar could have seen from this angle he would have laughed.

"You miscalculate the power of that petard, stripling. It will not perform the destruction you claim."

"Take a step closer to Januelus or me, and we will find out." Bluff called, that was almost too easy.

Treaman's senses jangled and he half-turned to see several gaunts shambling his way.

"Stop them, now! I'll drop it!"

The liche raised one hand, his face wrinkled with anger, and the undead stopped instantly.

"This is nonsense!" he snapped. "No mortal of this age could compose blasting powder of such efficacy. Tinker, where are you, stop skulking in the shadows and come here."

Treaman felt his hand shake a moment now, as Enict Moaro glided from the back of the hall and came closer to his new master. So Forge was still uncaught, a small blessing extended. Vrule looked at the revenant intently a few moments, and Treaman felt it must be a mental connection, such as he shared with his dragon.

{*"Hallah, can you come here please?"*}

{*"Hallah come."*}

The liche clucked in disbelief. "It is a fantasy! Your powder is formed from the waste of bats, I know, you cannot—"

Vrule jaw froze open, as Hallah flapped down to light on Treaman's shoulder. Absurdly, she hissed long and loud at the lord of undeath.

"I assure you," Treaman said lightly kicking the cask, "what we have here is of the highest quality."

Vrule stared and stared as his anger rose until his frame practically vibrated with it. Behind him at an angle, Treaman saw Vuthienne working her bonds again, but he dared not look on her fully. The din outside was truly loud now, like a rising wind that never fell, but slowly crept up the scale by indiscernible steps.

"Mortal fool!" the liche bellowed at last, still not moving. "I am the first among necromancers in all the Lands, thane of the Lieges of Despair, not to be delayed by an insect with a candle. My body has survived forty centuries and no further path to damage it exists, short of the power of heroes."

"Bring down the palace then! Murder all your friends, your pet, end your own life. It matters not. I will move every stone one by one, I will dig until I find the tomb and resurrect an army such as your pathetic kingdoms have never seen. And if you crushed my frame, what then? My spirit is immortal, moron! In a few days, a year, a decade, I would find another body to house it; yours, if there is a scrap of justice. Yes, let us see if your resolution matches such fine words. I shall make sure our bodies embrace in the rubble, and I shall be certain to raise you as my slave."

Treaman could see that first fatal step in his direction, and only wished he could have avenged his friend on the Earth Demon first. But this was the only way. Until he heard an unfamiliar voice ring out above the noise.

"Nay, you have raised your last corpse, Wolga Vrule!"

Treaman looked to the stairs then, and saw someone who appeared not in the least like Anteris.

"You!" the liche near her shrieked in apoplexy. "Solemn Judgement! Here! How?"

"Long have I sought ye, liche," the Man in Grey said as he slowly advanced down the steps, hat pulled low over his eyes and staff gripped in one hand.

"And I have fondly hoped to meet you again, dung monkey," returned the tall skeletal one, still with his back to Vuthienne as he flung out one hand loosing a bolt of blackfire at his foe. Judgement dodged with minimum effort at that range, and reached the bottom of the stairs. Vuthienne was ready to strike but held back, seeing such an uncharacteristic reaction in her foe. Vrule looked to the ceilings above and behind him, as if expecting attack from above. Whirling again to face the stranger he shouted, "No call to the heroes, boy? Have you lost your faith then?"

Judgement shook his head once and came on, his face ablaze with an intense anger fully under his own control. "Found it, rather," was his only reply.

"Is this the remote Percentalion, or the center of Conar!" Wolga Vrule shouted as he loosed another bolt which made his foe duck and roll. "I will not stomach another interruption today." Vrule signaled to his minions and more than a half-dozen surrounded the intruder before he could approach.

Vuthienne could not understand what interest the liche took in the grey stranger, but he was clearly absorbed, forgetting even Treaman's threat in his avid excitement and perhaps, she thought, a touch of fear. The man's staff whirled and flared with silver as he bowled down two gaunts in his path and tried to work his way closer to the liche.

"You should have stayed in your library, boy!" Vrule crowed as several undead held his foe by the cape and arms, nearly immobilizing him. "Here you have no hold on me, no oath or rules to restrain me from giving you what you deserve." The liche signaled to his revenant, who slid towards the foe with hand outstretched.

Nothing dismayed, the grey man called out in the Ancient tongue, and the silver holy symbol around his neck blazed with blue light that arced to suffuse the man who had been Enict Moaro, until he blazed forth from his fingers and eyes as if he'd swallowed a lantern. Before Vrule could start his howl of rage, the revenant was destroyed, falling in pieces to the floor as Solemn Judgement broke free and his staff resumed its weaving dance.

"*My revenant!* So it was you!"

"Aye, such small service am I happy to perform. May I do the same for you in a moment."

"Fool! Insect, dung monkey, you cannot harm me now. No mortal can end Wolga Vrule."

The stranger ceased to struggle a moment, his face still wild with fury. "Not even one who has mastered the secret? One who has crossed Ranebruh, and visited Thanazun."

The liche choked with surprise as his enemy continued.

"Who found the missing lore you murdered a mage of ancient days to keep secret, whose death was so important to you that you lost your freedom to bury it, and plotted all these years since to escape?"

The stranger took advantage of the monster's astonishment to break free of his unguided minions and point to him with dreadful, righteous anger.

"And now, all your plots have come to nothing, Wolga Vrule. I have composed the ritual, even now it is being copied to distribute to all the Lands. Your *kemetaria* will be put to rest, all future potential victims will be protected from your dread curse. And I shall lay you to rest if I can, tonight."

Wolga Vrule began howling and swearing as he gesticulated wildly for his undead to slay the intruder.

Finally, Vuthienne saw her moment.

Nerving herself for what must follow, she broke her rope's last cord, stepped forward behind the lord of the undead, and swept as hard as she could at the back of his feet.

As the skeletal frame went limbs-askew and down, Vuthienne could not tear her eyes from Januelus beyond him, standing there with jaws agape at the success of such a trick. She heard the clatter of bones, the grunt of the liche as his skull impacted the brick, and Vuthienne listened to one more sound she had longed for, ever since she knew she must die.

The silvered chime of the Scepter of Law, with the ruby Eye of Kog still atop it, rolling free of the liche's hand. No one was close enough to get it back, and he was already groping after it.

She shouted her last defiance to her enemy, with her eyes on her lover.

"You longed for my embrace, have it now!"

Over Januelus' anguished keen, she threw herself bodily onto Wolga Vrule, locking her limbs on his to prevent his arising.

Treaman spent a moment in complete shock, and then his spirit lurched into action with the chance for life.

"Anteris, get the scepter!"

Through the din of the red storm outside he could just make out the sound of human flesh cold-cooking, as every part of Vuthienne's body touching the liche's skin scarred and withered. Her scream was agonized but triumphant. Januelus lurched against his chains hard enough to draw blood from his wrists. The others broke into movement; Haltar swept the longsword through a skeleton's neck while Mhoral dashed for his weapons to one side and Linya threw a bolt of fire into a gaunt advancing on her.

Down the stairs, three at a time, came a man dressed in Anteris' garb and practically flying across the audience hall. Leaning down, he scooped up the silver scepter and continued on towards the archway. To one side, Forge darted between several lurching corpses and snagged up the tent-bag, angling to join him.

The grey stranger continued to pummel undead to all sides with great sweeps of his staff, creating more room to maneuver. A few words of an Elvish song did not lend the encouragement of its miracle. At the arch, Treaman saw the boys skid to a stop, and Anteris yelled the words in Ancient that invoked the power of the central kingdom.

"Ac nomin Regente Areghel!"

The golden gate suffused with a golden glow.

Vrule finally rose, throwing off the husk that had been Primara of Oncario.

"Stayyee!"

Treaman watched as the boys struggled to move, yet could not stir a step. To his horror, he realized the same was true for himself, and everyone else in the chamber. The grey paladin beat back one remaining undead, then stood with both hands on his staff.

"Enuff ov theez ahnoyyansses!" Without the scepter in hand, could only use his stump of a tongue to speak. "Oll ov yewwill survv mee noww, behgining wiv diss wun" His cruel eyes fixed on Januelus, Wolga Vrule reached down with one misshapen hand to the scar-laced corpse that had been a beautiful woman seconds ago. With a few muttered words and a cackle, he carved Vuthienne's heart from her chest. As the liche stood again Januelus was only whimpering, heaving breaths and pulling his chains taut in impotence.

"Waash kaerfuly, oll ov yew, yur fayt vollowss herz." Gesturing with his good hand, Vrule appeared to draw a curtain back in mid-air, revealing a deep darkened chamber where an enormous crystal globe hung already stuffed thick with uneven spheres of human meat. As he pushed his hand into and through the globe's surface, Treaman could see the corpse at his feet begin to stir. His legs convulsed with the attempt to flee, but his feet were welded to the floor. Treaman was helpless; the same fate awaited him, and all his friends, one by one. It was time to drop the wick and end this in fire. Even a few years' delay…

Suddenly, Solemn Judgement took three steps closer to Vrule, as free as ever. The energy of Vrule's spell had failed to affect him. Judgement smoothly drew the miniature powder-bow from his belt, aimed, clicked, and pulled the trigger.

A thunderous report broke glasses on the floor, and within the vision-cave Vrule's crystal globe shattered into a thousand shards.

The mid-air door winked out instantly, and Vrule staggered back shrieking in horror. With a single sigh, the body of Vuthienne sank back to lie on the floor, and every other undead creature in the room followed suit instantly.

Vrule turned on Judgement then, his face etched in rage as he drew to his fullest height, arms raised to bring down destruction. Judgement calmly rotated a second barrel to the top of the powder-bow, aimed and blasted again at point blank range. Vrule was blown back and down to the ground by the force of that pebble of silversteel.

Even as the liche rose to his hands and knees, just as Judgement aimed his final shot, the ceiling exploded.

Above the audience hall something huge, hard, spherical and firey skimmed past the palace, clipping off the top level as a scythe lops off the head of the wheat. Too fast to follow, it careened on towards the river and bridge just beyond the city walls. Enormous shards of glass and chunks of brickwork rained into the room; the floor writhed like a snake underfoot, dropping everyone to the ground. A hole opened beneath Braja's body, and he fell into darkness. The floor immediately in front of Treaman also broke through, and the keg dropped three man-lengths down into the basement level, followed by his fumbled tinder-wick. He clung to the pillar next to him and watched as the tiny spark of light fell, bounced, and caught on the wick of the cask. The reflections of its sparking light showed stacks of barrels to all sides.

"Everyone get out of here!" he roared, voices easier to hear now that the red star had fallen. The crimson light was now replaced by an ocean of bright moonlight falling across most of the hall, the twin-moons of winter at their fullest.

"Iee zhall zlaye ovry wun ov yew unseks!" Vrule screamed, staggering to his feet clearly wounded but not stopped. "Iee zhall, Iee—vot in oll da hellz?"

It was all happening quickly. Treaman saw Anteris and Forge continue through the portal, while Mhoral, Linya and Haltar grabbed what they could and followed close after. Solemn Judgement lingered, clearly unwilling to break the contact but on the far side of another great rent in the floor and uncertain what other damage might appear. The Woodsman started toward Januelus' pillar and its chains, but stopped at the call of the timber-man, which turned to a growl in mid-sentence.

"Treaman, go my friend! All of you go! This one is mine!"

Bathed in moonlight, Januelus seemed to grow larger from its shine, his muscles standing out, and now hair growing from all his parts. Treaman felt his hackles rise, as the creature snapped its chains and howled full up at the sky while it continued to transform.

"A zilverweer!" Vrule cried, his voice again showing fear through the mangled words. "No, stayy beck, keep uway vrom mee!" The liche blasted a bolt of blackfire into the beast rearing on its hind legs still twenty feet away; the wound was ragged and deep, but within seconds it began to close under the power of the creature.

Treaman shouted to the Man in Grey. "Come, grey man, we must leave now, come!"

He skipped backwards to keep Januelus in sight, and the stranger walked without haste in his direction as well. They both stopped by the gate, still glowing, and looked back into the room.

In a single bound, Januelus leapt the barrier of broken floor and over another bolt of blackfire, to pounce on the liche with both hands embedded in his chest. Treaman heard the sound of thick rotten sailcloth tearing as the silverwere who had been Januelus ripped the liche's body cavity wide open. While the liche screamed, the silver-furred beast ripped off his arms with the ease of a hungry man tearing a leg from a capon, then twisted his skull on his neck until with a loud pop it came free.

The silverwere raised his arms and howled in victory, a call that was cut off from the overwhelming concussion of four tons of blasting powder going up in rapid sequence. Hell rose to the level of the Lands in a wave of fire and flying stone; Treaman and Judgement instinctively hugged each other and huddled against the arch for shelter. A second hail of stones pounded down from high in the air. When the storm of rocks cleared, Januelus and the liche had vanished and the entire palace level was exposed and scraped out like a skeletal pumpkin. Barely three feet were left around most of the walls, columns collapsed into the basement along with the stairs and all the rest of the portico levels.

"That tomb will stay hidden," Treaman managed to say.

"Aye, well enough done," the stranger remarked.

"I don't believe I know your—"

"Hold," the Man in Grey interrupted, pointing out to the center of the room. Treaman followed that gaze, and his rapid-pumping blood was chilled to see a misty shape coalesce in the moonlight. It floated towards them, and the Woodsman could make out a tall, handsome mage in full resplendent robes and the prime of life, but a face etched in a totally familiar hatred.

Judgement stepped fearlessly in front of Treaman, and held out his holy symbol with a short cry in the Ancient tongue. The spirit stopped, and seemed to speak, but it was too faint to make out words.

Even as they watched in horror, Treaman perceived a second shape gliding up behind the first. It was female and its scream too was inaudible to the mortals. But Vrule's form quivered as if stabbed, and he held his hands to his ears from the sound. It seemed to Treaman that the face was suddenly older now, and Vrule started to speak, to hold out his hands, to cast a spell of some kind. But the female screamed again, not even a whisper of her voice reaching his ears but clearly a racket that drowned all attempt at order from Wolga Vrule. Pained and wrinkled, he turned to flee at the speed of a spore in a gentle breeze, and the female followed, her face carved in stone resolution and the need for vengeance. After a time the two shapes disappeared into shadow beyond the moonlight.

"Truly strange are the ways of Hope," the Man in Grey said. "No fate I could devise for mine enemy would have come close to that which he brought upon himself."

"My name is Treaman," the Woodsman said, holding out his arm to clasp. "Let's go, stranger, if you're willing. I still have a demon to settle with."

Treaman saw Linya first, tears in her eyes; as he went to stand with her she threw her arms around him and wept for Braja. The Woodsman felt the sting of tears himself. To his surprise Mhoral walked slowly over and just leaned his helm against the two of them, saying nothing. A few feet away he could see Forge staring up at his friend, gripping his arms as if to confirm what he saw, and then barking a laugh, a curse, a half-sentence. Anteris stood in his too-short clothes and tried to smile with tears also on his cheeks. Haltar of course seemed as unaffected as ever, casually looking at four oozing cuts on his arms and chest before striding over to eye the grey stranger. That's when Treaman noticed something about their surroundings that made him break away from his friends.

It was another enormous room, dwarfing the size of the audience hall in Oncario and much more opulent. Wherever there had been brick, there was now marble and porphyry. Windows showed the twin-moons setting to the south and the edge of a white dawn westward, which would come later in this city set at the western base of Skysword. Four more arches were set to the periphery, the balcony was built against the wall without glass flooring or other twists and turns, and the exits stood quite the same as he had seen in Oncario's palace now destroyed.

But Treaman noticed the other occupants of the room, which put him on alert. Very dimly in the predawn glow, movement on all sides, between columns, passing up the throne-steps where the man in black sat cross-legged on the floor with eyes closed, coming up and down stairs and sometimes through doors that did not open. Ghosts, scores of them, enough to fill a palace and make it bustle with a semblance of life lived out for centuries on another plane of existence.

"Everyone, stand still, no sudden moves." Treaman spoke too loud in the enormous chamber, but they noticed what he meant. Instinctively, the party went back-to-back with Anteris and Forge in the center, except for the Man in Grey who stood nearby with weapon ready. They watched the slow pageant of ghostly life in total silence, crab-scuttling one way to avoid a spirit coming too near.

"Let's go back, through the gate to Oncario," Linya suggested.

"There's nothing there anymore," Treaman told them. "Januelus… is gone. And that liche, and Vuthienne."

"But here there is only death," Mhoral insisted.

"We have been here some while," Haltar pointed out, "and all still alive."

"You can't be serious, Haltar!" Mhoral hissed. "You saw what these things did to—well, we all know ghosts can't be fought."

In the silence that followed, Treaman felt dismay but also a rising sense of humor.

"Well Haltar," he murmured, "you wanted us in Reghalion and here we are at last."

"Indeed we made it, Woodsman, thanks to you." Haltar's response seemed uncommonly gracious, and a voice inside Treaman remarked that he should do something brave now. That was when he noticed the Man in Grey still standing to one side, looking around and bearing himself as if either the ghosts or the party could attack him next.

"What is your name, stranger? We have you to thank for no small part of our success back there."

"I am Solemn Judgement, sir, a wanderer, a student. And Wolga Vrule's defeat lay on my side of the scale, certes. You spoke of a demon, mean you Kog?"

"We do," Treaman managed. "He has destroyed—he is attacking the world outside... he slew our comrade."

The grey man nodded saying "He too is a debt I must repay."

"We saw you destroy undead," Mhoral suggested.

"What can we do," Haltar asked, "about these ghosts?"

Solemn Judgement looked around him at the dim shapes. "Sooth, and I can have no surety. The ghost, in lore, is driven by a passion that will not let them die. But mark you how they seem not to notice us? And some whom I trow to discern more clearly, are dressed as for court, appearing up and about their business. I know little of ghosts, my studies are incomplete, focused elsewhere on necromancy of the first form. But I think mayhap these are unaware of their condition. Mayhap they are even still... Children of Hope."

Holding up a finger for waiting, he strode several paces away from the group, wending fearlessly between passing forms to a spot nearer the center of the massive hall. Raising both arms, he spoke in a strong voice that Treaman found shocking.

"I call upon Areghel to detect Despair!"

Blue waves of light radiated from the stranger, and as he turned slowly in a circle it created a spiraling ripple of magic moving across the hall. Wherever it touched a ghostly shape the magic energy clung a moment; Treaman could see it remained blue before fading. But one or two of the dim figures slowed and turned in Judgement's direction now, evidently his call being enough to attract their attention.

Treaman couldn't shake the image of what that girl had done to Wolga Vrule, and everyone's gaze stopped on Anteris as they looked around. But he swallowed hard and made a decision.

"Let's approach that fellow on the floor. Move slowly, and do nothing to attract their attention if you can."

Now the Man in Grey was in the lead as they walked toward the throne at the end of the room. One of the misty figures was trailing along behind him, evidently trying to ask a question. The Woodsman bit his lip and focused on keeping his pace slow but steady. They all arrived at the man in black sitting cross-legged, eyes closed and hardly breathing but sitting straight up.

"Has anyone thought," Mhoral whispered, "what we need to do now?"

Haltar shrugged. "If he is the heir—"

"I trow he is," said the Man in Grey, "mark you his black raiment, as was tradition for the descendants of Areghel before taking the throne."

"How did he, where was his family?" Linya asked. "And how could he have come all this way alone?"

"With no Woodsman to guide him." Haltar put in, exchanging a grin with Treaman.

"More proof," Judgement said.

"So you believe in a fate that guides us," Mhoral asked him. Judgement returned the gaze to that helmed faced, and the Elf flinched.

"I believe we all have a purpose, aye. It guides us, if we choose to be guided."

Treaman stepped across to face the stranger. "I don't know anything about the heroes, or our purpose in life," he said carefully. "But it cannot be a coincidence that we all find ourselves here. We should work together, for our mutual aid."

"For the restoration of the kingdom," Anteris offered, his deeper voice still startling.

Solemn Judgement nodded and held out a gauntleted hand. "And for the defeat of the Earth Demon Kog, if we can assay the task."

Treaman gripped his arm hard, and dropped his voice low. "Oh, yes. Yes indeed to that."

They returned then to contemplate the man in black at their feet.

This near the throne, the group was more closely in the path of several ghosts in their passing. Treaman noted some ascending the steps before them to address the empty throne. One held a scroll and read from it, seeming to await a reply before turning to walk back down. The one behind Judgement was still trying to get his attention; the Woodsman thought it better not to mention this, but on balance there was a definite pressure to move ahead in the room.

"Should we wake him?" Mhoral asked with his usual genius for identifying the wrong course.

Anteris spoke again. "Perhaps the Scepter and Sword will draw him. Somehow." He was holding the rod with his hands beneath his tunic, but it was clearly still painful for him. At Treaman's nod, he set it down, with the evil red jewel still attached to its top, within a foot of the man's knee. Forge opened the tent bag and carefully took out the sheathed Sword of Air, doing likewise before stepping back.

They contemplated the man some more, who did not move or even breathe.

"Does it seem to you," Linya asked, "that the Scepter and Sword are glowing a little?" No one answered as they strained to see.

"What was that prophecy again?" Haltar asked, and Anteris began to recite immediately.

"As Areghel's line sits the Kingdom's throne
Ways keep straight, Kog's day is done.
But failing the seat, hell's place repeat,
And no child of Hope alone
No branch of Conar's bone
May demon cheat, his eye align,
Or Tridium seat, till the heir assign
The fivescore castles his own."

"Lovely rhyme," Mhoral remarked. "But what does it mean to say 'no child of hope alone', is it hopeless then?"

"The next line," Linya said, "could mean someone who's not a Man, of Conar's kingdom. Like an Elf."

Mhoral raised his visor to this, blinking at the unusual attention. But the voice of Solemn Judgement cut in.

"Sooth, are the Elves not then among the Children of Hope?"

"We still need to find out if this is the heir," Haltar said, "and what it means to assign the castles."

"And we have to find the Crown, or we can't seat the Tridium," Treaman said. "Two references to the seat, maybe it's as simple as getting him on this throne here."

Treaman looked up at the marvelous wooden throne with gold inlay, and his voice choked off. All around the group, the ghosts were now standing in a circle with no gaps, staring hard at something in the center. A few glanced around with new awareness, or at themselves as if sensing their own immateriality now that warm bodies were in the chamber.

He managed a whisper with a gesture outward. "We have to hurry."

The man in black at their feet took a deeper breath and opened his eyes. Looking down to his feet he noted the Scepter and Sword, then his gaze swept up to Treaman in front of him. With his charge of fear redoubled, Treaman managed a bow.

"Majesty, or so we believe you to be. We wish to aid you to become king and dispel the curse over this land. Also, em, we might need your protection, from these ghosts around us."

The circle of ghosts was pressing smaller and closer now, some reaching out for either the group, or the items or the man in black. Treaman didn't know which and did not want to find out.

"Anteris!" He hissed, "Where is that damn Crown?"

"I, I don't know, sir." Anteris managed, shocked and stupid from all that had happened. Just holding the Scepter through cloth he had felt battered by a nameless desire, which only the need to save his life by running had dampened. He looked at Forge, who shrugged. "The words in Ancient were *super mentum ar loctu*, but I cannot—"

" 'Find the crown in its highest place' " Solemn Judgement interrupted, in a voice of simple confidences. Anteris stared as the grammar fell into order, and nodded to him. Then he remembered and cried out for joy, forgetting where he was.

"The palace! Remember, Areghel had things set up the same in both cities. I know where it is! I know how to get there!"

The man in black stood up, and everyone bowed to him now, Anteris thought, just to be on the safe side.

"You say I am a king."

"We believe so, sir." Treaman said, speaking for all. "May I know your name?"

"I am called Pol."

"Indeed," Solemn Judgement chimed in again. "Of the line of Pollus and Reghine, daughter of Areghel in ages past." And again Anteris nodded in agreement: this fellow frightened him but he knew his history. "You fostered in Mendel, near the sign of the sheltering oak," Judgement continued, "and then took study in the Crystal City."

Wonderingly Pol nodded at the Man in Grey, seemingly unaffected by the news that he was heir to a throne. "I came to the center," he said simply, "led the last league by your group, which I take to be a sign of destiny. And now you say these are mine," he looked down on the rod and sword.

The ghosts were pressing in very close now, and Anteris had no desire to experience their anger a second time. He knew where the Crown must lie but could not bear to take one step in their direction, now totally surrounded.

Pol seemed unconcerned with the misty shapes around him, perhaps did not see them at all. First he picked up the Sword of Air, hefting its weight in the scabbard, then drawing the hilt so that the lightning-blade flooded the chamber. Anteris could not see a thing for long moments, and expected to feel the chilling touch, hear the scream of a ghost any instant while blinded. His vision cleared as the light of the sword ebbed a little, still drawn but now responding to Pol's touch. He did not seem to feel any difficulty in holding the blade himself, and any doubts Anteris' reason might have suggested, about the improbability of what he saw, melted away in the calm demeanor of the man in black. The ghosts, meanwhile, had drawn back at the light of the blade. Maybe they had a few moments yet.

Pol sheathed the Sword, returning normal morning light to the chamber, and stooped to retrieve the Scepter. Again there were no sparks, such as Anteris had felt from trying to hold it. Pol frowned to note the palm-sized ruby fused to its top.

"What is this?" he asked with an edge like anger, offended in the way of someone who smells something rank.

"That," said Solemn Judgement laconically, "is the Eye of Kog, Majesty. Once set in the face of your ancestor's great enemy, it was struck from him in the Wars of Liberation, consigning the demon to the hell where he belongs. But now, it has been released, through my own fault," he continued without a hitch, as if quite accustomed, "and thus Kog has again been loosed upon the world. How it came here, I know not, except that his ally the liche Wolga Vrule had a part."

"And now?" Pol asked calmly.

"The liche, has been dealt with, Majesty. But Kog ravages the land and increases the curse."

"Just so," Pol said, "I can feel it calling to me, and whispering of power." He contemplated the Scepter, and Anteris remembered its call to him in the brief time he had held it. Now he thought he saw in Pol's face a complete lack of such earthly weakness and it shamed him. Pol held the Scepter of Law near the top in one hand, while the other curled into a fist that glowed with mystic energy.

"Stay back," Linya advised, and Anteris shrank away on instinct as the man in black brought his glowing fist down hard atop the Scepter directly onto the glowing red gem.

There was no explosion or shattering sound. Pol's fist came down to the top of the Scepter as if the jewel had disappeared in the last instant. But the agonized roar and blood-freezing howls behind him made clear that this was no illusion. Anteris fell to the ground at the unearthly racket.

At the other end of the throne room stood a massive being with shiny red, hard skin, three legs like tree trunks and many arms of various shapes and lengths. His chest-sized maw was open and braying with pain, exposing teeth the size of forearms and a cloven tongue. Down the ragged wound on one side of his face ran deep green blood, stemming from a thousand cuts in the gap of his missing eye, now studded with crystal crimson shards. On all sides of him were three massive hounds, missing a leg each and howling in sympathy with their master.

"Anteris!" Treaman shouted, "get the Crown now!"

Then the man who had been a scribe's assistant remembered his foot-speed, beginning the race of his life.

The demon roared again in an excess of agony, flames washing off his body but curiously flickering out almost as soon as they lost contact with his skin. Treaman felt as if he were still holding the Sword of Air, with every nerve tingling he started to move and shout orders.

"Scatter, everyone, don't give him a target. Hallah, fly up and stay safe. Your Majesty," to Pol, putting a hand to restrain him, "we need you on the throne."

Kog stared at the group before him now, focusing on Pol at first, but then glancing to one side at the two boys running away. He pointed them out to his helldogs who released an horrific baying and loped off after the pair. Then he began to stride up the center of the throne room towards Pol. The ghosts on all sides fell back, fading in dawn and firelight as the demon strode heedless through them.

Treaman had no hope at all anymore, that he could live through this. But his heart hardened and he thought again, of how well he could die. Putting his body between the heir and hell, he drew Gutter and said "Please be seated, Majesty. Once you have been invested, you'll have the power you need to defeat him."

Kog began to grow arms longer than saplings, reaching across the shortening distance to seize and crush. From one side, Haltar loped in and sliced completely through one with his silversteel longsword.

The flopping limb by itself knocked him down with its lashing, and Kog grabbed it up and ate it as he continued. Mhoral on the other side began to sing, barely audible above the clamor of the exiting helldogs and the stamp of Kog's feet. A lasso flew to entangle another limb, and as the Elf yanked it hard back, Treaman saw blood from where the metal-sharpened noose cut into the softer sinuous skin. But the weight of a pious warrior was no hindrance to an Earth Demon, who strode on and dragged him bodily along behind. New limbs grew to take the place of those lost.

Treaman raised his blade and shouted, "Come on you car—" and was struck aside in mid-curse, by the speed and unearthly reach of Kog's arm. He felt something in his ribcage give, and hit the marble floor fully eight feet from where he had been standing. No hope, then, for any of them.

Then he heard the gravel-voiced shout of the second Kog.

"Imposter!" His enemy whirled around behind him to confront once again his twin.

"This way!" shouted Forge, bearing to the right-hand archway behind the throne.

"No, to the left!" Anteris countered, running at the opposite angle. "No way up from the bedchamber, remember?"

Forge nodded and altered course, looking back into the melee and cursing. "Cark, move fast."

Anteris glanced back to see three beasts of hell pounding after them, and cried "Keep up!". The pair plunged into the left-side archway.

The décor and architecture were all changed, but Anteris was only looking for stairs leading up. They were prominent and the boys both took them. In the pounding, curving hill-climb, they were an even match; Forge used his hands to propel himself along the rails, but Anteris took the treads two at a time with his longer stride.

Yet the dogs were faster than either of them. After skidding on the marble floor at the bottom of the stairs, they aligned and came up, barking and growling with their red-coal eyes and gaining a step for every ten as the race went on. Three floors, four and Anteris was starting to feel it in his lungs now.

Suddenly the top, an empty guardroom with an open arch leading toward the other tower, and the end of all their hopes. Forge slammed into Anteris' back when he came to a full halt, even with death slavering a half-level behind them.

"Heroes, no," Anteris gasped.

There was no bridge between these towers.

Treaman held his side and tried to focus on the confrontation in the center of the room. There was an eerie sense of unreality here, the group was similarly scattered the first time this had happened. Get to the king, protect him; though his rib barked, Treaman staggered up, but could not move further, riveted as were ghosts to either side of him by the two colossi facing off in the center of the chamber.

"I do not recall creating you, son," the first, larger one beamed in glee.

"I-do-not-recall-creating-you," the latter answered in a copy for tone and accent, but just a bit halting in pace. In a flash, Treaman saw several feet behind the second demon was Linya, headband flaring and concentrating with closed eyes. She gestured with her arms and the demon in front of her imitated the action, as if feinting an attack.

Kog looked harder on the intruder then and Treaman figured the scam was exposed. Not enough time. Suddenly the new demon opened its maw and a flood of hellfire poured out in a column to strike Kog directly. He roared in surprise more than pain; Treaman saw behind the second demon Linya had fired the largest fire-bolt he had ever seen her throw, passing neatly through her own illusion from behind and looking for all the world as if emanating from Kog's doppleganger. The fire was brief, not a true flame-wash such as Kog himself could vomit up, but it was a convincing attack. Hardening his one good eye, the Earth Demon came on then to grapple.

Haltar was shaking his head and regaining his feet. Solemn Judgement stepped in and attacked the larger foe with his staff, parrying one of the arms while striking into its body to some effect. Treaman shuffled to the throne steps, pleading with one outstretched arm for Pol to remain seated.

"But your friends, sir," Pol said to him calmly.

"They know what they're doing," Treaman cried, not feeling at all certain, "you must stay, the Crown will be here."

Kog had come to grips with his son, and it was clear that this was no contest. The imposter sprouted no new limbs, only held off Kog's first two arms, took no bites, threw no insults, and steadily lost the war of leverage. With a cry of pain, Linya collapsed to the floor and the illusion dissolved into flaps and shreds in Kog's hands. He spent a long moment looking at the space, heedless how its limbs still fought Haltar, Judgement and Mhoral to a standstill, and then threw back his head for a round of horrible laughter.

"This was cleverly done!" Kog scooped up the mage's form in one new-grown tentacle and turned back to the throne speaking as if to Pol. "See, insect, how well she diverted me, most amusing." He tossed her bodily ten feet before him near the foot of the steps. "Now then, woman, since you were so concerned that I have a new son, let us begin here, and then settle with this stripling on my throne."

Treaman's ears rang with something red and hot, as he charged down to bat away a small tentacle from his unconscious comrade. Haltar stepped before the advancing demon and drove his blade with speed directly into his body, leaving several inches there when Kog roared and batted him away. The demon again tried to spew flame, but could not force the fire more than a foot from his mouth. Snarling with rage, Kog raised a massive foot to crush Haltar where he lay defenceless.

Solemn Judgement, dodging under an arm on the other side, spun into position and reaching high overhand, jammed his silver staff directly into Kog's splinter-strewn eye socket.

Treaman stood over Linya not six feet away and the sound of Kog's pain was enough to nearly knock him down, though still satisfying. He no longer cared a whit for his own life, not compared to Linya's, to Braja's or Bildon's or Hallah's. He just wanted to strike a blow like that one before the end. And then die well. The demon staggered back, then grew ten new limbs to smack the grey warrior back and finally down. The leviathan stood a moment, still bleeding from the eye socket and unable to decide which foe to destroy first.

"Treaman!" a deep voice cried behind him, "Now!"

Anteris could not think or move for a long second, staring into the winter sunshine outside the archway, seeing its twin on the opposite side. How could he have made such a mistake?

"Too far to jump," Forge shouted, "this is it, my friend."

But then Anteris decided he believed. In the heroes, in this palace, the force of Law and the power of Hope. He grabbed Forge by the collar and heaved forward with all his might as the first helldog broke upon the landing not a body's length behind him. Falling to his death was better than this anyway.

Just beyond the archway and bathed in light they both stumbled and fell on thin air. Anteris stared between his hands at more than a hundred feet of sheer drop to the palace roof. To his side, Forge saw the same sight and urinated. The drops spilling around the sides of his pant leg fell through like rain to the world below.

Behind them the helldogs barged up to the archway and halted as if slamming into a wall. Anteris and Forge scrambled further away on nothing; Forge's dagger came loose from his belt and also fell, through the space between his legs. The beasts now whined with urgency, looking down and shrinking back; though driven by their master's commands they could not stand the height where they found themselves.

"What the carking hells," Forge shouted, still scared.

"I don't know," Anteris replied, hauling to his feet and helping his friend to stand on a surface that returned no feeling of any kind to the soles of his feet, yet held them both up all the same. They moved further away, and the dogs, taunted by this, nerved themselves up to try, but failed with whines, howls and swipes of retribution at each other.

"The bridge in Oncario," Anteris said, "it was too long to hold up, remember?"

Forge looked at him in doubt, "So?"

Anteris laughed shakily and hit him on the back, as an adult would to a student. "Well, so is this one!"

Forge eyed him suspiciously and then kept looking down.

"Eyes ahead," Anteris told him. "Just the other end, is all. Let's go."

And a half-step at a time, they went, clinging to each other on a bridge that arced slightly up and slightly down again, and was made of nothing at all.

In the opposite chamber, there was only one podium, and on it lay the Order Brow. The thin gold circlet was elegantly simple, rising at four points to a symbol of Hope and otherwise unadorned with gem or inscription. His hands shaking, Anteris took it off the velvet and turned to Forge.

"You did it," the Stealthic said.

"I have lived to touch all three of the Tridium," Anteris whispered.

"We have to get back." Forge stated flatly.

Anteris looked at the growling pack across the way and thought a moment. He knew time was of the essence; his friends might already be dead, and a little voice inside him suggested he stay right here until he safely starved.

"We could try to climb down," Forge suggested, but the scribe shook his head. "Well then, how?"

Anteris grinned a little, just as he imagined Forge did sometimes. "I believe I know. Wait here."

Back onto the nothing-bridge, Anteris walked slowly but steadily to the other side with the Order Brow held behind his back. Unlike the other two it did not tingle or spark in his hand, and he hoped this was a good sign. From halfway on, every foot closer to those dogs seemed an impossibility. Their snarling, glowing eyes and black talons sparking off the marble floor were enough to kill him at this distance, he was sure. But Anteris murmured a prayer to Areghel for courage, and one to Astor for his help too, since Forge was nearby.

Somehow he edged his way close enough to smell their charnel, charcoal breath before he stopped with legs quivering. He drew a deep breath and tried to speak without stuttering.

"You think you want me, don't you. Huh? Don't you." He edged in another step and the helldogs burst into growls, shouldering each other to be the first to bite him. Anteris waited, and looked at them all one more moment.

"But you really want *this*!" He held the Order Brow directly in front of him the same way he held out a riddy for Folio back home.

With a starving howl of hatred, all three beasts lunged forward snapping at the crown. Anteris fell back, and heard their cries as they dropped all the way to the palace roof below. As Forge came running on behind, Anteris glanced down and saw them lying broken and bleeding below him.

The descending levels were a blur, he and Forge nearly tumbling forward in their haste to get back. Don't think about it, Anteris urged himself, just run. When they broke into the bottom landing and surged back into the throne room, Anteris saw everyone was down on the ground around the Earth Demon, excepting Treaman standing on the bottom stair thirty feet away. Kog was coming on; he was too close. Anteris whipped his arm around and threw with all his strength.

"Treaman! Now!"

Treaman saw the spinning circlet of gold and dropped Gutter to reach for it. The demon grew a dozen mouths all shouting his outrage, even as he sprouted another tentacle to reach out and strike down the Woodsman.

Treaman felt his hand snag the crown and quickly but gently placed it on the head of the man in black sitting in the throne.

Pol became the center of another sunrise, a single wave of bright argent light radiating from him in all directions. Treaman felt renewed as if from a long sleep; behind him Kog the massive Earth Demon stood frozen in mid-cry, his limbs unmoving and his body standing as if carved from bloody granite. Those who had been ghosts stood revealed plainly and gasped at their first breaths to draw air in centuries. The light rolled on, passing through the stone walls and open archways alike, undimmed and unslowed, and Treaman could not doubt it would reach the uttermost corners of the kingdom.

As the youths approached the King of the Percentalion stood, laying his Sword and Scepter down behind him to advance upon his enemy. He looked for a time upon the paralyzed leviathan, then worked his arms slowly in patterns not unlike a dance, while about him an aura of golden energy gathered. With a sudden cry, Pol launched himself at Kog, one foot striking the center of his chest and his body carrying through the demon's frame as if he kicked a wall made of parchment. In the same way a statue does, Kog's body fell into shards and pieces, leaving a thousand stones no larger than a hand piled high on the floor of the throne room. Pol's aura faded and he turned back to face his handiwork, first act of his reign, while Anteris could barely keep his breath in awe.

"The ways are again made straight," the King said quietly.

Anteris reached the throne and said to Treaman, "You have done it sir."

Treaman quietly whispered to no one, "Bildon, for you."

All around the newly restored court of Reghalion bowed low before their monarch. Haltar too, rose and bowed, as the comrades gathered around the stony pile that represented the demon's corpse.

"It seems too hard to believe," Anteris said breathlessly, clapping Forge on the back.

"Fools!" Kog's disembodied voice echoed through the chamber, causing many of the courtiers to gasp and fall. "I am immortal, not to be destroyed by the likes of you. So the prophecy has come true has it? You forget, my spirit simply returns to hell for a time. With or without my Eye, I can find another way to regain my strength. There is no way to defeat me, Child of Hope alone!"

Pol looked down on the body-rubble and frowned. "He may be correct. The prophecy must be complete, or why did the ancients write it thus?"

The Man in Grey stepped forward then, his voice shaking with emotion but strong. "I am no Child of Hope." He rested the end of his staff against the stony corpse. "And this, demon, is the mast of my father's skiff. It is no branch of Conar's bone."

As the Man in Grey began to incant, the stones reformed into a body they all knew, dead but once again of horn and bone and chitin. The language was unlike anything Treaman had ever heard, but the words rang with power, and energy began to form around Kog's body. The demon's wail was filled with unaccustomed terror, and started loud enough to make the others cover their ears.

The Man in Grey continued to chant, sweat standing out on his face and driving his weight down on the staff as with an attack. Steadily, energy gathered around Judgement's staff, the scream faded as if down an endless hall, until no one could hear it more above Judgement's chanting. Kog's millenia-old body crumbled to dust and the Man in Grey stumbled forward nearly falling. The whisper of something malevolent but powerless swept past Treaman's face, on its way out of the hall and into oblivion.

"What did you do?" Anteris asked in wonder.

Judgement sagged against his staff and shook his head in deprecation of the miracle. "I have gained some small mastery of lore useful against necromancy," he said quietly. "Kog's body has been given permanent rest, as even our enemies deserve. Another king taught me that."

Pol nodded and walked slowly back to his throne, where he took up again the Scepter and sat. Everyone in the hallway bowed and awaited his words.

"A great curse has today been laid aside. From this seat of Areghel I can see across a wide kingdom, whose wrack has been restored to health. A few villages and scattered folk survive; many more will come. Let all who would serve them come forward now to assist in the governance of this land."

Pol turned then to the adventurers and Treaman saw the calm, regal bearing he had imagined of kings since the tales of his youth.

"And what reward can a king offer to those who secured his throne?"

Treaman felt several sets of eyes on him, most attached to grinning faces. But he could only think of Braja, and Bildon and the others who had been lost. He bowed to Pol and said, "We didn't have such a high purpose, Your Majesty. Mainly, we wished to find all of the Tridium because… because we thought we might be able. For myself, I wanted to see that demon destroyed. Before he killed someone else, someone as valuable to another as my friend was to me. None of us, I would guess, object to money." Haltar and Mhoral chuckled behind him. "But if it please you, sir, I think we might chiefly like to rest a while."

Pol smiled saying "I shall see to it that chambers are prepared. As soon as I can ascertain which of my staff survive, and would be charged with such a task. Indeed, I sought the center and have found there is much here." He looked to Treaman's right, where the Man in Grey stood alone. "And what of you, grey wanderer whose lore made secure our victory. What would you have of me today?"

"Certes, Majesty, only that I might offer you my congratulations on your ascension, and your leave to go."

"Go? Will you not linger a day, that I might show my gratitude at some leisure."

"Nay, if Your Majesty offers me my will. I would be off and about my business once again."

"What business, pray, have you now?"

The Man in Grey returned the gaze of the king without flinching. "See you how I stand here, still alive? Then sooth, there is still work to do." He turned and walked in the direction of one of the archways, marked with the heraldry of Mendel.

"Solemn Judgement!" Treaman trotted to catch up and offered his arm to grip once more. "I, I want to thank you, and to say I hope we meet again someday."

Judgement ignored the proffered arm but bowed as low to Treaman as he had to the king. "Pray not, rather, Woodsman. For where'er I go there are people unhappy of my coming. But know that I am in your debt for such assistance as was rendered this day, which unburdens me of a great shame. You have helped me to honor my father's memory."

He turned to face the arch as if Treaman had already left. Behind them, Pol's voice rang out. *"Ac nomin Regente Areghel."* The Man in Grey stepped through and was gone.

Treaman turned back to his group and exchanged back-slaps and hugs with all of them. To Forge he said "Your contract has been fulfilled, young man." Turning to Anteris he put a hand on his shoulder and said "Let us see about getting you home."

Excerpt from the Kingdom Chronicles, 1995 ADR

All past editions of this chronicle have demarked the change of an age coincident with the start of a given year, as for example the beginning of the Age of Peace in 19 ADR. It is most likely, therefore, that the wisdom of sages will agree on the final day of 1995 as the end of this age. Yet those living in Trainertown in the final week of Raccoon saw an earlier end to peace.

With the morning sun on the 26th came a writhing cloud of carrion birds, darkening the day and hovering over the city causing panic by their very numbers and appearance. Most of the populace fled to basements or hidden nooks, but few chose to leave; thus many died apart from their fellows in ways unknown, even their bodies never discovered thereafter.

Close upon the birds came the army of the Earth Demon Kog, unseen upon the Lands since his defeat at the hands of Areghel in the Third Age. The chaos-lord stood taller than the entrance gates, and all screamed to behold his massive stature and multiple, changing limbs. The guards and veterans atop the walls quailed at the sight of that scarred, one-eyed face, laughing through new mouths grown before their eyes. The demon marshaled his forces at the edge of the chaos-lands, just east of the ancient way recently recovered, and studied the city before him for a time. Some cried it had been only the road which led him here, and called for the departed heroes to rescue them, without result.

Lashing with whip-grown arms, Kog drove forward a grotesque menagerie of deformed beasts, which he evidently judged expendable, to storm the walls of a city that had not known war since its construction.

Many guards routed from this initial onslaught, as insects the size of houses, plus horned or talon-bearing creatures clambered, flew and hopped over the walls to ravage the streets within. Some few veterans on the gate, either braver than other men or too slow to withdraw, essayed to defend their position and repulsed many beasts who approached too near, killing several. The demon, seeing this carnage, laughed and shouted in alternation, finally signaling his man-like legions forward.

On came the garruk and savage ape-men, with clubs and spears, hooked ropes and some swinging massive hammers, to take the southern and eastern gates in two columns. Men surmise that here the brave veterans on the south gate perished, judging from the bodies of several enemies found slain on the steps entwined with their own corpses.

Screams and smoke rose from the city now, and Kog at last advanced to pull down large sections of the wall in his glee, and to breath flame on the buildings of the southern quarter, when all were distracted by a great blast of horns from the eastern road. Young King Gareth of Shilar, at the van of some twenty-score knights and retainers, approached the city having come nearly a hundred leagues in less than three days of marching. Reports say that, observing the scene before him, Gareth drew his knights in line abreast protecting the rearguard wagons. Kog called back his garruk and brought up endless scores of cat-like, wolfish and spike-headed minions, plus some larger monsters that bounded or flew. In a ragged order and mainly from fear of their master they met the charge of Shilar's knights in the shadow of the town walls.

Various eyewitness accounts give that it was a splendid charge, and the men of Hope wrought wondrous execution with lance and sword upon the beasts of Despair. But as their charge played out, Shilar's forces slowed and the endless supply of their opponents began to tell a different tale. Kog, now outraged, called the garruk to return from plunder, and some obeyed, others did not hear, and still others were enamored of blood and did not mind him. Yet hearing Shilar's charge outside, some among the people's guards and townsfolk took heart, emerging to hurriedly consult, and attack stray ape-men, or try to put out some of the many fires that had been started. But there was no saving the tavern, nor its owner Fairnum who died within clutching great handfuls of promissory notes.

Enraged, Kog did lead his second wave of recalled minions personally into battle, pulling down knights with horses together and blasting fires of hell in three directions at once. The line of Shilar's cavalry wavered and began to fall back, and the King in the center with his bodyguard looked soon to be cut off, as surviving witnesses attest.

Further from the city flowed the line of battle, and now knights were falling in increasing numbers, though none yet had turned to flee. An elderly lord in the king's company wrought a great miracle drawing down a bolt from the heavens which struck in the midst of the evil horde slaying many in a blow, scattering others to flee and breaking also through the great cloud of carrion birds overhead, dispersing them. This knight, a seer and advisor to the previous king, fell prostrate from his mount after effecting this stroke of Hope, and his body was lost in the press of battle. Still the demon-horde thrust the knights back, and Kog destroyed whatever lay between himself and the king of Shilar, whether of his own army or the enemy, to be revenged for this delay to his will and damage to his forces.

Gareth the king, seeing Kog's approach awaited him gamely with those of his guard who remained, and at the last caused a flag with the watchful eye to be raised above his position. In the space of a moment some hundred or more knights appeared to the south and west, flanking and nearly surrounding the army of chaos. By their rustic lore the warriors of the Bordbeyonds had remained unseen until the signal was given, and now these more lightly-armed and swifter knights rode down the right wing of Kog's army, stampeding and slaying beasts and garruk alike with many savage cries and strange words.

Pressed on two sides, yet the hell-horde still was far larger than their foes. Many beasts fell under the onslaught of the plains and the renewed vigor of the Shilarians. Kog did scream for the carrion birds to join the attack and they wheeled down to vie with the living for meat, contrary to their custom. Then some among the Bordbeyonds flung glittering handfuls of some silt or powder, flaring to fire in the very air and routing many of the scavengers to flee south again and not return.

Still in the center was the lord of hell untouched, dragging down foes to trample underfoot and healing all wounds from lance and blade as the water closes over stones. Many in the bodyguard of the king were thrown down, either injured or dead. And Kog did summon his three helldogs, who bayed horrendously causing horses to founder and even the forces of hell to flee. These beasts plunged into the thin line of the Bordbeyonds and wrought havoc there, forcing them back and apart from the Shilarians and taking no wounds the while.

At this same time, roving bands of garruk were still plundering the town, setting fire to the church, and they also wantonly hammered the struts of the clock tower, so that it tilted and buckled half-way over, its bell ringing the hour for the final time. Then it was that most in the town believed their last hope extinguished and doom come upon them.

Beyond the torn walls and the smoking ruin upon the center of Trainertown, Kog at last reached the King, who showed himself not at all unwilling to meet the monster in combat. Their speech was brief, in the memories of those who were there, and ran its course with speed.

"And now the end, little king," the demon said, "you are not the heir of prophecy, so know fear of me before the end."

"We defy you, thane of evil," the King cried, "it was not for fear that we came, we followed instead the signs of heaven and our duty."

"No matter, brave little crownless boy, as now you are only a meal for Kog."

The demon then did lash down with a mighty arm. But one of the king's squires did interpose to take the blow, even as Gareth landed his sword square upon the demon's chest. Per usual the monster took little harm from the blade; yet suddenly he did cry out in agony and throw back his head in torment. And a witness did claim, without perfect surety, that there had appeared in Kog's cratered socket the shards of a ruby gem, most likely the source of the demon's wail.

Kog did upon that moment disappear from view, never to be seen by those who survived.

Still the legions of hell remained, and much too great were their number, so that the forces of Shilar and the Bordbeyonds were helpless to do more than defend themselves with tiring arms and horses. Within the town, bands of garruk still marauded, some chasing a group of children into the empty western quarter. Every portion of the town was visited by flame and ruin; those who survived thought not to live much longer.

The sounding of a bell rang clearly over the field of battle, as all attest though the tower of the town was already destroyed. Many in the king's army saw a bridge as if made of light appear to the west of town, behind the army of hell, and down the span came several score mounted men in armor wearing the tabards of the Order of Chosen Wanderers. With a trumpet blast they advanced full into the foe, which without leadership could form no orderly response to the threat. Great execution was wrought by these heavily armored knights, and the men of Shilar and the Plains rallied at the sight redoubling their efforts. Hell's horde quite dissolved, and within moments the land outside of town was covered in the slain of chaos. As the king did order his followers to pursue the rout south, the leader of the Wanderers took his men within the town to hunt out those engaged in sack and plunder.

Many townsfolk had been slain, and half the houses were in flames. But as the knights swept each street, survivors came forth with more confidence to fight the fires and offer condolences or aid to each other. All the Town Council survived, though it would be some days before they were all found. The smith was still alive, defending his forge with his hammer and using hot coals to keep a giant insect at bay until it could be surrounded and slain. In the western quarter of town, a marauding pack of garruk had been drawn after the children, who led them fleetly through empty streets until they became somewhat confused. The wily hostler of that quarter did release all his stock of horses, whose echoing hoofbeats created further distraction to the vandals; and when a squadron of

Wanderer knights approached, the garruk ignored the threat until too late, and all were slain.

Before the doors of the library other knights found the body of the town sage and scribe Valenthur, who had used a heavy chair with all his strength to strike a garruk warrior upon the skull so that it cracked and the chair shattered to pieces. They found his body beneath that of his foe, and a torch no doubt intended to fire the archives still in hand not six feet from the door.

Thus was the town largely saved despite the onslaught of hell, by the brave armies of its neighboring polities. Upon his return from the pursuit, Gareth did hold council with the Bordbeyonds and the Chosen Wanderers. By this hour all could see that the Pecentalion had been restored to its former shape, and many did wonder greatly at the rolling hills and forested horizon covered in snow that lay before them. It was decided to send a deputation at once south, in search of news.

Thus did the year 1995 conclude in Conar and may it never be again as filled with events as it was at the passing of the age.

In other lands too, the new year brought great change. In Conar, the noble classes began to meet anew and discuss changes to their order, with more knights seeking to travel, some to Novar, others to far kingdoms, and there find employment for their skills and a useful purpose to the advantaged lives they possessed. In Mendel, by some secret stratagem the Mark of Eldarport was able to ferret out the location of the pirate base, and sent his fleet against them, where in a great naval battle he was victorious and drove them from the sea forever. To the east the Bordbeyonds celebrated the unison of their royal houses with a binding treaty of friendship and alliance, trade and exchange, symbolized by a stone bridge between their countries across the River Sweeping.

The wisdom of sages in time will discern the best name for this new age. For the purposes of this entry, on provision only, it shall be called the Age of Adventure. May it be known that the ill omen many associate with that word is not lost on this humble chronicler. For many will find that unpleasant experience, fear and dread, and of course great uncertainty are the hallmark of change, even change for the better. We may not seek it, but in the plan of the heroes it may come nonetheless. Whether we do well or poorly is not to the purpose; only that in each day of whatever age or character, we do what we can.

Here endeth the chronicle of the year 1995 A.D.R.

It was a deeply cold winter's night, the last of the old year. Cedrith watched the thick, inaudible snowfall out the window and drew the comfort that comes to a man whose home is snugly made, whose outdoor chores are done, and who sits well fed by a fire. He turned back to his desk and contemplated the manuscript before him, still in its very early stages, an attempt to describe on paper the quest to the Hopeward which had brought him such unwonted fame and so many nightmares. A thought stole over him as he recalled being wet and chilled in the Halls of Glass, a sense of cold both like and unlike the night outside; he chuckled at the irony of writing about such a thing from the warmth of his fireside and reinforced by another sip of that matchless wine supplied by his distant relatives.

"My dear," he called out to his wife in the kitchen, "should a history confine itself to the deeds that were done, the causes and results, so forth. Or do you think it would be the proper place of a narrative to make the reader feel as if they had been there?"

Kia came to the entrance of the fire-room with her hands still covered by the oven-towel where she had put the pie in to bake. She gazed on him the way she often did, not as if thinking but more to show the answer was obvious and she merely paused to give him a chance to guess.

"I think," she replied carefully, "that you should write this tale in such a way that no one in their right mind would want to repeat it."

"Easily done, I should think!" He reached to take her hand and draw her to him. "Will you not let me help you with these chores, you make me feel like a Theme with your bustling."

"Away, you have done dishes and swept up here—fairly well anyway—and now you must have time to write or this horrid chore you've taken on will never be done. You'll keep complaining of it all winter, and that will be a chore for me to listen to."

Cedrith laughed and kissed her twice, asking, "What day now?"

She looked skyward to calculate, "Today's quota done, I reckon about the Tenth of the Fire Ant. Two months still behind."

"Tenth Fire Ant! Unlucky day, when this horrid adventure began. Let me get at least to mid-Lion then."

They both laughed and she leaned into him as he sat. Cedrith knew he could imagine no greater happiness.

But the knock on the door sent him back to the Hopeward in an instant.

He jumped, and his hand flexed as if reaching for a mace instead of his quill. All humor fled him and he felt a terrible sense of menace. Was the scar of that quest still so fresh, the memory so near the surface that a simple knock could send him back into fear of his life? He swallowed hard and stood, managing, "Who could that be in this storm?"

Kia clucked and moved to the door, muttering, "If this is some royal summons, after all this time, I swear by my Moments—"

"Kia wait!" Cedirth lurched forward, not in time to stop her opening, but able at the last second to interpose his body between her and the unknown outside.

There on the stoop, lightly dusted in snow, stood the Man in Grey.

Cedrith stared with jaw agape. The guest swept off his broad-brimmed hat, saying "I was selfish, Eldest, and thought only of myself when your letter wrote of an invitation to visit. I have no doubt inconvenienced you."

"My very dear Solemn Judgement! I am so surprised, that is I am delighted, simply delighted that you would travel to see me. Come in, come in at once, please! My dear, this is the Guildsman of our order I have spoken about."

"Indeed, so often and so well. Do come in sir."

Judgement remained rooted in place. "It is clear that you are busy."

"Nonsense, I am honored that you would come, and so relieved to see you again."

"Get in at once, sir," Kia ordered, "or you will freeze like a block and so will we." At last the Man in Grey complied.

He stood just within the door, as if ready to leave in a moment. Kia sighed hard and Cedrith was brushed back as she applied her talents to this hard case in hospitality. Firmly taking his arm she half-dragged him closer to the fire, pointed imperiously at the best armchair, and pried his fingers loose from his staff which she placed in the corner. She then took off his cloak without permission and hung it by the fire to dry.

Cedrith followed along behind and gripped his arm shaking it with honest vigor.

"Guildsman," he said, using the title he knew his guest accepted, "you have come through many trials if I know anything at all about you, but I've had no word since your letter from Shilar. To think, we were in the same room! You must tell me everything."

"Nonsense, he must eat," Kia countered.

"Many thanks, milady," Judgement replied evenly, "I have eaten."

"Hah, but when!" Cedrith cried. "Not yet today or I miss my guess."

Unwilling to lie, Judgement said nothing and shrugged a fraction.

"I am not hungry."

"Not much, I am sure. My dear, could you reheat some of that marvelous stew."

"Of course, and will you have ale or some wine, sir? My husband has opened a bottle of the Kira-Ashton, finest in the Lands."

"I'm afraid our guest will only take water, my dear. But use the pewter tankard, that may please him."

"You are too kind," Judgement said quietly. "It may be that tonight, a taste of your Kira-Ashton would go well."

Cedrith turned to his guest in astonishment. "Well then, another honor. Judgement please sit."

Under Kia's merciless instruction, the Man in Grey ate hearty fare, and drank cautiously of the finest wine ever vinted. Cedrith could not take his eyes off the silver-haired youth, watching him exercise these mundane functions of life. For his part, the guest looked carefully around at times, noting the location of furniture and stairs, utensils, shelves, beds, as if to memorize the way normal folk lived.

Cedrith felt a surge of sympathy near tears, for a friend who never knew these things. By slow degrees the guest seemed to relax, to feel and perhaps enjoy a fire's heat as well as the conversation.

After a time, Judgement's tongue became a bit more facile and he allowed himself to be drawn into conversation with his hosts. Cedrith told him a bit of his adventures on the road to Shilar, of his escape with the Rom and eventual reunion with Kia.

Judgement surprised him by asking after the health of several in the Gypsy band by name. With much urging, the guest spoke sparingly of his deeds, and as he sat in the chair Cedrith felt Kia clutching his arm, as if to prevent this stranger from being swept up into another such horror on the instant.

"And thus," he said quietly, "a second king was crowned, and his enemy defeated I believe for good." Cedrith watched as Judgement stared into the fire for a long time, with an intensity that made it seem another book he was reading.

"Well," Kia managed, "you have done wondrous things, Solemn, and I'm sure have earned the good repute of these rulers from many lands."

The Man in Grey shook his head once. "There is little to be done with a landless adventurer, milady. My time in this adopted world may be long or brief, but certes it shall hold nothing worthy of much praise."

"Oh, such nonsense," Cedrith said with feeling, reaching out to touch his friend's arm. "You saved my life, and Natasha's, poor woman, don't forget that, Guildsman. And now you have battled ghouls, recovered lore none of us knew was missing, defeated a liche from our history's nightmares, even restored a king and a kingdom. Yours shall be accorded the highest place in any chronicle I would write, rest assured."

The gaze Cedrith saw returned was softer than any he had previously seen.

"Ye shall write as ye wish, Eldest. Perhaps best of all, you would favor me by continued correspondence. With the heroes I encountered, there in Reghalion, I trow I saw such close comradery that I felt somewhat askew. Who knows what wonders the next year may hold, and it be not for one such as I to question my place in it. What work comes my way, I shall endeavor to do."

Cedrith stared with Judgement into the fire awhile. He stood and raised his glass. "Once I saluted you, Solemn Judgement, as a noble man. I learned from you that this is a word for a person's character, not the accident of their birth. Tonight, I affirm what I said then, to the most noble man I know."

Judgement slowly rose and raised his glass also. "Let us drink rather to Natasha, who gave so selflessly to save us, and who binds us to her future salvation, a better fit for such a title."

"I shall gladly toast them both," Kia said and everyone drank.

Judgement sat again and the conversation resumed. In a few hours the house known as Riarden's Rest would hold but two persons; the cape and staff would be gone from their place by the fire. But for now, there was still talk, and friendship old with young, and a new year coming in to the same life and hope as the old one left behind.

The Plane of Dreams

A standalone novel from the Lands of Hope

In the southern empire of Argens just roiled by the rebellion of Yula, a band of adventurers returns from the Shimmering Mindsea bearing enormous treasure and minus one of its members. The Tributarians, unaware of the growing threat to the waking world, embark on separate plans. But the spirit of the hero lives on in all of them, as their good deeds have consequences beyond their original intention. Will it be enough to avert the peril they have unwittingly brought about?

This first novel-length tale set in the Lands of Hope features a complex world and intelligent, dedicated characters whose actions entwine over distances and beyond their own comprehension. Like any world worth living in, the Lands have humor, mystery, horror and action to delight and entertain the reader.

Shards of Light Book I:
The Ring and the Flag
A Sword and Sorcery series from the Lands of Hope.

Newly-graduated imperial officer Justin is convinced he has no future, and hearing the details of the secret mission he's assigned for the Emperor won't change his mind. Civil War threatens the North Mark. Justin must race against time to form a company, and lead his men into the center of the web; but what happens when his loyalty to the Empire means the death of those who follow him?

Shards of Light Book II: Fencing Reputation

A Sword and Sorcery series from the Lands of Hope.

When the elven lords, preachers and merchants of Cryssigens need wrongs righted without clues, they look for the stealthic Feldspar to solve their problems. But the legend without a face is hard to find: and when Feldspar takes a commission from the most famous, and beautiful, priestess in the city, he finds problems of his own piling up, and is forced to choose between Hope and safety.

To be continued with "Perilous Embraces" & "Shards of Light".

www.ingramcontent.com/pod-product-compliance
Lightning Source LLC
Chambersburg PA
CBHW030551310726
48979CB00011B/2110/J
9783956810817